Christmas

BLOCKBUSTER 2023

LYNNE
GRAHAM

JULES
BENNETT

NINA
SINGH

CHARLOTTE
HAWKES

MILLS & BOON

CHRISTMAS BLOCKBUSTER 2023 © 2023 by Harlequin Books S.A.

A BABY ON THE GREEK'S DOORSTEP
© 2020 by Lynne Graham
Australian Copyright 2020
New Zealand Copyright 2020

First Published 2020
Second Australian Paperback Edition 2023
ISBN 978 1 867 29582 2

A TEXAN FOR CHRISTMAS
© 2018 by Jules Bennett
Australian Copyright 2018
New Zealand Copyright 2018

First Published 2018
Second Australian Paperback Edition 2023
ISBN 978 1 867 29582 2

CHRISTMAS WITH HER SECRET PRINCE
© 2018 by Nilay Nina Singh
Australian Copyright 2018
New Zealand Copyright 2018

First Published 2018
Second Australian Paperback Edition 2023
ISBN 978 1 867 29582 2

UNWRAPPING THE NEUROSURGEON'S HEART
© 2019 by Charlotte Hawkes
Australian Copyright 2019
New Zealand Copyright 2019

First Published 2019
Second Australian Paperback Edition 2023
ISBN 978 1 867 29582 2

Published by
Mills & Boon
An imprint of Harlequin Enterprises (Australia) Pty Limited (ABN 47 001 180 918), a subsidiary of HarperCollins Publishers Australia Pty Limited (ABN 36 009 913 517)
Level 19, 201 Elizabeth Street
SYDNEY NSW 2000
AUSTRALIA

MIX
Paper | Supporting responsible forestry
FSC
www.fsc.org   FSC® C001695

® and ™ (apart from those relating to FSC®) are trademarks of Harlequin Enterprises (Australia) Pty Limited or its corporate affiliates. Trademarks indicated with ® are registered in Australia, New Zealand and in other countries. Contact admin_legal@Harlequin.ca for details.

Printed and bound in Australia by McPherson's Printing Group

CONTENTS

A Baby On The Greek's Doorstep

Lynne Graham

MODERN

Power and passion

Visit the Author Profile page
at millsandboon.com.au for more titles.

Lynne Graham was born in Northern Ireland and has been a keen romance reader since her teens. She is very happily married to an understanding husband who has learned to cook since she started to write! Her five children keep her on her toes. She has a very large dog who knocks everything over, a very small terrier who barks a lot and two cats. When time allows, Lynne is a keen gardener.

CHAPTER ONE

TOR SARANTOS IGNORED his security head's frown at the news that he would require neither his car nor his usual bodyguards that evening.

'You know what day this is,' Tor said simply. 'I go out... I go alone.'

'With all due respect,' the older man began heavily, 'in your position, it is not safe.'

'Duly noted,' Tor breathed very drily. 'But it is what I do, as you well know.'

Every year without fail for the past five years, Tor had gone out alone on this particular date. It was an anniversary but not one to celebrate. It was the anniversary of his wife's and daughter's deaths. He considered himself to be neither an emotional nor sentimental man. No, he chose to remember what had happened to Katerina and Sofia because their sad fate was *his* worst-ever failure. His ferocious anger, injured pride and bitterness had led to that ultimate tragedy, which could not, in conscience, ever be forgotten. Out of respect for the family he had lost, he chose to remember them one wretched day a year and wallow in his shamed self-loathing. It was little enough, and it chastened him, kept him grounded, he acknowledged grimly. After all, he had screwed up, he had screwed up *so* badly that it had cost two human lives that could have been saved had he only been a more forgiving and compassionate man.

Tragically, the traits of compassion and forgiveness had never run strong in Alastor, known as Tor, Sarantos. Although he came from a kind and loving family, he was tough, inflexible and fierce in nature as befitted a billionaire banker, celebrated for his ruthless reputation, financial acumen and foresight, his advice as much sought by governments as by rich private investors. In business, he was a very high flyer. In his private life, he was appallingly aware that he had proved to be a loser. However, that was a secret he was determined to take to his grave with him, as was the truth that he would never remarry.

That was why he rarely went home now to his family in Greece. Not only did he have an understandable wish to avoid meetings with his Italian half-brother, Sevastiano, but he also didn't want to listen to his relatives talking with increasingly evangelical fervour about him 'moving on'. On his visits, a parade of suitable young women was served up at parties and dinners even though he had done everything possible to make it brutally obvious that he had no desire to find another wife and settle down again.

After all, he had long since transformed from the young man happily wed to his first love into a womaniser known throughout Europe for his passionate but short-lived affairs. At twenty-eight, he was generations removed from the naïve and idealistic man he had once been, but his family stubbornly refused to accept the change in him. Of course, his parents were as much in love now as they had been on the day of their marriage and fully believed that that happiness was achievable by all. Tor didn't plan to be the party pooper who told them that lies, deceit and betrayal had flourished, unseen and unsuspected, within their own family circle. He preferred to let his relatives live in their sunny version of reality where rainbows and unicorns flourished. He had learned the hard way that, once lost, trust and innocence were irretrievable.

Dressing for his night out, Tor set aside his gold cufflinks, his platinum watch, all visible signs of his wealth, and chose the anonymity of faded designer jeans and a leather jacket. He would go to a bar alone and drink himself almost insensible while he pondered the past and then he would climb into a taxi and come home. That was all he did. Allowing himself to forget, allowing himself to truly move on, would be, he honestly believed, an unmerited release from the guilt he deserved to suffer.

Eighteen months later

Tor frowned as his housekeeper appeared in his home office doorway, looking unusually flustered. 'Something wrong?'

'Someone's abandoned a baby on the doorstep, sir,' Mrs James informed him uncomfortably. 'A little boy about nine months old.'

'A...*baby*?' Tor stressed in astonishment.

'Security are about to check the video surveillance tapes,' the older woman told him before stiffly moving forward. 'There was a note. It's addressed to you, sir.'

'Me?' Tor said in disbelief as an envelope was slid onto his desk.

There was his name, block printed in black felt-tip pen.

'Do you want me to call the police?'

Tor was tearing open the envelope as the question was asked. The message within was brief.

This is your child.
Look after it.

Obviously, it couldn't possibly be *his* child. But what if it belonged to one of his family? He had three younger brothers, all of whom had enjoyed stays at his London town house within recent memory. What if the child should prove to be a nephew or niece? Clearly, the mother must have been desperate for help when she chose to abandon the baby and run.

'The police?' Mrs James prompted.

'No. We won't call them...yet,' Tor hedged, thinking that if one of his family was involved, he did not want a scandal or media coverage of any kind erupting from an indiscreet handling of the situation. 'I'll look into this first.'

'So, what do I do with it?'

'With what?'

'The baby, sir,' the housekeeper extended drily. 'I've no experience with young children.'

His fine ebony brows pleated. 'Contact a nanny agency for emergency cover,' he advised. 'In the meantime, I'll sort this out.'

A baby? Of course, it couldn't be his! Logic stirred, reminding him that no form of contraception was deemed entirely foolproof. Accidents happened. For that matter, *deliberate* accidents could also occur if a woman chose to be manipulative.

Like other men, he had heard stories of pins stuck in condoms to damage them and other such distasteful ruses, but he had never actually met anyone whom it had happened to.

Fake horror stories, he told himself bracingly. Yet, momentarily, unease still rippled through Tor, connected with the unfortunate memory of the strange hysterical girl who had stormed his office the year before...

Eighteen months earlier

Pixie used the key to let herself into the plush house that was her temporary home. Several glamorous, high-earning individuals shared the dwelling, and as a poor and ordinary student nurse she was fully conscious that she was enjoying a luxury treat in staying there. She was happy with that, simply grateful to be enjoying a two-week escape from living under the same roof with her brother and his partner, who, sadly, seemed to be in the process of breaking up.

Listening to Jordan and Eloise constantly fighting, when there was absolutely no privacy, had become seriously embarrassing in the small terraced home she shared with them.

For that reason, it had been a total joy to learn that Steph, the sister of one of her friends, had a precious Siamese kitten, which she didn't want to abandon to a boarding facility while she was abroad on a modelling assignment. Initially, Pixie had been surprised that Steph didn't expect her housemates to look after her pet. Only after moving in to look after Coco had she understood that it was a household where the tenants all operated as independent entities, coming and going without interest in their housemates in a totally casual way that had confounded Pixie's rosy expectations of communal life with her peers.

But in the short term, Pixie reminded herself, she was enjoying the huge indulgence of a private bathroom and a large bedroom with the sole responsibility of caring for a very cute kitten. As she was currently working twelve-hour shifts on her annual placement for her final year of nursing training, living in the elegant town house was a treat and she was grateful for the opportunity. A long bath, she promised herself soothingly as she stepped into the room and Coco jumped onto her feet, desperate for some attention after a day spent alone.

In auto mode, Pixie ran a bath, struggling greatly not to dwell on the reality that during her shift in A & E she had had to deal with her first death as a nurse. It had been a young, healthy woman, not something any amount of training could have prepared her for, she acknowledged ruefully. Put it in a box at the back of her brain, she instructed herself irritably. It was not her role to get all *personally* emotional, it was her job to be supportive and to deal with the practical and the grieving relatives with all the tact and empathy she could summon up.

Well, she was satisfied that she had done her job to the best of her ability, but the wounding reality of that tragic passing was still lingering with her. She was not supposed to bring her work or the inevitable fatalities she would see home with her, she reminded herself doggedly, striving to live up to the professional nursing standards she admired. But at twenty-one, still scarred as she was by her own family bereavement six years earlier, it was a tough struggle to take death in her stride as a daily occurrence.

Dressed in comfy shorty pyjamas and in bare feet because the house was silent and seemingly empty, it being too early in the evening for the partying tenants to be home while others were travelling for work or pleasure. At this time of day and in the very early morning, Pixie usually had the place to herself, her antisocial working hours often a plus. She lit only the trendy lamp hanging over the kitchen island, hopelessly thrilled with the magazine perfection of her surroundings. Moulded work surfaces, fancy units and a sunroom extension leading out into a front courtyard greeted her appreciative gaze. Pixie loved to daydream and sometimes she allowed herself to dream that this was *her* house and she was cooking for the special man in her life. Special man, that was a joke, she thought ruefully, wincing away even from the dim reflection she caught of herself in the patio doors, a short curvy figure with a shock of green hair.

Green! What had possessed her when she had dyed her hair a few weeks earlier? Her brother Jordan's lively and outspoken partner, Eloise, had persuaded her into the change at a moment when Pixie was feeling low because the man she was attracted to had yet to even notice that she was alive. Antony was a paramedic, warm and friendly, exactly the sort of man Pixie thought would be her perfect match.

But the hair had been a very bad idea, particularly when the cheap dye had refused to wash out as it was supposed to have done and she had then checked the instructions to belatedly discover that the lotion wasn't recommended for blond hair. She had hated her blond curls from the instant she was christened 'Poodle' at school, and not by her enemies but by her supposed friends. In recent weeks, she had learned that green curls were far worse than blond because everyone, from her nursing mentor to her superiors and work colleagues, had let her know that green hair in a professional capacity was a mistake. And she couldn't afford to go to a hairdresser for help. She might be working a placement, but it was unpaid, and because of her twelve-hour shifts it was virtually impossible for her to maintain a part-time job as well.

Still preoccupied with her worries, Pixie dragged out her toasted sandwich machine and put the ingredients together for a cheese toastie. It was literally all she could afford for a main meal. In fact, Coco the cat ate much better than she did. She put on the kettle, thought she heard a sound somewhere close by and blamed it on the cat she had left playing with a rubber ball in her room next door. Coco was lively but, like most kittens, she tired quickly and would fold up in a heap in her little princess fur-lined basket long before Pixie got to sleep.

While she waited for her toastie, Pixie contemplated the reality that she was returning to her brother's house that weekend. She hated living as a third wheel in Jordan's relationship with Eloise, but she didn't have much choice and, since he had lost his job over an unfortunate expenses claim that his employers had regrettably deemed a fraud rather than a mistake, Jordan was having a rough time. All his rows with Eloise were over money because he hadn't found work since he had been sacked and naturally, the bills were mounting up, which in turn made Pixie feel terrible because she was only an added burden in her brother's currently challenging existence.

Jordan had become her guardian when their parents died unexpectedly when she was fifteen and he was twenty-three. Pixie was painfully aware that Jordan could have washed his hands of her and let her go into foster care, particularly when they were, strictly speaking, only half-siblings, having been born from the same father but to different mothers, her father having been married and widowed before he met her mother.

Even so, Jordan hadn't turned his back on her as he could have done. He'd had to jump through a lot of hoops to satisfy the authorities that he would be an acceptable guardian for an adolescent girl. She owed Jordan a lot for the care and support he had unstintingly given her over the years, seeing her through her school years and then her nursing course.

'Something smells good...'

At the sound of an unfamiliar male voice, Pixie almost leapt a foot in the air, her head swivelling with a jerk to focus on the strange man slowly spinning round the recliner in the unlit sunroom, where he had apparently been seated unnoticed by her.

'Heaven must be missing an angel' was the cheesiest pickup approach Pixie had ever received, but for the very first time she was looking at a man who might legitimately have inspired such a line with his sleek dark fallen-angel beauty. He *was* otherworldly in his sheer masculine perfection. Her heart was still beating very fast with fright and, striving to crush those inappropriate thoughts, she stepped forward. She collided involuntarily with the eyes of an apex predator—sharp, shrewd, powerful and dark as the night sky. 'I didn't see you in there... who are you?' she asked as civilly as she could, fearful of causing offence to any of Steph's housemates or their friends.

'I'm Tor,' he murmured. 'I think I must have fallen asleep before I called a taxi to take me home.'

'I didn't know anyone was here. I've just come in from work and I was making some supper,' Pixie confided. 'Who are you visiting here?'

His brow furrowed. Slowly, he sank back down on the recliner. 'My apologies... I don't recall her name. A leggy redhead with an annoying giggle.'

'Saffron,' Pixie told him with concealed amusement. 'But why did she just leave you in here?'

He shrugged. 'She stormed off. I rejected her and it made her angry.'

'You rejected... *Saffron*?' Pixie queried in disbelief because

Saffron, a wannabe actress, resembled a supermodel and turned heads in the street.

'A misunderstanding,' he corrected smoothly. 'I thought I was coming to a party. She thought something else. I'm sorry. I'm rather drunk, not in proper control of my tongue.'

No way was he drunk!

Pixie was accustomed to dealing with surly drunks at A & E and usually they could barely vocalise or stand without swaying or cursing. He was speaking with perfect diction and courtesy and remained astute enough to smooth over the unfortunate impression he might have made in saying bluntly that he had rejected the other woman. All the same, she hadn't thought there was a man born who wouldn't jump at the chance of having sex with the gorgeous redhead. Presumably, Saffron had either sought the privacy of her own room upstairs to handle such a blow to her ego or she had gone out again, but Pixie could only be impressed by a man particular enough in his tastes to say no to a beauty like Saffron.

'What are you cooking?' he shot at her unexpectedly.

'A cheese toastie,' Pixie responded in an undertone as she lifted the lid, waved away the steam and reached for her plate.

'It smells incredible...'

'Would you like one?' she heard herself ask and she wanted to slap herself for being so impressionable.

He was a complete stranger and she owed him nothing but, as her brother's partner had warned her, she was a 'nurturer', the sort of woman whom men, according to Eloise, would take advantage of. And Pixie had seen the evidence for that condemnation in her own nature. She *did* like to feed people; she *did* like to take care of them. Pleasing people, tending to their needs, satisfied something in her, a something that Eloise believed she should suppress out of self-interest.

'I'd love that. I'm starving.' He smiled at her and that smile locked her knees where she stood because it was like a galaxy of golden warmth engulfing her, locking his lean bronzed features into shocking beauty, releasing a flock of butterflies low in her tummy. Stupid, stupid, *stupid*, she castigated herself with self-loathing as she reached for the bread and butter again before saying, 'Here…have this one… I'll have the next.'

As she pushed the plate with a knife and fork across the island, he tugged out one of the high stools and settled into it. She busied herself with the sandwich maker, her pale skin pink while he watched her, and she could feel the weight of his regard like a brand. Nothing she had felt in Antony's radius could compare to the thrumming level of awareness assailing her beneath the stranger's gaze.

The hair was weird, there was no other word for it, Tor was reflecting, his gaze locked to those tumbling pale green curls lying tousled on her narrow shoulders, but if a woman *could* rock green hair, she was rocking it. She had the brightest blue eyes he had ever seen, the softest, pinkest mouth, the most flawless skin, but she was so undersized he could barely see her behind the barrier of the island.

'What height are you?' he asked curiously.

Pixie cringed. 'About four ten…no tall genes in my family tree.'

'How old are you?'

'Why are you asking me that?'

'I'm in an unfamiliar house with unknown occupants. I don't want to find out that I'm keeping company with someone's child, and you don't look very old…'

'I'm twenty-one,' Pixie provided grudgingly. 'Almost a fully qualified nurse. Totally grown-up and independent.'

'Twenty-one is still very young,' Tor countered mildly.

'So, how old are you, old man?' Pixie enquired teasingly, putting down the lid on the second toastie and relaxing back against the kitchen cabinets to watch him eat. 'Coffee?'

'Black, sweet. I'm twenty-eight,' he told her.

'And married,' she noted without thought as the ring on his

wedding finger glinted under the light and she switched on the coffee machine again. 'What were you doing with Saffron? Sorry, none of my business… I shouldn't have asked,' she muttered, backtracking in haste from that unintentional challenge.

'No offence taken. I'm a widower,' Tor volunteered.

Pixie turned back to him, stirring the coffee and passing it to him. 'I'm sorry for your loss.'

'It's OK,' Tor said with a stiffness she recognised, the awkwardness of someone unaccustomed to dealing openly with the topic of grief. 'It's been five years since my wife and my daughter died.'

Pixie paled. 'You lost your child as well?'

Pixie felt even more awkward, painfully aware of how she had felt earlier that evening when she had dealt with her first death at the hospital. The finality of a passing and the grieving family left behind scarred the staff as well. For a man to have lost both a wife and a child together was an enormous double blow and her heart squeezed on his behalf at the idea of such a huge loss.

Pale too beneath his bronzed skin, Tor jerked his chin down in silent confirmation.

'I'm so sorry,' she whispered.

'Nobody ever mentions it now. For them it's like it happened a hundred years ago,' he muttered with perceptible bitterness.

'Death makes people uncomfortable. They avoid discussing it often out of fear of saying the wrong thing.'

'Or as if it might be contagious,' Tor slotted in drily.

'I know… My parents passed within a week of each other and even my friends avoided me at school when I went back,' she told him with a grimace of recollection.

'A car accident?'

'No, they caught legionnaires' disease on a weekend away. They were both diabetic with compromised immune systems and they didn't go for treatment soon enough. They thought they'd caught some harmless virus and none of us knew any different.' Pixie shifted a wordless shoulder in pained acceptance. 'My father went first and Mum a day later. I was devastated. I had no idea how ill they were until it was too late.'

'Is that why you're doing nursing?'

'Partially. I wanted to know more so that I could help people when they needed it and I like doing useful, practical stuff.' Pixie sighed, a rueful smile tugging at her generous mouth. 'And to be frank, I was also the sort of child who bandaged teddy bears and tried to raise orphaned baby birds. My brother calls it a save-the-world mentality.'

'I have a brother too but we're estranged,' Tor heard himself volunteer, and wondered for the first time if that old saying about alcohol loosening the tongue could actually be true because he was gabbling like a chatterbox, which he was not and never had been. He was innately reserved, rather quiet outside working hours. Or was it *her* affecting him? Unthreatening and studiously unsexy as she was in her pale grey pyjamas adorned with little pink flamingos? And no sooner had he thought that than he had to notice the stupendously sexy thrust and sway of a pair of firm full breasts beneath her top as she clambered up on the stool to eat her toastie.

'You're estranged?' Her big blue eyes clouded with sympathy. 'That's sad.'

'No, it's not. He *slept* with my wife!' Tor bit out, shocking himself with that revelation, which had never crossed his lips before, not to anyone, not for any reason, a sordid secret he had planned to keep buried until the day he died.

Pixie's eyes widened in shock. 'Oh, my goodness...' she gasped. 'Your brother did *that*?'

'He and I didn't grow up together. We are not close,' Tor acknowledged grudgingly. 'But I could never forgive him for that betrayal.'

'Of course, you couldn't.'

That first confession having leapt from his tongue, Tor was discovering that for some inexplicable reason he could not hold back the rest. 'On the night my wife died she admitted that she had fallen in love with Sev *before* we married but that she fought her feelings out of loyalty to me and assumed she would get over him.'

'She still shouldn't have married you,' Pixie opined feelingly. 'She should've told you she was having doubts before the wedding.'

'That would certainly have been less devastating than the end result.' His lean, bronzed face could have been sculpted out of granite, his dark-as-night eyes flinty and hard. 'Finding out several years down the road that our whole life together was a fake, a *lie*, was much worse and…and I didn't handle it well,' he completed in a raw undertone.

'I should think you were in shock.' Pixie sighed, retrieving his coffee mug and moving to refill it.

'Still doesn't excuse me.' The eyes she had believed were so dark focused on her absently and she saw the gleams of gold lightening them to bronze. Such beautiful eyes, fringed and enhanced by ridiculously long black lashes. He was shockingly attractive, she thought, struggling to concentrate and avert her attention from the perfect slash of his dark brows, the exotic slant of his high cheekbones and the fullness of his mouth.

'Why? What did you do?' she prompted.

'When I arrived home, she was putting cases into her car. That was when she told me about the affair…at the very last minute. I had no suspicion that there was another man in her life but, after three years of what I had believed was a happy marriage, she was just going to leave me a note.' His nostrils flared with disgust. 'We had a massive argument. It was…chaotic,' he selected roughly. 'I barely knew what I was saying.'

'Shock,' she told him again. 'It intensifies everything you feel but at the same time you're not yourself. You're not in control.'

'I said a great deal I regret… I was cruel,' Tor admitted unevenly, biting back the final shameful admission that Katerina had made, which had torn him apart: her insistence that the daughter he loved was *not* his child but had been fathered by her lover.

'You weren't prepared. You had no time to think.'

Warmed by her compassionate need to console him, he reached for her hand where it rested on the counter and squeezed it gently before withdrawing his touch again. 'You may be able to save the world, but you can't save me from a world of regret. Katerina raced upstairs to lift our daughter out of her cot. My wife was very worked up by that stage and in no condition to drive. I tried to reason with her, but she wouldn't listen to me. Sofia was screaming and upset...'

His voice had become gruff and he lifted his hands to scrub at his face, wiping away the dampness on his cheeks, and her heart went out to him in that moment because she knew that he was recalling the guilt and powerlessness that grief inflicted. 'It was all madness that night, madness and chaos,' he continued. 'Katerina drove off far too fast and the car skidded on the icy drive and careened into a wall.'

'So, you saw it happen.' Pixie was lost for words, full of sympathy for him, able to see that he was still torturing himself for what he had said and done that night in his own shock and distress.

'And it was too late to change anything,' he completed in a curt undertone.

Her eyes connected with his, awash with fellow feeling and understanding. 'You recall every wrong thing you ever did or said to the person. Every emotion is exaggerated. When my mother was passing, I was beating myself up for being cheeky to her when she had told me to clean my room. That's being human.'

Tor sat back tautly. 'I don't know why I've told you all this. I've never talked to anyone about it before.'

'No one?' Pixie pressed in surprise.

'I didn't want to tell anyone the truth about what happened that night. I didn't want anyone judging Katerina or thinking less of her. The truth wouldn't have eased the shock of her death and my daughter's for anyone, least of all her own family. It would only have caused greater distress.'

'But staying silent, forcing yourself to go on living a lie made it harder for *you*,' Pixie slotted in with a frown.

'I've got broad shoulders…and I really don't know what I'm doing here,' Tor confessed, the smouldering, breathtaking appeal of his bemused eyes and drowsy smile washing over her, imbuing her with a sense of connection she had never felt with any man before. 'It must be true that it's easier to talk to a stranger. But I think it's time for me to order that taxi.'

'Possibly,' Pixie muttered self-consciously, scrambling off the stool in haste and beginning to tidy up to keep her hands busy. She stacked the dishwasher, darting round the island at speed to gather up the dishes before opening the tall larder cupboard to stow away the clutter of condiments that had been left sitting out.

'What's the address?' he asked her as he paced several feet away with his phone in his hand, a deprecatory smile of great charm curving his mobile mouth at his having to ask that basic question that divulged the reality that he truly didn't know where he was.

For a split second she couldn't drag her eyes from him, that half-smile somehow enhanced by the black shadow of stubble framing it and defining his strong jawline, his eyes gleaming a glorious tigerish gold. There was a condensed power to him, a leashed energy that sprang out at her.

Pixie had to think for a second before trotting out the address in a rush, stumbling and correcting herself with the number, and she was already scolding herself for her reaction to him. He was a very, *very* good-looking guy and naturally she had noticed, but she had also immediately recognised that he was way, way out of her league. She was ordinary, he was something far superior, not only in the looks department, but also with his instinctive assurance and ingrained courtesy.

'The taxi will be here in five minutes.' Tor dug the phone back into his jeans and walked towards her.

'I'll wait outside. Thanks for feeding me…and for listening,' he murmured ruefully. 'I didn't even ask you for your name.'

She laughed. 'Pixie…'

His brows pleated as he stared at her. *'Pixie?'*

'I was a very small, premature baby. Mum thought it was cute.' Pixie wrinkled her tip-tilted nose, eyes blue as cornflowers gazing up at him.

Marvelling at the truth that she was barely tall enough to reach his chest, for he stood over six feet in height, he extended a lean brown hand. 'I'm Alastor Sarantos but I've always been called Tor.'

'Pleased to meet you.'

As he swung away to leave, he walked head first into the larder cupboard door and reeled back from it, sufficiently stunned by the blow to his temple to grab the edge of the island to steady himself and stay upright. Pixie gasped and rushed over to him.

'No…no, stay still, don't move,' she warned him. 'You hit your head hard.'

His hand lifted to his temple in a clumsy motion and he blinked in bemusement. 'That hurt,' he admitted.

Guilt assailed Pixie as she glimpsed the still-swinging door, which she had neglected to close. It was her fault that he had been injured. 'Can I check your head?' she asked.

'I'm fine,' he told her, even as he swayed, and he frowned at her because, she reckoned, he was having difficulty focusing on her.

'No, you're not. Nobody could be fine after smacking their head that hard,' she declared, running light fingers across his temple, feeling the bump in dismay while being relieved that he hadn't cut himself and there was no blood. 'You're not bleeding but you are going to have a huge bruise. I think you should have it checked out at A & E because you probably have a concussion.'

'I will be absolutely fine.' Tor swore impatiently as he attempted to walk away and staggered slightly.

'You're still very dizzy. Take a moment to get steady. You can lie down in my room until the taxi arrives,' Pixie murmured as she planted a bracing arm to his spine and directed him down the hall to the room next door. He towered over her, his big powerful frame rigid as he attempted to put mind over matter.

'Are you feeling sick?'

'No,' he told her very drily.

No, big masculine men didn't like to be knocked off balance by any form of weakness, she thought, feeling guiltier than ever about his plight and his doubtless aching head as she pushed open the door of her room and guided him over to the bed.

He lowered himself down and kicked off his shoes. Pixie set them side by side neatly on the rug. 'You can nap. You seem to be thinking coherently.'

From his prone position, Tor rested dazed, long-suffering dark golden eyes on her anxious face. 'I don't want to be saved right now. Go save someone else,' he urged.

It was a polite way of telling her that she was being irritating and she gritted her teeth on a sharp comeback.

CHAPTER TWO

'WHY GREEN?' Tor mumbled.

'The hair?' Embarrassed, Pixie touched a hand to her hair and grimaced. 'I wanted to be different.'

'It's different,' Tor confirmed, wondering when he had last seen a woman blush, and it looked like an all-over blush too, a slow tide of colour sweeping up from her throat to her hairline.

Pixie winced. 'There was a guy I was hoping would notice me at work. *And* he did notice,' she admitted with a slight grimace. 'Antony said I reminded him of a leprechaun.'

A spontaneous laugh broke from Tor. 'Not quite the effect you were looking for? I shouldn't tease you. *Diavole*... I am drunk,' he groaned, watching the ceiling revolve for his benefit. 'Where's my taxi got to?'

'It should be here soon,' she said soothingly. 'Just chill.'

'Don't have a lot of practice at just chilling. I'm naturally impatient.'

Pixie sat on her knees by the bed because there was nowhere else to sit in the room. She breathed in deep and slow. She was very tired but she had to stay awake until the taxi arrived and she saw him off. At least he had taken her mind off what had happened during her shift: the pointless death of a young life in a car accident, a young woman on the brink of marriage, deeply mourned by her heartbroken fiancé and her devastated family.

'What's he like? The guy you want to notice you?' Tor prompted without warning, startling her out of her reverie.

'What's it matter? Leprechauns aren't sexy,' she pointed out in a defeatist tone. 'Antony's a paramedic so I don't know much about him, only that he's a lovely guy. For all I know, he could have a girlfriend.'

'I think you look more like a forest fairy than a leprechaun,' Tor remarked, wondering when a woman had last told him that she was attracted to someone else rather than him. He didn't think it had *ever* happened to him. It was a startling, disconcerting novelty. He was used to walking into a bar and every beautiful woman there making a beeline for him. He was young, he was rich, he was single. That was how his world worked and casual sex was always easily available, not something he had to plan.

Before his marriage, though, he hadn't had much experience. He had grown up with Katerina. Their families had been and still were friends. He had known even as a teenager that he would marry Katerina and he had insisted on going ahead and marrying her when he was only twenty. Maybe his parents had been right when they had tried to talk him out of that, tried to tell him that they were too young. He had been ready for that commitment but evidently Katerina hadn't been. Yet he had honestly believed that she loved him the way he loved her.

Forest fairy? That sounded rather more complimentary than a leprechaun, Pixie was reflecting ruefully. OK, she was fishing for hope! What he had already taught her without even trying was that what she had regarded as attraction with Antony was a laughable shadow in comparison to the way in which Tor drew her. Perhaps she had only focused on Antony because there was nobody else around and she had yet to find a boyfriend.

'Maybe that depends on your point of view. If I still look

like I belong in a kid's storybook, it's not exactly seductive,' Pixie muttered. 'But you've definitely got the gift of the gab.'

'Gift of the gab? What's that?' he questioned.

'A ready tongue. You know the right thing to say. If you were interested in a woman, you would know better than to compare her to a leprechaun,' she guessed.

'That's true,' Tor acknowledged without hesitation.

Pixie studied him, liking his honesty in admitting that, where women were involved, he was as smooth and cutting edge as glass, instinctively knowing the right words to impress and please. That fitted. No guy as downright gorgeous as he was could be an innocent or clumsy with his words. He had already been married, which made her respect and trust him more because he had committed to *one* woman young when he must have had so many other options.

In his marriage, however, he had been badly burned, she reflected with fierce compassion, because the woman he had married had betrayed his trust and *hurt* him. And that was what he was *truly* struggling with, she decided thoughtfully. He wasn't only striving to handle the pain of loss, but he was also dealing with the pain of being betrayed by someone whom he had loved and trusted.

She went out to the front door to check for any sign of the taxi, but the street was quiet. She padded back into her room, colliding with watchful dark eyes shot through with accents of gold. He really did have the most beautiful eyes and the thickest, longest, blackest lashes and any woman would have noticed those attractions, she reasoned uncomfortably. The guy had dynamite sex appeal. 'Why were you on your own tonight?' she asked him curiously as she leant over him.

'I go out every year on this date and remember Katerina's and Sofia's deaths,' he confided, dismaying her.

'If you have to drink to handle those memories, it's a destructive habit,' Pixie told him gently. 'It would be wiser to talk about them and leave the booze out of it.'

Tor pushed himself up on his elbows. 'And what would you know about it?'

'I lost my parents six years ago,' she reminded him. 'I used my nursing course to work through those feelings of loss by helping other people. I have to deal with bereaved people at work on a regular basis. Sometimes their unhappiness makes me feel anxious and sad. Let me look at your head.'

She had the brightest blue eyes and a full soft pink mouth. Arousal slithered through Tor and he struggled to master it and concentrate on the conversation as he lowered his head. 'And how do you handle it?'

'I have a box with a lid at the back of my mind. At work I cram anything that makes me uncomfortable in there and then close the lid down tight. I don't allow myself to think about any of it until the end of my shift.'

He shivered as gentle fingertips brushed his brow and delicately traced the bump. He was already imagining those soft fingers smoothing over a far more sensitive part of his body and he castigated himself for his arousal because she had been kind to him and she was too young for him, possibly not that experienced either. She didn't deserve for him to take advantage of her sympathetic nature.

'All that restraint sounds rather too taxing for me.' Tor tilted his head back again to look up at her.

And her heartbeat pounded like a crazed drum as their eyes met again, a wild fluttering breaking free in her tummy even as an almost painful ache thrummed between her thighs. It was lust, instant and raw and nothing at all like the simple sexual curiosity Antony had stirred in her. A man had never made her feel anything that powerful before and that shocking intensity stopped her dead in her tracks. Long brown fingers reached up to lace with care into her curls, tugging her head down to his.

'I want to kiss you,' Tor murmured almost fiercely.

'Do it,' she heard herself urge without hesitation, so greedy was she for more of the new sensations he had awakened.

And his mouth tasted hers, gently parting and seeking, startling her with that sensual testing appeal and warm invitation. His mouth sent a curling flame of liquid heat to the heart of her, which made her lean down, instinctively seeking more of the same. Long, lazy arms extending, he brought her down on top of him and effortlessly turned them both over, flipping her down onto the bed beside him without her registering any sense of alarm.

In fact, as he slid partially over her, the weight of one masculine leg parting hers, a naked thrill of excitement raced through Pixie and her entire body tingled as the tip of his tongue skidded over the roof of her mouth. Nothing had ever felt so good or so necessary as the hot urgency of his mouth on hers. She was no innocent when it came to kissing but never before had she enjoyed kisses that set her on fire. Beneath her top she was ridiculously conscious of the heavy swell of her breasts and the prickling tightening of her nipples while in her pelvis a combustible mix of heat and craving seethed.

He eased a hand below her top and cupped her breast, his thumb rubbing an urgently tender nipple, and her back arched and her hips bucked, and a breathless moan was torn from her lips without her volition. He thrust the top out of his path and locked his mouth to the straining, tightly beaded tip of her nipple and her whole body rose against his on the surge of tormenting sensation that darted straight to the hollow between her legs.

'I love your body,' he husked. 'It's so sexy.'

And her lashes almost fluttered open on surprised eyes because she had never been told she was sexy before. No, she was always the girl the stray men locked on to and shared their life stories with. They told her about their past break-ups and what sort of girl they were hoping to meet. It was never ever a short curvy blonde who liked to listen and didn't like exercise much. No, it was always someone tall, slim and into the gym. She had more gay friends than heterosexual ones, friends who told her she needed to be more confident, outgoing and chatty if she wanted men to notice her. That instant of clear thought and surprise faded as Tor divided his attentions between her breasts with a single-minded intensity that destroyed any control she had over her sensation-starved body.

Tor was making her feel sexy. He was making her feel good about herself and her body and the burning, yearning ache at her feminine core, making her hips writhe, cutting through every other consideration she might have had. He touched her *there*, where she needed that touch most, tracing her slick folds with skilled fingertips, toying with her to make her gasp and then circling her unbearably sensitive core until she didn't know what she was doing any more, only knew that her body felt like one giant yawning scream in desperate need of release. She was shifting, moving, out of control, feverish with a need she had never felt so strongly before.

'Want me?' he groaned as he skimmed off her pyjama bottoms.

'*Yes!*' she exclaimed, longing for that gnawing hunger to be satisfied.

'*Thee mou*... I've never wanted anything the way I want you right now!' Tor growled, shifting over her, rearranging her willing body to push her legs up and back and higher.

And then he was surging into her, partially sating that desire for more with a compelling rush of new sensations. There was the burn as he stretched her tight channel and then a sudden sharp sting of pain as he plunged deeper. It made her grit her teeth but before she could linger on that development a whole host of new reactions was washing her memory of it away.

'So tight, so *good*, you feel amazing, *moraki mou*,' he framed raggedly, dark eyes sheer smouldering golden enticement as he looked down at her, shifting his lithe hips to send another cascade of sensual response travelling through her pliant body that made her breath catch on a gasp of wonder.

What had momentarily felt new and disconcertingly intense now felt absolutely right. Deep down inside, her body was tightening and tightening while his every passionate stroke inside her sent a sweet tide of rapturous sensation rippling through her. His urgency increased her breathless excitement. She thought her heart was about to burst from her chest. Only quick, shallow breaths came to her lungs and her body was rising up to his until finally the unbearable tension gripping her broke and she convulsed, her body clenching tight on his as an exquisite surge of release sent her over the edge and engulfed her in ecstasy.

In the wake of that shattering conclusion, Pixie stirred, shifting out awkwardly from beneath Tor's weight. 'Tor?' she whispered. *'Tor?'*

She scrambled out of bed, worriedly scanning him. Breathing normally, he was fast asleep. Her fingers grazed his brow, but his temperature was already cooling from his exertions on her behalf. Her face flamed hotter than hellfire.

Pixie was in shock as she eased back into her pyjama shorts with a wince because a part of her that she didn't want to think about just then was sore. Tor had kept on warning her that he was very drunk, but she hadn't really believed him. Some people retained better control under the influence of alcohol, and he was clearly one of those individuals, capable of having a normal conversation and putting up a front. His conduct, however, was more revealing, she conceded uneasily. Intoxicated people were less inhibited, more liable to succumb to impulsive, uncharacteristic behaviour.

And having sex with her could only have been a random impulse and something he wouldn't have done under any other circumstances. She could feel the blood draining from her shaken face as she made that deduction.

Saffron had brought him home for sex and he had said no. While respectfully engaged in remembering the death of his loved ones, Tor had not wanted a one-night stand with anyone. Pixie completely understood that, so she could not explain how she had lost control of the situation to the extent of actually having sex with Tor. How had that happened? How had she contrived to take advantage of a guy who was drunk and probably concussed and confused into the bargain?

She hurried into the compact en suite bathroom and went for a quick shower, registering in consternation as she undressed that neither one of them had thought to use contraception. She lifted chilled hands to her distraught face because she wasn't on the birth-control pill or the shot or anything, having deemed such advance precautions unnecessary when she had yet to have even a relationship with a man and had never felt any urge to try more casual encounters.

Of course, she could ask for the morning-after pill, she reminded herself, and tensed at the prospect of having to make that decision. Why was that the exact moment when she had to recall her late mother tugging her curls and saying, 'You were my little surprise baby!' Although she hadn't been planned by her parents, both of whom had been in their forties when she was unexpectedly conceived, she had been welcomed into the world and loved all the same. How could she do any less for any child she conceived?

Well, she *was* being a little theatrical in imagining such a challenging scenario in the immediate aftermath of her *first* sexual encounter, she told herself in exasperation.

But in truth, she was in shock at what she had done. She wasn't an impulsive person and yet from that first scorching kiss she had succumbed to Tor and had encouraged his every move. She hadn't made the smallest attempt to call a halt, she reminded herself crushingly. Her body and the fiery seduction of her own eager responses had enthralled her. All these years, it seemed, she had totally underestimated the fact that sexual arousal genuinely could lead to seriously bad choices.

Tor was gorgeous and he had got her all excited and everything that had happened from that point had been *her* fault. He had told her that he was drunk, and she had seen for herself that he was probably concussed. She had chosen to have sex with a drunk, grieving man and could only thank herself for the powerful sense of humiliation and shame that she was now enduring. *She* had taken advantage of *him*.

Pixie moved back into the bedroom, where Tor still slept. In only a couple of hours she had to get up again and go to work. She got back on the bed and clung to her side of it, eyes so heavy they ached. She felt sad, ashamed that she had been so foolish as to get carried away like a wayward teenager with the excitement of sex. She knew better, she knew the risks to her health and happiness and knew she would be visiting a clinic as soon as possible to be checked and go on some form of birth control. Although the guilt currently assailing her warned that she was highly unlikely to make such a mistake twice.

His phone was buzzing in his pocket and she drew it out with careful fingers and gently switched it off before replacing it. She was in no mood to be confronted by an angry, confused man because she couldn't explain what had happened between them either.

Dawn was lightening the skies when she rose again and quietly dressed for her shift. Tor was still heavily asleep, and she decided to leave him to let himself out. That approach would neatly sidestep any embarrassing conversations or partings. She never ever wanted to lay eyes on the guy again!

CHAPTER THREE

TEARS WERE BURNING the backs of Pixie's eyes as she sat stiffly in the waiting area of the opulent office building. The receptionist was exasperated with her for refusing to take a polite hint and leave: Tor Sarantos was not available for an appointment or even a phone conversation with anyone whose name wasn't on the 'approved' list.

So, how was she supposed to tell the man that he had got her pregnant? Putting such a confidential disclosure in a letter struck her as foolish and careless. It would be read by office staff and likely discarded as the ravings of some desperate wannabe striving to importune the boss. And if it *was* given to him, he would be embarrassed that employees had been made aware of information that he would probably prefer stayed private.

Yes, Tor Sarantos, banker extraordinaire, had certainly been hiding his light under a bushel, a virtual forest of bushels, according to everything that Pixie had learned about him on the internet and in the media in the months since their meeting. He was an incredibly rich and important banker and as far removed from her ordinary world as a gold nugget would be in a wastepaper bin. Only the craziest accident of fate could have ever let them meet in the first place, never mind conceive a child together.

It had taken Pixie quite a few months to decide that she *had* to tell Tor that she was pregnant. It was his right to know that he was going to be a father again. She would never forget the devastation she had seen in his haunted eyes when he told her about his wife and daughter dying. He had loved and cared for his daughter and it was that fact more than any other that had forced Pixie to listen to her conscience and seek him out.

He might not want any sort of relationship with her, but he might well want a relationship with their child, and she could not bring herself to deny either him or their unborn child that opportunity.

She was almost six months pregnant now. And, so far, pregnancy was proving to be a long, exhausting haul. She had finished her nursing training before she even allowed herself to acknowledge her symptoms and do a pregnancy test. She had wasted weeks running away from a looming truth that frightened her, she acknowledged shamefacedly, afraid to face the trial of being pregnant, alone and unsupported.

Her brother had been incredulous. 'You're a nurse!' he had exclaimed when she had told him. 'How could someone with your training fall pregnant? Why weren't you on birth control? And why haven't you gone for a termination yet?'

Yes, there had been loads of awkward, painful conversations between her sibling and her, conversations mostly bereft of Eloise's more sympathetic input because her brother and his partner had split up and Eloise had moved out. Sadly too, although Pixie still saw Eloise as a friend away from the house, Eloise's departure had worsened their financial situation and made meeting the mortgage payments an even bigger challenge.

Thankfully, however, Pixie was now able to work and contribute to the household bills, but the larger she got, the harder she was finding it to work a twelve-hour shift. Her exhaustion had been another factor that had persuaded her that she needed help and that she had to approach Tor for it even if it was the very last thing she wanted to do.

After all, it wasn't as though she had even been a one-night stand who had fallen inconveniently pregnant. Tor hadn't sought her out, hadn't personally selected her from any crowd of available women, he had simply kissed her and ended up having sex with her because he had fallen asleep in the wrong kitchen. Proximity had been their downfall and every step of the way she had encouraged him with her willingness. She should have said no, she should have called a halt but, controlled by that crazy excitement, she had been greedy, immature and selfish.

Pixie was still convinced that Tor would not have chosen to have sex with her had he been in full control of himself. But alcohol, grief and a nasty blow to the head had made him vulnerable and she, who should have known better, had urged him on.

Even worse, she didn't want to be another problem in his life. She didn't want to upset him. But once she'd realised that false pride was keeping her from reaching out for the assistance she needed, she had finally seen common sense. Unhappily, getting a personal meeting with Tor was probably as easy as getting to have tea with the Queen.

'Miss Miller, I've called Security to show you the way out,' the receptionist informed her with a fixed, unnatural smile. 'There's no point in you sitting here waiting when Mr Sarantos is unavailable.'

And that was when Pixie appreciated that by following the rules she had got as close to Tor as she was ever likely to get. As soon as the receptionist returned to her desk, Pixie rose and began walking down the wide corridor that led to the imposing double doors, behind which she had estimated lay Tor's office.

A shout hastened her steps. 'Hey! You can't go in there! Security... *Security!*' The receptionist was screeching at the top of her voice.

Pixie thrust down the door handle and stalked right in. Tor swung round with a phone gripped in one hand. Impossibly elegant and tall, he wore a dark pinstriped suit teamed with a white shirt and a snazzy red tie. He looked indescribably sophisticated and intimidating, not remotely like the man who had sat at the kitchen island and eaten a cheese toasted sandwich with every evidence of normal enjoyment.

'What is the meaning of this interruption?' Tor demanded imperiously, studying her with frowning intensity.

And Pixie held her breath and waited…and waited…for recognition to colour that cool, distant stare. It didn't happen, and that absence of recognition flustered her even more.

'Don't you remember me, Tor?' she murmured almost pleadingly, cringing inwardly from that note in her own voice.

'I don't know who you are. How could I remember you?' he enquired cuttingly, his attention lowering to the prominent swell of her abdomen, his wide sensual mouth tightening when he registered that she was pregnant.

'That night you were with me last year,' she whispered uncertainly, tears involuntarily stinging her eyes at having to voice that lowering reminder. 'I came to tell you that I'm pregnant.'

Derision hardened his lean, darkly handsome features. 'I've never seen you before and if you want to make fanciful allegations of that nature, I suggest you approach my lawyers in the usual fashion.'

'Sorry about this, sir. She wouldn't listen to reason!' the receptionist snapped, a hand closing over Pixie's forearm to prevent her from moving deeper into the office. 'Security are on their way.'

Pixie had never felt so humiliated in her life.

I don't know who you are… I've never seen you before.

Perhaps it had been naïve of her not to expect that sort of rejection. Perhaps it had been ridiculously optimistic, even vain, for her to expect Tor Sarantos to remember her after a casual sexual encounter. To be strictly fair though, she supposed her appearance had changed since her green hair had faded and eventually washed out entirely.

Even so, she just hadn't been prepared for him to look through her as if she didn't exist, and then perceptibly wince when the tears her pregnancy hormones couldn't hold back flooded down her cheeks and a noisy sob was wrenched from her.

An older man began easing her back out of the office again and by then she was crying so hard, she could hardly see to walk. And what a terrible irony it was for her to hear Tor intervene loudly with the words, 'Be careful with her...she's pregnant!' As if he were the only person who might have noticed the vast swell of her once-flat stomach.

'Well?' Jordan had demanded expectantly, when he'd come home from his barista job that evening. 'What did he say?'

And for the first time she had told her brother a little more of the truth of how very fleeting her intimacy with Tor had been. Jordan had simply shrugged and said that such facts were irrelevant and that the father of her child still had obligations to meet.

'Not until the baby is born,' Pixie had protested, cutting through Jordan's insistence that she needed a solicitor to fight for her rights.

Jordan generally got aggressive and argumentative in difficult situations but that wasn't Pixie's way. It took her weeks to get over that distressing encounter in Tor's office, when he had denied all knowledge of her. She had wondered if Tor was telling the truth, or if indeed he remembered her perfectly well but just didn't want to be bothered or embarrassed or reminded of what had happened between them that night. And that wounding suspicion had cut her to the quick.

Admittedly, she wasn't a beauty like the women she had seen him with in the media. She wasn't a socialite, a model or an actress who swanned around in designer clothing and posed for photos. She was a very ordinary young woman. A handful of small, unexpected events and coincidences had put her on intimate terms with Tor and resulted in her ending up in bed with him.

He had been special to her, but she hadn't been special to him. They had both walked away afterwards, both of them probably feeling the same: that it shouldn't have happened. So, it didn't really matter whether Tor genuinely didn't remember her, she told herself, or whether he was simply *pretending* not to remember her. At the end of it, his distaste and derision that day in his office stayed with her and understandably coloured her attitude to him. After that experience, she was pretty convinced that even though she was pregnant by him, Tor would prefer *not* to know, and her conscience quietened. She decided that she didn't need his help and that she didn't want his financial assistance either, no matter what arguments her aggrieved brother put up!

Present day

Pixie wakened and revelled in the quietness of the house, smothering a yawn as she sat up and wondered if Jordan had taken Alfie out to the park.

She smiled as she thought of her son. He was nine months old, big and strong for his age, hitting every developmental target ahead of time and already trying to walk.

Coco slunk up the stairs to greet her with delighted purrs and she petted the cat with a warm smile. Steph had begun leaving Coco with Pixie whenever she went abroad, and weeks would pass before she finally reappeared to collect the little animal again. In the end, she had asked if Pixie would like to keep the Siamese because she was finding pet ownership too much of a tie.

Pixie crossed the landing to the bathroom and went for a quick shower before dressing. Everything she did was done by rote because she had been working night shifts since Alfie was born. In the morning she came home, fed and dressed her son and then went immediately to bed while Jordan took charge of Alfie for a few hours.

Working nights as a nurse, combined with Jordan's freedom to choose his shifts as a barista, meant that she didn't have to pay for childcare. Considering the amount of debt that her brother seemed to have acquired since he had lost his insurance job, that was fortunate. Clad in cropped jeans and a long-sleeved cotton top in raspberry pink and white stripes, she descended the creaking narrow staircase.

The terraced house was small, but she had managed to squeeze a cot into her bedroom and there was a little backyard she was currently cleaning up to serve as a play area for Alfie once he became more mobile. She was taken aback to find her brother sitting at the tiny breakfast bar with a beer.

'Where's Alfie?' she asked. 'And why are you drinking at this time of day?'

Jordan shot her a defiant look. 'I've sorted things out for you,' he said, compressing his lips.

As she took after her mother in looks, Jordan took after their father. He was tall with dark hair and a beard and spectacles, which gave him a slightly nerdy look.

'What things?' she questioned with a frown as she glanced into the cramped lounge, expecting to see her son playing on the floor with his toys. The room, however, was empty and the toy box sat untouched by the wall.

'Your situation, the mess you made having that child… against *all* my advice!' her brother complained loudly.

'Jordan…where's Alfie?' Pixie exclaimed, cutting across his words.

And then he told her, and she couldn't believe her ears, was already snatching up her coat and her bag in sheer panic at the danger he had put her son in. 'Were you out of your mind?' she demanded in disbelief.

'Alfie's his kid. *He* should be looking after him and taking care of all his needs!' Jordan countered heatedly.

'You abandoned my son in the street, where anything could have happened to him?' Pixie yelled at him full blast.

'No, I stood out of sight and watched to see that he was taken into the house before I walked away. I'm not an idiot and he *is* my nephew. He may be a nuisance, but I do care about the little tyke!'

'What house?' she demanded in sudden sincere bewilderment.

There was another wildly frustrating hiatus while Jordan explained how he had paid some man he met in a pub to find out Tor's London address. By the time she'd dug that information out of her sibling she'd already ordered a taxi—because no way, no how, when her baby boy was in danger, was she heading out on a bus or a train to reclaim him!

Jordan pursued her right out onto the street, heatedly arguing his point of view, which was that her attitude towards caring for Alfie had been wrong from the start.

'You could've made a killing out of having that child and now you *will*,' Jordan declared, striking horror into her bones. 'And it'll be all thanks to me for looking out for your interests.'

'Not everything is about money, Jordan,' Pixie breathed in disgust. 'And I did *not* have Alfie to feather anyone's nest!'

She slumped in the taxi, sick to her stomach. When had money come to mean more to Jordan than his own flesh and blood? Had she always been blind to that side of her brother? How had she contrived to ignore the fact that Jordan had only begun supporting her desire to have her baby *after* he had grasped that Alfie's father was a very rich man? Even back then, had Jordan been viewing her little boy as a potential source of profit? As the ticket towards an easier life? Her stomach shifted queasily. And what on earth was her brother expecting to happen now that he had confronted Tor Sarantos with the child he didn't want to know about?

Was Jordan hoping that Tor would pay handsomely for her and Alfie to go away and not bother him again? What other scenario could he be picturing? And how could she continue living with and entrusting Alfie's care to a man who could behave as he had done and put an innocent child at risk?

Still in a panic, Pixie leapt out of the taxi and rushed up the steps of the imposing town house. It was a three-storey Georgian building in a grand city square with a private park in the centre. She rang the bell and thumped the door knocker as well, so desperate was she to reach her son.

An older woman with an expressionless face answered the door.

'My son was left here…accidentally,' Pixie said with a shaky smile. 'I'm here to collect him.'

In silence the door widened, allowing her to step into a cool, elegant hall. A fleeting glance was all it took for Pixie to feel shabby, poor and out of her comfort zone as she stood there clad in her cheap raincoat and scuffed trainers. The aromatic scent of beeswax polish lingered in the air, perfectly matching the gracious interior of polished antiques and a truly splendid classical marble sculpture that looked as though it should be in a museum.

'I will ask if Mr Sarantos is free to see you,' the woman said loftily.

As Pixie hovered, she saw two men in suits standing almost out of sight down a short side corridor, both men avidly studying her, and she flushed and turned her head away, relieved when the older woman reappeared and asked her to follow her.

A clammy feeling of disquiet engulfed Pixie's body, quickening both her heartbeat and her breathing as she contemplated the unpleasant prospect of meeting Tor Sarantos again. A man who had utterly rejected her during her pregnancy, who insisted he didn't recall ever even meeting her before? Of course, she didn't want to see him again.

But, sadly for her, Jordan had made it impossible for her to continue sitting on the fence and avoiding the issue of Alfie's existence and his father's responsibility towards him. Now she had to come clean about events eighteen months earlier, regardless of how embarrassing or humiliating that might be. Pixie lifted her chin and reminded herself that all she should still feel guilty about was surrendering to a meaningless sexual encounter while neglecting to protect herself from the risk of a pregnancy.

That horrid little scene in Tor's office had clawed away the finer feelings of guilt that he had once induced in her. Going through a pregnancy and the delivery of her child with only Eloise's occasional support as a friend had made Pixie less self-critical. She had done all right alone; she might not have done brilliantly but there were many who would have coped worse and complained a great deal more. She had nothing to apologise for, she told herself bracingly.

Tor was in a very grim mood. He didn't like mysteries or unexpected developments and the instant the same woman who had forced her way into his office the previous year appeared in his office doorway, a chill of foreboding slid down his rigid spine. Who the hell was she? Stymied by the lack of information about her that day, he had failed to establish her identity after the event and had waited impatiently to see if any claim for child support arrived with his lawyers. When no such claim had arrived, he had written off her visit to a possible mental-health issue. But if she was the child's mother, who was the man surveillance had on tape who had left the child on the doorstep?

'I'm here to pick up my son,' Pixie announced stiffly, her slim shoulders rigid because being even the depth of a room away from Tor Sarantos was too close for comfort. 'I'm sorry you've been dragged into this…er…situation.'

There he stood, tall, poised, predatory dark eyes locked to her like grappling hooks seeking purchase in her tender skin. He was angry, suspicious, everything she didn't want to be forced to deal with but, even with him in that mood, she wasn't impervious to how gorgeous he was, clad in an impossibly elegant dark grey designer suit, sharply tailored to his lean, powerful frame. And while still being that aware of his movie-star-hot looks annoyed her, it also reminded her of how very strange it was that she could ever have conceived a child with a man so far out of her league.

That night they had been together so briefly loomed like a distant and surreal fantasy in the back of her mind and her face heated with mortification because *that* night was the very last thing she wanted to think about in his presence.

'You need to come in, take a seat and explain what you describe as a "situation" to me,' Tor said coolly, watching her like a hawk.

She was incredibly tiny and curvy with a torrent of golden curls that framed her heart-shaped face and enhanced her crystal-blue eyes. Something about her eyes struck him as weirdly familiar; there was something too about that soft, full, pink mouth and the stirring of that vague chord of familiarity spooked Tor as much as a gun held to his head. Because Pixie Miller, whoever she was, was *not* his type. He had always gone for tall brunettes and certainly not a tiny blonde, who from a distance could probably still be mistaken for a child.

'I don't want to talk to you… I just want to collect my son,' Pixie told him truthfully.

'I'm afraid it's not that simple. I need to know what's going on here and then I need to contact social services.'

'Why would you need to contact them?' Pixie gasped in dismay, the colour draining from her face.

'Come in, sit down,' Tor repeated steadily, wondering why she was so skittish and reluctant to speak up when presumably the baby had been dropped as a most effective way of grabbing his attention and forcing such a meeting. 'And then we can talk.'

Pixie clenched her teeth together hard and steeled herself to walk into the book-lined room. He planted a seat down in front of his desk and tapped it.

Pixie slung him a mutinous glance. 'I'm not sitting down while you stand over me,' she warned him. 'Where's my son?'

'In a safe environment being cared for by a nanny. If it makes you feel more secure, I will sit down as well,' Tor breathed impatiently, stepping back behind his desk and dropping down into the leather office chair there.

'You mentioned social services,' Pixie reminded him tautly. *'Why?'*

Tor ignored the question. First, he wanted some facts. 'Who was the man who left the baby outside this house?'

Pixie stiffened. 'My half-brother, Jordan. We had an argument…er…a misunderstanding,' she corrected uncomfortably.

'Why here? Why this house?' Tor pressed.

'Jordan knows you're Alfie's father,' Pixie murmured flatly, focusing on a gold pen lying on the desktop.

'And how could he possibly know that when *I* don't know it?' Tor enquired very drily. 'Am I the victim of some silly story you have told your brother about how you got pregnant?'

Pixie compressed her lips and paled. 'No. I tried to tell you last year at your office, but I bottled out when you didn't even remember me,' she admitted plainly, feeling the shame and sting of that moment warming her cheeks afresh. 'That was a bit too much of a challenge for me.'

His sleek ebony brows had drawn together as he studied her, dark eyes flaming like melted caramel below his outrageous lashes, those beautiful eyes that she had been seduced by that unforgettable night. 'Let's get this straight.' In shock at her simple explanation, Tor regressed a step. 'You are saying that that baby is *mine*?'

'Yes,' Pixie said simply.

'I am finding that hard to credit when I don't remember you. Yes, there is a certain familiarity about your eyes, possibly your face, but that's *all*.'

'So sorry I wasn't a more memorable event,' Pixie countered thinly. 'But facts are facts. You were with me and you got me pregnant.'

'I never have sex without contraception.'

Pixie flung her head back, anger in her gaze. 'Well, you did with me and Alfie is the result. Maybe it was wrong of me not to see a solicitor while I was still pregnant and make some sort of formal approach to you but it's bad enough having to tell you about it, never mind some total stranger! But there it is, that night happened even though we both regret it.'

Tor sprang upright, outraged by the words spilling from her lips. He didn't sleep around indiscriminately, and he was always careful and responsible when sex was involved. 'I still find this story almost impossible to credit and think it may be wiser for us to proceed through legal channels...'

'Oh, for goodness' sake,' Pixie groaned, tipping her head forward and then pushing her hands through her tumbled curls to push the strands off her face again. 'I'm not being fair to you, am I? If you honestly don't remember, it's *because* you were drunk and grieving...although, in my defence, I have to say that I didn't realise how drunk you were until afterwards.'

Tor had frozen in place, a darkening expression of consternation tightening his lean, dark features. 'Drunk? *Grieving?* I rarely drink to excess.'

'It was the anniversary of your wife and child's accident,' Pixie filled in heavily. 'You told me that you went out every year on that date and drank while you remembered them.'

With difficulty, Tor forced himself back down stiffly into his chair. Inside he was reeling with shock, but that she knew that much about him literally confirmed his worst fears and struck him like a hammer blow. How much had he told her? *All* of it or only some of it? He was affronted by his own failure to keep his secrets where they belonged.

'And it's probably very rude to say it...but when you're drunk, you're a much nicer, more approachable guy,' Pixie whispered apologetically. 'If you'd been like you are now, I probably wouldn't have made love with you, which of course would have been wiser for all of us...although I couldn't ever give up Alfie, even to make you feel better.'

'Make *me* feel better?' Tor echoed in disbelief. 'Nothing you have so far told me could make me feel better!'

'Yes, you're one of those glass half-empty rather than half-full types, aren't you?' Pixie sighed. 'Look, now we've got the embarrassing stuff out of the way, can I please see my son?'

'I'm afraid it isn't that straightforward.'

'Why not?' Pixie demanded. 'What's the problem?'

'Where were *you* when your brother took your son and left him in the street?'

'I was in bed.' Pixie flushed beneath his censorious gaze. 'I'm a nurse and I'd just come off night shift. I come home, feed and dress Alfie and then I leave him in Jordan's care while I sleep. I'm usually up by lunchtime. I can get by on very little sleep. And Jordan didn't leave Alfie in the street.'

'He *did*,' Tor interposed flatly.

'Yes, but he hung around somewhere nearby to ensure that Alfie was taken into the house before he left. Look, I *know* that what Jordan did was totally wrong and dangerous and that he shouldn't have done it. I'm still very angry about it too,' Pixie declared tautly. 'But the point is, Jordan has been helping me to look after Alfie and letting us live with him ever since Alfie was born. I owe my brother a lot.'

'I can understand that.'

'No, not really, how could you? You can't understand when you live like *this*…' Pixie shifted an expressive, almost scornful hand that encompassed all the opulent designer touches that distinguished the decor even in a home office setting. 'You and me? We live in very different worlds. In my world it's a struggle to keep a roof over our heads and pay the bills.'

'We will deal with all those problems at a more appropriate time,' Tor cut in. 'Right now I am more concerned about the child's present welfare and security.'

'Alfie's none of your business,' Pixie told him curtly, compressing her lips so hard they went white. 'Do you think I don't appreciate how you feel about this situation? Do you really think I want anything from a man who would prefer that neither I nor my child even exists? '

'This is all getting very emotional and again it is not the

right time for this discussion,' Tor countered grimly. 'If your child is also *my* child, I obviously don't want to involve the social services in this issue. But neither am I prepared to hand over custody of a baby to someone who may not keep him safe from harm.'

'How dare you?' Pixie gasped, leaping up out of her seat in angry disbelief at that condemnation.

'Whether you like it or not, you have given me the right to interfere. Either I'm acting as a concerned citizen or as a possible father to ensure that the baby is protected. You can see your son but I will *not* allow you to remove him from this household or take him anywhere near your brother until I am convinced that that is in *his* best interests,' Tor completed with harsh conviction.

'You can't do that...' Pixie whispered shakily.

'Either you accept my conditions, or I contact the authorities, explain what has happened and allow them to make the decisions. If you choose the second option, be aware that neither of us can control events in that scenario,' Tor warned her.

'You don't even believe that Alfie is yours yet,' she protested tightly. 'Why are you trying to screw up our lives? Alfie's a happy child.'

'I want your permission to carry out DNA testing,' Tor admitted. 'I want irrefutable proof of whether or not he is my child.'

'Of course, you're not going to take my word for it,' Pixie remarked stiffly.

Tor was tempted to say that once, without even asking the question, he had blithely assumed that a child was his and had then learnt, very much to his shock, that it was not an assumption any man could afford to make. Now he took nothing for granted and he checked and double-checked everything and trusting anyone had become a serious challenge.

'Will you agree to the testing?' he prompted.

Pixie nodded jerkily for she could think of no good reason to avoid the process. He had the right to know to his own satisfaction that Alfie was his son and it would be wrong of her to deny him that validation, wouldn't it be? Unhappily, however, events were moving far too fast in a direction she had not foreseen.

She had been foolishly naïve when she'd raced to Tor's home to collect her son, too distraught to appreciate that there would be long-term consequences to such exposure. Tor would not let either of them walk away again until his questions were answered. And evidently, she had misjudged him that day at his office. He *had* forgotten her as entirely as though she had never existed and that was an unwelcome truth that could only hurt.

As she watched, he pulled out a phone, selected a number and began speaking to someone in a foreign language. She wondered if it was Greek while she scanned the eloquent movement of a lean brown hand, fingers spreading and then curling as he talked. For such a tall, well-built guy he was very graceful, but all his movements were tense and controlled, hinting at the darkness of his mood.

The night they had met Tor had been so natural, so relaxed and open with her. Sober, however, he was a very different person with his freezing politeness and disciplined reserve. But she could still read him well enough to recognise that her appearance and that of a potential child in his life were a huge surprise and a disaster on his terms. He didn't *want* Alfie. He might be talking impressively about needing to ensure that Alfie was safe, but he wasn't personally interested in her son, excited at the possibility of being his father, or indeed anything positive that she could see.

'I've organised the DNA testing,' he informed her grimly. 'Now I want you to sit back down and tell me about the night we met.'

'No...' Pixie's refusal leapt straight to her lips.

'But obviously I want to know what happened between us!' Tor slung back at her between gritted teeth.

'Why should you need to know anything when Alfie's the evidence?' Pixie dared, lifting her chin.

'So, you expect me to just live with this blank space in my memory?' Tor breathed with incredulous bite.

'Yes, I'm quite happy to exist in that blank and I don't see any advantage to raking over an encounter that upsets you so much.'

'I'm *not* upset,' Tor responded icily.

'Angry, ashamed, whatever you want to call it. It doesn't matter to me now,' Pixie told him truthfully, wishing he could bring himself to be a little more honest with her. 'All I want now is to see my son.'

Tor released his breath in a soundless hiss of frustration. He wasn't accustomed to dealing with opposition from a woman. Women invariably went out of their way to please and flatter him, keen to attract and retain his interest. But Pixie Miller?

She was more likely to raise her stubborn chin and challenge him with defiant crystal-blue eyes. And he wondered, *of course*, he wondered if it had been that difference in her that had attracted him to her in the first place. Was he attracted to stronger, more independent women? Certainly, he never had been in the past, had always played safe by choosing quiet, discreet lovers who understood that sex with him didn't ever lead to anything deeper.

But that he should have slept with another woman that night of all nights? That shook him, but it also filled him with intense curiosity. He might not know her, but he knew himself. Either Pixie had been extraordinarily seductive, or she was something a great deal more special than she was willing to admit or he was able to remember...

CHAPTER FOUR

'I THINK YOU could at least take your coat off before I take you upstairs to your son,' Tor told Pixie drily. 'You won't be returning home until we sort this out.'

With a stiff little twist of her shoulders, Pixie removed her coat. 'There's nothing to sort and I have to be back at work by seven.'

'Leaving the baby in your brother's tender care? Not on my watch,' Tor spelt out curtly, watching her bend to drape the coat over the chair and reveal an awesomely curvy bottom covered in tight denim. Grabbable, squeezable, touchable, every word that occurred to him startled him because he was no longer a sexually libidinous teenager and he didn't leer at women's bodies like one either, did he? Well, so much for Pixie Miller not being his type, a little devil piped up in the back of his brain, infuriating him even more as a throbbing pulse at his groin stirred.

She was sexy, *very* sexy, that was all it was, and her appeal was all the stronger because she didn't work at it. No, there was nothing remotely inviting or sensual about her presentation of herself, he conceded grudgingly, nothing in her appearance that sought attention. She looked like what she was: a young mother on a restricted income. But that description did not encompass the whole of her or reveal the charm of those tousled golden curls, the clarity of her bright anxious eyes, the soft pink pout of her mouth.

Angrily aware of his burgeoning erection, Tor led the way out of the room and up the sweeping staircase. He hadn't even looked at the child, hadn't gone near it. If he was honest with himself for once, that was because he tended to avoid young children and the memories they roused of Sofia.

Now in many ways, though, he was being confronted by his worst nightmare: another child and a relationship with a woman that could not be denied, the sort of bonds he had been resolutely determined to avoid since the death of his wife and daughter.

Of course, her son could not be his! At the very least it was highly unlikely. Had he even *had* sex with her that night? There was still room for doubt on that score. He had few memories of that anniversary, had already acknowledged that he had behaved irresponsibly by getting dangerously drunk. He had wakened with an aching head in an unfamiliar bedroom, but he had *still* been fully clothed. That he could have had sex with anyone had not once occurred to him, only that he shouldn't have been reckless enough to get that intoxicated. As he had left that strange house in haste, someone had been coming downstairs behind him and he hadn't even turned his head because all he had wanted to do was get home. He had known even at that point that he would not be drowning himself in alcohol for that anniversary ever again. It had been a foolish, juvenile habit he had naturally decided not to repeat.

'They're in here…' Tor thrust open the door.

Pixie surged over the threshold. Standing up, Alfie was holding on to the side of a travel cot and bouncing with his usual irrepressible energy. He was the strangest mix of his parental genes, she thought fondly, because he had inherited her golden curls with his father's dark eyes and olive skin tone.

'Mm…mm…mm!' Alfie burbled excitedly, his sturdy little arms lifting as soon as he saw his mother.

'I think he's trying to say Mum,' the smiling young woman

hovering said. 'Hello, I'm Emma and I've been looking after your...son?'

Alfie clawed up the front of Pixie's body in his desperation to reach her and held on as tight as a clam with his whole body wrapped round her, burying his little face fearfully in her shoulder, still muttering, 'Mm...mm.'

It was the moment when Pixie would have happily killed her brother for having subjected her child to such a frightening experience. Alfie wasn't normally clingy, and she had never seen him frightened before because he was one of those unnerving kids who jumped unafraid into unfamiliar situations and left her with her heart in her mouth.

'Alfie,' Pixie sighed, hugging him close. 'Hello, Emma. I'm Pixie and, yes, I'm his mum and this little boy got lost this morning and I was frantic!' She punctuated those remarks by tickling Alfie under the ribs in an effort to break him free of his anxiety and it worked. Alfie went off into paroxysms of giggles and leant back, the weight of him forcing Pixie to kneel down and brace him on the floor before he toppled both of them.

'He's a real little charmer,' Emma commented. 'How old is he?'

'Nine months.'

'And already getting ready to walk. My goodness, that'll be a challenge for you,' Emma chattered. 'The younger they are, the less sense they have.'

Tor had frozen where he stood as Alfie flung his head back, laughing, and his dancing dark eyes and slanting mischievous grin reminded Tor powerfully of his youngest brother, Kristo, who was only seventeen. Unnerved by that instantaneous sense of familial recognition, he looked hastily away, reminding himself that the child was very unlikely to be related to him. But if he *was*?

A faint shudder raked through Tor's tall, powerful frame because *that* would be a game-changer, the ultimate game-changer, forcing him to embrace everything he had turned his back on. Choice would have nothing to do with it.

'This is Alfie,' Pixie said simply as she looked up at Tor, so impossibly tall from that angle as she knelt. He looked pale, or as pale as someone as sun bronzed as he was could look, she adjusted uncomfortably.

Alfie settled back on the floor to explore a plastic truck with his fingers and his mouth, his attention unnervingly locked to Tor as if he was sizing him up. Tor wanted to back away. Countless memories of Sofia at the same age were engulfing him but he fought them off and got down on his knees, careless of his suit and his dignity.

'Shall I leave now, Mr Sarantos?' the nanny enquired.

'No, we still need you, but you can take a break while Alfie has his mother here,' Tor murmured, quite proud of the steadiness of his voice as Emma nodded and left the room.

Alfie settled the truck down on Tor's thigh and sat back expectantly, big chocolate-coloured eyes unerringly pinned to Tor, almost as though he could sense his discomfiture.

'Let me,' Pixie began to intervene awkwardly.

'No, I've got this.' Alfie chuckled as Tor ran the truck along the floor with the appropriate *vroom-vroom* noises even though his eyes stung like mad as he did it and he cursed himself for being a sentimental fool.

Alfie grinned and patted Tor's thigh to indicate that he wanted his truck back now that its magic had been demonstrated to his satisfaction. Tor handed it back and hastily backed away, vaulting back upright again.

'I'm sorry… I'm out of practice. I've avoided young children since, well, since Sofia's death,' he admitted grittily, determined to be frank because he had evidently been more than frank with this young woman when they first met and for once there was no reason for him to put up a front.

Pixie almost winced because that likelihood hadn't occurred to her, and she scolded herself for not appreciating that Alfie would resurrect memories that Tor probably preferred to bury. Even so, on another level and one she didn't want to examine, his sensitivity saddened her because Alfie was his child too. Of course, he wouldn't accept that until he had the official proof of it.

With a knock on the door the woman who appeared to be the housekeeper appeared and announced that Tor had a visitor downstairs.

'I'll send him up when he's done with me. It'll be the DNA testing I requested.'

'My goodness, how did you get it organised this quickly?' Pixie exclaimed in surprise.

'To put it simply…money talks,' Tor replied drily. 'But I'm afraid we'll still have to wait twenty-four hours for the results.'

'Well, I'm not going to be in suspense,' Pixie pointed out.

'You haven't the slightest doubt?'

Pixie reddened and then lifted her head high, her crystal-blue eyes awash with censure.

'No. You were my first and only, so there isn't the smallest chance that anyone else could have fathered Alfie.'

His lean, darkly handsome features tightened as though she had struck him, and she might as well have done, Tor acknowledged. He paused at the door and glanced back at her. 'How old are you?'

'Twenty-two,' Pixie answered. 'You asked me the same question the night we met. It's infuriating. It's because I'm small and people always assume I'm younger than I am.'

Tor went downstairs to have the swab done for the DNA testing with an inescapable sense of guilt. If that little boy was his child, he had hit on a twenty-one-year-old virgin, left her to struggle through her pregnancy alone, denied all knowledge of her when she'd approached him for support and generally treated her in the most unforgivable manner. The idea that he could have behaved like that shattered him and left him reeling with shock because the whole nightmare situation was making him appreciate that he hadn't been living in the *real* world for over six years.

He had been living in the past, seeing the world and the people around him through toxic lenses, believing that he was standing tall and strong in the face of adversity when in fact he was continually backing away from the wounding truth that his wife and his half-brother had betrayed him. He hadn't come to terms with it, hadn't dealt with it, hadn't put it behind him the way he should have done.

And in reacting in that inflexible way, it seemed he might have caused one hell of a lot of damage to an innocent bystander. He breathed in deep and slow as he made those deductions and hoped that the child turned out not to be his, because at that moment the alternative was just too much for him to contemplate.

The DNA test was carried out in minutes and Pixie was left alone with her son. After some energetic play, Alfie went down in the travel cot for a nap. She had put her phone on mute because Jordan had called her repeatedly and she wasn't in the mood to talk to him and didn't know what she would say when she did. He had destroyed her trust in him but to a certain extent she understood his frustration with her.

She had leant on her brother when she should've been seeking the support of Alfie's father because her pride had got in the way and that stubborn pride of hers hadn't done her any favours.

For months, Jordan had been forced to stay home most evenings while she was at work, a considerable sacrifice for a young, single man. Worse still, he was unable to look for other employment because only casual barista work allowed him to choose his hours and mind Alfie for his sister. Her decision to go ahead and have her child had adversely affected Jordan's life. It was pointless to say that she had never meant to do that when she had still gone ahead and done what *she* wanted to do, which was to give birth to a child without a partner and depend on her brother's help.

If she could have gone back and changed things she knew

she would have done it all differently, she conceded heavily. She had taxed her brother's patience for too long, forcing him to act in an effort to make her confront Tor. Yes, dumping Alfie on Tor's doorstep had been absolutely the wrong way to go about achieving that, but had she gone to a solicitor to claim child support from Tor, Jordan might have been released from the responsibility of having to help her look after her child months ago.

'Mr Sarantos would like you to come downstairs for a meal,' Emma told her, sliding into the room on quiet feet. 'I'll keep an eye on Alfie.'

Pixie checked the time and suppressed a sigh. Soon she would need to get home to get ready for work. As she came down into the hall the housekeeper was waiting to show her into a formal dining room, where a polished table set with silver cutlery and crystal wine glasses awaited her. Tor strolled forward, all lithe contained power, vibrant energy radiating from his dark golden eyes.

'I assumed you'd be hungry.'

'I've haven't got much time before we have to leave,' Pixie responded uncomfortably.

'I still want to know what happened that night between us,' Tor admitted, disconcerting her.

'But it's not important now,' Pixie reasoned stiffly.

'If you're telling me the truth and that night led to the conception of my son, it's *very* important,' Tor contradicted as a man in a short white jacket entered and proceeded to pour the wine, mercifully silencing him on that subject.

'Not for me, thank you,' Pixie said, refusing the wine while watching the man leave again with wide eyes. 'You are surrounded by staff here.'

'I have to concentrate on work. Domestic staff take the irritating small stuff out of my day. How do you feel about leaving Alfie here in Emma's care tonight?'

Pixie paled. 'I'd prefer to take him home.'

'Which would mean your brother taking charge of him again. Give your brother a night off,' Tor urged.

Her slight shoulders stiffened. She had to talk to Jordan before she could feel that she could trust him again with her child. 'If I didn't have to go to work, I wouldn't agree,' she muttered ruefully. 'But just one night, and I'll have to go home and get Alfie's things before.'

'Anything the baby needs can be bought.'

'Bunny, his toy rabbit, can't be, and he won't go down for the night without it. Babies like familiar things around them. It makes them feel secure.' Pixie sighed. 'I also need to feed my cat and if Alfie stays, when am I supposed to get him back tomorrow?'

'I'm expecting you to return here in the morning and stay. A room beside his will be prepared for your use. It would also mean that you'll be here when the DNA results become available.'

He already had her movements and Alfie's all worked out on his schedule, but letting him interfere in their lives to that extent disturbed Pixie. On the other hand, Tor contacting the authorities to share his concern about Alfie's safety in her brother's custody would cause a firestorm, which would be a great deal worse, she conceded wryly. In truth, with that 'concerned citizen' threat of his, Tor Sarantos had trapped her between a rock and a hard place and deprived her of choice.

'That night…' Tor said again, shimmering dark golden eyes locking to her and making it hard for her to find her voice.

And Pixie gave way but stuck to the bare bones, telling him about their meeting in the kitchen, the cheese toasted sandwich she had given him and the accidental collision he had had with the cupboard door. While she talked, a deliciously cooked meal was served, and she began to eat.

'Yes… I had a bruise above my eye,' Tor commented with a frown. 'I wondered if I'd fallen or got into some sort of altercation.'

'The taxi didn't arrive and that was my fault too,' Pixie explained in a rush. 'I was only staying there for two weeks and when you asked me for the house number I got it wrong. I only realised that a couple of days afterwards.'

'These are dry facts,' Tor remarked, cradling his wine glass elegantly in one lean brown hand as he lounged back in his chair like a king surveying a recalcitrant subject. 'You've stripped everything personal out of this account. Nothing you have yet shared explains how we ended up in bed together.'

'I should think your imagination could fill in that particular blank,' Pixie dared.

'Surprisingly not. That particular night I wouldn't have been looking for sex with anyone,' Tor asserted coolly. 'It was out of character.'

'Blame the alcohol.'

'And as you were a virgin, presumably it was out of character for you as well.'

Pixie went red as fire and hated him for throwing that in her teeth. 'Obviously, I was overwhelmingly attracted to you.'

An entirely spontaneous grin slashed Tor's wide sensual mouth, chasing the gravity from his startlingly handsome features. 'OK.'

'Was that *personal* enough for you?' Pixie slammed back at him sharply as she rose from the table, furious that he had embarrassed her and that she had been that honest with him in her response.

As Tor also sprang up, smouldering dark golden eyes collided with hers and she stopped breathing and froze in her retreat to the door. She couldn't drag her attention from him as he stalked towards her, all lean predatory grace and masculine power.

'No, in the interests of research I'd like to get a lot more personal,' Tor confided. 'I want to kiss you.'

Pixie was knocked off balance entirely by that familiar phrase. 'You said that that night.'

'And what did you say?'

'*Do it,*' she recalled weakly as he reached for her.

The tip of his tongue licked along the closed seam of her mouth and she shivered violently, wanting more, craving more, outraged by the flood of instant awareness cascading through her treacherous body. She didn't know what he did to her self-discipline, but it was lethal because with one touch her whole body switched on as though he had pressed a magic button. Her skin felt too tight round her bones, her breath shortened in her throat and her heart began to pound. The light play of his splayed fingers across her spine somehow made her breasts swell and stir inside her bra, letting her feel the straining taut-ness of her nipples. Her lips parted and he took advantage, delving between to explore the moist interior of her mouth.

The immediate rush of heat and dampness between her thighs took her by storm, prickling, tingling awareness shoot-ing through every nerve ending she possessed. She jerked in helpless response. It was one kiss and her body leapt on it as though it were her first meal after a famine.

He pressed her back against the table and her hands lifted up, her fingers spearing into his springy black hair to hold him fast while his firm lips moved with compelling hunger on hers. The bottom could've fallen out of the world at that moment and she wouldn't have noticed. Her surroundings had fallen away. All she was aware of was him, the hard, demanding bar of his erection against her stomach, the passion of his mouth on hers, the glorious heat and strength of him that close.

Breathing raggedly, Tor dragged his mouth from her and pulled back from her, dark eyes flaring with bright golden in-tensity and full of new knowledge. 'Well, I don't need to ask *how* it happened, do I? We have explosive chemistry…and I'm remembering things now. The taste of you…and green hair? *Diavole*…where does *green* hair come into it? And I said that you reminded me of a forest fairy? *Thee mou*…spouting non-sense of that calibre, I must've been incredibly drunk!'

Pixie reeled back from him, deeply shaken by the passion

that had betrayed her in his arms, exposing a vulnerability that mortified her. She didn't even feel relieved that he was starting to remember stuff, only more mortified and exposed than ever.

'I had dyed my hair before we met...it stayed sort of pale green until it finally washed out,' she muttered tightly. 'And you *did* compare me to a forest fairy, but only because someone else said I reminded them of a leprechaun with my green hair and I told you that.'

Tor shot her a glance of concealed wonderment because she was on another plane entirely, too naïve to even register how unusual it was to find a sexual connection that strong. He had gone up in flames with her. She was a dynamite charge in a tiny package and all he had wanted to do was spread her out on the table and thrust inside her hard and fast.

The ache of having to deny and control his libido was new to him. Sex had become something Tor snapped his fingers and received with minimal effort. Persuading or coaxing had never been required from him. But no woman had ever aroused him to the extent that Pixie did. Her effect on him, however, certainly explained what must have happened that night and his own unusual recklessness...

But he had recalled enough of his own reactions to be thoroughly disconcerted by what he was both learning and remembering. *Best sex I ever had...* That was what he had fallen asleep thinking that night, satiated by the glory of her silken, tight depths. He breathed in deep and slow, tamping down those thoughts and forcing himself back to the present.

'A limo will take you home and bring you back here again. Do you want me to accompany you? At some stage, I will need to speak to your brother,' Tor imparted, while thinking that within a couple of days he would know everything he needed to know about the siblings because he had told his head of security to have them checked out.

'Why would you need to speak to Jordan?'

Tor compressed his lips. 'Because you don't appear to have sufficient control over him.'

Her face flamed with annoyance because she was in no position to argue after what Jordan had done with Alfie.

'Look, with Emma here I'll let Alfie stay here tonight and I'll come back in the morning as you asked but, to be frank, once the emergency is over, I hope we can all settle back down and get on with our lives,' Pixie admitted, hoping that if she gave a little, he would too. 'But I don't want you to speak to Jordan. I'll take care of that.'

'How?' Tor challenged.

'I can't defend what Jordan did this morning when he left Alfie here,' Pixie conceded. 'But he's my half-brother, my only surviving family and he's been good to both of us when there was nobody else willing to help, so please cut him some slack…'

'If that baby *is* my son, it's going to change your lives,' Tor retorted in a growling undertone, ignoring her plea on her brother's behalf. 'I'd be a liar if I said anything else.'

Pixie set her teeth firmly together on a hasty and ill-judged response to that statement. She saw no reason why he should interfere with *her* life. She was willing to accept him as a masculine role model in Alfie's world and hopefully a better one than Jordan had so far proved to be. Presumably, Tor would expect to spend time with Alfie. He would also expect to contribute towards his support, she assumed, but she hoped that that would be as far as his interference went because there was nothing more personal between them than that single night and Alfie's unintentional conception.

Really? a little voice sniped, unimpressed, deep inside her. What about that kiss? What about that response you gave him? That had gone way beyond masculine role models and child support, that had been personal and intimate to a level that filled Pixie with guilt and discomfiture. That kiss had smashed through the defensive barriers she had forged and blown her away.

'Why did you call him Alfie?'

'I named him after my grandfather. He was a wonderful character. He died when I was six, but I never forgot him.'

Tor accompanied her to the front door, waiting there in silence until a sleek black shiny limousine pulled up outside. 'I have an appointment now, so I won't see you before you leave for work. Hopefully, I'll see you in the morning for breakfast,' he murmured silkily.

Pixie nodded and went down the steps, wide-eyed as the driver climbed out to open the passenger door of the limousine for her. She got in, sinking into the pearl-grey leather upholstery and scanning the embellishments in front of her, wondering what the various buttons and switches she could see did, but restraining herself from experimenting lest she embarrass herself.

The house was empty when she got back. Jordan had gone out, probably to avoid dealing with her recriminations, she reflected with a wry shake of her head. She rushed around, gathering up her son's belongings, and changed for work, conscious that she didn't have much time to waste.

If that baby is my son, it's going to change your lives.

That declaration had aggravated her. Tor Sarantos could only change what she *allowed* him to change, she reminded herself bracingly. He didn't own her; he didn't own either of them. He couldn't force her to do *anything* she didn't want to do…

CHAPTER FIVE

ELOISE SAT ACROSS the table in the hospital canteen from Pixie during their break and said, 'About the only thing your brother got right was when he advised you to take what you can get to make raising Alfie easier. His father *should* be sharing the responsibility.'

Pixie stiffened and blinked, taken aback by the pretty brunette's frankly offered opinion. Since the other nurse and her brother had broken up, by mutual agreement both women had avoided discussing Jordan. 'I never thought you'd say that.'

'It's gloves-off time. The best thing for both you and Alfie would be to get as far away from Jordan as you can because if you don't, he'll rob you blind like he did me.' Eloise sighed. 'I'm sorry to be that blunt, Pixie, but Jordan left me broke. Although I could never get the truth out of him, money was always disappearing, and I didn't believe the stories he told me. I suspected he was gambling but he laughed in my face when I accused him, and I couldn't prove anything. If Alfie's father gives you financial help, grab it with both hands and step away from your brother.'

'*Gambling?*' Pixie whispered, aghast.

'What else could he be at? Where do you think the debts he's always complaining about are coming from?' Eloise prompted in an undertone, mindful of the diners at tables nearby. 'He doesn't live the high life or smoke or use drugs. The money has to be going somewhere and, if you're not careful, you and Alfie will end up on the street because when I moved out that mortgage was already in serious arrears.'

Pixie frowned. 'But I give him most of the money to cover it every month.'

'Check it out for yourself. Your name's on the mortgage too,' Eloise reminded her drily. 'Stop trusting Jordan to take care of the budget because I suspect he's been pulling the wool over your eyes as well.'

'You think he's dishonest. That's why you dumped him,' Pixie finally grasped and that new knowledge made her feel grossly uncomfortable. 'But if he *was* that kind of cheating, lying person, why would he have looked after me for so long?'

The brunette rolled her eyes ruefully. 'Everyone's a mix of good and bad. But you had better believe that your brother dumped your son on his rich father's doorstep because he decided that there was something in it for *him*!'

'I wish you'd told me what you suspected sooner,' Pixie admitted heavily, having been given a lot to think about. It was an empty wish, but she found herself wishing that her parents were still alive because she would have turned to them for advice. She felt gutted by the suspicion that Jordan might have been up to no good behind her back and that he could not be trusted with money.

'Jordan and I split up and bad-mouthing him to his sister afterwards struck me as bitchy and unnecessary because I've moved on now.'

After that conversation, it was a struggle for Pixie to concentrate on work and when she was leaving the hospital, with her brain buzzing with conjecture, she was dismayed to see Jordan waiting for her outside the door because she still wasn't ready to deal with him. At the same time, though, she knew it was necessary.

Her brother gave her a sad-eyed sideways glance. 'I'm sorry,' he said awkwardly as he walked by her side. 'But I didn't have a choice—'

'There's *always* a choice, Jordan!' Pixie cut in thinly.

'No, on this occasion there truly wasn't,' Jordan told her, dropping down onto a stone bench that overlooked the busy car park. 'You ignored all my advice. You refused to go to a solicitor and apply for child support.'

'I know *but*—' Pixie deemed it too early in the conversation to admit that she now accepted she had leant too heavily on him for support.

'The house is about to be repossessed,' Jordan told her heavily.

Pixie turned bone white. 'That's not possible. There would have been letters.'

'I've been hiding the letters. I hoped that I could stop it happening, but I can't, and I *had* to force you to deal with Sarantos some way, so that he could be there to look after you and Alfie. I didn't want you ending up in some homeless shelter because I've been stupid!'

Pixie's knees finally gave way and she sat down beside him, plunged deep into shock by that blunt confession. 'But I've been giving you money towards the payment every month.'

'It's all gone. I'm sorry but we're going to lose the house,' Jordan muttered heavily.

As he confirmed Eloise's misgivings, Pixie was reeling in horror and disbelief at such a betrayal of her trust. 'But how could that happen?'

Her brother sprang up again, refusing to meet her stricken gaze. 'I'm very sorry,' he said again and he walked away at speed.

Pixie splurged on another taxi to return to Tor's town house. She was in a state and her exhaustion wasn't helping. Worry about her brother's state of mind and the fear of impending homelessness had overloaded her brain. Only a couple of days ago she had been secure and now all of a sudden, and without warning, her life was falling apart. Once again she craved parental support. Jordan had lied to her and could no longer be trusted. In the aftermath of that acknowledgement, walking into the gracious luxury of Tor's home gave her a surreal feeling and, more than ever, the sense that she did not belong in such a setting.

She went straight upstairs and found Emma bathing Alfie. That reunion got her very damp, but she insisted on taking over because early mornings had always been her fun time with Alfie, and she treasured those moments when he was fresh for the new day and full of energy and nonsense.

She took him downstairs for breakfast, wincing at the formality of the dining room and the prospect of Alfie's mealtime messiness, but Mrs James, the housekeeper, did at least have a smile for her as a high chair was brought in—complete, she was amused to see, with a protective mat for it to sit on.

Tor, it seemed, was already long gone from the house, which was a relief for Pixie in the mood she was in.

After she and Alfie had both eaten their fill from an array of breakfast dishes that would not have shamed a top-flight hotel, she handed her son back to Emma and retired to the beautiful room next door to them, smothering a yawn.

Nothing would seem so bad after she had had a decent sleep, she soothed herself as she climbed into the wonderfully comfortable bed and set the alarm on her phone. Perhaps some solution would come to her while she slept, she thought hopefully, striving not to stress about the future but knowing in her gut that she did not want to be dependent on Tor.

She could share Alfie with him, but she wanted any other connection between them to be remote and unemotional and most definitely *not* physical. The last thing she needed was to get attached to a man still in love with his dead wife, even though she had cheated on him. She hoped she had more sense than that, but a hot, sexy Greek like Tor Sarantos played merry hell with a woman's common sense. She had made a huge mistake once with Tor, but she had no intention of repeating that mistake, she assured herself firmly.

The results of the DNA testing had been delivered to Tor at his office, but he resisted the urge to rip open the envelope. On another level, he knew he didn't really need to open the envelope to know that Alfie was *his* child. That truth had shone out of Pixie when he'd realised that she had no doubts about who had fathered her child, but, even more potently, Tor had felt the family connection the instant he saw Alfie's smile and was reminded of his little brother. The preliminary file he received on Pixie and her brother, however, posed more of a problem. The contents bothered Tor and while he also appreciated that those same facts would make Pixie more reliant on him for assistance, Tor didn't really want to be the bearer of such bad news when his relationship with Alfie's mother was already strained and difficult. On the other hand, he couldn't see that he had much of a choice on that score.

He went home at lunchtime, needing to be within reach of the child he believed to be his, before the results confirmed it. Telling a flustered Mrs James, taken aback by his sudden appearance, that he didn't need lunch, only coffee, he strode into his home office. He tore into the envelope then, and breathed in deep before he looked down at the page in his hand.

Ninety-nine point nine per cent likelihood that he was Alfie's father. Ironically, the shock wave of confirmation left him light-headed and then galvanised him into heading straight upstairs. He glanced down at his immaculate city suit and silk tie and frowned, striding into his bedroom to change.

He was a father, genuinely a father, for the first time. It shook him how much that meant to him. Of course, the first time around he had taken fatherhood for granted. He hadn't realised that until the night Katerina and Sofia died.

Katerina had put the little girl into the car against his wishes while informing him that he had no right to object because Sofia wasn't *his* daughter, but her lover's. Rage had burned in Tor's gut like a bushfire. Never again would he allow a woman to put him in so powerless a position, he'd sworn to himself.

He was a father, and fathers had rights...didn't they? He was an unmarried father, though. That was a different situation. He needed to talk to his legal team to find out exactly where he stood.

But that wasn't an immediate priority, he told himself impatiently, heading straight off to see his son.

Frustratingly, however, Alfie was sound asleep, his little flushed face tucked up against a battered rabbit soft toy, his bottom in the air. Tor studied the slumbering child intently, wanting to pick him up, wanting to hold him, knowing he could not. Phone the lawyers, his ESP was urging as the recollection of his own family history returned to haunt him.

His elder brother, Sevastiano, had grown up outside Tor's family circle because his Italian mother, Francesca, had changed her mind about marrying Tor's father to marry another man instead. Tor's father, Hallas, had moved heaven and earth to try to gain access to the child he had known Francesca was already carrying, but he had failed because a child born within marriage was deemed to be the husband's child and DNA testing had been in its infancy back then. Without evidence that there was a blood tie, the law and an antagonistic stepfather had excluded Hallas from his son's life. That sobering story in mind, Tor phoned his lawyers and, from them, he learned facts that startled him. In the UK, an unmarried father had virtually no rights. He had no right to either custody or even visitation with his child without the mother's consent.

Pixie was emerging from the en suite bathroom wrapped in a capacious towel when a knock sounded on the bedroom door. She had slept like a log but the instant she wakened her mind began seething with anxiety again. If the house was to be repossessed, where was she going to live? How was she going to manage to work without Jordan to rely on for childcare? Checking the towel was secure, she opened the door a crack.

'It's Tor...can we talk?'

'Right now?' Pixie muttered doubtfully, stepping back a few feet without actually meaning him to take that retreat as an invitation.

Tor strode in without skipping a beat. 'Give me five minutes,' he urged.

His gorgeous black-lashed dark eyes locked to her, golden as heated honey, and she froze, scanning his appearance in faded jeans and a black top with almost hungry eagerness. He looked so good in denim he stole her breath from her lungs, the jeans showcasing lean hips and long powerful thighs. She dredged her attention from him again with pink spattering her cheeks and said uneasily, 'I need to get dressed.'

'You're pretty much covered from head to toe,' he pointed out gently.

It was true. The large towel stretched from above her breasts to her feet and she sank down on the side of the bed and endeavoured to relax and behave less awkwardly around him.

'I got the DNA results,' he volunteered. 'And as you said, Alfie's my son.'

'So?' Pixie prompted.

'We have a lot to talk about.'

'I suppose we have...that is *if* you're planning to play an active part in his life,' Pixie responded.

'So far I may not have made much of a showing in the father stakes, but I plan to change that,' Tor swore with impressive resolve.

'I believe that would benefit Alfie,' Pixie commented quietly.

'I hope that it will benefit *both* of you,' Tor countered with assurance, his attention welded to her because she was so tiny and dainty in the towel, her curls damp from the shower, bare pink toes peeping out from beneath it. Impossibly pretty, incredibly cute and sexy. All of a sudden, this tiny blonde was becoming the most fascinating woman he had come across in years. It was *because* she was Alfie's mother, he reasoned with himself, nothing at all to do with the fact that he wanted to rip the towel off her and spread her across the bed. That was just lust, normal, natural lust. It didn't relate to anything more complex.

Colouring at the tenor of his appraisal, Pixie shifted uneasily. 'I'm not sure I understand what you mean...obviously we can learn to be civil to each other,' she murmured. 'It's probably a blessing that we were never in an actual relationship. We've got none of the baggage that can go with that scenario. That's a healthy start.'

Tor didn't agree at all. He didn't want to be reminded that they had never been in a relationship. Nor did he want to be held at arm's length like a stranger.

'I'd like to have my name put on Alfie's birth certificate, but I understand you have to fill in forms and go to court to achieve that.'

'Then you already know more than I do,' Pixie admitted, stiffening a little at that reference to going to court, nervous of that legal step without even knowing why. 'I only know that when I registered his birth I couldn't put your name on the certificate without you being there and agreeing to it.'

'We'll look into it.'

'Look, can I get dressed now?' Pixie pressed. 'I'll come downstairs straight away.'

Tor departed, thinking about the contents of that file and the brother she semi-idolised for his supposed sacrifice in becoming her guardian. What he had to tell her would hurt, but he could not conceal the truth from her when her safety and his son's could be at risk.

Pixie got dressed, pulling on ankle boots, a flouncy skirt and a long loose sweater. She was off work for a few days and she liked to make the most of her downtime, usually commencing her break with a trip to the park with Alfie and a fancy coffee somewhere. But she didn't have the money to cover fancy coffees any longer, she reminded herself, feeling guilty about the taxis she had employed in recent days. Now she had to carefully conserve what money she had because she had to be prepared to find somewhere else to live. And there and then, the whole towering pack of cards on which her life and security were built began to topple, she acknowledged with a sinking in the pit of her stomach. Her salary was good, but it wouldn't stretch to cover both rent *and* childcare.

Tor awaited her in the opulent drawing room, which had oil paintings on the walls and sumptuous contemporary seating. A tray sat on the tiered coffee table. 'We'll serve ourselves,' he told the housekeeper smoothly.

Tor scanned the outfit Pixie wore, which was eclectic to say the very least, his gaze lingering on her slender, shapely legs and then whipping up to her flushed face beneath the curls she had haphazardly caught up in a knot on top of her head, the hairstyle accentuating her brilliant blue eyes. Natural, artless, everything he had never looked for in a woman, everything he had never guessed he would find appealing.

Pixie dished out the coffee, remembering that he took his black and sweet and handing it to him. She sank down into the depths of a capacious sofa, one knee neatly hooked over the other, her legs slanted to one side while tension thrummed through her, making her small body rigid while she wondered what he wanted to say and what demands he might try to make of her. His name on the birth certificate? She saw no reason to object to that.

'As soon as I realised that you were saying that I was the father of your child yesterday I asked my head of security to have your background investigated—'

'Investigated?' Pixie repeated, cutting in, her dismay unhidden.

'I'm sorry if that annoys you, but I needed to know more

about you. It's standard in my life to take that sort of precaution,' Tor proffered unapologetically.

Pixie forced an uneasy little smile. 'I've got nothing to hide.'

'No, but unfortunately your brother did,' Tor revealed ruefully.

'If you're about to tell me that the house is about to be repossessed because of Jordan's debts, I already know. He came to see me after I finished work at the hospital today. It was a major shock because I wasn't aware that there was even a problem. He had hidden that from me.'

'His web of deception goes much deeper than that, I'm afraid,' Tor told her reluctantly.

Fully focused on his tall, powerful figure by the fireplace, Pixie sat forward with a frown. 'What do you mean?'

'When your parents passed away, your mother's house was left entirely to you.'

'No, the house was left to both Jordan and me,' Pixie corrected.

'Obviously, it was in your brother's interests to make you believe that, but that house, which originally belonged to your mother's parents, was left solely to *you*. In fact, so keen was your mother to ensure that the house went to you only that she wrote her will soon after she married Jordan's father, in the event that they should have any children. Social services were aware that the house belonged to you but at the time that Jordan applied to become your guardian he was decently employed and would have seemed to be a fine upstanding citizen, capable of taking care of his little half-sister…'

Her brow furrowed in growing surprise. 'Jordan didn't get a share of the house *too*?'

'No. But by taking on caring for you he gained access to a free roof over his head and as soon as you were old enough he got you to sign documents which enabled him to take out a large loan against the house.'

Pixie frowned. 'The bathroom and kitchen were badly in need of an update. We both had to sign for the loan.'

'I suspect he gave you forged documents. You were young, inexperienced. I doubt that it took much effort for him to fool you, and at the same time he got you to put him on the mortgage, which enabled him to do a great deal behind your back.'

Pixie blinked rapidly. What he was telling her was much worse than anything she could have dreamt up because he was suggesting that her brother had defrauded her, had taken advantage of her ignorance and *used* her to try to steal *her* inheritance. 'The loan was honest. There was nothing questionable about it,' she argued tightly, seeking a strand of comforting truth to cling to in her turmoil. 'The work needed to be done and there was no other way of paying for it.'

'But Jordan pocketed most of the loan and, I imagine, spent only a small part of it on home improvements. From what I understand that's when the gambling started. He bet, he lost, he borrowed more and more money from various sleazy sources, and he sank deeper and deeper into debt. He's a gambling addict.'

'Then he needs professional help,' she whispered painfully, appalled that Jordan could have sunk so low without her even noticing and wondering what could possibly be done to cure him of such an addiction. She was gutted and she felt horribly alone, for he was her only relative. Yet in her heart her fondness for Jordan still lingered deep down, even though the man he was now wasn't the man he had been a few years earlier.

'He should be punished for what he's done to you,' Tor contradicted, his firm mouth compressing into a taut line.

'Mum *should* have left the house to both of us,' she protested on her brother's behalf. 'It must've been very hurtful for Jordan to realise that he'd been left out.'

'He wasn't her son, he was her stepson,' Tor pointed out drily. 'Generally parents do choose to leave their worldly goods to blood relatives.'

'And you think Jordan targeted me because I was left the house?' Pixie demanded angrily, jumping to her feet. 'Well, I think that's nonsense! Maybe he did cheat to get his hands on the money, but he cared about me.'

'I'm not saying that he didn't, but using you to get his hands on more money quickly became his main motivation. Before he got involved you had a secure future with the ownership of that house. Instead he ensured you were loaded down with mortgage payments and student loans,' Tor sliced in in a harsh undertone. 'And now some very dangerous men are chasing him for repayment, which puts both you and Alfie at risk. You *can't* go back to that house. You can't risk meeting up with Jordan in public again either.'

'You can't tell me that!' Pixie gasped. 'You can't tell me where I can live and what I can and can't do!'

'When it comes to your security I will tell you, particularly if it affects my son.'

'You didn't want to know about your son when I was pregnant last year!' Pixie slung at him vengefully. 'Don't expect me to have faith in you now!'

'You know now that I didn't remember you and that I'm only telling you what you don't want to hear because you need to know those facts,' Tor countered in his measured level drawl. 'But you *can* have faith in my determination to ensure that neither you nor my son are further affected by Jordan's bad choices.'

'But I *have* to go back to the house… I've got a cat to look after…and then there's all my stuff.' Pixie gasped, the ramifications of what he was telling her finally beginning to sink in.

'I'll make arrangements for you to remove your cat and your possessions immediately. There's a good chance that your brother's creditors will ransack the property and take anything that they can sell.'

Pixie went pale and broke out in nervous perspiration. 'Oh… my…word,' she whispered in horror. 'This is a nightmare.'

'With my support it doesn't have to be.' Tor pulled his phone out and began to make calls while she stared at him wordlessly.

He was on the phone for about ten minutes and it sounded as though he was rattling off instructions to someone. 'When you go to the house you will take my security team with you to protect you and you will leave Alfie here.'

Slowly, painfully, it was dawning on Pixie that, faced with impending homelessness, she was in no position to call any shots. 'But I can't move in here!' she exclaimed.

'I am more than happy to have you and Alfie here.'

'Well, possibly for a few days until I can move on. I'll have to find somewhere I can rent. Maybe there's someone at work I can share with. Thank goodness I'm not due back at work until next week,' she gabbled, covering her clammy face with her spread hands in an expression of near desperation as the true meaning of her position hit her hard.

'I'd prefer for you to stay on here,' Tor admitted. 'It will make it easier for me to get to know Alfie.'

'That's important to you, is it?'

'The most crucial thing in my life right now,' Tor disconcerted her by declaring. 'I can't begin to tell you how much his existence matters to me.'

And Pixie almost scoffed at that turnaround in attitude on his part until she recalled the man with the haunted eyes telling her about his daughter's death, and she compressed her lips and said nothing, shame silencing her because she recognised sincerity when she saw it. Tor had only needed confirmation that Alfie was his to develop a serious interest in his son.

'You and I have had a very troubled start…but we don't have to continue in the same vein,' Tor framed almost roughly.

'We don't,' she agreed, welded to his beautiful eyes, bronzed by golden highlights and strong emotion.

'In time I genuinely believe that we could make something of this…attraction between us, potentially even marriage,' Tor spelt out almost curtly, so tough did he find it to broach the

concept of a new relationship, particularly when he had promised himself that never again would he make such an attempt
with a woman.

Pixie flushed and froze, not quite sure she had heard those
words but keen to nip any such toxic notion in the bud. 'Oh,
no...you and me? We're *not* going there,' she told him without
hesitation.

His fine ebony brows drew together. He was not vain, but he
was confident and arrogant, and he knew his own worth. He was
richer than sin, reasonably good-looking and most women loved
him. He wasn't remotely prepared for Pixie's blunt and wound-
ingly *instant* rejection. 'Why not?' he asked equally bluntly.

A strangled laugh that was not one of amusement was
wrenched from Pixie. She stared back at him wide-eyed, as if
his proposition had been shocking.

'*Why not?* How can you ask me that?' she exclaimed. 'Five
years after you lost your unfaithful wife you're *still* not over her
and you're *still* wearing your wedding ring. No woman in her
right mind would risk getting involved with you!'

For once in his life, Tor was silenced because it was a direct
strike he hadn't been expecting. His ultimate goal was to marry
Pixie and legitimise his son's birth and he had expected to proceed to that desirable conclusion by easy stages; the possibility
of rejection had not once crossed his mind. Now it dawned on
him that he could well be facing a long and stony road, toiling
uphill every step of the way, because this was a woman who
knew stuff no other woman had ever known about him and
there would be no fooling her, no fobbing her off with something less than she felt she deserved.

'So, to sum up, you and me...well, you bury that idea,' Pixie
advised him briskly. 'You and Alfie? Speed ahead...and I'll stay
here until I get sorted out.'

It was a tragedy that he was so emotionally unavailable, so
wrapped up in the past, she acknowledged unhappily. Marriage to Tor would have changed her life and Alfie's out of

recognition but marrying a man still unhealthily attached to a past love would be a daily punishment for her. She could still remember the love between her parents and their relationship had struck her as a shining example of what marriage should be. She cringed at the prospect of being Tor's second-best and the likelihood that she would always be compared to her predecessor, whom he had loved. No, she had made the right decision, putting her own need for security and happiness above her son's needs...*hadn't she?*

CHAPTER SIX

IT WAS THE middle of the night or at least the early hours of the morning, Pixie guessed, when Tor shook her awake.

'Your brother's in hospital,' he told her grittily.

Pixie forced herself up on her elbows, shaken out of a sound sleep, and stared up at Tor, fully dressed and formidable. 'He's... *what*?'

'He's been beaten up by his creditors,' Tor divulged thinly. 'I wasn't sure whether or not to tell you.'

Pixie searched his lean dark features in wonderment. 'Of course, you tell me,' she protested. 'He's my brother and he screwed up, but I still love him!'

That bold statement of affection seemed to unnerve Tor slightly. His shimmering golden eyes hooded and cloaked as if she was showing him a softness that he didn't want to see in her. 'Does that mean that you want to see him?'

'Of course, I do,' she confirmed, clambering out of bed, suddenly uneasily conscious of the reality that she was only clad in pyjamas and of how incredibly uncomfortable Tor could make her feel when she was anything less than fully dressed.

In recent nights, she had encountered Tor in the nursery when teething was making Alfie fractious and unwilling to settle and he would cry and cry. She usually told Emma to go back to bed and that she would take care of her son, but Tor had proved to be surprisingly invested in Alfie being upset, persisting with his presence when she had expected him to lose patience and leave them alone. And gradually, it had dawned on her that Tor was a father prepared to take the rough with the smooth and willing to help out when Alfie was less than his cheerful smiling self. Was that the result of his previous experience with young children or simply his drive to make up for that poor start in fatherhood that he had acknowledged? Whichever, Pixie was unwillingly impressed by Tor's ability to cope with his son even when he was whiny and miserable. Add in the reality that Tor was half-naked during those encounters, clad, as he was, in only a pair of faded jeans, and she was a woman, heaven forgive her for that truth, but suddenly she was fully on board with him pushing in where before she had had nobody but herself to depend on.

There was Tor, a six-pack of impressive musculature on parade, all bronzed and lethally built and sensual. With that temptation before her, being got out of bed in the middle of the night had, without warning, become a thrilling kind of adventure. She had to struggle to keep her attention on Alfie when Tor was there, bare-chested and sleepy, those gorgeous eyes drowsy and somehow even more compelling, the black spiky lashes strikingly noticeable and his eyes on her. Hot, hungry, interested. But she wasn't stupid and she wasn't going there—wasn't going to make that mistake *again*.

She was a pushover for Tor, she reckoned unhappily. One hint that he wanted something more and she was ready to jump on the chance. But that would only complicate things between them, she warned herself sagely. Tor was open to having sex with her, nothing more lasting, nothing deeper, she reckoned ruefully. She believed the idea of marrying her had been his knee-jerk conventional overreaction to the discovery that he was a father again, not a proposition that he was properly serious about. In the short term, however, Tor was a typical male, programmed to seek sexual satisfaction, and for the present he didn't seem to be seeking that outlet with any other woman, so she was convenient and available, but his apparent interest didn't mean anything more than that. It was wiser to keep her distance, retain her barriers and stay uninvolved while letting him build his relationship with Alfie separate from hers.

'A car will be waiting for you when you're ready.'

'You're not coming with me?' she heard herself say and reddened fiercely.

'I want to punch your brother too. He put you and Alfie in danger. You could've been in that house with him. You could've been hurt, and it would've been his fault,' Tor breathed rawly.

Pixie compressed her lips. It was several days since she had returned to the empty house and packed up their belongings and Coco. The move had been executed at frightening speed because Tor's aid had included a professional removal team and a van as well as a squad of Tor's security men to protect her. Within little more than an hour and a bit, everything she possessed had been transferred, much of it now stowed in an attic room on the top floor of the town house. Some day she would have to go through it all and she would probably dump a lot of what she had grabbed in haste, stuff that Jordan wouldn't value but she did. There had been the family photo albums, and her mother's treasured bits and pieces as well, items she would never part with, the objects that reminded her of her happy childhood and favourite moments, which she would, one day, share with Alfie.

'But Alfie and I have been with you, *safe*, and Jordan's my brother,' she muttered ruefully.

'Your *half*-brother,' Tor stressed.

'He was eight when I was born. He's been with me all my life. He might as well be my full brother,' Pixie countered steadily.

'A family connection isn't a forgive-all escape clause,' Tor objected, marvelling at her ongoing loyalty to a male who had let her down so badly. His half-brother, Sev, had betrayed him and Tor knew that he would never pardon him for his behaviour. Of course, his outlook had always been very black and white on such matters, he conceded, and clearly Pixie's was not.

And Pixie instantly knew that he was thinking of *his* brother, who had slept with his wife and whom he could not forgive.

'Jordan loves us. He's got nobody else,' Pixie stated almost apologetically in the face of Tor's disapproval. 'I need to be the bigger person here and try to help him.'

'Even if he's already burned all his boats?'

'He tried to tell me, warn me away to keep Alfie and me safe, but I think he was too ashamed to tell me the whole story.' Pixie sighed.

In spite of his attitude, Tor joined her in the waiting limo. It was barely dawn and the drive to the hospital was accomplished in silence. 'You don't need to do this,' she said awkwardly on the way in.

'If you're here, I'm here.'

Jordan was in a cubicle in A & E. He had been badly beaten, his face swollen, his eyes black. He had a broken arm and cracked ribs too and he couldn't meet her eyes. 'I knew they'd be coming for me,' he said thickly. 'That's why I wanted you and the baby out.'

'You can come back from this,' she told him.

He twisted his head away, a tear leaking from one eye before he closed it and shuddered. 'It's too late. I've lost everything—the house, you and Alfie…there's nothing left. It's all my own doing.'

'You can come back from this,' she repeated.

'Jordan needs help, he needs therapy,' Pixie muttered to Tor, who had remained in the waiting room, an island in a distant corner, surrounded by security men and normal humanity. 'He's at his lowest ebb.'

'He's got what he deserves,' Tor opined unsympathetically, walking her back outside and tucking her into the waiting limo.

Her gaze was full of reproach. 'Do you have to be so hard?'

'That's who I am. And after what Jordan did to you, you shouldn't be feeling sorry for him,' Tor told her grimly as he swung in beside her.

'You don't have an ounce of compassion in you,' Pixie complained.

'You could persuade me otherwise,' Tor informed her, dark eyes bright as gold ingots below the velvet sweep of his black lashes. 'But I wouldn't advise you to try.'

The power of those eyes holding hers unleashed a flock of nervous butterflies low in her tummy. 'Why not?'

'The world turns on negotiations and agreements. If you want me to help your undeserving brother, there would be a price... and you wouldn't *want* to pay it.'

Bewilderment gripped her. 'Try me...' she invited.

'You're appealing to my dark side and that's not a good idea,' Tor warned her.

'You mentioned negotiation,' she reminded him.

'Essentially, you give me what I want and in return I give you what you want.'

'I'm not stupid. I understood that without the explanation!' Pixie slung back impatiently. 'Jordan needs help.'

'He needs therapy, his debts paid off, a fresh start,' Tor enumerated without skipping a beat. 'You're asking me for money and that's easy because I've got a lot of it, even though I don't believe that Jordan *should* be dug out of the hole he dug for himself.'

'Shut up!' Pixie cried, out of all patience with that unemotional assessment. 'What do you want from me? And *no*, you can't have *that*.'

Rare amusement lightened Tor's gaze, making his eyes sparkle and dance and his firm mouth slant upward. *'That?'* he queried sardonically. 'Are you referring to sex?'

'Yes,' Pixie retorted tightly. 'And you can't have that in return because I'm not for sale and I'm not the sort of person who would trade sex for anything.'

Tor's self-discipline cracked and he grinned. 'I'm glad to hear that and I can work with what you've just told me.'

Pixie shot him an unconvinced glance. 'You...*can*?'

'I wouldn't want a woman who would use sex as a bargaining chip,' Tor traded smoothly. 'For the right price, I want *more* than sex.'

Pixie studied him in complete shock.

'You're so innocent. Why do you look so surprised?' Tor quipped. 'Virtually everything has a price.'

'Jordan's my family.'

'Who stole from you and put you and our son at risk of harm.'

'What did you mean about "the right price"?'

'My terms would be simple. That you agree to visit Greece with me to introduce Alfie to my family and consider marrying me.'

'Marrying you?' She gasped incredulously.

'You only have to consider the idea. When I first broached the idea, after all, you dismissed it without even considering it. I'm not going to try and force you into anything,' Tor proclaimed defensively. 'But I do want my family to meet Alfie.'

'I have to go back to work tomorrow.'

'Give me that trip to Greece and you'll never have to work again,' Tor murmured sibilantly. 'Seriously, the world will become your oyster.'

Breathless, Pixie whispered, 'And Jordan?'

'He gets therapy and a new start, but he has to be in the mindset to change, otherwise, I warn you, you're wasting your time,' he warned her flatly.

'I want him to have that chance...'

'Marry me and we'll be a family,' Tor told her.

And it was the perfect promise because Pixie longed to be part of a family again more than she wanted anything else. Jordan's deception had hit her hard and, while she still regarded her brother as family, he was now somewhere on the outside of that charmed circle until he could prove himself decent again.

'OK… I'll go to Greece with you for a visit and I'll apply for unpaid leave from my job. I don't want to just give it up. I *like* working,' she admitted, while scarcely able to credit that she was willing to take that leap of faith into the unknown with him.

But her world and its boundaries had changed irrevocably, she acknowledged ruefully. She could no longer trust Jordan because, clearly, he was addicted to gambling. He had stolen her inheritance from her, frittered away her hard-earned cash, destroyed her trust. Even if Jordan recovered, it could be years before she could have faith in him again because addiction was a slippery slope and he would always be fighting temptation. And Jordan had put both her and Alfie at risk. Tor, at the very least, was keen to put Alfie's best interests first, and that Tor was keen to introduce their son to his family impressed her. He could've kept Alfie as a dark little secret and visited him discreetly and nobody would ever have known that the little boy existed.

Instead, Tor had chosen to be open and honest with his relatives and he was making room for his son everywhere in his life. Only, what did that mean for her? Not marriage, she couldn't marry a man simply because he had got her pregnant, could she? But everything in her once stable world was shifting, she conceded apprehensively, and it was happening so fast that it left her breathless.

'You and Alfie will need new clothes. It's much warmer out there,' Tor completed. 'A shopping trip is on the cards.'

But Pixie was still thinking over his insistence that she consider marrying him. She had noticed that he had finally removed his wedding ring but naturally she hadn't said anything about it. 'Why do you want me to consider marrying you?' she asked bluntly.

'Two parents would be better than one for Alfie. I want him to have my name and my family, to become part of that support system. I want to be fully involved in his upbringing, not standing on the sidelines. Without taking him away from you,

I want to share him,' he delineated tautly. 'But that's all for him and me. For us—well, we'd be a work in progress but we'd be a family and the attraction between us is strong.'

'I would need love.'

'I have to be honest. I don't think I could do love again.'

'Because you're scared,' Pixie breathed in a softer tone of understanding.

'It's nothing to do with fear,' Tor asserted between gritted teeth of repudiation, insulted by that interpretation of his natural reservations. 'I grew up with Katerina. She was my first love. I was young, naïve and idealistic. I'm not that boy any more. I'm a man and my expectations of a woman are much more practical and prosaic. You have abilities that I respect and value. Loyalty to your brother, in spite of the fact that he's let you down badly. You have compassion for the weak because, make no mistake, Jordan *is* weaker than you and in trying to help him you could be setting yourself up for a world of hurt and disappointment.'

'I'm willing to take that chance and, even though some of what you've said makes sense, I'd want more than practicality in marriage. I'd want passion.'

'I can give you passion,' Tor told her boldly, shimmering eyes welded to hers, and all the oxygen in the car suddenly seemed to be sucked up. 'I can give you as much passion as you can handle.'

'Passion *and* love from a guy who's willing to take a risk on me.'

'Successful bankers estimate the risks they take in advance and without emotion getting involved.'

Pixie nodded in acceptance and sighed. 'I'm not a cold person.'

'No, you're not...and my family are not cold either. For Alfie's sake, I'm glad you are the way you are, but that doesn't change the fact that you and I are very different. We would only work as a couple if you could accept those differences.'

'I'd always be wanting more,' Pixie told him, wondering why

her eyes were prickling and stinging, why she suddenly felt all worked up about a perfectly innocent and unthreatening conversation. Aside of that sexual sizzle between them, they didn't suit and that was that—better by far to see and accept that now than try to fight it. So, Katerina had been his first love, his *only* love, which was probably why her treachery had been so massively damaging. After all, if he couldn't trust the girl he had grown up with, who could he trust?

'I have every hope that you'll change your mind,' Tor murmured. 'Should I have lied and said that I could give you what you want?'

'You can't fake emotion. I'd have seen through you.'

'Most people can't read me.'

'I saw you at your lowest. You have certain tells,' she told him gently, thinking of his body language that night when Alfie had been conceived: the haunted dark eyes, his lean, restless hands shifting with the grace and eloquence that were so much a part of him, the emotion that seethed inside him, the emotion that he denied and suppressed.

Tor elevated a fine ebony brow. 'We're definitely going to have to discuss the tells.'

Emerging from that disturbing recollection of their first meeting, Pixie went pink, trembling a little as that unavoidable flood of physical awareness shifted like melted honey down deep inside her, warming her from the inside out as she pressed her thighs together and stiffened defensively. She wanted to slap herself for even those few moments of remembrance, for an indulgence she no longer allowed herself. To maintain boundaries, she too needed to put that intimate past knowledge of Tor behind her.

'No, we're not arguing about this any longer…you are *not* buying me clothes!' Pixie told Tor heatedly. 'You can pay for Alfie's clothes, but *not mine*.'

'Have you any idea how much money I must owe you in terms of child support?' Tor enquired calmly.

And it was precisely that calm and lack of embarrassment that riled Pixie. She didn't want to discuss money with Tor. She didn't want to admit that she was pretty much broke because she'd never had sufficient cash to manage to save. Paying what she had believed to be her share of the mortgage and buying food every month had cleaned her out and reduced her wardrobe to 'must-have' slender proportions.

She had forgotten what it felt like to buy something just because she liked it or fancied something new because, nine times out of ten, Alfie had needed something more. And now Tor was trying to hand her credit cards, open accounts for her, put her in the hands of some fancy stylist so that she could do him proud in Greece, and it was all too much for her to handle. Registering that she was on the brink of silly tears because he wasn't listening to her, Pixie pushed her trembling hands down on the arms of her chair and stood up.

'I can't listen to any more of this… I'm out,' she said thinly, and walked out of the dining room.

Tor released his breath in a groan and drained his wine glass, pushing away the plate in front of him because his appetite had died. For long minutes he sat and pondered his dilemma. How was she planning to buy clothes without money? Why was she so resistant to his financial help when it came to her personal needs? Had he ever even heard of a woman refusing a new wardrobe before?

When the table was being cleared, and after he had politely refused his housekeeper's suggestion that she make something else for him to eat, Tor vaulted upright and followed Pixie upstairs. There was nothing more frustrating than someone who walked away from a dispute, he registered in frustration, although he could not recall *ever* having an argument with a woman before the night on which Katerina had died. He and Katerina had never argued prior to that, had had no differences of opinion, minor or major. In essence they had not talked that much. Maybe those had been revealing signs of an unhealthy or, at the very least, boring relationship, he conceded grimly. How did he know? He hadn't had a single relationship since then and if he had ever had any skills in that field, they had to be distinctly rusty.

He knocked on her bedroom door and scowled. That was another problem: the whole 'separate bedrooms' thing was tying him up in knots. Why did she make such a big deal of sex? Sex was physical, not a pursuit anyone needed to imbue with magical properties or meaning. Was it because the only time she had indulged in sex she had ended up pregnant? Or could she simply be resistant to his advances because that one-off experience with him had been lousy? That drunk, how considerate could he have been? Tor clenched his teeth together and wondered if he could bring himself to ask. He knocked again. He *needed* to know, he *needed* details. He recalled sufficiently to be aware that he had enjoyed himself thoroughly, but that did not mean that his partner had also enjoyed the experience.

'What?' Pixie demanded aggressively as she flung the door wide on him. Dragged out of the shower by the knocking on the door, she was in a thoroughly bad mood.

There she was, not even five feet tall and barefoot and wrapped in a stupid towel, which covered her delectable curves from neck to toe. Why did his housekeeper buy such *huge* towels in his household? Tor wondered absently. And why did the angry fire of challenge in Pixie's bright blue eyes turn him on?

'We need to talk.'

'No, we don't,' Pixie argued, trying to close the door on him.

'Yes, we *do*,' Tor decreed, stalking over the threshold, automatically gathering her up into his arms, a warm, struggling, fragrant bundle of damp femininity that fiercely aroused him. He was shocked by that reaction as he carefully laid her back down on the bed. 'You explain to me now why you won't allow me to buy you clothes when you need them…'

'Where's your furry loincloth? You're behaving like a guy who just walked out of a Stone Age cave!' Pixie snapped back at him.

'I need to understand the problem before I can fix it,' Tor breathed in a raw undertone.

'I don't need you to fix *everything* in my life,' Pixie muttered. 'I mean, you've already spent a fortune trying to sort out Jordan. Isn't that enough?'

'That was our agreement and I haven't spent a fortune. You wouldn't let me buy the house for him.'

'No, because that would have cost too much and Jordan needs to rebuild his life somewhere new,' Pixie reasoned. 'He has to become self-sufficient again and he shouldn't be rewarded for what he's done. You don't need *all* of us hanging on your sleeve like scroungers.'

Tor gave up the ghost and groaned out loud in frustration, sinking down on the edge of the bed and raking impatient fingers through his cropped black hair. 'Why would you think for one moment that I would look on the mother of my child as a scrounger? Have I done or said anything to give you that impression?'

'Well, no,' she conceded grudgingly. 'But it's how I feel… Why is the clothes thing so important to you?'

'I want you to feel comfortable with my family and friends. I don't want you to feel inappropriately dressed or out of place.'

'Are you afraid my appearance is going to embarrass you?' she whispered, thinking that if she flew out with her well-worn winter wardrobe there was a good chance that it would, and that there was an even stronger chance that she might be mistaken for one of the cleaners that came into the town house to clean several times a week. And that would definitely embarrass everybody, not just her. He was winning the argument, she thought ruefully—he was winning without even trying.

Tor closed a large hand over hers. 'Nothing you could do

would embarrass me. I'm thinking of your comfort, your ability to relax.'

'Maybe it would help if you told me about where you're taking me.'

'An island called Milnos. I bought it a few years ago. The property I built is large enough to house my family when they come to visit. They live on Corfu. One of my brothers, Kristo, is still at school. Dimitri is at university and the eldest, Nikolaos, works for my father in his shipping company.'

'No sisters?'

'None. And so far I'm the only son who has married. Sofia was my parents' first grandchild and her death hit my family as hard as it hit me,' Tor confided tautly, trying to ignore the small fingers gently smoothing over his thigh in a gesture that he knew was intended to offer comfort but which was, instead, travelling straight to his groin and winding him up. 'That's why I want them to meet Alfie. My family are overdue for a glimpse of a brighter future.'

'Yes, I'm pretty sure you haven't been a bundle of laughs to be around,' Pixie mumbled, and then flushed at having made that tactless comment. 'Sorry—'

Tor grinned down at her, relishing the flushed triangle of her animated face beneath the tousled curls. 'You could be right... I've been all about work and nothing else for a long time, but I'm lighter-hearted around you...when we're not arguing, of course.'

'OK. I'll see the stylist and pick clothes,' Pixie muttered with a slight grimace. 'But I'd much prefer not to have to let you pay.'

Tor stared down at her, dark golden eyes unashamedly hungry. 'Do you think you could include some sexy underthings in the selection?' he murmured thickly.

Her cheeks burned. 'What would be the point?'

'My imagination thrives on fuel,' Tor husked, bending down slowly.

Her fingers skimmed up from his wide shoulders into his luxuriant black hair. He smelt amazing to her, fresh and earthy and male, a faint hint of citrus fruit in his designer cologne, that scent achingly familiar to her, achingly evocative. It was the same cologne he had worn *that* night. Her brain was telling her with increasing urgency to push him away, to sit up, to *stop* touching him, but her body was rebelling against common sense with Tor that close. She could feel the heat of his big body through the towel she was wrapped in, the stinging sensation of her nipples snapping taut, the warm damp ache making her feel hollow between her thighs. Every nerve ending was sitting up and taking screaming notice. It was like a wave of physical insanity taking her over.

'I like your fingers on me,' Tor muttered raggedly as he lowered his mouth to hers, let those sensual lips play across hers in a wildly arousing fashion that brought her out in a fever of awareness and damp heat. 'I'd like them all over me, your mouth as well—'

'We said we weren't doing this.'

'*You* said. I didn't make any promises,' Tor said urgently against her parted lips before his tongue delved between, and suddenly speech of any kind was beyond her. And she was bargaining shamelessly with herself: a few kisses. Where was the harm in that? And he was such an amazing kisser, it would be foolish to deny herself the experience.

Her hand slid off his thigh over his crotch, tracing the hard thrust of his erection, and he shuddered against her, his mouth hotter and harder than ever on hers, and she wanted nothing so much as for him to whip off the towel, lay her back and sate the unbearable longing as he had once before. She wanted him and he wanted her, no denying that. But when it went wrong, she thought frantically, Alfie would be caught up in the fallout and her relationship with Tor would become fatally toxic. Having sex with Tor again would come with a price tag attached and a series of risks. One or both of them would ultimately be disappointed and that would lead to discord.

'We can't do this,' she groaned against the urgency of his mouth.

'I can do this fine,' Tor contradicted.

And discomfiture washed over her because she had encouraged him, given him expectations, and she didn't like to be provocative. 'You shouldn't touch me,' she told him.

'You shouldn't touch me either.'

Her face burned so hot she was afraid that she would spontaneously combust. 'I'm acting like a tease and that's not me.'

'No, you need time to decide what you want and I'm not giving you space the way I promised because you're too damn tempting,' Tor growled, setting her back from him, scorching golden eyes smouldering over her discomfited face. 'I'm just naturally impatient and assertive when I want something. You need to push back hard to handle me when I get too enthusiastic.'

'But how does that work when I'm enthusiastic too?'

'You marry me,' Tor said simply.

CHAPTER SEVEN

'NOT WITHOUT LOVE,' Pixie protested.

'I've got lust covered,' Tor said almost insouciantly as he re-clined back on her bed, completely unashamed of the arousal tenting his tailored trousers. 'I've got lust in spades.'

And Pixie thought about it in that moment—seriously thought about marrying a man because she couldn't keep her hands off him—until all her common sense stood up and screamed at her to get her brain back in gear.

'We need more,' she told him heavily.

'We've got Alfie, and Alfie will benefit from having an equal share of both of us. Two parents together, *united*.'

'You're still hung up on Katerina.'

'No. I've taken the ring off. That's behind me. I can't prom-ise love because that's an emotional state and I don't know if I'm capable of feeling like that again,' Tor told her frankly. 'But I can tell you that I'll be faithful and trustworthy and secure.'

And she wanted him, dear heaven, Pixie had never wanted anything as she wanted Tor at that moment because she saw that he was willing to try, she saw that he had moved himself on, indeed that the eruption of her and Alfie into his life had fundamentally changed his outlook. But was it enough?

'I'd be taking a chance on you…and I don't do that,' she whispered honestly. 'I always play safe.'

'I'll *make* it work. You marry me and I'll make it work,' Tor intoned fiercely. 'We can be married within a couple of days and you can meet my family as my wife.'

And that offer had undeniable power because she had naturally been nervous of meeting his family. Being a wife would give her more status than merely being his illegitimate son's mother, a position that would only leave his family questioning exactly what their relationship encompassed. If she went to Greece with him, the two of them would be very much under scrutiny, which made her uneasy. She had watched Tor with Alfie, watched him being patient and caring. She could look for no more than that in the father of her son.

Even though it had gone against the grain, Tor had extended a helping hand to Jordan because that was what *she* wanted him to do. Even if she only married him for Alfie's sake and security, she would be making the right choice, she reasoned. But that wouldn't be the only reason she married him, her conscience piped up, and her face heated. She could have him in bed, if she married him, no worries about what he might think of her for succumbing, no worries about where that intimacy could be heading because marriage would give them the solid framework that they lacked.

Pixie breathed in deep and fast. 'OK… I'll marry you, so that we can be a real family.'

Tor lowered lush black lashes over stunned eyes at that seemingly snap decision, wondering what he had said right, *done* right to ultimately convince her round to his point of view. 'I'll get it organised.'

Pixie nodded slowly. 'I want a proper wedding though,' she warned him. 'I know you've already done it before, but this is my first time.'

'*Last* time,' he qualified. 'And I understand. If you have no objection, my mother will be ecstatic to be asked to organise a wedding reception and we'll get married in Greece.'

'You're looking for trouble,' Eloise pronounced after Pixie had finished breathlessly sharing her insecurities on the topic of marrying Tor. 'Why are you doing that?'

Pixie's smooth brow furrowed as yet another model strolled out wearing a dream wedding dress, only unfortunately, not one she had seen so far matched *her* dream. She lacked the height and shape to do puffy or elaborate or dramatic. But concentrating even on something as superficial as choosing her wedding gown was a challenge when her brain was eaten up by so many other worries.

'Am I?'

'Yes,' Eloise confirmed without hesitation. 'Tor is hotter than sin and richer than an oil well. So, he comes with some baggage like a first wife he may not be over... Well, who *doesn't* have baggage? Start appreciating what you've got, Pixie. Even if he gets bored and dumps you a few years down the road, you'll be left financially secure and Alfie will still have his father. You can't expect to get a man like Tor, a wedding ring and undying love too. Life isn't a fairy tale.'

'I know it's not, but do you think he can be faithful?' Pixie whispered. 'I mean, from everything I've read online about him, he's been quite a womaniser.'

'I think if Tor plays away, he's clever enough to be discreet and you'll never know about it,' Eloise countered cynically. 'And I know that's not what you want to hear but if you can content yourself with what you've got you'll be far happier.'

Pixie swallowed hard, well aware that the brunette was not the person to turn to for reassurance because Eloise had been hurt and disappointed by men too many times. She was a good friend, but she always spoke her mind and she was correct—she had yet to say anything that Pixie had wanted to hear. Eloise had already pointed out that she was boxing above her weight with Tor, that she had landed the equivalent of a super tanker when by rights on the strength of her attractions she had only been due a tugboat. Pixie hadn't needed those reminders of her own essential insignificance, her ordinariness and her lack of any surpassing beauty or talent.

Perhaps unwisely, she had researched Tor's first wife online and had read about the tragic accident that had occurred at their London home, which had later been sold. And she had seen what Katerina looked like: a truly beautiful slender brunette with almond-shaped dark eyes and a mane of dark, glossy hair. She had been on board a yacht, her wonderful hair blowing, looking all athletic and perfect and popular with a bunch of friends around her. After that first glimpse, something inside Pixie had died along with curiosity and she had looked for no further photos.

Tor was in Brussels attending a banking conference and Pixie had been kitting herself out with a new wardrobe and her wedding gown. In the end she had only invited three people to the Greek wedding, Eloise and a couple of gay friends, male nurses she had trained with, who had accompanied her to the stylist and laughed her out of her attempts to go light on Tor's wallet. Jordan had refused to come to Greece, which had hurt, but at the same time she had understood that, in his current mood as he underwent counselling for his addiction and was forced to face all his mistakes, the idea of having to put on a front for strangers at her wedding was more than he could bear. Tor's comments on the same score had, predictably, been a good deal more critical.

Pixie had also had to find and engage a new nanny because Emma was only temporary and preferred moving between different jobs. Actually, having to interview potential employees had been nerve-racking for her, but Tor had pointed out quite rightly on the phone that she wouldn't be happy leaving the task to him. She had found Isla, a cheerful young Scot, who had struck up an instant connection with Alfie that impressed her and who couldn't wait to make a trip to Greece.

'Oh, that's *it*,' Pixie said warmly, focusing appreciatively on the slender sheath dress with the pretty scalloped neckline that the current model was displaying. 'That's definitely the dress.'

'But it's very plain. A bride needs more pizzazz,' Eloise opined in surprise at the choice.

'It's got enough pizzazz for me.' Pixie laughed, knowing that the dress probably cost a small fortune even though it was unadorned, because they were in a designer bridal salon.

'Don't you think you should go for something fancier for a big society wedding?' Eloise made one last attempt to sway her.

'No, it's not going to be a large event. Tor said it would be small and it's my day and I'm not going to worry about trying to impress people.' *As if she could*, she was thinking ruefully, having decided that the only sensible way to behave was to be herself without any false airs or graces.

Three days later, Pixie flew out of London with her friends and Alfie and Isla on board Tor's private jet. It was her wedding day and all she had to do was show up with her dress and a magic wand would take care of all the other necessities—at least according to Tor, that was. In reality, she was pretty apprehensive about what was coming next. They landed in Athens to VIP treatment and they were ushered straight onto a helicopter to complete the journey to Milnos. She had her friends to comment out loud on the luxury and ease of their journey and what life was like on the five-star side of the fence. And all she could think, thoroughly intimidated as she was by the champagne offered on boarding by attractive stewardesses and the constant service, was how on earth was she ever going to fit into this new world where wealth provided so many of the extras she had never enjoyed before?

For that reason, arriving in the lush landscaped grounds of the Sarantos property on the island, a massive white villa with wings radiating out from it, and meeting up with her future in-laws came as a huge relief. Pandora Sarantos was reassuringly motherly and friendly, and she lit up like a firework display the instant she laid eyes on Alfie. Alfie suddenly became the eighth wonder of the world and Pixie could not be uncomfortable with an older woman that keen to admire and appreciate her son. By her side, Hallas, a shorter, greying version of his sons, was less vocal but truly welcoming. He apologised for the absence of his younger sons, who were with Tor, he explained, and he asked if he could have the honour of walking her down the aisle. Pixie agreed, pleased not to have to undergo the stress of having to walk that aisle alone in front of strangers and touched by the offer, a pang of pain arrowing through her as she thought how much her father would have enjoyed fulfilling that role for her. It would have been wonderful to have her parents with her to share the day, she conceded, but Tor's parents were a comfort and their enthusiasm for Alfie was very welcome.

'Alfie is so beautiful, with your hair and Tor's eyes,' Pandora enthused in fluent English as Alfie tottered upright, gripping the edge of a metallic coffee table in the foyer. 'Tor will have to tackle childproofing everything here. Let me show you up to the nursery…'

As Pixie left her friends being shown to their rooms with wide eyes fixed to their palatial surroundings, she followed Pandora Sarantos upstairs with Alfie and the nanny, Isla.

'Wow, this is some place,' the nanny remarked in a shaken undertone.

Pixie was relieved to have someone else comment on the sheer splendour of the marble stairs and hallways and the airy grandeur of the sunlit walkways left open to balconies and fabulous island and sea views.

'This is *your* home now,' Tor's mother announced, disconcerting Pixie. 'I may be here to host your wedding but I'm not the interfering type. I won't be visiting without invitation or anything of that nature. Tor's father, Hallas, and I are really happy that Tor is settling down again.'

Because that's the agreement, Pixie reflected, thinking that she and Tor really were going to have a marriage based on the most practical rules. He would settle down in order to gain regular access to his son and have Alfie become a Sarantos by name. Alfie's mother, Tor's bride, was more or less an afterthought, a necessary step towards reaching those all-important goals. Clearly, Tor's chatty mother had assumed that their marriage was of a more personal, normal nature and she could hardly be blamed for that when most couples married because they were in love with each other, Pixie reasoned ruefully.

Pandora spread open the door of a room furnished as a nursery but not the usual nursery, Pixie adjusted, scanning in wonderment shelves of new toys and every luxury addition known to early childhood. It was a nursery arranged for a little prince, not a normal toddler. 'I can't tell you what a thrill I had furnishing this room for Alfie,' the older woman explained volubly. 'I was so excited to find out about him and you and Tor. You and Alfie are exactly what I was hoping would arrive in his life…a new family.'

And you couldn't get much more of a welcome mat than that, Pixie conceded, warmed to the heart by that little speech and finally appreciating, as her soon-to-be mother-in-law looked yearningly at Alfie and smiled, that her son was so welcome and that she was equally welcome because obviously Tor's parents had assumed that he had fallen in love again. Any parents that loved their son and had seen him heartbroken by the tragic end to his first marriage would want to see him embark on a fresh relationship. Yet even they didn't know the truth of how very tragic and soul-destroying that prior marriage had been for Tor, she acknowledged ruefully, because they didn't know about the infidelity and heartbreak involved.

'I mustn't keep you back from your bridal beautifying,' the older woman remarked with a sudden smile. 'It's a wonderfully exciting day for all of us.'

'She's lovely,' Pixie told Eloise when she arrived in the suite of rooms designated as the bridal suite.

'"Mothers-in-law" and "lovely" don't go together in the same sentence,' Eloise told her in dismay at the statement. 'There's probably a hidden agenda there and it'll take time for you to work it out.'

'I don't think that's true this time,' Pixie said with assurance, because she had recognised the genuine warmth in Tor's mother. 'Wait until you meet her properly. I think she's just happy that her son has found someone and that there's a grandchild. Alfie's going to be spoilt rotten.'

A pair of strangers entered, accompanied by a young, very pretty brunette, who seemed to be there to act as an interpreter and who introduced herself as Angelina Raptis, a friend of the family. One of her companions was a hairstylist, Pixie learned, and the other a make-up artist.

'I don't wear a lot of make-up,' Pixie began uncertainly.

'But today you *do*,' Eloise whispered in her ear. 'Today is special. You want to look your very best and feel good.'

Pixie acquiesced, wanting to at least fit nominally with Tor's expectations. The stylist wanted to cut and straighten her hair and she mustered the courage to say that she preferred her curls and simply wanted to wear her hair up in some fashion.

'I love curls. They're *so* natural,' Angelina commented. 'How brave of you to leave them like that for a formal occasion.'

Encountering the steely glint in the brunette's eyes and noting the scornful curve of her lips, Pixie reddened and turned her head away again, recognising that Angelina was a bit of a shrew while conceding that she couldn't expect everyone she met at her wedding to be a genuine friendly well-wisher.

'I can't wait to meet your son,' Angelina told her brightly. 'Does he look like Tor?'

'Yes, although he's fair-haired like me. He has Tor's eyes though.'

'A very handsome little boy, then. I admire you for being so calm.'

In the background, Eloise was grimacing but, mercifully, her other friends Denny and Steve had come in to join the bridal preparation team and lighten the mood.

'Pixie's looking forward to enjoying a wonderful day,' Denny said cheerfully, earning a relieved smile from Pixie, who loved his positive attitude.

'Even with that awful story in the press?' Angelina burbled, startling Pixie. 'I really admire your strength, Pixie.'

'What press? What awful story?' Pixie repeated in consternation. 'What are you referring to?'

Denny groaned out loud while Eloise stared at Angelina as though she wanted to strangle her where she stood. 'Until you spoke up, we were keeping that story to ourselves, flower,' Denny told Angelina.

'What story?' Pixie whispered afresh, her heart sinking although she had done nothing that she knew that she should be ashamed of.

'Some viper called Saffron sold a story to a tabloid newspaper about the night you met Tor,' Steve explained. 'And the newspaper did a little digging and made a fluffy story out of it.'

Saffron—the wannabe actress who had brought Tor back to that house Pixie had temporarily stayed in; Saffron, the redhead he had rejected and a woman who would probably relish publicity exposure. What on earth could she have to say about anything? Had she seen Tor leaving the bedroom the next morning? That was the only explanation, Pixie decided unhappily.

'Let me see it,' she said to Denny, who was already tapping his phone.

'I'm so sorry. I didn't mean to upset anyone,' Angelina said plaintively.

'You don't dump that sort of stuff on a bride,' Steve said stiffly.

'I'm sure you didn't mean anything by it,' Pixie said politely, forgivingly, her heart racing until Denny had handed her his phone and she glimpsed a very glamorous photo of Saffron next to a brief article about the billionaire banker about to marry the nurse he had got pregnant on a one-night stand. News of her pregnancy had probably got back to Saffron by way of her housemate, Steph, who had given Pixie her cat, Coco. Steph was also the sister of one of Pixie's former colleagues. A stray piece of gossip had probably exposed Pixie's secret pregnancy, she thought heavily, and Saffron had put two and two together to register that they made a very neat four.

'Then I suppose that I shouldn't say that Tor is absolutely furious,' Angelina revealed. 'Look, I feel awkward now... I'll leave you to get dressed with your friends.'

'And you'll not be making a friend of that toxic piece,' Eloise breathed wrathfully.

'If there's nothing untrue in the article I'll just have to live with it,' Pixie pronounced with a stiff smile as she struggled to conceal how mortified she was that Tor's family and friends should have access to the bare shameless facts of their first meeting. 'Let's just forget about it for now.'

'Why on earth would Tor be furious?' Eloise scoffed.

'Because I expect he likes his private life to stay private, like me.' Pixie sighed as the make-up artist fluttered around her, one soft brush after another tickling her brow bone and her cheeks and every other part of her face.

'You're going to look totally amazing,' Eloise told her bracingly.

Denny gave her a fond appraisal. 'A complete princess...'

'A trophy bride,' Steve completed, not to be outdone on the soothing-compliment front.

After presenting her with a beautiful bouquet of roses, Hallas Sarantos accompanied her down to the church in the village down by the harbour. They travelled in a flower-bedecked vintage car that he confided belonged to him as he admitted to a passion for classic cars. Pixie thanked him for all that he and his wife had done to make the wedding possible, and then she was stepping out with a smile into the warmth and brightness of the day outside the small village church. Her smile lurched a little when she saw how packed the church was and the sea of faces that turned to look at her because being so much the centre of attention unnerved her.

Instead, she chose to gaze down the aisle at Tor and, reassuringly, he didn't look angry, only his usual cool self-possessed self. And so incredibly handsome that he stole her breath away at that moment just as he had the very first time she saw him, her attention lingering on the slashing black sweep of his brows, the sculpted high cheekbones that lent his features that perfect definition, the straight nose and the masculine fullness of his sensual mouth. It was as if looking at him lit a whole row of little fires inside her, flushing her face with warmth, filling the more sensitive areas of her body with heat and sexual awareness.

There was a smile in the stunning bronzed eyes that met hers at the altar, no, not absolutely furious about anything, Pixie decided, liberated from that apprehension. If he even knew about the newspaper piece, and she doubted that he did, it evidently hadn't annoyed him in the slightest. He eased the wedding ring over her knuckle and the ceremony was complete. Tor had become her husband and she was now his wife, a conclusion that still shook her.

'You look ravishing,' he murmured on the way out of the church, dark eyes sliding over the shapely silhouette that the elegant gown somehow accentuated, noting the way the fine silk defined the lush plumpness of her breasts and the full curve of her derrière, and more than a little surprised to realise that he was categorically aroused by the prospect of taking his bride to bed, even though he *was* furious with her for the choices she had made. Bad choices, wrong decisions, the sort of mistake he had to expect from someone as youthful and inexperienced in the world as she was, he reminded himself grimly.

'Your parents are brilliant,' she told him chirpily. 'You lucked out there. Neither one of them asked me a single awkward question.'

'Wait until you meet my three brothers, none of whom are known for their tact,' Tor parried smoothly.

And the car swept them back to the enormous villa, where a throng far larger than Pixie had anticipated awaited them in a vast room with ornamental pillars that could only have been described as a modern ballroom. 'You married someone who's got a freaking ballroom!' Denny gasped in her ear. 'And his mother is *still* calling this affair "a very small do"!'

Possibly by Sarantos standards it was small, Pixie conceded as she was tugged inexorably into a receiving line to meet their guests and the long procession of names and faces quickly became a blur. Personal friends, business acquaintances, family friends and relatives. Tor's three brothers were remarkably like him in looks. There truly was a very large number of people present and the only light moment of the experience for Pixie was when Isla appeared with her son and Alfie made a mad scramble out of her arms to reach his mother, smiling and chattering nonsense. Dressed in the cutest little miniature suit she had ever seen, Alfie was overjoyed at the reunion and it was a shock to her when, after giving her a hug, he twisted and held out his arms to greet Tor as if it was the most natural thing in the world.

Her baby boy was growing up and there was room in his little heart for a father now, and the immediacy of Tor's charismatic smile and pleasure at that enthusiastic greeting from his son warmed Pixie as well. It was just at that moment that a tall dark man appeared in front of them and Tor froze, his grasp on Alfie tightening enough that the baby complained and squirmed in his hold.

'Pixie, this is my half-brother, Sevastiano Cantarelli... I didn't realise you were attending,' he said flatly.

'I was determined to drop in and offer my congratulations.

I can't stay for long,' Sevastiano responded in his low-pitched drawl. 'It means a lot to Papa.'

'Yes, yes, it would,' Tor acknowledged with a razor-edged smile as the other man moved on past, as keen to be gone, it seemed, as Tor was to see him go.

'If you would simply tell your family the truth, you wouldn't have been put in the position of having to entertain him,' she whispered helplessly.

'Don't interfere in what you don't understand!' Tor countered with icy bite and she paled with hurt and surprise and looked away again, suddenly appreciating that she had spoken too freely on what was a controversial topic in Tor's life. He might have spilled his guts the night they first met, but alcohol had powered those revelations, she reminded herself doggedly. His reaction now was a disquietingly harsh reminder that she was *still* an outsider, a virtual newcomer in Tor's world, not someone who should have assumed that she had the right to wade in and offer an opinion on a matter that private and personal.

CHAPTER EIGHT

A PERFECTLY CATERED MEAL was served by uniformed staff. Speeches were made by some of Tor's relatives and he translated them for her.

'You're very quiet,' Tor murmured then. 'I was rude earlier. I'm sorry.'

'No, sometimes I have no filter and it was a sensitive subject.'

'Let me explain,' Tor urged, skating a fingertip across the back of her clenched fingers, letting her know that *he* knew that she was still as wound up as a clock by his rebuke. 'For various reasons, Sev didn't get to know our father until he had grown up and their relationship now means a lot to Hallas. My mother has become very fond of him as well. If I spoke up, it would tear them all apart. My father is a very moral man and he would feel he had to choose between his sons and exclude Sev. What good would that anguish and disappointment do any of us now?'

'Your attitude is generous.' Pixie was impressed by his unselfish, mature outlook while recognising the sense of family responsibility that he had allowed to trap him into silence. 'But if your family had understood what you were *really* going through back then, they might have been able to offer you better support.'

'All of that is behind me now,' Tor insisted with impressive conviction. 'Meeting you gave me something of a second chance.'

'No, Alfie did that,' Pixie contradicted without hesitation.

Tor gritted his teeth at that response but said nothing. Knowing that he was to blame for every low point in their relationship was a new experience for him and not one anyone could have said he enjoyed. His bride wasn't in love with him, didn't think he was the best thing ever to happen to her and didn't even particularly crave what he could buy her either. His rational mind argued with that appraisal, reminding him that Katerina's supposed love, which, ironically, he had never once doubted, had been an empty vessel. Love didn't need to have anything to do with his marriage. And Pixie was naïve, honest though, loyal, everything Katerina had not been. For the very first time, he mulled over the truth that Katerina had lied to him and conducted an affair with another man that had begun even before their marriage. Three years of lies including Sofia's birth, he reflected angrily, and even the anger was new because he was making comparisons and he saw now so clearly that his first marriage had been all wrong from the very outset.

So, this time around, Tor reflected grimly, he wasn't compromising, he wasn't making any allowances for misunderstandings or mistakes. He was going to be who he was, tough, and when it came to telling his wife that she had gone wrong he was going to grasp that hot iron and go for the burn.

'Where are we going?' Pixie questioned breathlessly some hours later as she climbed out of the car down at the small harbour. 'And what about Alfie?'

'Alfie and his nanny will join us tomorrow. We can manage one night without him...*right?*' Tor arrowed up a questioning black brow as he bent down, curving an arm to her spine, and even in moonlight she felt the heat of embarrassment at being exposed as an overprotective mother.

As her gaze clashed in the moonlight with those stunning

dark glittering eyes of his, her heart jumped inside her chest and her lower limbs turned liquid. His fierce attraction rocked her where she stood and almost instinctively she leant into him for support, literally mortified by the effect he could have on her because the feelings he inspired in her were so powerful and so far removed, she believed, from his reaction to her.

'It would be cruel to lift Alfie out of his cot at this hour,' she agreed, deliberately stepping back a few inches from him, striving to act cooler.

'Especially after he was exhausted by his social whirl.' Tor's expressive mouth quirked as he recalled his son being passed around like a parcel between groups of cooing women during the reception. Alfie certainly wasn't shy, and his unusual combination of golden curls and dark eyes attracted attention as much as his smiles and chuckles. 'At least he wasn't scared and shaken up like he was the day Jordan abandoned him,' Tor completed, knowing he would never forget the sight of his son clawing his way up his mother's body and clinging in the aftermath of an ordeal that had visibly traumatised him.

Pixie gasped a little in surprise as he bent and simply lifted her off her feet to lower her down into the launch tied up by the jetty. She winced at his words though, wishing he wouldn't remind her of her brother's lowest moment and worst mistake. 'You still haven't said where we're going… You said I didn't need to get changed and now I'm wearing a wedding dress in a boat.'

'To board a much larger vessel,' Tor sliced in, indicating the huge yacht anchored out in the bay and silhouetted against the starry night sky.

'You own a yacht?'

'No. It belongs to a family friend and his wedding present is the use of it. If you like cruising we can always buy one,' he told her as the launch bounced over the sea at speed, driven by the crew member in charge of the wheel.

Pixie studied the yacht with wide eyes, struggling to accept that she was now living in a world where her bridegroom could talk carelessly about purchasing such an enormous luxury. 'Why haven't you bought one already?'

'To date, I haven't taken much time away from work and a yacht would have been a superfluous purchase for a workaholic. But that has to change with you and Alfie in my life now,' Tor traded calmly.

She wanted to ask him if he had been an absentee husband and father during his first marriage, but on their own wedding day it felt as if that would be tacky and untimely. He had made her wary of impulsive speech as well when he had reacted badly to a tactless question earlier that day. For that reason, she made no comment and bore up beautifully to being hoisted on board the enormous yacht in her fancy gown and greeted by the captain and a glass of champagne before being guided up to the top deck and a bedroom that took her breath away.

'I'm afraid that we now need to have a serious discussion about your brother,' Tor murmured levelly then, utterly taking her aback with that announcement.

Bright blue eyes widening in bewilderment, Pixie slowly swivelled, silk momentarily tightening across her slender, shapely figure to draw his magnetic gaze. 'What on earth are you talking about?'

'Today of all days, I don't want you to be upset,' Tor informed her smoothly. 'But I believe that Jordan was the source of a rather sleazy story about our first night together and Alfie that appeared in a British newspaper this morning—'

A fury unlike anything Pixie had ever felt, or indeed had even guessed she *could* feel, burned up her backbone like a licking flame and she went rigid with the force of it. 'Is that so?' she almost whispered.

'Who else could it be but Jordan?' Tor derided. 'He'll do anything for money. He has no decency, no backbone.'

'Shut up!' Pixie practically spat at him in her outrage at that denunciation.

His brows knotted, a look of incredulity in his smouldering golden eyes, such incivility not having featured very often in his experience. '*Diavolos*, Pixie. There is no reason for you to treat this as though it is some kind of personal attack on *you*. It is not intended as such.'

And Tor stood there, smokingly handsome, thrillingly sexy and towering over her. He was utterly sure of his ground in a fashion that she supposed came entirely naturally to him and yet she wanted to kill him in that instant, smite him down with heavenly lightning for blaming her poor brother for the tabloid article as well. As though Jordan had not already sinned enough and *paid* the price for his mistakes! He had lost her respect and the only home he had ever known, and his self-esteem was at basement level. And yes, he had deserved that punishment, but right now he was trying very hard to fix himself and pick himself up again, only he hadn't yet mustered sufficient strength to make more than a couple of tottering steps back towards normality. At present, in her view, Jordan was more to be pitied than condemned.

'Yes, shut up and stop talking down to me in that patronising way!' Pixie let fly at Tor angrily again. 'I gather you haven't actually *seen* that article. Well, before you hang, draw and quarter my brother for the story, acquaint yourself with the article and the facts first.'

'Have you seen it? I assumed you didn't know about it,' Tor confided in disconcertion. 'I didn't mention it because I didn't want to destroy the day.'

'So, you just destroyed it now instead by assuming that Jordan is to blame when in fact it is *your own choices* that brought the humiliation of that article down on the two of us!' Pixie flung back at him in a furious counter-attack.

'How could it be anything to do with *my* choices?' Tor shot back at her icily, his own temper rising because he had not been prepared for either her attitude or the argument that had erupted. Unsurprisingly, he would never have chosen to mention the article on their wedding night had he foreseen her response.

'Look it up online and find out, as I had to,' Pixie urged him curtly.

Tor did nothing so basic. He shot an order to one of his personal assistants to send him an exact copy of the item, still outraged that *his* assumptions, *his* conclusions, were being questioned.

First, a photo of a woman he had never seen in his life before arrived on his screen, and he turned it towards Pixie and breathed, 'Who is she?'

'Saffron Wells—an actress. The beauty who brought you back to the house that night. You allowed her to pick you up and bring you back there and I suspect that she saw you leaving the room I was using the next morning.'

'I don't know what you're talking about and you know it!' Tor thundered at her, while grudgingly recalling that vague memory of someone coming down the stairs in that house that morning. Disorientated and in a bad mood, he hadn't even turned round to see who it was. 'Because you flatly *refused* to tell me everything about that night!'

Pixie was in no mood to compromise when she was still so angry with him. On a level she didn't want to examine, some of her anger related to the weirdest current of possessiveness inside her. It still annoyed her that he had allowed Saffron to pick him up, even if he hadn't done anything with the other woman, and even though she knew she would never have met him otherwise, that annoyance went surprisingly deep.

'Saffron brought you back to the house in the first place. You apparently believed you were accompanying her to a party, but she thought she was bringing you home for the night. You rejected her because supposedly you weren't in the mood and she stormed off… At least that's what *you* told me happened. But for all I know,' Pixie breathed with withering bite, 'you slept with her too before I came into the kitchen, where you were waiting for a taxi!'

Tor swore in vicious Greek at being slapped in the face with that character assassination. 'I may have been drunk, I may have slept with you that night, but I'm no playboy and you know it.'

'According to your online images, you've been around...*a lot,*' Pixie emphasised, unimpressed. 'However, I'd say it's unlikely anything happened between you because I think you offended her and that's one good reason why she sold that story. Her being passed over for someone as ordinary as me would have been the last straw. The other reason is that, being a media person, she lapped up the opportunity to get her picture into a newspaper.'

Tor was frowning now. 'But if she was some random woman in that house, how could she possibly have known about you getting pregnant and all the rest of it when you left the property only a couple of days later?'

'There were other connections involved. I was using Steph's room that night. Steph was one of the other tenants and I worked with her sister. I had ongoing contact with Steph because of my cat, Coco. Steph only finally gave Coco to me when I was pregnant,' Pixie recited wearily, the fury draining from her without warning. 'Someone somewhere talked and connected the dots and that's how the story about us got out. It had nothing at all to do with my brother, who knew less than you did about what happened that night until very recently.'

His lean dark features hard and forbidding, Tor jerked his chin in acknowledgement of that likelihood. He was angry because he had got it badly wrong again with his bride. He was angry because he had been so *sure* of his facts when a thieving, dishonest, greedy character, such as he regarded Jordan to be, had been in the mix and available to blame. But he was still stunned by the level of her loyalty to her brother, her childhood memories of the other man evidently sufficient to restore some measure of her faith and affection for him.

Her attitude made him think of his own response to Sevastiano, the older brother he had only met when they were both adults. Tor had found it an unnerving experience to go from being the eldest son in the family to the discovery that his father's eldest child had actually been born to another woman before his marriage to Tor's mother. If he was honest, he had never really given Sevastiano a fair crack of the whip and learning that Katerina had been unfaithful to him *with* Sev had been the last nail in the coffin. No semblance of sibling affection had ever developed.

Shaking off that momentary attack of self-examination, Tor straightened his broad shoulders. 'I owe you an apology,' he breathed between gritted teeth. 'But make some allowances for the difference between our natures. When it comes to your brother, I'm less forgiving of his wrongs towards you and my son and much more about punishment, while you're overflowing with compassion and a desperate desire to rehabilitate him. But please accept that *my* strongest motivation is to protect you from Jordan and ensure that he cannot take advantage of you or hurt you again.'

Pixie nodded jerkily, tears stinging the backs of her eyes because this was not how she had imagined her wedding night would turn out, with them at loggerheads, angry words having been exchanged and now all the subsequent discomfiture of the aftermath. 'Apology accepted,' she said stiffly, crossing the room to explore through a door and discover to her relief that it led into a bathroom where she could excusably escape for long enough to regroup. 'I'm going to treat myself to a bath... if you don't mind?'

'Of course not,' Tor murmured tautly, wondering how to dig himself back out of the hole he had dug for himself and coming up blank from lack of practice in that field.

'I need your help to undo the hooks on this dress,' Pixie admitted even more stiffly. 'I don't want to damage it. Being a sentimental sort, I want to keep it.'

Tor breathed in deep and slow, questioning how the hell he had once again screwed up with her when such errors and misunderstandings had never occurred with any other woman. He was all over the place inside his head: he could *feel* it and it unnerved him more than a little to appreciate that, with her, he lost his focus, his self-discipline and his logical cool. She had shouted at him and he had not even known she was *capable* of shouting because in so many ways she was his exact opposite, being gentle and caring and softer in every way. Softer but *not* weak, he grasped, grateful for that distinction, because her weasel-like brother's weakness had turned his stomach.

'I like that,' he admitted honestly. 'You're not thinking of me having a successor.'

Pixie twisted her head round to survey him in shock. 'You thought that might have been likely?'

'It's not uncommon in my world for a woman to use her first marriage as a stepping stone to better.'

'You're Alfie's father. I couldn't get better,' she insisted awkwardly.

'Even though I messed up?'

'Everyone does that occasionally,' Pixie pointed out, shooting him a sideways smile as he embarked on the hooks on her silk gown. 'Sooner or later I'm going to do it too...nothing surer.'

'You always say the right forgiving thing, don't you?'

'Well, it's better than being all bitter and cynical and always expecting the worst from people, which seems to be your MO... *not* trying to start another argument!' she added in haste.

'I see the world through a different lens. I'm not bitter,' Tor asserted.

Pixie would have begged to differ on that score, but she compressed her lips and said nothing at all. Of course, Tor was bitter that his first love had let him down so badly, but if he was determined not to recognise the fact, that was *his* business, not hers. It wasn't his fault that he didn't know enough about his own emotions to label them, was it? Because she had decided that *that* was what she was dealing with: a guy utterly unable to recognise his own feelings for what they were, blind as a bat to his own emotional promptings. He had concentrated on the guilt he'd experienced at his wife and daughter's deaths, beat himself up for his mistakes rather than on the huge betrayal that had preceded and powered that tragic loss.

Tor's usually nimble fingers began to get inexplicably clumsy as he unhooked the back of Pixie's dress. Pale pearly shoulder blades, narrow and delicate, were revealed, and as the hooks worked down, something frilly and lacy and absolutely Tor's favourite sort of lingerie began to appear and he snatched in a startled breath, wondering why it felt vaguely indecent to find his bride quite so sexually potent. It was a tiny corset, as tiny as she was as long as she didn't turn round and show off the front view, which he imagined would be spectacular. He reminded himself that she was heading for a bath and that the last thing she needed now was to be mauled by a sexually voracious bridegroom, who had already infuriated her. He spread the corners of the gown back and succumbed involuntarily to temptation, pressing his lips softly against an inch of pale porcelain skin.

'Tor...?' Pixie prompted, but only after a helpless little quiver as that unsought kiss on her skin travelled through her.

'Working on the hooks,' Tor ground out thickly, watching the corset hooks appear, the pulse at his groin speeding from interested to crazed because he was realising just what he had wrecked. The fancy lingerie had been for *his* benefit because he had made that remark about how much he liked such adornments.

'I find you incredibly tempting,' he breathed with a ragged undertone as he traced the line of her shoulder to her nape with the tip of his tongue and lingered there, drinking in the fruit scent of her skin, some kind of peachy scent that absolutely did it for him. 'I'm sorry.'

Pixie wasn't really speaking to Tor, not in a childish way but in a grown-up-quiet way. She had been en route to a bath and a serious rethink about where she stood with him, but nobody had ever told her that she was incredibly tempting before. No man's hand had ever trembled before against her shoulder and that she could have the power to affect Tor to that extent was a dream come true for her. Slowly, Pixie turned round and let the silk dress drop down her arms to her wrists and fall, so that the whole thing dropped round her ankles and he was gratifyingly entranced. It was written all over him, brilliant dark golden eyes locked to her like magnets, and she liked that, really, *really* liked that.

'Kiss me,' she said abruptly, not thinking about it, *refusing* to think about it, just acting on natural instinct.

'That's where we started out before.'

'Nothing wrong with a repeat,' Pixie told him squarely. 'But you're far too tall to kiss standing upright, so I think we should move…er…lie down, whatever.'

'You were going for a bath.' Tor husked the reminder reluctantly.

'A lady can change her mind,' Pixie told him, drowning in the dark golden smouldering depths of his black-fringed eyes, revelling in the truth that the gorgeous guy was actually *her* gorgeous guy and not someone else's.

'Did I say sorry *that* well?' Tor asked, sucking in a quick shallow breath, quite unbelievably enthralled by her change of heart and shocked by himself.

'I'm softer than you but selfish too,' Pixie whispered shakily. 'I want you. I probably want you more than I ever wanted anything in my life.'

And that was the green light that Tor needed to snatch her up out of her fallen gown and carry her over to the bed, where he laid her out to admire her in all the glory of the white corset, panties and white stockings she had worn for his benefit. He couldn't take his eyes off her tiny figure lying on display, the full mounds of her breasts cupped in lace for his delectation, the tight white vee of silk between her thighs, the slender graceful line of her thighs. He was enchanted by that view. Dimly, he registered that sex had, evidently, been rather boring before he met Pixie, something only his strong libido had driven him to do on a regular basis, and that was a fine distinction he had not recognised before. *She* made him burn with lust, *she* added another entire dimension to his concept of sexual desire.

Without warning, Pixie scrambled up and off the bed and began to help him out of his jacket. 'You've got too much on,' she mumbled, half under her breath, belatedly embarrassed by her own boldness.

Tor smiled, shed the tie, the jacket, peeled off his shirt and toed off his shoes. He was getting rid of the socks and unzipping his trousers when he saw her seated at the foot of the wide divan watching him as though he were a film. 'What?' he queried with a raised brow.

'You didn't undress the first time,' Pixie admitted starkly.

And in that single admission, Tor knew how badly he had got it wrong the night his son had been conceived and he almost grimaced. 'Precautions?'

Pixie winced and reddened. 'No, neither of us thought of that, so that wasn't entirely your fault. I was foolish too.'

His black brows drew together. 'I was fully clothed when I woke up the next day, which is why I had no idea I had been intimate with anyone,' he breathed in a driven undertone, because nothing that he was discovering was raising his opinion of himself when he was under the influence of alcohol and he knew it would be a cold day in hell before he got in that condition again.

Pixie dropped her curly head with a wincing motion of her slight shoulders. 'I...er...tidied you up. I was... I was embarrassed... If I'm honest, I didn't want you to know or remember me. I felt I had let myself down and taken advantage of you.'

'Of...*me*?' Tor cited in disbelief.

'Well, you'd been quite clear about not wanting to be with

anyone after you had rejected Saffron,' she reminded him rue-fully. 'I should've heeded that and drawn back.'

Tor set his teeth together. 'We both got carried away and I know why. You turn me on fast and hard and neither of us was able to call a halt.'

Pixie nodded in a rush, seeing that he had grasped what had happened, the sheer explosion of hunger that had seized her. But while they had been talking, Tor had also been getting naked and her mind was wandering because she was very much enjoy-ing the view. Stripped down to black boxers, he had the build of a Greek god garbed in living flesh instead of marble and the lean, powerful lines of muscle etching his chest and abdomen made her mouth run dry. He was amazingly perfect and beau-tiful. In Eloise's parlance, it was a case of the super tanker and the tugboat comparison again. What on earth had he *ever* seen in her ordinary self? Or was that kind of physical attraction sim-ply unquantifiable and impossible to explain? she wondered. The pull between them that night had been so strong, so irre-sistible and already she could feel the same thing happening to her again, her body warming and quickening down deep inside and her heartbeat speeding up.

'Tonight will be different from that first night,' Tor swore with an edge of raw anticipation and masculine resolve that sent butterflies cascading through her stomach while a hot, tight feeling clenched her pelvis.

CHAPTER NINE

'IT WASN'T A bad experience…er…you and me,' Pixie reassured him with hot cheeks. 'Physically it worked for me.'

'I can do better than that,' Tor husked, staring down at her, at the high plump mounds peaking from the lace edge of the corset. 'I love this lingerie, *hara mou.*'

'You're acting like it's something special to you…me wearing this stuff,' Pixie muttered tensely. 'When we both know it's *not* special because you've had many women in your life and a great deal of experience.'

'After Katerina I never stayed with anyone for more than a few days, so I was never around long enough for anyone to make the effort to dress up for me,' he countered bluntly as he gazed down at her with heavily lashed, half-hooded, dark brooding eyes. 'We're married now. This is a whole different relationship.'

Yes, very different from the one he must once have had with the woman he loved, Pixie's brain sniped, and she stifled that thought, knowing that such thoughts, such pointless, tasteless comparisons, would drive her mad if she let them in. Katerina was his past and *she* was his present and she had to be sensible and view their marriage in that positive light, not give way to envy. *Envy?* That was what she was discovering inside herself, a sense of envy relating to his late wife, who had had it all with him and simply thrown it away. Why *was* she envious? Why was she feeling more than she should about an old relationship that was none of her business?

But that knotty question fled her mind as Tor brought her down on the bed and crushed her mouth under his. If there was one thing she had learned the first time Tor kissed her, it was that Tor knew how to kiss, indeed, Tor knew so well how to kiss that he made her head spin and sent a ripple of craving shooting through her with every dancing plunge of his tongue. Her fingers laced into the thick silk of his hair and held him to her, smoothing down over his wide, strong shoulders, exploring over the satin skin of his back because that first night she hadn't been able to touch him while he was still clothed.

Tor came up on an elbow, a long forefinger skimming back an edge of lace to bare a rounded breast crowned by a straining pink nipple. 'You excite the hell out of me,' he admitted gruffly, hungrily closing a mouth to that tempting peak, using the tip of his tongue, the tug of his teeth and his warm sensual mouth to pleasure her.

The motion of his mouth on her breasts tightened her, as if there were a chain leading to the hot, liquid centre of her body, and her hips shifted upwards, all of her awash with more craving. He sat her up with easy confidence and began to unhook the corset. Her cheeks flushed and she looked away from him, wanting so much to own that confidence of his. It had been dim that first night, never mind his lack of awareness: he had not been looking for flaws.

'What's wrong?' he asked her, disconcerting her by noticing her anxiety.

'It was sort of darkish that night and now I feel like I'm under floodlights.' With one hand she made an awkward motion towards the fancy lights above, the mirrors on the units adding their myriad reflections to the brightness.

Tor shifted up and hit a switch above the bed and the illumination dimmed. 'Better?'

'It's really stupid being shy when we've already got a kid,' Pixie muttered guiltily, wishing she could get a grip on her self-consciousness before it wrecked the atmosphere.

'No, it's not.' Tor tugged her back down to him, moulding his big hands to her full breasts. 'But you do stress a lot, don't you?'

'Yes,' she admitted ruefully.

'So, it's up to me to ensure you have more to think about, *latria mou*…' Tor skated a fingertip across the taut triangle of her panties and she gasped, the pulse of arousal between her slender thighs kicking on to an intense high.

In that moment everything else melted away along with her insecurities. Suddenly, she was twisting round to find that wicked mouth of his, so sensually full and yet hard and soft at the same time, that so enthralled her. He was peeling off her panties and she quivered at the prospect of him touching her again, for the merest instant mortified by her own eagerness, but then she was already maddeningly conscious of the swollen, slick readiness of her own body.

Even the lightest brush of his fingertips aroused her, and she was knocked off balance when he slid down the bed and began to use his mouth on that most tender area. Of course, she knew about that, knew the specifics of everything sexual, but she hadn't ever imagined that anything could feel as good as what he made her feel then. Every nerve ending in her body seemed to be centred there and before very long she was quivering with little reflexive tremors running through her and breathless little sounds she couldn't silence falling from her parted lips as her head thrashed back and forth on the pillow.

As the pressure in her pelvis rose and tightened, her hips began to writhe to a spontaneous rhythm and the great gathering whoosh of sensation surged and she cried out and then lay there, discovering her fingers were knotted in his hair and slowly withdrawing them, a great lassitude sweeping her.

'No, you don't get to sleep now, *moraki mou*,' Tor told her with a slashing grin that banished every shred of dark, forbidding tension from his lean, darkly handsome features. He kissed her with devouring hunger as he stretched up over her with the lean, powerful, predatory grace of a stalking panther. She tasted herself on his lips and still moaned beneath that sensual assault as he hooked up her knees and settled her back, pushing his hot, sleek shaft against the still-tingling entrance to her body and plunging in hard enough to make her gasp in delight.

He angled down his hips and sank so deep into her that she didn't know where he began and she ended and that was only the beginning, the wildly arousing beginning while she was still in control. But the excitement of his fluid, driving thrusts into her sensitised body smashed her control, smashed it and broke it into tiny pieces until she was rising against him with her heart pounding and her body arching, craving his every move. She could barely breathe, she could certainly not speak, but had she had her voice she would only have urged him *not to stop*. The burning rise to orgasm began all over again, forcing her higher and higher, stimulated almost beyond bearing and seething with a physical sensual energy she had not known she possessed. And then at the zenith of sensation she shattered, electrified by the blazing excitement that convulsed her every limb, and she was utterly captivated by the drenching slow, sweet pleasure that flooded her in the aftermath.

Tor froze as Pixie cuddled into him, her little hand spreading across the centre of his damp heaving chest, and for an instant he almost lost control and pushed her away from him in a knee-jerk reaction. For five years, he had been pushing women away the instant they tried to be affectionate because, rather than pleasing him, it chilled him. It had always reminded him of Katerina's superficial affection, which had, in the end, proved to be so false, not only towards him, but towards her daughter as well, he acknowledged grimly. But he would not make vile comparisons that Pixie did not deserve, and he would make a really big effort to pretend that this was his first marriage *before* he learned to question almost everything a woman said and did.

That sounded bitter, he conceded in surprise as he extended an arm round Pixie's slight, pliant body and pulled her close. But he wasn't bitter—*was he? Thee mou*, his bride was as good as a witch when it came to slotting odd ideas into his mind! Only, she didn't need a book to cast a spell, only her body, her response, her warmth, all of which she offered so freely. If he wasn't very careful he would hurt her again, because she was much more fragile than the women he was accustomed to dealing with and he wasn't of a sensitive persuasion.

'Is it always that amazing?' Pixie whispered.

'No, it's not,' Tor answered truthfully, and he was almost but not quite tempted to tell her that it had never been that good for him before, but she didn't need to know that, did she? Theirs was a marriage of convenience and practicality and that was *all* he wanted it to be. He didn't want the legendary highs or the fabled lows, he would be content with his son and a marriage on an even keel.

Pixie felt blissfully relaxed, relieved that the silly newspaper story had been dealt with and set aside without causing more trouble. Being in a relationship, being one half of a whole, was very new to her and she was beginning to see that there were no hard and fast rules and that she had to learn to compromise and smooth over the rough spots where she could. Even now, though, she was aware that even if Tor didn't see it, he was still damaged by what Katerina had done to him.

Pixie had felt him freeze when she'd snuggled up to him and she had held her breath, waiting to see what he would do, and she had only relaxed when he'd pulled her the rest of the way into his arms. But that didn't mean that she wasn't aware that she had married a wary, bitter, suspicious man with a tendency to expect everything to blow up in his face when he least expected it. Hopefully, time and experience would teach him differently when it came to having her and Alfie as a family. Should how he felt matter to her as much as it did? Well, she knew what her problem was: she was halfway to falling madly in love with Tor, possibly even further than halfway, she conceded ruefully.

Almost a month later, Pixie watched Tor climb, still dripping, from the pool, after the acrobatics he had performed there to entertain Alfie, and cross the main deck to speak to the yacht captain, a bearded man currently sporting an apologetic smile.

While they were chatting she lifted Alfie, who was already half-asleep, and moved down to the cabin where her son was sleeping to change him and put him in his crib for a nap. Their nanny, Isla, was probably sunbathing on the top deck because Pixie and Tor usually kept Alfie with them in the mornings. She went for a shower and was towelling herself dry when Tor reappeared in the doorway.

'We have an unscheduled stop to make this evening to take on supplies. While the crew are dealing with stocking up, we'll be enjoying a sheltered cove and dining in a restaurant which the captain assures me is a hidden gem,' he related lazily as he peeled off his shorts.

Heat mushroomed in her pelvis as she watched and dimly wondered if she would ever become accustomed to Tor's utterly stunning masculine beauty. His gleaming bronzed gaze struck hers and she stilled, her heartbeat quickening, her breath catching in her throat. *'Se thelo,'* he breathed, thick and low.

I want you—one little Greek phrase she had become hugely familiar with over the past four weeks.

Hunger lightening his eyes to gold, he reached for her, disposing of the towel with an aggressive jerk to release her small body from its folds and hauling her up against his hard, hot length.

'I *always* want you,' he breathed with a slight frown, as if he couldn't quite work out why that should be so. 'You're turning me into a sex addict.'

Pixie flushed, knowing that she matched him there. She couldn't keep her hands off him, couldn't back off from the allure of that raw masculine magnetism he emanated if her life depended on it. It flared in her every time she looked at him, every time he reached for her, like a flame that had only been fed into a blaze by constant proximity. A month was a long time for a couple to be alone together, she acknowledged, just a little sad that they would be returning to London the following day. It had been a wonderful holiday though, *her* honeymoon, something she had not been quite sure it was when they'd first set sail on their wedding night. But they had both needed that time and space to get to know each other on a deeper level and it had worked. Tor had probably planned it that way, she conceded, having finally come to understand that Tor planned most things. It was just the way he operated. Only with sex was Tor spontaneous or impulsive.

'What's wrong?' Tor husked as he backed her into the cabin again, all hungry predatory resolve and indescribably sexy in the role.

'Absolutely nothing,' she told him truthfully, because she reckoned that she would have to be a very demanding person to want more from him than she already had, and she refused to allow herself to feel discontented.

He spread her out on the bed and she tingled all over, her skin prickling with high-voltage awareness and anticipation as he feathered his sensual mouth over her protuberant nipples, making her moan. He stroked a provocative fingertip between her legs, where she was already swollen and damp, and a fierce smile of satisfaction slanted his lean, darkly handsome features. Without any further preamble, he thrust into her hard and fast and a shot of dynamite pleasure ravaged her pliant body. His compelling rhythm sent her to a stormy height of need faster than she would have believed. It was good, it was *so* good she climaxed crying out his name…and something else. 'I love you!' she gasped, just seconds before her brain could kick in again and make her swallow those words.

And Tor said…*nothing*. Pixie told herself that possibly he

hadn't heard or that he was just politely ignoring that accidental word spillage of hers and that that was better than forcing
her to discuss the issue. For Tor would see that declaration as an
issue, not a benefit, not a compliment, not something he should
treasure and be grateful for. In turmoil, she turned away from
him, her face literally burning with mortification and a sense of
humiliation. Why? *Why* had she had to let those words escape?

Maybe it was pathetic to be so happy with a guy who didn't
love her when deep down inside her there was still this dangerous nagging need to have *more* from him and, of course, it
bothered her. After all, love couldn't be turned on like a magic
tap by anyone but perhaps, over time, Tor would come to care
for her more, she had recently soothed herself. Life wasn't a
fairy tale, Eloise had warned her, but, in truth, Pixie couldn't
help still yearning for the fairy tale.

Yet at the same time, honesty lay at the very heart of her
nature and she had wanted to share her feelings with Tor, give
him that warmth and validation. After all, she knew for a fact
that life could change in a moment with an accident, an illness,
some other terrible event, and she needed to live in the moment.
Secrets weren't her style.

It was true though that there were still little black holes in
their relationship where she didn't dare travel. He never ever
talked about Katerina or Sofia, not even accidentally. It was as if
he had locked that all up in some underground box on the night
of the crash when he'd lost his wife and child and, sadly, only
an excess of alcohol had unleashed his devastating emotional
confessions the evening he and Pixie had first met. The rest of
the time? Tor might as well have been a single man rather than
a widower when she'd married him.

Yet Tor had asked her so much about her parents and her
childhood memories, had freely satisfied his own curiosity and
it had brought them closer, of course it had. Why couldn't he
do the same for her when it came to his first marriage? His silence was a barrier that disturbed her. Why was he still holding

back? It was because of her honesty that Tor now understood a great deal better why she was so attached to her half-brother, the boy who had stood up for her in the playground when other children had teased her about her diminutive size, the adult male who had comforted her after the death of their father and her mother by promising that he would always be there for her.

'Need a shower,' she muttered, pulling free of the arms anchored round her and heading for the bathroom as though her life depended on it because his silence hurt her. Was it possible that he was still in love with his dead wife? Or was she being fanciful?

Tor rolled over and punched a pillow, perfect white teeth clenching now that Pixie was out of view. For a split second he was furious with her for putting him in that position. Just because he wasn't prepared to lie, wasn't prepared to pretend! Those three words were so easy to say, had routinely featured between him and Katerina and they had been absolutely meaningless and empty on her side.

But was it fair to punish Pixie for Katerina's lies and pretences?

He froze as that possibility penetrated his brain for the very first time. He wasn't punishing anybody, he roared defensively inside himself. He was simply insisting on a higher standard of honesty in their marriage, which meant that there would be a smaller chance of misunderstandings occurring between them. They needed a lot of things in a successful marriage, but love wasn't a necessity, not as respect and loyalty and caring were, he reasoned in exasperation. Pixie was just young and rather naïve and had yet to grasp such fine distinctions. And it wasn't as though believing that she loved him was likely to do her any harm, he rationalised, denying the warmth spreading through his chest and the smile tugging at the corners of his mouth.

That evening Pixie dressed to go ashore for dinner in a glorious white sundress that flattered her new tan, her blond curls tumbling round her shoulders in abundance. Her wardrobe had expanded over the month because Tor had taken her to more than one exclusive shopping outlet where he had insisted on buying her stuff. Jewellery such as she had never expected to own sparkled in the diamonds at her ears and throat, the slender gold watch on her wrist, the glittering rings on her fingers. On the outside she looked like a rich woman; on the inside, though, she still felt like an imposter, she acknowledged unhappily. She had won Katerina's place only by the other woman's death and an accidental conception. She was basically just Katerina's imperfect replacement and even Alfie was only a replacement for the little girl who had died.

The launch delivered her and Tor to a beach, where he insisted on carrying her across to the steps that wound up the cliff to where the restaurant sat. Pixie examined her feelings for him as he set her carefully down on the steps, so attentive, so honourable, so everything but *not* loving. How could she condemn him for that lack? she scolded herself sharply, annoyed that she was letting her own humiliation linger and twist her up to the detriment of their marriage. That was foolish, short-sighted, and in the light of that reflection she linked her arms round his neck before he could straighten and stretched up to kiss him. He didn't have to love her because she loved him; they could get by fine as they were.

Relief coursed through Tor, who had remained insanely conscious of how quiet and muted Pixie had become throughout the day. He didn't know when he had become so attuned to her moods, but he noticed the instant the sparkle died in her eyes and she withdrew from him. It had disconcerted him to appreciate how much she could put him on edge. He smiled at her as he urged her up the steps, careful to stay behind her in case she stumbled in her high heels. They took seats out on the terrace with its panoramic view of the sea and had only received their menus when Tor swore softly in surprise under his breath.

An older couple had walked out onto the terrace.

'My godparents,' he breathed. 'Basil and Dimitra...*not* a happy coincidence.'

'I think I dimly remember them from the wedding...but we didn't actually speak,' Pixie whispered. 'Don't you like them?'

'It's not that,' Tor parried with a frown before he stood up to greet the other couple.

Pixie rose as well, walking into a hail of Greek being exchanged and smiling valiantly. Dimitra introduced herself in easy English, explaining that she had grown up in London before moving to Greece in her teens, where she had gone to school with Tor's mother, Pandora. Their meeting was not quite the coincidence Tor had stated, Pixie thought once she learned that the other couple owned a holiday home nearby. Tor insisted that the couple join them for their meal, and it passed pleasantly with talk of their cruise round the Greek islands until Tor became increasingly involved in talking business with his godfather. By the coffee stage, the men had shifted to the outside bar across the terrace and the two women were alone.

'I feel guilty that we've intruded on your last night away.' Dimitra sighed.

'I'm really surprised that I didn't get talking to you at the wedding when you're so close to Hallas and Pandora,' Pixie confided, wondering how that oversight had come about.

'I suppose because we felt it would've been inappropriate to put ourselves forward too much. I wasn't even sure about us accepting the invitation to your wedding,' Dimitra admitted and, seeing Pixie's frowning, puzzled look, added, 'You don't know, do you? Tor's first wife was *our* daughter...'

'Oh...' Pixie whispered, bereft of breath by that revelation but equally quickly grasping the difficulties of that situation. 'But you're all still good friends, aren't you?'

'Of course, although it's a shame that Tor chose to conceal the truth about their marriage,' Dimitra shared in a troubled undertone. 'After what he'd endured, we've never wanted to tackle that subject with him directly, but we're straight-talking people and it would've been easier for us had he just admitted that our daughter was having an affair and that Sofia was not his. At first I was grateful for that silence but with such close friends I would've preferred the truth rather than feeling forced to live a lie.'

Pixie settled startled eyes on the other woman, swiftly suppressing the shock of learning that Sofia had *not*, after all, been Tor's child. 'I don't think Tor realises that *you* know.'

'We knew. We tried hard to stop it, but we got nowhere. Katerina was obsessed with Devon.'

Pixie's brow furrowed. 'Devon?' she queried.

'Sevastiano's half-brother, Devon. Katerina called him Dev. Ironically, they met at a prewedding party Hallas and Pandora threw for Tor and my daughter. Devon was already married with two young children,' Dimitra revealed heavily. 'But once Tor and Katerina moved to London, where Devon lived, the fact that they were both married didn't influence either of them and we didn't know it was happening until two years after the marriage when we caught them together. It was on that horrible day that my daughter admitted that she was pregnant with Devon's child. I won't go into our feelings, but you can imagine how treacherous I felt when Pandora wept over the passing of a child who was not of their blood. But it was not *our* secret to tell.'

And Tor hadn't revealed that final secret even when he *could* have told it that first night they met, Pixie reflected painfully. Even more revealing was his silence on that score, a silence so complete, so unyielding over the entire sordid business that he had been erroneously blaming his brother, Sevastiano, for being his late wife's lover when in fact it had not been him. How on earth had he contrived to get *that* wrong? Yet it served Tor right, a part of Pixie declared *without* sympathy. He had been far too busy hugging his damaged ego and his secrets, and Tor and his family had remained in dangerous ignorance long after the event. And that was very unhealthy, wasn't it?

A welter of differing thoughts and deductions assailed Pixie on the launch that wafted them back to the yacht. What she had learned from Dimitra had put her in an awkward position. She had to tell Tor not only that his former in-laws were already fully acquainted with their late daughter's peccadilloes, but also that he had misjudged his brother, Sevastiano, who had not been Katerina's lover. How could she keep quiet about such matters? They were too important to ignore yet too personal for her to want to tackle them…aside of that revelation about Sofia, who had not been Tor's daughter, as he had led her to believe.

But did Tor even know that Sofia had not been his child? It was perfectly possible that he didn't know, Pixie reasoned uneasily. On the other hand, if he *did* know, Pixie believed that Tor should have told *her*—because such an issue *did* matter to the mother of the baby she had assumed to be his second child.

However, if Dimitra was to be believed, Alfie was Tor's firstborn, and if he had known that all along and kept quiet about it, deliberately misleading Pixie in relation to her son's status, she *did* have a bone to pick with him. Just at that moment Pixie felt very tired of following in Katerina's footsteps and suspecting that her beloved Alfie was a mere replacement for Tor's lost daughter. All of a sudden that felt like a burning issue for her. But at the same time she was consumed by the awareness of what Tor must have suffered when he'd realised that the child he loved was not his child, and she felt quite sick at the prospect of having to broach that topic with him.

'You're very quiet. Did Dimitra say something that upset you? I didn't intend to leave you alone. Basil had a tricky financial problem he wanted my advice on and I lost track of time.'

'No, nothing she said upset me,' Pixie lied, because she didn't want him misinterpreting her meaning. 'Although I could've done with you just biting the bullet and telling me that your godparents are your former in-laws. It's not such a big deal.'

'It feels awkward now that I've remarried,' Tor countered a little stiffly. 'Especially with all that happened five years ago.

I've known them all my life but I'm aware that they feel uncomfortable as well. It's unfortunate. They're a lovely couple.'

'Yes. I liked them,' Pixie confided, on surer ground.

'It's a mystery to me why their daughters turned out as they did. Maybe they spoilt them, never told them no... I don't know. I feel like I should know, though, when I grew up with them running around my home, but you have a different viewpoint as a child.'

'I didn't know there was another daughter.'

'Angelina. Didn't you meet her at the wedding?' Tor asked casually.

'Oh, yes, I met her, but I didn't realise the connection.' Pixie understood Angelina's bad attitude then, or thought she did: a sister being confronted by her dead sibling's replacement bride and child. The brunette had been unpleasant but her identity granted her some excuse for her behaviour, in Pixie's opinion.

Her mind moved on as she mulled over Tor's remark about it being a mystery how the Raptis daughters had turned out as they had. That was the closest he had ever come to criticising Katerina and it surprised her, for she had assumed that he still viewed his first wife as some kind of misunderstood martyr.

'We have to talk when we get back,' she breathed softly as Tor settled her down in a seat on the launch, having carried her across the beach to save her from the task of removing her shoes.

'About what?'

'Stuff,' she framed flatly.

His ebony brows pleated, bronzed eyes narrowing with a dark glitter in the moonlight, and she thought how gorgeous his sculpted bone structure was and of the marvel that she was actually married to such a man. All that electrifying sexiness and caring and she was still finding fault? Was she crazy?

CHAPTER TEN

TOR HAD SPENT much of the evening lazily watching his wife across the depth of the terrace, drinking in her natural animation, the shine of her naturally blond curls below the lights, the deep ocean blueness of her eyes and the amazing curves hinted at even below that perfectly modest sundress. Where she was concerned, he was like a junkie in constant need of a fix, he reflected grimly, because that lack of control, that burning hunger that continually seethed in him, bothered him. Something about Pixie revved his libido to absurd heights and, always a fan of everything in moderation, he had already tried and failed abysmally to switch off that reaction or at the very least turn it down to a more acceptable level.

And what did she want to talk about? He could think of nothing amiss and that put him on edge as well because he didn't like surprises. In his past experience a surprise had rarely led to anything good and yet Pixie regularly surprised him in the most positive of ways. She was a terrific mother to his son, protective without overdoing it, loving and caring and willing to share Alfie. She was unsophisticated, naïve, utterly ignorant of the exclusive world he inhabited and yet she moved through that same world with disconcerting grace and assurance, relying on ordinary courtesy to smooth her path. When he least expected it, she impressed him, and she had done it over and over again.

On board the yacht again, Pixie walked ahead of him up to their master cabin, where most of their luggage had already been packed ready for their departure back to London. First thing in the morning they were being picked up by a helicopter, which would deliver them straight to the airport.

'We can talk when we get back to London,' she suggested rather abruptly, apprehensive about the confrontation that she knew awaited her. It cut her to the heart that Tor had *not* chosen to confide in her about the truth that he had not been Sofia's father. That revelation on top of Katerina's infidelity must have devastated him. Yet Pixie had believed that she and Tor were getting really close, but how could she go on believing that comforting conviction when he continued to hide such a dreadful secret from her? His silence on that score hurt her a great deal, showing a dangerous fault line in their relationship, making her feel more insecure than ever about how he still viewed Katerina.

Tor was frowning now, his lean, strong features taut and a little forbidding. 'No, say whatever you have to say now.'

'I'll just spit it out, then,' Pixie murmured reluctantly. 'I found out some pretty shocking things listening to Dimitra this evening.'

'But you said—'

'I couldn't explain unless we had privacy,' Pixie interposed wryly. 'For a start, Katerina's parents are fully aware that their daughter was having an affair and was in the process of leaving you when she died. They tried to stop the affair, but she wouldn't listen to them.'

Tor was stunned.

'I can't credit that…are you sure?'

'Unequivocally. Dimitra actually said that pretending everything was fine in your marriage put more of a strain on them because they felt as though they were being forced to lie. But at the same time, she acknowledged that it was your right to maintain that pretence if that's what you preferred. She didn't have any axe to grind. I appreciate that you believed you were protecting them from distress by not telling them the truth but, really, I think it would have been easier all round if you'd just spoken up at the time,' she confided gently.

'You know nothing about it. I told you about the situation with Sev though,' Tor bit out angrily, taking her aback because that anger seemed to come out of nowhere at her.

'According to your ex-mother-in-law, Sev *wasn't* Katerina's lover,' Pixie stated even more uneasily. 'It wasn't him, it was his brother, Devon.'

Tor stared back at her, his eyes dark with seething incredulity. 'That's not possible. Dimitra must have misunderstood.'

'I don't think so. They knew about the affair before you did and presumably, if they tried to stop it, they did discuss the man involved with their daughter,' Pixie pointed out quietly. 'Look, I know you hate all this being raked up again and I appreciate how difficult all of this is for you, Tor—'

'How the hell could you?' Tor demanded with ferocious bite. 'You're standing there giving forth about issues that are nothing to do with you and naturally I resent that.'

'I resent being plunged into the middle of your secret, sordid past when I didn't want to be involved in any way!' Pixie fired back at him, embarrassment and pain at his attitude combining to send her temper over the edge as well. 'As far as I'm concerned, I feel like Katerina might as well still be alive because you still think of her as your wife and protect her good name so carefully. Well, what about me? Where do *I* come in? I've only been married to you for a month and already I feel like I'm living in her shadow!'

'*Thee mou*...that's rubbish!' Tor blistered back at her, bronzed eyes shot through with smouldering lights of gold disbelief at that charge.

Pixie raised a doubting brow. 'Is it? Why are you still so

guilty about her death that you took all the blame for it on your own shoulders? Were you a rotten husband? Were you unfaithful as well? And why didn't you tell me that Alfie was your *first* child? I feel that that's something that I should have known. Maybe because it's the only thing out of all of this mess that relates to me personally. But you should've told me that Sofia wasn't your daughter by blood. I understand and fully accept that you loved her and that you probably didn't discover that truth until Katerina was leaving you, but I do believe that you *could* have shared that with me.'

Tor had frozen where he stood, shaken at that hail of spontaneously emotional censure emerging from mild-tempered Pixie. 'I wasn't a rotten husband and I wasn't unfaithful. As to why I didn't tell you about Sofia's paternity…?' He spread lean brown hands. 'I can't really answer that. Maybe because it was the last straw, the ultimate humiliation for a man to learn that the child he has been raising and loving is not his. Maybe I was still in denial because, yes, I did love that little girl a great deal. But I still don't see how Sofia's paternity has anything at all to do with you or Alfie.'

'Well, that news doesn't surprise me,' Pixie retorted tight-lipped in her distress, furiously swallowing back the thickness in her throat and the warning sting at the backs of her eyes. 'All along you haven't once understood how I feel about anything because you don't really care about me. So, let's leave it there for tonight, Tor. I'm exhausted and I'm going to bed.'

'That's not true,' Tor declared as she snatched up her toiletries bag and cosmetics from the en suite and walked to the door. 'Where are you going?'

'I don't want to share a bed with you tonight. I don't want to be anywhere near you,' Pixie countered stiffly, determined not to reveal her distress in front of him. 'I'll sleep in one of the other cabins.'

'That's ridiculous… I don't want that. You're blowing this nonsense up out of all proportion,' Tor proclaimed rawly.

But Pixie didn't believe that. She was horribly upset, all her feelings flailing with pain inside her and he was the blind focus of them. And she didn't even know exactly what she wanted from him, only that she wasn't receiving it. Was she blaming him for not loving her as he had loved Katerina? She stopped dead in the empty cabin next door, stricken by that suspicion because that would be absolutely unfair to Tor. And she thought of what she had thrown at him without warning and almost cringed where she stood. When had she ever acted with so little compassion before? Where had her sympathy, her understanding gone?

Dear heaven, she had thrown in his teeth the reality that his poor little daughter had not been fathered by him. Had he even known that fact before she'd hurled it at him? Or had he only suspected that he might not be Sofia's father and had she confirmed his misgivings with her attack? Her stomach tightened and swirled with nausea at that possibility. She was horrified. Kicking off the high heels now pinching her toes, she trekked back barefoot to the master cabin.

A dim light glowed on the deck terrace beyond the French windows.

Through them she could see Tor leaning up against the rail, luxuriant black cropped hair ruffling in the breeze, his jacket discarded, the fine fabric of his shirt rippling against his lean, powerful torso, and her mouth ran dry the way it always did when the sheer beauty of him punched her afresh. Lifting her chin and suppressing that reaction, Pixie went outside to join him.

'Were you already aware that Sofia wasn't yours?' she pressed bluntly, her troubled face pale and tight in the low light.

Tor gritted his teeth. 'Yes… Yes, I knew. When I tried to prevent her mother from removing her from the house that night she told me then that Sofia wasn't my daughter. At first I didn't believe her because she was hysterical. But afterwards…' He breathed with difficulty. 'I had the tests done because I had to know the truth and it was confirmed.'

'I'm still really sorry I hurled it at you like that though,' Pixie muttered shakily. 'I also think that that little girl was very fortunate to have your love and care while she was alive. Like you, she didn't know the truth, but you loved each other anyway. You were still her father, Tor, in every way that mattered.'

Tor drained the tumbler in his clenched hand, whiskey burning down into the chill inside him because he was still in shock from their exchange. 'That's a really kind thing for you to say in these circumstances. But I'm sorry that you were inadvertently dragged into my secret, sordid past tonight. Just go to bed now, Pixie. I've got nothing else to say to you right now...'

And that was true. The tormenting belief that he could have wrongly believed his half-brother, Sevastiano, had betrayed him for so many years sickened Tor. In retrospect it struck him as unbelievable that he had chosen not to confront Sev. Did he blame his pride for that silence? His desire to let sleeping dogs lie for the sake of family unity?

Yet the instant Pixie had named Devon, pieces that had never made sense to Tor had locked together neatly to provide a much clearer picture of that secret affair. And suddenly, for the first time, it had all made sense.

Devon was Sev's English half-brother and he would already have been a married man when Katerina had first met him. No doubt that was why she had gone ahead and married Tor, because she had been unable to foresee and trust in a future with a lover who already had a wife and children. Easier access to Devon would explain why she had been so keen to live in London as well.

And Sevastiano?

Tor swore under his breath, recognising that his older brother would have been placed in an impossible situation, stuck in the middle between two half-brothers: one who had never really made an effort with him—Stand up, Tor, and own your mistakes, he urged himself—the other whom presumably he'd had a warmer relationship with because he had grown up with Devon.

How could Sevastiano possibly have chosen loyalties between them?

Dismissed, and feeling like a sleepwalker, Pixie went back next door, undressing where she stood, deciding that, yes, she could go to bed with make-up on because she didn't care, she really didn't care just at that moment. Her eyes were prickling and throbbing, the tears she had been holding back burning through her defences and finally overflowing, a painful sob tearing at her throat. He had thrown her own unjust words back at her... his 'secret sordid past'. And she should never have said such words to him when the sordid aspect had related to his wife's behaviour and had had nothing at all to do with his.

Why had she done it? Why had she dragged up all that messy stuff from the past and thrown it at him as though he were the worst husband in the world? And the easy answer twisted inside her like a knife and made her groan out loud because there was nothing very adult or admirable about her envy of Katerina, her possessive vibes about her son's status or her embittered attitude to Tor's grief over the death of his first wife.

In reality, she was a nasty jealous cow and now he knew it too. She had unveiled herself in all her immature, selfish glory for his benefit, all because she had admitted she loved him and he had ignored that confession. That disappointment had wounded her and put her in the wrong state of mind, releasing turbulent emotions that had quickly got out of her control. She had said things she didn't believe, demanded truths she wasn't entitled to receive and roused memories of a tragedy she truly hadn't wanted to bring alive for him again. And she had told him that she loved him and then acted in a very unloving way. Her eyes burned and ached as she recalled his tense chilliness towards her out on the terrace. Well, what had she expected from him? Bouquets and praise?

* * *

Tor stayed up thinking for most of the night and when dawn lightened the skies, he felt amazingly light as well. It had been so many years since he had felt like that that it was almost like being reborn. Reborn? Tor winced at that fanciful concept, but he was still smiling, still wondering how he had got everything so wrong for so very long and if it was even possible that he could have set a new record for sheer stupidity.

Pixie rose heavy-eyed in spite of the exhaustion that had finally sent her to sleep and grimaced at the tackiness of waking up without having removed her make-up. It sucked to have mascara ringing her eyes and smears of make-up on her pillow and she fully understood too late why she shouldn't have done it in the first place. She was in a funereal mood, eyes swollen and red behind strategically worn sunglasses, mouth tight, a wintry outfit chosen to suit her mood.

Tor surveyed her approach for an early breakfast, noting the jeans and the black sweater and how much they enhanced her petite yet curvy figure that drove him crazy with desire. Then there was the glorious glitter of her silky curls in sunlight and the sweet delicate lines of her troubled face. An uphill climb then, he recognised grimly, exactly what he deserved because he had done everything wrong, got everything wrong, merited nothing better.

In comparison to both parents, Alfie was brimming with energy and love. He bounced in his high chair with a huge smile at them both, held out his arms pleadingly to his mother, who for the very first time failed to notice his need, and succumbed to his father instead, who not only noticed but also swept him up and made him giggle and smile and gave him kisses.

'He needs to eat, Tor,' Pixie breathed curtly.

'He wanted a cuddle,' Tor breathed with perfect assurance. 'He's a very affectionate child. Sofia was much more reserved in nature.'

Disconcerted by that reference, Pixie lifted her head. 'She was?'

'Yes. Katerina kept us apart. I thought she was a possessive mother. Even when she kept me out of the delivery room when she was born I assumed the wrong things,' he told her, taking her utterly aback with those revelations. 'I didn't smell a rat.'

'A rat?' she echoed, nonplussed.

'I wasn't a suspicious husband,' he clarified wryly. 'But right from the beginning, she tried to keep me apart from Sofia. She knew she wasn't mine and she felt guilty.'

'Oh…' Pixie replied, her confusion only deepening at what could be driving his desire to be disclosing such facts when he had never been that confiding in relation to Katerina before.

'I didn't see it at the time. I didn't even see it afterwards,' Tor admitted starkly. 'I wasn't very good at seeing that sort of thing…in advance, as it were…or even in retrospect.'

'No, you're not very switched on that way…empathy-wise,' Pixie extended awkwardly. 'You're obviously very efficient in the business line, but in personal relationships you kind of lose the plot a little.'

'Or maybe don't even see the plot to begin with,' Tor added.

Pixie steeled herself to say what she still felt she had to say. 'I wasn't fair to you last night.'

'No, you got it right,' Tor broke in grimly. 'I got it wrong.'

That silenced Pixie, who had been trying to make amends without embarrassing herself. She didn't understand. She didn't want to get it wrong again either, though, and it was the fear of doing that that kept her quiet throughout their trip to the airport and their subsequent flight back to London.

'I want you to think about whether this house is right for us,' Tor remarked as the limo drew up outside the town house. 'I didn't buy it as a family house.'

'It's a blasted amazing house,' Pixie told him sniffily, because it was enormous and fancy and everything she believed suited him to perfection. 'It's even got a garden out back. What are you talking about?'

Tor mustered his poise and a decided amount of valour and breathed in deep and slow to say, 'Some day we may think of extending the family.'

Pixie sent him a wide blue-eyed glance of naked disbelief. 'Oh, you can forget that,' she said helplessly. 'Seriously, just forget that idea!'

Another baby? Was he kidding? Whatever, his expectations were seriously out of line with her own. She would be perfectly happy just to settle for Alfie…and…er…what? she asked herself. And she couldn't come up with a single goal because, in truth, without the love she craved, Tor had nothing to offer her. She was an unreasonable woman, she told herself squarely. He was gorgeous, amazing in bed and he did all the right things as if they had been programmed into him at birth. Seriously, he was the sort of guy who would never ever forget your birthday. It wasn't love but it was the best he could offer.

So, who was she to say it wasn't enough? Who was she in her belief that she ought to have more than the basics? This was a guy who had told her from the start that he didn't think he could fall in love again…that he could give her everything else but that.

Tor had been honest.

She had been dishonest, accepting him on those terms while secretly yearning for exactly what he had told her that he couldn't deliver. Appreciating that, she swallowed hard and struggled to suppress all the powerful hurt reactions that were making it virtually impossible for her to behave normally again with Tor. She had to stop acting that way, concentrate on the future he was holding out to her, not dwell on the downside, because everything had a downside to some extent. And that future Tor was suggesting included a larger family, which was something she would eventually want too, so why had she snapped at him when he admitted it?

Isla already had Alfie tucked in his crib when she entered the nursery.

The nanny was going home to stay with her own family for a few days and while Pixie loved and relied on having help with her son, she was, conversely, looking guiltily forward to having him all to herself again for a few days. Wishing the other woman a happy break, she went into the master bedroom, stiffening into immobility a few steps in when she glimpsed Tor poised by the tall windows.

'I have something I need to tell you,' he breathed as he swung round.

And Pixie wanted to run, didn't want any more stress, any more bad news. She was full to the brim and overflowing with insecurity, regret and worry as it was.

'This is important. Perhaps you should sit down,' Tor told her tautly. 'I may not be great in the empathy stakes, but I do know that we need to clear the air.'

And he was right, of course, he was, Pixie conceded, sinking down on the foot of the bed and folding hers arms defensively on her lap while watching him like a hawk to try and read his mood. But all she could read was his tension because his beautiful eyes were screened and narrowed in concentration. His uneasiness screamed at her because not since their very first meeting had she seen Tor look less than confident.

'What's wrong?'

'I finally worked some things out and it's changed the way I see everything,' he volunteered almost harshly. 'Try not to interrupt me. I'm not good at talking about this sort of stuff and I don't want to lose the thread of what I need to explain...'

'You're scaring me,' she whispered and then she clamped a guilty hand to her lips because she realised she had said that out loud even though she didn't intend to do so. 'Sorry.'

And for a split second his wide charismatic smile flashed across his serious features and her heart jumped inside her before steadying again, because nothing could be that serious if he could still smile like that. 'There's nothing to be scared of.'

Pixie nodded rather than speak again.

But the silence stretched way beyond her expectations as Tor paced with the controlled but restive aspect of a man who would rather be anywhere than where he was at that moment. His lean, impossibly handsome face went tight. 'I feel ashamed even saying it, but I can see now that Katerina and I didn't love each other the way we thought we did when we married, but that she had the misfortune of finding that out long before I did...'

Pixie was transfixed because whatever she had been expecting, it had not been that admission. She had always believed that Katerina had been his childhood sweetheart, his first deep love, his everything.

'There was no great passion between us. I didn't think that mattered. I assumed that being friends, getting on well, the similarity between our backgrounds and even our parents being so close was more than enough to make a really good marriage.' Tor shifted a pained lean brown hand. 'I was only twenty but considered mature beyond my years because I wanted to settle down and marry young. I thought I knew it all on the basis of very little experience. My parents tried to stop me, but I wouldn't listen to them either. I believed that what I felt for Katerina was love, but I can see now that it was more of a friendship, familiarity, admiration, loyalty, many decent things but not necessarily what a husband and wife need to stay together. I can only assume that it was the same for her and that when she met Devon, she quickly realised the difference.'

'Presumably, Devon wasn't initially prepared to leave his wife for her, or their affair wouldn't have lasted so long,' Pixie murmured uncertainly.

Tor shrugged. 'Who knows? But being able to finally see that different picture has made those events easier for me to accept. I think I felt so guilty about Katerina for so many years because in my brain somewhere, I knew I didn't love her the way she deserved to be loved.'

'But it was mutual, so you can't take on all the blame for that,' Pixie interposed soothingly, worried by his continuing tension. 'It's a very positive thing for you to be able to take a less judgemental view.'

'The guilt made it impossible for me to let go of the past. I felt responsible. I did care for her, but I shouldn't have argued with her that night.'

'No, stop it,' Pixie urged anxiously. 'No more blaming, no wishing you could change it all when you can't. Katerina made her choices as well and she chose to lie about everything. She chose not to tell you beforehand that she had fallen for another man or about Sofia. She drove off late at night in an emotional state of mind and that was the fatal decision which caused the accident.'

'I agree with you,' Tor admitted, startling her. 'It would never have happened as it did if she had not lied. I would have let her go, with great misgivings, but I would never have tried to keep her with me when she was unhappy and Sofia's paternity would have settled that. Be warned though…' Dark golden eyes locked to her hard and fast and her mouth ran dry. 'I would lock you up in a tower and lock myself in with you. I wouldn't be reasonable or compassionate or responsible. I would be possessive and enraged and jealous as hell!'

Pixie flushed and tilted her head back to look at him, blond curls tumbling back from her cheeks. 'And why would I get the tough treatment? Not that I'm thinking of straying,' she hastened to add.

Tor laughed half under his breath. 'The reason I finally understood that I didn't love Katerina was because I know what love feels like now. I've never been in love before, but it knocked me for six. For weeks since you came back into my life, I've been acting oddly because I didn't understand how I felt about you. So, while I was telling you that I couldn't fall in love again,

I was actually falling in love for the first time, with you.' He grimaced. 'No prizes for my failure to recognise that happening. I'm not the introspective type. I don't analyse feelings, I just react, which is why I've been all over the place…emotionally speaking,' he completed with a harsh edge of discomfiture in his voice.

Pixie blinked, so shocked she wasn't quite sure what to say. He was telling her he loved her, a little voice screamed inside her head.

'I thought telling you would fix things!' Tor bit out in frustration. 'You love me… I love you. Isn't that enough?'

Pixie glided up out of paralysis like a woman in a dream because she was still telling herself off inside her head. He might not have known what he was feeling but she felt that she should have recognised in his desire to constantly be with her, to constantly touch her and connect, that he was feeling far more for her than a man merely striving to be an attentive partner. 'I've been blind,' she whispered. 'I was so envious of what I believed you must've felt for Katerina. It made me irrational. And yet I loved you anyway. I was always just wanting more.'

'Nothing wrong with wanting more.' Tor closed strong arms round her, dragging her close with the fierceness of his hold. 'But at the end of the day I just want you any damned way I can have you and it's much more powerful than anything I ever felt in my life before. I can't stand seeing you hurt or upset or unhappy,' he confided, crushing her soft parted lips under his with a revealing hunger that shot through her like a re-energising drug.

Clothes were discarded in a heap. His mouth still hungrily ravishing hers, he tugged her down onto the bed and drove into her hard and fast. The wild excitement engulfed her but there was a softer, more satisfying edge to it now because she knew he loved her. She felt safe, secure, happy, no longer sentenced to crave what she had believed she couldn't have because that had decimated her pride. Completion came in a climax of physical pleasure that shot through her in an electrifying high-voltage charge.

Afterwards, Tor cradled her close. 'I'll never forgive myself for not remembering you that day in my office.'

'No negative thoughts,' Pixie urged, fingers tracing his wide sensual mouth in reproach. 'We can't change the way we started out.'

'I think the absence of the green hair didn't help,' Tor teased. 'And I was more fixated by the fact that you were very pregnant, so I didn't look at you as closely as I should have done. But what I do understand is that we were incredibly lucky to find each other that first night because, for me, you are that one-in-a-million woman, who sets me on fire with a look. I love you so much...'

One in a million? That made Pixie feel good and she smiled up into the dark golden eyes welded to her with such fierce appreciation. 'Why didn't you respond when I told you I loved you?'

Tor laughed. 'Because I was a very late arrival to the party. I only realised last night. You talked of being in Katerina's shadow when you had never been and I sat up thinking about all of it, the past and the present. That's when what was really happening became clear to me. I understood how I truly felt after Katerina's death and why I hadn't got over that guilt. I also understood what I was feeling for you.'

'I probably would like another baby in a year or two,' Pixie told him, gently shooing away Coco, who was trying to climb into bed with them. 'Sorry I snapped over that idea. It's been a very emotional twenty-four hours.'

'But worth it,' Tor countered with a scorching smile, and he was bending his tousled dark head to toy with her lips again when a faint sound alerted Pixie and made her pull away from him.

'Alfie's awake.' Pixie slid off the bed and began to dress in haste. 'Isla's on holiday...remember?' she prompted.

'So, we get to be real parents,' Tor teased, rolling off the bed, naked and bronzed.

'Yes, Tor,' Pixie said with eyes filled with amusement. 'And the first lesson in being real parents is, you have to put on clothes.'

'Did I tell you how much I love you?' Tor asked, hitching an ebony brow.

'It was practically love at first sight for me.' Pixie held up a finger in unashamed one-upmanship. 'I win hands down.'

'I'm not so sure. I was a pushover for you and I'm not a push-over,' Tor declared. 'But maybe it was the green hair...'

'Well, we're never going to know for sure because I'm not going green again,' Pixie assured him with a chuckle, bending forward to kiss him as he pulled up his jeans and dallying there, Alfie having quieted again, her keen hearing assured her.

'And I'm never ever going to be without you again, *agapi mou*,' Tor husked, gathering her to him with all the possessiveness of a male determined never to let her go.

EPILOGUE

OVER TWO YEARS LATER, Pixie was presiding over a busy Christmas gathering at the mansion she and Tor had moved to overlooking the Thames. Surrounded by acres of gardens and possessed of numerous bedrooms, it was the perfect home for a family who enjoyed entertaining. Tor's relatives were frequent visitors.

Although that had not been her original intention, Pixie had never returned to work. At first, she had revelled in the luxury of being able to be with her son whenever she liked. But as she had begun to adapt to her new life, she had also become much busier. Having taken an interest in the charities that Tor supported, she had become actively involved with one in a medical field. She had soon realised that she could do a lot of good helping to raise funds and that fired up greater interest in such roles.

Moving from the town house into a much larger property had consumed a lot of her time as well, although she had thoroughly enjoyed the opportunity to decorate and furnish her first new home. That her first new home should be a virtual mansion still staggered her.

And now she was pregnant again, six months along and glowing with an energy she had not benefited from the first time around. Of course, she acknowledged, everything was different now for her. She was incredibly happy and secure and supported every step of the way. Tor's love had changed her, lending her new confidence and boosting her self-esteem. Discovering that she was carrying non-identical twins had been a bit of a shock at first, but a shock she and Tor had greeted with pleasure because they got so much joy out of Alfie, who was now a lively little boy of three.

Now she watched as Alfie dragged his grandfather, Hallas, outside to show the older man his ride-on car where it was parked on the terrace. Tor's father grinned as he visibly tried to explain in dumbshow to the little boy that he was far too big to get into the vehicle and take the wheel. Looking long-suffering with an expression that was pure Tor, Alfie climbed in instead to demonstrate his toy. Pixie smiled, feeling very fortunate that Tor's parents were so loving.

Tor had finally stopped being secretive about his first marriage and, although his revelations had roused shock and consternation, Pixie was inclined to believe that everyone was much more relaxed now that the truth was out and they were able to understand how Tor had felt for the five years that he had endured being treated like a heartbroken widower. Of course, he *had* been heartbroken in many ways, just not in the way that people had naturally assumed. She was particularly fond of her husband's half-brother, Sev, whom she had only got to know after Tor had cleared the air with him.

Just then she was wondering if Sev would manage to spend Christmas with them. Or if he was off somewhere else with some gorgeous beauty on a beach, drinking champagne and carousing, for Tor's Italian half-brother Sev was an unashamed womaniser, chary of any form of commitment and deeply cynical. Even so, he and Tor had eventually grown closer, in spite of the fact that at the start that development had looked unlikely.

A huge Christmas tree embellished the front entrance hall while a log fire crackled in the grate. Richly coloured baubles twirled at the end of branches decorated with glittering beaded strings, multicoloured reflections dancing off the marble hearth. It looked beautiful and so it should, Pixie conceded, because she had spent so much time seeking out special ornaments since her very first precious Christmas with Tor and Alfie. And every year she would bring them out and hang them, enjoying the memories that particular decorations evoked. Here and there on the branches hung the less opulent ornaments she had inherited from her late parents, enabling the tree to remind her of her happy childhood as well.

Her attention roamed to her brother, Jordan, where he was kneeling on the floor beside a little girl of about five. Tula was his girlfriend Suzy's daughter. It was a fairly new relationship, but Pixie was crossing her fingers and praying that it would work out for Jordan—because although he had rebuilt his life, she knew he needed someone to do it for and to ground him, and hopefully Suzy was that woman.

Jordan had suffered a long hard road in rehabilitation. There had been relapses and episodes of depression and various other obstacles for him to overcome, but in the end he had succeeded. He had found somewhere to live at his own expense and, a year ago, he had found work in a charitable organisation where he had no access to money. He had met Suzy through his job soon afterwards. Tor was very slowly warming up towards her sibling and generally becoming, under Pixie's influence, a little more compassionate with regard to other people's failings.

Tor came through the door with Alfie clinging to him like a limpet while his father chatted to him, but Tor's stunning bronzed eyes sought out and instantly settled on his wife. There was a welter of talk and greetings as his entire family converged on him, for they had only arrived earlier that day and he had been at the office.

'My son adores you,' her mother-in-law, Pandora, pronounced with satisfaction at Pixie's elbow. 'You are the woman I always wanted for him and every woman deserves to be adored.'

'I adore him back,' Pixie whispered chokily.

'And another two grandchildren on the way together,' Pandora teased, fanning her face to lighten the atmosphere. 'What more can I say?'

'Three's enough!' Pixie laughed.

'We will see...'

Tor finally made it to Pixie's side. 'I need a shower and to change,' he groaned, raking his fingers up over his unshaven jaw with the attitude of a man suggesting that he resembled a down-and-out.

'Off you go,' his mother urged, her smile emerging as her son ensnared his wife's hand and tugged her upstairs with him.

'A shower?' Pixie lifted a dubious brow.

'Afterwards,' Tor suggested meaningfully, guiding her straight into their bedroom and peeling off his jacket in almost the same motion.

A pulse stirred between her thighs and turned into an ache as she saw his arousal through the fine expensive cloth of his trousers. It was a hunger that never quite dimmed, never ever got fully satisfied, she acknowledged, studying him from the crown of his cropped black hair to his shimmering dark golden eyes to the electrifyingly sexy dark shadow of stubble on his jawline. And something gave within her and she just stepped forward and flung herself at him with all the exuberant passion that he revelled in.

'*Thee mou...* You are beautiful, *agapi mou*,' Tor husked raggedly, struggling for breath as he emerged from that kiss.

Not half as beautiful as he was, she thought, but she had long since learned not to embarrass him with such words of appreciation. 'This is going to be a wonderful Christmas,' she told him happily. 'I feel so lucky. We've got everybody who matters to us here to celebrate with us.'

'I really only need you,' Tor told her truthfully. 'And Alfie... and our twins,' he extended as he turned her round and splayed large possessive hands over the swell of her stomach. 'I never realised I could love anyone the way I love you.'

'It was the green hair,' she teased.

'No, it was the first dynamite kiss. I'm a very physical guy,' Tor breathed hungrily, divesting her of her dress. 'Do you think we're having boys or girls this time? I think boys because they seem to run in my family.'

'I think girls.'

They were both right. Three months later, Pixie gave birth to a boy and a girl, whom they christened Romanos and Zoe.

* * * * *

A Texan For Christmas

Jules Bennett

DESIRE

Scandalous world of the elite.

USA TODAY bestselling author **Jules Bennett** has published over sixty books and never tires of writing happy endings. Writing strong heroines and alpha heroes is Jules's favorite way to spend her workdays. Jules hosts weekly contests on her Facebook fan page and loves chatting with readers on Twitter, Facebook and via email through her website. Stay up-to-date by signing up for her newsletter at julesbennett.com.

Books by Jules Bennett

Harlequin Desire

What the Prince Wants
A Royal Amnesia Scandal
Maid for a Magnate
His Secret Baby Bombshell

Best Man Under the Mistletoe

The Rancher's Heirs

Twin Secrets
Claimed by the Rancher

Taming the Texan

A Texan for Christmas

Texas Cattleman's Club: Bachelor Auction

Most Eligible Texan

Visit her Author Profile page at millsandboon.com.au, or julesbennett.com, for more titles.

Dear Reader,

If you've been keeping up with my Rancher's Heirs series, you have already met Colt, Nolan and Hayes. Who's next? Oh, that's right. The mysterious Hollywood heartthrob, Beau Elliott.

I hope you'll forgive that I skipped ahead in this fictitious world and picked up where Hayes's book left off, but I made the season Christmas. What's more magical than Christmas? Believe me, these characters needed some magic in their lives!

Scarlett has suffered so much heartache, and being thrust into this nanny position is just another layer of pain. But working with Beau Elliott does help take out the sting. Who wouldn't want to be under the same roof with an A-list actor for three weeks?

Beau can't believe this is his nanny. Maybe he should've specified a warty, gray-haired grandmother, because the second the sultry Scarlett shows up on his doorstep, he knows he's in trouble. Poor Beau.

Once these two break past the barriers of heartache and pain, they quickly realize they have more in common than they ever thought possible. And with the magic of Christmas and a beautiful little baby girl, well, maybe this will be one holiday to remember!

I hope you all enjoy the final installment of The Rancher's Heirs. The Elliott brothers have been a joy to write!

Happy reading,

Jules

CHAPTER ONE

SCARLETT PATTERSON CLUTCHED the handle of her small suitcase and waited.

And waited.

She'd knocked twice on the door, but still no answer. She knew this was the address she'd been given—a small cabin nestled in the back of the sprawling, picturesque Pebblebrook Ranch. She'd been told exactly who she'd be working for and her belly did flips just thinking of Beau Elliott—deemed Hollywood's Bad Boy, the Maverick of Movies, Cowboy Casanova... the titles were endless.

One thing was certain, if the tabloids were correct—he made no apologies about his affection for women. Scarlett wasn't sure she'd ever seen an image of him with the same woman.

That is, until his lover turned up pregnant. Then the two were spotted out together, but by then the rumors had begun— of drugs found in his lover's carry-on, of affairs started...or maybe they'd never stopped.

Why he'd come back home now, to this quiet town in Texas and his family's sprawling ranch, was none of her concern.

With a hand blocking her eyes from a rare glimpse of winter sun, Scarlett glanced around the open fields. Not a soul in sight.

In the distance, a green field dotted with cattle stretched all the way to the horizon. This could easily be a postcard.

The Elliott land was vast. She'd heard there were several homes on the property and a portion of the place would soon become a dude ranch. In fact, this cabin would eventually be housing for guests of said dude ranch.

So why was Beau Elliott staying here instead of one of the main houses, with his brothers? Was he even planning to stick around?

So many mysteries…

But she wasn't here to inquire about his personal life and she certainly wouldn't be divulging any extra information about hers.

She was here to help his baby.

Even if that meant she had to come face-to-face with one of the sexiest men on the planet.

The snick of a lock had her turning her attention back around. When the door swung wide, it was all Scarlett could do to hold back her gasp.

Beau Elliott, Hollywood's baddest boy, stood before her sans shirt and wearing a pair of low-slung shorts. Scrolling ink went up one side of his waist, curling around well-defined pecs and disappearing over his shoulder.

Don't stare at the tattoos. Don't stare at the tattoos.

And, whatever you do, don't reach out to touch one.

"Who are you?"

The gravelly voice startled her back into reality. Scarlett realized she'd been staring.

Beau's broad frame filled the doorway, his stubbled jaw and bedhead indicating he hadn't had the best night. Apparently, according to the information she'd received, his last nanny had left last evening because of a family emergency.

Well, Scarlett wasn't having the best of days, either, so they were at least on a level playing field—other than the whole billionaire-peasant thing.

But she could use the extra money, so caring for an adorable five-month-old baby girl shouldn't be a problem, right?

Tamping down past hurts that threatened to creep up at the thought of caring for a child, Scarlett squared her shoulders and smiled. "I'm Scarlett Patterson. Your new nanny."

Beau blinked and gave her body a visual lick. "You're not old or frumpy," he growled.

Great. He'd already had some visual image in his head of who she should be. Maggie, the original nanny, was sweet as peach pie, but she *could* be best described as old and frumpy. Obviously, that was what Hollywood's Golden Child had thought he would be getting this morning, as well.

Beau Elliott, raised a rancher and then turned star of the screen, was going to be high maintenance. She could already tell.

Why would she expect anything less from someone who appeared to thrive on stardom and power?

Unfortunately, she knew that type all too well. Knew the type and ran like hell to avoid it.

She'd grown up with a man obsessed with money and getting what he wanted. Just when she thought she'd eliminated him from her life, he went on and became the governor. Scarlett was so over the power trip. Her stepfather and her mother weren't happy with her choices in life and had practically shunned her when they realized they couldn't control her. Which was fine. She'd rather do life on her own than be controlled…by anybody.

"Not old and frumpy. Is that a compliment or an observation?" She waved her hand to dismiss his answer before he could give her one. "Forget it. My looks and age are irrelevant. I am Maggie's replacement for the next three weeks."

"I requested someone like Maggie."

He still didn't make any attempt to move or to invite her inside. Even though this was Texas, the morning air chilled her.

Scarlett wasn't in the mood to deal with whatever hang-ups he had about nannies. Coming here after a year away from nanny duties was difficult enough. If she'd had her way, she would've found someone else to take this assignment, but the agency was short staffed.

This job was only for three weeks. Which meant she'd spend Christmas here, but the day after, she'd be heading to her new life in Dallas.

After the New Year, she'd start over fresh.

She could do this.

So why did she already feel the stirrings of a headache?

Oh, right. Because the once-dubbed "Sexiest Man Alive" was clearly used to getting his own way.

A bundle of nerves curled tightly in her belly. He might be sexy, but that didn't mean she had to put up with his attitude. Maybe he needed to remember that he was in a bind. He'd hired a nanny and Scarlett was it.

"Maggie, and everyone else at Nanny Poppins, is unavailable during the time frame you need."

Scarlett tried like hell to keep her professional smile in place—she did need this money, and she'd never leave a child without care. Plus, she wouldn't do a thing to tarnish the reputation of the company she'd worked for over the past several years.

She tipped her head and quirked a brow. "You do still need help, correct?"

Maggie had told Scarlett that Beau was brooding, that he kept to himself and only really came out of his shell when he interacted with his baby girl. That was all fine and good. Scarlett wasn't here to make friends or ogle the superstar, no matter how delicious he looked early in the morning.

A baby's cry pierced the awkward silence. With a muttered curse, Beau spun around and disappeared. Scarlett slowly stepped through the open door and shut it behind her.

Clearly the invitation wasn't going to happen.

"I feel so welcome," she muttered.

Scarlett leaned her suitcase against the wall and propped her small purse on top of it. The sounds of a fussy baby and Beau's deep, calming voice came from the bedroom to the right of the entryway.

As she took in the open floor plan of the cabin, she noted several things at once. Beau was either neat and tidy or he didn't have a lot of stuff. A pair of shiny new cowboy boots sat by the door and a black hat hung on a hook above the boots. The small kitchen had a drying rack with bottles on the counter and on the tiny table was a pink-and-white polka-dot bib.

She glanced to the left and noted another bedroom, the one she assumed would be hers, but she wasn't going to put her stuff in there just yet. Across the way, at the back of the cabin, was a set of patio doors that led to another porch. The area was cozy and perfect for the soon-to-be dude ranch.

The lack of Christmas decorations disturbed her, though. No tree, no stockings over the little fireplace, not even a wreath on the door. Who didn't want to celebrate Christmas? The most giving, joyous time of the year?

Christmas was absolutely her favorite holiday. Over the years she'd shared many Christmases with various families…all of which had been more loving and fulfilling than those of her stuffy, controlled childhood.

Scarlett continued to wait in the entryway, all while judging the Grinch's home. She didn't want to venture too far from the front door since he hadn't invited her in. It was obvious she wasn't what he'd expected, and he might ask her to leave.

Hopefully he wouldn't because she needed to work these three weeks. Those extra funds would go a long way toward helping her afford housing when she left Stone River to start her new life.

Even so, the next twenty-one days couldn't pass by fast enough.

Beau came back down the hall and Scarlett's heart tightened as a lump formed in her throat. A full assault on her emotions took over as knots in her stomach formed.

She couldn't do this. No matter how short the time span,

she couldn't stay with this man, in this confined space, caring for his daughter for three weeks and not come out unscathed.

She wasn't sure which sight hit her hardest—the well-sculpted shirtless man or the baby he was holding.

Being this close to the little girl nearly brought her to her knees. Scarlett knew coming back as a hands-on nanny would be difficult, but she hadn't fully prepared herself for just how hard a hit her heart would take.

She'd purposely given up working in homes only a year ago. She'd requested work in the office, even though the administrative side paid less than round-the-clock nanny services. She'd been Nanny Poppins's most sought-after employee for eight years, but after everything that had happened, her boss completely understood Scarlett's need to distance herself from babies and families.

Fate had been cruel, stealing her chance of having kids of her own. She wasn't sure she was ready to see another parent have what she wanted. Working for Beau Elliott would be difficult to say the least, but Scarlett would push through and then she could move on. One last job. She could do this…she hoped.

The sweet baby continued to fuss, rubbing her eyes and sniffling. No doubt she was tired. From the looks of both of them, they'd had a long night.

Instinct had Scarlett reaching out and taking the baby, careful not to brush her fingertips against the hard planes of Beau's bare chest.

Well, she had to assume they were hard because she'd stared at them for a solid two minutes.

The second that sweet baby smell hit Scarlett, she nearly lost it. Her eyes burned, her throat tightened. But the baby's needs had to come first. That's why Scarlett was here. Well, that and to get double the pay so she could finally move to Dallas.

She could've turned down this job, but Maggie was in a bind, the company was in a bind, and they'd been so good to Scarlett since she'd started working there.

Scarlett simply couldn't say no.

"Oh, sweetheart, it's okay."

She patted the little girl's back and swayed slowly. Maggie had told her the baby was a joy to be around.

"Madelyn."

Scarlett blinked. "Excuse me?"

"Her name is Madelyn."

Well, at least they were getting somewhere and he wasn't ready to push her out the door. Scarlett already knew Madelyn's name and had read all the pertinent information regarding this job, but it was nice that Beau wasn't growling at her anymore.

Still, she wished he'd go put a shirt on. She couldn't keep her eyes completely off him, not when he was on display like that. Damn man probably thought he could charm her or distract her by flexing all those glorious, delicious muscles. Muscles that would no doubt feel taut beneath her touch.

Scarlett swallowed and blinked away the erotic image before she could take it too far. At least she had something else to think of other than her own gut-clenching angst and baby fever. Hunky heartthrob to the rescue.

Scarlett turned away from the distracting view of her temporary boss and walked toward the tiny living area. The room seemed a little larger thanks to the patio doors leading onto the covered porch, which was decorated with a cute table and chair set.

The whole cabin was rather small, but it wasn't her place to ask why a billionaire film star lived in this cramped space on his family's estate. None of her business. This would just be a quick three weeks in December—in and out—in the most unfestive place ever.

Maybe she could sneak in some Christmas here and there. Every child deserved some twinkle lights or a stocking, for heaven's sake. Definitely a tree. Without it, where would Santa put the presents?

"She's been cranky all night," Beau said behind her. "I've

tried everything, but I can't make her happy. I've never had that happen before."

The frustration in his voice softened Scarlett a bit. Beau might be a womanizer and a party animal, if the tabloids were right—which would explain his comfort level with wearing no shirt—but he obviously cared for his daughter.

Scarlett couldn't help but wonder where the mother was, but again, it was none of her concern. She'd seen enough tabloid stories to figure the mother was likely in rehab or desperately needing to be there.

Madelyn let out a wail, complete with tears and everything. The poor baby was miserable, which now made three of them, all under the same roof.

Let the countdown to her move begin.

How the hell had his nanny situation gone from Mrs. Doubtfire to Miss December?

The sultry vixen with rich skin, deep brown eyes, and silky black hair was too striking. But it was those curves in all the right places that had definitely woken him up this morning. His entire body had been ready to stand at attention, so perhaps he'd come across a little gruff.

But, damn it, he had good reason.

He'd been assured a replacement nanny would arrive bright and early, but he'd expected the agency to send another grandmother type.

Where was the one with a thick middle, elastic pants, sensible shoes and a gray bun? Where the hell did he order up another one of those? Warts would help, too. False teeth, even.

Beau stood back as he watched Scarlett comfort his daughter.

Scarlett. Of course she'd have a sultry name to match everything else sultry about her.

Not too long ago she would've been exactly his type. He would've wasted no time in charming and seducing her. But now his entire life had changed and the only woman he had time for was the sweet five-month-old he'd saved from the clutches of her partying, strung-out mother.

Money wasn't something he cared about—perhaps because he'd always had it—but it sure as hell came in handy. Like when he needed to pay off his ex so he could have Madelyn. Jennifer had selfishly taken the money, signed over the rights, and had nearly skipped out of their lives and onto the next star she thought would catapult her career.

The fact that he'd been used by her wasn't even relevant. He could care less about how he'd been treated, but he would not have their baby act as a pawn for Jennifer's own vindictive nature.

Beau couldn't get Madelyn out of Hollywood fast enough. His daughter was not going to be brought up in the lifestyle that too many fell into—himself included.

He'd overcome his past and the ugliness that surrounded his life when he'd first gotten into LA. He'd worked damn hard and was proud of the life he had built, but now his focus had to shift and changes needed to be made.

Coming home hadn't been ideal because he knew exactly the type of welcome he'd get. But there was nowhere else he wanted to be right now. He needed his family, even if he took hell from Colt, Hayes and Nolan for showing up after years of being away...with a kid in tow.

Thankfully, his brothers and their women all doted over Madelyn. That's all he wanted. No matter how people treated him or ignored him, Beau wanted his daughter to be surrounded with love.

His life was a mess, his future unknown. Hell, he couldn't think past today. He had a movie premiere two days before Christmas and he'd have to go, but other than that, he had no clue.

All that mattered was Madelyn, making sure she had a solid foundation and family that loved her. The calls from his new agent didn't matter, the movie premiere didn't matter, all the press he was expected to do to promote the film sure as hell didn't matter. To say he was burned out would be a vast understatement.

Beau needed some space to think and the calming serenity of Pebblebrook Ranch provided just that.

Unfortunately, concentrating would be rather difficult with a centerfold look-alike staying under his roof. Well, not his roof exactly. He was only using one of the small cabins on the land until the dude ranch officially opened in a few months. His father's dream was finally coming to fruition.

Beau wondered how he'd come to this moment of needing someone. He prided himself on never needing anyone. He had homes around the globe, cars that would make any man weep with envy, even his own private island, but the one place he wanted and needed to be was right here with his family—whether they wanted him here or not.

Beau had turned his back on this land and his family years ago. That was the absolute last thing he'd intended to do, but he'd gotten swept away into the fortune and fame. Eventually days had rolled into months, then into years, and the time had passed too quickly.

But now he was back home, and as angry as his brothers were, they'd given him a place to stay. Temporary, but at least it was something. He knew it was only because he had Madelyn, but he'd take it.

"She's teething."

Beau pulled his thoughts from his family drama and focused on the nanny. "Teething? She's only five months old."

Scarlett continued to sway back and forth with Madelyn in her arms. His sweet girl sucked on her fist and alternated between sniffles and cries. At least the screaming wasn't so constant like last night. Having his daughter so upset and him feeling so helpless had absolutely gutted him. He would've done anything to help her, but he'd been clueless. He'd spent the night questioning just how good of a father he really was.

Madelyn's wide, dark eyes stared up at the new nanny as if trying to figure out where the stranger had come from.

He was having a difficult time not staring, as well, and he knew full well where she came from—every single one of his erotic fantasies.

"Her gums are swollen and she's drooling quite a bit," Scarlett stated. "All perfectly normal. Do you happen to have any cold teething rings in your fridge?"

Cold teething rings? What the hell was that? He was well stocked with formula and bottles, diapers and wipes, but rings in the fridge? Nope.

He had an app that told him what babies should be doing and what they needed at different stages, but the rings hadn't been mentioned yet.

"I'm guessing no from the look on your face." Scarlett went into the kitchen area and opened the freezer. "Can you get me a napkin or towel?"

Beau wasn't used to taking orders, but he'd do anything to bring his daughter some comfort. He grabbed a clean dishcloth from the counter and handed it to her. He watched as she held on to the ice through the cloth and rubbed it on his daughter's gums. After a few minutes the fussing grew quieter until she finally stopped.

"I'll get some teething rings today," Scarlett murmured as if talking to herself more than him. "They are wonderful for instant relief. If you have any children's pain reliever, we can also rub that on her gums, but I try natural approaches before I go to medicine."

Okay, so maybe Miss December was going to be an asset. He liked that she offered natural options for Madelyn's care. He also liked that she seemed to be completely unimpressed with his celebrity status. Something about that was so refreshing and even more attractive.

Watch it. You already got in trouble with one sexy woman. She's the nanny, not the next bedmate.

He told himself he didn't need the silent warning that rang in his head. Scarlett Patterson would only be here until the day after Christmas. Surely he could keep his libido in control for that long. It wasn't like he had the time anyway. He couldn't smooth the ruffled feathers of his family, care for his child and seduce a woman all before December 26.

No matter how sexy the new nanny was.

Besides, he thought, it couldn't get more clichéd than that—the movie star and the nanny. How many of those stories had he read in the tabloids of late?

No, there was no way he was going to make a move on the woman who was saving his sanity and calming his baby. Besides, he respected women; his mother had raised Southern gentlemen, after all. The media liked to report that he rolled out of one woman's bed and right into another, but he wasn't quite that popular. Not to mention, any woman he'd ever been with had known he wasn't looking for long-term—and agreed with it.

Beau had a feeling Scarlett would be a long-term type of girl. She likely had a family—or maybe she didn't. If this was her full-time job, she probably didn't have time to take care of a family.

Honestly, he shouldn't be letting his mind wander into the territory of Scarlett's personal life. She was his nanny, nothing more.

But damn it, did she have to look so good in her little pink capris and white sleeveless button-up? Didn't she have a uniform? Something up to her neck, down to her ankles and with sleeves? Even if she was completely covered up, she still had those expressive, doe-like eyes, a perfectly shaped mouth and adorable dimples.

Damn it. He should not be noticing each little detail of his new nanny.

"Why don't you go rest?" Scarlett suggested, breaking into his erotic thoughts. "I can take care of her. You look like hell."

Beau stared across the narrow space for a half second before he found his voice. Nobody talked to him like that except his brothers, and even that had been years ago.

"Are you always that blunt with your clients?"

"I try to be honest at all times," she replied sweetly. "I can't be much help to you if you just want me here to boost your ego and lie to your face."

Well, that was a rarity…if she was even telling the truth now. Beau hadn't met a woman who was honest and genuine. Nearly everyone he'd met was out for herself and to hell with anyone around them. And money. They always wanted money.

Another reason he needed the simplicity of Pebblebrook. He just wanted to come back to his roots, to decompress and figure out what the hell to do with his life now. He wanted the open spaces, wanted to see the blue skies without buildings blocking the view. And he needed to mend the relationships he'd left behind. What better time than Christmas?

"I'm Beau." When she drew her brows in, he went on. "I didn't introduce myself before."

"I'm aware of who you are."

He waited for her to say something else, but clearly she'd formed an opinion of him and didn't want to share. Fine. So long as she kept his daughter comfortable and helped him until Maggie returned, he could care less what she thought.

But she'd have to get in line because his brothers had already dubbed him the prodigal son and were eager to put him in his place. Nothing less than he deserved, he reasoned.

As he watched Scarlett take over the care of Madelyn, Beau knew this was what he deserved, too. A sexy-as-hell woman as his nanny. This was his penance for the bastard he'd been over the past several years.

He'd do well to remember he was a new man now. He'd do well to remember she was here for his daughter, not for his personal pleasure. He'd also do well to remember he had more important things to do than drop Scarlett Patterson into each and every one of his fantasies…even if she would make the perfect lead.

CHAPTER TWO

MADELYN HAD CALMED down and was now settled in her crib napping. There was a crib in each of the two bedrooms, but Scarlett opted to put Madelyn in the room Maggie had vacated. This would be Scarlett's room now and she simply didn't think going into Beau's was a smart idea.

After she'd put her luggage and purse in her room, Beau had given her a very brief tour of the cabin, so she'd gotten a glimpse into his personal space. The crib in his room had been nestled next to the king-size bed. Scarlett tried not to, but the second she recalled those messed sheets, she procured an image of him lying there in a pair of snug boxer briefs...or nothing at all.

Scarlett groaned and gently shut the bedroom door, careful not to let the latch snick. She wasn't sure how light of a sleeper Madelyn was, so until she got to know the sweet bundle a little better—

But she couldn't get to know her too much, could she? There wasn't going to be time, and for Scarlett's sanity and heart, she had to keep an emotional distance. Giving herself that pep talk and actually doing it were two totally different things.

Before her surgery, she'd thrown herself into each and every job. Before her surgery, she'd always felt like one unit with the families she worked with.

Before her surgery, she'd had dreams.

The hard knot in her chest never eased. Whether she thought of what she'd lost or was just doing day-to-day things, the ache remained a constant reminder.

Scarlett stepped back into the living area and found Beau standing at the patio doors, his back to her. At least he'd put a T-shirt on. Even so, he filled it out, stretching the material over those chiseled muscles she'd seen firsthand. Clothes or no clothes, the image had been burned into her memory bank and there was no erasing it.

"Madelyn's asleep," she stated.

Beau threw her a glance over his shoulder, then turned his attention back to the view of the open field.

Okay. Clearly he wasn't chatty. Fine by her. He must be a lonely, miserable man. She'd always wondered if celebrities were happy. After all, money certainly couldn't buy everything. Her stepfather was proof of that. He'd been a state representative for years before moving up to governor. He'd wanted his children—he included her in that mix—to all enter the political arena so they would be seen as a powerhouse family.

Thanks, but no thanks. She preferred a simpler life—or at least one without lies, deceit, fake smiles and cheesy campaign slogans.

"If there's something you need to go do, I'll be here," she told Beau. Not surprisingly, he didn't answer. Maybe he gave a grunt, but she couldn't tell if that was a response or just indigestion.

Scarlett turned toward the kitchen to take stock of what type of formula and baby things Madelyn used. Being here a short time, she wanted to make sure the transitions between Maggie and her then back to Maggie went smoothly. Regardless of what Scarlett thought of Beau, Madelyn was the only one here who mattered.

Before Scarlett could step into the kitchen, a knock sounded on the front door.

Beau shifted, his gaze landing on the closed door. He looked like he'd rather run in the opposite direction than face whoever was on the other side. Given that they were on private property, likely the guest was just his family, so what was the issue? Wasn't that why he'd come home? To be with his family for the holidays?

When he made no attempt to move, Scarlett asked, "Should I get that?"

He gave a curt nod and Scarlett reached for the knob. The second she opened the door, she gasped.

Sweet mercy. There were two of them. Another Beau stood before her, only this one was clean shaven and didn't have the scowl. But those shoulders and dark eyes were dead on and just as potent to her heart rate.

"Ma'am," the Beau look-alike said with a drawl and a tip of his black cowboy hat. "I'm Colt Elliott, Beau's twin. You must be the replacement nanny."

Another Elliott and a *twin*. Mercy sakes, this job was not going to be a hardship whatsoever if she had to look at these men each day.

She knew there were four Elliott sons, but wow. Nobody warned her they were clones. Now she wondered if the other two would stop by soon. One could hope.

"Yes," she said when she realized he was waiting on her to respond to his question. "I'm Scarlett."

Colt's dark eyes went from her to Beau. "Is this a bad time?"

Scarlett stepped back. "Not at all. I just got the baby to sleep. I can wait outside while you two talk. It's a beautiful day."

She turned and caught Beau's gaze on her. Did he always have that dramatic, heavy-lidded, movie-star stare? Did he ever turn off the act or was that mysterious, sexy persona natural?

"If you'll excuse me." She turned to Colt. "It was a pleasure meeting you."

"Pleasure was mine, ma'am."

Somehow Scarlett managed to get out the front door without

tripping over her own two feet, because that sexy, low Southern drawl those Elliott boys had was rather knee-weakening.

Once she made it to the porch, she walked to the wooden swing on the end in front of her bedroom window. She sank down onto the seat and let the gentle breeze cool off her heated body. December in Texas wasn't too hot, wasn't too cold. In this part of the state, the holiday weather was always perfect. Though the evenings and nights could get chilly.

Good thing there were fireplaces in this cabin. Fireplaces that could lead one to instantly think of romantic talks and shedding of clothes, being wrapped in a blanket in the arms of a strong man.

Scarlett shut her eyes as she rested her feet on the porch and stopped the swaying swing. There would be no romance and no fires…at least not the passionate kind.

Raised voices filtered from inside. Clearly the Elliott twins were not happy with each other. Two sexy-as-hell alphas going at it sounded like every woman's fantasy, but she couldn't exactly barge in and interrupt.

Then she heard it. The faint cry from her bedroom, right on the other side of the window from where she sat. Well, damn it.

Scarlett pushed off the swing and jerked open the front door. Hot men or not, powerful men or not, she didn't take kindly to anyone disturbing a sleeping baby.

As she marched toward her bedroom, she shot a warning glare in the direction of the guys, who were now practically chest to chest. She didn't have time to worry about their issues, not when Madelyn had barely been asleep twenty minutes.

Scarlett crossed to the crib and gently picked up the sweet girl. After grabbing her fuzzy yellow blanket, Scarlett sank into the nearby rocking chair and patted Madelyn's bottom to calm her.

Madelyn's little sniffles and heavy lids were Scarlett's main focus right now. She eased the chair into a gentle motion with her foot and started humming "You Are My Sunshine." Madelyn didn't take long to nestle back into sleep and Scarlett's heart clenched. She'd just hold her a tad longer... It had been so long since she'd rocked a little one.

She had no idea what happened with Beau and the baby's mother, but the tabloids and social media had been abuzz with a variety of rumors over the past few weeks.

Well, actually, the couple had been quite the fodder for gossip a lot longer. It was over a year ago when they were first spotted half naked on a beach in Belize. Then the pregnancy seemed to send shock waves through the media. Of course, after the baby was born, there was all that speculation on the state of the mother and she was seen less and less.

Chatter swirled about her cheating, then her rehab, then the breakup.

Then there was talk of Beau. One online source stated he'd been passed over for a part in an epic upcoming blockbuster. One said he'd had a fight with his new agent. Another reported that he and his ex had been spotted arguing at a party and one or both had been inebriated.

Honestly, Beau Elliott was a complication she didn't want to get tangled with, so whatever happened to send him rushing home was his problem. That didn't mean, however, that a child should have to suffer for the sins of the parents.

Once Madelyn was good and asleep, Scarlett put her down in the crib. There was a light tap on the door moments before it eased open.

Scarlett turned from the sleeping baby to see Beau filling the doorway.

"Is she asleep again?" he whispered.

Stepping away from the crib, Scarlett nodded. "Next time you want to have a family fight, take it outside."

His eyes darkened. "This isn't your house," he stated, taking a step closer to her.

Scarlett stood at the edge of the bed and crossed her arms. "It isn't exactly your house, either," she retorted. "But Madelyn is my job now and I won't have her disturbed when she's been fussy and obviously needs sleep. Maybe if you put her needs first—"

In a second, Beau had closed the gap and was all but leaning over her, so close that she had to hold on to the bedpost to stay upright.

"Every single thing I do is putting her needs first," he growled through gritted teeth. "You've been here less than two hours, so don't even presume to know what's going on."

Scarlett placed her hand on his chest to get him to ease back, but the heat from his body warmed her in a way she couldn't explain…and shouldn't dwell on.

She jerked her hand back and glanced away, only to have her eyes land on the pile of lacy panties she'd thrown on her bed when she'd started unpacking earlier.

There went more of that warmth spreading through her. What were the odds Beau hadn't noticed?

She risked glancing back at him, but…nope. He'd noticed all right. His eyes were fixed on her unmentionables.

Beau cleared his throat and raked a hand over the back of his neck before glancing to where his baby slept peacefully in the crib on the other side of the room.

When his dark eyes darted back to her, they pinned her in place. "We need to talk." Then he turned and marched out, likely expecting her to follow.

Scarlett closed her eyes and pulled in a breath as she attempted to count backward from ten. This was only the first day. She knew there would be some bumps in the road, right?

She just didn't expect those bumps to be the chills rushing over her skin from the brief yet toe-curling contact she'd just had with her employer.

Beau ground his molars and clenched his fists at his sides. It had been quite a while since he'd been with a woman and the one currently staying under his roof was driving him absolutely insane…and it wasn't even lunchtime on her first day of employment.

Those damn panties. All that lace, satin…strings. Mercy, he couldn't get the image out of his head. Never once did he think his nanny's underwear would cause his brain to fry, but here he was with a silent seductress helping to take care of his daughter and he couldn't focus. Likely she didn't even have a clue how she was messing with his hormones.

Scarlett honestly did have Madelyn's best interest in mind. She was none too happy with him and Colt earlier and he wasn't too thrilled with the situation, either. Of all the people angry with him for his actions and for being away from home so long, Colt was by far the most furious. Ironic, he thought. He'd figure his own twin would try to have a little compassion.

Unfortunately, there was so much more contention between them than just the missing years. Coming home at Christmas and thinking things would be magical and easily patched up had been completely naive on his part. But damn it, he'd been hopeful. They'd been the best of friends once, with a twin bond that was stronger than anything he'd ever known.

Delicate footsteps slid across the hardwood floor, interrupting his thoughts. Beau shored up his mental strength and turned to face Scarlett. Why did she have to look like a walking dream? That curvy body, the dark eyes, her flawless dark skin and black hair that gave the illusion of silk sliding down her back.

Damn those panties. Now when he saw her he wondered what she wore underneath her clothes. Lace or satin? Pink or yellow?

"What do you want to talk about?" she asked, making no move to come farther into the living area.

Beau gestured toward the oversize sectional sofa. "Have a seat."

She eyed him for a moment before finally crossing the room and sitting down on the end of the couch. She crossed her ankles and clasped her hands as if she were in some business meeting with a CEO.

Beau stood next to her. "Relax."

"I'd relax more if you weren't looming over me."

Part of him wanted to laugh. Most women would love for him to "loom" over them. Hell, most women would love him under them, as well. Perhaps that's why he found Scarlett of the silky panties so intriguing. She truly didn't care that he was an A-list actor with more money than he could ever spend and the power to obtain nearly anything he ever wanted.

Beau didn't want to make her uncomfortable and it certainly wasn't his intention to be a jerk. It pained him to admit it, but he needed her. He was only a few weeks out on his own with Madelyn and he really didn't want to screw up this full-time parenting job. This would be the most important job he'd ever have.

"We probably need to set some rules here," he started.

Rules like keeping all underwear hidden in a drawer at all times. Oh, and maybe if she could get some long pants and high-neck shirts, that would certainly help. Wouldn't it?

Maggie sat straighter. "I work for you, Mr. Elliott. Just tell me the rules you had for Maggie."

Beau nearly snorted. Rules for Maggie were simple: help with Madelyn while Beau was out working on the ranch and trying to figure his life out. The rules for Scarlett? They'd go beyond not leaving your lingerie out. He mentally added a few more: stop looking so damn innocent and sexy at the same time, stop with the defiant chin that he wanted to nip at and work his way down.

But of course he couldn't voice those rules. He cleared his throat and instead of enumerating his expectations, he took a different approach.

"I'm a hands-on dad." He started with that because that was the most important. "Madelyn is my life. I'm only going to be at Pebblebrook for a short time, but while I'm here, I plan on getting back to my roots and helping to get this dude ranch up and running."

That is, if his brothers would let him in on realizing their father's dream. That was still a heated debate, especially since Beau hadn't been to see Grant Elliott yet.

His father had been residing in an assisted-living facility for the past few years. The bad blood between them couldn't be erased just because Beau had made a deathbed promise to the one man who had been more like a father to him than his real one.

Still, Beau was man enough to admit that he was afraid to see his dad. What if his dad didn't recognize him? Grant had been diagnosed with dementia and lately, more often than not, he didn't know his own children. Even the sons who'd been around the past few years. Beau wasn't sure he was strong enough to face that reality just yet.

"Beau?"

Scarlett's soft tone pulled him out of his thoughts. Where was he? Right, the rules.

"Yeah, um. I can get up with Madelyn during the night. I didn't hire a nanny so I could be lazy and just pass her care off. I prefer a live-in nanny more because I'm still…"

"Nervous?" she finished with raised brows. "It's understandable. Most first-time parents are. Babies are pretty easy, though. They'll pretty much tell you what's wrong, you know, just not with actual words."

No, he actually didn't know. He just knew when Madelyn cried he wanted her to stop because he didn't want her unhappy.

Beau had spent the past five months fighting with his ex, but she'd only wanted Madelyn as a bargaining chip. He'd finally gotten his lawyer to really tighten the screws and ultimately, Jennifer James—wannabe actress and worthless mother— signed away her parental rights.

As much as he hated the idea of Madelyn not having a mother around, his daughter was better off.

Beau studied his new, refreshing nanny. "I assume you don't have children since you're a nanny full-time."

Some emotion slid right over her, taking away that sweet,

calm look she'd had since she'd arrived. He could swear an invisible shield slid right between them. Her lips thinned, her head tipped up a notch and her eyes were completely unblinking.

"No children," she said succinctly.

There was backstory behind that simple statement. He knew that for sure. And he was curious.

"Yet you know so much about them," he went on. "Do you want a family of your own one day?"

"My personal life is none of your concern. That's my number-one rule that you can add to your list."

Why the hell had he even asked? He didn't need to know her on a deeper level, but now that she'd flat-out refused to go there, he wanted to find out every last secret she kept hidden. He hadn't asked Maggie personal questions, but then Maggie hadn't pulled up emotions in him like this, either.

Even though he'd just vowed to stay out of Scarlett's personal business, well, he couldn't help himself. If she was just standoffish, that would be one thing, but hurt and vulnerability had laced her tone. He was a sucker for a woman in need.

Scarlett, though, clearly didn't want to be the topic of conversation, something he not only understood but respected. He told himself he should focus on his purpose for being back home and not worry about what his temporary nanny did in her off time.

Beau nodded in affirmation at her demand. "Very well. These three weeks shouldn't be a problem, then."

He came to his feet, most likely to get away from the lie he'd just settled between them. Truthfully, everything about having her here was a problem, but that was on him. Apparently she didn't care that his hormones had chosen now to stand up and pay attention to her. She also didn't seem to care who he was. He was just another client and his celebrity status didn't do a damn thing for her.

While he appreciated her not throwing herself at him, his ego wasn't so quick to accept the hit. This was all new territory for him where a beautiful woman was concerned.

"I'm going to change and head to the main stable for a bit." He pulled his cell from his pocket. "Give me your cell number and I'll text you so you have my number. If you need anything at all, message me and I'll be right back."

Once the numbers were exchanged, Beau picked up his boots by the front door and went to his room to change. He slipped on a pair of comfortable old jeans, but the boots were new and needed to be broken in. He'd had to buy another pair when he came back. The moment he'd left Pebblebrook years ago, he'd ditched any semblance of home.

Odd how he couldn't wait to dig right back in. The moment he'd turned into the long white-fence-lined drive, he'd gotten that kick of nostalgia as memories of working side by side with his brothers and his father came flooding back.

Right now he needed to muck some stalls to clear his head and take his mind off the most appealing woman he'd encountered in a long time…maybe ever.

But he doubted even grunt work would help. Because at the end of the day, he'd still come back here where she would be wearing her lacy lingerie…and where they would be spending their nights all alone with only an infant as their chaperone.

CHAPTER THREE

"You're going to get your pretty new boots scuffed."

Beau turned toward the open end of the stable. His older brother Hayes stood with his arms crossed over his chest, his tattoos peeking from beneath the hems of the sleeves on his biceps.

"I need to break them in," Beau replied, instinctively glancing down to the shiny steel across the point on the toe.

If anyone knew about coming home, it was Hayes. Beau's ex-soldier brother had been overseas fighting in Afghanistan and had seen some serious action that had turned Hayes into an entirely different man than the one Beau remembered.

Whatever had happened to his brother had hardened him, but he was back at the ranch with the love of his life and raising a little boy that he'd taken in as his own. He'd found a happy ending. Beau wasn't so sure that would ever happen for him—or even if he wanted it to.

"So, what? You're going to try to get back into the ranching life?" Hayes asked as he moved to grab a pitchfork hanging on the inside of the tack room. "Or are we just a stepping stone?"

Beau didn't know what the hell he was going to do. He knew in less than three weeks he had a movie debut he had to attend, but beyond that, he'd been dodging his new agent's calls because there was no way Beau was ready to look at another script just yet. His focus was needed elsewhere.

Like on his daughter.

On his future.

"Right now I'm just trying to figure out where the hell to go." Beau gripped his own pitchfork and glanced to the stall with Doc inside. "Nolan ever come and help?"

Hayes headed toward the other end of the row. "When he can. He stays busy at the hospital, but he's cut his hours since marrying and having a kid of his own. His priorities have shifted."

Not just Nolan's priorities, but also Colt's and Hayes's. All three of his brothers had fallen in love and were enjoying their ready-made families.

Beau had been shocked when he'd pulled into the drive and seen his brothers standing on Colt's sprawling front porch with three ladies he didn't know and four children. The ranch had apparently exploded into the next generation while he'd been gone.

Beau worked around Nolan's stallion and put fresh straw in the stall before moving to the next one. For the next hour he and Hayes worked together just like when they'd been kids. Teamwork on the ranch had been important to their father. He'd instilled a set of ethics in his boys that no formal education could match.

Of course they had ranch hands, but there was something about getting back to your roots, Beau knew, that did some sort of reset to your mental health. At this point he needed to try anything to help him figure out what his next move should be.

He actually enjoyed manual labor. Even as a kid and a teen, he'd liked working alongside his father and brothers. But over time, Beau had gotten the urge to see the world, to find out if there was more to life than ranching, and learning how to turn one of the toughest professions into a billion-dollar lifestyle. The idea of being in charge of Pebblebrook once his father retired held no shred of interest to Beau. He knew Colt had always wanted that position so why would Beau even attempt to share it?

"So you all live here on the estate?" Beau asked when he and Hayes had completed their stalls and met in the middle of the barn.

Hayes rested his hand on the top of the pitchfork handle and swiped his other forearm across his damp forehead. "Yeah. I renovated Granddad's old house back by the fork in the river and the creek. I've always loved that place and it just seemed logical when I came back."

The original farmhouse for Pebblebrook would be the perfect home for Hayes and his family, providing privacy, but still remaining on Elliott land.

When they'd all been boys they'd ventured to the back of the property on their horses or ATVs and used it as a giant getaway or a man cave. They'd had the ultimate fort and pretended to be soldiers or cowboys in the Old West.

Once upon a time the Elliott brothers were all close, inseparable. But now...

Beau was virtually starting over with his own family. That deathbed promise to his former agent was so much more difficult to execute than he'd originally thought. But Hector had made Beau vow he'd go home and mend fences. At the time Beau had agreed, but now he knew saying the words had been the easy part.

He leaned back against Doc's stall and stared blankly.

"Hey." Hayes studied Beau before slapping a large hand over his shoulder. "It's going to take some time. Nolan is hurt, but he's not pissed. Me? I'm just glad you're here, though I wonder if you'll stay. So I guess that makes me cautious. But Colt, well, he's pissed and hurt, so that's the one you need to be careful with."

Beau snorted and shook his head. "Yeah, we've already had words."

Like when Colt swung by earlier to talk, but ended up going off because of the new nanny. Colt claimed Beau was still a wild child and a player, hiring a nanny looking like that. Beau had prayed Scarlett hadn't heard Colt's accusations. She was a professional and he didn't want her disrespected or made to feel unwelcome. Not that his brother was disrespecting Scarlett. No, he was aiming that all at Beau.

Even if the choice had been his, Beau sure as hell wouldn't have chosen a woman who looked like Scarlett to spend twenty-four hours a day with inside that small cabin. Even he wasn't that much of a masochist.

Beau had no idea what had originally brought Colt over to see him, but he had a feeling their morning talk wasn't the last of their heated debates.

"You'd think my twin would be the most understanding," Beau muttered.

"Not when he's the one who held this place together once Dad couldn't," Hayes retorted. "I was overseas, Nolan was married to his surgery schedule and you were gone. Colt's always wanted this life. Ranching was it for him, so I guess the fact you wanted nothing to do with it only made the hurt worse. Especially when you rarely called or came back to visit."

Beau knew coming back would rip his heart open, but he'd had no clue his brother would just continually pour salt into the wound. But he had nobody to blame but himself. He was man enough to take it, though. He would push through the hard times and reconnect with his family. If losing Hector had taught him anything, it was that time was fleeting.

"I can't make up for the past," Beau started. "And I can't guarantee I'll stay forever. I just needed somewhere to bring Madelyn, and home seemed like the most logical place. I don't care how I'm treated, just as long as she's loved. I can work on Colt and hopefully mend that relationship."

"Maybe you should start with seeing Dad if you want to try to make amends with anyone."

The heavy dose of guilt he'd been carrying around for some time grew weightier at Hayes's statement. His older brother was absolutely right, yet fear had kept Beau from reaching out to his father since he'd been home.

"Will he even know me?" Beau asked, almost afraid of the answer.

Hayes shrugged. "Maybe not, but what matters is that you're there."

Beau swallowed the lump of emotions. Everything he'd heard over the past year was that their father barely knew anything anymore. The Alzheimer's had trapped him inside his mind. He and Beau may have had major differences in the past, but Grant Elliott was still his father and Beau respected the hell out of that man...though he hadn't done a great job of showing it over the years.

His father had been a second-generation rancher and took pride in his work. He'd wanted his sons to follow in that same path of devotion. Beau, though, had been a rebellious teen with wandering feet and a chip on his shoulder. Pebblebrook hadn't been enough to contain him and he'd moved away. On his own for the first time, he'd wanted to experience everything that had been denied him back home, and ended up in trouble. Then he was discovered and dubbed "a natural" after a ridiculous commercial he wanted to forget.

Beau threw himself into the acting scene hard. His career had seemed to skyrocket overnight.

At first he'd been on a path to destruction, then a path to stardom. And through it all, he hadn't even thought of coming home. He'd been too wrapped up in himself. No excuses.

Then one day he'd realized how much time had passed. He had come home but the cold welcome he'd received had sent him straight back to LA.

But this time was different. This time he was going to stay, at least through the holidays, no matter how difficult it might be.

"I'll go see him," Beau promised, finally meeting Hayes's eyes. "I'm just not ready."

"Always making excuses."

Beau and Hayes turned to the sound of Colt's angry voice. Just what he needed, another round with his pissed brother.

Colt glanced to the pitchfork in Beau's hand. "Are you practicing for a part or actually attempting to help?"

"Colt—"

"No." Beau held out his hand, cutting Hayes off. "It's not your fight."

Hayes nodded and took Beau's pitchfork and his own back to the tack room, giving Beau and Colt some privacy.

"I came home because I needed somewhere safe to bring my daughter," Beau stated, that chip on his shoulder more evident than ever. "I came home because it was time and I'd hoped we could put aside our differences for Christmas."

Did he think he could just waltz back onto the ranch and sing carols around the Christmas tree and all would be well? Had he been gone so long that he could just ignore the tension and the hurt that resided here?

"You won't find a red-carpet welcome here," Colt grunted. "We've gotten along just fine without you for years. So if you're just going to turn around and leave again, don't bother with all this show now. Christmas is a busy time for Annabelle at the B and B. I don't have time to figure out what the hell you're doing or not doing."

Seeing his twin back here where they'd shared so many memories…

Every part of Colt wished this was a warm family reunion, but the reality was quite different.

Beau had chosen to stay away, to make a new family, a new life amidst all the Hollywood hoopla, the parties, the women, the money and jet-setting.

Bitterness had settled into Colt long ago and showed no sign of leaving.

"What did you want when you came by this morning?" Beau asked. "Other than to berate me."

Hayes carried a blanket and saddle down the stable and passed them, obviously trying to get the hell out of here and not intervene.

Colt hooked his thumbs through his belt loops. "I was going to give you a chance to explain. Annabelle told me I should hear your side, but then I saw your replacement nanny and realized nothing about you has changed."

Of course Beau would have a stunning woman living under his roof with the guise of being a nanny. Was his brother ever going to mature and just own up to his responsibilities?

"Replacement nanny?" Hayes chimed up.

Beau's eyes narrowed—apparently Colt had hit a nerve. But they both ignored Hayes's question.

The resentment and turmoil that had been bubbling and brewing over the years was best left between him and his twin. Colt didn't want to drag anybody else into this mix.

Though his wife had already wedged herself into the drama. He knew she meant well, he knew she wanted one big happy family, especially considering she lost her only sibling too early in life. But still, there was so much pain in the past that had only grown like a tumor over the years. Some things simply couldn't be fixed.

Beau kept his gaze straight ahead to Colt. "Who I have helping with Madelyn is none of your concern and I didn't decide who the agency sent to replace Maggie. Her husband fell and broke his hip so she had to go care for him for a few weeks until their daughter can come help. If you have a problem, maybe you'd like to apply for the job."

"Maybe you could worry more about your daughter and less about your dick—"

Beau didn't think before his fist planted in the side of Colt's jaw. He simply reacted. But before he could land a second shot, a restraining hand stopped him. Hayes stood between the brothers, his hands on each of their chests.

"All right, we're not doing this," Hayes told them both.

"Looks like I missed the official work reunion."

At the sound of the new voice, Beau turned to see Nolan come striding in. No fancy doctor clothes for his oldest brother. Nolan looked like the rest of them with his jeans and Western shirt and boots and black hat.

There was no mistaking they were brothers. Years and lifestyles may have kept them apart, but the Elliott genetics were strong. Just the sight of his three brothers had something shifting in Beau's chest. Perhaps he was supposed to be here now, for more than Madelyn.

"Throwing punches took longer than I thought," Nolan growled, closing the distance. "You've been here a whole week."

Beau ignored the comment and glared back at Colt. "You know nothing about me anymore, so don't presume you know what type of man I am."

"Whose fault is that?" Colt shouted. "You didn't let us get to know the man you grew into. We had to watch it on the damn movie screen."

Guilt...such a bitter pill to swallow.

"Why don't we just calm down?" Hayes suggested as he stepped back. "Beau is home now and Dad wouldn't want us going at each other. This is all he ever wanted, us together, working on the ranch."

"You haven't even been to see him," Colt shot at Beau, his dark eyes still judgmental.

"I will."

Colt shook his head in disgust, but Beau didn't owe him an explanation. Beau didn't owe him anything. They may be twins, but the physical appearance was where their similarities ended. They were different men, with different goals. Why should Beau be sorry for the life he'd created for himself?

Nolan reached them then and diverted his attention. "Pepper wanted me to invite you and Madelyn for dinner," he stated in that calm voice of his. "Are you free this evening?"

Beau blew out the stress he'd been feeling and raked a hand along the back of his neck. "Yeah. I'm free. Madelyn's been a little cranky. Scarlett thinks she's cutting teeth, but we should be able to make it."

"Scarlett?" Nolan asked.

"His new nanny," Colt interjected. "She's petite, curvy, stunning. Just Beau's type."

Beau wasn't going to take the bait, not again. Besides, already he knew that Scarlett was so much more than that simple description. She was vibrant and strong and determined…and she'd had his fantasies working overtime.

"You're married," he said instead to his twin. "So my nanny is none of your concern."

"Just stating the facts." Colt held his hands out and took a step back. "I'm happily married with two babies of my own, so don't worry about me trying to lay claim. I'm loyal to my wife."

"Scarlett can come, too, if you want," Nolan added, clearly ignoring his brother's argument. "Pepper won't mind."

Scarlett joining him? Hell no. That would be too familial and definitely not the approach he wanted to take on day one with his temporary help. Not the approach he'd want to take on any day with her, actually.

Not that long ago he would've jumped at the excuse to spend more time with a gorgeous woman, but his hormones were just going to have to take a back seat because he had to face reality. The good times that he was used to were in the past. His good times now consisted of a peaceful night's sleep and a happy baby.

Damn, he was either getting old or finally acting like an adult.

He'd always tried to keep himself grounded over the years, but now that he was home, he realized just how shallow Hollywood had made him. Shallow and jaded. Yet another reason he needed to keep himself and his daughter away from that lifestyle.

"It will just be Madelyn and me," he informed his brother. Then he shifted his attention back to Colt. "Do you want my help around here or not?"

"From the prodigal son?" Colt's jaw clenched, and Beau could see a bruise was already forming there. Colt finally nodded. "I've got most of the guys on the west side of the property mending fences. I'll take your free labor here."

Well, that was something. Maybe there was hope for them after all. Beau decided since they weren't yelling or throwing more punches, now would be as good a time as any to pitch his thoughts out there.

"I want in on the dude ranch, too."

Beau didn't realize he'd wanted that until they all stood here together. But there was no denying his wishes now. Whether he stayed on the ranch or not, he wanted to be part of his father's legacy with his brothers.

Colt's brows shot up, but before he could refuse, Beau went on. "I'm part of this family whether you like it or not and Dad's wish was to see this through. Now, I know you plan to open in just a few months and a good bit of the hard work is done, but that doesn't mean you couldn't use me."

Hayes shrugged. "Wouldn't be a bad idea to have him do some marketing. He'd have some great connections."

Colt's gaze darted to Hayes. "Are you serious?"

"Hayes is right," Nolan added. "I know none of us needs the extra income, but we want Dad's dream to be a success."

Colt took off his hat, raked a hand over his hair and settled the hat back in place. "Well, hell. Whatever. We'll use you until you take off again, because we all know you won't stick."

Beau didn't say a word. What could he say? He knew full well he likely wasn't staying here long-term. He'd returned because of a deathbed promise and to figure out where to take his daughter. Pebblebrook was likely a stepping stone…nothing more. Just like Hayes had said.

CHAPTER FOUR

SCARLETT SWIPED ANOTHER stroke of Cherry Cherry Bang Bang on her toes. Beau had taken Madelyn to dinner at his brother's house and told her she didn't need to come.

So she'd finished unpacking—getting all of her panties put away properly. Then she'd caught up on social media, and now she was giving herself an overdue pedicure with her new polish. She wasn't a red type of girl, but she figured with the new move coming and another chapter in her life starting, why not go all in and have some fun? Now that she was admiring it against her dark skin, she actually loved the festive shade.

And that's about as wild as she got. Red polish.

Could she be any more boring?

She never dreamed she'd be in this position at nearly thirty-five years of age: no husband, no children and a changing career.

She was fine without the husband—she could get by on her own, thank you very much. But the lack of children would always be a tender spot and the career change hurt just as much. Not that her career or lack of a family of her own defined her, but there were still dreams she'd had, dreams she'd had to let go of. These days she tried to focus on finding a new goal, but she still scrambled for something obtainable.

Scarlett adored being a nanny, but she simply couldn't continue in that job. Seeing all that she could've had but never would was just too painful.

Ultimately, she knew she had no choice but to walk away from that career. And because she had no family, no ties to this town of Stone River, she'd decided to move away, as well. In a large city like Dallas, surely there would be opportunities she didn't even realize she wanted.

As she stretched her legs out in front of her on the bed, Scarlett admired her toes. If Christmas wasn't the perfect time to paint her toes bright red, she didn't know when would be.

She settled back against her thick, propped pillows and reached for her laptop. In three weeks she'd be starting her new job as assistant director of activities at a nursing home in Dallas. While she was thrilled about the job and the prospect of meeting new people, she had yet to find proper housing. The one condo she'd hoped to rent had fallen through, so now she was back to the drawing board. Her Realtor in the area kept sending listings, but most were too expensive even with her pay raise.

While her toes dried, she scrolled through page after page of listings. She preferred to be closer to the city so she could have some social life, but then the costs just kept going up. She also preferred a small home instead of a condo or apartment, since privacy was important to her. But there was no way her paycheck would stretch enough to make a mortgage payment on a house. The condo she'd wanted to rent had an elderly lady living on the other side, so Scarlett had been comfortable with that setup.

She was switching to a new website when she heard the cabin door open and close. She eased her laptop aside and, after checking that her toes were nice and dry, she padded barefoot toward the living room.

As soon as she stepped through the door, Beau held his finger up to his lips and Scarlett noticed the sleeping baby cradled in his arm…against one very flexed, very taut biceps.

Down, girl.

She'd seen him on-screen plenty of times, but seeing him in person was quite a different image. She didn't know how he managed it, but the infuriating man was even sexier.

Wasn't there some crazy rule that the camera added ten pounds? Because from her vantage point, she thought maybe he'd bulked up since being on-screen because those arms and shoulders were quite something.

Scarlett clenched her hands, rubbing her fingertips against her palms at the thought of how those shoulders would feel beneath her touch.

She seriously needed to get control of her thoughts and focus. The only person she needed to be gripping, touching or even thinking about was Madelyn.

Scarlett motioned toward her room and whispered, "Let her sleep in here tonight since you didn't sleep last night."

He looked like he wanted to argue, but Scarlett quirked a brow, silently daring him to say one word. He may be the big, bad billionaire, but she wasn't backing down. Part of being a good nanny was to not only look after the child, but also take note of the parent's needs.

When Beau took a step toward her room, Scarlett ushered ahead and pulled the blinds to darken the space over the crib. The moon shone bright and beautiful tonight, but she wanted Madelyn to rest peacefully.

Scarlett took her laptop and tiptoed out of the room while Beau settled Madelyn in her crib. After taking a seat on the leather sofa in the living room, Scarlett pulled up those listings again. The sleeping baby didn't need her right now and she figured Beau had things to do. So, until he told her differently, she wouldn't get in the way.

Moments later, he eased from her room and closed the door behind him.

"I have food for you."

His comment caught her off guard. "Excuse me?"

Beau came around the couch and stood in front of her. That

black T-shirt and those well-worn jeans may look casual, but the way they fit him made all her girly parts stand up and take note of just how perfectly built he truly was. Not that she hadn't noticed every other time she'd ever looked at him.

"Pepper, Nolan's wife, insisted I bring you food and she was angry I didn't invite you."

Scarlett smiled, but waved a hand. "No reason to be angry. You didn't need me."

Something flared bright and hot in his eyes, but before she could identify what she'd seen, he asked, "Have you eaten?"

"I had a granola bar, but I'm not really that hungry." She was too concerned with being homeless when she moved to Dallas.

Beau muttered something about needing more meat on her bones before he headed back out the front door. An instant later he came back in with containers and headed toward the open kitchen.

Scarlett set her laptop on the raw-edged coffee table and figured it would be rude if she didn't acknowledge the gesture.

"I could eat a little more," she commented just as her belly let out a low grumble. "What do you have?"

He gestured to the stool opposite the island where he stood. "Have a seat and I'll get you a plate before your stomach wakes my daughter."

As Scarlett eased onto the wooden stool, she couldn't believe her eyes. Hollywood heartthrob Beau Elliott was essentially making her dinner. There wasn't a woman alive who wouldn't want to be in her shoes right now.

Beau pried lids off the plastic storage containers and Scarlett's mouth watered at the sight of mashed potatoes with gravy, green beans, and meatloaf he heaped onto a plate. Mercy sakes, a real home-cooked meal. There was no way she could eat all of that and still button her pants.

"Don't tell me you're one of those women who count every carb," he growled as he spooned a hearty dose of potatoes onto a plate.

"Not every carb, but I can't exactly afford to buy bigger clothes."

He shook his head as he once he filled the plate he placed it in front of her. He pulled open a drawer and grabbed a fork, passing it across, too.

"What would you like to drink? I haven't been the best at keeping food in here for me," he stated as he walked to the fridge. "I have formula, cereal, organic baby juice or water."

Wasn't it adorable that everything in the kitchen was for a five-month-old? But, seriously, what on earth was the man going to live on? Because someone as broad and strong as Beau needed to keep up his stamina…er, energy.

Do not think about his stamina—or his broad shoulders. Or tracing those tattoos with your tongue.

"Water is fine, thanks."

She decided the best thing to do was just shovel the food in. She may regret overeating later, but at least her mouth would be occupied and she couldn't speak her lascivious thoughts.

"I'll take Madelyn and make a grocery run tomorrow," she offered as she scooped up another bite of whipped potatoes.

Beau opened one cabinet after another, clearly looking for something. "I don't expect you to do the work of a maid."

"Then who will do it?" she countered before she thought better of it. But then she opened her mouth again and charged forward. "Either you have to go or I have to, unless you want the media to chase you through aisle seven and see what type of toilet paper you buy."

Beau stopped his search and turned to face her. He flattened his palms on the island and leaned in.

Maybe she'd gone too far, but seriously, who would do the shopping? Surely not his brothers, who were obviously not taking Beau's homecoming very well, for reasons that were none of her concern but still inspired her curiosity. Still, she probably should've left that last part off, but she'd never had a proper filter.

"Are you always this bold and honest?" he asked.

Oh, he didn't want her complete honesty. Was this a bad time to tell him she'd been holding back?

Scarlett set her fork down and scooted her plate back. Resting her arms on the counter, she cocked her head.

"I believe in honesty at all times, especially in this line of work. But I really am just trying to make things easier for you."

He stared at her another minute and she worried that she had a glob of gravy in the corner of her mouth or something, but he finally shook his head and pushed off the counter.

"You don't have to go," he told her. "I can ask one of my sister-in-laws to pick some things up for me."

As much as she wanted to call him out on his bullheadedness, she opted to see a different side. She may not know the dynamics of his family or the stormy past they'd obviously had, but she recognized a hurt soul when she saw one.

"I'm perfectly capable of grocery shopping," she stated, softening her tone. "I've lived on my own for some time now and besides, you wouldn't be the first client I've shopped for."

Beau folded his arms across his broad chest and leaned back against the opposite counter. "And where do you live?"

Her appetite vanished, pushed out by nerves as she pondered her upcoming move.

"Currently here."

"Obviously." His dry tone left no room for humor. "When you're not taking care of children, where do you call home?"

Between his intense stare and the simple question that set her on edge, Scarlett slid off the bar stool and came to her feet.

"I have no home at the moment," she explained, sliding her hands in the pockets of her jeans. "I'm still looking for a place."

Beau's dark brows drew in, a familiar look she'd seen on-screen, but in person… Wow. That sultry gaze made her stomach do flips and her mouth water. She didn't care if that sounded cliché, there was no other way to describe what happened when he looked at her that way.

"You're only here three weeks," he stated, as if she'd forgotten the countdown.

Scarlett picked up her plate and circled the island. She covered the dish up and put it inside the fridge. She needed to do something to try to ignore the fact that she wasn't only under the same roof as Beau Elliott, she was literally standing within touching distance and he was staring at her as if he could see into her soul.

No, that wasn't accurate at all. He was staring at her as if she stood before him with no clothes.

Maybe she should've kept that island between them.

"I'm moving to Dallas," she explained, trying to stay on topic. "This is my final job with the Nanny Poppins agency."

The harsh reality that this was it for her never got any easier to say. But, hey, if she had to leave, at least she was going out on the highest note of her nanny career. Staying with Hollywood Bad Boy Beau Elliott and taking care of his precious baby girl.

"Why the change?" he asked. "You seem to love your job."

The burn started in her throat and she quickly swallowed the emotions back. This was the way things had to be, so getting upset over it would change absolutely nothing. She might as well enjoy her time here, with the baby and the hunk, and move on to the new chapter in her life.

New year, new start, and all that mumbo jumbo. This was the second time in her life she'd started over on her own. If she did it when she was younger, she could certainly do it now.

"Why don't you get me a grocery list and I'll take Madelyn when she wakes in the morning," she said.

Scarlett started to turn, but a warm, strong hand curled around her bare biceps. She stilled, her entire body going on high alert and responding to the simplest of touches.

But this wasn't a simple touch. This was Beau Elliott, actor, playboy, rancher, father. Could he be more complex?

When he tugged her to turn her around, Scarlett came face-to-face with a sexy, stubbled jawline, firm mouth, hard eyes.

No, not hard, more like…intense. That was by far the best adjective to describe her boss. There was an intensity that seemed to radiate from him at all times, and that powerful stare, that strong, arousing grip, had her heart pounding.

"Women don't walk away from me."

No, she'd bet not. Most likely he gave them one heavy-lidded stare or a flash of that cocky grin and their panties melted off as they begged him for anything he was willing to give.

"I'm not walking away from you," she defended. "I'm walking away from this conversation."

"That's not fair." He still held on to her arm and took a half step closer until his torso brushed against hers. "I guarantee you know more about me than I know about you."

Scarlett laughed, more out of nerves than humor. "That's not my fault you parade your life in front of the camera. You know all you need in order for me to do my job."

The hold he had on her eased, but he still didn't let go. No, now he started running that thumb along the inside of her elbow.

What the hell?

She'd say the words aloud, but then he might stop and she wanted to take this thrill and save it deep inside her memory. So what if this was all wrong and warning flags were waving in her head?

"You don't look like a nanny," he murmured, studying her face. "Maggie looked like a nanny. You…"

Her entire body heated. With each stroke of that thumb she felt the zings down to her toes.

"What do I look like?" she asked. Why did that come out as a whisper?

"Like trouble."

Scarlett wanted to laugh. Truly she did. Of all the words used to describe her, *trouble* certainly had never been a contender.

This had to stop before she crossed the professional boundary. She'd never had an issue like this before, and by issue she meant a client as potent and as sexy as Beau Elliott. No wonder women flocked to him and wanted to be draped over his arm. If she were shallower and had no ambitions, she'd probably beg to be his next piece of arm candy.

But she wasn't shallow and she most definitely had goals... goals that did not include sleeping with a client.

"Make me that grocery list and text it to me," she told him as she took a step back. "Madelyn and I will head out in the morning."

She didn't wait on him to reply. Scarlett turned and fled to her room. She didn't exactly run, but she didn't walk, either. There was no way he wasn't watching her. She could practically feel that heavy gaze of his on her backside.

No doubt Beau knew just how powerful one of his long looks were. He'd gotten two big awards for his convincing performances and she couldn't help but wonder just how sincere he was with his affection or if he was just trying to find another bedmate.

Scarlett gently closed the door behind her and leaned against it. Over in the corner Madelyn slept. That little girl was the only reason Scarlett was here. There was no room for tingles or touching or...well, arousal.

There, she'd admitted it. She was so turned on by that featherlight touch of Beau's she didn't know how she'd get any sleep. Surely if she so much as closed her eyes, she'd dream of him doing delicious things to her body. That was the last image she needed on this final nanny assignment.

Scarlett moved away from the door and started changing for bed.

One day down, she told herself. Only twenty more to go.

CHAPTER FIVE

WHAT THE HELL had he been thinking touching her like that?

Beau slid his cowboy boot into the stirrup and swung his other leg over the back of Starlight, the newest mare to Pebblebrook.

He'd gotten up and out of that house this morning before seeing Scarlett. A niggle of guilt had hit him when he'd slunk out like he was doing some walk of shame, but damn it. He couldn't see her this morning, especially not all snuggly with Madelyn.

He hated not kissing his daughter good morning, but one day would be all right. Perhaps when he got back to the cabin he'd have a little more control over his hormones and unwelcome desires.

Damn it. He'd been up half the night, restless and aching. Likely Scarlett had been sleeping and not giving him another thought. This was all new territory for him, wanting a woman and not being able to have her.

With a clack of his mouth and a gentle heel to the side, Beau set Starlight off toward the back of the property.

Last night, his thoughts volleyed all around. He couldn't help wondering what Scarlett planned on doing when she left the agency, or why she was even leaving in the first place, but what kept him up all night was wondering what the hell she slept in.

Maybe she had a little pair of pajamas that matched that bright red polish she'd put on her toes. Mercy, that had been sexy as hell. He was a sucker for red.

Beau gripped the reins and guided the beautiful chestnut mare toward Hayes and Alexa's house. Beau hadn't been to the old, original farmhouse nestled in the back of the ranch since coming home. It was time he ventured out there and started making amends with his brothers. So what if he was starting with the one least pissed at him?

When Hector had been diagnosed with the inoperable brain tumor, Beau had known things weren't going to end well for them. Hector had been so much more than an agent. He'd been like a father figure, pulling Beau from the mess he'd gotten himself into when he'd first hit LA. For years they'd been like one unit, and then Beau's foundation was taken away.

But Hector had made Beau promise to go home and work on the relationships with his brothers and father. So, here he was. Having a sexy woman beneath his roof was just added penance. It was like fate was mocking him by parading Scarlett around like some sweet dream that would never become reality.

Which was why he'd been scolding himself all morning.

He couldn't touch her again. First of all, he'd put her in an uncomfortable position. That wasn't professional and he probably owed her an apology…but he wasn't sorry. He wasn't sorry that he'd finally gotten to touch her, to inhale that sweet, floral scent and see the pulse at the base of her neck kick up a notch.

Second of all, he couldn't touch her again because last night he'd been about a half second from jerking that curvy body against his to see exactly how well they'd fit.

He felt his body react to that thought, and forced his mind onto something else. The weather. That was innocuous enough. He looked around. The morning sun was warming up and already burning off the fog over the ranch.

He hoped the ice around Colt's heart would burn off just as easily. Granted, the cold welcome Beau had received was his own fault. Still, Colt acted like he didn't even want to try to forgive. Maybe that was just years of anger and resentment that had all built up and now that Beau was home Colt felt justified to unload.

But Christmas was only a few weeks away, and Beau wondered if he'd even be welcome at the table with the rest of the family. Hopefully by then, the angry words would be out of the way and they could start moving forward to a more positive future.

Beau had a movie premiere just two days before Christmas, but he planned on being gone only two days and returning. There was nothing he wanted more than to have his daughter at the ranch during the holiday and with the rest of the family.

Beau's cell vibrated in his pocket, but he ignored it. Instead, he kept Starlight at a steady pace and let himself relax as they headed to the back of the estate. He'd ridden horses for movie roles, but nothing was like this. No set could compare to being on his own land, without worrying about what direction to look or how to tip his hat at just the right angle for the camera, but not to block his eyes.

Being out here all alone, breathing in the fresh air and hoping to sew up the busted seams of his relationships kept Beau hopeful.

And really, his future depended on how things went over the next few weeks. Apologizing and crawling home with his proverbial tail between his legs wasn't easy. Beau had his pride, damn it, but he also had a family that he missed and loved.

If Christmas came and there was still no further progress made with Colt, Beau would go. He'd take Madelyn and they would go…somewhere. Hell, he had enough homes to choose from: a mansion in the Hollywood Hills, a cabin in Montana, a villa in France, his private island off the coast of Italy. Or he could just buy his own spread and build a house if that's what he chose. Maybe he'd start his own ranch and show Madelyn the way he was brought up.

But he wanted Pebblebrook.

The cell continued to vibrate. Likely his new agent, worried Beau had officially gone off-grid. Maybe he had. Maybe he wouldn't emerge until the premiere in a few weeks—maybe not even then. He didn't necessarily want to go to the premiere, but this was the most anticipated holiday movie and the buzz around it had been bigger than anything he'd ever seen.

Apparently *Holly Jolly Howards* struck a chord with people. The whole family falling apart and finding their way back together after a Christmas miracle saved one of their lives was said to be the next holiday classic. Move over *White Christmas* and *It's a Wonderful Life*.

Getting his on-screen family back together had been easy. All he'd had to do was act out the words in the script. But in real life, he was on his own.

Beau had only been back in Pebblebrook a short time, but already there was a peacefulness that calmed him at times like this. Just being out in the open on horseback helped to clear his mind of all the chaos of the job, the demands of being a celebrity, and the battle he waged with himself.

These past several months since becoming a parent had changed his entire outlook on life. He wanted the best for Madelyn, and not just the best material things. Beneath the tailormade suits, the flashy cars and extravagant parties, he was still a simple man from a Texas ranch. He'd always had money, so that wasn't anything overly important to him.

He wanted stability. He knew it was vital in shaping the future of a child. The simplicity of routine may sound ridiculous, but he'd found out that having a schedule made his life and Madelyn's so much easier. She needed to have a life that wasn't rushing from one movie set, photo shoot, television interview or extravagant party to another. That whirlwind lifestyle exhausted him; he couldn't imagine a baby living like that.

Beau may have a nanny now, but that's not how he wanted to live his entire life. He wasn't kidding when he said he wanted to be a hands-on father. He wouldn't be jetting off to various locales just to have someone else raise his daughter.

As Hayes's white farmhouse came into view, guilt reacquainted itself with Beau. His parents had done a remarkable job of providing security and a solid foundation for the four Elliott boys.

Once their mother passed, that foundation was shaken and everyone had to figure out their purpose. Beau had started getting that itch to see if there was something else out there for him. Since money hadn't been an issue, he'd taken a chunk out of his college fund and headed to Hollywood, despite his father's demands to stay.

The cell in Beau's pocket vibrated once again as he pulled his horse up to Hayes's stable. He dismounted and hooked the rein around the post. When he turned toward the house, Alexa stepped out the back door and her son, Mason, came barreling out past her.

Beau smiled, loving how his brother had found this happiness. They'd even decorated the house for the holidays. Sprigs of evergreen seemed to be bursting from the old wagon in the yard, a festive wreath hung on the back door, and red ribbons were tied on the white posts of the back porch.

"Hope you don't mind me stopping by," Beau said as he approached the steps. "I figured I should get to know my new family members a little better."

Alexa crossed her arms and offered a welcoming grin. "Never in my life did I think I'd meet a movie star, let alone have one for a soon-to-be brother-in-law."

Mason stopped right in front of Beau and stared up at him. "Hi."

Beau tipped his hat back and squatted down to the little guy. "Hey, buddy," he greeted. "How old are you?"

Mason held up one finger and smiled. Beau had already been educated on the ages of his nieces and nephews. This was just another reason he wanted Madelyn here. This new generation

of Elliotts should be close, because when your life went to hell
and got flipped upside down, family was invaluable.

Beau thought of his brother Colt's reaction yesterday. Part
of him knew that if Colt didn't care, he wouldn't be acting like
a wounded animal right now. The ones you loved most had the
ability to cause the most pain.

"Why don't you come on in," Alexa invited. "Mason and
I were just about to make some muffins to take to Annabelle
this afternoon. She's got her hands full at the B and B, so I offered to help. I'm not a great baker, but I can make muffins."

"I don't want to interrupt."

Alexa raised her brows. "Yet you rode out here without calling or texting?"

She offered a wide smile and waved her hand. "Get in here.
Family doesn't interrupt."

Beau could see how Hayes hadn't stood a chance with this
one. She was sassy and headstrong…pretty much like the sultry seductress down in his cabin.

Granted, Scarlett didn't have a clue how his stomach knotted up just thinking of her, how he'd been in a tangle of sheets
all night because…well, the fantasies wouldn't let him sleep.

Mason lifted his arms toward Beau. Without hesitation, Beau
picked up his…well, this would be his nephew. He hadn't been
around children until he'd had his own. Oh, there were a few
on some sets that he worked with, but they weren't his responsibility or they were a little older and so professional, they didn't
act like regular kids.

But this little guy didn't care that Beau had two shiny acting
awards back at his Hollywood Hills mansion. He didn't even
know who Beau was or why he was here. Mason wanted affection and he was open and trusting and ready to accept the
comfort of a stranger.

If only the rest of the family could be as welcoming as a child.

"Hayes actually just ran into town to get more supplies at
the store," Alexa stated as she stepped into the house and held

the door open for him. "I offered, but he keeps saying he needs to get out more."

Which was a huge accomplishment in itself. Suffering from PTSD had kept Hayes hidden away and everyone shut out for too long. Alexa had pulled him out of the rubble he'd buried himself in. The love of a good woman, Beau reckoned, was clearly invaluable. All of his brothers had found their perfect soul mate and secured a happy future.

There was clearly something in the water on Pebblebrook Ranch. No way in hell was he drinking from the well. The last thing he needed was more commitment or a relationship to worry about. Maybe one day—maybe—but not now.

Beau stepped into the kitchen and stilled. "Wow."

Alexa smiled. "I know. Hayes did an amazing job of renovating this place, though he did take my advice on the kitchen and use some of my Latino heritage as inspiration."

Judging by the bold colors from the blue backsplash to the yellow and orange details in random tiles on the floor, there was no doubt Hayes had made his fiancée feel part of this renovation.

"I haven't been back," he murmured as he held on to Mason and stepped farther into the room. "I'm going to need a tour."

Alexa reached for an apron on the hook by the pantry doors. "I'm going to let Hayes do that," she stated. "I'd say you two need some time alone."

The back door opened and Beau spun around to see his brother step in carrying bags of groceries.

"That place was pure hell," he growled as he set everything on the raw-edge kitchen table. "Remind me never to go in the morning again. Every senior citizen from town was there, all wanting to talk or shake my hand."

Beau knew his brother was grateful for the people who appreciated his service to their country, but Hayes had never been one for accolades.

"That's because they're thankful for your service." Alexa laughed and crossed to Beau. She lifted Mason from his hands.

"Your brother wants a tour of the house. Now, go do that and let me work on these muffins so Annabelle doesn't have to do everything for her guests."

Annabelle, Colt's wife and owner of the bed-and-breakfast next door, was not only the mother of nearly two-year-old twin girls, rumor had it she was also a phenomenal chef. Beau had the utmost respect for her because he could barely make a bowl of cereal and care for Madelyn at the same time.

Hayes eyed his brother and Beau slid off his cowboy hat and hooked it on the top of a kitchen chair. "Care to show me what you did to the place?"

"Are we rebuilding the brotherly bond?" Hayes asked.

"Something like that."

Hayes stared another minute before giving a curt nod. "Let's go, then."

Beau followed Hayes out of the kitchen and caught Alexa's warm smile and wink as he left.

They stepped into the living room, and Beau noticed the old carpet had been replaced with wide-plank wood flooring. The fireplace and mantel had been given a facelift. The room glowed with new paint, new furniture.

The fireplace had garland and lights draped across it, as well as three knitted stockings. A festively decorated Christmas tree sat in the front window. Presents were spread all beneath and Beau figured Hayes may have gone a bit overboard with the gifts for Mason.

Everything before him, from the renovations to the holiday decor, was the sign of a new chapter in his brother's life.

Beau wanted to start a new chapter, but he couldn't even find the right book for his life.

"We'll start upstairs," Hayes said over his shoulder. "That way I can grill you without Alexa overhearing."

Beau mounted the steps. "Why do you think I came here instead of Colt's? I'm easing into this re-bonding process."

Hayes reached the landing before making the turn to the

second story. "Heard you went to Nolan's last night. Does that mean Colt is tomorrow?"

Beau shrugged. "We'll see."

"And Dad?"

Beau stood on the narrow strip with his brother and stared into familiar dark eyes. "I'll get there," he promised.

Hayes seemed as if he wanted to say more, but he turned and continued on upstairs. "Then we can discuss your nanny while I show you what I did with the place."

Great. As if she hadn't been on his mind already. She actually hadn't gotten *off* his mind since she'd showed up at his door looking like she'd just stepped off a calendar for every male fantasy. The fake women in LA didn't even compare to the natural beauty of Scarlett Patterson.

"There's nothing to know about her," Beau stated, hoping that would end the conversation, but knowing better.

"Here's the guest bath." Hayes motioned toward the open doorway, but remained in the hall. "We gutted it and started from scratch. So, Scarlett replaced Maggie. That was quite a change."

"That wasn't a very smooth transition from the bath to the nanny."

Hayes merely shrugged and leaned against the door frame, clearly waiting for an answer.

Returning his attention to the renovated bath, Beau glanced around at the classy white and brushed nickel decor. He was impressed with all the work that went into the restoration, but he couldn't focus. Just hearing Scarlett's name had his body stirring. It had simply been too long since he'd been with a woman, that's all. It wasn't like he had some horny hang-up over his nanny. For pity's sake, he was Beau Elliott. He could have any woman he wanted.

Yet he wanted the one with a killer body, doe-like eyes, a layer of kickass barely covering a heavy dose of vulnerability. The fact that she cared for his daughter above all else and wasn't throwing herself at him was just another piece in the puzzle that made up this mystery of emotions.

His cell buzzed again and this time Beau pulled his phone out, grateful for the interruption so he could stop the interrogation.

The second he glanced at the screen, though, he barely suppressed a groan at the sight of four voice mails and three texts. The texts, all from his new agent, were frantic, if the wording in all caps was any indicator.

"Problem?" Hayes asked.

Beau read the messages, but ignored the voice mails. "The movie I have coming out is getting in the way of my sabbatical."

Hayes crossed his arms and leaned against the wall. "Is that what this is? You're just passing through until something or someone better comes along?"

Beau muttered a curse and raked his hand through his hair. "Hell, that didn't come out right. I just… I have no clue what I'm doing and it's making me grouchy. My agent and publicist have scheduled so many media slots for me to promote this movie, but I've told them I need to cancel. I'll do call-ins, but I'm not going to LA or New York right now to appear on talk shows."

He simply couldn't handle it. First, he wasn't dragging Madelyn to every event because they lasted from early morning until late at night. Second, well, he needed a damn break.

"You're a good dad."

Beau jerked his attention to Hayes, surprised by his brother's statement. "Thanks. My agent, he tried to get me to take Madelyn and basically use her for more publicity. I won't do that. Jennifer tried and I won't have it. I want Madelyn as far away from the limelight as possible."

Hayes nodded, whether in understanding or approval Beau didn't know. Perhaps a little of both.

"Maybe now you can see a little where Dad was coming from."

Hayes muttered the statement before moving on down the

hall like he hadn't just delivered a jab straight to the heart of the entire matter.

Beau respected the hell out of his brothers and his father. Perhaps because they all had chosen one path and been happy with their lives. Beau had thought he'd been happy and on the right path, until he became a father and his ex had decided drugs and wild parties and a future as a star were much more important.

"Show me what else you've done with the house," Beau said, shoving his cell back in his pocket.

"Don't you need to call someone?"

"This is more important."

Hayes offered a half grin, which was saying something for his quiet, reserved brother. "There's hope for you yet. But we're still going to circle back to Scarlett."

Of course they were, because why not? He'd left the house to dodge her for a bit, but now he was forced to discuss her. There was no end in sight with that woman.

Well, in less than three weeks there would be an end.

But he had a feeling she'd haunt his thoughts for some time.

CHAPTER SIX

SCARLETT HANDED MADELYN another fruit puff while she sat in her high chair. She wasn't surprised Beau wasn't here when she'd gotten home from the store.

Home. No. Pebblebrook wasn't her home by any means.

Yet she'd gone a tad overboard purchasing Christmas items to decorate the place. But she couldn't pass them by. She only hoped Beau didn't mind.

She busied herself putting together one of her favorite dishes. She'd come here in such a hurry and at the last minute, she had no clue if Beau had food allergies or what he liked.

Madelyn smacked her hands against the high chair tray and made little noises then squeals. Her little feet kicked and Scarlett smiled.

As much as being with a baby hurt her heart, Scarlett couldn't deny it was something she'd missed. Madelyn was such a sweetheart and so easy to care for. The few times she'd fussed with her swollen gums had passed quickly, thanks to cold teething rings.

Once the casserole was assembled and put into the oven, Scarlett unfastened Madelyn from the high chair. Madelyn let out high-pitched happy squeals and Scarlett's heart completely melted. Babies had their own language, no doubt about it.

"You need a bath," Scarlett crooned. "Yes, you do. You have sticky fingers and crazy hair."

The click of the front door had Scarlett shifting her focus from the baby to the sexy man who filled the doorway. The second he stepped inside, his dark eyes met hers. Even from across this space, she felt that intense stare all through her body. Those eyes were just as potent as his touch.

For a moment, Beau didn't move and she wondered what he was thinking. She really wished he'd say something to ease the invisible charge that crackled between them.

Scarlett finally broke eye contact, needing to get beyond this sexual tension because suddenly she was getting the idea that it wasn't one-sided anymore. And that could be trouble.

Big trouble.

"I just put dinner in the oven," she stated as she held on to Madelyn and circled the island. "I'm about to give Madelyn a bath."

The front door closed, then the lock clicked into place. Beau slid his black hat off his head and hung it on a peg by the door. Finally, his gaze shifted from her and roamed around the open cabin.

"What's all that?" he asked, nodding toward the sacks lining the sofa and dotting the area rug.

Madelyn reached for Scarlett's hair and tugged. "Just some Christmas decorations," she said, pulling her hair from the baby's sticky grasp.

Beau propped his hands on his hips and shook his head. "Give her to me. I'll give her a bath."

"Are you sure? I don't mind at all."

Beau stepped toward her, that long stride closing the distance between them pretty quickly. "I'll do it."

He slid Madelyn from Scarlett's arms and once he had his daughter, he lifted her in the air and a complete transformation came over him. He smiled, he made silly noises and had the craziest baby-talk voice she'd ever heard.

Well, Maggie had been right on this. Beau was completely different with Madelyn. He may be dealing with his own personal battles, but he wasn't letting that get in the way of his relationship with his baby.

When he went into his room and closed the door, Scarlett figured she might as well tidy up the kitchen. She'd put groceries away, then fed Madelyn when he brought her out, and laid her down for a nap. With time on her hands, she knew she should continue the house hunt. Each day that passed took her closer to her move and it was looking more and more like she'd be in a hotel for longer than she'd anticipated.

But she pushed those worries aside for now, eschewing the laptop for the bags of decorations. She got to work taking the holiday items out of the sacks and figuring where to put them. Considering she was watching every penny, she hadn't bought too much, but now that she was looking at everything in this small space, maybe it was a good thing she'd limited her impromptu spree. But there had been sales and, well, she was a savvy woman who couldn't turn down a bargain—or those little rustic cowboy boot ornaments.

Live garland nestled perfectly on the thick wood mantel. Once the two plaid stockings were in place, Scarlett stood back and smiled. This was already starting to look like home. Not for her, but for the little family in the other room.

She tried to take into consideration Beau's tastes, though she didn't know him well. At least she'd kept the decor more toward the masculine side. Though it had been difficult to leave behind the clearance garland with kissing reindeer and red sparkly snowflakes.

For reasons she couldn't explain, there wasn't a tacky Christmas decoration she didn't love.

Before Scarlett could go through the other bags, the oven timer went off.

She'd just set the steaming casserole dish on the stovetop when Beau stepped from his bedroom. He had Madelyn in a red sleeper with little reindeer heads on the feet. The baby looked so cute, but it was the man who drew her eyes like a magnet. Beau looked so sexy, his chest bare and his jeans indecently low on his narrow hips.

She licked her lips, then realized that wasn't the smartest move when his eyes dropped to her mouth. There went that tug on the invisible string pulling them together.

Why did he have to put those tattoos on display? The image of wild horses obviously paid homage to his roots, but she couldn't help it they also encompassed his true spirit of wanting to be wild and free...or maybe he used to be.

Either way, the ink was a distraction she didn't need, yet she desperately wanted to explore. Along with the lean muscles and six-pack abs.

Scarlett cleared her throat. "Dinner is ready."

Beau moved closer, his eyes locked on hers as if he could read her thoughts. "Is that why you're staring at my chest?"

Scarlett blinked and snapped her eyes to meet his. "I was not."

"You're a liar, but I won't report that to your employer." As he handed Madelyn over, he leaned in close and inhaled right by her neck. "Dinner smells good."

That low, gravelly tone sent shivers throughout her body and she nearly gave in to the temptation to close the two-inch gap and touch that gorgeous chest that beckoned her. But before she could move, he turned away and went back into his bedroom. Scarlett just stood there, stock still, wondering what the hell had just happened. What was he doing and why had she almost let herself get caught up in it? Damn it. That behavior was not at all professional.

Done berating herself, she took Madelyn to the portable swing in the living area and fastened her in. Once the music and swing were on, Scarlett went back to the kitchen and started dishing up the casserole. There was no way she was knocking on Beau's door to see if he was coming out to eat. She'd simply make a plate and he could eat when he wanted.

Scarlett had just poured two glasses of sweet tea when Beau stepped from his room. With his wet hair glistening even darker than she'd seen and a fresh T-shirt stretched across his broad shoulders, it was all she could do to force her eyes away.

He eyed the two plates sitting on the island, then he glanced to her. "You don't have to cook for me."

"You're welcome." The snarky reply just came out, so she added, "I had to cook for myself anyway. Hope you like cabbage."

He didn't say a word, but came over and sank onto one of the stools on the bar side of the island. As he dug in, she watched for a moment and figured he must not hate it. Part of her was relieved, though she didn't know why. What did it matter if he liked her cooking? She wasn't here to impress him with her homey skills.

Scarlett remained on the kitchen side of the island and started eating. The cabbage, bacon and rice casserole was one of her favorites. It was simple, filling, and rather healthy.

"You can have a seat," he told her without looking up from his plate. "I only bite upon request."

Why did she have to shiver at that? Just the idea of his mouth on her heated skin was enough to have her keeping this island between them. She may only "know" Beau from what she'd read online over the years, but she knew enough to realize he was a ladies' man and an endless flirt. And she was just another female in what she was sure was a long line of forgettable ladies.

So the fact that she lit up on the inside and had those giddy nerves dancing in her belly was absolutely ridiculous. She was leaving soon and he'd go on to more women and probably more children.

"I'm fine," she told him. "I'm used to eating standing up anyway."

That wasn't a lie. In fact, when she'd worked in other homes with small children, she'd been happy simply to get her meal hot. Besides, there was no way she'd get close to him. It wasn't so much him she was afraid of but her growing attraction, and she worried if she didn't keep some distance...

Well, she'd keep her distance so they didn't find out.

"I can keep an eye on Madelyn this way," she went on.

Beau glanced over his shoulder to where his daughter continued to swing. Then he jerked around, his fork clattering to the plate.

"What the hell is all that?" he barked.

Scarlett nearly choked on her bite. She took a drink of her sweet tea and cleared her throat. "Christmas decorations. I told you earlier."

His dark eyes shifted straight to her. "I know what you said earlier, but I didn't realize you were taking over the entire cabin. I thought you were putting stuff in your room. Why the hell is it all over my living room?"

"Because it's Christmas."

Why did he keep asking the most ridiculous questions?

"I didn't ask you to do that," he grumbled.

"Well, you didn't ask me to cook for you, either, but you're clearly enjoying it."

He muttered something else before going back to his plate, but she couldn't make it out. And she didn't ask him to repeat it. Instead, they finished eating in awkward silence. Only the sound of the nursery rhyme chiming from the swing broke through the space.

"There's no reason to get cozy here."

His words sliced right through her and she pulled in a deep breath before addressing him.

Scarlett propped her hands on her hips. "Are you talking to me or yourself?"

His dark eyes darted to hers once more. "Both."

"Well, I don't know what's going on in your personal life,

but this is Madelyn's first Christmas. She deserves to have a festive place, whether it's temporary or not."

Madelyn started to fuss and Scarlett ignored her plate and went to the baby.

"Eat," Beau stated as he came to stand beside her. "I can give her a bottle and get her ready for bed."

Scarlett unfastened Madelyn and turned off the swing. "I've got her. You worked all day, so finish your dinner."

She didn't wait for his reply or give him an opportunity to argue. She started to make a bottle, but Beau beat her to it.

"Lay her in my room." He kissed Madelyn's head and glanced up to Scarlett. "I'll keep her tonight."

He stood so close, too close. His arm brushed hers, those eyes held her in place. She'd thought they were dark brown, but now she could see almost golden flecks. They were nearly hypnotic, pulling her in as if in a trance she couldn't resist.

But you have to.

The silent warning broke the spell and she cleared her throat.

"You're paying me to watch her," Scarlett told him, pleased when her voice sounded strong. "If you're going to the stables early, then you need your rest."

She should take a step back, but she didn't want to. He smelled too good and looked even better.

"I also said I'm a hands-on dad." He handed over the bottle. "So leave her in my room after she eats."

Scarlett wasn't going to argue with him. She worked for him and this was his child. If he wanted to be woken up during the night, that was his call.

She clutched the bottle in one hand and held the baby in the other as she headed toward his room, leaving him in the kitchen to finish his dinner. The second she stepped into his bedroom, a full-on assault hit her senses. If she thought he smelled good a moment ago, that was nothing compared to the masculine, fresh-from-the-shower scent that filled his space.

The sheets were rumpled and she found herself transfixed

by the sight. Just the thought of Beau Elliott in a tangle of dark navy sheets would fuel her nighttime fantasies for years. He was a beautiful man, all sculpted and tan, with just a little roughness about him.

Was it any wonder Hollywood had pulled him into its grasp and cast him in that first film set in the Wild West? He'd been perfect. Captivating and sexy, riding shirtless on his horse. A handsome cowboy straight from a Texas ranch. He didn't just play the part; he was the part.

Scarlett hated to admit how many times she'd watched that exact movie.

She closed her eyes and willed herself to stop the madness of these mind games. Hadn't she vowed not to focus on the man and remain dedicated to the child?

She fed Madelyn and soothed her until she was ready to be laid down. Once she had the baby in her crib, Scarlett turned to leave, but once again her eyes went to that messy king-size bed.

How many days did she have left?

Scarlett closed her eyes and pulled in a deep breath. She would get through this and keep her lustful desires out of the picture.

She tiptoed from the room and gently shut the door behind her. When she came back into the open area, she noted the kitchen had been cleaned up and the dishes were all washed.

She was stunned. Not only at the idea of a celebrity getting dishpan hands, but a billionaire who had employees who likely did everything from his laundry to making his reservations with arm candy dates.

Scarlett nearly laughed at herself. She wasn't going to date Beau; she wasn't even going to be friends with the man. This relationship, if it could be called such, was strictly professional.

She turned from the kitchen and spotted Beau standing in front of the fireplace. With his back to her, Scarlett had a chance to study him...as if she needed another opportunity or reason to ogle. But that shirt stretched so tightly across his shoulders and that denim hugged his backside in all the perfect places.

"I used to want this."

His low words cut through her thoughts and she realized she'd been caught once again staring. He'd known she was back here.

Scarlett took a few cautious steps forward and waited for him to continue. Clearly he was working through some thoughts.

"Christmas as a kid was always a big deal," he went on as he continued to stare at the stockings. "My mom would bake and I remember coming in from the barns and smelling bread or cookies. There was always something in the oven or on the counter."

She continued to listen without interrupting. Whatever he was working through right now had nothing to do with her. But the fact she was getting a glimpse into his personal life only intrigued her more. Scarlett had a feeling not many people saw this side of Beau.

"Mom would pretend that she didn't see Colt and me sneak out a dozen cookies before dinner." He let out a low rumble of laughter. "That poor woman had a time raising four boys and being a loving wife to my dad. She never worried about anything and was so relaxed. I guess she had to be, considering she was in a house full of men."

Beau paused for a moment before he went on. "Christmas was her time to shine. She had every inch of that house covered in garland and lights. I always knew when I married and settled down I wanted my house to be all decked out. I wanted my kids to feel like I did."

Scarlett's heart did a flip and she realized she'd closed the distance and stood so close, close enough to reach out and touch him. She fisted her hands at her sides.

Beau turned to face her. The torment on his face was something she hadn't seen yet. The man standing before her wasn't an actor. Wasn't a billionaire playboy. The man before her was just a guy who felt pain and loss like anyone else.

"I appreciate what you did here for Madelyn," he told her.

Scarlett smiled. "I did it for both of you."

His lips thinned and he glanced down as if to compose himself. "You didn't have to," he said, his gaze coming back up to hers.

"I wanted to."

Before she thought twice, Scarlett reached out, her hand cupping his cheek. She meant to console, to offer support, but his eyes went from sad to hungry in a second.

Scarlett started to pull away, but he covered her hand with his and stepped into her. Her breath caught in her throat at the brush of his torso on hers.

If she thought his stare had been intense before, it was nothing compared to what she saw now. Raw lust and pure desire.

"Beau."

He dipped his head and she knew exactly what was coming. She also knew she should move away and stop this before they crossed a line neither of them could come back from.

But she couldn't ignore the way her body tingled at his touch, at the passion in his eyes. She desperately wanted him to put that tempting mouth on hers. She didn't care if she was just another woman to him. She wasn't a virgin and she knew exactly what this was and what this wasn't.

It was just a kiss, right?

Beau feathered his lips over hers. The instant jolt of ache and need shot through every part of her body. But then he covered her mouth, coaxing her lips apart as he teased her with his tongue.

He brought their joined hands between their bodies and the back of his hand brushed her breast.

She'd been wrong. So, so wrong.

This was so much more than a kiss.

CHAPTER SEVEN

BEAU HAD LOST his damn mind, yet there was no way he could release Scarlett now. He'd wanted to taste her since she showed up at his doorstep looking like some exotic fantasy come to life.

Alarm bells went off in his head—the ones that usually went off when he was about to make a mistake. He ignored them.

Scarlett's curvy body leaned in, her nipple pebbled against the back of his hand. The way she groaned and melted into him had Beau ready to rip off this barrier of clothing and take exactly what they both wanted.

Beau took his free hand and settled it on the dip in her waist, curling his fingers and pulling her in tighter. She reached up and gripped his biceps as she angled her head just enough to take more of the kiss.

Kiss. What a simple word for a full-body experience.

Beau eased his fingertips beneath the hem of her shirt and nearly groaned when he came in contact with silky skin.

Scarlett tore her lips away and stepped back. Coolness instantly replaced the heat where her body had been. Beau had to force himself to remain still and not reach for her.

She covered her lips with her shaky hand and closed her eyes. "We can't do that."

"We just did." Like hell he'd let her regret this. They were adults with basic needs. "Did you not want me to kiss you?"

She pulled in a breath and squared her shoulders before she pinned him with that stunning stare. "I wanted it. No use in pretending I didn't, considering I nearly climbed up your body."

Beau couldn't help the twitch of a smile. "Then what's the problem?"

"The problem is that I'm your nanny," she volleyed back. "The problem is I won't be another woman in your long line of panty-droppers."

Panty-droppers? Beau laughed. Full from the belly laughter. Well, at least now he knew exactly what she thought.

Scarlett narrowed her dark eyes. "I don't see what's so funny."

"You can't believe the tabloids," he told her. Because he really wanted her to understand, he explained further. "I know everyone thinks I'm a major player, but that perception is fueled by the tabloids. They like to come to their own conclusions and then print assumptions. Just because a woman was on my arm or in my car doesn't mean she was in my bed."

"I won't be in your bed, either."

That smart mouth of hers kept him smiling. "Well, no, because Madelyn is in there. We should use your bed."

Scarlett let out an unladylike growl and turned away. "We are not discussing this."

"What? Sex? Why not?"

Beau started after her, but stopped when she spun back around. "Other than the obvious reason of me being your daughter's nanny, and I really hate clichés, I'll repeat that I won't be another girl in your bed."

Now she was just pissing him off. "You're really hung up on who's in my bed."

"Or maybe I'm just reminding myself not to get caught up in your charm." She propped her hands on her hips and tipped her head. "I realize I may be a challenge and you're not used to people saying no, but we kissed, it's over. Can we move on?"

She had to be kidding. That heat wasn't just one-sided. She'd damn well melted against him. She claimed to always be honest, but she wasn't just lying to him, she was lying to herself.

"Move on?" he asked. "Not likely."

Her dark eyes flared wide. The pulse at the base of her throat continued to beat faster than normal.

Yeah, that's right. He wasn't one to hide the truth, either. There was no way he could just move on now that he'd tasted her and felt that lithe body against his.

"I have no interest in a fling or to be bullied by someone just because they have money and power," she sneered. "I'm going to bed. I'll keep the monitor on in case you need me."

Money and power? What the hell did that have to do with anything? Clearly she had other issues that went well beyond him, this moment and her attraction.

The second Scarlett turned from him, Beau closed the gap between them and curled his arm around her waist, pulling her side against his chest.

"I never make a woman do anything," he corrected. Above all, she had to know he wasn't like that. "We were both very involved in that kiss. If I thought for a second you weren't attracted to me, I never would've touched you, Scarlett."

She shivered beneath him when he murmured her name in her ear. His thumb eased beneath the hem of her shirt and slid over that dip in her waist.

"Tell me who hurt you," he demanded, his tone firm, yet low.

He didn't like the idea of any woman being hurt by a man, but something about Scarlett made him want to protect her, to prevent any more pain in her life.

Scarlett stiffened and turned those dark eyes up to his. There was a weakness looking back at him that he recognized. He'd seen that underlying emotion every single day in the mirror for the past year. Whatever she was battling, she was desperately trying to hide it. Damn it, he knew how difficult it was to keep everything bottled up with no one to talk to, to lean on.

Circumstances as of late had led him to that exact vulnerable point in his life.

Beau hadn't expected a layer of admiration to join the physical attraction, but slowly his take on Scarlett was evolving into something he couldn't quite figure out.

"I won't be here long enough for my personal life to matter to you," she whispered.

"So I can't care about your feelings while you're here?"

Her eyes darted away, looking in the direction of the fireplace. Maybe the holidays were difficult for her, as well. Did she have family? She hadn't mentioned being with them or buying presents or anything that came with sharing Christmas with someone special.

Everything in him screamed that he was walking a fine line with her. He had a sinking feeling she was alone or she'd lost someone. Whatever the reason, the holiday was difficult on her.

Something twitched in his chest, but Beau refused to believe his heart was getting involved here. There was nothing wrong with caring or worrying about someone, even if that person was a virtual stranger. He'd been raised to be compassionate, that's all. Just because he was concerned didn't mean he wanted a relationship.

He stroked his thumb along her bare skin again, reminding himself anything between them should and would stay physical.

Finally, her eyes darted back to his. "I don't think this is a good idea."

The goose bumps beneath his touch told a different story. He feathered another swipe across her waist.

"What part isn't a good idea?"

"The kiss, the touches." She shook her head and stepped away from him. "I'm going to my room. I still need to find housing before my move so I'm not stuck in a hotel forever…and I need some space from you."

"I'll give you space," he vowed. "That still won't make the

ache go away. You know ignoring this will only make the pull even stronger."

She took another step away, as if she could escape what was happening here.

"Then we both better hope we can control ourselves until my time here is up."

Well, so far she'd managed to find eight places to rent, all over her budget, she'd done some yoga trying to calm her nerves, and she was now browsing through social media but not really focusing on the posts.

And it was one in the morning.

Scarlett kept telling herself to go to sleep because the baby would need her undivided attention tomorrow and she may even wake during the night.

Honestly, though, there was just no way she could crawl between the sheets when her body was still so revved up. She didn't even have to concentrate to feel his warm breath tickling the sensitive spot just below her ear or the way he kept that firm yet gentle touch just beneath the hem of her shirt. He tempted, teased…left her aching for more of the forbidden.

How dare Beau put her in this position?

Granted, she hadn't exactly resisted that toe-curling kiss. She'd thoroughly enjoyed Beau. She knew he would never force himself on her. No, he'd kissed her because she hadn't been able to hide her desire and that made her just as easy as all the other women he'd charmed. Damn it, she'd told herself to hold it together. It was only three weeks, for pity's sake.

The last thing she needed was a temporary, heated fling with her movie star boss. Other than the obvious working relationship that should keep them apart, she valued herself as more than someone forgettable—because she knew once she was gone, Beau wouldn't remember her.

Scarlett's heart clenched. Her family had forgotten her, as well. When she didn't bow to their wishes or aim to fulfill any political aspirations to round out the powerhouse family, they'd dismissed her as easily as a disloyal employee.

She slid off her bed and stretched until her back popped. She'd like to grab a bottle of water, but if he was out in the living room, then she really should stay put. She hadn't heard him on the monitor, so either he was incredibly stealthy or he hadn't gone to bed yet.

Scarlett eased over to her closed door and slowly turned the knob to peek out. There was a soft glow from the Christmas lights she'd strung on the mantel, but other than that, nothing. She didn't see him anywhere.

Tiptoeing barefoot, she crossed the living area and went into the kitchen. She tried her best to keep quiet as she opened the fridge and pulled out a bottle of water. When she turned, she spotted the bags of Christmas decor she hadn't done anything with yet.

She wasn't sure if she should mention a tree to Beau or just have one appear. Even if it was a small one, everyone needed a little Christmas cheer. She'd seen a tree farm in town earlier and had heard good things about the family-owned business. Maybe she'd check it out tomorrow just to see if they had something that would work in this small space.

Growing up she'd never been allowed to decorate. Her stepfather always had that professionally done. After all, what would their guests say when they showed up for parties and the tree had been thrown together with love by the children who lived there?

Not that Scarlett got along with his kids. They were just as stuffy and uptight as he was. The one time Scarlett tried to have a little fun and slide down the banister from the second floor to the entryway, her step-siblings were all too eager to tattle.

Scarlett crossed the small area and sank down onto the rug. Glancing from one shopping bag to the next, she resisted the urge to look inside. The rattling of bags would definitely make too much noise—besides, she knew exactly what she had left.

Little nutcracker ornaments, a few horses, some stars. Nothing really went together, but she'd loved each item she'd seen so she'd dumped them into her cart.

Scarlett uncapped her water and took a sip.

"Can't sleep?"

She nearly choked on her drink, but managed to swallow before setting her bottle on the coffee table beside her.

Beau's footsteps brushed over the hardwood floors as he drew closer. Scarlett didn't turn. She was afraid he'd be in something like boxer briefs and all on display. Not that she was much better. She had on her shorts and a tank, sans bra and panties because that was just how she slept. At least she'd thrown on her short robe, so she was covered. Still, her body tingled all over again at the awareness of him.

She didn't answer him. The fact that she sat on the floor of the living room at one in the morning was proof enough that she couldn't sleep.

When Beau eased down beside her, Scarlett held her breath. Were they going back for round two? Because she wasn't so sure she could keep resisting him if he didn't back off a little.

Or perhaps that was his plan. To keep wearing her down until he could seduce her. Honestly, it wouldn't take much. One more tingling touch and she feared she'd strip off her own clothes and start begging for more.

There really was only so much a woman could handle.

"I still won't apologize for that kiss."

And here they went. Back at it again.

"But I also won't make this more difficult for you," he quickly added. "I need you and Madelyn needs you."

She exhaled that breath she'd been holding. That was what she'd wanted him to say, yet now that she knew he was easing off, she almost felt cheated.

Good grief. Could she be any more passive-aggressive? She just… Well, she just wanted him, but that wasn't the issue. The issue was, she *shouldn't* want him.

"I'm not sorry we kissed," she admitted. Might as well go for honesty at this point. "But I need this job, so we have to keep this professional."

Now she did risk turning to look at him. He had on running shorts, not boxers, thank God. But then she raised her eyes and saw that he wore shorts and nothing else.

Why could men get away with wearing so little? It simply wasn't fair. It sure as hell wasn't fair, either, that he looked so perfectly...well, perfect.

"You have somewhere to put all of this?" he asked, nodding toward the bags.

Scarlett nodded, pulling her attention from that bare chest to the sacks. "On the tree."

"I don't have a tree."

"I plan on fixing that very soon."

When he continued to stare at her, she didn't look away. Scarlett stretched her legs out in front of her and rested her hands behind her, daring him to say something negative about Christmas or decorations.

"I assume you saw the Christmas tree farm down the road?" he asked.

Scarlett nodded. "I believe Madelyn and I will go back into town tomorrow and check it out. I'll just get something small to put in front of the patio doors."

"Were you going to ask?"

"Like you asked about kissing me?"

Damn it. She hadn't meant to let that slip, but the snark just came out naturally. The last thing she could afford was for him to know she was thinking of him, of that damn kiss that still had her so restless and heated.

"Forget I said that." She shook her head and looked down at her lap. "I'm—"

"Right," he finished. "I didn't ask. That's because when I see what I want, I just take it. Especially since I saw passion staring back at me."

He didn't need to say he wanted her—she'd gotten that quite clearly. Most likely she appealed to him because she hadn't thrown herself at him or because she was the only woman around, other than his brothers' women.

Beau slid his finger beneath her chin and forced her to look at him. Oh, that simple touch shouldn't affect her so, but it did. She was human, after all.

"What makes you so different?" he muttered beneath his breath, but she heard him.

Scarlett shifted fully to face him. "What?"

Beau shook his head, almost as if he'd been talking to himself. That fingertip beneath her chin slid along her jawline, gentle, featherlight, but she felt the touch in every part of her body. The stillness of the night, the soft glow of the twinkling lights just above Beau's head had her getting wrapped up in this moment. She told herself she'd move away in a second. Really, she would.

Beau didn't utter a word, but his eyes captivated her, held her right in this spot. He feathered his fingertips down the column of her neck and lower to the V of her robe. She pulled in a deep breath and tried not to stare at those tattoos on his chest that slid up and disappeared over his shoulder. If she looked at his body, then she'd want to touch his body.

Scarlett clenched her fists in her lap. The robe parted slightly, and her nipples puckered in anticipation.

"Beau," she whispered.

His eyes dropped to where his hand traveled and explored, then he glanced back up to her. "I want you to feel."

The raw statement packed a punch and Scarlett wasn't sure what he wanted to happen, but she definitely felt. Just that soft touch had her body tingling and burning up.

He dropped that same hand to the top of her bare thigh and she stilled. Those dark eyes remained locked on hers as he slid his palm up her leg and beneath the hem of her robe.

Scarlett's breath caught in her throat as she glanced down

to watch his hand disappear. Beau leaned in closer, his lips grazed her jaw.

"You promised no more kissing," she whispered.

"I'm not kissing you." His warm breath across her skin wasn't helping. "Relax."

Relax? He had to be kidding. Her body was so revved up, there was no relaxing. She trembled and ached and it took every bit of her willpower not to strip her clothes off, lie down on this rug and beg him for every single thing she'd been denying them both.

His fingertips slid beneath her loose sleep shorts. If he was shocked at her lack of panties, he didn't say so and his fingers didn't even hesitate as they continued their journey to the spot where she ached most.

She shifted, easing her legs apart to grant him access...all while alarms sounded and red flags waved trying in vain to get her attention. All that mattered right now was his touch. Who they were didn't matter. They were beyond that worry and clearly didn't give a damn.

There was only so long a woman could hold out and Beau wasn't an easy man to ignore. Damn it, she'd tried.

Scarlett spread her legs wider, then before she knew it, she was lying back on that rug with Beau propped on his elbow beside her. He slid one finger over her before sliding into her. She shut her eyes and tipped her hips to get more. Did he have to move so agonizingly slow? Didn't he realize she was burning up with need?

"Look at me," he demanded.

He slid another finger into her and Scarlett opened her eyes and caught his intense gaze. The pale glow from the Christmas lights illuminated his face. This wasn't the movie star or the rancher beside her. Right at this moment, Beau Elliott was just a man with basic needs, a man who looked like he wanted to tear off her clothes, a man who was currently priming her body for release.

"Don't hold back." It was half whisper, half command.

Considering she'd had no control over her body up until this point, let alone this moment, holding back wasn't an option.

The way he continued to watch her as he stroked her was both arousing and intimidating. What did he see when he looked at her? Was he expecting more? Would they carry this back into her room?

Scarlett's thoughts vanished as her body spiraled into release. She couldn't help but shut her eyes and arch further into his touch. He murmured something, perhaps another demand, but she couldn't make out the words.

Wave after wave rushed over her and Scarlett reached up to clutch his thick biceps. He stayed with her until the tremors ceased, and even then, he continued to stroke her with the softest touch.

How could she still be aroused when she'd just been pleasured?

After a moment, Beau eased his hand away and smoothed her shorts and robe back into place. Scarlett risked opening her eyes and found him still staring down at her.

"You're one sexy woman," he told her in that low, sultry tone that seemed to match the mood and the dark of night.

Scarlett reached for the waistband of his shorts, but he covered her hand with his. "No. Go on to bed."

Confused, she drew back and slowly sat up. "You're not—"

Beau shook his head. "I wanted to touch you. I *needed* to touch you. I'm not looking for anything in return."

What? He didn't want more? Did men like that truly exist? Never would she have guessed Beau to be so giving, so selfless.

Scarlett studied his face and realized he was completely serious.

"Why?" The question slipped through her lips before she could stop herself.

Beau answered her with a crooked grin that had her stomach doing flips. "It's not important. Go on, now. Madelyn will be ready to go early and I need you rested."

When she didn't move, Beau came to his feet and extended his hand. She slid her fingers into his palm and he helped her up, but didn't release her.

"I'll be busy all day," he told her. "I look forward to seeing that Christmas tree when you're done with it."

He let her go, but only to reach up and smooth her hair behind her ears. His eyes held hers a moment before he turned and headed back to his room and silently closed the door.

Scarlett remained in place, her body still humming, and more confused than ever.

Just who was Beau Elliott? Because he wasn't the demanding playboy she'd originally thought. He was kind and passionate, giving and self-sacrificing. There was so much to him that she never would've considered, but she wanted to explore further.

Which would only prove to be a problem in the long run. Because a man who was noble, passionate and sexy would be damn difficult to leave in a few weeks.

CHAPTER EIGHT

COLT EASED BACK onto the patio sofa and wrapped his arm around Annabelle. Lucy and Emily were happily playing on the foam outdoor play yard he'd just put together. With the padded sides and colorful toys in the middle, the two seemed to be perfectly content.

"You're home earlier than usual," Annabelle stated, snuggling into his side. "Not that I'm complaining."

"I knew you would be in between cleaning the rooms and checking new guests in."

She rested her delicate hand on his thigh. Those gold bands on her finger glinted in the late-afternoon sunshine.

"We are actually free for the night," she replied. "The next several days are crazy, but I love it."

He knew she did. Annabelle's goal had always been to have her own B and B where she could cater to guests and showcase her amazing cooking skills.

Colt never could've imagined how much his life would change when this beauty came crashing onto his ranch...literally. She took out the fence in her haste to leave after their first meeting and he had been smitten since.

"You've not talked much about Beau."

Her statement brought him back to the moment and the obvious situation that needed to be discussed…even though he'd rather not.

"What do you want me to say?"

Lucy patted the bright yellow balls dangling on an arch on one side of the play yard. Annabelle shifted in her seat and eased up to look him directly in the eye.

He knew that look…the one of a determined woman.

"I can't imagine how difficult this is for you," she started, then patted his leg. "But think about Beau. Can you imagine how worried he was coming back, not knowing if he'd be accepted or not and having a baby?"

Colt doubted Beau had ever been worried or afraid in his life. He'd likely come home because… Hell, Colt had no idea the real reason. He hadn't actually asked.

"I can see your mind working."

Colt covered Annabelle's hand with his and gave her a slight squeeze. Lucy let out a shriek, but he glanced to see that she was laughing and nothing was actually wrong.

"This is tough," he admitted, hating the vulnerability, but he was always honest with his wife. "Having him back is all I'd ever wanted for so long. I guess that's why I'm so angry now."

"Then maybe you should talk to him about your feelings."

Colt wanted to. He played various forms of the conversation over and over in his mind, but each time he approached Beau, something snapped and the hurt that had been building inside Colt seemed to snap.

"Do you trust me?"

Colt eased forward and kissed Annabelle's forehead. "With everything."

"Then let me take care of this," she told him with that grin of hers that should scare the hell out of him. She was plotting.

Colt wasn't so far gone in his hurt that he wouldn't accept help and he trusted his wife more than anyone.

"I love you," he told her, then glanced to their twin girls. "And this life we've made."

Annabelle settled back against his side and laid her head on his shoulder.

"Let's see if we can make it just a bit better," she murmured.

If anyone could help repair the relationship between him and Beau, he knew it was Annabelle.

Maybe there was hope, because all he'd ever wanted was a close family. That was the ultimate way to honor their father.

Beau glanced over the blueprints of the dude ranch. The cabins, one of which he was using, were in perfect proportion to the river, the creek, the stables. His brothers couldn't have chosen a better spot for the guests to stay.

The mini-prints hung in raw wood frames on the wall of the office in the main stable closest to Colt's house. Beau's eyes traveled from one print to the next. The four original surveys of the land from when their grandfather purchased the ranch were drawn out in quarters. So much was the same, yet so different since he was home last.

A lump of guilt formed in Beau's throat. His brothers had designed this and started construction while he'd been in LA living his own life and dealing with Jennifer and her pregnancy. His father's main goal for his life was to see a dude ranch one day on the Elliott Estate. Now the dream was coming to fruition, but Grant couldn't even enjoy it because he was a prisoner in his own mind. Even if Beau or his brothers managed to bring their father here to see the progress, he'd likely never realize the sight before him, or the impact he had on his boys.

"I was hoping to find you here."

Beau glanced over his shoulder at the female voice. Annabelle, Colt's wife, stood in the doorway with a sweet smile on her face. Her long, red hair fell over both shoulders and she had a little girl on her hip.

"Which one is this?" he asked, smiling toward the toddler.

"This is Emily. Lucy is back at the house for a nap because she didn't sleep well last night."

Emily reached for him and Beau glanced to Annabelle. "May I?"

"Of course."

Beau took the child in his arms, surprised how much different she felt than his own. Granted, there was nearly a year between the two.

"I imagine having twins is quite a chore," he stated. "Do you ever get sleep?"

Annabelle laughed. "Not at first, but they're pretty good now. Lucy is getting another tooth, so she was a bit fussy during the night."

Apparently teeth were a huge deal in disrupting kids' sleep habits.

Emily smacked her hands against his cheeks and giggled. Such a sweet sound. "What brings you to the stables?" he asked Annabelle. "If you're looking for Colt, I haven't seen him today."

Likely because his brother was dodging him, but Beau wouldn't let that deter him. He was here to try to repair relationships and he couldn't give up.

"I'm actually looking for you," Annabelle stated. "I'd like you to come to dinner this evening. Well, you, Madelyn and Scarlett."

Beau stilled. Dinner with his disgruntled twin brother? Dinner with his baby and his nanny? Why the hell would he want to torture himself?

When he and Colt got a chance to speak about their past, Beau sure as hell didn't want an audience.

There was so much wrong with this dinner invitation. First of all, he wasn't quite ready to settle around a table with his brother and second, he couldn't bring Scarlett. Having her there would make things seem too familial and that would only give her the wrong impression.

Damn it. Beau could still feel her against him, still hear her soft pants and cries of passion. Last night had been a turning point, though what they'd turned to he had no idea. All he knew was they were far beyond nanny and boss—which was the reason she couldn't come to dinner.

"I can tell by your silence you're not thrilled." Annabelle smiled. "Let me rephrase. You will come to dinner and bring your daughter and your nanny."

"Why are you so determined to get me to dinner?" he asked.

Emily reached for her mother and Annabelle took the little girl back. "Because you and Colt need to keep working on this relationship. My husband is agitated and he's keeping his feelings bottled up. The more time you two can spend together, the better off you both will be."

He nodded, not necessarily in agreement, but in acknowledgment of what his sister-in-law had just said.

Beau tipped back his hat. "Why does Scarlett need to join us?"

Annabelle rolled her eyes. "Because it's rude to leave her at the cabin and I imagine she wants some female companionship."

Did she? He'd never asked. Granted, it was difficult to talk about her needs when he'd only been worried about his own—which basically involved touching her, tasting her.

Annabelle's intense stare held him in place and he wrangled in his errant thoughts and let out a deep sigh.

"Does Colt ever win an argument with you?"

A wide smile spread across her face. "Never. We'll see you all at six." Then she turned and headed out of the office.

Beau stared after her until he realized he was still staring at the open doorway. That was one strong-willed woman, which was exactly what Colt needed in his life.

The Elliott men were headstrong, always had been. A trait they'd all inherited, right along with their dark eyes and black hair. Beau figured there would never be a woman who matched him, but that was all right. He had Madelyn and she was more than enough.

He turned back to the blueprints on the opposite wall and continued to admire what would become of this property. Beau didn't know if his father would ever be able to come see this, but he couldn't help but wonder if he should take a copy of these blueprints to show him. Maybe seeing something that meant so much to him his entire life would trigger some memory.

Beau just wanted to do something, to make it possible for his dad to have some semblance of his past to hopefully trigger the present.

In all honesty, Beau wondered if his dad would even recognize him.

He did know one thing. He couldn't keep putting that visit off. He pulled his cell from his pocket and figured it was time to set up a time to see his father.

Scarlett adjusted the tree once again, but no matter how much she shifted and tilted it, the stubborn thing still leaned…and by leaned she meant appeared as if it was about to fall.

She let out the most unladylike growl, then startled when she heard chuckling behind her.

"Problem?"

Turning toward the doorway, Scarlett tried to keep her heart rate normal at the sight of Beau. First of all, she'd thought she was alone, save for Madelyn. Second, she hadn't seen him since he'd sent her to her room last night, though she'd thought of him all day.

Okay, she'd actually replayed their erotic encounter over and over, which was quite a leap ahead of just thinking of her hunky roommate. Had Beau thought about what happened? Did the intimacy mean anything to him at all or was this just one-sided?

"The damn tree is crooked," she grumbled.

Beau tilted his head to the side and narrowed his eyes. "Not if I stand like this."

She threw up her hands. "This doesn't happen in the movies. Everything looks perfect and everyone is happy. Christmas is magical and everyone has matching outfits and they go sleigh riding in some gorgeously decorated sled pulled by horses."

Beau laughed as he slid his hat off his head and hung it on the peg by the door. "That's quite a jump from worrying about a tree. Besides, everything is perfect in the movies because decorators are paid a hefty sum to make that happen. Real life isn't staged."

Scarlett turned to stare back at the tree. "It was the only one they had that would fit in this space. I thought I could make it work. Now what am I going to do?"

Beau's boots tapped across the hardwood, then silenced when he hit the rug…the very rug where she'd lain last night and on which she'd been pleasured by this man. She'd tried not to look at it today. Tried and failed.

"Decorate it."

She glanced over her shoulder at his simple, ridiculous answer, but he wasn't looking at her. He only had eyes for his little girl who sat in her swing, mesmerized by the spinning bumblebee above her head.

"How's she been today?"

"Pretty happy." Scarlett stepped around the bags of ornaments and lights she had yet to unpack. "I made some organic food for her so you have little containers in the fridge we can just grab whenever. It's better than buying jars."

Beau jerked his dark eyes to her. "You made her food?"

"I know you want to keep things simple and healthy for her." Now she felt silly with the way he seemed so stunned. "I mean, if you don't want to use it, that's fine, I just—"

"No."

He reached for her arm and Scarlett tried not to let the warmth from his touch thrust her into memories of the night before. But considering they were standing right where they'd made the memory, it was rather difficult not to think of every single detail.

"I'm glad you did that for her," he added, sliding his hand away. "I just didn't expect you to go above and beyond."

Scarlett smiled. "Taking care of children is my passion. There's nothing I wouldn't do for them."

Beau tipped his head. "Yet you're not going to be a nanny anymore when you leave here."

There was no use trying to fake a smile, so she let her face fall. In the short time she would be here, Scarlett really didn't want to spend their days rehashing her past year and the decisions that led to her leaving her most beloved job.

Scarlett stepped around him and turned the swing off. She unfastened Madelyn and lifted her up into her arms. When she spun around, Beau faced her and still wore that same worried, questioning gaze. Not what she wanted to see because he clearly was waiting on her to reply.

Also not what she wanted to see because she didn't want to think about him with those caring feelings. Things were much simpler when she assumed him to be the Playboy Prince of Hollywood.

"Let me get Madelyn settled into her high chair and I'll start dinner." Maybe if she completely dodged the topic, then maybe he wouldn't bring it up again. "Do you like apricots? I found some at the farmer's market earlier and I want to try a new dessert."

Before she could turn toward the kitchen, Beau took a step and came to stand right before her.

"Actually, Annabelle is making dinner tonight," he told her. "She came to the stables earlier and invited me."

"Oh, well. No worries. I'll make everything tomorrow." She brushed her hand along the top of Madelyn's baby curls. "Should I put Madelyn to bed while you're gone or are you taking her?"

Beau cleared his throat and rocked back on his boot heels. "We're all going."

"Okay, then I'll just clean her up and—" Realization hit her. "Wait. We're all going. As in *all* of us?"

Beau nodded and Scarlett's heart started that double-time beat again.

Why on earth would she go to Colt and Annabelle's house? She wasn't part of this family and she wasn't going to be around long enough to form a friendship with anyone at Pebblebrook Ranch. She was trying to cut ties and move on, not create relationships.

"There's really no need," Scarlett stated, shaking her head. "I can make myself something here."

"Annabelle didn't exactly ask," he told her. "Besides, why wouldn't you want to come? The only person Colt will be grouchy with is me."

"It's not that."

Silence nestled between them. She couldn't pinpoint the exact reason she didn't want to go. There wasn't just one; there were countless.

"One meal. That's all this is."

Scarlett stared up at him as she held on to Madelyn. Beau's dark eyes showed nothing. No emotion, no insight into what he may be thinking, but his words were clear. Just dinner. Meaning there was no need to read any more into it.

Was that a blanket statement for what happened between them right here last night? Was he making sure she knew there was nothing else that could happen? Because she was pretty sure she'd already received that message. A message she needed to keep repeating to herself.

"We should discuss last night." As much as she didn't want to, she also didn't want this chunk of tension growing between them, either. "I don't know what you expect of me."

"Expect?" His dark brows drew together.

Why did he have to make this difficult? He had to know what she was talking about.

"Yes," she said through clenched teeth. "You don't think I believe you don't want…something in return."

Beau's eyes darkened as he took a half step closer, his chest brushing her arm that held his daughter. "Did I ask you for anything in return? Did I lay out ground rules?"

Scarlett shook her head and patted Madelyn when the baby let out a fuss. She swayed back and forth in a calming motion.

"Then I expect you to listen to your body," he went on in that low, whisky-smooth tone. "I expect you to take what you want and not deny the pleasure I know you crave. I expect you to come to me when you're ready for more, because we both know it will happen."

Scarlett licked her lips and attempted to keep her breathing steady. He painted an erotic, honest image. She did want him, but would she act on that need?

"You sent me away last night," she reminded him. "If you know what I want, then why did you do that?"

He reached up and slid a fingertip down Scarlett's cheek, over her jaw and around to just beneath her chin. He tipped her head up and leaned in so close his lips nearly met hers.

"Because I want you to ache just as much as I do," he murmured in a way that had her stomach tightening with need. "Because I knew if we had sex last night, you'd blame it on getting caught up in the moment. But now, when you come to me, you'll have had time to think about what you want. There will be no excuses, no regrets."

Her entire body shivered. "You're so sure I'll come to you. What if I don't?"

Beau's eyes locked onto hers and he smiled. "If you weren't holding my daughter right now, I'd have you begging for me in a matter of seconds. Don't try to lie to me or yourself. You will come to me."

"And if I don't?"

She fully expected him to say he'd eventually come to her, but Beau eased back and pulled Madelyn from her arms. He flashed that high-voltage smile and winked. That man had the audacity to wink and just walk away.

That arrogant bastard. He thought he could just turn her on, give her a satisfying sample, then rev her up all over again and she'd just…what? Jump into his bed and beg him to do all the naughty things she'd imagined?

Scarlett blew out a sigh. That's exactly what she wanted to do and he knew it. So now what? They'd go to this family dinner and come back to the cabin, put Madelyn down and…

Yeah. It was the rest of that sentence that had nerves spiraling through her.

Beau Elliott was a potent man and she had a feeling she'd barely scratched the surface.

CHAPTER NINE

BEAU WAS HAVING a difficult time focusing on the dinner set before him. Between his brother's glare at the opposite end of the table, the noise from the three kids, and Scarlett sitting right across from him, Beau wondered how much longer he'd have to stay at Colt's.

He'd left Scarlett with something to think about back at the cabin, but he hadn't counted on getting himself worked up and on edge. That flare of desire in her eyes had given him pause for a moment, but he had to be smart. Wanting a woman wasn't a new experience, but wanting a woman so unattainable was.

The temporary factor of her presence didn't bother him. After all, he wasn't looking for anything long-term. He actually hadn't been looking for anything at all…but then she showed up on his doorstep.

What bothered him was how fragile she seemed beneath her steely surface. He should leave her alone. He should, but he couldn't.

Scarlett wasn't playing hard to get or playing any other games to get his attention. No, she was guarded and cautious—traits he needed to wrap his mind around before he got swept up into another round of lust.

"Scarlett, what are you going to be doing in Dallas?"

Annabelle's question broke into Beau's thoughts. He glanced across the table as Scarlett set her fork down on the edge of her plate.

"I'll be an assistant director of recreational activities at a senior center."

She delivered the answer with a smile, one that some may find convincing. Even if Beau hadn't been an actor, he knew Scarlett enough to know the gesture was fake.

"I'm sad to leave Stone River," she went on. "But Dallas holds many opportunities, which is what I'm looking for. I'm excited. More excited as my time to leave gets closer."

"What made you decide on Dallas? Do you have family there?"

Beau was surprised Colt chimed in with his questions. But considering Beau was curious about more of her life, he turned his focus to her as well, eager to hear her answers.

Her eyes darted across the table to him, that forced smile frozen in place. "I have no family. That's one of the reasons being a nanny was so great for me. But circumstances have changed my plans and I'm looking for a fresh start."

Colt leaned back in his seat and smiled. "Well, good for you. I wondered if my brother would convince you to stick with him."

Beau clenched his teeth. Was Colt seriously going to get into this now? Did every conversation have to turn into an argument or a jab?

"There's no convincing," Scarlett said with a slight laugh. "I've already committed to the new job. Housing has turned into a bit of a chore, though. I didn't realize how expensive city living was."

"Small towns do have perks." Annabelle came to her feet and went to one of the three high chairs they'd set up. She lifted one of her twins—he still couldn't tell the difference—and wiped the child's hands. "Miss Emily is messy and I need to clean her up and get her changed. I'll be right back."

Scarlett took a drink of her tea and then scooted her chair

back. "I can start taking these dishes to the kitchen. Dinner was amazing."

"Sit down." Colt motioned to her. "Annabelle wanted to make a good impression so she made everything herself, but our cook will clean up."

Scarlett didn't sit, but she went to Madelyn who played in her high chair, patting the top of the tray, then swiping her hands in the water puddles she'd made by shaking her bottle.

"Let me get her," Beau said as he rose and circled the antique farm-style table to extract her from the high chair. "I haven't seen her much today and when we get back she'll need to go to bed."

Which would leave them alone again. Night after night he struggled. Last night had barely taken the edge off. No, that was a lie. Last night only made him want her even more. She'd come to him tonight, that much he was sure of.

"Never thought I'd see you back at the ranch," Colt stated. "Let alone with a child."

Beau patted Madelyn's back as she sucked on her little fist. "I knew I'd come back sometime, but I never had intentions of having children."

When Lucy started fussing, Colt immediately jumped to get her.

"You plan on settling down anytime soon?" he asked as he picked up his daughter. "Maybe have more kids?"

Beau wasn't sure what his next move was, let alone if there was a woman somewhere in his future. "I have no idea," he answered honestly. "Believe it or not, I did love growing up here and having a large family. I'm not opposed to having more kids one day. Being a parent changes you somehow."

Scarlett cleared her throat and turned away. "Excuse me."

She fled the room and Beau glanced over his shoulder to see her heading toward the front of the house. What was wrong with her? Was it something he'd said? Was she that uncomfortable being at this family dinner?

She didn't owe him any explanations, but that wouldn't stop him from finding out what he could do to make her stay here a little easier. The pain that she kept bottled up gnawed at his gut in a way he couldn't explain, because he'd never experienced such emotions before.

"She okay?" Colt asked.

Beau stared at the empty doorway another minute before turning to his twin and lying to his face. "She's fine. We can head on out if you'd rather. I know Annabelle probably forced your hand into this dinner."

Lucy plucked at one of the buttons on Colt's shirt. "She didn't, actually. I wanted you here and she offered to cook."

Shocked, Beau shifted Madelyn in his arms and swayed slowly back and forth as she rubbed her eyes. "So she jumped at the chance when she saw an opening?"

Colt shrugged. "Something like that. Listen, I don't want—"

"Sorry about that." Scarlett whisked back into the room and Beau didn't miss the way her eyes were red-rimmed. "Let me take Madelyn back home and put her to bed. You two can talk and maybe Colt can bring you back to the cabin later."

"I'll come with you," he offered.

She eased a very tired baby from his arms and shook her head. "I'll be fine," Scarlett said, then turned to Colt. "Please tell Annabelle everything was wonderful."

"I will, though I'm sure she'll have you over again before you leave town," Colt assured her. "I'll make sure Beau has a ride back."

Scarlett nodded and then turned to go, catching Beau's eyes before she did so. Her sad smile and that mist in her eyes undid him. She took Madelyn and left, leaving Beau torn over whether he should stay or go.

"You're really just going to let her go?" Colt asked. "She's clearly upset."

Shoving his hands in his pockets, Beau weighed his options.

"She wants to be alone. I can talk to her once I'm back and Madelyn is asleep. Besides, you and I need to talk, don't we?"

Staring at his brother had Colt really taking in the moment. He loved Beau—that was never in question. He loved him in a completely different way than Hayes or Nolan. Not more, just different. Perhaps because of the special bond from twins; he wasn't sure.

Colt knew no matter how much anger and resentment tried to push them apart, their connection could never be completely severed.

"I'm surprised you don't have plans set in place to leave the ranch," Colt stated after a moment.

Or if Beau did, Colt didn't know. And he wanted to…no, he needed to know. He had to steel his heart if his brother was just going to hightail it out of town again and not be heard from for years.

"I came back for Madelyn," Beau replied.

"You came back for you," Colt tossed back, unable to stop himself. "You may have had a change of heart from whatever you were doing in LA, but you needed to be here because something or someone has made you face us again. You didn't come back because you actually wanted to."

Beau stared at him for a minute. Silence settled heavy between them and Colt waited for his brother to deny the accusation. He didn't.

"I've wanted you home for so long." Colt softened his tone. He didn't want to be a complete prick, but he also had to be honest. "When you left, I was upset, but I understood needing to do your own thing. But then you didn't come back and… I resented you. I felt betrayed."

Beau muttered a curse and glanced down to his still-shiny boots before looking back to Colt. "I wanted to see just how far I could get," he admitted. "I knew I was good at acting. So once I did that commercial, then my agent landed that first movie, things exploded. I admit I got wrapped up in my new lifestyle. But I never forgot where I came from. Not once. It just wasn't me anymore."

Colt gritted his teeth and forced the lump of emotions down. "And now? Is this ranch life still not you?"

Beau's lips thinned as he hooked his thumbs through his belt loops. "I want a simpler life for my daughter. I don't want her growing up around pretentious people and worrying if she fits in and all the hustle and bustle. Becoming a parent changed everything I thought about life."

On that, Colt could agree one hundred percent. "Being a father does change you."

But Beau still hadn't answered the question completely.

Before Colt could dig in deeper, Annabelle came back into the room without Emily. "Well, Little Miss was happy lying in her crib in her diaper, so I left her there chatting with her stuffed elephant."

His wife stopped her chatter as she came to stand next to Colt. "What's going on?" she asked as she slid Emily from Colt's arms.

"Just talking with my brother," Colt stated.

"I'm glad to hear it." She rocked Emily back and forth and patted her back. "Where is Scarlett?"

"She took Madelyn back to the cabin for bed," Beau told her. "She wanted me to tell you thanks for everything."

Annabelle shot a glance to her husband. "And did she leave because you guys were bickering or to give you space to actually talk?"

"She really was putting Madelyn to bed," Beau added. "I'm sure she wanted to give us space, too."

"And how has the talking gone?" Annabelle asked, her gaze darting between them. "I lost my sister in a car accident not long ago. We had our differences, we said things we thought we meant at the time, but I'd give anything to have her back. I just don't want you guys to have regrets."

Colt's heart clenched as Annabelle's eyes misted. When he stepped toward her, she eased back and shook her head. Such a strong woman, his Annabelle. He admired her strength and her determination to repair this relationship between brothers.

"You're getting another chance, so work on it," she added. "It's Christmas, guys. Just start a new chapter. Isn't that what your parents would've wanted?"

Beau stepped forward and wrapped an arm around her shoulders. "They would've," Beau agreed before releasing her.

Annabelle sniffed and swiped a hand beneath her eye.

"Babe, don't cry." Colt placed his hand on her shoulder and looked to his twin. "We're making progress. It's slow, but it's coming. Right, Beau?"

He nodded. "We're better than we were, but we're working on years of animosity, so it might take a bit."

Something settled deep within Colt—something akin to hope. For the first time in, well, years, Colt had a hope for the future with his brother.

Did Beau ultimately want that? Colt truly believed fatherhood had changed him, but they'd have to see because words were easy…it was the actions that were difficult to execute.

"I'll let you guys finish your chat," Annabelle said with a soft smile and left the room.

Colt nodded toward the hallway and Beau followed him to the living room. They truly had taken a giant leap in their relationship.

Once they were in the spacious room with a high-beamed ceiling and a stone fireplace that stretched up to those vaulted beams, Beau took a seat on the dark leather sofa.

They had a full, tall Christmas tree in this room, as well. He couldn't help but laugh. As beautiful as the perfectly decorated tree was, he suddenly found himself longing for the tiny cabin with the crooked, naked tree.

If he were honest with himself, he longed more for the woman in the cabin who was determined to give his daughter a nice first Christmas.

How could he not feel a pull toward Scarlett? Sexual, yes, but there was more. He couldn't put his finger on it…or maybe he didn't want to. Either way, Scarlett was more than Madelyn's nanny.

"Are you planning on leaving Hollywood?" Colt asked as he stood next to the fireplace.

Beau eyed the four stockings and shrugged. "No idea, honestly. I know I don't want that lifestyle for Madelyn. There's too much in my world there that could harm her. I couldn't even take her to a park without the paparazzi attacking us. I just want a normal life for her."

"You gave up the normal life when you chose to pursue acting," Colt sneered. "You had a life here, on the ranch."

Beau shook his head and rested his elbows on his knees. "I'm not rehashing the past or defending myself again. I'm moving on. I won't stay at Pebblebrook, though. There's clearly no room and I'm still not sure what my place is."

"What the hell does that mean?" Colt demanded. "Your place is as an Elliott. You're still a rancher whether you want to be or not. It's in our roots."

Yes, it was. Being back here had been like a balm on his tattered heart and soul. But even with coming home and diving right back into the life he'd dodged for years, something was still missing. His world still seemed as if there was a void, a huge hole he'd never fully be able to close.

Perhaps it was Hector's death. Losing his best friend, his father figure, his agent, was hell. But Beau wondered if being home and not seeing his actual father riding the perimeters or herding cattle was the main reason he felt so empty.

"I'm just trying to figure things out," Beau admitted. "I have a movie premiere a few days before Christmas. I'll have to attend that, and then I'd like to be here for the holidays. I'll go after that."

"And when will you fit a visit to Dad in there?" Colt propped his hands on his hips.

"I'm hoping to go see him tomorrow."

That shut Colt up. Beau knew his brother hadn't expected that comeback and Beau would be lying if he didn't admit he was scared as hell to see his dad. He didn't know how he would feel if he walked into the room and Grant Elliott had no clue who he was.

Ironic, really. He was an award-winning movie star, but the one person in the world he wanted to recognize him was his own father.

"Do you want me to come with you?"

Colt's question shocked him. Beau never expected his twin to offer. Maybe this was the olive branch that Beau wondered if he'd ever see.

He swallowed the lump of emotions clogging his throat and nodded. "Yeah, sure."

Colt gave a curt nod, as well. They may not be hugging it out and proclaiming their brotherly love, but this was a huge step in what Beau hoped was just the first phase in repairing their relationship. Because this process wouldn't be quick and it wouldn't be easy. But it was a start.

CHAPTER TEN

SCARLETT CONTINUED TO stare at the tree mocking her in the corner. The one in Colt and Annabelle's house had looked just like the perfect ones she'd described to Beau. There had even been ornaments on the tree of twin babies with a gold ribbon across that said "Babies' First Christmas."

Scarlett hadn't been able to handle another moment. As much as she wanted to be the woman for Beau, she also knew she could never fully be the woman he wanted...not if he wanted more children and a family.

And this little cabin may not be her home, but Scarlett was determined to give Beau and Madelyn a nice Christmas. Too bad she felt she was failing miserably.

Madelyn had taken a bottle and gone right to sleep, leaving Scarlett alone with her thoughts...thoughts that drifted toward the man who would walk through that door any minute.

So she'd opted to try to decorate this tree. Once the lights went on and she plugged them in, she decided to stop. Maybe this was the best this poor thing would look. The crooked trunk didn't look so bad on the tree lot, but now that it was in the small cabin the imperfection was quite noticeable.

Maybe if she turned it slightly so the leaning part faced the patio doors?

Scarlett groaned. Perhaps she should bake some cookies instead. That would help liven up her holiday spirit, plus the house would smell better than any potpourri or candle she could've bought.

But it was late, so she decided to postpone that until tomorrow. Now she headed to her room to change her clothes, figuring on making some tea with honey to help her relax. She really should make it quickly and get back to her room before Beau came home.

Beau...

He'd tempted her in ways that she'd never been tempted before. Never had a man had her so torn up and achy and...damn it, confused.

She shouldn't want him. There was no good ending to this entire ordeal. They clearly led different lives and he was so used to getting what he wanted, yet another reason why they couldn't work. If she stayed and tried at a relationship, even if he was ready for that, she couldn't ultimately give him what he wanted.

But there were so many turn-ons—so, so many.

Scarlett pulled on a tank and a pair of cotton shorts as she mentally argued with herself. She could either continue to dodge the pull toward Beau or she could just give in to this promised fling. After all, she was leaving in a few weeks. She could have the fling and then move, start her new life and not look back.

He'd already pleasured her, so she knew what awaited her if she surrendered to him. And she knew it would be even better when they actually made love, when his body was taking her to those heights instead of just his hand.

Just thinking about that orgasm caused her cheeks to flush. Yes, that was an even bigger reason to want to agree to everything he'd been ready to give. If that had been part of his master plan the entire time, well then, he'd won this battle.

Fanning her heated cheeks, Scarlett opened her bedroom door...and froze. Beau stood just on the other side, his raised fist poised to knock.

She gripped the doorknob in one hand and tried to catch her breath. Between the surprise of seeing him here and the intense look in his eyes, Scarlett couldn't find a reason to ignore her needs any longer.

Not that she could ignore them even if she wanted to. Not with this gorgeous, sexy, intense man looking at her like he was.

She did the only thing she could do at that moment. She took a step toward him and closed the gap between them.

She kept her eyes locked onto his as she framed his face with her hands. That dark stubble along his jaw tickled her palms, the simple touch sending waves of arousal and anticipation through her, fanning the flames her fantasies had ignited.

"Scarlett—"

She slid her thumb along his bottom lip, cutting off his words. "Do you still want me?"

She had to take charge. She had to know the power belonged to her or he wouldn't just win the battle between them…he'd win the war.

Beau's tongue darted out and slid across her skin as he gripped her hips and pulled her to him, aligning their bodies. There was no mistake how much he wanted her, no mistake in what was about to happen.

She needed this distraction, needed to forget how much she'd hurt earlier seeing all those babies and the happy family. Maybe she shouldn't use him for her need to escape, but she'd wanted him all along and why shouldn't she take what she wanted?

"Why now?" he asked, studying her face. "What changed?"

Scarlett's heart thumped against her chest as she swallowed and went for total honesty…well, as much as she was willing to share about her pain.

"Sometimes I want to forget," she murmured. "Make me forget, Beau."

The muscle clenched in his jaw and for a moment she wondered if he'd turn her down and leave this room. But then he covered her mouth with his and walked her backward until her back came in contact with the post of the bed.

His denim rubbed her bare thighs, only adding to the build of the anticipation. As much as she loved how he looked in his cowboy wardrobe, she desperately wanted to see him wearing nothing but her.

Beau's hands were instantly all over her, stripping her of her shorts, then her tank. He only broke the kiss long enough to peel away the unwanted material and then he wrapped her back in his strong arms and made love to her mouth.

That was the only way to describe his kisses. He didn't just meet her lips with his; he caressed them, stroked them, laved them, plundered them. And she felt every one of those touches not only on her mouth but in the very core of her femininity.

Needing to touch him the same way, Scarlett reached between them for the hem of his T-shirt. She'd lifted it slightly when his hands covered hers and he eased back.

"In a hurry?" he asked.

She nodded. "I'm the only one ready for this."

"Baby, I've been ready since you walked in my door."

She shivered at his husky tone and glanced down to their joined hands. Her dark skin beneath his rough, tanned hands had her wondering why this looked so…right. Was it just because she hadn't been with someone in so long? Was it because this was *the* Beau Elliott?

She didn't think so, but now wasn't the time to get into why she had these unexplainable stirrings at just the sight of them coming together.

"Someone is thinking too hard. Maybe this will keep your thoughts at bay."

Beau stepped back and pulled off his shirt, tossing it aside. He was playing dirty and he damn well knew it.

As if to drive the point home, he quirked his dark brows as a menacing, sexy smile spread across his face.

"What did you want when you came to my room?" she asked, surprised she even had the wherewithal to speak.

He went to the snap of his pants and shoved them off as he continued to stare at her. He stood before her in only his black boxer briefs and she couldn't keep her eyes from roaming every inch of muscle and sinew on display before her. His body was pure perfection. The sprinkling of dark chest hair and the dark tattoos over his side, pec and shoulder were so sexy. Who knew she was a tattoo girl?

"I wanted to talk," he replied.

"That look in your eye doesn't look like you wanted to talk."

His lips thinned. "Maybe I needed to forget, too."

She crossed her arms and glanced down, suddenly feeling too vulnerable standing before him completely naked as he let a crack open so she could glimpse into his soul.

Beau reached out, unhooking her arms. "Don't hide from me. I've been waiting to see you."

Scarlett swallowed and looked up at him. "You saw me last night."

"Not enough."

His fingertips grazed down the slope of her breasts and around to her sides. She shivered when his hands slid down the dip in her waist, then over the flare of her hips.

"Not nearly enough."

He lifted her by her waist and wrapped his arms around her. Scarlett wrapped her legs around his waist as he carried her to the bed. She slid her mouth along his as she tipped back, then found herself pressed firmly into the thick comforter, Beau's weight on her. She welcomed the heaviness of this man.

The frantic way his hands and mouth roamed over her made her wonder if he was chasing away some demon in his own mind.

Maybe for tonight, they were just using each other. But right now she didn't care. She wanted him. She needed him. Right now.

When Beau sat up, Scarlett instinctively reached for him to pull him back to her.

"I need to get protection," he told her as he grasped his jeans.

Scarlett hadn't even thought of that. Of course pregnancy wasn't an issue for her, but she didn't know his history and he didn't know hers. Safety had to override hormones right now. She was just glad one of them was thinking straight.

She watched as he removed his boxer briefs and sheathed himself, relishing the sight of his arousal. Nothing could make her turn away or deny this need that burned through her. Well... if Madelyn started crying, but other than that, nothing.

Beau eased his knee down onto the bed next to her thigh. Scarlett rose up to her elbows, her heart beating so fast as desire curled all through her.

He trailed his fingertips up her thigh, teasing her as he went right past the spot she ached most, and on up her abdomen.

"You're one sexy woman," he growled. "It was all I could do to hold back last night."

Which only made him even more remarkable. He wasn't demanding and selfish. Even now, he was taking his time and touching, kissing, enjoying...all while driving her out of her mind.

Those fingertips circled her nipples and Scarlett nearly came off the bed.

"Beau."

"Right here," he murmured as he leaned down and captured her lips.

She opened to him and shifted her legs restlessly. Beau settled between her thighs and she lifted her knees to accommodate him. He hooked one hand behind her thigh and lifted her leg at the same time he joined their bodies.

Scarlett cried out against his mouth as she tilted her hips to meet his. He seemed to move so slow in comparison to the frantic need she felt. The man was maddeningly arousing.

She clutched at his shoulders and arched against him, pulling her mouth from his as she tipped her head back. Beau's lips traveled a path down her neck to her breast and Scarlett wrapped her legs around his waist, locking her ankles behind his back.

Beau never once removed his lips from her skin. He moved all over her, around her, in her, and in minutes that familiar coiling sensation built up within her and Scarlett bit her lip to keep from crying out again.

But Beau gripped her backside, his large powerful hand pulling her to him as he quickened the pace and Scarlett couldn't stop the release from taking over, nor could she stop the cry.

Beau's body tightened against hers as he surged inside her, taking his own pleasure. After a moment, that grip loosened and he eased down onto the bed, shifting his weight so he wasn't completely on top of her.

When the pulsing stopped and her heartbeat slowed, and she was able to think once again, Scarlett realized she was in new territory. She wasn't sure what she was supposed to say or do here. Anyone she'd ever slept with had been someone she was committed to. What did she do now, naked, sated and plastered against a man who was nothing more—could be nothing more—than a fling?

"Someone is thinking too hard again," he said, trailing his finger over her stomach and up the valley between her breasts. "Maybe I didn't do my job well enough."

Scarlett laughed. "You more than did your job. I'm just confused what to do now."

Beau sat up and rested his head in his hand as he stared down at her. The entire moment seemed so intimate, more than the act of sex itself.

"This doesn't have to be anything more than what it was," he told her. "You needed to escape something and so did I. Besides, this was bound to happen."

His words seemed so straightforward and matter-of-fact. They were all true, but she wished he'd…

What? What did she wish? That they'd start a relationship

and see where things went? She knew full well where they'd go. She'd be in Dallas and he'd be back in LA. There was nothing for them other than a brief physical connection.

Scarlett shifted from the bed and came to her feet. Being completely naked now made her feel too vulnerable, too exposed emotionally.

She started putting her sleep clothes back on, trying to ignore the confident cowboy stretched out on her bed.

"Care to tell me what had you running from Colt's house?"

Scarlett pushed her hair away from her face and turned to face him. "I told you. Madelyn was tired and I was letting you guys talk."

He lifted one dark brow and stared, silently calling her out on her lie.

"Could you cover up?" she asked. "I can't concentrate with you on display like that."

Beau laughed and slowly came to his feet…which maybe was worse because now he was closing in on her with that naughty grin. "I like the idea of you not concentrating."

Scarlett put her hands up and shook her head. "Don't touch me. We're done for the night."

He nodded. "Fine, but I still want to know what had you scared or upset."

From his soft tone, she knew he truly meant every word. He didn't care that they weren't diving back in for round two and he genuinely wanted to know what had bothered her.

Scarlett didn't want to get into her emotional issues. Dredging them all up wouldn't change anything, and the last thing she wanted was pity from Beau. Besides, he'd said he was dealing with his own issues.

"I think it's best if we don't get too personal," she told him and nearly laughed. This was Beau Elliott and women all around the world would give anything to trade places with Scarlett right now.

"We're already personal," he countered, reaching for her.

When she tried to back away, he cupped her elbow. "You're taking care of my daughter, living with me and we just had sex. Not to mention my sisters-in-law have all taken to you. We're temporarily bonded, so stop trying to push me away. I can listen and be a friend right now."

Scarlett raked her eyes over him. "With no clothes on?"

He cursed beneath his breath as he spun around and grabbed those black boxer briefs. As if putting on that hip-hugging underwear helped.

The second he turned his focus back to her, she crossed her arms and decided to give the interrogation right back at him.

"Do you want to tell me what's got you so torn up here?" she asked. "Other than your brothers?"

He stared at her for a moment before he shrugged. "I'm not sure what future I have to offer my daughter because I have no clue what I want to do. I'm mending relationships with my brothers, hopefully my father, and figuring out if I even want to go back to LA."

Scarlett couldn't believe he'd said anything, let alone all of that.

"My life is a mess," he went on. "My former agent was more like a father figure and best friend. He recently passed away."

Scarlett put her hand over her heart. "Oh, Beau, I'm sorry."

"Thank you. It's been difficult without him, but each day is a little easier than the last. But the next step is so unclear." He pursed his lips for a moment before continuing. "I have a feeling someone with her new life laid out before her isn't so worried about the future."

"Not when I'm constantly haunted by my past," she murmured.

She rubbed her arms, hating how he was somehow managing to break down her walls. He'd easily opened and didn't seem to care that she saw his vulnerability. Could she do the same?

"I could guess and I bet I'd be right."

She shook her head. "You don't know me."

Beau stepped into her and reached up, smoothing her hair from her face. "You love Christmas and more decorations than anyone needs. You chose the most hideous tree I've ever seen, yet you're determined to make this a good holiday. You're passionate in bed and let yourself lose all control, which is the sexiest thing I've ever seen, by the way."

She stared at him, listening as he dissected her from the nuggets of information he'd gathered over the past few days. Beau was much more perceptive than she gave him credit for. No selfish man would've taken every moment into consideration and parsed each portion of their time together to understand her better.

"I also know that my daughter and I are lucky you're here," he went on, inching even closer until she had to tip her head to look up at him. "And I know too much discussion on babies or families makes you shut down and get all misty-eyed, yet you're a nanny."

Scarlett tightened her lips together and tried to ignore that burn in her throat and eyes.

Beau slid his finger beneath her chin and tipped her head up. "Shall I keep going?" he asked. "Or maybe you could just tell me what you're running from."

Scarlett pulled in a shaky breath and closed her eyes. "I can't have children."

CHAPTER ELEVEN

BEAU'S SUSPICIONS WERE RIGHT. He wished like hell he'd been wrong because he could see the pain in her eyes, hear it in her voice.

Just as he started to reach for her again, she opened her eyes and held up one hand. "No. I don't need to be consoled and please, don't look at me like that."

He didn't know what she saw in his eyes, but how could he not comfort her? He may have the reputation of a playboy, and perhaps he didn't do anything to rectify that with the media, but he did care.

Even though he'd only known Scarlett a short time, it was impossible to ignore the way he felt. Attraction was one thing, but there was more to this complex relationship.

Unfortunately, he had to ignore the pull and remain closed off from tapping into those unwanted, untimely feelings. He had a future to figure out and he'd already screwed up with one woman.

"I love being a nanny," she went on, her voice still laced with sadness and remorse. "But my life changed about a year ago, and I just can't do this job anymore."

"That's why you're leaving."

Beau crossed to the bed and sat down. Maybe she'd feel more

apt to talk if he wasn't looming over her in only his underwear. He never wanted her to feel intimidated or insecure. He doubted she really had anyone she could talk to and the fact that she chose him—after he'd somewhat forced her hand—proved she was more vulnerable than he'd first thought.

But he actually wanted to listen and he wanted to know how he could help...even if that only came in the form of making her forget.

"I can't be in Stone River." Scarlett's words cut through his thoughts. "There are too many memories here of my life, my hopes and dreams. Starting over somewhere fresh will be the best healer for me."

He understood all too well about needing to start over. The need to find a place that would be comforting and not pull you down further. Her reasons for leaving Stone River were the exact reasons he'd left LA. They both needed something new, something that promised hope for an unknown future.

"I'm sure that wasn't an easy decision to make," he stated.

She turned to face him and shrugged one slender shoulder. "There wasn't much else I could do. After my surgery, I took a position out of the field, in the office. I love the people I work with. I just couldn't be a nanny anymore. I thought working in the office would be easier, but it wasn't. I was still dealing with families and listening to the stories of my coworkers. Then Maggie asked me to fill in for these few weeks before I leave and I couldn't tell her no."

"I'm glad you didn't."

Scarlett stared at him for a minute. The lamp on her bedside table set a soft glow on her mocha skin. Skin he ached to touch again. Scarlett was one of the sexiest, most passionate women he'd ever known, and after hearing a bit of her story, he knew she was also one of the strongest.

"Me, too," she whispered.

He did reach for her now and when her hand closed in his,

he pulled her toward him. Scarlett came to stand between his legs and she rested her hands on his shoulders.

"What surgery did you have to have?" he asked.

When she pulled in a shaky breath, he placed his hands on her waist and offered a comforting squeeze.

"I had a hysterectomy," she explained. "The short version of my story is I had a routine checkup. The test results came back showing I had some abnormal cells and the surgery was necessary. Unfortunately, that took away any chance I had at my own family, but in the end, the threat of uterine cancer was gone."

He couldn't imagine wanting something, dreaming of having it your whole life and then not obtaining it. There was nothing Beau didn't covet that he couldn't get through money or power. That's how he'd been raised. Yes, his parents had instilled in him a strong work ethic, but he also knew that at any given time he could reach for anything and make it his.

Yet with all his money, power and fame, he couldn't make his own future stable when he was so confused where he should land. And if he had the ability, he'd sure as hell do something to make Scarlett's life easier.

With a gentle tug, Beau had Scarlett tumbling onto his chest. He gripped her thighs and helped her straddle his lap. As he looked up into her eyes, he realized that if there was any woman who could make him lose his heart, it could be her.

Which was absolutely crazy. Why was he even having such thoughts? He'd screwed things up before when he'd let his heart get involved. Wanting a woman physically and thinking of deeper emotions were two totally different things and he needed to refocus before he found himself even further from where he needed to be.

Between all of this with his family and now his mixed feelings for Scarlett, he needed to remain in control before he completely lost himself.

"Let's keep our painful pasts out of this room, out of this

bed," he suggested as he nipped at her chin. "For as long as you're here, stay with me."

Her eyes widened as she eased slightly away. "You want to continue this fling?"

"'Fling'? That's such a crass word." He let his hands cover her backside and pull her tighter where he needed her most. "We don't need a title for this. Just know I want you, for however long you're here."

Scarlett laced her hands behind his neck and touched her forehead to his. "I swore I wouldn't do this with you," she murmured.

"Yet here we are."

She laughed, just as he'd hoped. "I guess I'm wearing too many clothes."

He stripped her shirt off, sliding his hands and eyes over her bare torso, her breasts. "Let's make each other forget."

Scarlett pushed Madelyn in the child swing that had been hung on the back patio. Even though winter had settled in and they were closing in on Christmas, the sun was shining bright in the cloudless sky and with a light jacket and pants, the day was absolutely beautiful.

Madelyn cooed and grinned as the swing went back and forth. Scarlett couldn't help but return the smile. It was impossible to be unhappy around Madelyn. Even when she'd fussed about her sore gums, Scarlett cherished the time. Madelyn was such a special little girl and having a father who cared so deeply made her very fortunate.

Beau had made a difficult decision to leave his Hollywood home and find out what life he and his daughter should lead.

Maybe he'd go back to his home in LA, but for now he seemed to be in no hurry. After spending the past several nights in his bed—well, hers—Scarlett wasn't in too big of a hurry to leave, either.

But she had to. She couldn't stay here forever playing house.

There was no happily-ever-after for them, no little family. No, Scarlett wasn't going to get that family…at least not with Beau.

Maybe one day she'd meet a man and he might have kids already or maybe they'd adopt. She still couldn't let go of that dream. A new dream had replaced the old one and Scarlett had a blossom of hope.

Strong arms wrapped around her from behind, pulling her out of her thoughts, and Scarlett squealed.

"It's just me," Beau growled in her ear. "Unless you were expecting someone else."

Scarlett eyed him over her shoulder. "My other lover was supposed to come by because I thought you were out."

He smacked her butt. "There are no other lovers as long as I'm in your bed," he said with a smile.

Which would only be for another two weeks.

Scarlett didn't want to think of the end coming so soon. Only a few days ago she was counting down until she could hightail it out of town, but now…

Well, falling into bed with Beau had changed everything.

"I thought you were with Colt and Hayes looking over résumés for guides for the dude ranch."

The new business venture of the Elliott brothers was due to start in early spring. Scarlett had heard Beau discussing how much still needed to be done, she was only sorry she wouldn't be around to see how magnificent all of this would be. Pebblebrook was a gorgeous, picturesque spread and no doubt they would draw in thousands of people a year.

Scarlett wondered if Beau and Colt had told their dad about the ranch, about the way they were closing in on making his dream a full reality, when they'd gone to see him yesterday morning. But Beau had been closed off when he'd returned. Scarlett hadn't wanted to press him on a topic that was obviously so sensitive. She couldn't imagine that bond father and son had shared growing up and how much this must be hurting Beau.

Growing up, she did everything to avoid her stepfather and

mom. They'd been so caught up in their own worlds anyway, so she went unnoticed.

"We finished early," Beau told her. "I told my brothers I needed to get back home to see Madelyn."

Scarlett gave the swing another gentle push and turned to face Beau. Those dark eyes, framed by thick lashes, all beneath a black brim only made him seem all the more mysterious. Over the last week she'd found out that there were several sides to him, and she had to admit she liked this Beau.

The man before her wasn't the actor she'd seen on-screen or the playboy the media portrayed. This Beau Elliott was a small-town rancher.

Albeit a billionaire.

She glanced over at Madelyn. "She woke from a nap about twenty minutes ago, so you're just in time."

Beau slid his hands up her arms, over the slope of her shoulders, and framed her face. "I may have wanted to see you, too."

Scarlett couldn't help the flutter in her chest. The more time she spent with him and his daughter, the more she realized how difficult leaving would be. But she'd be fine. She had to be.

"I also left because I have a surprise planned for you."

"A surprise?" she repeated, shocked he'd think to do anything for her. "What is it?"

Beau slid his lips softly over hers, then stroked her cheeks with the pad of his thumbs. "If I tell you then it won't be a surprise."

"Oh, come on," she begged. "You can't tease me like that."

He thrust his pelvis toward hers and smiled. "You weren't complaining about being teased last night, or the night before, or the night before that."

Scarlett slapped him on the chest. "Fine. But you'll pay for that."

Beau grazed his mouth along her jaw and up to the sensitive area just behind her ear. "I'm counting on it."

Madelyn let out a fuss, which quickly turned into a cry. Before Scarlett could get the baby from the swing, Beau had moved around her and was unbuckling her.

Scarlett stepped away and watched as he cooed and offered sweet words and patted her back. Something stirred inside her. An unfamiliar feeling. An undeniable feeling.

She was falling for Beau.

How ridiculous that sounded even inside her own mind. But there was no denying the fact. Beau Elliott had worked his way past her defenses and into her personal space, quite possibly her heart. There was no future here and she was a fool for allowing this to happen.

Of course she didn't *allow* anything. There had been no stopping these feelings. From the second Beau showed her just how selfless he was, how caring, Scarlett couldn't help but fall for him.

Beau lifted Madelyn over his head and spun in a circle. With the sun off in the distance and the soft rolling hills of the ranch as the backdrop, Scarlett had to tamp down her emotions. The father/daughter duo was picture perfect and maybe neither of them realized how lucky they were to have each other.

Scarlett let them have their moment as she slipped inside the tiny cabin. As silly as it was, she'd come to think of this little place like home. This was nothing like the massive home she'd grown up in. The place might as well have been a museum with the expensive furniture, priceless art and cold atmosphere.

Maybe that's why this cozy cabin touched her so much. There was life here, fun, a family. All the things she'd craved as a child and all the things she wanted as an adult.

But they weren't hers...and she needed to remember that.

Instead of dwelling on those thoughts, Scarlett moved to the kitchen where she'd baked sugar cookies earlier. They were ready to be iced and taken to Annabelle, Alexa and Pepper.

Scarlett didn't proclaim to be the best baker, but she did love her sugar cookie recipe. In fact, she'd made extra just for Beau. Maybe part of her wanted to impress him still, which was silly, but she hadn't been able to help herself. She cared for him, so much. Much more than she should be allowed.

The man came through the doorway just as her thoughts turned to him once again. Of course, he was never far from her thoughts, just as he was never far from her in this tiny space.

"I thought I smelled cookies when I came in earlier." He held Madelyn with one strong arm as he came to stand on the other side of the island. "But it looks as if you have enough to feed a small army. Are we expecting company?"

Scarlett started separating the icing she'd made into smaller bowls so she could dye it in different colors. "I'm taking a dozen each to your brothers' houses later. I just… I don't know. I thought I should do something and I love to bake. I think Christmas just demands the house smell like warm sugar and comfort."

She applied two drops of yellow food coloring into the icing for the star cookies, then she put green drops into another bowl for the tree cookies. The silence had her unsettled so she glanced up to find Beau staring at her with a look on his face she'd never seen before.

"What?" she asked, screwing the lids back on the small bottles of food coloring.

"You watch my baby all day, you cook, you decorate—"

"Don't call that tree in the corner decorating," she grumbled. "Maybe I baked because I need a chance to redeem myself."

He chuckled and shifted Madelyn around to sit on the bar and lean back against his chest. He kept one firm hand on her belly.

"The mantel is beautiful and way more than I'd ever think of doing, and the front porch looks like a real home with the wreath and whatever you did to that planter by the steps." He slid his hat off and dropped it onto a bar stool. "I don't know how you do it all. Maybe women are just born with that gene that makes them superhuman."

"We are."

His smile widened. "And a modesty gene, too, I see."

"Of course," she said without hesitation.

"Regardless of how you get everything done, I'm grateful."

The sincerity of his statement just pulled back another layer of defense she'd tried to wrap herself in. Unfortunately, every time the man opened his mouth, he stripped away more and more. She was losing this fight with herself and before these next couple of weeks were up, she had serious concerns about her heart.

"How long until the cookies are ready to deliver?" he asked.

"I just need to ice three dozen." She glanced behind her to the trays lining the small counter space. "I can ice the dozen for us after I get back."

"You made cookies for us, too?"

Scarlett laughed. "You think I'm baking and not thinking of myself?"

Madelyn let out a jumble of noises as she patted her father's hand. Was there anything sexier than a hunky rancher caring for his baby? Because she was having a difficult time thinking of anything.

"Well, as soon as you get those iced, you'll get your surprise," he told her. "This will all work out quite well."

"What will?"

"The deliveries, your surprise." He leaned in just a bit as his eyes darted to her mouth. "Coming back here later and pleasuring you."

Her body heated, not that she needed his promise for such a reaction. Simply thinking of him incited her arousal. But all of the emotions swirling around inside her were so much more than sexual. Her heart had gotten involved in this short span of time. She hadn't seen that coming. She'd been so worried about not falling for his seduction, she hadn't thought of falling for the man himself.

Damn it. She was sinking fast and not even trying to stop herself. Why bother? Why not just enjoy the ride as long as this lasted?

She deserved to go after what she wanted, no matter how temporary, and she wanted Beau Elliott. Considering he wanted her just as much, there was no reason to let worry in now.

For the time they had left, she planned on enjoying every single moment of her last job as a nanny.

As for her heart, well, it had been broken before. But she hadn't experienced anything like Beau Elliott. Would she ever be able to recover?

CHAPTER TWELVE

SCARLETT PUT THE final lid on the gold Christmas tin. She stacked the festive containers in a tote and went to get Madelyn from her swing in the living room. Thankfully, she wasn't so fussy with her swollen gums now. The teething ring had helped.

"All ready?"

She turned to see Beau. "I'm ready." Giddiness and anxiousness spiraled through her. "Just what is this surprise?"

That familiar, naughty smile spread across his face. Beau could make her giddy like a teenager with her first crush and arouse her like a woman who knew exactly what she was getting into. She'd never met a man who could elicit such emotions from her.

"You're about to find out," he promised with a wink. "Let me take the cookies out and I'll be right back."

"I can carry them," she argued.

Beau put his hand up. "No. Stay right there with Madelyn. Actually, she'll need a jacket and hat. It's cool this evening and we'll be outside for a bit."

Scarlett narrowed her eyes. "We're not driving to your brothers' houses?"

The estate had a ridiculous amount of acreage—she thought she'd heard the number of five thousand thrown out—so the only way around the place was on tractors, four-wheelers, horses or cars.

With only a smile for her answer, Beau adjusted the wide brim of his black hat before he grabbed the bag stuffed with cookie tins and headed out the front door.

Scarlett glanced to Madelyn and tapped the tip of her nose. "Your daddy is driving me crazy."

By the time Scarlett grabbed the jacket and hat for Madelyn from the peg by the door, Beau swept back inside.

"I'll finish getting her ready," he said, taking his daughter. "Take a jacket and hat for yourself, too. I can't have you shivering or you won't appreciate the surprise."

Scarlett laughed. "You're making me nervous, Beau."

He reached up and stroked one finger down the side of her face. "Trust me."

How could she not? She trusted him with her body…and he was closing in on her heart.

Scarlett smiled, mentally running from the unfamiliar emotions curling through her. "You know I do."

She went to her room to get her things. Whatever Beau had planned, he seemed pretty excited about what he'd come up with.

Warmth spread through her at the thought of him thinking of a way to surprise her. Was this a Christmas present or just because? Or did this surprise involve something he liked, as well? The questions and the unknowns were driving her crazy.

It was difficult not to read more into this situation because they'd agreed to have just these last couple of weeks of intimacy before she left. So why was he going that extra mile? Why was he treating this like…well, like a relationship?

Scarlett groaned as she tugged on her red knit hat. Her thoughts were trying to rob her happy time here. She had one of the sexiest men in the world waiting to give her something he'd planned just for her. And she'd simply enjoy it.

She slid on her matching red jacket, perfect for the holiday season and delivering Christmas cookies. For another added bit of flair, she grabbed her black-and-white snowflake scarf and knotted it around her neck.

When she stepped back into the living room, Beau held Madelyn in one hand and extended his other toward her. He kept that sneaky grin on his face and she just knew he was loving every minute of torturing her.

Giddy with anticipation, Scarlett slid her hand in his. She had to admit, she liked the look of her darker skin against his. Her bright red nails were quite the contrast with his rough fingertips from working on the ranch.

Beau tugged her forward until she fell against his side and he covered her mouth with his. The short yet heated kiss had her blinking up at him and wondering how he kept knocking her off her feet. She never knew what he'd do next, but he continued to have her wanting more.

"Everything's ready," he told her. "Go on outside."

She couldn't wait another second. Scarlett reached around him and opened the door. The moment her eyes focused on the sight before her, she blinked, wondering if this was a dream.

"Beau," she gasped. "What did you do?"

Directly in front of the porch were two chocolate-brown horses in front of a wide wooden sled. A sled decorated with garland and lights. On the seat she saw plaid blankets. There was evergreen garland wrapped around the reins, and the horses stood stoic and stared straight ahead as they waited for their orders.

Scarlett spun back around and threw her arms around Beau, careful of how she sandwiched Madelyn in the middle.

"I can't believe you did this," she squealed. "How on earth did you manage it?"

Beau took her hand in his and led her to the sled. "I have my ways and that's all you need to know."

Scarlett didn't hesitate as she carefully climbed into the sled.

Once she nestled against the cushioned seat, she reached down for Madelyn.

The sled jostled slightly as Beau stepped up into it and folded his long, lean frame next to her. He gripped the reins in hand as Scarlett pulled the cozy blanket up over their laps. She laced her hands around Madelyn and glanced to Beau as he snapped the reins to set the sled in motion.

"Why did you do all of this?" she asked.

"Why not?" he countered, shooting her that toe-curling grin and dark gaze. "You mentioned loving Christmas and sleigh rides. I'm just giving you a bit of extra cheer."

Scarlett wasn't quite sure what to say. Beau had put so much thought into this, even though he tried to brush the sweet gesture aside. This full-on reality was so much better than anything she'd ever seen in the movies.

"I'm glad I made you a dozen cookies, then," she joked as he headed in the direction of Nolan's house. "You may even get extra icing."

"Is that a euphemism?"

Scarlett's body heated, but she laughed because she didn't want to get all hot and bothered when she was in the midst of this festive family moment.

The breath in her throat caught and was instantly replaced with thick emotions. Family. This fantasy moment she was living in had thrust her deeper into her job than she'd ever been.

Feeling like part of the family was often just a perk of being a nanny. But nothing had ever prepared her for falling for the man she worked for, or for his daughter. And how could she not fall for him? He'd been attentive since day one...which really wasn't all that long ago.

Still, Beau actually listened to her. He met her needs in the bedroom and out, and she was an absolute fool if she thought she'd walk away at the end of this without a broken heart.

"So you'll be leaving at the end of next week for your movie premiere," she stated, more reminding herself and making sure this stayed out in the open. "Are you sure you'll be home Christmas Eve?"

"Positive," he assured her. "Nobody else is playing Santa to my girl but me."

"I wondered if you'd bought presents."

He shot her a side glance. "Of course I have. You think I'd let my baby's first Christmas come and go and not have presents?"

"Well, you didn't have a tree or a stocking," she reminded him with an elbow to his side.

Beau guided the horses as Nolan's home came into view. The large log resort-type home looked like something from a magazine. Not surprising, though, since the Elliotts had the lifestyle of billionaire ranchers and Nolan was a surgeon. He and Pepper lived here with their little one and their home was beautifully decorated, with wreaths adorning every window and a larger one with a red bow on the front door.

"Maybe I didn't have a tree or stockings," Beau added. "But I'm not a complete Scrooge."

Scarlett shifted in the seat and glanced down at the baby. "I think we're putting her to sleep," she stated. "Next time her gums are bothering her, just hitch up the sled and take her for a ride."

"Sure." He snorted. "No problem."

Within another minute, Madelyn was fast asleep. There were so many questions Scarlett had for Beau regarding his future, but she wasn't sure if she had a right to ask...or if she even truly wanted to know the answers.

She decided to wait until they left Nolan's house to bring up her thoughts. Nolan and Pepper weren't home, so Beau left the tin on the porch swing and sent his brother a text.

As they took off again, this time toward Hayes and Alexa's house, Scarlett figured this was the perfect time. If he didn't want to answer, then he didn't have to, but she couldn't just keep guessing.

"When you go back for the movie premiere, do you think you'll want to stay?"

"No. I'll definitely be back here for Christmas."

Scarlett pulled the plaid blanket up a little further. "I mean, will being back there make you miss that life?"

He said nothing. Only the clomping of the horses through the lane broke the silence. Scarlett wondered if she'd gone too far, simply because he hadn't talked much about the movie and she got the impression that topic was off the table.

"Forget it," she said after waiting too long for his reply. "None of my concern. It's not like I'll be here or part of your life."

"It's okay." He shifted in his seat, his thigh rubbing against hers. "Honestly, I doubt it. I'm not looking forward to going back."

"Do you hate that world so much?"

Beau's brows dipped as he seemed to be weighing his words. "I hate how people can get so swept up in their own lives they forget there's a world around them. The selfishness runs rampant out there. Everyone is out for themselves, but they're never happy because when they get what they want, they still want more."

He pulled in a deep breath and shook his head. "I can say that because I'm that person."

Scarlett slid her left hand over Beau's denim-clad thigh. "You're not that person at all."

The muscles in his jaw clenched. "I am," he volleyed back. "I left here because I wanted more. I made it in Hollywood, had a career people would kill for and still wanted more. Then I won two big acting awards, and that wasn't enough, either. I met Jennifer and thought we might have had a future together, but that went to hell. I have a gorgeous baby, yet I'm still looking for more."

Scarlett didn't like the defeated tone in his voice. "You're not looking for more," she scolded. "You're looking for the right place to raise your daughter and trying to reconnect with your family. That's not selfish. And it sure as hell wasn't selfish that you surprised me with a horse-drawn sleigh ride."

"Oh, the sleigh ride was just so I'd get laid."

Scarlett squeezed his thigh until he yelped.

"I'm joking," he laughed. "Well, not really. I still want in your bed tonight."

"You didn't have to do this to get there," she reminded him. "I haven't been complaining, have I?"

He pulled back on the reins until the horses and sleigh came to a stop. When Beau shifted in his seat to face her, Scarlett's heart kicked up.

"I've been thinking…" He gripped the reins in one hand and slid his other beneath the blanket to cover hers. "I don't want to cheapen this to just sex or for you to ever think I'll forget you when you leave."

A burst of light filled the cracks in her heart. What exactly was he trying to say?

"I know you're moving and I have no idea where I'll be," he went on. "But I don't want to just hide in the cabin and keep you naked."

Scarlett rolled her eyes and glared. "Really?"

His lips quirked into a half grin. "Okay, that's exactly what I'd like, but I want you to know you're more important to me than Madelyn's nanny or my temporary lover."

Scarlett pulled in a breath and held his dark gaze. "So what are you saying?"

"I want to take you on a date."

"A…a date?"

Not what she thought he'd say, but she wasn't exactly opposed to the idea.

"I didn't think you wanted to be seen in town or anywhere because of privacy."

He squeezed her hand and leaned forward to graze his lips across hers. There was no chill in the December air at all when she had Beau next to her. Just one simple touch, just one promised kiss had her entire body heating up.

When Beau eased back, he stroked the back of her hand with his fingertip. "Some things are worth the risk."

Well, that sealed the deal. There was no coming back from this because her heart tumbled, flipped, flopped, did all the amazing things that had her wanting to squeal and yell that she'd fallen completely in love with Beau Elliott.

Unfortunately, there was no room in this temporary relationship for such emotions. There would be no love, no family Christmas cards and definitely no happy-ever-after.

She only had a week left with Beau and then she'd be out of his life for good.

CHAPTER THIRTEEN

BEAU WASN'T SURE what had made Scarlett shut down after he'd asked her on a date. Honestly, he hadn't planned on that impromptu invitation, but he'd needed her to know that she wasn't just some woman he'd seduced and conquered. He'd never thought of any woman in that manner, and he sure as hell had more respect for Scarlett than that.

She was special. Not because of how she cared for Madelyn and not because she was so easy to talk to. Scarlett presented the entire package of an honest woman, one who genuinely cared.

Part of him wanted to give her the world, but what part of his world could he actually give? He couldn't even figure out his own plan. Though after being at Pebblebrook for a few weeks, he knew he wanted a ranch of his own. The hands-on approach he'd taken each day had turned something inside of him. The fact that he wasn't interested in looking at scripts now was rather telling.

Maybe one day he'd look to the screen again, but for now, Beau truly felt this was his destiny. He'd gone and explored like he'd wanted. He'd made himself one of the biggest names in Hollywood, but like he'd told Scarlett, something had still been missing.

Beau nearly laughed at himself for his *Wizard of Oz* epiphany. Everything he'd ever wanted was right here in his own backyard…literally.

He stood in front of the crazy Christmas tree in the corner of the cabin. Scarlett's soft singing voice filtered in from his bedroom as she got Madelyn to sleep for the night.

They'd delivered cookies and both Annabelle and Alexa were thrilled with the surprise. Beau loved the praise they gave Scarlett, and the fact that they treated her like family had him wanting to explore more with her. He'd never wanted someone like this before. Not just for sex, but to see if they could grow together.

But she was moving to Dallas.

Beau's mind raced in too many directions to try to keep up with, but he figured he didn't have a set place he wanted to be. He was quite literally free to do anything.

Was he even ready for something like this? He'd come back home to mend relationships, not to try to build a new one. Added to that, he hadn't known Scarlett very long. Was he honestly considering this? He'd made such a terrible judgment call with Jennifer, but Scarlett was so different than his ex. Scarlett wasn't out to gain anything for herself or trying to use him for anything other than a job before she left.

As one idea formed into another, Beau found himself smiling while still staring at the undecorated tree—save for the lights.

"She's out."

Scarlett's words had him turning to face her. When he met her gaze across the room, she stopped and set the bottle on the kitchen island.

"What?" she asked, tipping her head. "You're smiling and you've been staring at my tree. You're plotting something, aren't you? Are we burning it and roasting marshmallows?"

Beau shook his head and circled the couch to head toward the kitchen. She never glanced away and he figured he looked like a complete moron because he couldn't wipe the smile off his face.

If she thought the sleigh ride was nice, she'd be utterly speechless when he presented her with the next surprise.

"We aren't burning it," he told her as he drew closer. "But in continuing your festive holiday cheer, I say we break out our cookies and get them iced."

She narrowed her dark eyes. "Why do I have a feeling this will end with my clothes on the kitchen floor?"

Beau shrugged. "Because you're realistic."

Scarlett shook her head as she laughed. "You don't have to talk me into getting naked, you know?"

Beau slid his hands over the dip in her waist. "Maybe not, but I'm in the mood for dessert."

He backed her up until they circled the island. Scarlett gripped his biceps when she stumbled.

"What are you doing?" she asked, smiling up at him.

Beau planted a kiss on the tip of her nose. Her freakin' nose. Now he knew he'd gone and lost his mind. He'd never done such an endearing action before, but he couldn't help himself. For as sexy as Scarlett was, she was also quite adorable.

"We're going to ice those cookies," he told her. "You did promise."

She jerked back, her brows shooting up. "You seriously want to ice cookies? Does this mean I'm melting Scrooge's heart?"

He smacked her on the butt before releasing her. "I'm hardly Scrooge, but I'll admit I've never iced cookies. My mom did all of that. Baking and cookie decorating was serious business at Christmastime in my house and she wanted it to be perfect."

Beau grabbed the icing from the counter next to the stove and set it on the island. Then he reached back around for the tin of cookies.

"I guess Christmas baking was the one time she wasn't about to let a bunch of boys ruin her creations." Beau glanced at the spread before him and laughed as he turned to Scarlett. "So I guess your work is cut out for you."

Scarlett went to pull off all of the lids, revealing the yellow, green and red food coloring. The instant smell of sugar hit him and he couldn't wait to take a bite.

Beau picked up a bare cookie and dipped it in the yellow icing before taking a bite. "You're right. These are good."

"Beau," she exclaimed, smacking his chest. "The icing isn't a dip."

He chewed his bite and went back in for more icing—red this time. "I think I'm onto something here."

"You're impossible." She reached into a drawer and pulled out a plastic spatula. "Let me show you how you should ice cookies."

As he continued to dip, Beau watched her expertly smooth the frosting over the tree cookie. When she was finished, she laid it aside on the wax paper and grabbed another.

"Want to try?" she asked.

"Sure."

He took the cookie and the utensil, then dipped the spatula into the red icing. With a quick move, he streaked a stripe across her shirt.

"Oops." He smiled and shrugged. "That didn't work. You might want to take your shirt off before that stains."

Scarlett propped a hand on her hip and narrowed her eyes. "That's not very original."

He gave another swipe. "Maybe not, but I bet you take that shirt off."

She kept her eyes on his as her fingers went to the top button. One slow release at a time, she revealed her dark skin and festive red bra.

Once she dropped her shirt to the floor, she reached around him and picked up another cookie. She grabbed the spatula from his hand and proceeded to decorate.

"Just because you act childish doesn't mean the lesson is over," she informed him. "Do you see how I'm using nice, even strokes?"

"I can use even strokes, too."

Scarlett rolled her eyes and laughed. "I'm talking about icing."

Beau leaned in and nipped at her ear. "Maybe I was, too."

Scarlett leaned slightly into him. "I can't concentrate when you're doing that."

Good. He slid his hand along the small of her back, around the dip in her waist, and covered her flat abdomen. She shivered beneath his touch, just as he'd expected.

"I can't concentrate when you're not wearing a shirt," he whispered in her ear.

She tipped her head back to meet his gaze. "And whose fault is that?"

"You're the one who took it off."

Beau spun her slightly and gripped her hips. He lifted her onto the counter, away from the mess. "Let's see what else we can do with this icing."

Her eyes darkened as she raised a brow. "You didn't really want to learn how to decorate cookies, did you?"

He flashed her a smile. "Not at all."

But he did make use of all of the icing and by the end of the night, Scarlett wasn't complaining.

Scarlett lifted Madelyn out of the car seat and adjusted the red knit cap. Downtown Stone River may be small, but people bustled about and businesses thrived like in a major city.

The sun was high in the sky, shining down on this picturesque square. The large tower clock in the middle struck twelve. Benches in a circle around the clock were filled with couples eating lunch. Every single lamppost had garland and lights wrapped around it. Oversize pots sat on each corner and overflowed with evergreens and bright red poinsettias.

Scarlett would miss this place.

"Hey. You okay?"

Beau came to stand beside her, his hand resting on her back. She offered him a smile and nodded.

"I'm fine," she told him. "And ready to eat. I used too much energy last night."

"We could've had more cookies for breakfast," he offered with a naughty grin and a wink.

"Considering you ate every cookie and, um…we finished the icing, that wasn't an option."

Mercy, her body still tingled just thinking about what they had done with those colors. The extra-long shower to cleanse their bodies of the sticky mess had only led to even more intimacy. And more intimacy led to Scarlett wishing she didn't have to leave.

"I think we should try that café on the corner," he said, pointing over her shoulder. "It looks like you."

"I've eaten there before," she told him, without looking to see which place he referred to. "And what do you mean it looks like me?"

Beau shrugged and looked back down at her. His wide-brim hat shielded a portion of his face from the sun. She didn't know if he wore the hat because he'd gotten used to it since he'd been back or if he'd brought it to be a little discreet. Either way, he looked like the sexy cowboy she'd come to know and love.

Fine. There it was. The big L word she'd been dancing around and not fully coming to terms with. She knew she was falling, but she could admit now that she was there.

"It's all festive with the gold-and-red Christmas signs out front," he told her, oblivious to her thoughts. "The big wreath on the doorway, the candles in the windows. It just looks like you."

She figured that was a compliment, but she wasn't quite sure.

Madelyn let out a yawn and rubbed her eyes. Scarlett patted her back and eased her head down onto her shoulder.

"We should eat so we can get this one to take a nap on the car ride home," she told him.

Beau's cell went off and he groaned. "I'm not answering that."

"You should," she retorted. "It could be about your dad."

Which he'd still never talked about. She wanted to know his feelings and help him if she could. Maybe when they got back home she'd address the topic.

Beau pulled his cell from his pocket and stared at the screen, then a wide smile spread across his face.

"I take it that's not your agent?" she asked.

He pocketed the cell and leaned in, covering her mouth with his. The kiss ended as quickly as it started, leaving her a bit unbalanced.

"What was that for?" she asked.

"I have a surprise for you."

Her heart warmed. "Another one?"

"I promise, this one is much better than the last."

Scarlett's face lit up. "Tell me."

He kissed her once again, lingering a bit longer this time. "When we get home."

"Then we're getting our food to go."

Beau laughed as he steered her toward the café. "No, we're not. I promised you a date and that's what we're doing."

CHAPTER FOURTEEN

SCARLETT WASN'T SURE whether to be nervous or not with Beau's mysterious surprise. They stepped into the cabin and Madelyn was wide-awake now after a brief nap in the car.

Beau had only been asked about twenty times at the café for his autograph, and with each person who approached him, he took the time to talk and sign. He might be a star, but he was also humble and so far removed from the celebrity she'd originally thought him to be.

Christmas was coming quickly and he'd be leaving in just a few days for his premiere. Their time together had been rocky at first, but then it had become an absolute fantasy. She'd never, ever gotten involved with someone she worked for. Beau had made that personal ethic impossible, though, and she wasn't the least bit sorry.

"Wait right there," he told her.

Scarlett stood in the living area and obeyed. She couldn't imagine what could top the horse-drawn sleigh, but she couldn't wait.

She took Madelyn to the little play mat on the floor. Carefully, Scarlett eased down to her knees and laid Madelyn beneath the arch where random plush animals swung back and forth. At the sight of them, she started kicking her feet and making adorable cooing noises.

Scarlett stood back up and smiled. She was seriously going to miss this sweet little nugget.

"Are you ready?"

She spun around and her smile widened as Beau came back in with his laptop. "I don't know what I'm ready for, but bring it."

He took a seat on a bar stool and patted the other one for her. Once his computer was up, he clicked through several screens before pulling up a page with several images of a beautiful old white farmhouse. There was a stone path leading up to the door, four gables on each side of the house, a pond in the back. The landscaping had to have been professional and there was even a white porch swing with colorful pillows. The entire place looked straight out of a magazine.

"If you like the outside, I can move on and show you the inside," he told her.

Scarlett gasped. "Beau, did you buy this?"

He clicked on the next screen and pulled up the entryway photo. "I knew it was the one the second my real estate agent sent options."

Joy consumed her and she reached for his hand. "Beau, I'm so happy for you. I didn't know you were that close to finding a permanent home."

She glanced back to the screen and looked at the thumbnail photos. "Click on that one," she said, pointing. "I think that will make a perfect room for Madelyn. Does it overlook the pond?"

"Wait." He squeezed her hand until she shifted her focus to him. "I bought this house for you."

Scarlett jerked back. "What? For me?"

He released her hand and clicked on another tab. "See? It's just outside of Dallas and only a twenty-minute commute to your new job."

Shock and denial replaced happiness. She stared at him for a moment before looking back to the image of the route from the new house to her new job. She didn't even know where to start with the questions because there were so many swirling around in her head.

"If you don't like it, I can put this on the market and find another," he went on.

She snapped her attention back to him. "Do you hear yourself? When people give gifts they usually give a scarf or a candle, sometimes jewelry. Who buys gift houses on a whim?"

Those dark brows drew in as if he were confused. "It wasn't necessarily a whim. I mean, I knew you were having trouble finding a place to live and I wanted to help you out. Besides, you've done so much for Madelyn and me, plus it's Christmas. I thought you'd like this."

Scarlett shook her head and slid off the stool. How in the world had this last job run the gamut of every single emotion she'd ever had? Worry, anxiety, stress, giddiness, love, anger... betrayal.

"You can't do this," she snapped as she turned back around. "You can't just send me on my way with a parting gift, as if that will replace what has happened here."

Damn it. She hadn't meant to let that sliver of her feelings out. She didn't want him to know how much she'd valued and cherished every second of their time together. When it was time for her to go, she'd have to make a clean break in an attempt to keep her heart intact...if that was even possible.

"You think that's what I'm doing?" he asked. "I bought this for you to make your transition easier, because you deserve a damn break. Why are you angry?"

Maybe her anger stemmed from confusion and hurt and the loss of a hope that maybe they could've been more. Which was ridiculous considering who he was, how they met and how little they'd known each other.

But still, how could she just ignore all that had transpired up until this moment? They'd shared a bed almost every night, he took her on a sleigh ride, he asked her on a date…they'd crammed a lifetime of memories into a few short weeks.

"I can't accept this gift," she told him. "I can't live in a house that you bought when you were thinking of me. When I leave here, I need to be done with what we had, and living there would only remind me of you. Besides, I couldn't accept something so extravagant. It's just not normal, Beau."

"It's not normal to want to help?" he tossed back. "Who's to say I wouldn't come visit?"

Oh, now that was just being cruel. "For what? To extend the affair? What happens if you meet someone else or I do? What happens when one of us decides to get married? We can't drag this affair on forever."

No, because that would be a relationship and they'd both agreed this fling was temporary. Besides, after she left, she didn't want to know who he was seeing or what was going on in his personal life. No doubt she'd see another piece of arm candy at his side. She certainly wouldn't follow him on social media, but his face would be on every tabloid at the supermarket checkout line. It would be difficult to dodge him completely.

Beau opened his mouth, but a pounding on the cabin door stopped him. Scarlett propped her hands on her hips and stared at him across the room. More pounding on the door had Beau cursing.

He went to the door and jerked it open. "What?" he barked.

Colt stood on the other side holding his cell up for Beau to see a photo. Scarlett couldn't make out exactly what it was, but Beau's shoulders went rigid and he let out a string of curses.

"Want to explain what the hell this is?" Colt demanded. "I believed you when you said she was only your nanny."

Scarlett went nearer to see the image on the phone Colt held out. An image of Beau, Madelyn and Scarlett on the street earlier when he'd leaned in to kiss her. Above it was the headline: "A New Leading Lady for Hollywood's Favorite Cowboy."

Scarlett stilled. Was nothing sacred anymore? It just took one person to snap a picture on their phone and send it to the masses.

Colt's eyes went to her, then back to Beau.

"I am his nanny," Scarlett started. "We just—"

"It's not like that," Beau said, cutting her off. He kept his back to her and his focus on his brother. "She is my nanny and when I leave for the premiere, she'll stay here and care for Madelyn. Scarlett is moving next week and we went out for lunch. I leaned in and kissed her, so what? It's nobody's business."

"Nobody's business?" Colt roared as he pushed his way inside. "You do realize we are trying to honor our father and work on the opening of this dude ranch. Now you're back in town and making headlines like this. What about two weeks from now when it's another woman, or another? We're a close family, with strong core values Dad taught us. Those are the values we want to promote in this new business."

"Calm down," Beau demanded. "Scarlett and I kissed. Don't read anything more into that. It was an innocent kiss. I didn't think anything of it. The only person who will make a big deal about this is you."

Innocent kiss? He didn't think anything of it?

The air whooshed from her lungs and her throat clogged with emotions. She turned from the dueling brothers and went to Madelyn. Blinking against the tears gathering in her eyes, Scarlett bent down and lifted Madelyn in her arms. Then she headed toward her room.

"I'll let you two talk," she said without glancing their way.

She couldn't let Beau see her hurt. She couldn't let him see just how his words had cut her down. What happened to the man she'd come to know? To pretend their kisses meant nothing was flat out a bastard move.

So she'd hide out in her room and gather her strength. Because there was going to be a showdown and there was no way in hell she'd confront him with tears in her eyes.

CHAPTER FIFTEEN

"YOU BETTER GET your head on straight," Colt commanded through gritted teeth. "Scarlett isn't one of your random women."

Beau glanced to the closed bedroom door and wanted to punch something. He fisted his hands at his sides to prevent decking his own twin.

"I never said she was." Beau faced Colt and pulled in a deep breath. "I said this was nobody's business. And the dude ranch won't suffer because I kissed someone in public. Don't be so dramatic."

Colt adjusted his hat and pocketed his phone. "That's not what I'm saying. You claimed you've changed, but all of the media wrapped their claws around you and what woman you'd be with on any given day. I don't want that carried over here."

"It's not."

Damn it. He didn't want to have this conversation with Colt. He wanted to be in that bedroom because he knew he'd hurt Scarlett with his careless attitude. In his defense, he hadn't wanted to let Colt in on the relationship. He'd been trying to save her reputation. Instead, he'd left her thinking what they had wasn't special.

Only a jerk would purposely hurt a woman.

"If you're done berating me like a disappointed parent, you are free to go."

Colt clenched his jaw and nodded. "If you want to prove you've changed, then start by doing right with Scarlett."

His brother turned and left the cabin, closing the door with a hard click that echoed through the tiny space. Beau muttered a string of curses and raked his hand over the back of his neck. He should've seen this coming. One of the reasons he'd been staying in the cabin was because he'd wanted to dodge the press and any outsiders while he tried to find some semblance of normalcy.

Of course then Scarlett landed on his doorstep and everything snowballed from there. Somehow he needed to fix this—all of it. Her anger toward the home he'd purchased for her, hurting her and having Colt witness everything.

This morning he'd been full of hope and the possibility of exploring a future with her. Now...hell, he didn't have a clue what lay on the other side of that door.

Beau made his way across the cabin and tapped his knuckles on Scarlett's bedroom door. Without waiting for an answer, he tried the knob, surprised she hadn't locked him out.

Easing the door open, he peeked his head through. Scarlett sat cross-legged on her bed reading a book to Madelyn, who lay in front of her on the plaid quilt.

"What you heard out there—"

"Was the truth," Scarlett said as she closed the book and laid it on the bedside table. "You didn't say anything but the truth. There's nothing more to us than a few weeks of passion and a good time. We've made memories, but that's where it ends."

Beau slipped into her room, but remained by the open door. Her words shocked him. Her steely demeanor seemed so out of character, and he wasn't sure what to say.

Scarlett swung her legs off the side of her bed and came to her feet. She made sure to keep distance between them.

"Since we are so close to the end of our time together," she said, "it's probably best to end the intimate side of things. I'm sure you understand why. And I'm sure you can see why I cannot accept the house. I appreciate the gesture, but you should have your agent put it back on the market."

Well, wasn't her speech all neat and tidy and delivered with an iciness he never expected from someone so warm and caring.

Beau had never experienced this before. Rejection. But it wasn't the rejection that stung. No, what really sliced him deep was the fact that he had caused Scarlett so much suffering that she'd resorted to this as her defensive mechanism.

"Maybe I'm not ready to end things," he stated, folding his arms over his chest.

She stared at him across the room and finally took a step toward him. "There's no reason to prolong this, Beau. I will continue to care for Madelyn and watch her while you're gone to your premiere. But Maggie will be back next week and I'll be gone. This had to come to an end sometime."

Beau couldn't penetrate this wall she'd put up so quickly around herself. She'd need time and he needed to respect her enough to give it to her. Unfortunately, time wasn't on their side. He could give her today, but that's all he could afford.

"Scarlett, I never want you to believe that kiss, and everything before that, meant nothing." He needed her to know this above all else. "Anything I said to Colt was to protect you. Maybe I didn't go about it the right way, but don't think that I don't care for you."

Scarlett crossed her arms over her chest and nodded. "I'm going to feed Madelyn and take her for a walk to the stables. Then I'll come back and fix dinner."

She didn't extend the invite to the stables. Beau would stay behind, to give her time to think. Because there was no way she could just turn off this switch. If she felt half of what he felt for her, she couldn't ignore such strong emotions.

"I'll make dinner," he volunteered.

"Fine." She reached down and lifted Madelyn in her arms. "If you'll take her for a minute, I need to change my clothes."

"Scarlett—"

"Please."

Her plea came out on a cracked voice and he finally saw a sheen of tears in her eyes. She was struggling to hold everything together.

Beau reached for his baby and held her tight against his chest. Scarlett continued to stare at him, blinking against her unshed tears.

Without another word, he turned and left her alone in her room. After he shut the door firmly behind him, Beau went to his own room to contact his agent.

Not his real estate agent about the house. No, Beau had every intention on keeping that.

He laid Madelyn down in her crib and handed her a plush toy to chew on. With a deep sigh and heavy dose of guilt, he pulled his cell from his pocket and dialed his agent.

"Beau," he answered. "You're one hell of a hard man to get ahold of."

There wasn't much to say and this conversation was long, long overdue. But it was time for some changes and they were going to start right now.

Beau gripped the phone as he watched his daughter play.

"We need to talk."

Scarlett didn't know what was more difficult, having Beau in the cabin or knowing he was miles away and gearing up for a fancy movie premiere tomorrow.

The past few days had been strained, to say the least. They'd been cordial to each other, like strangers who were stranded together and forced to cohabitate.

Scarlett had just put Madelyn down for her morning nap and was heading to the sink to wash bottles when a knock sounded on the front door.

She wore only leggings and an oversize sweatshirt, and her hair was in a ponytail—compliments of insomnia, anxiety, and a broken heart. But she ignored her state of dress and went to see who the unexpected visitor was.

After glancing through the peephole, Scarlett pulled in a long, slow breath and blew it out before flicking the dead bolt and opening the door.

"Annabelle," she greeted. "What brings you by?"

His beautiful sister-in-law offered a sweet smile and held up a basket. "I brought fresh cranberry apple muffins. Can I come in?"

"I would've let you in without the bribe, but I won't turn it down." Scarlett laughed as she stepped aside to let Colt's wife in.

Annabelle set the basket down on the island. "The muffins were just an excuse," she said as she turned back to face Scarlett. "Can we talk for a minute?"

Scarlett didn't know why Annabelle wanted to talk, but she wasn't stupid. Likely this had to do with Colt and Beau, but if the woman thought Scarlett had any hold over Beau or could sway him to work on the relationship with his brother, well, that couldn't be further from the truth.

"Sure," Scarlett replied. "Have a seat."

She hadn't seen or talked to any of Beau's family since Beau had left a couple of days ago. Scarlett didn't think Beau counted their kisses as nothing, but hearing the words had hurt just the same. And hearing those words only gave her the smack of reality that she'd needed in order to see that this wasn't normal. What normal, everyday woman fell in love with a movie star and had him reciprocate those feelings? The idea was simply absurd.

Annabelle took a seat on the leather sofa and Scarlett sat on the other end. "What's up?" Scarlett asked.

"I'm going to cut out the small talk because it's pointless." Annabelle crossed her legs and leveled her gaze at Scarlett. "I know you have feelings for Beau. Don't deny it. I saw the two of you together. And I can also tell you that he has feelings, too."

Scarlett wanted to deny both statements, but she simply didn't have the energy. Maybe if she let Annabelle talk, she'd get this off her chest and then leave. Scarlett preferred to sulk in private.

"I also know my stubborn husband came down pretty hard on Beau and you, by default," Annabelle went on. "This ranch is absolutely everything to him and he sometimes speaks before he thinks."

Scarlett smiled. "You didn't have to come down here to apologize for him."

"I'm not," Annabelle corrected. "He needs to apologize on his own. I'm here to tell you that you need to ignore what Colt says, what the media speculate and what you're afraid of."

She let out a soft sigh as she scooted over a bit farther. "What I'm trying to say is, your time here is almost up and I'd hate for you to go when you have so much unresolved."

Scarlett glanced down to her clasped hands and swallowed. "How do you know what's unresolved?"

Annabelle reached over and offered a gentle squeeze of her hand. "Because Colt and Hayes commented on Beau's broodiness before he left for LA and he was so happy before that. You make him happy. When he came back here he was broken and scared. He'd never admit that, so don't tell him I said it. But he was so worried for Madelyn and how his relationships with his brothers would pan out…or even if they would."

Scarlett glanced back up. "Beau and I aren't anything. I mean, I won't lie and say things didn't progress beyond a working relationship, but that's over."

"Is it?"

Nodding, Scarlett chewed the inside of her cheek before continuing. "He hasn't fully let me in. I know about the reasons he left here when he was eighteen. I know the issues with his brothers and his dad. But when he and Colt went to see their dad the other day, Beau shut down and wouldn't let me help. I don't even know what happened."

Annabelle leaned back on the couch and released Scarlett's

hands. "Grant didn't remember his sons," she stated. "Colt said Beau took it pretty hard and wouldn't even talk to him on the ride home."

Oh, Beau.

"He has let you in," Annabelle went on. "And I'm here to tell you that if you want to give it a try with him, I'm going to help. Alexa and Pepper are ready to join in, too."

Stunned, Scarlett eased back and laughed. "Excuse me?"

Annabelle's smile spread wide across her face. "We all three figured if you want to make a statement, it's going to have to be bold."

"The three of you discussed this?" Scarlett asked, still shocked. "What do you all think I should be doing?"

That smile turned positively mischievous and the gleam in her eye was a bit disconcerting. Annabelle reached for her hand once again.

"What do you say about going to your first movie premiere?"

CHAPTER SIXTEEN

THIS ENTIRE THING WAS ABSURD. The fact that she'd let Annabelle, Alexa and Pepper not only talk her into using the Elliotts' private jet to fly to LA, but they'd given her a makeover on top of that. Somehow, in a whirlwind of deciding she couldn't let Beau go without a fight and getting her hair curled and lips painted, she'd ended up at a Hollywood movie premiere.

Scarlett sat in the back of a limo—somehow the dynamic trio managed to get her that as well—and looked over at Madelyn in the carrier car seat. She'd guarantee this was the only limo arriving tonight with a car seat in the back.

Somehow the ladies had not only procured a dress for Scarlett, along with shoes and a fashionable bag, they'd found a red sparkly dress and matching headband for Madelyn.

As the limo slowed, Scarlett turned her attention to the tinted window. Bright lights flooded the night, cameras flashed, the roar of the crowd filtered in and nerves swirled through her belly at the sight and sound.

What was she thinking coming here? She was so far out of her element. She didn't do crowds or glam or dressing up in a fitted, sequined emerald green gown with her hair curled and in bright red lipstick. She was more of a relaxed kind of girl who made homemade baby food and decorated with clearance Christmas decor.

"Ma'am, I'm going to pull closer to the red carpet entrance," the driver informed her. "Please wait until a guard opens your door and escorts you out."

Oh, mercy. She was really going through with this. Scarlett didn't know how the incredible Elliott women managed the jet, the wardrobe, the limo and a last-minute invite to the red carpet to arrive just after Beau's car. No doubt money talked and they had tapped into some powerful resources to make all of this happen in less than twenty-four hours.

The car came to a stop and Scarlett unfastened a sleepy baby from her car seat. She cradled Madelyn against her chest and adjusted the headband, which had slipped down over one eye like a pirate's patch.

"You'll just be around the block?" she asked the driver. "I'm leaving the rest of Madelyn's things in here."

"Yes, ma'am. You call me and I'll be right back. I'm only driving for you tonight."

Scarlett's stylish clutch was just large enough for a couple of diapers, a travel pack of wipes, her cell and her wallet. She'd just fed the baby before Madelyn fell asleep so they should be good for a few hours. Besides, who's to say Beau wouldn't publicly reject her and she'd be right back in this car in just a few moments?

But what if he asked her to stay? What if he wanted to take her and Madelyn into the premiere and whatever party after?

She'd worry about that when the time came. Right now, her car had eased up and came to another stop. The lights and the screams intensified and Scarlett had to concentrate on the sweet child in her arms, still sleeping and oblivious to this milestone moment.

The door opened and the warm California air hit her. She already missed Texas and the laid-back life with cool evenings. Maybe city life wasn't for her. Maybe she hadn't only found the man—she'd found a piece of herself that clicked right into place. Perhaps the next chapter she was going to start was the wrong one. She had so many questions…and they were all about to be answered.

Scarlett laid a protective hand over Madelyn's ears to protect her from the thundering noise, but she stirred and her eyes popped open.

Questions and microphones were shot in her direction, but Scarlett looked ahead, beyond the men in black suits with mics attached to their lapels. She ignored the questions of who she was, what part she had in the film, who was the cute baby.

Scarlett spotted a flash of the wide, familiar grin then broad shoulders eased away from one set of reporters to another. Beau was flanked by those men in suits who were unsmiling and whose eyes were always scanning the area.

A hand slid over her elbow and Scarlett jerked to see who was beside her.

"Right this way, ma'am." One of the suited men clearly recognized the newbie on the red carpet and tried to usher her along. "There is extra security tonight with all the hype. I'll make sure you and your little one get to the entrance of the theater."

She had to strain to hear him over the white noise of the crowd and she didn't even bother to tell him this child wasn't hers, but rather belonged to the star of the premiere. Had she made a mistake bringing Madelyn? Would Beau be upset? She wanted to show him they could all be a family—they could be one unit and build something solid together.

One thing she knew for certain: she wasn't about to stop and talk to the different media outlets. For one thing, she had nothing to say that she'd want printed or quoted. For another, she was here for only one reason and it wasn't to be interviewed.

Scarlett shifted Madelyn in her arms, still shielding the baby's ears from the chaos. She leaned toward the security guard as she tried to keep up with the pace he'd set.

"I don't need to talk to any reporters. I'm here with Mr. Elliott," she informed him. Then she realized how stalker-like that sounded, so she quickly added, "And this is his baby."

The guard looked at her then down to Madelyn, but Scarlett smiled, hoping he'd move this process along. She had a right to be here—she assumed since Annabelle assured her this was okay—and she couldn't wait.

The man finally nodded and gripped his lapel as he talked out the side of his mouth and ordered the guards up ahead to stop Beau from moving to the next set of reporters.

Scarlett pushed through, ignoring the yells from either side of the roped-off area. If she tried to take in all the lights, all of the questions, all of the chaos around her, she would give in to the fear and the anxiety that had accompanied her all the way from Texas.

She never should have let Beau walk out of that cabin thinking he didn't mean more to her. Their time together since she'd shut down had been so strained and she'd ached for him in ways she'd never imagined possible.

In her defense, she'd been hurt and thought it best if they made a clean break since their temporary arrangement was coming to an end anyway. Unfortunately, that clean break didn't work.

Because she loved him.

There was no way to ignore such strong emotions and if she had to make a fool of herself and take the biggest risk of her life, then she was willing to try for the man she'd fallen for so helplessly.

One of the escorts next to Beau tapped on his shoulder and intervened, pulling him from a current interview. Then the man leaned in and told Beau something that had Beau darting his gaze straight in her direction and their eyes instantly locked.

Scarlett wasn't sure if it was the shock in his eyes or the wide smile on his face that had her nerves kicking in even more. She watched as he raked that sultry dark gaze over her body. Even at this distance and despite the chaos around them, the visual lick Beau gave her had her body instantly responding.

His eyes snapped back to hers and then he was taking long strides to come back down the red carpet. Scarlett didn't think she'd ever seen him smile this much.

"Scarlett."

Beau reached her and shook his head, as if still processing what she was doing here. That went for her, too. She felt as if this whole night was surreal.

"How did you… What… Annabelle texted me and asked if I could get a couple of passes and a limo. My agent pulled everything together, but I just assumed she and Colt were coming."

Well, that explained how the quick red carpet treatment happened.

"Mr. Elliott, who's the lady?"

"Beau, is that your little girl?"

"Is Jennifer James no longer part of your life?"

Reporters shot off so many questions, so prying and so demanding. Part of Scarlett wished she would've waited until he got home, but the other part was glad she'd allowed herself to be talked into coming. Standing here, supporting him, was the only way she knew to truly show him how sorry she was and how much he meant to her.

"I wanted to surprise you," Scarlett told him. "This wasn't my idea, but I needed to tell you—"

He slid his hands up her bare arms and stepped farther into her, with Madelyn nestled between them.

"Say it," he demanded. "I need to hear it."

Scarlett stared up into those dark eyes. "What do you need to hear?"

"That you love me." A corner of his mouth quirked into a grin. "That's why you're here, isn't it?"

She shifted Madelyn, but Beau ended up easing his daughter up into his arms. He palmed her back with one large hand and held her secure against his chest.

Questions roared even louder, but his eyes never left Scarlett's. The media might as well not even exist; all his attention was on her.

How did she ever think that his words weren't genuine? That he didn't think they were something special? He'd shown her over and over again just how much she meant to him and she'd shied away in fear. She firmly believed that everything he told Colt was to save her reputation, which only added another layer of respect and love.

"Scarlett."

She smoothed her hand down her emerald beaded gown and tucked the clutch beneath her arm.

"I wanted to be the one to tell you." Scarlett smiled, though her nerves were at an all-time high. "But you stole the words from my mouth."

Beau's hand went to her hip and he leaned down. If she thought the crowd was loud before, that was nothing compared to the roar now. They were yelling so much. She couldn't make out full questions, but she did pick up on "romance" and "love." Yes, they had all of that and so much more.

"Say it," he told her again.

Her eyes darted away, but he raised his hand to cup her face, drawing her attention back to him.

"I'm right here," he stated. "They don't exist. It's just the three of us."

His sweet girl was a package deal and she absolutely loved how he always put Madelyn first. And she wanted them as a package because she couldn't think of a better present.

"I love you," she told him as she reached up to lay her hand over his. "I'm sorry I didn't have the courage to say it before, but I got scared the other day. All of this happened so fast, but everything I feel is so, so real."

He closed the distance between them and touched his lips to hers. And that set the media into a tizzy.

"Beau, is this your new leading lady from the picture?"

"Does she have a name?"

"Is this the rumored nanny?"

"Are you planning a Christmas proposal?"

Beau pressed his forehead to hers. "Are you sure you're ready for all of this tonight?"

Scarlett wasn't sure, but if this was what Beau's life consisted of, she'd find a way to make things work.

"If you love me, then I'm ready for anything," she said, easing back to glance up at him.

"I love you, Scarlett. As crazy as it is, as little time as we've known each other, I love you more than I ever thought I could love any woman."

Her heart swelled and she knew the risk she'd taken had paid off.

"I know I could've waited for you to get back to Texas, but Annabelle thought I should make a statement."

Beau chuckled as he slid an arm around her waist. "Baby, that dress is quite the statement and I plan on showing you when we get back to my place tonight."

She hadn't thought that far, but the idea of ending the night at his house in the Hollywood Hills, of seeing even more into his world had her giddy with anticipation.

Scarlett smoothed a hand over Madelyn's dark curls. "You mentioned wanting a big family and you know that I can't give you that."

"Adoption," he said, using one simple word to put her worries at ease and further prove just how amazing he was. "We'll have that large family when the time is right."

She chewed on her bottom lip and then smiled. "Is it too late to tell you that the farmhouse you bought is perfect for us?"

Beau tapped her forehead with a quick kiss. "That place was always for us," he explained. "I just didn't get a chance to tell you before Colt showed up and then you kicked me out of your room."

He'd planned that house to be for the three of them all this time? Scarlett's eyes welled with tears, but she couldn't cry. It had taken a small army to get this makeup so perfect.

"I think we need to give the reporters something to chew on before they break the barriers."

Scarlett nodded. "Whatever you think."

Beau cradled Madelyn in one arm and kept his other firmly around Scarlett's waist. He angled them toward the front of the red carpet so both sides of the aisle could see them. As soon as they were facing forward, the crowd seemed to hush, waiting for that next golden kernel of a story.

"I'm happy to announce that Scarlett Patterson is in fact my next leading lady," Beau declared. "And my future wife."

Wife? Scarlett jerked her gaze to his, which warranted her a toe-curling wink that set butterflies fluttering in her stomach.

"Is that a proposal?" she asked, shocked her voice was strong.

Beau kept that wide grin on his face. "What do you say? Be my leading lady for life, Scarlett."

"Yes." As if any other answer was an option. "There's nobody else I'd ever want for the star in my life."

Flashes went off, one after another, causing a strobe light effect. As people started yelling more questions, Beau waved and smiled. Scarlett wasn't sure what world she'd stepped into, but the strong man at her side would help her through.

She never thought she'd have the title of leading lady, but as Beau escorted her into the venue, Scarlett realized there was no greater role she could think of—besides wife and mother, of course.

Once inside, Beau ushered her down a hallway to find some privacy.

"I'm taking a break from Hollywood," he told her when they stopped in a quiet place. "I decided that before you came, but now that I see a better future, I'm not sure I'll want to come back here at all."

She didn't know how to respond, but she didn't get a chance. Beau backed her up a step until she came in contact with the wall. He held Madelyn in one arm and reached up with his free hand to stroke the side of her face, then sifted his fingers through her hair.

"You take my breath away, Scarlett. I want you forever, so if we need to take things slow before we marry, I'll do whatever you want."

He kissed her, pouring out his promise and love. When he eased back, he kept his lips barely a whisper away.

"This is the greatest Christmas present I could have ever asked for," he told her.

Scarlett rested her hand over his on Madelyn's back. "Me, too, but I don't know what to wrap up and put beneath our crooked tree."

He nipped at her bottom lip. "How about more of that cookie dip?"

She wrapped her arm around his waist and smiled. "I think I can manage that, but first we have a movie premiere to get to."

"And then we have the rest of our lives to plan."

EPILOGUE

"WHAT THE HELL IS THAT?" Colt demanded.

Scarlett smiled and held up her hands in an exaggerated fashion toward the tree. "It's our Christmas tree," she exclaimed.

"Why is it crooked?"

Beau stepped into the room after putting Madelyn down for the night. "Don't ask. Just go with it."

Scarlett rolled her eyes. "He loves it, don't let him fool you."

Colt's brows drew in before he shook his head and shrugged. "Whatever makes you two happy."

Oh, she was most definitely happy. Christmas Eve was magical here at the ranch and tomorrow was Christmas where all of the Elliotts—spouses, fiancées, and children—would gather and start a new chapter.

"I just wanted to come by and let you guys know that I spoke with the nursing home and they're okay with us bringing Dad home for the day tomorrow."

Beau's eyes went from his brother to Scarlett, then back again. "Seriously?"

Colt nodded. "They said as long as he's having a good day. They offered to send a nurse, but I truly think once he's home, he might see something that triggers some memories, and we can care for him well enough. Even if he's only there an hour. I think we all need it."

Scarlett's heart swelled as tears pricked her eyes. She crossed the room to Beau and wrapped an arm around him.

"This is great news for you guys," she stated. "I think it's exactly what this family needs for a fresh start."

"I just hope he remembers," Beau added.

Colt nodded. "I have a feeling he will. I think this is definitely a Christmas for miracles."

He drifted his gaze toward the leaning tree. "I mean, if you can call that a Christmas tree, I think anything is possible."

Beau laughed as he hugged Scarlett tighter against him. "That tree embodies our lives. We're not perfect, but we're sure as hell trying."

Scarlett smiled as she watched the twins share an unspoken message with their eyes and their matching grins.

Yes, this was a season for miracles.

* * * * *

Christmas With Her Secret Prince

Nina Singh

Forever

Glamorous and heartfelt love stories.

Nina Singh lives just outside of Boston, Massachusetts, with her husband, children and a very rambunctious Yorkie. After several years in the corporate world, she finally followed the advice of family and friends to "give the writing a go, already." She's oh-so-happy she did. When not at her keyboard, she likes to spend time on the tennis court or golf course. Or immersed in a good read.

Books by Nina Singh

Harlequin Romance

9 to 5

Miss Prim and the Maverick Millionaire

The Marriage of Inconvenience
Snowed in with the Reluctant Tycoon
Reunited with Her Italian Billionaire
Tempted by Her Island Millionaire

Visit the Author Profile page
at millsandboon.com.au.

Dear Reader,

My home city of Boston knows how to do Christmas right. In fact, all of New England turns into a magical winter wonderland around the holidays. It's the perfect location to fall in love. So I knew I had to set Mel and Ray's story in just such a wonderland.

The two literally meet by accident. And as they get to know each other, the attraction is strong and undeniable. But can they both let go of their respective pasts enough to give in to that attraction?

Rayhan al Saibbi is a crown prince who's always done what was expected of him, taking his responsibilities seriously. For once in his life, can Ray bring himself to ignore that responsibility and go after the woman he's fallen in love with?

Mel has been burned once already by giving her heart to a man who ultimately crushed it. She's not sure she can be brave enough to do so again. To a real-life prince of all people!

But with a little help from the magic of Christmastime, Mel and Ray eventually realize true love is worth taking a few chances.

I had so much fun writing these characters. I hope you enjoy their romantic journey as much as I did.

Happy reading!

Nina

To my two very own princes.
And my two princesses.

Praise for
Nina Singh

"Singh's latest has a love story that will make readers swoon, 'ooh,' and 'ahh'... *Snowed in with the Reluctant Tycoon* is a great read any time of year."

—*RT Book Reviews*

CHAPTER ONE

PRINCE RAYHAN AL SAIBBI was not looking forward to his next meeting. In fact, he was dreading it. After all, it wasn't often he went against his father—the man who also happened to be king of Verdovia.

But it had to be done. This might very well be his last chance to exert any kind of control over his own life. Even if it was to be only a temporary respite. Fate had made him prince of Verdovia. And his honor-bound duty to that fate would come calling soon enough. He just wanted to try and bat it away one last time.

The sun shone bright and high over the majestic mountain range outside his window. A crisp blue stream meandered along its base. The pleasant sunny day meant his father would most likely be enjoying his breakfast on the patio off the four-seasons room in the east wing.

Rayhan found his father sitting at the far end of the table. Piles of papers and a sleek new laptop were mixed in with various plates of fruits and pastries. A twinge of guilt hit Rayhan as he approached. The king never stopped working. For that matter, neither did the queen, his mother. A fact that needed to be addressed after the events of the past year. Part of the reason Rayhan was in his current predicament.

This conversation wasn't going to be easy. His father had

been king for a long time. He was used to making the rules and expected everyone to follow them. Particularly when it came to his son.

But these days the king wasn't thinking entirely straight. Motivated by an alarming health scare Rayhan's mother had experienced a few months back and prompted by the trouble-some maneuverings of a disagreeable council member, his father had decided that the royal family needed to strengthen and reaffirm their stability. Unfortunately, he'd also decided that Rayhan would be the primary vehicle to cement that stability.

His father motioned for him to be seated when he saw Ray-han approach.

"Thank you for seeing me, Father. I know how busy you are."

His father nodded. "It sounded urgent based on your mes-sages. What can I assist you with, son? Dare I hope you're closer to making a decision?"

"I am. Just not in the way you might assume."

Rayhan focused his gaze on his father's face. A face that could very well be an older version of his own. Dark olive skin with high cheekbones and ebony eyes.

"I don't understand," his father began. "You were going to spend some time with the ladies in consideration. Then you were to make a choice."

Rayhan nodded. "I've spent time with all three of them, cor-rect. They're all lovely ladies, Father. Very accomplished—all of them stunning and impressive in their own unique way. You have chosen well."

"They come from three of the most notable and prominent families of our land. You marrying a prominent daughter of Verdovia will go far to address our current problems."

"Like I said, you have chosen well."

The king studied him. "Then what appears to be the issue?"

Where to start? First of all, he wasn't ready to be wedded to any of the ladies in question. In fact, he wasn't ready to be wedded at all.

But he had a responsibility. Both to his family and to the kingdom.

"Perhaps I shall choose for you," the king suggested, his annoyance clear as the crisp morning air outside. "You know how important this is. And how urgent. Councilman Riza is preparing a resolution as we speak to propose studying the efficacy and necessity of the royal family's very existence."

"You know it won't go anywhere. He's just stirring chaos."

"I despise chaos." His father blew out a deep breath. "All the more reason to put this plan into action, son."

The *plan* his father referred to meant the end of Rayhan's life as he knew it. "It just seems such an archaic and outdated method. A bachelor prince choosing from qualified ladies to serve as his queen when he eventually ascends the throne."

His father shrugged. "Arranged marriages are quite common around the world. Particularly for a young man of your standing. Global alliances are regularly formed through marriage vows. It's how your mother and I wedded, as you know. These ladies I have chosen are very well-known and popular in the kingdom."

Rayhan couldn't argue the point. There was the talented prima ballerina who had stolen the people's hearts when she'd first appeared on stage several years ago. Then there was the humanitarian who'd made the recent influx of refugees and their plight her driving cause. And finally, a councilman's beautiful daughter, who also happened to be an international fashion model.

Amazing ladies. All of whom seemed to be approaching the king's proposition more as a career opportunity than anything else. Which in blatant terms was technically correct. Of course, the people didn't know that fact. They just believed their crown prince to be linked to three different ladies, and rumors abounded that he would propose to one of them within weeks. A well-calculated palace publicity stunt.

"As far as being outdated," the king continued, "have you

seen the most popular show in America these days? It involves an eligible bachelor choosing from among several willing ladies. By giving them weekly roses, of all things." His father barked out a laugh at the idea.

"But this isn't some reality show," Rayhan argued. "This is my life."

"Nevertheless, a royal wedding will distract from this foolishness of Riza's."

Rayhan couldn't very well argue that point either. The whole kingdom was even now in the frenzied midst of preparing for the wedding of the half century, everyone anxious to see which young lady the prince would choose for himself. Combined with the festivities of the holiday season, the level of excitement and celebration throughout the land was almost palpable.

And Rayhan was about to go and douse it all like a wet blanket over a warming fire.

Bah humbug.

Well, so be it. This was his life they were talking about. He wanted to claim one last bit of it. He wouldn't take no for an answer. Not this time. But this was a new experience for him. Rayhan had never actually willingly gone against the king's wishes before. Not for something this important anyway.

"Well, I've come to a different decision," he told his father. Rayhan made sure to look him straight in the eye as he continued, "I've decided to wait."

The king blinked. Several times. Rapidly. "I beg your pardon?"

"I'd like to hold off. I'm not ready to choose a fiancée. Not just yet."

"You can only postpone for so long, son. The kingdom is waiting for a royal wedding… We have announced your intention to marry. And then there's your mother."

Rayhan felt a pang of guilt through his chest at the mention of the queen. She'd given them all quite a scare last year. "Mother is fine now."

"Still, she needs to slow down. I won't have her health jeopardized again. Someone needs to help take over some of the queen's regular duties. Your sisters are much too young."

"All I'm asking for is some time, Father. Perhaps we can come to a compromise."

The king leaned toward him, his arms resting on the table. At least he was listening. "What sort of compromise did you have in mind?"

Rayhan cleared his throat and began to tell him.

"Honestly, Mel. If you handle that invitation any more, it's going to turn into ash in your hands."

Melinda Osmon startled as her elderly, matronly employer walked by the counter where she sat waiting for her shift to begin. The older woman was right. This had to be at least the fifth or sixth time Mel had taken the stationery out simply to stare at it since it had arrived in her mailbox several days ago.

The Honorable Mayor and Mrs. Spellman request the pleasure of your presence...

"You caught me," Mel replied, swiftly wiping the moisture off her cheeks.

"Just send in your reply already," Greta added, her back turned to her as she poured coffee for the customer sitting at the end of the counter. The full breakfast crowd wasn't due in for another twenty minutes or so. "Then figure out what you're going to wear."

Melinda swallowed past the lump in her throat before attempting an answer. "Greta, you know I can't go this year. It's just not worth the abject humiliation."

Greta turned to her so fast that some of the coffee splashed out of her coffeepot. "Come again? What in the world do you have to be humiliated about?"

Not this again. Greta didn't seem to understand, nor did

she want to. How about the fact that Mel hadn't yet moved on? Unlike her ex-husband. The ex-husband who would be at the same party with his fashionable, svelte and beautiful new fiancée. "Well, for one thing, I'd be going solo. That's humiliating enough in itself."

Greta jutted out her chin and snapped her gum loudly. "And why is that? You're not the one who behaved shamefully and had the affair. That scoundrel you were married to should be the one feeling too ashamed to show his face at some fancy-schmancy party you both used to attend every year when you were man and wife."

Mel cringed at the unfiltered description.

"Now, you listen to me, young lady—"

Luckily, another customer cleared his throat just then, clearly impatient for a hit of caffeine. Greta humphed and turned away to pour. Mel knew the reprieve would be short-lived. Greta had very strong opinions about how Mel should move along into the next chapter of her life. She also had very strong opinions about Mel's ex. To say the older woman was outraged on Mel's behalf was to put it mildly. In fact, the only person who might be even angrier was Greta's even older sister, Frannie. Not that Mel wasn't pretty outraged herself. A lot of good that did for her, though. Strong emotions were not going to get her a plus-one to the mayor's Christmas soiree. And she certainly was nowhere near ready to face the speculation and whispery gossip that was sure to greet her if she set foot in that ballroom alone.

"She's right, you know," Frannie announced, sliding into the seat next to Mel. The two sisters owned the Bean Pot Diner on Marine Street in the heart of South Boston. The only place that would hire her when she'd found herself broke, alone and suddenly separated. "I hate to admit when that blabbermouth is right but she sure is about this. You should go to that party and enjoy yourself. Show that no-good, cheating charlatan that you don't give a damn what he thinks."

"I don't think I have it in me, Frannie. Just to show up and then have to stare at Eric and his fiancée having the time of their lives, while I'll be sitting there all alone."

"I definitely don't think you should do that."

Well, that was a sudden change of position, Melinda thought, eyeing her friend. "So you agree I shouldn't go?"

"No, that's not what I said. I think you should go, look ravishing and then confront him about all he put you through. Then demand that he return your money."

Melinda sighed. She should have seen that argument coming. "First of all, I gave him that money." Foolishly. The hard-earned money that her dear parents had left her after their deaths. It was supposed to have been an investment in Eric's future. Their future. She had gladly handed it to him to help him get through dental school. Then it was supposed to be her turn to make some kind of investment in herself while he supported her. Instead, he'd left her for his perky, athletic dental assistant. His much younger, barely-out-of-school dental assistant. And now they happily cared for teeth together during the day, while planning an extravagant wedding in their off-hours. "I gave it to him with no strings attached."

"And you should take him to court to get some of it back!" Frannie slapped her palm against the counter. Greta sashayed back over to where the two of them sat.

"That's right," Greta declared. "You should go to that damn party looking pretty as a fashion model. Then demand he pay you back. Every last cent. Or you'll see him in front of a judge."

Mel sighed and bit down on the words that were forming on her tongue. As much as she longed to tell the two women to mind their own business, Mel just couldn't bring herself to do it. They'd been beyond kind to her when she'd needed it the most. Not to mention, they were the closest thing to family Mel could count since her divorce a year ago.

"How? I barely have the money for court fees. Let alone any to hire an attorney."

"Then start with the party," Greta declared as her sister nodded enthusiastically. "At the very least, ruin his evening. Show him what he's missing out on."

Nothing like a couple of opinionated matrons double-teaming you.

Mel let out an unamused laugh. "As if. I don't even have a dress to wear. I sold all my fancier clothes just to make rent that first month."

Greta waved a hand in dismissal. "So buy another one. I tell you, if I had your figure and that great dark hair of yours, I'd be out shopping right now. Women like you can find even the highest-end clothing on sale."

Mel ignored the compliment. "I can't even afford the stuff on sale these days, Greta."

"So take an advance on your paycheck," Frannie offered from across the counter. "We know you're good for it."

Mel felt the immediate sting of tears. These women had taken her in when she'd needed friendship and support the most. She'd never be able to repay their kindness. She certainly had no desire to take advantage of it. "I can't ask you to do that for me, ladies."

"Nonsense," they both said in unison.

"You'd be doing it for us," Greta added.

"For you?"

"Sure. Let two old bats like us live vicariously through you. Go to that ball and then come back and tell us all about it."

Frannie nodded in agreement. "That's right. Especially the part about that no-good scoundrel begging you for forgiveness after he takes one look at ya."

Mel smiled in spite of herself. These two certainly knew how to cook up a good fantasy. Eric had left her high and dry and never looked back even once. As far as fantasies went, she was more likely to turn a frog into a prince than receive any kind of apology from her ex-husband.

"I don't think that's going to happen anytime soon." Or ever. Mel reached down to tighten the laces of her comfortable white tennis shoes. She had a very long shift ahead of her, starting with the breakfast crowd and ending with the early-evening dinner guests.

"You won't know unless you go to this ball."

She couldn't even tell which of the ladies had thrown that out. Mel sighed and straightened to look at them both. Her bosses might look like gentle, sweet elderly ladies, complete with white hair done up in buns, but they could be relentless once they set their minds to something.

"All right. I give."

They both squealed with delight. "Then it's settled," Frannie declared and clasped her hands in front of her chest.

Mel held a hand up. "Not so fast. I haven't agreed to go just yet."

Greta's smile faded. "Come again?"

"How about a deal?"

"What kind of deal?"

"I'll go out after my shift and look for a dress." Though how she would summon the energy after such a long day was a mystery. But she was getting the feeling she'd hear about this all day unless she threw her two bosses some kind of bone. "If, and only if, I come across a dress that's both affordable and appropriate, I'll reconsider going."

Frannie opened her mouth, clearly about to protest. Mel cut her off.

"It's my only offer. Take it or leave it."

"Fine," they both said in unison before turning away. Mel stood just as the bell for the next order up rang from the kitchen. She had a long day ahead of her and it was only just starting. She was a waitress now. Not the young bride of an up-and-coming urban dentist who attended fancy holiday balls and went shopping for extravagant ball gowns. That might have been her reality once, but it had been short-lived.

Little did the Perlman sisters know, she had told them something of a fib just now when making that deal. She had no expectation that she'd find any kind of dress that would merit attending that party in a week.

The chances were slim to zero.

His driver-slash-security-guard—who also happened to be a dear childhood friend—was very unhappy with him at the moment. Rayhan ignored the scowl of the other man as he watched the streets of downtown Boston outside his passenger-side window. Every shop front had been decorated with garlands and glittery Christmas decorations. Bright lights were strung on everything from the lamp poles to shop windows. Let his friend scowl away, Rayhan thought. He was going to go ahead and enjoy the scenery. But when Saleh took yet another turn a little too fast and sharp, he found he'd had enough. Saleh was acting downright childish.

To top it off, they appeared to be lost. Saleh had refused to admit he needed the assistance of the navigation system and now they appeared to be nowhere near their destination.

"You know you didn't have to come," Rayhan reminded the other man. "You volunteered, remember?"

Saleh grunted. "I clearly wasn't thinking straight. Why are we here, again? At this particular time, no less."

"You know this."

"I know you're delaying the inevitable."

He was right, of course. Not that Rayhan was going to admit it out loud. "I still have a bit of time to live my life as I see fit."

"And you decided you needed to do part of that in Boston?"

Rayhan shrugged, resuming his perusal of the outside scenery. "That was completely coincidental. My father's been eyeing property out here for months now. Perfect opportunity for me to come find a prime location and seal the deal."

"Yes, so you say. It's a way to… How do the Americans say it? To kill two birds with one stone?"

"Precisely."

"So why couldn't you have come out here with the new soon-to-be-princess after your engagement?"

Rayhan pinched the bridge of his nose. "I just needed to get away before it all gets out of control, Saleh. I don't expect you to understand."

Not many people would, Rayhan thought. Particularly not his friend, who had married the grade-school sweetheart he'd been in love with since their teen years. Unlike Rayhan, Saleh didn't have to answer to nor appease a whole country when it came to his choice of bride.

Rayhan continued, "Everywhere I turn in Verdovia, I'm reminded of the upcoming ceremonies. Everyone is completely preoccupied with who the heir will choose to marry, what the wedding will be like. Yada yada. There are odds being placed in every one of our island casinos on everything from the identity of the next queen to what flavor icing will adorn the royal wedding cake."

Saleh came to a sudden halt at a red light, a wide grin spread across his face.

"What?" Rayhan asked.

"I placed my wager on the vanilla buttercream."

"I see. That's good to know." He made a mental note to go with anything but the vanilla buttercream when the time came. If he had any say on the matter, that was. Between his mother and the princess-to-be, he'd likely have very little sway in such decisions. No doubt his shrewd friend had made his bet based on the very same assumption.

"I don't understand why you refuse to simply embrace your fate, my friend. You're the heir of one of the most powerful men in the world. With that comes the opportunity to marry and gain a beautiful, accomplished lady to warm your bed. There are worse things in life."

Saleh overlooked the vast amount of responsibility that came with such a life. The stability and prosperity of a whole kingdom full of people would fall on Rayhan's shoulders as soon as he ascended. Even more so than it did now. Few people could understand the overwhelming prospect of such a position. As far as powerful, how much did any of that mean when even your choice of bride was influenced by the consideration of your position?

"How easy for you to say," he told Saleh just as the light turned green and they moved forward. "You found a beautiful woman who you somehow tricked into thinking marrying you was a good idea."

Saleh laughed with good-natured humor. "The greatest accomplishment of my life."

Rayhan was about to answer when a screeching noise jolted both men to full alert. A cyclist veered toward their vehicle at an alarming speed. Saleh barely had time to turn the wheel in order to avoid a full-on collision. Unfortunately, the cyclist shifted direction at precisely the same time. Both he and their SUV were now heading the same way. Right toward a pedestrian. Saleh hit the brakes hard. Rayhan gripped the side bar, waiting for the inevitable impact. Fortunately for them, it never came.

The cyclist, however, kept going. And, unfortunately for the poor pedestrian woman, the bicycle ran straight into her, knocking her off her feet.

"Watch where you're going!" the rider shouted back over his shoulder, not even bothering to stop.

Rayhan immediately jumped out of the car. He ran around to the front of the SUV and knelt down where the woman still lay by the sidewalk curb.

"Miss, are you all right?"

A pair of startled eyes met his. Very bright green eyes. They reminded him of the shimmering stream that lay outside his windows back home. Not that this was any sort of time to notice that kind of thing.

She blinked, rubbing a hand down a cheek that was rapidly bruising even as they spoke. Saleh appeared at his side.

"Is she okay?"

"I don't know. She's not really responding. Miss, are you all right?"

Her eyes grew wide as she looked at him. "You're lovely," she said in a low, raspy voice.

Dear heavens. The woman clearly had some kind of head injury. "We have to get you to a doctor."

Saleh swore beside him. "I'm so terribly sorry, miss. I was trying to avoid the bike and the cyclist was trying to avoid me but he turned right toward you—"

The woman was still staring at Rayhan. She didn't acknowledge Saleh nor his words at all.

He had a sudden urge to hold her, to comfort her. He wanted to wrap her in his arms, even though she was a complete stranger.

Rayhan reached for his cell phone. "I'll call for an ambulance."

The woman gave a shake of her head before he could dial. "No. I'm okay. Just a little shaken." She blinked some more and looked around. Her eyes seemed to regain some focus. Rayhan allowed himself a breath of relief. Maybe she'd be all right. Her next words brought that hopeful thought to a halt.

"My dress. Do you see it?"

Did she think somehow her clothes had been knocked off her upon impact? "You…uh…you are wearing it still."

Her gaze scanned the area where she'd fallen. "No. See, I found one. I didn't think I would. But I did. And it wasn't all that pricey."

Rayhan didn't need to hear any more. Unless she was addled to begin with, which could very well be a possibility, the lady had clearly suffered a blow to the head. To top it all off, they were blocking traffic and drawing a crowd. Kneeling closer to the woman sprawled in front of him, he lifted her gently into his arms and then stood. "Let's get you to a hospital."

"Oh!" she cried out as Rayhan walked back toward the SUV with her embraced against his chest.

Saleh was fast on his heels and opening the passenger door for them. "No, see, it's all right," she began to protest. "I don't need a doctor. Just that gown."

"We'll make sure to get you a dress," Rayhan reassured her, trying to tell her what she clearly needed to hear. Why was she so focused on clothing at a time like this? "Right after a doctor takes a look at you."

He gently deposited her in the back seat, then sat down next to her. "No, wait," she argued. "I don't need a doctor. I just want my dress."

But Saleh was already driving toward a hospital.

The woman took a panicked look out the window and then winced. The action must have hurt her injuries somehow. She touched a shaky finger to her cheek, which was now a dark purple, surrounded by red splotches.

Even in the messy state she was in, he couldn't help but notice how striking her features were. Dark, thick waves of black hair escaped the confines of some sort of complicated bun on top of her head. A long slender neck graced her slim shoulders. She was curvy—not quite what one would consider slim. Upon first glance, he would never consider someone like her his "type," so to speak. But he had to admit, he appreciated her rather unusual beauty.

That choice of words had him uncomfortably shifting in his seat. He stole a glance at her as she explored her facial injuries with shaky fingers.

Now her right eye had begun to swell as an angry, dark circular ring developed around it. Rayhan bit out a sharp curse. Here he was trying to enjoy what could very well be his last trip to the United States as a free man and he'd ended up hurting some poor woman on his first day here.

Perhaps Saleh was right. Maybe this whole trip had been a

terrible idea. Maybe he should have just stayed home and accepted his fate.

There was at least one person who would be much better off right now if he had.

CHAPTER TWO

SHE WOULD HAVE been much better off if she'd just ignored that blasted invitation and thrown it away as soon as it arrived in her mailbox. She should have never even opened it and she definitely should have never even considered going to that godforsaken party. Her intuition had been right from the beginning. She no longer had any kind of business attending fancy balls and wearing glamorous gowns.

But no, she had to go and indulge two little old ladies, as well as her own silly whim. Look where that had got her—sitting on an exam table in a cold room at Mass General, with a couple of strange men out in the hallway.

Although they had to be the best-looking strangers she'd ever encountered. Particularly the one who had carried her to the car. She studied him now through the small window of her exam room door. He stood leaning against the wall, patiently waiting for the doctor to come examine her.

Even in her stunned shock while she lay sprawled by the side of the road, she hadn't been able to help but notice the man's striking good looks. Dark haired, with the barest shadow of a goatee, he looked like he could have stepped out of a cologne advertisement. Though there was no way he was some kind of male fashion model. He carried himself with much too much authority.

His eyes were dark as charcoal, his skin tone just on the darker side of dessert tan. Even before they'd spoken, she'd known he wasn't local.

His looks had taken her by surprise, or perhaps it had been the blow she'd suffered, but she distinctly remembered thinking he was lovely.

Which was a downright silly thought. A better description would be to say he looked dangerous.

Mel shook off the fanciful thoughts. She had other things to worry about besides the striking good looks of the man who had brought her here. They'd called the diner after she'd been processed. Presumably, either Greta or Frannie was on her way to join her at the hospital now. Mel felt a slight pang of guilt about one of them having to leave in the middle of closing up the diner for the night.

She would have frowned but it hurt too much. Her face had taken the brunt of the collision with the reckless cyclist, who, very rudely, had continued on his way. At least the two gentlemen out there hadn't left her alone and bleeding by the side of the road. Though now that meant she would be saddled with an ER bill she couldn't afford. Thinking about that expense, coupled with what she'd paid for the evening dress, had her eyes stinging with regret. In all the confusion and chaos right after the accident, her shopping bag had been left behind. Mel knew she should be grateful that the accident hadn't been worse, but she couldn't help but feel sorry for herself. Would she ever catch a break?

A sharp knock on the door was quickly followed by the entrance of a harried-looking doctor. He did a bit of a double take when he saw her face.

"Let's take a look at you, Miss Osmon."

The doctor wasted no time with his physical examination, then proceeded to ask her a series of questions—everything from the calendar date to what she'd had for breakfast. His unconcerned expression afterward told her she must have passed.

"I think you'll be just fine. Though quite sore for the next several weeks. You don't appear to be concussed. But someone will need to watch you for the next twenty-four hours or so. Just to be on the safe side." He motioned to the door. "Mind if I let your boyfriend in? He appears to be very concerned about you."

"Oh, he's not—they're just the—"

The doctor raised an eyebrow in question. "I apologize. He took care of the necessary paperwork and already settled the fees. I just assumed."

He had settled the bill? A nagging sense of discomfort blossomed in her chest. This stranger had paid for her care. She would have to figure out how to pay him back. Not that it would be easy.

The physician continued, "In any case, if he's the one who'll be watching you, he'll need to hear this."

"He won't be watching me. I have a friend—"

Before she got the last word out, Greta came barreling through the door, her springy gray hair still wrapped tight in a kitchen hairnet.

"Yowza," the older woman exclaimed as soon as her gaze landed on Mel's face. "You look like you went a couple rounds with a prizefighter. Or were ya fighting over a discounted item at The Basement? Their shoppers can be brutal!"

"Hi, Greta. Thanks for coming."

"Sure thing, kid. I took a cab over as soon as we heard. You doin' okay?" She'd left the door wide-open behind her. The two strangers hovered uncertainly out in the hallway, both of them giving her concerned looks.

Mel sighed. *What the heck? May as well make this a standing room–only crowd.* After all, they were nice enough to bring her in and take care of the processing while she was being examined. She motioned for them to come in. The taller, more handsome one stepped inside first. His friend followed close behind.

"The doctor says I'll be fine," she told them.

The doctor nodded. "I also said she needs to be monitored overnight. To make sure there are no signs of concussion or other trauma." He addressed the room in general before turning to Mel directly. "If you feel nauseous or dizzy, or if over-the-counter medications don't seem to be addressing the pain, you need to come back in. Understood?"

"Yes."

He turned to the others. "You need to watch for any sign of blacking out or loss of balance."

Greta nodded. As did the two men for some reason.

The doctor gave a quick wave before hastily walking out.

Mel smiled awkwardly at the two men. It occurred to her she didn't even know their names. "Um… I'm Mel."

They exchanged a glance between them. Then the taller one stepped forward. "I'm Ray. This is Sal." He motioned to his friend, who politely nodded.

More awkwardness ensued as all four of them stood silent.

"I'm Greta," the older woman suddenly and very loudly offered.

Both men said hello. Finally, Greta reached for Mel's arm. "C'mon, kiddo. Let's get you dressed. Then we'll call for a cab so we can get you home."

Ray stepped forward. "That won't be necessary. We'll take you anywhere you need to go."

Ray sighed with relief for what must have been the hundredth time as the old lady directed them to the front of a small eatery not far from where the accident had occurred. Thank goodness that Mel appeared to be all right. But she was sporting one devil of a shiner on her right eye and the whole side of her face looked a purple mess.

For some inexplicable reason, his mind kept referring to the moment he'd picked her up and carried her to the car. The softness of her as he'd held her, the way she'd smelled. Some delicate scent of flowers combined with a fruity shampoo he'd noticed when her head had been under his nose.

"This is our stop," Greta declared and reached for the door handle.

Ray immediately got out of the car to assist Mel out onto the street. After all, the older woman looked barely able to get herself moving. She'd actually dozed off twice during the short ride over. Ray hadn't missed how Mel had positioned herself to allow Greta to lean against her shoulder as she snored softly. Despite her injury. Nor how she'd gently nudged her friend awake as they approached their destination.

Who was taking care of whom in this scenario?

How in the world was this frail, seemingly exhausted older lady supposed to keep an eye on her injured friend all night?

Ray would never forgive himself if Mel had any kind of medical disaster in the middle of the night. Despite his reassurances, the doctor had made it clear she wasn't completely out of the woods just yet.

"My sister and I live in a flat above this diner, which we own and manage," Greta informed him around a wide yawn as the three of them approached the door. She rummaged around in her oversize bag for several moments, only to come up empty.

"Dang it. I guess I left my keys behind when I rushed over to the hospital."

She reached for a panel by the side of the door and pressed a large button. A buzzer could be heard sounding upstairs. Several beats passed and...nothing.

Mel offered him a shy smile. Her black hair glistened like tinsel where the streetlight hit it. The neon light of the diner sign above them brought out the bright evergreen hue of her eyes. Well, the one that wasn't nearly swollen shut anyway. The poor woman probably couldn't wait to get upstairs and lie down.

Unfortunately, she would have to wait a bit longer. Several more moments passed. Greta pressed the button at least half a dozen more times. Ray wasn't any more reassured as they continued to wait.

Finally, after what seemed like an eternity, the sound of shuffling feet could be heard approaching as a shadow moved closer to the opposite side of the door. When it finally opened, they were greeted by a groggy, disheveled woman who was even older than Greta. She didn't even look fully awake yet.

It was settled. There was no way he could leave an injured woman with the likes of these two ladies. His conscience wouldn't allow it. Especially not when he was partly responsible for said injury to begin with.

"I'm glad that's over with." Saleh started the SUV as soon as Ray opened the passenger door and leaned into the vehicle. "Let's finally get to our hotel, then. I could use a long hot shower and a tall glass of something strong and aromatic." He reached for the gearshift before giving him a quizzical look. "Why aren't you getting in the car?"

"I've decided to stay here."

Saleh's eyes went wide with shock. "What?"

"I can't leave the young lady, Saleh. You should see the older sister who's supposed to watch Mel with Greta."

"You mean Greta's the younger one?"

"Believe it or not."

"Still. It's no longer our concern. We've done all we can. She'll be fine." He motioned with a tilt of his head for Rayhan to get in the car.

"I'm going to stay here and make sure of it. You go on ahead and check us into the hotel."

"You can't be serious. Are you forgetting who you are?"

Ray bit down on his impatience. Saleh was a trusted friend. But right now, he was the one close to forgetting who he was and whom he was addressing.

"Not in the least. I happen to be part of the reason that young lady is up there, sporting all sorts of cuts and bruises, as well as a potential head injury, which needs to be monitored. By someone who can actually keep an eye on her with some degree of competence."

"Your Highness, I understand all that. But staying here is not wise."

"Don't call me that, Saleh. You know better."

"I'm just trying to remind you of your position. Perhaps I should also remind you that this isn't an announced state visit. If these ladies were to find out who you are, it could leak to the rest of the world before morning. The resulting frenzy of press could easily result in an embarrassing media nightmare for the monarchy. Not to mention Verdovia as a whole."

"They won't find out."

Saleh huffed in exasperation. "How can you be sure?"

Ray ignored the question as he didn't really have any kind of adequate answer. "I've made up my mind," he said with finality.

"There's more to it. Isn't there, Rayhan?"

Ray knew exactly what his friend meant. The two had known each other their whole lives, since they were toddlers kicking around a sponge soccer ball in the royal courtyard. He wouldn't bother to deny what his friend had clearly observed.

"I saw the way you were looking at her," Saleh threw out as if issuing a challenge. "With much more than sympathy in your eyes. Admit it. There's more to it."

Ray only sighed. "Perhaps there is, my friend." He softly shut the car door.

Ray was asleep on Frannie and Greta's couch. Mel popped two anti-inflammatory pills into her mouth and then took a swig of water to swallow them down. Her borrowed nightgown felt snug against her hips. It belonged to Greta, who could accurately be described as having the figure of a very thin teenage boy. A description that didn't fit Mel in any way.

The feel of her nightwear wouldn't be the only thing bothering her tonight, Mel figured. The man lying in the other room only a few feet away would no doubt disrupt her sleep. Had she ever felt so aware of a man before? She honestly couldn't say, despite having been married. He had such a magnetism, she'd be hard-pressed to put its impact on her into words. Everything about him screamed class and breeding. From the impeccable and, no doubt, expensive tailored clothing to the SUV he and his friend were driving around in, Ray was clearly not lacking in resources. He was well-mannered and well-spoken. And judging by what he'd done earlier tonight, he was quite kindhearted.

Ray had feigned being too tired to travel with his friend to their hotel across town and had asked the Perlman sisters if he could crash on their couch instead. Mel wasn't buying it in the least. First of all, he didn't seem the type of man to lack stamina in any way. No, his true intention was painfully obvious. He'd taken one look at Frannie, studied Greta again and then perused Mel's battered face and decided he couldn't leave her in the care of the elderly sisters. None of them questioned it. Sure, Ray was barely more than a stranger, but he'd had ample opportunity if his motives were at all nefarious.

Besides, he hardly appeared to be a kidnapper. And he definitely wasn't likely to be a thief looking to take off with the Perlman sisters' ancient and cracked bone china.

No, he was just a gentleman who'd not only made sure to take care of her after she'd got hurt, he'd insisted on hanging around to keep an eye on her.

She crawled into the twin bed the Perlman sisters kept set up in their spare room and eyed the functional sleigh-bell ornament taken off the diner Christmas tree that Greta had handed her before going to bed. She was supposed to ring it to arouse their attention if she felt at all ill during the night. As if either sister had any chance of hearing it. Frannie hadn't even heard the much louder door buzzer earlier this evening. No wonder Ray had insisted on staying.

She felt oddly touched by his thoughtfulness. Not every man would have been so concerned.

She tried to imagine Eric going out of his way in such a fashion under similar circumstances. Simply to help a stranger. She couldn't picture it. No, Ray didn't seem at all like her ex. In fact, he was unlike any other man she'd ever met. And his looks! The man was heart-stoppingly handsome. She still didn't know where he was from, but based on his dark coloring and regal features, she would guess somewhere in the Mediterranean. Southern Italy perhaps. Maybe Greece. Or even somewhere in the Middle East.

Mel sighed again and snuggled deeper into her pillow. What did any of her speculation matter in the overall scheme of things? Men like Ray weren't the type a divorced waitress could count among her acquaintances. He would be nothing more than a flash of brightness that passed through her life for a brief moment in time. By this time next week, no doubt, he wouldn't give the likes of Melinda Osmon more than a lingering thought.

"So did she even find a dress?"

"I guess so. She says she lost the shopping bag 'cause of the accident, though."

"So no dress. I guess she definitely isn't going to the ball, then."

"Nope. Not without a dress. And not with that crazy shiner where her eye is."

What was it about this dress everyone kept talking about? Ray stirred and slowly opened his eyes. To his surprise it was morning already. He'd slept surprisingly well on the lumpy velvet-covered couch the sisters had offered him last night. Said sisters were currently talking much too loudly in the kitchen, which was off to the side of the apartment. Clearly, they didn't entertain overnight guests often.

His thoughts immediately shifted to Mel. How was she feeling? He'd slept more soundly than he'd expected to. What if she'd needed something in the middle of the night? He swiftly strode to the kitchen. "Has anyone checked on Mel yet?"

Both ladies halted midspeech to give him curious looks. "Well, good morning to you, too," Greta said with just a touch of grouchiness in her voice. Or maybe that was Frannie. In matching terry robes and thick glasses perched on the ends of their noses, they looked remarkably similar.

"I apologize. I just wondered about our patient."

The two women raised their eyebrows at him. "She's *our* patient now, huh?" one of the women asked.

Luckily, the other one spoke before Ray could summon an answer to that question. "She's sleeping soundly. I sneaked a peek at her as soon as I woke up. Breathing nice and even. Even has some color back in her face. Well, real color. Aside from the nasty purple bruise."

Ray felt the tension he wasn't aware he held slowly leave his chest and shoulders. One of the women pulled a chair out for him as another handed him a steaming cup of coffee. Both actions were done with a no-nonsense efficiency. Ray gratefully took the steaming cup and sat down.

The small flat was a far cry from the majestic expanse of the castle he called home, but the sheer homeliness and coziness of the setting served to put him in a comfortable state of ease, one that took him a bit by surprise. He spent most of his life in a harried state of rushing from one activity or responsibility to another. To be able to simply sit and enjoy a cup of coffee in a quaint New England kitchen was a novel experience. One he was enjoying more than he would have guessed.

"Damn shame about the dress," Greta or Frannie commented as she sat down across him, the other lady joining them a moment later after refreshing her mug. He really needed one of them to somehow identify herself or he was bound to make an embarrassing slip before the morning was over about who was who.

"Can someone tell me what the deal is with this dress?" he asked.

"Mel was coming back from shopping when you and your friend knocked her on her keister," the sister right next to him answered.

"Frannie!" the other one exclaimed. Thank goodness. Now he just had to keep straight which was which once they stood. "That's no way to talk to our guest," she added.

Ray took a sip of his coffee, the guilt washing over him once more. Though technically they hadn't been the ones to actually run into Mel—the cyclist had done that—he couldn't help but feel that if Saleh had been paying better attention, Mel wouldn't be in the state she was in currently.

"She lost the shopping bag in all the confusion," Frannie supplied.

"I'm terribly sorry to hear that," Ray answered. "It must have been some dress. I'll have to find a way to compensate for Mel's losing it."

"It's more what she needed it for."

Ray found himself oddly curious. When was the last time he cared about why a woman needed an article of clothing? Never. The answer to that question was a resounding *never*.

"What did she need it for?"

"To stick it to that scoundrel husband of hers."

Ray found himself on the verge of sputtering out the coffee he'd just taken a sip of. Husband. Mel was married. It really wasn't any of his business. So why did he feel like someone had just landed a punch in the middle of his gut? He'd met the woman less than twelve hours ago for heaven's sake. Had barely spoken more than a few words to her.

"He's her ex-husband," Greta clarified. "But my sister's right about the scoundrel part."

"Oh?" Ray inquired. For the second time already this morning, he felt like a solid weight had been lifted off his shoulders. So she wasn't actually married currently. He cursed internally as he thought it. What bit of difference did it make where he was concerned?

"Yeah, he took all her money, then left her for some flirty flirt of a girl who works for him."

That did sound quite scoundrel-like. A pang of sympathy blossomed in his chest. No woman deserved that. What little he knew of Mel, she seemed like she wouldn't hurt another being if her life depended on it. She certainly didn't deserve such treatment.

"Before they got divorced, Mel and her ex were always invited to the mayor's annual charity holiday ball. The mayor's daughter is a college friend of both of theirs. This year that no-good ex of Mel's is taking his new lady. Word is, he proposed to her and they'll be attending as doctor and fiancée."

Frannie nodded as her sister spoke. "Yeah, we were trying to convince her to go anyway. 'Cause why should he have the satisfaction? But she had nothing to wear. We gave her an advance on her paycheck and told her to find the nicest dress she could afford."

Ray sat silent, taking all this in. Several points piqued his interest, not the least of which being just how much these ladies seemed to care for the young lady who worked for them. Mel was clearly more than a mere employee. She was family and so they were beyond outraged on her behalf.

The other thing was that she'd been trying to tell him right there on the sidewalk about how important the dress was, and he hadn't bothered to listen. He had just assumed that she'd hit her head and didn't know what she was talking about. He felt guilt wash over him anew.

"I still wish there was a way she could go." Greta shook her head with regret. "That awful man needs to know she don't give a damn about him and that she's still going to attend these events. With or without him."

A heavy silence settled over the room before Frannie broke

it with a clap of her hands. "You know, I got a great idea," she declared to her sister with no small display of excitement.

"What's that?"

"I know she don't have anything to wear, but if she can figure that out, I think Ray here should take her." She flashed a brilliant smile in his direction.

Greta gasped in agreement, nodding vehemently. "Ooh, excellent idea. Why, he'd make for the perfect date!"

Frannie turned to him, a mischievous sparkle in her eyes. "It's the least you can do. You did knock her on her keister."

Greta nodded solemnly next to him.

This unexpected turn proved to take him off guard. Ray tried to muster what exactly to say. He was spared the effort.

Mel chose that moment to step into the room. It was clear she'd heard the bulk of the conversation. She looked far from pleased.

Mel pulled out a chair and tried to clamp down on her horror. She could hardly believe what she'd heard. As much as she loved the Perlman sisters, sometimes they went just a tad too far. In this case, they'd traveled miles. The last thing she wanted from any man, let alone a man the likes of Ray, was some kind of sympathy date. And she'd be sure to tell both the ladies that as soon as she got them alone.

For now, she had to try to hide her mortification from their overnight guest.

"How do you feel, dear?" Greta asked.

"Fine. Just fine."

"The swelling seems to be going down," Frannie supplied.

Mel merely nodded. She risked a glance at Ray from the corner of her eye. To his credit, he looked equally uncomfortable.

Frannie stood suddenly. "Well, the two of us should get downstairs and start prepping for the weekend diner crowd." She rubbed Mel's shoulder. "There's still fresh coffee in the pot. You obviously have the day off."

Mel started to argue, but Frannie held up a hand to stop her. Greta piped up from across the table. "Don't even think about it. You rest and concentrate on healing. We can handle the diner today."

Mel nodded reluctantly as the two sisters left the kitchen to go get ready for their morning. It was hard to stay aggravated with those two.

Except now she was alone with Ray. The awkwardness hung like thick, dense fog in the air. If she was smart, she would have walked away and pretended not to hear anything that was said.

Of all the...

What would possess Greta and Frannie to suggest such a thing? She couldn't imagine what Ray must be feeling. They had put him in such a sufferable position.

To her surprise, he broke the silence with an apology. "I'm so terribly sorry, Mel."

Great, he was apologizing for not taking her up on the sisters' offer. Well, that got her hackles up. She wasn't the one who had asked him to take her to the ball.

"There's no need to apologize," she said, perhaps a little too curtly. "I really had no intention of attending that party anyway. I hardly need a date for an event I'm not going to. Not that I would have necessarily said yes." Now, why had she felt compelled to add that last bit?

Ray's jaw fell open. "Oh, I meant. I just—I should have listened when you were trying to tell me about your dress. I didn't realize you'd dropped your parcel."

Mel suddenly realized her mistake. He was simply offering a general apology. He wasn't even referring to the ball. She felt the color drain from her face from the embarrassment. If she could, she would have sunk through the floor and into another dimension. Never to be seen or heard from again. Talk about flattering oneself.

She cleared her throat, eager to change the subject. Although this next conversation was going to be only slightly less cringeworthy. "I was going to mention this last night, but you ended up staying the night."

"Yes?"

"I know you paid for my hospital visit. I have every intention of paying you back." Here was the tough part. "I, um, will just need to mail it to you. It's a bit hard to reimburse you right at this moment."

He immediately shook his head. "You don't need to worry about that."

"I insist. Please just let me know where I can mail a check as soon as I get a chance."

"I won't accept it, Mel."

She crossed her arms in front of her chest. "You don't understand. It's important to me that I pay back my debts." Unlike her ex-husband, she added silently.

He actually waved his hand in dismissal. "There really is no need."

No need? What part about her feeling uncomfortable about being indebted to him was he unable to comprehend? His next words gave her a clue.

"Given your circumstances, I don't want you to feel you owe me anything."

Mel felt the surge of ire prickle over her skin. She should have known. His meaning couldn't be clearer. Ray was no different than all the other wealthy people she'd known. Exactly like the ones who'd made her parents' lives so miserable.

"My circumstances? I certainly don't need your charity, if that's what you mean."

His eyes grew wide. "Of course not. I apologize. I meant no offense. I'm fluent, but English is my second language, after all. I simply meant that I feel responsible for you incurring the fees in the first place."

"But you weren't responsible. The cyclist was. And he's clearly not available, so the responsibility of my hospital bill is mine and mine alone."

He studied her through narrowed eyes. "Is it that important to you?"

"It is."

He gave her a slight nod of acquiescence. "Then I shall make sure to give you my contact information before I leave so that you can forward reimbursement at your convenience."

"Thank you."

Ray cleared his throat before continuing, "Also, if you'll allow me, I'd love to attend the Boston mayor's annual holiday ball as your escort."

CHAPTER THREE

MEL BLINKED AND gave her head a small shake, the action sending a pounding ache through her cheek straight up to her eye. In her shock, she'd forgotten how sore she was. But Ray had indeed just shocked her. Or maybe she hadn't actually heard him correctly. Maybe she really did have a serious head injury that was making her imagine things.

"I'm sorry. What did you just say?"

His lips curved into a small smile and Mel felt a knot tighten in the depths of her core. The man was sinfully handsome when he smiled. "I said I'd like to attend the ball with you."

She gently placed her coffee cup on the table in front of her. Oh, for heaven's sake. She couldn't wait to give Frannie and Greta a speaking-to. "You don't need to do that, Ray. You also didn't need to cover my expenses. And you didn't need to stay last night. You've done more than enough already. Is this because I insist on repaying you?" she asked. How much of a charity case did he think she was? Mel felt her anger rising once more.

But he shook his head. "Has nothing to do with that."

"The accident wasn't even your fault."

"This has nothing to do with the accident either."

"Of course it does. And I'm trying to tell you, you don't need to feel that you have to make anything up to me. Again, the accident yesterday was not your fault."

He leaned closer to her over the table. "But you don't understand. It would actually be something of a quid pro quo to take me to this ball. You'd actually be the one doing me a favor."

Okay, that settled it. She knew she was hearing things. In fact, she was probably still back in Frannie and Greta's guest room, soundly asleep. This was all a strange dream. Or maybe she'd accidentally taken too many painkillers. There was no way this could actually be happening. There was absolutely nothing someone like Mel could offer a man such as Ray. The idea that accompanying her to the ball would be a favor to *him* was ridiculous.

"Come again?"

"Allow me to explain," Ray continued at her confused look. "I'm here on business on behalf of the king of Verdovia. He is looking to acquire some property in the Boston area. The type of people attending an event that the mayor is throwing are precisely the type of people I'd like to have direct contact with."

"So you're saying you actually want to go? To meet local business people?"

He nodded. "Precisely. And in the process, we can do the two-birds-killing."

She was beginning to suspect they both had some kind of brain trauma. Then his meaning dawned on her. He was misstating the typical American idiom.

"You mean kill two birds with one stone?"

He smiled again, wider this time, causing Mel's toes to curl in her slippers. "Correct. Though I never did understand that expression. Who wants to kill even one bird, let alone two?"

She had to agree.

"In any case, you help me meet some of these local business people, and I'll make sure you stick your ex-husband."

She couldn't help it. She had to laugh. This was all so surreal.

It was like she was in a completely different reality than the one she'd woken up in yesterday morning. "You mean stick it to."

"That's right," he replied, responding to her laugh with one of his own.

For just a split second, she was tempted to say yes, that she'd do it. But then the ridiculousness of the whole idea made her pause. It was such a harebrained scheme. No one would believe Mel and someone like Ray were an actual couple. An unbidden image of the two of them dancing close, chest to chest, flashed in her mind. A curl of heat moved through the pit of her stomach before she squelched it. What a silly fantasy.

They clearly had nothing in common. Not that she would know with any real certainty, of course. She didn't know the man at all.

"What do you think?" Ray prompted.

"I think there's no way it would work. For one thing, we've barely met. You don't know a thing about me and I don't know a thing about you. I have no idea who you are. How would we even begin to explain why we're at such an event together?"

A sly twinkle appeared in his eye. "That's easy to fix. We should spend some time getting to know each other. Can I interest you in breakfast? I understand there's an excellent eating establishment very nearby. Right downstairs, as a matter of fact."

Greta seated them in a corner booth and handed him a large laminated menu. The giant smile on the older woman's face gave every bit the impression that she was beyond pleased at seeing the two of them at breakfast together. Though she did initially appear quite surprised.

Well, Ray had also surprised himself this morning. He'd had no idea that he'd intended to ask to take her to the mayor's ball until the words were actually leaving his mouth. Saleh would want to throttle him for such a foolish move. Oh, well, he'd worry about Saleh later. Ray's reasons were sound if one really thought about it. So he'd exaggerated his need to meet local business leaders, considering he already had the contacts in Boston that he needed. But Mel didn't know that or need to know that. And what harm would it do? What was so wrong about wanting to take her to the ball and hoping she'd have a good time there? Between the terrible accident yesterday and what he'd found out this morning about her past history, she could definitely use some fun, he figured. Even if it was only for a few hours.

Why he wanted to be the one to give that to her, he couldn't quite explain. He found himself wishing he'd met her under different circumstances, at a different time.

Right. He would have to be a completely different person for it to make an iota of difference. The reality was that he was the crown prince of Verdovia. He'd been groomed since birth to be beholden to rules and customs and to do what was best for the kingdom. He couldn't forget this trip was simply a temporary respite from all that.

This ball would give him a chance to do something different, out of the norm, if he attended as an associate of the royal family rather than as the prince. After all, wasn't that why he was in the United Sates? For one final adventure. This was a chance to attend a grand gala without all the pressures of being the Verdovian prince and heir to the throne.

He asked Mel to order for them both and she did so before Greta poured them some more coffee and then left their booth, her smile growing wider by the second.

"All right," Mel began once they were alone. "Tell me about yourself. Why don't you start with more about what you do for a living?"

Ray knew he had to tread carefully. He didn't want to lie to her, but he had to be careful to guard his true identity. Not only for his sake, but for hers, as well.

"You said something about acquiring real estate for the Verdovian royal family. Does that mean real estate is your main focus?" she asked.

Ray took a sip of his steamy beverage. He'd never had so much coffee in one sitting, but the Boston brew was strong and satisfying. "So to speak. I'm responsible for various duties in service of the king. He'd like to expand his American property holdings, particularly in metropolitan cities. He's been eyeing various high-end hotels in the Boston area. I volunteered to fly down here to scope out some prospects and perhaps make an agreement." Technically, he was telling her the complete truth.

Mel nodded. "I see. You're definitely a heavy hitter."

That wasn't an expression that made immediate sense to him. "You think I hit heavy?"

"Never mind. Do you have a family?"

"My parents and two younger sisters."

"What would you tell me about them?"

This part could get tricky if he wasn't careful. He hated being on the slim side of deceitful but what choice did he have? And in the overall scheme of things, what did it hurt that Mel didn't know he was a prince? In fact, he'd be glad to be able to forget the fact himself for just a brief moment in time.

"My father is a very busy man. Responsible for many people and lots of land. My mother is an accomplished musician who has studied the violin under some of Europe's masters and composes her own pieces."

Mel let out a low whistle. "Wow. That's quite a pedigree," she said in a near whisper. "How'd you end up picking such a high-profile career?"

He had to tread carefully answering that one. "It was chosen for me," he answered truthfully.

She lifted an eyebrow. "You mean the king chose you?"

He nodded. Again, it was the complete truth. "There were certain expectations made of me, being the only son of the family."

"Expectations?"

"Yes. It was a given that I would study business, that I would work in a career that led to the further wealth and prosperity of our island kingdom. Otherwise…"

The turn in conversation was throwing him off. Mel's questions brought up memories he hadn't given any consideration to in years.

She leaned farther toward him, over the table. "Otherwise what?"

He sighed, trying hard to clamp down on the years-old resentments that were suddenly resurfacing in a most unwelcome way. Mel stared at him with genuine curiosity shining in her eyes. He'd never discussed this aspect of his life with anyone before. Not really. No one had bothered to ask, because it was all such a moot point.

"Otherwise, it wasn't a career I would have chosen for myself. I was a bit of an athlete. Played striker during school and university. Got several recruitment offers from coaches at major football clubs. Though you would call it soccer here."

She blinked. "So wait. You turned down the opportunity of a lifetime because the king had other plans?"

Ray tapped the tip of his finger against the tabletop. "That about sums it up, yes."

She blew out a breath. "Wow. That's loyalty."

"Well, loyalty happens to be a quality that was hammered into me since birth."

"What about your sisters?" she asked him. "Are they held to such high standards, as well?"

Ray shook his head. "No. Being younger, they have the luxury of much fewer demands being made of them."

"Lucky for them. What are they like?"

"Well, both are quite trying. Completely unbearable brats," he told her. But he was unable to keep the tender smile off his face and his affection for his siblings out of his voice despite his words.

That earned him a small smile. "I'm guessing they're quite fortunate in having you as a brother." She sighed. "I don't have any siblings. I grew up an only child." Her tone suggested she was somewhat sad about the fact.

"That can have its advantages," he said, thinking of Saleh and the rather indulgent way the man's family treated him. "What of your parents?"

Mel looked away toward the small jukebox on the table, but not before he caught the small quiver in her chin. "I lost them about three years ago. They passed within months of each other."

"I'm so terribly sorry."

"Thank you for saying that."

"To lose them so close together must have been so difficult."

He couldn't help but reach for her hand across the table to comfort her. To his surprise and pleasure, she gripped his fingers, taking what he offered her.

"It was. My father got sick. There was nothing that could be done. It crushed my mom. She suffered a fatal cardiac event not long after." She let go of his fingers to brush away a tiny speck of a tear from the corner of her eye. "It was as if she couldn't go on without him. Her heart literally broke. They'd been together since they were teens."

Ray couldn't help but feel touched. To think of two people who had decided at such a young age that they cared for each other and stayed together throughout all those years. His own parents loved each other deeply, he knew. But their relationship had started out so ceremonial and preplanned. The same way his own marriage would begin.

The king and queen had worked hard to cultivate their affection into true love. He could only hope for as much for himself when the time came.

A realization dawned on him. Mel had been betrayed by the man she'd married within a couple of years of losing her parents. It was a wonder the woman could even smile or laugh.

He cleared his throat, trying to find a way to ask about her husband. But she was way ahead of him.

"You should probably know a little about my marriage."

"Aside from the knowledge that Frannie and Greta refer to him as 'that scoundrel,' you mean?"

This time the smile didn't quite reach her eyes. "I guess that would be one way to describe him."

"What happened?" He knew the man had left his wife for another woman. Somehow he'd also left Mel to fend for herself without much in the way of finances. He waited as Mel filled in some of the holes in the story.

She began slowly, softly, the hurt in her voice as clear as a Verdovian sunrise. "We met at school. At homecoming, our first year there. He was the most attentive and loving boyfriend. Very ambitious, knew from the beginning that he wanted to be a dentist. Husband material, you would think."

Ray simply waited as she spoke, not risking an interruption.

"When I lost my parents, I couldn't bear to live in their house. So I put it on the market. He invited me to live with him in his small apartment while he attended dental school. Eventually, he asked me to marry him. I'd just lost my whole family…"

She let the words trail off, but he could guess how the sentence might end. Mel had found herself suddenly alone, reeling from the pain of loss. A marriage proposal from the man she'd been seeing all through college had probably seemed like a gift.

"My folks' house netted a good amount in the sale. Plus they'd left me a modest yet impressive nest egg."

She drew in a shaky breath.

"Here's the part where I demonstrate my foolishness. Eric and I agreed that we would spend the money on his dentistry schooling after college graduation. That way we could start our lives together free of any school loans when he finished. I handed over all my savings and worked odd jobs here and there to cover any other costs while he attended classes and studied. When he was through, it was supposed to be my turn to continue on to a higher degree. I studied art history in my undergrad. Not a huge job market for those majors." She used one hand to motion around the restaurant. "Hence the waitressing gig. At the time, though, I was set on pursuing a teaching degree and maybe working as an elementary school art teacher. Once we had both achieved our dreams, I thought we would start a family." She said the last words on a wistful sigh.

Ray didn't need to hear the rest. What a foolish man her former husband was. Mel was quite a beautiful woman, even with the terrible degree of bruising on her face. Her injuries couldn't hide her strong, angular features, nor did they diminish the sparkling brightness of her jewel-green eyes.

From what he could tell, she was beautiful on the inside, too. She'd given herself fully to the man she'd made marriage vows to—albeit with some naïveté—to the point of generously granting him all the money she had. Only to be paid back with pure betrayal. Her friends obviously thought the world of her. To boot, she was a witty and engaging conversationalist. In fact, he wouldn't even be able to tell how long they'd been sitting in this booth, as time seemed to have stood still while they spoke.

"Frannie and Greta are sorely accurate in their description of this Eric, then. He must be a scoundrel and a complete fool to walk away from you."

Mel ducked her head shyly at the compliment, then tucked a strand of hair behind her ear. When she spoke again, she summoned a stronger tone. He hoped it was because his words had helped to bolster some of her confidence, even if only a little.

"I have to take some of the blame. I moved too quickly, was too anxious to be a member of a family again."

"I think you're being too hard on yourself."

"Enough of the sad details," she said. "Let's talk about other things."

"Such as?"

"What are your interests? Do you have any hobbies? What type of music do you like?"

She was trying valiantly to change the subject. He went along. For the next several minutes, they talked about everything from each other's favorite music to the type of cuisine they each preferred. Even after their food arrived, the conversation remained fluid and constant. It made no sense, given the short amount of time spent in each other's company, but Ray was beginning to feel as if he knew the young lady across him better than most of the people in his regular orbit.

And he was impressed. Something about her pulled to him unlike anyone else he'd ever encountered. She had a pure authentic quality that he'd been hard-pressed to find throughout his lifetime. Most people didn't act like themselves around the crown prince of Verdovia. Ray could count on one hand all the people in his life he felt he truly knew deep down.

As he thought of Saleh, Ray's phone went off again in his pocket. That had to be at least the tenth time. If Mel was aware of the incessant buzzing of his phone, she didn't let on. And Ray didn't bother to reply to Saleh's repeated calls. He'd already left a voice message for him this morning, letting his friend know that he'd be further delayed.

Besides, he was enjoying Mel's company too much to break away simply for Saleh's sake. The other man could wait.

"So just to be sure we make this official." He extended his hand out to her after an extended lull in their lively conversation. "May I please have the pleasure of accompanying you to the mayor's annual holiday ball?"

She let out a small laugh. "You know what? Why not?"

Ray held a hand to his chest in mock offense. "Well, that's certainly the least enthusiastic acceptance I've received from a lady. But I'll take it."

It surprised him how much he was looking forward to it. Even so, a twinge of guilt nagged at him for his duplicity. He'd give anything to completely come clean to Mel about who he was and what he was doing here in the city. Something shifted in his chest at the possibility of her finding out the truth and being disappointed in him. But he had no choice. He'd been groomed to do what was best for Verdovia and its people.

As Mel had phrased it earlier, though, the king had other plans for him.

CHAPTER FOUR

A LIGHT DUSTING of snow sprinkled the scenery outside the window by their table. Mel couldn't remember the last time she'd had such a lighthearted and fun conversation. Despite his classy demeanor, Ray had a way of putting her at ease. Plus, he seemed genuinely interested in what she had to say. He had to be a busy man, yet here he still sat as the morning grew later, happy to simply chat with her.

She motioned to Ray's plate. She'd been a little apprehensive ordering for him. He didn't strike her as the type who was used to diner cuisine. But he'd done a pretty nice job of clearing his plate. He must have liked it a little. "So, what did you think? I know baked beans first thing in the morning is an acquired taste. It's a Boston thing."

"Hence the name 'Boston Baked Beans'?"

"Correct."

"I definitely feel full. Not exactly a light meal."

She felt a flutter of disappointment in her stomach. Of course, she'd ordered the wrong thing. What did she know about what an international businessman would want for breakfast? She was completely out of her element around this man. And here she'd just agreed to attend a grand charity gala with him. Pretending she was his date. As if she could pull off such a thing.

"But it definitely—how do you Americans say it?—landed in the spot."

His mistake on the expression, along with a keen sense of relief, prompted a laugh out of her. "Hit the spot," she corrected.

"Yes, that's it. It definitely hit the spot."

His phone vibrated for the umpteenth time in his pocket. He'd been so good about not checking it, she was starting to feel guilty. He was here on a business trip, after all.

She also hadn't missed the lingering looks he'd received from all the female diner patrons, young and old alike. From the elderly ladies heading to their daily hair appointments to the young co-eds who attended the city's main university, located a shuttle ride away.

"I know you must have a lot to do. I probably shouldn't keep you much longer."

Ray sighed with clear resignation. "Unfortunately, there are some matters I should attend to." He started to reach for his pocket. "What do I owe for the breakfast?"

She held up a hand to stop him. "Please, employee privilege. It's on me."

"Are you sure? It's not going to come out of your wages or anything, is it?"

Not this again. It wasn't like she was a pauper. Just that she was trying to put some money away in order to finally get the advanced degree she'd always intended to study for. Before fate in the form of Eric Fuller had yanked that dream away from her.

"It so happens, Greta and Frannie consider free meals part of my employee package." Though she normally wouldn't have ordered this much food for herself over the course of a full week, let alone in one sitting. Something told her the two ladies didn't mind. Not judging by the immensely pleased smirks they kept sending in her direction when Ray wasn't looking.

"Well, thank you. I can't recall the last time I was treated to a meal by such a beautiful woman."

Whoa. This man was the very definition of *charming*. She

had no doubt that had to be one doozy of a fib. Beautiful women probably cooked for him all the time.

"But you're right, I should probably be going."

She nodded and started to pile the empty plates in the center of the table. Waitress habit.

"Can I walk you back upstairs?" Ray asked.

She wanted to decline. Lord knew he'd spent enough time with her already. But a very vocal part of her didn't want this morning to end. "I'd like that," she found herself admitting.

He stood and offered her his arm. She gently put her hand in the crook of his elbow after he helped her out of the booth. With a small wave of thanks to her two bosses, they proceeded toward the side door, which led to the stairway to the apartment.

"So I'll call you tomorrow, then?" Ray asked. "To discuss further details for Saturday night?"

"That sounds good. And I'll work on finding a plan B for what my attire will be."

His mouth furrowed into a frown, causing deep lines to crease his forehead. "I'd forgotten about that. Again, I'm so terribly sorry for not paying more attention as you were telling me about your parcel."

She let out a small laugh. "It's okay. It wasn't exactly a situation conducive to listening."

"Still, I feel like a cad."

"It's all right," she reassured him. "I'm sure Frannie and Greta won't mind if I do some rummaging in their closet. They might have something bordering on suitable."

He paused on the foot of the stairs right as she took the first step up. The difference in height brought them eye to eye, close enough that the scent of him tickled her nose, a woodsy, spicy scent as unique as he was.

"I'm afraid that won't do at all." His eyes looked genuinely troubled.

"It's all right. I'm very creative. And I'm a whiz with a sewing machine."

"That may be, but even creative geniuses need the necessary tools. Not to mention time. Something tells me you're not going to find anything appropriate in any closet up in that apartment." He pointed to the ceiling.

It wasn't like she had much choice. She'd already spent what little she could afford on the now-missing dress. All her closest friends had moved out of the New England area, so it wasn't as if she could borrow something. She was out of options. A jarring thought struck her. Could this be Ray's subtle way of trying to back out of taking her? But that made no sense. He was the one who had insisted on going in the first place. Could he have had a sudden change of heart?

"There's only one thing to do. I believe I owe you one formal ball gown, Miss Osmon. Are you up for some shopping? Perhaps tomorrow?"

Mel immediately shook her head. She absolutely could not accept such an offer. "I can't allow you to do that, Ray. Thank you, but no."

"Why not?"

She would think it was obvious. She couldn't allow herself to be this man's charity case. He'd done enough when he'd paid for her hospital bill, for goodness' sake. A sum she still had to figure out how to pay back. Further indebting herself to Ray was absolutely out of the question. She opened her mouth to tell him so.

He cut her off before she could begin. "What if I said it was more for me?"

A sharp gasp tore out of her throat. He had to be joking. That notion was so ridiculous, she actually bit back a laugh. He didn't look like the type, but what did she know? Looks could be deceiving. And she certainly wasn't one to judge.

He responded with a bark of laughter. "I see I've given you the wrong impression. I meant it would be for me in that if I'm trying to make an impression at this event with various people, I would prefer to have my date dressed for the occasion."

That certainly made sense, but still, essentially he would be buying her a dress. She cleared her throat, tried to focus on saying the right words without sounding offended. He really couldn't be faulted for the way he viewed the world. Not with all the material privilege he'd been afforded. She understood that better now after the conversation they'd just had together. Lord, it was hard to concentrate when those deep dark eyes were staring at her so close and so intently.

"If it makes you feel better, the gown can become the property of the royal family eventually. The queen is always looking for donated items to be auctioned off for various charities. I'll have it shipped straight to her afterward. I can pretend I was considerate enough to purchase it for that very purpose."

That cracked her resolve somewhat. Essentially, she'd only be borrowing a dress from him. Or more accurately, from the royal family of Verdovia. That was a bit more palatable, she supposed. Especially if in the end it would result in a charitable donation to a worthy cause.

Or maybe she was merely falling for his easy charm and finding ways to justify all that Ray was saying. Simply because she just couldn't think straight, given the way he was looking at her.

Saleh was already outside, idling on the curb in the SUV by the time Ray reluctantly left the diner. His friend did not look happy.

Ray opened the passenger door only to be greeted by a sigh of exasperation. No, definitely not happy in the least.

"After yesterday, maybe I should drive," Ray said before entering the car, just to further agitate him.

It worked. "You have not been answering your phone," Saleh said through gritted teeth.

"I was busy. The ladies treated me to an authentic New England breakfast. You should try it."

Saleh pulled into the street. "If only I hadn't already eaten a gourmet meal of warm scones made from scratch and fresh fruit accompanied by freshly squeezed orange juice at my five-star hotel."

Ray shrugged. "To each his own. I'm happy I got to try something a little different." Who would have thought that there were parts of the world where people had baked beans for breakfast?

"Is breakfast the only thing you tried?" Saleh removed his hands from the steering wheel long enough to place air quotes on the last word.

"What you're alluding to is preposterous, my friend. I simply wanted to make sure the young lady was all right after the accident. Nothing more."

Saleh seemed satisfied with that answer. "Great. Now that you've made sure, can we move on and forget all this unpleasantness of the accident?"

Ray shifted in his seat. "Well, not exactly."

Saleh's hands gripped the steering wheel so tightly, his knuckles whitened. "What exactly does 'not exactly' mean, my prince?"

"It means I may have made a commitment or two to Miss Osmon."

"Define these commitments, please."

"I'll be taking her shopping at some point."

"Shopping?"

"Yes. And, also, I'll be accompanying her to the Boston mayor's holiday charity ball on Saturday."

Saleh actually hit the brake, eliciting a loud honk from several cars behind them. "You will do what?"

"Perhaps I should indeed drive," Ray teased.

Saleh took a breath and then regained the appropriate speed. "If you don't mind my asking, what the hell has got into you?"

"I'm simply trying to enjoy Christmastime in Boston."

"There are countless ways you can do that, Prince Rayhan. Ways that don't involve risking embarrassment to Verdovia and the monarchy behind it."

"I've already committed. I fully intend to go."

"But why?" the other man asked, clearly at a loss. "Why would you ever risk your identity being discovered?"

Ray pinched the bridge of his nose. He didn't want to have to explain himself, not about this. The truth was he wasn't sure even how to explain it. "I'll be careful to avoid that, Saleh. I've decided the risk is worth it." Mel was worth it.

"I don't understand. Not even a little."

Ray sighed, searched for the perfect words. If he couldn't confide in Saleh, there really was no one else on this earth he could confide in. He had to try. "I'm not sure how to put it into words, Saleh. I felt something when I lifted her into my arms after she was hurt. The way she clung to me, shivering in my embrace. And since this morning, the more time I've spent with her, the more I want to. You must understand that. You must have felt that way before."

Saleh bit the inside of his cheek. "My wife and I were seven when we met."

Okay. Maybe Saleh wasn't the person who would understand. But he had to see where Ray was coming from.

"I just don't understand how this all came about. How in the world did you end up agreeing to attend a charity ball of all things? You always complain about having to frequent such affairs back home."

"It's a long story."

"We have a bit of a drive still."

Ray tried to summon the words that would make his friend understand. "It's different back home. There I'm the crown prince. Everyone who approaches me has some ulterior motive." Most especially the ladies, be it a photo opportunity or something more involved. "Or there's some pressing financial or property matter." Ray halted midspiel. He was bordering on being perilously close to poor-little-rich-prince territory.

"So we could have hit a few clubs in the evening," Saleh responded. "I don't see how any of that leads you to your decision to take this Mel to a holiday ball."

Ray sighed. "Also, her ex-husband will be attending. A very nasty man. She had no one to go with. She wants to prove to him that she's content without him."

Saleh nodded slowly, taking it in. "I see. So she has feelings for her former spouse."

"What? No. No, she doesn't." At least Ray didn't think she did.

"Then why would she care about what he thinks?"

It was a possibility Ray hadn't considered. He felt himself clench his fists at his sides. The idea rankled more than he would have thought.

Saleh continued, "I urge you to be careful. This is simply to be a brief reprieve, coupled with a business transaction. Do not forget you still have a duty to fulfill upon your return."

Ray turned to stare out the window. Traffic had slowed down and a light dusting of snow filled the air.

"I haven't forgotten."

CHAPTER FIVE

MEL DIDN'T COME to Newbury Street often. By far one of the ritziest neighborhoods in downtown Boston, it housed some of the city's most premier shops and restaurants, not to mention prime real estate. Many of New England's sports stars owned condos or apartments along the street. High-end sports cars, everything from Lamborghinis to classic Bentleys rolled down the pavement. Being December, the street was currently lined with faux mini Christmas trees, and big red bows adorned the old-fashioned streetlights.

When she did come out this way, it certainly wasn't to visit the type of boutique that she and Ray were about to enter. The type of boutique that always had at least one limousine sitting out front. Today there were two. And one sleek black freshly waxed town car.

When Ray had suggested going shopping, she'd fully expected that they'd be heading to one of the major department stores in Cambridge or somewhere in Downtown Crossing.

Instead his friend Sal had picked her up and then dropped both her and Ray off here, at one of the most elite shops in New England. A place she'd only heard of. The sort of place where a well-heeled, well-manicured associate greeted you at the door and led you toward a sitting area while offering coffee and refreshments.

As soon as they sat down on the plush cushioned sofa and the saleslady walked away, Mel turned to Ray. "This is not what I had in mind. It's totally wrong. We shouldn't be here," she whispered.

Ray lifted one eyebrow. "Oh? There are a couple of other spots that were recommended to me. This was just the first one on the street. Would you like to continue on to one of those stores?"

He was totally missing the point. "No, that's not what I mean."

"Then I don't understand."

"Look at this place. It has to be beyond pricey. This is the sort of place queens and princesses buy their attire."

Ray's face grew tight. Great. She had no doubt insulted him. Obviously he could afford such extravagance or whoever his acquaintance was wouldn't have recommended this to him.

"Please do not worry about the expense," he told her. "We have an agreement, remember?"

"But this is too much. I doubt I'd be able to afford so much as a scarf from a place like this." She looked down at her worn jeans and scruffy boots. It's a wonder the saleslady hadn't taken one look at her and shown her the door. If Ray wasn't by her side, no doubt she would have done exactly that.

"It's a good thing we are not in the market for a scarf today."

"You know what I mean, Ray."

"I see." He rubbed his chin, studied her. "Well, now that we're here, let's see what's available. Don't forget, we are not actually buying you a dress. It will go up for bidding at one of the queen's auctions, remember."

That was right. He had said that yesterday. When one considered it that way, under those conditions, it really didn't make sense for her to argue. Essentially, she was telling Ray how to spend his money and what to present to his queen. Who was she to do that? "I suppose it won't hurt to look."

As soon as she made the comment, the young lady who'd greeted them stepped back into the room.

"Miss, our designer has some items she would have you look at. Come right this way." With no small amount of trepidation, Mel followed her. She wasn't even sure quite how to act in a place like this. She certainly didn't feel dressed for the part. The slim, fashionable employee leading her down an elegant hall looked as if she'd walked straight off a fashion runway. Her tight-fitting pencil skirt and stiletto heels were more stylish than anything Mel owned.

The saleslady must have guessed at her nervousness. "Our designer is very nice. She'll love working with a figure such as yours. I'm sure there are several options that will look great on you."

Mel had the urge to give the other woman a hug. Her kind words were actually serving to settle her nerves, though not by much.

"Thank you."

"I think your boyfriend will be very pleased with the final choice."

"Oh, he's not my boyfriend. We're attending an event together. Just as friends. And I had nothing to wear because I lost my bag. It's why I have this black eye and all this bruising—" She forced herself to stop talking and to take a deep breath. Now she was just rambling. "I'm sorry. I'm not used to seeing a designer to shop for a dress. This is all so unreal." She probably shouldn't have added that last part. Now the poor lady was going to think she was addled in addition to being talkative.

The other woman turned to her with a smile. "Then I think you should pretend."

"I don't understand."

"Pretend you are used to it."

Mel gave her head a shake. "How do I do that?"

She shrugged an elegant shoulder. "Pretend you belong here, that you come here often. And pretend he is your boyfriend." She gave her a small wink before escorting her inside a large dressing room with wall-to-wall mirrors and a big standing rack off to the side. On it hung a dozen dazzling evening gowns that took her breath away. And even from a distance, she could see none of them had a price tag. This wasn't the type of place where tags were necessary. Customers who frequented a boutique like this one knew they could afford whatever the mystery price was.

"Deena will be in to see you in just a moment."

With that, the greeter turned on her high, thin heels and left. All in all, her suggestion wasn't a bad one. Why shouldn't Mel enjoy herself here? Something like this was never going to happen to her again. What if she really was here on one of her regular shopping trips? What if this wasn't a completely novel experience and she knew exactly what she was doing? There was nothing wrong with enjoying a little fantasy. Lord knew she could use a bit of it in her life these days.

And what if the charming, devilishly handsome man sitting in the other room, waiting for her, really was her boyfriend?

Ray stared at the spreadsheet full of figures on his tablet, but it was hard to focus. If someone had told him a week ago that he'd be sitting in a fashion boutique in the heart of Boston, waiting for a woman to pick a gown, he would have laughed out loud at the notion. Not that he was a stranger to being dragged out to shop. He did have two sisters and a mother, after all. In fact, one of his sisters had been the one to suggest this particular boutique. Those two knew the top fashion spots in most major cities. The only problem was, now he was being hounded via text and voice mail about why it was that he needed the recommendation in the first place. He could only hold them off for so long. He would have to come up with an adequate response. And soon.

He felt Mel enter the room more than he heard her. The air seemed to change around him. When he looked up and saw her, his breath caught in his throat. The slim tablet he held nearly slipped out of his hands. Even with a nasty purple bruise on her cheek, she was breathtakingly stunning in the red gown. The color seemed to bring out every one of her striking features to their full effect.

Mel took a hesitant step toward him. She gestured to her mid-section, indicating the gown she wore. "I wanted to see what you thought of this one," she said shyly.

He couldn't seem to get his tongue to work. He'd spent his life around some of the most beautiful women in the world. Everything from actresses to fashion models to noble ladies with royal titles. Yet he couldn't recall ever being this dumbstruck by a single one of them. What did that say about his sorry state of affairs?

"Do you think it will work?" Mel asked.

Think? Who would be able to think at such a moment? She could only be described as a vision, perhaps something out of a romantic fairy-tale movie. The dress hugged her curves in all the right places before flaring out ever so slightly below her hips. Strapless, it showed off the elegant curve of her necks and shoulders. And the color. A deep, rich red that not many women would be able to wear without the hue completely washing them out. But it only served to bring out the dark blue hint of her hair and accent the emerald green of her eyes. The fabric held a sheer hint of sparkle wherever the light hit it just so.

Since when had he become the type of man who noticed how an article of clothing brought out a woman's coloring or features?

He'd never felt such an urge to whistle in appreciation. Hardly suitable behavior for someone in his position.

What the hell, no one here actually knew who he was. He whistled.

A smile spread across Mel's face. "Does that mean you like it?"

Someone cleared their throat before Ray could answer. Sweet heavens, he hadn't even noticed the other woman in the room with them. She had a long tape measure hanging from her neck and gave him a knowing smile.

"This one was the top choice," the woman said. "If you're okay with it, we can start the necessary alterations."

He was way more than okay with it. That dress belonged on Mel; there was no way they were walking out of here without it.

"I think it's perfect," he answered the designer, but his gaze was fixated on Mel's face as she spoke. Even with the angry purple bruising along her cheek and jaw and the black eye, she was absolutely stunning.

"Are you sure?" Mel asked. "If you'd like, I can show you some of the other ones."

Ray shook his head. He couldn't be more sure. "I have no doubt you'll be the most beautiful woman to grace that ballroom with that dress."

Mel ducked her head, but not before he noticed the pink that blossomed across her cheeks. "Even with my black eye?"

"I've never seen anyone look so lovely while sporting one."

"I'll be in the dressing room when you're ready, miss," the designer offered before leaving them.

Ray found himself stepping closer to her. He gently rubbed his finger down her cheek, from the corner of her eye down to her chin. "Does it still hurt very much?"

She visibly shivered at his touch, but she didn't pull away. In fact, she turned her face ever so slightly into his caress. It would be so easy for him to lean in closer, to gently brush her lips with his. She smelled of jasmine and rose, an intoxicating mix of scents that reminded him of the grand gardens of his palatial home.

He'd been trying to deny it, but he'd been thinking about kissing her since having breakfast with her. Hell, maybe he'd been thinking about it much before that. He had no doubt she would respond if he did. It was clear on her face, by the quickening of her breathing, the flush in her cheeks.

The loud honk of a vehicle outside pulled him out of his musings and back to his senses. He couldn't forget how temporary all this was. In a few short days, he would return to Verdovia and to the future that awaited him. One full of duty and responsibility and that would include a woman he wasn't in love with.

Love. For all the earthly privileges he'd been granted by virtue of birth, he would never know the luxury of falling in love with the woman he was to marry. He just had to accept that. He couldn't get carried away with some kind of fantasy while here in the United States. And he absolutely could not lead Mel on romantically. He had nothing to offer her. Other than a fun night celebrating the holiday season, while also proving something to her ex. That was all this whole charade was about.

With great reluctance, he made himself step away.

"You should probably go get the dress fitted and altered. I'll go settle the charge."

It took her a moment to speak. When she did, her voice was shaky. "So I guess we're really doing this, huh?"

"What exactly are you referring to?"

"Going to the ball together. I mean, once the dress is purchased, there'll be no turning back, will there?"

Ray could only nod. He had a nagging suspicion that already there would be no turning back.

Not as far as he was concerned.

CHAPTER SIX

As far as transformations went, Mel figured she'd pulled off a major one. The image staring back at her in the mirror couldn't really be her. She hardly recognized the woman in the glass.

She was in Frannie and Greta's apartment. The two women had spent hours with her in order to get her ready. A lot of the time had been spent camouflaging the discolored bruising on her face. But the effect was amazing. These ladies knew how to use makeup to cover up flaws. Even upon close inspection, one would be hard-pressed to guess Mel had met the broadside of a set of steel handlebars only days before.

As far as soreness or pain, she was way too nervous to take any notice of it at the moment.

Her bosses had also helped do her hair in a classic updo at the crown of her head. Greta had found some sort of delicate silver strand that she'd discreetly woven around the curls. It only became visible when the light hit it just so. Exactly the way the silver accents in her dress did. Frannie had even managed to unearth some antique earrings that were studded with small diamond chips. They provided just enough sparkle to complement the overall look. All in all, the older women had done a notable job helping her prepare.

It was like having two fairy godmothers. Albeit very chatty

ones. They'd both gone on incessantly about how beautiful Mel looked, how she should act flirty with Ray in order to get under Eric's skin and because they thought Ray was the type of man who definitely warranted flirtatious behavior. Mel had just stood silently, listening. The butterflies in her stomach were wreaking havoc and made it hard to just breathe, let alone form a coherent sentence.

She was trying desperately not to think about all the ways this night could turn into a complete disaster. Someone could easily ask a fairly innocuous question that neither Ray nor she had an adequate answer to. They'd never even discussed what story to tell about how they'd met or how long the two of them had known each other. The whole scenario was ripe for embarrassing mistakes. If Eric ever found out this was all some elaborate pretend date merely to prove to him that she'd moved on, he'd never let Mel live it down.

His fiancée would also have an absolute field day with the knowledge. Not to mention the utter embarrassment it would cause if her other acquaintances found out.

"I believe your ride is here," Frannie declared, peeking around the curtain to look outside.

Greta joined her sister at the window. She let out a shriek of appreciation. "It's a stretch."

"Not just any stretch," Frannie corrected. "A Bentley of some sort."

Greta gave her sister's arm a gentle shove. "Like *you* would know what a Bentway looks like."

"Bentley! And I know more than you, obviously."

The butterflies in Mel's stomach turned into warring pigeons. He was here. And he'd gone all out apparently, hiring a stretch limo. He so didn't need to do that. She'd never been quite so spoiled by someone before—certainly not by a man. If she wasn't careful, this could all easily go to her head. There would be no recovering from that. She had to remind herself throughout the night how unreal all of it was, how temporary and short-lived it would all be. Tomorrow morning, she'd go back to being Mel. The woman who had no real plans for her future, nothing really to look forward to until she managed to get back on her feet somehow. A task she had no clue how to accomplish just yet.

Taking a steadying breath, she rubbed her hand down her midsection.

"How do I look?"

The sisters turned to her and their faces simultaneously broke into wide grins. Was that a tear in Greta's eye?

"Like a princess."

The buzzer rang just then. "I guess I should head downstairs."

"I say you make him wait a bit," Frannie declared. "In the diner. It's not often our fine establishment gets a chance to entertain such an elegant, handsome gentleman in a well-tailored tuxedo."

"Not often?" Greta countered. "More like never."

That comment earned her a scowl from her sister. Mel slowly shook her head. "I think I should just get down there, before I lose all my nerve and back out completely." It was a very real possibility at this point. She wasn't sure she could actually go through with this. The more she thought about it, the more implausible it all seemed.

"Not a chance we would let you do that," both sisters said in unison with obvious fear that she actually might do such a thing.

Mel willed her pulse to steady. Slowly, she made her high-heeled feet move to the door. Without giving herself a chance to chicken out, she yanked it open to step out into the stairway. Only to come face-to-face with Ray.

"I hope you don't mind. The street door was open so I made my way upstairs." He handed her a single red rose. "It matches the color of your dress."

Mel opened her mouth to thank him but wasn't able to. Her mouth and tongue didn't seem to want to work. They'd gone dry at the sight of him. The dark fabric of his jacket brought out the jet-black of his hair and eyes. The way the man looked in a tuxedo could drive a girl to sin.

What had she got herself into?

The woman was a stunner. Ray assisted Mel into the limousine waiting at the curb as the driver held the door open for them. He had no doubt he'd be the most envied man at this soiree from the moment they entered. If he thought she'd looked beautiful in the shop, the completed product was enough to take his breath away. He would have to find a way to thank his sisters for recommending the boutique; they had certainly come through.

He had half a mind to ask the limo driver to turn around, take them to an intimate restaurant instead, where he could have Mel all to himself. And if that didn't make him a selfish cad, he didn't know what would. He had no right to her, none whatsoever. By this time tomorrow, he'd be walking out of her life for good. A pang of some strange sensation struck through his core at the thought. A sensation he didn't want to examine.

Within moments, they were pulling up to the front doors of the Boston World Trade Center grand auditorium. The aromatic fishy smell of Boston Harbor greeted them as soon as they exited the car. An attendee in a jolly elf hat and curly-toed shoes greeted them as they entered through the massive glass doors.

Mel suddenly stopped in her tracks, bringing them both to a halt.

"Is something the matter?" She'd gone slightly pale under the bright ceiling lights of the lobby. The notes of a bouncy rendition of "Jingle Bells" could be heard from the ballroom.

"I just need a moment before we walk in there."

"Take your time."

"I know this is no time to get cold feet," she began. "But I'm nervous about all that could go wrong."

He took her gently by the elbow and led her away from the main lobby, to a more private area by a large indoor decorative fountain. "I know it's not easy right now, but why don't you try to relax and maybe even have a good time?" She really did look very nervous.

"I'll try but… Maybe we should have rehearsed a few things."

"Rehearsed?"

"What if someone asks how we met? What will we say? Or how long we've known each other. We haven't talked about any of those things."

Ray took in the tight set of Mel's mouth, the nervous quivering of her chin. He should have been more sensitive to her possible concerns under these circumstances. He hadn't really given any of it much thought himself. As prince of Verdovia, he was used to being questioned and spoken to everywhere he went. As a result, he'd grown masterful at the art of delivering nonanswers. Of course, someone like Mel wouldn't be able to respond so easily.

He gave her elbow a reassuring squeeze. "I find that under situations like these, the closer one sticks to the truth, the better."

She blinked at him. "The truth? You want to tell them the truth?"

"That's right. Just not all of it. Not in its entirety."

"I'm gonna need an example of what you mean."

"Well, for instance, if someone asks how long we've known each other, we can tell them we've only met very recently and are still getting to know one another."

The tightness around her eyes lessened ever so slightly. "Huh. And if they ask for details?"

"Leave that part up to me. I'll be able to come up with something."

That earned him a grateful nod. "What if they ask about how we met?" She thought for a moment and then answered her own question. "I know, I can tell them I was knocked off my feet before I'd barely laid eyes on you."

He gave her a small laugh. "Excellent. See, you'll do fine." He offered her his arm and motioned with his head toward the ballroom entrance. When she took it, her grasp was tight and shaky. Mel was not a woman accustomed to even the slightest deception. But some of the tension along her jawline had visibly eased. Her lips were no longer trembling. Now, if he could just get her to smile, she might actually look like someone about to attend a party.

He slowly walked her to the ballroom. The decor inside had been fashioned to look like Santa's workshop in the North Pole. Large replicas of wooden toys adorned various spots in the room. A running toy train traveled along a circular track hanging from the ceiling. Several more staffers dressed up as elves greeted and mingled with the guests as they entered. Large leafy poinsettias served as centerpieces on each table.

"How about we start with some Christmas punch?" he asked Mel as he led her toward a long buffet table with a huge glass punch bowl in the center. On either side was a tower of glass flutes.

"I'd like that."

Ray poured hers first and handed her the glass of the bubbly drink. After grabbing a glass for himself, he lifted it in a toast. "Shall we toast to the evening as it's about to start?"

She tapped the rim of her glass to his. To his happy surprise, a small smile had finally graced her lips.

"I really don't know how to thank you for this, Ray. For all of it. The dress, the limo. That was above and beyond."

"It's my pleasure." It surprised him how true that statement was. They'd only just arrived and already he was having fun and enjoying all of it: the bouncy music, the fun decor. Her company.

"I wish there was some way I could really thank you. Aside from a diner meal, that is," she added, clearly disturbed. Ray had no doubt that even now she was racking her brain to come up with ways to "repay" him somehow. The concept was clearly very important to her.

He wanted to rub his fingers over her mouth, to soften the tight set of her lips with his touch. He wished there was a way to explain that she didn't owe him a thing. "Look at it this way, you're helping me to enjoy Boston during Christmastime. If it wasn't for you, Sal and I would just be wandering around, doing the same boring old touristy stuff I've done before."

Complete with a droll official tour guide and the promise of hours-long business meetings afterward. No, Ray much preferred the anonymity he was currently enjoying. Not to mention the delight of Mel's company.

"You have no idea how refreshing this all is," he told her.

Before Mel could respond, a grinning elf dressed all in green jumped in front of them. She held her hand whimsically above Mel's head. In her grasp was a small plant of some sort.

Mistletoe.

"You know what this means," the young lady said with a cheery laugh.

A sudden blush appeared on Mel's skin. She looked at him with question. "You needn't—" But he wasn't listening.

Ray didn't hesitate as he set his drink down and leaned closer to Mel. As if he could stop himself. What kind of gentleman would he be if he didn't kiss her under the mistletoe at a Christmas party?

They were no longer in a crowded ballroom. Mel's vision narrowed like a tunnel on the man across from her, the man leaning toward her. Ray was about to kiss her, and nothing else in the world existed. Nothing and no one. Just the two of them.

How would he taste? What would his lips feel like against hers?

The reality was so much more than anything she could have imagined. Ray's lips were firm against hers, yet he kept the kiss gentle, like a soft caress against her mouth. He ran his knuckles softly down her cheek as he kissed her. She reached for him, ran her free hand along his chest and up to his shoulder. In response, he deepened the kiss. The taste of him nearly overwhelmed her.

But it was over all too soon. When Ray pulled away, the

look in his eyes almost knocked the breath from her. Desire. He wanted her; his gaze left no doubt. The knowledge had her off balance. He was looking at her like he was ready to carry her off to an empty room somewhere. Heaven help her, she would let him if he tried. She gulped in some much-needed air. The mistletoe-wielding elf had left, though neither one of them had even noticed the woman walk away. How long had they stood there kissing like a couple of hormonal teenagers?

"Mel." He said her name like a soft breeze, his breath still hot against her cheek. She found herself tilting her head toward him once more. As foolish as it was given where they were, she wanted him to kiss her again. Right here. Right now.

He didn't get a chance. A familiar baritone voice suddenly interrupted them.

"Melinda? Is that you?"

Her ex-husband stood less than a foot away, staring at her with his mouth agape. He looked quite surprised. And not at all happy. Neither did the woman standing next to him. Talley, his new fiancée.

"Eric, hello." Mel flashed a smile in Talley's direction. "Talley."

Eric unabashedly looked her up and down. "You look nice, Mel." It was a nice enough compliment, but the way he said it did not sound flattering in the least. His tone was one of surprise. Ray cleared his throat next to her.

"Excuse my manners," Mel began. "This is Ray Alsab. He's visiting Boston on business."

Talley was doing some perusing for herself as the men shook hands. She seemed to appreciate what she saw in Ray. But who wouldn't? The man looked like something out of *Billionaire Bachelors* magazine.

"Is that so?" Eric asked. "What kind of business would that be?"

"Real estate." Ray answered simply.

"Huh. What exactly do you do in real estate, Ray?"

Mel wanted to tell him that it was none of his business, and exactly where he could go with his questions. But Ray gave him a polite smile. "I work for the royal government of Verdovia. It's a small island nation in the Mediterranean, off the Greco-Turkish coast. His Majesty King Farood is looking to expand our US holdings, including in Boston. I've been charged with locating a suitable property and starting the negotiations on his behalf."

Eric's eyebrows rose up to near his hairline. He gave a quick shake of his head. "I'm sorry, how does someone in that line of work know Mel?"

The condescension in his voice was so thick, Mel wanted to throw her drink in Eric's face.

But her date merely chuckled. "We met purely by accident." Ray turned to her and gave her a conspiratorial wink, as if sharing a private joke only the two of them would understand. Her laughter in response was a genuine reaction. The masterful way Ray was handling her ex-husband was a talent to behold.

"We'll have to tell you about it sometime," he continued. He then took Mel's drink from her and set it on the table. "But right now, this lady owes me a dance. If you'll please excuse us."

Without waiting for a response, he gently took Mel by the hand and walked with her to the dance floor.

Talley's voice sounded loudly behind them. "I wouldn't mind a dance, Eric. Remember, you promised."

"Nicely done, sir," Mel giggled as she stepped into Ray's arms. The scent of his skin and the warmth of his breath against her cheek sent tiny bolts of lightning through her middle.

"He's still staring. At you. The way he looks at you..." He let his sentence trail off, his hand on her lower back as he led her across the dance floor.

Mel could hardly focus on the dance. She was still enjoying how he'd just handled Eric. But the grim set of Ray's lips and the hardness in his eyes left no question that he was upset. Interactions with her ex often had that effect on people.

"He's just arrogant. It's one of his defining traits."

He shook his head. "It's more than that. He looks at you like he still has some sort of claim," Ray bit out. "As if you still belong to him." His tone distinctly told her that he didn't like it. Not in the least.

Mel had never been much for dancing, but she could hold her own with the steps. Plus, she'd done her fair share of clubbing in her university days. Having Ray as her partner however was a whole new experience. She felt as if she was floating on clouds the way he moved her around the dance floor, perfectly in tune with whatever beat the current song carried.

"You're a man of many talents, aren't you? Quite the talented dancer."

He tilted his head to acknowledge her compliment. "I started taking lessons at a very young age. My parents were real sticklers about certain things they wanted me to be proficient at. It's expected of the pr—" He suddenly cut off whatever he was about to say.

Mel didn't bother to ask for clarification. Whatever the reason, he was the most fluid dance partner a woman could ask for. Whether classic ballroom dances or modern holiday music, he moved like a man who was comfortable with himself. As the kids who ate at the diner would say, the man had the rhythm and the moves.

The impact of the unpleasant encounter with Eric was slowly beginning to ebb, and she decided to throw herself into this experience fully. Remembering what the assistant in the store had told her helped. Sometimes it was all right just to pretend.

And it wasn't exactly difficult to do just that as she leaned into his length once a slower song had begun to play. He was lean and fit, the hard muscles of his chest firm and hard against hers. It took all her will to resist leaning her head against his shoulder and wrapping her arms around his neck.

And she couldn't help where her mind kept circling back to: the way he'd kissed her. Dear heavens, if the man kissed like that while out in public in front of a crowd of partygoers, what was he like in private? Something told her that, if they hadn't come to their senses, the kiss might very well have lasted much longer, leading to a thrilling experience full of passion. Her mind went there, to a picture of the two of them. Alone. Locked in a tight embrace, his body up against hers. His hands slowly moving along her skin. A shiver ran all the way from her spine down to the soles of her feet.

Stop it!

That train of thought served no purpose. The man lived thousands of miles away, never mind the fact that he was part of a whole different world. Women like her didn't date millionaire businessmen. She had him for this one evening, and she'd make the most of it before he walked out of her life for good.

But someone had other plans. Eric approached from the side and tapped Ray on the shoulder. "May I cut in?"

Ray gave Mel a questioning look, making sure to catch her eye before answering. Mel gave him a slight nod. If she knew anything about her ex, he wasn't going to take no for an answer, not easily anyway. The last thing she wanted was some sort of scene, even a small one. Ray didn't deserve that. And neither did she.

"I'll just go refresh our glasses," Ray told her before letting her out of his arms and walking to the beverage table. "Come find me when you're ready."

Reluctantly, she stepped into the other man's embrace, though she made sure to keep as good a distance as possible. "This was one of your favorite Christmas carols," Eric commented as soon as Ray was out of earshot. "I remember very well."

He remembered wrong. The song currently in play was "Blue Christmas," one she wasn't even terribly fond of. He was confusing it with one she did like, "White Christmas." She didn't bother to correct him. She just wanted this dance to be over.

It was ironic really, how this evening was supposed to be about proving something to the man who currently held her in his arms. But right now, she didn't even want to give him a moment of her attention. In fact, all of her attention was currently fully focused on the dark, enigmatic man, waiting alone for her by the punch bowl. A giddy sense of pride washed over her at the thought. Authentic date or not, Ray was here with her. She could hardly wait to be dancing in his arms again.

Though judging by the looks several ladies were throwing in his direction, he might not be alone for long.

"So is he your boyfriend?" Eric asked with characteristic disregard for any semblance of propriety.

"We are getting to know each other," she answered curtly.

"Right. Is that what you were doing when we first walked in? It looked like you were getting to know his face with your lips."

That was more than enough. "Honestly, Eric. I don't see how it's any of your business. We are divorced, remember?"

He winced ever so slightly. "Don't be that way, Mel. You know I still care about you. I don't want to see you get hurt."

"That's rich. Coming from you."

Eric let out a low whistle. "Harsh. But fair. You've grown a bit…let's say *harder*, in the past several months."

"I've had to grow in all sorts of ways since we parted."

"Just be careful, all right. That's all I'm saying." He glanced in Ray's direction. "Where's he from anyway? Exactly? *Vanderlia* doesn't ring a bell."

"Verdovia," she corrected. "We haven't really had a chance to discuss it." A sudden disquieting feeling blossomed in her chest. She really didn't know much about Ray's homeland. Why hadn't she thought to ask him more about where he was from?

"Why does it even matter, Eric?"

He shrugged. "Just trying to discover some more about your friend." He let go of her just long enough to depict air quotes as he said the last word. "He who's here to investigate potential properties and begin negotiations," he uttered the sentence in an exaggerated mimic of Ray's accent. Mel felt a surge of fury bolt through her core like lightning. Even for Eric, it was beyond the pale. Boorish and bordering on straight elitism.

"Are you actually making fun of the way he speaks?"

"Maybe."

Tears suddenly stung in her eyes. More than outrage, she felt an utter feeling of waste. How could she have given so much to this man? She wasn't even thinking of the money. She was thinking of her heart, of the years of her youth. He'd made it so clear repeatedly that he hadn't deserved any part of her. How had she not seen who he really was? She'd been so hurt, beyond broken, when he'd betrayed her with another woman and then left. Now she had to wonder if he hadn't done her an immense favor.

She pulled herself out of his grasp and took a steadying breath, trying to quell the shaking that had suddenly overtaken her. "I think I'm ready to go back to Ray now. I hope you and Talley have a great time tonight."

Turning on her heel, she left him standing alone on the dance floor. She wouldn't give him anything more, not even another minute of her time.

"You look like you could use some air," Ray suggested before she'd even come to a stop at his side. The grim expression in her eyes and the tight set of her lips told him her interaction with her ex-husband hadn't been all that pleasant. Not that he was surprised. He didn't appear to be a pleasant man in any way.

Which begged the question, how had someone like Mel ever ended up married to him in the first place? He was more curious about the answer than he had a right to be.

She nodded. "It's quite uncanny how well you know me after just a few days."

The comment was thrown out quite casually. But it gave him pause. The truth was, he *had* begun to read her, to pick up on her subtle vibes, the unspoken communications she allowed.

Right now, he knew she needed to get away for a few minutes. Out of this ballroom.

"But first—" She reached for the drink he held and downed it all at once.

"It went that well, huh?"

She linked her arm with his. "Let's go breathe some fishy Boston air."

Within moments they were outside, behind the building, both leaning on a cold metal railing, overlooking the harbor. She'd certainly been right about the fishy smell. He didn't mind. He'd grown up near the Mediterranean and Black Sea.

And the company he was with at least made the unpleasant stench worthwhile.

The air held a crisp chill but could be considered mild for this time of year. Still, he shrugged off his jacket and held it out to her.

She accepted with a grateful nod and hugged the fabric around her. She looked good wearing his coat.

Mel drew out a shaky breath as she stared out over the water. "Hard to believe I was ever that naive. To actually think he was good husband material."

"You trusted the wrong person, Mel. You're hardly the first person to do so." His words mocked him. After all, here he was leading her to trust *him*, as well. When he wasn't being straight with her about who he was, his very identity. The charade was beginning to tear him up inside. How much longer would he be able to keep up the pretense? Because the longer it went on, the guiltier he felt.

"I should have seen who he really was. I have no excuses. It was just so hard to be alone all of a sudden. All my friends have moved away since graduation. On to bigger and better things."

He couldn't help but reach for her hand; it fitted so easily into his. Her skin felt soft and smooth to the touch. "What about extended family?"

Her lips tightened. "There's no one I really keep in touch

with. Neither did my parents. It's been that way for as long as I can remember."

"Oh?"

"My father had no one. Grew up in foster homes. Got into quite a bit of trouble with the law before he grew up and turned his life around."

"That sounds quite commendable of him."

"Yeah. You'd think so. But his background is the reason my mother was estranged from her family. She came from a long line of Boston Brahmin blue bloods, who didn't approve of her marriage. They thought my father was only after her for their money. They never did come around. Not even decades of my parents being happy and committed could change their minds. Decades where neither one asked for a single penny."

Her declaration went a long way to explain her feelings about the hospital fee payment. No wonder she'd insisted on paying him back. It also explained her pushback and insistence on donating the dress, rather than keeping it.

"I never met any of them," she continued. "Supposedly, I have a grandmother and a few cousins scattered across the country."

He gave her hand a gentle squeeze. "I believe it's their loss for not having met you," he said with sincerity. It sounded so trite, but he wholeheartedly meant it.

"Thank you, Ray. I mean it. Thank you for all you've done tonight. And I'm sorry. I realize you haven't even had a chance to do any of the networking you had planned."

"I find myself caring less and less about that," he admitted.

She tilted her head and looked at him directly. "But it was your main reason for wanting to come."

"Not any longer."

She sucked in a short breath but didn't get a chance to respond. A commotion of laughter and singing from the plaza behind them drew both their attention. Several male voices were butchering a rendition of "Holly Jolly Christmas."

Ray turned to watch as about a dozen dancing men in Santa

suits poured out of a party van and walked into one of the sea-food restaurants.

He had to laugh at the sight. "You saw that, too, right? I haven't had too much of that champagne punch, have I?"

She gave him a playful smile and a sideways glance. "If it's the punch, then there's some strange ingredient in it that makes people see dancing Santas." She glanced at the jolly celebrators with a small laugh.

"Only in Boston, I guess."

She turned to face him directly. "You mentioned you wanted to experience the city, but not as a tourist. I may have an idea or two for you."

"Yeah? Consider me intrigued."

Ducking her chin, she hesitated before continuing, as if unsure. "If you have the time, I can show you some of the more interesting events and attractions. There's a lot to see and do this time of year."

He was more intrigued by the idea than he would have liked to admit. "Like my very own private tour guide?"

"Yes, it isn't much, but it would be a small thank-you on my behalf. For all that you've done to make this such a magical evening."

Ray knew he should turn her down, knew that accepting her offer would be the epitome of carelessness. Worse, he was being careless with someone who didn't deserve it in the least. Mel was still nursing her wounds from the way her marriage had dissolved and the heartless way her ex-husband had treated her. He couldn't risk damaging her heart any further by pursuing this charade any longer. This was supposed to be a onetime deal, just for one evening. To try to make up for the suffering and pain she'd endured after the accident he and Saleh had been indirectly responsible for.

But even as he made that argument to himself, he knew he couldn't turn down her offer. Not given the way she was looking at him right now, with expectation and—heaven help him—

longing. He couldn't bring himself to look into her deep green eyes, sparkling like jewelry in the moonlight, and pretend he wasn't interested in spending more time with her. He might very well hate himself for it later, and Saleh was sure to read him the riot act. The other man was already quite cross with him, to begin with, about this whole trip. And especially about attending this ball. But Ray couldn't bring himself to pass on the chance to spend just one more day in Mel's company. Damn the consequences.

"That's the best offer I've had in a long while," he answered after what he knew was too long of a pause. "I'd be honored if you'd show me around your great city."

CHAPTER SEVEN

"I DON'T SEE any frogs."

"You do realize it's mid-December, right?" Mel laughed at Ray's whimsical expression. He was clearly teasing her.

"I don't see any frozen frogs either."

"That's because they aren't here any longer. And if they were, they'd most definitely be frozen." She handed him the rented skates.

"But I thought you said we were going to a pond of frogs. Boston does have a very well-known aquarium."

"I figured you must have already been to the aquarium. And besides, they don't harbor any frogs there."

Okay. She obviously hadn't been very clear about exactly what they'd be doing. Mel had decided an authentic winter experience in Boston wouldn't be complete without a visit to the Frog Pond. It was the perfect afternoon for it: sunny and clear, with the temperature hovering just near freezing. Not a snowflake to be seen. She'd figured they could start their excursion with a fun hour or so of skating, then they would walk around the Common, Boston's large inner-city park, which housed the ice rink in the center.

"I said we'd be going to the Frog Pond."

"So where are the frogs?" he asked, wanting to know.

"They're gone. This used to be a swampy pond years ago. But now it's a famous Boston attraction. During the hot summer months, it's used as a splashing pool. In the winter, it turns into an ice-skating rink. I figured it would be fun to get some air and exercise."

"I see." He took the skates from her hands and followed her to a nearby park bench to put them on. "Well, this ought to be interesting."

An alarming thought occurred to her. "Please tell me you know how to skate."

He sat down and started to unlace his leather boots. "I could tell you that. But I'd be lying to you."

Mel would have kicked herself if she could. Why had she made such an assumption about a businessman from a Mediterranean island? She'd planned the whole day around this first excursion, neglecting to ask the most obvious question.

"Oh, no. I didn't realize. I'm so sor—"

He cut her off with a dismissive wave of her hand. "How difficult could it be? I'm very athletic, having played various sports since I could walk. I almost turned pro, remember?"

There was no hint of bragging or arrogance in his tone; he was simply stating a fact.

He motioned toward the rink with a jut of his chin. "If those tiny tots out there can do it, so can I."

Ray quickly proved he was a man of his word. After a couple of wobbly stumbles, where he managed to straighten himself just in time, he was able to smoothen his stride and even pick up some steam.

"Color me impressed," she told him as they circled around for the third time. That was all it took for Ray to complete a full pass around the rink without so much as a stumble. Just as he said, he'd been able to pick it up and had done so with a proficiency that defied logic. "I don't know if you're quite ready to a triple lutz in the center of the rink, but you seem to have got the hang of it."

He shrugged. "It's not all that different from skiing, really."

"Do you ski often?"

"Once or twice a year. My family owns an estate in the Swiss Alps."

Mel nearly lost her balance and toppled onto her face. An estate. In the Alps.

Not only was Ray a successful businessman in his own right—he would have to be to be working directly for the king of his nation—he came from the kind of family who owned estates. There was no doubt in her mind that there was probably more than just one.

Oh, yeah, she was so far out of her league, she might as well have taken a rocket ship to a different planet.

She was spared the need to respond when a group of school-age children carelessly barreled into her from the side. The impact sent her flying and threw her off balance. Unable to regain her footing, she braced herself for the impact of the hard ice. But it never came. Suddenly, a set of strong, hard arms reached around her middle to hold her steady.

"Whoa, there. Careful, love."

Love. Her heart pounded like a jackhammer in her chest, for reasons that had nothing to do with the startle of her near fall.

For countless moments, Mel allowed herself to just stand and indulge herself in the warmth of his arms, willing her pulse to slow. His breath was hot against her cheek. He hadn't bothered to shave or trim down his goatee this morning. The added length of facial hair only served to heighten his devilish handsomeness. She'd never been attracted to a man with a goatee before. On Ray, it was a complete turn-on. He managed to pull it off somehow in a sophisticated, classic sort of way.

"Thanks," she managed, gripping him below the shoulders for support. It was surprising that her tongue even functioned at the moment.

"Sure thing."

"I guess I should have thought this out more." In hindsight, ice-skating wasn't such a good idea, given that Ray hadn't even done it before and how disastrous it would be if she suffered another stumble. "Maybe I should have chosen a different activity."

He glanced down at her lips. "I'm very glad you did choose this. I'm enjoying it more than you can imagine."

She couldn't be misreading his double meaning. They were standing still in the outer ring of the rink, with other skaters whisking by them. The same group of kids skated by again and one of them snickered loudly as they passed. "Jeez, get a room."

Mel startled back to reality and reluctantly removed her hands from Ray's biceps. A quick glance around proved the kids weren't the only ones staring at them. An elderly couple skating together gave them subtle smiles as they went by.

How long had they been standing there that way? Obviously, it had been long enough to draw the attention of the other skaters.

"Just be careful," he said and slowly let go of her, but not before he tucked a stray strand of her hair under her knit cap. "We can't have you falling again. Not when your bruises appear to be healing so nicely."

She wanted to tell him it was too late. She was already off balance and falling in another, much more dangerous way.

They decided they'd had enough when the rink suddenly became too crowded as the afternoon wore on. Ray took Mel by the elbow and led her off the ice. In moments, they'd removed their skates and had settled on a park bench. Someone nearby had a portable speaker playing soulful R & B. Several middle school–age children ran around the park, pelting each other with snowballs.

All in all, it was one of the most relaxing and pleasurable mornings he'd spent. No one was paying the slightest attention to him, a rare experience where he was concerned. Mel sat next to him, tapping her leather-booted toe in tune with the music.

"Those kids have surprisingly good aim," he commented, watching one of the youngsters land a clumpy snowball directly on his friend's cheek. Mel laughed as the "victim" made an exaggerated show of falling dramatically to the snow-covered ground. After lying there for several seconds, the child spread out his arms and legs, then moved them up and down along the surface of the snow. He then stood and pointed at the snow angel he'd made, admiring his handiwork.

"I haven't made a snow angel in years," Mel stated, still watching the child.

"I haven't made one ever."

She turned to him with surprise clearly written on her expression. "You've never made a snow angel?" She sounded incredulous.

He shrugged. "We don't get that much snow in our part of the world. And when we're in the Alps, we're there to ski."

She stood suddenly, grabbing him by the arm and pulling him up with her. "Then today is the day we rectify that sad state of affairs."

Ray immediately started to protest. Anonymity was one thing, but he couldn't very well be frolicking on the ground, in the snow, like a playful tot. He planted his feet, grinding them both to a halt. "Uh, I don't think so."

Her smile faded. "Why not? You have to do it at least once in your lifetime! What better place than the snow-covered field of Boston Common?"

He gave her a playful tap on the nose. "Making a snow angel is just going to have to be an experience I'll have to forgo."

She rolled her eyes with exaggeration. "Fine, suit yourself."

To his surprise, she strolled farther out into the park and dropped to the ground. She then lay flat on her back. He could only watch as she proceeded to make an impressive snow angel herself.

Ray clapped as she finished and sat on her bottom. "That's how it's done."

He walked over, reached out his hand to help her up.

And realized too late her sneaky intention. With surprising strength, she pulled him down to the ground with her.

"Now that you're down here, you may as well make one, too," she told him with a silly wiggle of her eyebrows.

What the hell? Ray obliged and earned a boisterous laugh for his efforts. By the time they stood, they were both laughing like children.

Suddenly, Mel's smile faltered and her eyes grew serious. She looked directly at him. "You didn't grow up like most boys, did you? Making snow angels and throwing snowballs at friends."

Her question gave him pause. In many ways, he had been a typical child. But in so many other aspects, he absolutely had not. "Yes. And no."

"What does that mean?"

"It means I had something of a very structured upbringing."

She studied him through narrowed eyes. "That sounds like you never got in any kind of trouble."

He shook his head. "On the contrary. I most definitely did."

"Tell me."

Ray brushed some of the snow off his coat as he gathered the memories. "Well, there was the time during my fifth birthday party when an animal act was brought in as the entertainment."

"What happened?"

"I insisted on handling the animals." Of course, he was allowed to. People didn't often turn down the request of the crown prince, even as a child.

"That doesn't sound so bad."

He bit back a smile at the memory. "There's more. See, I didn't like how the poor creatures were confined, so I set them free. Just let them loose in the garden. Several reptiles and some type of rodent."

Mel clapped a hand to her mouth and giggled at his words. Ray couldn't bring himself to laugh, for he vividly recalled what had happened in the immediate aftermath.

His father had pulled him into his office that evening as soon as he'd arrived home from a UN summit. Ray distinctly remembered that event as his first lesson on what it meant to be a prince. He was expected to be different from all the other children, to never make any mistakes. To never break the rules. He would always be held to a higher standard, as the world would always be watching him. It was a lesson that had stayed with him throughout the years. On the rare occasions he'd forgotten, the repercussions had been swift and great.

"What about as a teen?" Mel asked, breaking into his thoughts.

The memory that question brought forth was much less laughable. "I got into a rather nasty fistfight on the field, during one particularly heated ball game. Walked away with a shiner that could compete with the one you've recently been sporting."

Mel bit her lip with concern.

"But you should have seen the other guy," he added with a wink.

Again, he wouldn't tell her the details—that the mishap had led to a near-international incident, where diplomats were called in to discuss at great length what had essentially been a typical teen tantrum over a bad play. As expected, the press had gone into a frenzy, with countless speculative articles about the king's lack of control over his only son and whether said son even had what it would take to be a competent king when the time came. His father had been less than happy with him. Worse, he'd been sorely disappointed. Yet another memorable lesson that had stayed with Ray over the years. Suddenly, the mood in the air had turned heavy and solemn.

"Come," Mel said after a silent pause, offering him her hand. "I think we could both use some hot cocoa."

He took her hand and followed where she led.

He hadn't been quite sure what to expect out of today. But Ray could readily admit it had been one of the most enjoyable days he'd ever spent. Now he stood next to Mel on the second level of Faneuil Hall, one of the city's better-known attractions.

"So this is Faneuil, then," he asked. He'd heard about the area several times during his research on Boston and on previous visits to Massachusetts. But he'd never actually had the chance to visit for himself. Until now.

"The one and only," Mel answered with a proud smile.

Ray let his gaze wander. He'd be hard-pressed to describe the place. It was an outdoor plaza of sorts, with countless shops, restaurants and pubs, all in one center area. But it was so much more. Several acts of entertainment performed throughout the square while adoring crowds clapped and cheered. Music sounded from every corner, some of it coming from live bands and some from state-of-the-art sound systems in the various establishments. Holiday decorations adorned the various shop fronts and streetlights. The place was full of activity and energy.

He and Mel had the perfect view of it all from above, where they stood.

"You're in for a real treat soon," Mel announced. "And we're in the perfect spot to see it." Even as she spoke, several people began to climb up the concrete steps to join them. Before long, a notable crowd had gathered.

"What kind of treat?"

She motioned with her chin toward the massive, tall fir tree standing on the first level. Even at this height, they had to look up to see the top of it. "They're about to light it in a few minutes. As soon as it gets dark."

They waited with patient silence as the night grew darker. Suddenly, the tree lit up. It had to have been decorated with a million lights and shiny ornaments.

Several observers cheered and clapped. Mel placed her fingers in her mouth and let out an impressive whistle.

"So what do you think?" she asked him after they'd simply stared and admired the sight for several moments. "I know Faneuil can be a bit overwhelming for some people."

Quite the opposite—he'd found it exciting and invigorating. "Believe it or not, it reminds me of Verdovia," he told her.

She glanced at him sideways, not tearing her gaze from the majestic sight of the tree as lights blinked and pulsed on its branches. "Yeah? How so?"

"In many ways, actually. We're a small country but a very diverse people. Given where we're located in the Mediterranean, throughout the years, settlers from many different cultures have relocated to call it home. From Central Europe to Eastern Europe to the Middle East. And many more." He motioned toward the lower level. "Similarly, there appears to be all sorts of different cultures represented here. I hear foreign music in addition to the English Christmas carols and American pop music. And it's obvious there are visitors here from all over the world."

Her eyes narrowed on the scene below in consideration of what he'd just told her. "I never thought of it that way. But you're right. I guess I just sort of took it all for granted. I've been coming here since I was a little girl."

"From now on, when you come, you can think about how it's a mini version of my home country."

Her smile faltered, her expression growing wistful. "Maybe I'll be able to see it someday."

Taking her hands, he turned her toward him. "I'd like that very much. To be able to show you all the beauty and wonder of my nation. The same way you've so graciously shown me around Boston."

"That'd be lovely, Ray. Really."

A wayward snowflake appeared out of nowhere and landed softly on her nose. Several more quickly followed, and before long, a steady flurry of snow filled the air.

Thick white flakes landed in Mel's hair, covering her dark curls. Ray inadvertently reached for her hair and brushed the snow off with his leathered fingers. He heard her sharp intake of breath at the contact.

Then she leaned in and surprised him with a kiss.

Stunned, he only hesitated for a moment. He wasn't made of stone, after all. Moving his hands to the small of her waist, he pulled her in closer, tight up against his length. She tasted like strawberries and the sweetest nectar.

He let her set the pace—she'd initiated the kiss, after all—letting her explore with her lips and tongue. And when she deepened the kiss and leaned in even tighter against him, he couldn't help but groan out loud. The touch and feel of her was wreaking havoc on his senses.

This was no way to behave. They were in public, for heaven's sake. What was it about this particular woman that had him behaving so irrationally? This was the second time in one day he'd wanted to ravage her in the plain view of countless strangers.

Grasping a strand of sanity, he forced himself to break the kiss and let her go. Like earlier at the ice-skating rink, they'd managed to attract the attention of observers.

"Mel."

She squeezed her eyes shut and gave a shake of her head. "I know. I'm sorry, I shouldn't have kissed you in public like that. Again. I can't seem to help myself."

"I believe the first kiss was my doing. But I had a mistletoe excuse."

She rubbed her mouth with the back of her hand and it took all his will not to take those lips with his own again. He really had to get a grip.

"Why don't we grab a bite?" he suggested, to somehow change the momentum and where this whole scenario might very well be headed: with him taking Mel behind one of the buildings and plundering her mouth with his. "The least I can do after you've entertained me all day is buy you dinner."

"I know just the place."

Within moments, they were down the stairs and seated at an outdoor eatery with numerous heat lamps to ward off the chill. Mel had chosen an authentic New England–style pub with raw shellfish and steaming bowls of clam chowder for them to start with.

Ray took one spoonful of the rich, creamy concoction and sighed with pleasure. He'd had seafood chowder before, but this was a whole new taste experience.

"This chowder is delicious," he told her.

"It's pronounced *chowdah* around here," she corrected him with a small laugh.

"Then this *chowdah* is delicious." Only, with his accent, he couldn't quite achieve the intended effect. The word came out sounding exactly as it was spelled.

Mel laughed at his attempt and then nodded in agreement. "It's very good. But I have to tell you, it doesn't compare to the chowder they serve in the town where I grew up. They somehow make it taste just a bit more home-style there. Must be the small-town charm that adds some extra flavor."

"You didn't grow up in the city?"

She shook her head. "No. About forty minutes away, in a coastal town called Newford. I moved to Boston for school and just ended up staying. Things didn't exactly turn out the way I'd intended after graduation, though."

The spectacle of her failed marriage hung unspoken in the air.

"Tell me more about your hometown," Ray prompted, in an attempt to steer the conversation from that very loaded topic.

A pleasant smile spread across her lips. "It was a wonderful place to grow up. Overlooking the ocean. Some of the small islands off the coast are so close, you can swim to them right from the town harbor. Full of artists and writers and creative free spirits."

"It sounds utterly charming."

She nodded with a look of pride. "It is. And we can boast that we have more art studios per block than most New England towns. One of which I could call a second home during my teen years, given all the hours I spent there."

That took him back a bit. "Really? At an art studio?" There was so much about her he didn't know.

"We had a neighbor who was a world-renowned sculptor. A master at creating magical pieces, using everything from clay to blown glass. He took me under his wing for a while to teach me. Said I had a real talent."

"Why haven't you pursued it? Aside from studying art history in college, that is."

She shrugged, her eyes softening. "I thought about maybe creating some pieces, to show in one of the galleries back home, if any of the owners liked them. But life got in the way."

Ray fought the urge to pull her chair closer to him and drape his arm around her. Her dreams had been crushed through no fault of her own. "Do you still see this sculptor who mentored you? Maybe he can offer some advice on how to take it up again."

Mel set her spoon down into her bowl. "Unfortunately, he passed away. These days, if I go back, it's only to visit an old friend of my mom's. She runs the only bed-and-breakfast in town. They also serve a chowder that would knock your socks off."

"I've never actually stayed at one of those. I hear they're quite charming."

"I'm not surprised you haven't frequented one. They're a much smaller version of the grand hotels your king probably likes to invest in. Tourists like them for the rustic feel while they're in town. It's meant to feel more like you're staying with family."

He was definitely intrigued by the prospect. A hotel stay that felt more like a family home. He would have to find time to stay in one on his next visit to New England. A pang of sorrow shot through his chest at that thought. He might very well be a married man at that time, unless he could convince the king otherwise. The idea made him lean closer to Mel over the table. He gripped his spoon tighter in order to keep from reaching for her.

Mel continued, "In fact, I should probably check in on her. The owner, I mean. Myrna has been struggling to make ends meet recently. She's on the market for a buyer or investor who'll take it off her hands and just let her run the place."

Ray's interest suddenly grew. The whole concept definitely called to him. But it wasn't the type of property the royal family of Verdovia would typically even take the time to look at. They'd never invested in anything smaller than an internationally known hotel in a high-end district of a major metropolitan city.

Still, he couldn't help but feel an odd curiosity about the possibilities. And wasn't he officially part of the royal family, who made such decisions?

CHAPTER EIGHT

"Whatever you've been up to these past couple of days, I hope you've got it out of your system."

"And a good morning to you, as well." Ray flashed Saleh a wide smile as the two men sat down for coffee the next morning in the main restaurant of their hotel. Not even his friend's sullen attitude could dampen his bright mood this morning. Between the way he'd enjoyed himself yesterday with Mel and the decision he'd made upon awakening this morning, he was simply too content.

"Must I remind you that we're only here for a few more days and we haven't even inspected any of the hotels we've come out all this way to visit?" Saleh asked, pouring way too much cream into his mug. He chased it with three heaping spoonfuls of sugar, then stirred. How the man stayed so slim was a mystery.

"You're right, of course," Ray agreed. "At this point, we should probably split up the tasks at hand. Why don't you go visit two of the hotels on the list? I believe a couple of them are within a city block of each other."

"And what will you be doing, Rayhan? If you don't mind my asking," he added the last part in a tone dripping with sarcasm.

"I'll be visiting a prospect myself, in fact, if all goes as planned."

Saleh released a sigh of relief. "Better late than never, I guess, that you've finally come to your senses. Which one of those on the list would you prefer to check out?"

"It isn't on our list."

Saleh lifted an eyebrow in question. "Oh? Did you hear of yet another Boston hotel which may be looking for a buyout?"

"Not exactly. Though the place I have in mind is indeed interested in locating a buyer. Or so I'm told." He couldn't wait to run the idea by Mel, curious as to what her exact reaction might be. He hoped she'd feel as enthusiastic about the prospect as he did.

Saleh studied his face, as if missing a clue that might be found in Ray's facial features. "I don't understand."

Ray took a bite of his toast before answering, though he wasn't terribly hungry after the large dinner he and Mel had shared the evening before. He'd definitely overindulged. The woman certainly knew what he might like to eat. In fact, after just a few short conversations, she already knew more about him than most people he'd call friends or family. He'd never quite divulged so much of himself to anyone before. Mel had a way of making him feel comfortable enough to talk about himself—his hopes, the dreams he'd once had. Around her, he felt more man and less prince. Definitely a new experience. He knew better than to try to explain any of it to the man sitting across the table. Best friend or not, he wouldn't understand. Ray couldn't quite entirely grasp what was happening himself.

"I'm considering, perhaps, looking at smaller options," he answered Saleh. "Something different than the grand international hotel chains."

"Smaller? How much smaller?"

"So small that the guests feel like they're actually staying with family."

Back to reality. Mel smoothed down the skirt of her waitress uniform and tried to force thoughts of Ray and the time they'd spent together yesterday out of her mind. Her shift would be starting in a few minutes and she had to try to focus. Customers really didn't like it when their orders were delayed, or if they mistakenly got the wrong dish.

It was time to pull her head out of the clouds. She'd done enough pretending these past few days.

"You look different," Greta declared, studying her up and down.

"Probably because my face is almost completely healed."

Frannie jumped in as she approached them from behind the counter. "No, that's not it. Greta's right. You look more—I don't know—sparkly."

Mel had to laugh. What in the world did she mean by that? "Sparkly?"

Both the older ladies nodded in unison. "Yeah, like there's more brightness in your eyes. Your skin is all aglow. You even had a spring in your step when you walked in. Can't say I've seen you do that before."

Frannie suddenly gasped and slapped her hand across her mouth. "Dear sweetmeat! You said you were spending the day with that businessman. Please tell me you spent the night with him, too!"

Mel looked around her in horror. Frannie's statement had not been made in a low voice. Neither woman seemed to possess one.

"Of course not! We simply did some skating, walked for a bit around the Common and then had a meal together." Try as she might, Mel knew she couldn't quite keep the dreaminess out of her voice. For the whole day had been just that…something out of a dream. "He dropped me off at my apartment at the end of the evening like a true gentleman."

Greta humphed in disappointment. "Damn. That's too bad."

"You two know me better than that."

"We know you're due for some fun and excitement. You deserve it."

"And that you're not an old maid," the other sister interjected. "Not that there's anything wrong with being one."

"I think you should have seduced him!" Again, the outrageous statement was made in a booming, loud voice. Mel felt a blush creep into her cheeks. Though she couldn't be sure if it was from embarrassment or the notion of seducing Ray. A stream of images popped into her head that spread heat deep within her core, intensifying into a hot fire as she recalled how brazenly she'd kissed him on the walkway overlooking the tree above Faneuil.

"He's leaving in a few days, Greta."

Greta waved a hand in dismissal. "Lots of people have long-distance relationships. Think of how much you'll miss each other till you can see one another again."

"Thousands of miles away, along the Mediterranean coast, is quite a long distance," she countered, fighting back a sudden unexpected and unwelcome sting of tears. Just like her to be foolish enough to go and fall so hard for a man who didn't even live on the same continent.

Not that it really mattered. Where they each lived was beyond the concept of a moot point. The fantasy of Ray was all well and good. But they weren't the type of people who would ever end up together in the long term.

Her family had never owned a European estate. What a laugh. She could barely afford the rent in her small studio apartment on the south side. She could only imagine how elegant and sophisticated Ray's parents and sisters had to be. Mel didn't even want to speculate about what they might think of someone like her. Look at the way her own father had been treated by his wife's family.

"So have some fun in the meantime," Greta argued. "He's still got a few more days in the States, you said."

"And I repeat, you know me better than that. I'm not exactly the type who can indulge in a torrid and quick affair." Though if any man could tempt her into doing so, it would most certainly be the charming man with the brooding Mediterranean looks who'd haunted her dreams all last night.

"Then maybe he should be the one who tries to seduce you," Frannie declared, as if she'd come up with the entire solution to the whole issue. Mel could only sigh. They clearly had no intention of letting the matter drop. She really did have to keep repeating herself when it came to the Perlman sisters.

"I already mentioned he was a gentleman."

The pocket of her uniform suddenly lit up as her phone vibrated with an incoming call.

Her heart jumped to her throat when she saw whose number popped up on the screen. It was as if her thoughts had conjured him. With shaky fingers, she slid the icon to answer.

The nerves along her skin prickled with excitement when she heard his deep, silky voice. Oh, yeah, she had it pretty bad.

And had no idea what to do about it.

"I wanted to thank you again for taking me to so many wonderful spots yesterday." Ray's voice sounded smooth and rich over the tiny speaker.

Mel had to suppress the shudder of giddiness that washed over her. She realized just how anxious she'd been that he might not reach out to her again, despite his assurances last night that he'd be in touch before leaving the United States. "I had a lot of fun, too," she said quietly into the phone. Greta and Frannie were unabashedly leaning over the counter to get close enough to hear her end of the conversation.

"Believe it or not, I'm calling to ask you for yet another favor," Ray said, surprising her. "One only you would be able to help me with."

"Of course," she answered immediately, and then realized that she should at least inquire what he was asking of her. "Um. What kind of favor?"

"You gave me an idea last night. One I'd like to pursue further to see if it might be worthwhile."

For the life of her, she couldn't imagine what he might be

referring to. Was she forgetting a crucial part of the evening? Highly unlikely, considering she'd run every moment spent with him over and over in her mind since he'd left her. Every moment they'd spent together had replayed in her mind like mini movies during her sleepless night. She'd felt light-headed and euphoric, and she hadn't even had anything to drink last night.

"I did?"

"Yes. Are you free later today?"

For him? Most certainly. And it wasn't like she had an active social life to begin with. She could hardly wait to hear what he had in mind. "My shift ends at three today, after the lunch crowd. Will that work?" It was impossible to keep the joy and excitement out of her voice. Something about this man wreaked havoc on her emotions.

"It does. Perfectly."

Mel's heart pounded like a jackhammer in her chest. She'd be spending the afternoon with him. The next few hours couldn't go by fast enough.

"I'm glad. But I have to ask. What is this idea I gave you?"

She could hardly believe her ears as he explained. Her off-the-cuff remark about the bed-and-breakfast in Newford had apparently had more of an impact on him than she would have guessed. She'd actually forgotten all about it. Ray's proposal sent a thrill down her spine. By the time she slid her phone back into her pocket, her excitement was downright tangible.

"Well, what was that all about?" Frannie demanded to know. "From the dreamy look on your face, I'd say that was him calling. Tell us what he said."

"Yeah. Must have been something good," Greta added. "You look like you're about ready to jump out of your skin."

All in all, it was a pretty apt description.

"Why, Melinda Lucille Osmon, let me take a look at you! How long has it been, sweetie?"

Ray watched with amusement as a plump, short older woman

with snow-white hair in a bun on top her head came around the check-in counter and took Mel's face into her palms. "Hi, Myrna. It's been way too long, I'd say."

"Now, why have you been such a stranger, young lady?"

"I have no excuses. I can only apologize."

"Well, all that matters is that you're here now. Will you be staying a few days?"

It was endearing how many little old ladies Mel had in her life who seemed to absolutely adore her. She might not have any more living blood relatives, but she seemed to have true family in the form of close friends. Ray wondered if she saw it that way.

Right now, this particular friend was making a heroic effort to avoid glancing in his direction. No doubt waiting for Mel to introduce him and divulge what they were doing there together on the spur of the moment.

Not too hard to guess what conclusion the woman had jumped to about the two of them arriving at the bed-and-breakfast together. The situation was bound to be tricky. Both he and Mel had agreed on the ride over that they wouldn't mention Ray's intentions about a potential purchase. Mel didn't want to get the other woman's hopes up in case none of it came to fruition.

Mel hesitantly cleared her throat and motioned to him with her hand. "This is a friend of mine, Myrna. His name is Ray Alsab. He's traveling from overseas on business. He wanted to see an authentic bed-and-breakfast before leaving the States."

"Why, I'm honored that mine is the one he'll be seeing," the other woman said with a polite smile.

Ray reached over and took her hand and then planted a small kiss on the back, as was customary in his country when meeting older women. "The honor is all mine, ma'am."

Myrna actually fanned herself. "Well, you two happen to have great timing. It's the night of the annual town Christmas jamboree. To be held right here in our main room."

Ray gave Mel a questioning look. "It's a yearly get-together for the whole town," Mel began to explain. "With plenty of food, drink and dancing."

"Another ball, then?"

Myrna giggled next to him. "Oh, no. It's most definitely not a ball. Nothing like it. Much less fancy. Just some good old-fashioned food and fun among neighbors." She turned to Mel, her expression quite serious. "I hope you two can stay."

This time it was Mel's turn to give him a questioning look. She wasn't going to answer without making sure it was all right with him. *Why not*, Ray thought. After all, the whole reason he was here was to observe the workings and attraction of a small-town lodge. To see if it might make for a worthwhile investment.

Yeah, right. And it had absolutely nothing to do with how it gave him another excuse to spend some more time with Mel. He gave her a slight nod of agreement.

"We'd love to stay and attend, Myrna. Thank you."

Myrna clasped her hands in front of her chest. "Excellent. Festivities start at seven o'clock sharp."

"We'll be there."

"I'm so happy you're here. Now, let's get you two something to eat." She laid a hand on Mel's shoulder and started leading her down the hall. "Ruby's thrown together a mouthwatering beef stew, perfect for the cold evening." She turned to Ray. "Ruby's our head cook. She does a fine job."

Ray politely nodded, but his mind was far from any thoughts of food. No, there was only one thought that popped into his head as he followed the two women into a dining area. That somehow he was lucky enough to get another chance to dance with Mel.

"So, what do you think of the place?" Mel asked him as he entered the main dining room of the Newford Inn with her at precisely 7:00 p.m.

"It's quite charming," Ray answered truthfully. The estab-lishment was a far cry from the five-star city hotels that made up most of his family's resort holdings. But if he was to deviate from that model, the Newford Inn would be a fine choice to start with. It held a New England appeal, complete with naval decor and solid hardwood floors. And the chef had done an amazing job with the stew and fixings. He still couldn't believe just how much of it he'd had at dinner. But Myrna had put bowl after bowl in front of him and it had been too good to resist.

"I'm so glad to hear it." She gave him a genuine smile that pleased him much more than it should have.

"Mel? What are you doing here?"

They'd been approached by a tall, lanky man who appeared to be in his thirties. He had a fair complexion and was slightly balding at the top of his head. The smile he greeted Mel with held more question than friendliness.

"Carl," Mel answered with a nod of her head. Her smile from a moment ago had faded completely.

"Wow, I wasn't expecting to see you here tonight."

"It was something of an unplanned last-minute decision."

The other man looked at Ray expectedly, then thrust his hand in his direction when Mel made no effort to introduce them. "I'm Carl Devlin. Mel and I knew each other growing up."

"Ray. Nice to meet you."

Carl studied him up and down. "Huh. Eric mentioned you were seeing someone," he said, clearly oblivious to just how rude he was being.

Mel stiffened next to him. "You and Eric still talk about me?"

Carl shrugged. "We talk about a lot of things. We're still fantasy-ball buddies."

Yet another American term Ray had never really understood the meaning of. It definitely didn't mean what it sounded like. As if American sports fans sat around together fantasizing about various sports events. Though, in a sense, he figured that was how the gambling game could be described.

Mel gave him a sugary smile that didn't seem quite genuine for her part either. "I'm so terribly happy that the two of you have remained friends since I introduced you two at the wedding. After all this time."

"Yeah. I'm really sorry things didn't work out between you two."

Ray felt the ire growing like a brewing storm within his chest. The blatant reminder that Mel had once belonged to a man who so completely hadn't deserved her was making him feel a strange emotion he didn't want to examine.

Luckily, Mel cut the exchange short at that point. She gently took Ray's arm and began to turn away. "Well, if you'll excuse us then, I wanted to introduce Ray to some friends."

Ray gave the other man a small nod as they walked away.

"I'm sorry if that was unpleasant," she said as she led him toward the other corner of the room. "I should have remembered that he and Eric still keep in touch."

"No need to apologize," he said and put his arm around her waist. "Though it occurs to me that we have the same predicament as we had the other evening at the holiday ball."

Her eyebrows lifted in question. "How so?"

"Looks like we'll have to put on a good show for your old friend Carl." He turned to face her. "Shall we get started?"

She responded by stepping into his embrace and giving him just the barest brush of a kiss on the lips.

CHAPTER NINE

"THIS MIGHT VERY well be the silliest dance I've ever done."

Mel couldn't contain her laughter as Ray tried to keep up with the line dance currently in play in the main room. Had she finally found the one thing Ray might not be good at? He was barely keeping up with the steps and had nearly tripped her up more than once when he'd danced right into her.

She had to appreciate the lengths he was going to simply to indulge her.

"You'll get the hang of it," she reassured him. "You're used to dancing at high-end balls and society events. Here at the Newford Inn, we're much more accustomed to doing the Electric Slide."

"It appears to be more complicated than any waltz," he said with so much grim seriousness that she almost felt sorry for him.

The song finally came to an end before Ray had even come close to mastering the steps. The next song that started up was a much slower love ballad. The dancers on the floor either took their leave and walked away, or immediately started to pair up. Ray reached for her hand. "May I?"

A shiver meandered down her spine. With no small amount of hesitation, she slowly stepped into his arms.

She wasn't sure if her heart could handle it. The lines between pretending to be a couple for Carl's benefit and the reality of her attraction to him were becoming increasingly blurry.

She had no doubt she was beginning to feel true and strong emotions for the man. But for his part, Ray's feelings were far from clear. Yes, he seemed to be doing everything to charm her socks off. But how much of that was just simply who he was? His charm and appeal seemed to be a natural extension of him. Was she reading too much into it all?

And that kiss they'd shared the night before while they'd watched the tree lighting. She'd felt that kiss over every inch of her body. She wanted to believe with all her heart that it had meant something to him as well, that it had affected him even half as much as it had affected her. The way he'd responded to her had definitely seemed real. There had been true passion and longing behind that kiss—she firmly believed that. But she couldn't ignore the fact that she'd initiated it. How many men wouldn't have responded? She didn't exactly have the best track record in general as far as men were concerned. Look at how badly she'd read Eric and his true intentions. In her desire to belong to some semblance of a family again, she'd gone ahead and made the error of a lifetime.

She couldn't afford to make any more such mistakes.

At the heart of it, there was only one thing that mattered. Ray would be gone for good in a few short days. She had to accept that. Only, there was no denying that he'd be taking a big part of her heart with him.

How foolish of her to let that happen.

Even as she thought so, she snuggled her cheek tighter against his chest, taking in the now-familiar, masculine scent of him. It felt right to be here, swaying in his arms to the romantic music.

Any hope she had that he might feel a genuine spark of affection died when he spoke his next words. "We definitely seem to have your friend Carl's attention. He seems convinced I can't keep my hands off you. If Eric asks, I'm sure he'll get the answer that we're very much enamored with each other."

Something seemed to snap in the vicinity of her chest. She yanked out of his arms, suddenly not caring how it would look. To Carl or anyone else.

"I don't care."

He blinked at her. "Beg your pardon?"

"I don't care what Eric thinks anymore. It was childish and silly to go through so much trouble just to prove a point to a selfish shell of a man." She swallowed past the lump that had suddenly formed in her throat. "A man I should have never fallen for, let alone married."

There was a sudden shift behind his eyes. He reached for her again and took her gently by the upper arms. "Come here."

Mel couldn't allow herself to cry. Since they'd walked into the room, all eyes had been focused on them. There was zero doubt they were being watched still. It would be disastrous to cause a scene right here and now. The last thing she wanted was gossip to follow her on this visit.

She couldn't even explain why she was suddenly so emotional. Only that her heart was slowly shattering piece by piece every time she thought of how temporary this all was. A month from now, it would be nothing more than a memory. One she would cherish and revisit daily for as long as she lived. More than likely, the same could not be said for how Ray would remember her.

Or if he even would.

The thought made her want to sob, which would definitely cause a scene.

"Please, excuse me," she pleaded, then turned on her heel to flee the room. She ran into the outer hallway, making her way past the desk and toward the small sitting area by the fireplace. Ray's footsteps sounded behind her within moments. He reached her side as she stood staring at the crackling flames. She wasn't quite ready to turn and face him just yet.

"What's the matter, Mel?" he asked softly, his voice sounded like smooth silk against the backdrop of the howling gusts of wind outside.

She took too long to answer. Ray placed a gentle hand on her shoulder and turned her around. The concern in his eyes touched her to her core.

"Nothing. Let's just get back and enjoy the dancing." She tried to step to the side. "I guess I'm just being silly."

He wasn't buying it. He stopped her retreat by placing both hands on either side of her against the mantel. Soft shadows fell across his face from the light of the fire and the dim lighting in the room. With the heat of the flames at her back and that of his body so close to hers, she felt cocooned in warmth. Ray's warmth. Her stomach did a little quiver as he leaned closer.

"*Silly* is the last word I would use to describe you."

She wanted to ask him how he would describe her. What were his true, genuine thoughts as far as she was concerned?

The sudden flickering of the lights, followed by a complete blackout, served to yank her out of her daze. Now that the music from the other room had stopped, the harsh sound of the howling wind sang loudly in the air.

She'd been a New Englander her whole life and could guess what had just happened. The nor'easter storm forecast for much later tonight must have shifted and gained speed. The roads were probably closed or too treacherous to risk. Attempting the forty-minute ride back into Boston would be the equivalent of a death wish.

They were almost certainly snowbound for the night.

"I'm sorry, dear. Unfortunately, the one room is all I have. Between the holidays, the storm warnings and this annual holiday jamboree, we've been booked solid for days now. I only have the one small single due to a last-minute weather-related cancelation."

Mel had been afraid of that. She stood, speaking with Myrna in the middle of the Newford Inn's candlelit lobby. Most of the partygoers had slowly dispersed and headed back to their rooms or to their houses in town. Ray stood off to the side, staring in awe at the powerful storm blowing outside the big bay window. The power wasn't expected to come back on in the foreseeable future and Myrna's backup generators were barely keeping the heat flowing. "I understand. I'm not trying to be difficult. I hope you know that."

Myrna patted her hand gently. "Of course, dear." She then leaned over to her and spoke softly into her ear so that only Mel could hear her. "Are you scared in any way, dear? To be alone in a room with him? If you are, even a little bit, I'll figure something out."

Mel felt touched at her friend's concern. But fear was far from being the issue. She didn't know if she had the emotional stamina to spend a night alone in a small room with Ray.

She shook her head with a small smile. "No, Myrna. I'm not even remotely in fear of him. It's just that we haven't known each other that long."

"I'm so sorry, Mel," Myrna repeated. "Why don't you sleep with me in my room, then? It will be tight, but we can make do."

That offer was beyond generous. Mel knew Myrna occupied a space barely larger than a closet. Not to mention she looked beyond exhausted. Mel knew she must have been running around all day to prep for the jamboree. Then she'd had to deal with the sudden power outage and getting the heat restored before it got too cold. All on top of the fact that Mel and Ray hadn't been expected. She felt beyond guilty for causing the other woman any inconvenience.

Ray suddenly appeared at her side and gently pulled her to the corner of the room. "Mel, I must apologize. I feel responsible that you're stranded here. With me."

The number of people suddenly apologizing to her was beginning to get comical. All due to a storm no one could control or could have predicted.

Ray continued, "Please accept whatever room the inn has available for yourself. I'll be perfectly fine."

"But where will you sleep?"

He gave her hand a reassuring squeeze. "You don't need to concern yourself with that."

"I can't help it," she argued. "I am concerned." The only other option he had was the SUV. "You're not suggesting you sleep in your car, are you?"

"It won't be so bad."

"Of course it will. You'd have to keep it running all night to avoid freezing. You probably don't even have enough gas to do that after our drive here."

"I can handle the cold," he told her. "I have roughed it in the past."

She quirked an eyebrow at him.

Ray crossed his hands in front of his chest. "I'll have you know that military service is a requirement in my country. I spent many months as a soldier training and surviving in worse conditions than the inside of an SUV during a storm. I can survive a few hours trying to sleep in one for one night."

He'd been a soldier? How much more was there about this man that she had no clue about?

Nevertheless, they had more pressing matters at the moment.

Mel shook her head vehemently. She couldn't allow him to sleep outside in a car during a nor'easter. Especially not in a coastal town. Plus, she felt more than a little responsible for their predicament. She was the native New Englander. If anything, she should have been prepared for the storm and the chance that it might hit sooner than forecast.

"Ray, setting aside your survival skills learned as a soldier, making you sleep outdoors is silly. We can share a room for one night."

He studied her face and then tipped his head slightly in acceptance. "If you insist."

She turned back to Myrna, glad to be done with the argument. What kind of person would she be if she allowed herself to sleep in a nice, comfortable bed while he was outside, bent at odd angles, trying to sleep all night in a vehicle? Military service or not.

"We'll take the room, Myrna. Thank you for your hospitality."

The other woman handed her an old-fashioned steel key. "Room 217. I hope you two stay warm."

"Thank you," she said with a forced smile, trying to convey a level of calm she most certainly didn't feel.

"Have a pleasant sleep," her friend added, handing her two toothbrushes and a minuscule tube of toothpaste.

That was doubtful, Mel thought as she motioned for Ray to follow her. It was highly unlikely she'd get much sleep at all. Not in such close quarters with a man she was attracted to like no one else she'd ever met.

Not even the man she had once been married to.

Ray placed his hand on Mel's as she inserted the key to open the door to what would be their room for the night. "My offer still stands," he told her, giving her yet another chance to be certain. "I can go sleep outside in the vehicle. You don't need to do anything you're not completely comfortable with."

He'd never forgive himself for the predicament he'd just put Mel in. Who knew the weather along the northeastern coast could be so darn unpredictable? He wasn't used to accommodating unexpected whims of the forecast where he was from.

"I appreciate that, Ray. I do." She sighed and turned the key, pushing open the wooden door. "But we're both mature adults. I've spent enough time with you to know you're not a man to take advantage. Let's just get some sleep."

"You're sure?"

She nodded. "Yes. Completely."

Grateful for her answer—he really hadn't been looking forward to being sprawled out in the back seat of an SUV for hours in the middle of a storm—he followed her in. The room they entered wasn't even half the size of one of his closets back home in his personal wing of the castle. But the real problem was the bed. It was barely the size of a cot.

Mel must have been thinking along the same lines. Her eyes grew wide as they landed on it. He could have sworn he heard her swear under her breath.

"I'll sleep on the floor," he told her.

She immediately shook her head. "There's only the one comforter. That wouldn't be much better than sleeping in the car."

He took her by the shoulders and turned her to face him. "Again. I'm sorry for all of this. I can assure you that you can rest easy and fall asleep. I won't do anything to make you uncomfortable. You don't have to worry about that."

She gave him a tight nod before turning away. Again, she muttered something under her breath he couldn't quite make out.

Despite his unyielding attraction to her, he'd sooner cut off his arm than do anything to hurt her. It was hard to believe how much he'd come to care about her in just the short time since they'd met. She had to know that.

They both got ready for bed in awkward silence. Mel climbed in first and scooted so close to the wall she was practically smashed up against it. Ray got into bed and lay on his side, making sure to face the other way.

"Good night, Mel."

"Good night."

Wide-awake, he watched as the bedside clock slowly ticked away. The wind howled like a wild animal outside, occasionally rattling the singular window. Had Mel fallen asleep yet? The answer came when she spoke a few minutes later.

"This is silly," she said in a soft voice, almost near to whispering. "I'm close to positive you aren't asleep either. Are you?"

Just to be funny, he didn't answer her right away. Several beats passed in awkward silence. Finally, he heard Mel utter a chagrined "Oh, dear."

He allowed himself a small chuckle, then flipped over onto his other side to face her. "Sorry, couldn't resist. You're right. I'm awake, too."

"Ha ha. Very funny." She gave him a useless shove on the shoulder. The playful motion sent her body closer against him for the briefest of seconds, and he had to catch his breath before he could speak again.

"I've never experienced a New England snowstorm before," he told her.

"It's called a nor'easter. We get one or two every winter, if we're lucky. If not, we get three, maybe even four."

"They're pretty. And pretty loud."

He felt her nodding agreement in the dark. "It can be hard to fall asleep, even if you're used to them."

"Since neither of us is sleeping," he began. "I was wondering about something."

"About what?"

"Something you said tonight."

"Yes?"

"When you told me you no longer cared about what Eric thought. Did you mean it?"

The sensation of her body so near to his, the scent of her filling his nostrils compelled him to ask the question. He realized he'd been wanting to all night, since she'd spoken the words as they'd danced together earlier.

He felt the mattress shift as she moved. "Yes. I did mean it. And I realize I haven't cared about his opinion for quite a while."

He wanted to ask her more, was beyond curious about what had led to their union. She seemed far too good for the man Eric appeared to be—she was too pure, too selfless. But this was her tale to tell. So he resisted the urge to push. Instead, he waited patiently, hoping she would continue if she so chose.

She eventually did. "I honestly don't know exactly what drew me to Eric. I can only say I'd suffered a terrible loss after my parents' passing. It's no excuse, I know."

"A person doesn't need an excuse for how they respond to grief," he told her.

"You speak as if you're someone who would know." She took a shaky breath. "Have you lost someone close to you?"

That wasn't it. He wouldn't be able to explain it to her. As the heir to the crown, he'd been to more ceremonial funerals than he cared to remember. Words had always failed him during those events, when confronted with the utter pain of loss that loved ones experienced.

"I haven't," he admitted. "I've been quite fortunate. I never knew my grandparents. Both sets passed away before I or my sisters were born."

She stayed silent for a while. "I lost the two most important people in the world to me within a span of a few months," she said, reminding him of their conversation from the other day. "I guess I longed for another bond, some type of tie with another person. So when Eric proposed…"

"You accepted." But she'd gone above and beyond the commitment of her marital vows. "You also put him through school."

"I never wanted finances to be an issue in my marriage. Money was the reason I had no one else after my parents died."

"And you never fought to get any of it back? To get your life back on track or even to pursue your own dreams?"

He felt her tense up against him. Maybe he was getting too personal. Maybe it was the effect of the dark and quiet they found themselves in. Not to mention the tight and close quarters. But he found he really wanted to understand her reasoning. To understand *her*.

"It's hard to explain, really. I didn't have the stomach to fight for something I readily and voluntarily handed over."

"Is that the only reason?"

"What else?"

"Perhaps you're punishing yourself. Or maybe trying to prove that you can be independent and rebound. All on your own."

He felt her warm breath on his chest as she sighed long and

deep. "I thought I was in love. To me, that meant a complete commitment. Materially and emotionally." The statement didn't really answer his question. But he wasn't going to push.

She didn't need to explain anything to him. And he suddenly felt like a heel for making her relive her grief and her mistakes. Gently, softly, he rubbed his knuckles down her cheek. She turned her face into his touch and he had to force himself not to wrap his arms around her and pull her closer, tight up against him. As difficult as it was to do so, he held firm and steady without moving so much as a muscle. For he knew that if he so much as reached for her, it would be a mistake that could only lead to further temptation.

Temptation he wasn't sure he'd be able to control under the current circumstances.

Mel couldn't believe how much she was confiding about herself and her marriage. To Ray of all people—a man she'd just recently met and barely knew. But somehow she felt more comfortable talking to him than anyone else she could name.

She was curious about things in his past, also.

"What about you?" she asked, not entirely sure she really wanted to know the answer to what she was about to ask him. "There must have been at least one significant relationship in your past. Given all you have going for you."

"Not really. I have had my share of relationships. But none of them amounted to anything in the long run. Just some dear friendships I'm grateful for."

"I find that hard to believe."

He chuckled softly. The vibration of his voice sent little bolts of fire along her skin. "You can believe it."

"Not even at university? You must have dated while you were a student."

"Sure. But nothing that grew serious in any way."

She had no doubt the women he was referring to would have much rather preferred a completely different outcome.

Ray seemed to have no idea the trail of broken hearts he must have left in his wake. Her eyes stung. She'd soon be added to that number.

After pausing for several moments, he finally continued, "I never really had much of a chance to invest any kind of time to cultivate the kind of relationship that leads to a significant commitment. As the oldest of the siblings, familial responsibilities far too often fell solely on my shoulders. Even while I was hundreds of miles away, studying in Geneva."

Ray sounded like he bore the weight of an entire nation on those shoulders. "Your family must be very important in Verdovia."

That comment, for some reason, had Ray cursing under his breath. "I'm sorry, Mel," he bit out. "For all of it."

He had to be referring to all the pain and anguish of her past that she'd just shared. Mel couldn't help but feel touched at his outrage on her behalf. The knowledge that he cared so deeply lulled her into a comfortable state of silence. Several moments went by as neither one spoke.

She wasn't sure how she was supposed to sleep when all she could think about was having Ray's lips on hers.

So it surprised her when she opened her eyes and looked at the clock, only to see that it read 7:30 a.m. A peaceful stillness greeted her as she glanced outside the window at the rising sun of early morning. The only sound in the room was the steady, rhythmic sound of Ray breathing softly next to her.

At some point, the winds had died down and both she and Ray had fallen asleep.

The air against her face felt frigid. Her breath formed a slight fog as she breathed out. The generators must not have been able to quite keep up with the weather, as the temperature in the room had gone down significantly. She came fully awake with a start as she realized exactly how she'd fallen asleep: tight against Ray's chest, snuggled securely in his arms. She hadn't even been aware of the cold.

CHAPTER TEN

THE AWKWARDNESS OF their position was going to be unbearable once Ray woke up. Mel racked her mind for a possible solution. She didn't even know what she would say to him if he woke to find her nestled up against his chest this way.

There was no doubt she'd been the one to do the nestling either. Ray remained in exactly the same spot he'd been when they'd got into the bed. She, on the other hand, was a good foot away from the wall.

She did the only thing she could think of. She pretended to snore. Loudly.

At first he only stirred. So she had to do it again.

This time, he jolted a bit and she immediately shut her eyes before he could open his. Several beats passed when she could hear him breathing under her ear. His body's reaction was nearly instantaneous. Heaven help her, so was her response. A wave of curling heat started in her belly and moved lower. Her fingers itched to reach for him, to pull him on top of her. Electricity shot through her veins at the images flooding her mind. She didn't dare move so much as an inch.

Mel heard him utter a soft curse under his breath. Then he slowly, gently untangled himself and sat up on the edge of the mattress. She felt his loss immediately. The warmth of his skin, the security of his embrace—if she were a braver, more reckless woman, she would have thrown all caution to the wind and reached for his shoulder. She would have pulled him back toward her and asked him for what she was yearning for so badly.

But Mel had never been that woman. Especially not since her divorce and the betrayal that had followed. If anything, the fiasco had made her grow even more guarded.

Ray sat still for several more moments. Finally, she felt his weight leave the mattress.

She wasn't proud of her mini deception, but what a relief that it had worked. The sound of the shower being turned on sounded from behind the bathroom door. There was probably no hot water. But Ray probably didn't need it.

She rubbed a shaky hand down her face. Hopefully he would take his time in there. It would take a while for her heart to steady, judging by the way it was pounding wildly in her chest.

Before long, the shower cut off and she heard him pull the curtain back.

Mel made sure to look away when Ray walked out of the bathroom, wearing nothing but a thick terry towel around his midsection. But it was no use, she'd seen just enough to have her imagination take over from there. A strong chiseled chest with just enough dark hair to make her fingers itch to run through it. He hadn't dried off completely, leaving small droplets of water glistening along his tanned skin. She had to get out of this room. The tight quarters with him so close by were wreaking havoc on her psyche. Not to mention her hormones. She sat upright along the edge of the mattress.

"You're awake," he announced.

She merely nodded.

"I…uh… I'll just get dressed."

"Okay." She couldn't quite meet him in the eye.

He began to turn back toward the bathroom.

"Do you want to take a walk with me?" she blurted out.

"A walk?"

"Yes. The wind and snow has stopped. We won't be able to start driving anywhere for a while yet. The salt trucks and plows are probably just now making a final run to clear the roads."

"I see. And all that gives you a desire to walk?" he asked with a small smirk of a smile gracing his lips.

"The aftermath of a snowstorm in this town can be visually stunning," she informed him. "I think you'd enjoy the sight of it."

He gave her an indulgent smile. "That sounds like a great idea, then."

She gave him a pleasant smile. "Great, you get dressed. I'll try to scrounge us up some coffee from the kitchen and meet you up front."

"I'll be there within ten minutes," he said with a dip of his head.

It was all the cue Mel needed to grab her coat and scarf, and then bolt out of the room.

As soon as she shut the door behind her, she leaned back against it and took several deep breaths. A walk was definitely an inspired idea. The air would do her good. And she knew just where to take him. Newford was home to yet another talented sculptor who put on a stunning display of three or four elaborate ice statues every year, right off the town square. At the very least, it would give them something to talk about, aside from the strange night they'd just spent in each other's arms.

But first, caffeine. She needed all the fortitude she could get her hands on.

Ray made sure to be true to his word and took the center staircase two steps at a time to find Mel waiting for him by the front doors. They appeared to be the only two people up and about—in this part of the hotel anyway.

"Ready?" she asked and handed him a travel mug of steaming hot liquid. The aroma of the rich coffee had his mouth watering in an instant.

He took the cup from her with a grateful nod and then motioned with his free hand to the doors. "Lead the way."

He saw what she'd meant earlier as soon as they stepped outside. Every building, every structure, every tree and bush was completely covered in a thick blanket of white. He'd never seen so much snow in a city setting before, just on high, majestic mountains. This sight was one to behold.

"It looks like some sort of painting," he told her as they started walking. The sidewalks still remained thick with snow cover, but the main road had been plowed. He was thankful for the lined leather boots he was wearing. Mel was definitely more accustomed to this weather than he was. She maintained a steady gait and didn't even seem to notice the cold and brisk morning air. He studied her from the corner of his eye.

Her cheeks were flushed from the cold, her lips red and ripened from the hot brew she was drinking.

His mind inadvertently flashed back to the scene this morning. He'd awoken to find her snuggled tight in his embrace. Heaven help him, it had taken all the will he possessed to disentangle her soft, supple body away from his and leave the bed.

In another universe, upon waking up with her that way, he would have been the one to put that blush on her cheeks, to cause the swelling in those delicious ruby red lips.

He blinked away the thoughts and continued to follow her as she made her way to what appeared to be the center of town.

"Do we have a destination?" he asked, trying to focus on the activity at hand and not on the memory of how she'd felt nestled against him earlier.

"As a matter of fact, we do," she replied. "You'll see soon enough."

As he'd thought, they reached the center of town and what seemed to be some sort of town square. The sound of the ocean in the near distance grew louder the farther they walked. There was nothing to see in the square but more snow. How in the world would all this get cleaned up? It seemed an exorbitant amount. Where did it all go once it melted?

Verdovia's biggest snowstorm in the past decade or so had resulted in a mere light covering that had melted away within days.

"This way," Mel said.

Within moments, she'd led them to a small alleyway between two long brick buildings, a sort of square off to the side of the main square. In the center sat a now quiet water fountain of cherubic angels holding buckets.

But the true sight to behold was the handful of statues that surrounded the cherubs. Four large ice sculptures, each an impressive display of craftsmanship.

"Aren't they magnificent?" Mel asked him with a wide smile.

"Works of art," Ray said as they walked near to the closest one. A stallion on its hind legs, appearing to bray at the sky.

"They certainly are," Mel agreed. "This spot is blockaded enough by the buildings that the sculptures are mostly protected from the harsh wind or snow, even during nasty storms like the one last night," she explained.

True enough, all four of them looked none the worse for wear. He couldn't detect so much as a crack in some of the most delicate features, such as the horse's thick tail.

After admiring the statue for several moments, they moved on to the next piece. A mermaid lounging on a rock. The detail and attention on the piece was astounding. It looked like it could come to life at any moment.

"One person did all these?"

Mel nodded. "With some minor help from assistants. She does it every year. Arranges for large blocks of ice to be shipped in, then spends hours upon hours chiseling and shaping. From dusk till dawn. Regardless of how cold it gets."

He smiled at her. "You New Englanders are a hearty lot."

"She does it just for the enjoyment of the town."

"Remarkable," he said. Mel took him by the arm and led him a few feet to the next one.

"Take a look at this piece. This one's a repeat she does every time," she told him. "It's usually my favorite." She ducked her head slightly.

It was a couple dancing. That artist's talent was truly notable, she had managed to capture the elegance of a ballroom dance, even depicting an expression of sheer longing on the faces of the two entwined statues. With remarkable detail, the man's fingers were splayed on the small of the woman's back. She was arched on his other arm, head back atop a delicately sculpted throat. Icy tendrils of hair appeared to be blowing in the wind.

"She's really outdone herself with this one this year," Mel said, somewhat breathless as she studied the frozen couple.

Ray was beyond impressed himself. And he knew what Mel had to be thinking.

They'd danced that way together more than once now. He couldn't help but feel touched at the thought of it.

Mel echoed his thoughts. "It sort of reminds me of the holiday ball. I think you may have dipped me just like that once or twice."

Mel hadn't exaggerated when speaking of the artistic talent of her small town. These pieces were exquisitely done, even to his layman's eye. He'd never seen such artwork outside of a museum. Yet another memory he would never have gained had he never met the woman by his side.

He turned to her then. "I don't know how to thank you, Mel. This has truly been the most remarkable holiday season I've spent."

She blinked up at him, thrill and pleasure sparkling behind her bright green eyes, their hue somehow even more striking against the background of so much white. "Really? Do you mean that?"

"More so than you will ever know."

"Not even as a child?"

"Particularly not as a child."

She gripped his forearm with genuine concern. "I'm really sorry to hear that, Ray."

He took a deep breath. How would he explain it to her? That Christmas for him usually consisted of endless events and duties that left no time for any kind of appreciation for the holiday. By the time it was over, he was ready to send the yuletide off for good.

In just the span of a few short days, she'd managed to show him the excitement and appeal that most normal people felt during the season.

He was trying to find a way to tell her all of that when she surprised him by speaking again. She took a deep breath first, as if trying to work up the courage.

"If you end up buying the Newford Inn," she began, "do you think you'll come back at all? You know, to check on your investment?"

The tone of her question sounded so full of hope. A hope he would have no choice but to shatter. He'd allowed this to happen. Mel was conjuring up scenarios in her head where the two of them would be able to meet up somehow going forward. Scenarios that couldn't have any basis in reality. And it was all his fault.

What had he done?

Ray might not have spoken the words, but his stunned silence at her question was all the answer Mel needed.

He had no intention of coming back here, regardless of whether he purchased the property or not. Not to check on an investment. And certainly not to see her. His expression made it very clear. Another thing made very clear was that he was uncomfortable and uneasy that she'd even brought up the possibility.

She'd done it again.

How much battering could a girl's pride take in one lifetime?

If there was any way to suck back the words she'd just uttered, she would have gladly done so.

Foolish, foolish, foolish.

So it was all nothing but playacting on his part. She no longer had any doubt of that. Both at the ball and last night at the party. He'd never told her otherwise. She'd gone and made silly, girlish speculations that had no basis in reality.

"Mel," Ray uttered, taking a small step closer to her.

She held a hand up to stop him and backed away. "Please. Don't."

"Mel, if I could just try to ex—"

Cutting him off again, she said, "Just stop, Ray. It's really not necessary. You don't have to explain anything. Or even say anything. It was just a simple question. I'm sorry if it sounded loaded in any way with an ulterior motive. Or as if I was expecting anything of you with your answer."

Something hardened behind his eyes, and then a flash of anger. But she had to be imagining it. Because anger on his part would make no sense. He was the one rejecting her, after all.

"I didn't mean to imply," he simply stated.

"And neither did I."

She lifted her coffee cup and took a shaky swig, only to realize that the beverage had gone cold. The way her heart just had. Turning it over, she dumped the remaining contents onto the white snow at her feet. It made a nasty-looking puddle on the otherwise unblemished surface. Matched her mood perfectly.

"I appear to be out of coffee. I'd like to head back and get some more, please."

He bowed his head. "Certainly."

Suddenly they were being so formal with each other. As if they hadn't woken up in each other's embrace earlier this morning.

"And we should probably make our way back into Boston soon after. With our luck, another storm might hit." She tried to end the sentence with a chuckle, but the sound that erupted from her throat sounded anything but amused.

For his part, Ray looked uncomfortable and stiff. She had only herself to blame. The forty-minute ride back into the city was sure to be mired in awkward silence. So different from the easy camaraderie they'd enjoyed on the ride up. How drastically a few simple words could change reality overall. Words she had no business uttering.

The walk back to the hotel took much less time than the one to get to the statues, most of it spent in silence. In her haste, she almost slipped on a hidden patch of ice in the snow and Ray deftly reached out to catch her before she could fall. Tears stung her eyes in response to his touch, which she could feel even through her thick woolen coat. It was hard not to think of the way he'd spent the night touching her, holding her.

"Thanks," she uttered simply.

"You're welcome."

That was the bulk of their conversation until they reached the front doors of the bed-and-breakfast. Ray didn't go in; instead, he pulled the car keys out of his pocket. "I'll just go start the car and get it warmed up. Please, go get your coffee."

"You've seen all you need to see of the hotel, then?"

He nodded slowly. "I believe I have. Please thank Myrna for me if you see her. For all her hospitality and graciousness."

"I'll do that. It might take me a few minutes."

"Take your time. Just come down when you're ready."

Mel didn't bother to reply, just turned on her heel to open the door and step into the lobby. So it was that obvious that she needed some time to compose herself.

Clearly, she wasn't as talented at acting as Ray appeared to be.

CHAPTER ELEVEN

RAY REALLY NEEDED a few moments alone to compose himself.

He knew she was angry and hurt. And he knew he should let it go. But something within his soul just couldn't let the issue drop. He hadn't misread her intention when she'd asked about him returning to the United States sometime in the future. He couldn't have been that mistaken.

Regardless, one way or another, they had to clear the air.

Ray gripped the steering wheel tight as Mel entered the passenger seat and shut her door. Then he backed out of the parking spot and pulled onto the main road. It was going to be a very long ride if the silent awkwardness between them continued throughout the whole drive back.

She didn't so much as look in his direction.

They'd traveled several miles when he finally decided he'd had enough. Enough of the silence, enough of the tension, enough of all the unspoken thoughts between them.

He pulled off the expressway at the next exit.

"Where are we going?"

"I'd like a minute, if you don't mind."

She turned to him, eyes wide with concern. "Is everything all right? I can take over the driving if you'd like to rest your legs. I know you're not used to driving in such weather." Even in her ire, she was worried about his state. That fact only made him feel worse.

"It's not my legs," he said, then turned into an empty strip mall. The lone shop open was a vintage-looking coffee stop. "Did you mean what you said back in Newford? That you really don't expect anything of me?"

Mel stared at him for several beats before running her fingers along her forehead.

"Yes, Ray. I did. You really don't need to concern yourself." She let out a soft chuckle. "It really was a very innocuous question I asked back by the ice statues."

He studied her face. "Was it?"

"Absolutely."

He could prove her wrong so easily, he thought. If he leaned over to her right now, took her chin in his hand and pulled her face to his. Then if he plunged into her mouth with his tongue, tasted her the way he'd so badly wanted to this morning, it would take no time at all before she responded, moaning into his mouth as he thrust his fingers into her hair and deepened the kiss.

But that would make him a complete bastard.

She deserved better than the likes of him. The last thing he wanted was for her to feel hurt. Worse, to be the cause of her pain.

Instead, he sighed and turned back to look out the front windshield. "Well, good," he said. "That's good."

A small hatchback that had seen better days pulled up two spots over. The occupants looked at him and Mel curiously as they exited their car. It occurred to Ray just how out of place the sleek, foreign SUV must look in such a setting. Especially with two people just sitting inside as it idled in a mostly empty parking lot.

"Fine," Mel bit out.

She certainly didn't sound as if she thought things were fine. He inhaled deeply. "I'd like to clear the air, Mel, if I could. Starting with the bed-and-breakfast."

"What about it?"

"I should have been clearer about Verdovia's potential investment in such a property. Please understand. A small-town bed-and-breakfast would not be a typical venture for us. In fact, it would be a whole different addition to the overall portfolio of holdings. I would have to do extensive research into the pros and cons. And then, if the purchase is even feasible or even worth the time and effort, I'd have to do some real convincing. I haven't even run the idea by my fa—" He caught himself just in time. "I haven't run it by any of the decision makers on such matters. Most notably, the king and queen."

"I understand. That sounds like a lot of work."

"Please also understand one more thing—I have certain responsibilities. And many people to answer to." An entire island nation, in fact. "A certain level of behavior is expected of me. With a country so small, even the slightest deviation from the norms can do serious damage to the nation's sovereignty and socioeconomic health."

He refrained from biting out a curse. Now he sounded like a lecturing professor. To her credit, Mel seemed to be listening intently, without any speculation.

He watched as she clenched her hands in her lap. "You can stop trying to explain, Ray. See, I do understand. In fact, I understand completely," she told him through gritted teeth. "You mean to say that I shouldn't get my hopes up. About the Newford Inn, I mean." Her double meaning was clear by the intense expression in her blazing green eyes and the hardened tone of her voice. "I also understand that Verdovia is much more accustomed to making bigger investments, and that nothing gets decided without the approval of the royal couple. Who have very high expectations of the man who obtains property and real estate on their behalf. Does that about sum it all up?"

Ray had to admire her thought process. It was as clear as day. She had just given him a perfect out, a perfect way to summarize exactly what he needed to say without any further awkwardness for either of them. He couldn't decide if he was relieved, annoyed or impressed. The woman was unlike anyone he'd ever met.

"I'm sorry." He simply apologized. And he truly was. She had no idea. The fate and well-being of an entire nation rested on his shoulders. To do what was best for Verdovia had been ingrained in him for as long as he could remember. He couldn't turn his back on that any more than he could turn his back on his very own flesh and blood. Verdovia needed a princess, someone who had been groomed and primed for such a position.

Even if he could change any of that, even if he turned to Mel and told her the complete truth about who he was at this very moment, then called his father and asked him to scrap the whole marriage idea, what good would any of it do?

Mel wasn't up to withstanding the type of scrutiny that any association with the Verdovian crown prince would bring into her life. Not many people could. If the international press even sniffed at a romantic involvement between Rayhan al Saibbi and an unknown Boston waitress, it would trigger a worldwide media frenzy. Mel's life would never be the same. He couldn't do that to her. Not after all that she'd been through.

He resisted the urge to slam his fist against the steering wheel and curse out loud in at least three different languages. The real frustration was that he couldn't explain any of that to her. All he had left were inadequate and empty apologies.

Mel finally spoke after several tense beats. "Thank you, but there's no need to say sorry. I'll get over it."

She turned to look out her side window. "And Myrna will be fine, too. The Newford Inn will find a way to continue and thrive. You said it yourself this morning. We New Englanders are a hearty lot."

Again, her double meaning was clear as the pure white snow piled up outside. With no small degree of reluctance, he pressed the button to start the ignition once more.

"I should get you home."

He had no idea what he would say to her or do once he got her there.

Mel plopped down on her bed and just stared at the swirl design on the ceiling. She felt as if she'd lived an entire year or two in the last twenty-four hours. Ray had just dropped her off and driven away. But not before he'd looked at her with some degree of expectation. She suspected he was waiting for her to invite him up so they could continue the conversation that had started when he'd pulled over to the side of the road.

She couldn't bring herself to do it. What more was there to discuss?

Not a thing. Once Ray left, she would simply return to her boring routine life and try to figure out what was next in store for her.

Easier said than done.

It occurred to her that she hadn't bothered to look at her cell phone all day. Not that she expected anything urgent that might need her immediate attention. Frannie and Greta weren't expecting her at the diner and no one else typically tried to contact her usually.

But this time, when she finally powered it on, the screen lit up with numerous text messages and voice mail notices. All of them from one person.

Eric.

Now what?

Against her better judgment, she read the latest text.

Call me, Mel. I'd really like to talk. I talked to Carl last night.

That figured. She should have seen this coming.

She had to admit to being somewhat surprised at his level of interest. He'd wasted no time after speaking with Carl to try to get more information out of her about the new man he thought she was seeing. What a blind fool she'd been where Eric was concerned. The man clearly had the maturity level of a grade-schooler.

No wonder she'd fallen for Ray after only having just met him.

But that was in itself just as foolish. More so. Because Ray wasn't the type of man a lady got over. Mel bit back a sob as she threw her arm over her face. Ray had certainly put her in her place during the car ride. He'd made it very clear that she should harbor no illusions about seeing him again.

She'd managed to hold it together and say all the right things, but inside she felt like a hole had opened up where her heart used to be.

She might have been able to convincingly act unaffected in front of Ray, but she certainly wasn't able to kid herself. She fallen head over heels for him, when he had no interest nor desire in seeing her again once his business wrapped up in the States.

She couldn't wallow in self-pity. She had to move on. Find something, anything that would take her mind off the magical days she'd spent with the most enigmatic and attractive man she was likely to ever meet.

She hadn't done anything creative or artistic in nearly two years. This might be an ideal time to ease herself back into using her natural talent for sculpting and creating something out of a shapeless slab of raw material. The idea of getting back into it sent a surge of nervous anticipation through the pit of her stomach.

She called up the keypad and dialed the number of the glass studio in Boston's Back Bay. A recorded voice prompted her to leave a message. She did so, requesting a date and time for use of the studio and materials. Then she made her way to the bathroom and hopped in the shower.

Studio time wasn't much in the way of adventurous, but at least it gave her some small thing to look forward to.

Her cell rang ten minutes later as she toweled off. Mel grabbed the phone, answering it without bothering to look at the screen. The studio had to be returning her call.

Mel realized her mistake as soon as she said hello. The caller wasn't the studio at all. It was her ex-husband.

"Mel? I've been calling you all day."

"What can I do for you, Eric?"

She had an urge to simply disconnect and hang up on him. She really was in no mood for this at the moment. But he'd simply keep calling and hassling her. Better to just have it out and get this over with.

"Carl called me last night. He mentioned you were visiting Newford. And that you weren't alone."

Well, he'd certainly gone and cut to the chase. Mel released a weary sigh. "That's right. I don't see how it's any of your business. Or Carl's, for that matter."

"I told you, Mel. I still care about you. We were man and wife once. That has to mean something."

"As much as it did the day you took off with your dental assistant, Eric?"

He let out an audible, weary sigh. "That's kind of why I'm calling. I've been giving this a lot of thought. I messed up, Mel. I shouldn't have walked away from our marriage."

What?

She nearly lost her grip on the phone. She had no idea where all this was coming from. But she had to nip it in the bud without delay. The whole idea of faking a pretend boyfriend in front of her ex-husband had backfired big-time. She'd simply meant to prove she'd moved on, and that she could attend a yearly event, even though he'd left her. The disaster happening right now hadn't even occurred to her as a remote possibility. Her ex-husband had made it more than clear two years ago that he had moved on and would be spending his life with another woman.

Or so Mel had thought.

She gripped the phone tight and spoke clearly. "Eric, you

don't know what you're saying. I'm guessing you and Talley had a fight. And now you're simply overreacting."

He chuckled softly. "You're right about one thing."

"What's that?"

"We had a fight, all right. She became upset because I couldn't stop talking about you. And why you were with that businessman."

Mel had been ready to tell him the complete truth about Ray—she really had. If only just to end this nightmare of a phone call and return Eric's wayward thoughts back to where they belonged, to his wife-to-be.

But the way he said it, with such an insulting and derisive tone, made her change her mind. She didn't owe this man anything, not an explanation, not any comfort. Nothing. Eric wasn't even worth her anger. He simply wasn't worth her time. No, she didn't owe him anything. But the truth was, he did owe *her*.

"Please, Mel. Can we just get together and talk?"

Ray's words from last night echoed in her mind. "Actually, maybe there is something we can talk about."

"Anything."

Mel figured he wouldn't be so enthusiastic once she brought up the subject matter. But Ray was right. She needed to stand up for herself and ask for what was rightfully hers. "I think we need to discuss some ways for you to pay me back, Eric. At least partially."

A notable silence ensued over the speaker. She'd shocked him.

She continued before he could say anything, "Other than that, you really need to stop concerning yourself with me and go resolve things with your fiancée. Now, if you'll excuse me, I'm waiting for an important phone call."

She didn't give him a chance to respond before continuing. "I wish you well, Eric," she said and meant it.

Then she disconnected the call.

CHAPTER TWELVE

MEL HUNG UP her apron and reached for her handbag atop the freestanding cabinet in the back kitchen. It had seemed a particularly long shift. Probably because she hadn't been able to focus on a thing to do with her job. Her mind kept replaying scenes from the past week over and over. Scenes which starred a handsome, dark-haired businessman who sported a shadow of a goatee on his chin and a smile that could charm a demon.

Hard to believe three days had gone by since Newford and the nor'easter that had stranded them overnight. It didn't help matters that she relived the entire experience every night in her dreams, as well as several times during the day in her imagination.

Suddenly Greta's scratchy voice sounded from the dining area. "Well, lookie who's here."

Mel's mouth went dry and her blood pounded in her veins. She wasn't sure how, but she knew who her friend was referring to. *Ray.* He was here.

The suspicion was confirmed a moment later when Greta yelled yet again. "Mel, you should come out here. Someone to see you."

Mel threw her head back and closed her eyes. Taking a steadying breath, she grasped for some composure. She could do this. Even if the chances were high that he was simply here to tell her goodbye. For good.

Masking her emotions as best she could, she pushed open the swinging door and went out of the kitchen. Her breath stopped in her throat when she saw him. Again, he hadn't bothered with a coat. A crisp white shirt brought out the tanned color of his skin and emphasized his jet-black hair. His well-tailored dark gray pants fitted him like a glove.

She smoothed down the hem of her unflattering waitress uniform and went to approach him, her bag still clutched in her hands and a forced smile plastered on her face.

"Ray, I didn't expect to see you."

He jammed his hands in his pockets before speaking. "I took a chance you may be at work. I was going to try your apartment if you weren't here."

"I see. Did you want to sit down?" As luck would have it, the only clean booth was the one they'd sat at together for breakfast that morning not so long ago—though now it seemed like another lifetime.

She'd been well on her way then, but hadn't yet quite fallen in love with him. Because that was exactly what had happened. She could no longer deny it. She'd fallen helplessly, hopelessly in love with Ray Alsab.

"I came to tell you that I've come to a decision. And it looks like we'll be moving forward."

She had to rack her brain to figure out exactly what he was talking about. Then it occurred to her. The bed-and-breakfast.

"You'll move forward with buying the Newford Inn, then?"

He nodded with a smile. "I wanted to tell you myself. We haven't even contacted Myrna yet."

Her heart fluttered in her chest, though whether it was the result of hearing the good news or seeing Ray's dashing smile again, she couldn't be sure.

"I've been speaking to all the appropriate people for the past three days," he added. "We've all decided to move ahead. The attorneys are drawing up the paperwork as we speak."

She was happy to hear it, she really was. Particularly for Myrna, who would have so much of the burden of owning the inn taken off her shoulders. But she couldn't just ignore the fact that all she wanted to do right now was to fling herself into his arms and ask him to take her lips with his own. Did he feel even a fraction the same?

It didn't appear so. Because here he was, and all he could talk about was the business deal he'd come to Boston for in the first place.

"It wouldn't have happened without you, Mel. I mean that. And this is just the start."

"The start?"

"That's the best part of it all. I told you the inn was much too small compared to Verdovia's hotel holdings. So we've decided to make it part of something bigger. We'll be investing in several more. A chain of resorts and inns throughout New England, all bearing the royal name. And you were the catalyst for it all."

She didn't know what to say. As much as she appreciated the credit he was giving her, all she could think about was how much she'd missed him these past few days, how she hadn't been able to get him out of her mind. There was no way she was going to tell him that, of course. But, dear heavens, she had to say something.

The words wouldn't form on her tongue, so she just sat there and continued to smile at him stupidly.

"Well, what do you think?" he finally prompted.

If he only knew.

"I think it's wonderful news, Ray. Really. I'm so glad it will work out. Sounds like your business trip will be a success. I'm happy for you."

His eyes suddenly grew serious. He reached across the table and took her hand in his. "There's something else I need to talk to you about."

Mel's pulse quickened and her vision suddenly grew narrow, her only focus at the moment being Ray's handsome face.

"I need to return home to get some things settled once and for all."

Mel felt the telltale stinging behind her eyes and willed the tears not to fall. She was right. This was simply a final goodbye. But his next words had her heart soaring with renewed hope.

"But then I'm going to call you, Mel. Once the dust is settled after I take care of a few things."

That was it, she couldn't hold back the tears, after all. He wasn't giving her the complete story, clearly, but neither was he shutting the door on the two of them. She would take it. With pleasure. She swiped at her eyes with the back of her arm, embarrassed at the loss of control.

He let out a soft chuckle and gripped her hand tighter. "Why are you crying, sweet Mel?"

She didn't get a chance to answer. Ray's phone lit up and vibrated in his front shirt pocket. With a sigh of resignation, he lifted it out. "I have to take this. I'm sorry, but it's about the inn and we're right in the middle of setting up the deal."

She nodded as he stood.

"I'll be right back."

Something nagged at the back of her mind as she watched Ray step outside to take the phone call. She'd got a brief look at the screen of his phone just now as his call had come through. The contact had clearly appeared on the screen as a call from someone he'd labeled as *Father*.

But he'd just told her the call was about the offer he was making to buy Myrna's bed-and-breakfast.

Why would his father be involved in a deal he was doing for the king?

Ray had never mentioned his father being in the same line of work. It didn't make any sense.

She gave her head a shake. Surely she was overthinking things. Still, the nagging voice continued in the back of her mind. The fact was, she'd had the same curious sense before. There seemed to be too many holes in the things Ray had told her about himself. Too many random pieces that didn't quite fit the overall puzzle.

She'd resisted looking at the questions too closely. Until now.

With trembling fingers, she reached into her handbag for the mini electronic tablet she always carried with her to work and logged on to the diner Wi-Fi. Ray was still outside, speaking on the phone.

Mel clicked on the icon for the search engine.

Ray rushed back to the booth where Mel still sat waiting for him, anxious to get back to their conversation.

Something wasn't right. Mel's fists were both clenched tight on the table in front of her. Her lips were tight, and tension radiated off her whole body. One look at the screen on the tablet in front of her told him exactly why.

"Mel."

She didn't even bother to look up at him, keeping her eyes fixed firmly on what she was reading. Ray had never considered himself to be a violent man, save for that one youthful indiscretion on the ball field. But right now, he had a near-overwhelming desire to put his fist through a wall. The gossip rags never failed to amaze him with the unscrupulous ways they so often covered his life.

Mel had gone pale. She used her finger to flip to another page on the screen. Ray didn't need to read the specific words to know what she was seeing. The international tabloid Mel currently stared at was a well-known one. One that featured him just often enough. Ray didn't bother lowering his voice as he bit out a vicious curse.

"Mel. Hear me out."

She still refused to look at him, just continued to read and then clasped a shaky hand to her mouth. Her gasp of horror sliced through his heart.

"Oh, my God," she said in a shaky whisper. "You don't just work for the royal family. You *are* the royal family."

"Mel." He could only repeat her name.

"You're the prince!" This time she raised her voice. So loud that the people around them turned to stare.

"It's what I was trying to explain." Even as he spoke, Ray knew it was no use. Too much damage had just been done. She was going to need time to process.

"When?" She pushed the tablet toward him with such an angry shove, it nearly skidded off the table before he caught it. "When exactly were you going to explain any of this?"

One particular bold headline declared that the Verdovian prince had finally chosen a bride and would be married within months. Somehow they'd snapped a picture of him with a young lady Ray didn't even recognize.

Damn.

"What's there to explain anyway?" she bit out through gritted teeth. "You lied to me. For days."

She was right. He'd been fooling himself, telling himself that not telling Mel the complete truth was somehow different from lying to her.

That itself was a lie.

He had no one to blame but himself. He rammed his hand through his hair and let out a grunt of frustration.

"Is it true?" she demanded to know. "That you're due to be engaged soon?"

He refused to lie yet again. "Yes."

"I need to get out of here," Mel cried out and stood. Turning on her heel with a sob that tore at his soul, she fled away from the table and toward the door.

Ray didn't try to chase after her. He didn't have the right.

And what would he tell her if he did catch up to her? That what she'd seen was inaccurate? The fact was he *was* the crown prince of Verdovia. And he had deceived her about it.

Greta and Frannie stood staring at him from across the room

with their mouths agape. For that matter, the whole diner was staring.

"You'll make sure she's not alone tonight?" he asked neither sister in particular. They were both giving him comparably icy glares.

"You bet your royal patootie."

"Don't you worry about it," Frannie added. At least he thought it was Frannie. Not that it really mattered. All that mattered was that Mel was looked after tonight. Because of what he'd done to her.

As he left, Ray heard one of the diner patrons behind him.

"Told you this place was good," the man told his dining companion. "We got dinner and a show."

Ray was the prince. The actual heir to the crown. An heir who was due to marry a suitable, noble young woman to help him rule as king when the time came for him to take over the throne. Mel felt yet another shiver of shock and sorrow wash over her. Greta rubbed her shoulder from her position next to her on the couch. Frannie was fixing her a cup of tea in the kitchen. She didn't know what she'd do without these women.

"How could I have been so clueless, Greta?" she asked for what had to be the hundredth time. "How did I not even guess who he might have been?"

"How would you have guessed that, dearie? It's not every day a prince runs you over in the middle of a busy city street, then insists on buying you a dress to make up for it."

Mel almost laughed at her friend's summary. In truth, that accident had simply been the catalyst that had set all sorts of events in motion. Events she wasn't sure she would ever be able to recover from.

Her doorbell rang just as Frannie set a tray of cookies and steaming tea on the coffee table in front of them.

All three of them looked up in surprise. "Who could that be?"

Greta went over to look through the peephole. She turned

back to them, eyes wide. "It's that fella that was with your prince. The one who was at the hospital that day."

Her prince. Only, he wasn't. And he never would be.

Mel's heart pounded at the announcement. "What could he possibly want?"

"Only one way to find out," Greta declared and then pulled open the door without so much as checking with Mel.

The gentleman stepped in and nodded to each of them in turn. He pulled an envelope out of his breast pocket.

"Sal?"

He gave her a slight bow. "My full name is Saleh. Saleh Tamsen."

Okay. "Well, what can I do for you, Mr. Saleh Tamsen?"

"It's more what I'm here to do for you," he informed her. What in the world was he talking about?

"The kingdom of Verdovia is indebted to you for your recent service in pursuing a business contract. This belongs to you," he declared and then stretched his hand out in her direction.

Mel forced her mouth to close, then stood up from the couch and stepped over to him. He handed her the envelope. "What is it?"

"Please open it. I'm here to make sure you're satisfied and don't require a negotiation."

Negotiation? Curiosity piqued, Mel opened the envelope and then had to brace herself against Greta once she saw what it contained.

"Yowza!" Greta exclaimed beside her.

She held a check in her hand for an exorbitant sum. More money than she'd make waitressing for the next decade.

"I don't understand."

"A finder's fee. For bringing the prince to the Newford Inn, which he is in the process of acquiring on behalf of the king and the nation of Verdovia."

"A finder's fee? I hardly found it. I grew up near it." None of this made any kind of sense. Was this some type of inspired attempt on Ray's part to somehow make things up to her? That thought only served to spike her anger. If he was trying to buy her off, it was only adding salt to her wounds.

"Nevertheless, the check is yours."

Mel didn't need to hesitate. She stuck the check back in the envelope and handed it back to Saleh. "No, thank you."

He blinked and took a small step back. "No? I assure you it's standard. We employ people who do the very thing you accomplished. I can also assure you it's no more or less than they receive. Take it. You've earned the fee."

She shook her head and held the envelope out until he reluctantly took it. "Nevertheless, I can't accept this. Thank you, but no."

Saleh eyed her up and down, a quizzical gleam in his eye. "Fascinating. You won't accept the money, even though you've earned it."

"No, I won't. And please tell His Royal Highness I said it's not necessary."

Saleh rubbed his chin. "You know what? Why don't you just tell him yourself? He's waiting downstairs for me to return."

CHAPTER THIRTEEN

To HIS CREDIT, Ray looked pretty miserable when he walked through her door. Though she doubted his misery could even compare to the way she was feeling inside—as if her heart had been pulled out of her chest, torn to shreds and then placed back inside.

Greta and Frannie had gone into the other room in order to give them some privacy. No doubt they had their ears tight against the wall, though, trying to hear every word.

Ray cleared his throat, standing statue still. "Mel. I didn't think you'd want to see me."

She didn't. And she did.

She gave him a small shrug. "It just didn't feel right. You know, leaving a prince waiting alone in a car. The last time I did that, at the inn, I didn't actually realize you were a prince. So you'll have to forgive me," she added in a voice dripping with sarcasm.

"You have every right to be upset."

If that wasn't the understatement of the century. "How could you, Ray?" She hated how shaky her voice sounded. "How could you have not even mentioned any of it? After all this time?"

He rubbed his forehead in a gesture so weary that it nearly

had her reaching for him. She wouldn't, of course. Not now. Not ever again.

"It wasn't so straightforward. You have to understand. Things seldom are for someone in my position."

"Not even your name? You're Rayhan al Saibbi. Not Ray Alsab."

"But I am. It's an anglicized version of my name. I use it on business matters in North America quite often." He took a hesitant step toward her. "Mel, I never purposely lied to you."

"Those are merely semantics and you know it, Ray." She wanted to sob as she said the last word. She wasn't even sure what to call him now, despite what he was telling her about anglicized business aliases.

"It would have served no purpose to tell you, love. My confiding it all would have changed nothing. I'm still heir to the Verdovian throne. I still have the same duties that came with my name. None of my responsibilities would have changed. Nor would the expectations on me."

Mel had to gulp in a breath. Every word he uttered simply served to hammer another nail into her wound. She felt the telltale quiver in her chin, but forced the words. "The purpose it would have served is that I would have preferred to know all that before I went and fell in love with you!" Mel clasped a hand to her mouth as soon as she spoke the words. How could she have not contained herself? How could she have just blurted it out that way? Well, there was no taking it back now. And what did it matter anyway? What did any of it matter at this point?

Ray took a deep breath, looked down at his feet. When he tilted his head back up to gaze at her, a melancholy solace had settled in the depths of his eyes. "Then allow me to tell you the honest truth right now. All of it."

Mel wanted to run out of the room. She wasn't sure if she could handle anything he was about to tell her. Nothing would ever be the same again for her. No matter what he said right now. Her broken heart would never heal.

Ray continued, "The truth is that I completely enjoyed every moment you and I spent together. In fact, it might very well be the first time I actually spent a Christmas season having any fun whatsoever. In a different universe, a different reality, things would be very different between you and me. You are a bright light who also lights up everyone you're near. You certainly lit a light inside me. You should never forget that, Mel." He stepped over to her and rubbed the tip of his finger down her cheek in a gentle caress. "I assure you that I never will."

She couldn't hold on to her composure much longer. Mel knew she would break down right there in front of him if he said so much as one more word.

"I think you should leave now," she whispered harshly, resisting the urge to turn her cheek into his hand.

He gave her a slight tilt of his head. "As you desire."

She held back her tears right up until the door closed behind him. Then she sank to the floor and simply let them fall.

"Well, that went about as well as could be expected."

Ray slid into the passenger side of the car and waited as Saleh pulled away and into traffic.

"Your lady is definitely not a pushover, as the Americans say."

Ray didn't bother to correct his friend. Mel certainly couldn't be referred to as his lady in any way. But he so badly wished for the description to be accurate.

"Did you even convince her to take the fee?" Saleh asked.

"No. I know there's no use. If she refused it from you, she will most definitely refuse it from me."

Saleh clicked his tongue. "Such a shame. The young lady is being stubborn at her own expense and detriment."

Ray nodded absentmindedly. He couldn't fully focus on Saleh's words right now. Not when he couldn't get Mel's face out of his mind's eye. The way she'd looked when she'd told him she'd fallen in love with him. What he wouldn't give to have the luxury of saying those words back to her.

But his friend kept right on talking. "Sometimes one should simply accept what he or she is owed. Or at least be adamant about asking for what they're owed, I would think. Don't you agree?"

Ray shifted to look at the other man's profile. "Is there a point you're trying to make?"

Saleh shrugged. "I simply mean to remind you that you are a prince, Rayhan. And that your father is the current ruling king."

"I think you should have taken the money!" Greta declared and popped one of the now-cold cookies into her mouth. The whole cookie. She started chewing around it and could hardly keep her mouth closed.

Frannie turned to her sister. "Why don't you go make us tea, Greta? It's your turn."

Greta gave a grunt of protest but stood and walked to the kitchen.

"You doin' all right, kid?" Frannie asked, taking Greta's place on the couch.

Mel leaned her head against the back of the couch and released a long sigh. "I don't know, honestly. It feels like there's a constant stabbing pain around the area of my heart and that it will never feel better." She sniffled like a child who'd just fallen and skinned her knee.

"It will. Just gonna take some time, that's all." Frannie patted Mel's arm affectionately. "Tell me something?"

"Sure."

"What's makin' you hurt more? That he didn't tell you who he was? Or that you can't have him?"

Mel blinked at the question. A friend like Frannie deserved complete honesty. Even if the question was just now forcing her to be honest with herself.

"I think you know the answer to that," she replied in a low, wobbly voice. Now that she was actually giving it some thought, she realized a crucial point: it was one thing when there had still been a chance for her and Ray, regardless of how miniscule. When she thought he was a businessman who might change his mind and return to the States because he couldn't bear to live without her. But he was a prince. Who had to marry someone worthy of one. Someone who was the polar opposite of a divorced, broke waitress who now lived in South Boston. It was almost exactly how her parents' relationship had started out. Only without the happy ending and loving marriage they'd shared.

"You didn't tell him that," Frannie declared. "You didn't even ask him how he felt. Don't you think you deserved to know? From his own mouth and in his own words, I mean?"

Mel closed her eyes. This conversation was making her think too hard about things she just wanted to forget. In fact, thinking at all simply made the hurt worse. "Well, as he pointed out himself, Frannie, none of it would have made any sort of difference." She knew her voice had taken on a snarky tone, but she couldn't summon the will to care. Hopefully the older woman would just drop the subject.

No such luck. Frannie let out a loud sigh. "Not so sure about that. Now, I may be old but I can count to two."

Mel gave her friend a confused look. "Is that some sort of South Boston anecdote?"

"All I'm saying is there appears to be at least two instances in your adult life where you didn't come out and ask for what was rightfully yours. Damn the consequences."

Mel couldn't be hearing this right. "You can't be including my ex-husband."

"Oh, but I am."

"Are you suggesting that I shouldn't have walked away from Eric? That I should have fought for him, despite his betrayal?" The question was a ridiculous one. She'd sooner have walked through the tundra in bare feet than give that man a second chance. Especially now, after these past few days with Ray.

Frannie waved her hand dismissively. "Oh, great heavens, no. Getting away from that scoundrel was the best thing that could have happened to you."

"Then what?"

Frannie studied her face. "He took your money, dear. Just took it and walked away with another woman."

"I gave him that money, Frannie. It was my foolish mistake."

"Your biggest mistake was trusting that he would honor his vows and his commitment. He didn't."

Of course, the older woman had a valid point. But this train of conversation was doing nothing for her. She loved both Frannie and Greta, and she was beyond grateful for all the support and affection they'd consistently shown her. But Frannie had no idea what it was like to come home one day and find that your husband wouldn't be returning. That he'd found someone else, another woman he preferred over you. Frannie was a widow, whose husband had adored her right up until he'd taken his last breath. They'd had an idyllic marriage, much like her own parents'. The type of union that was sure to elude Mel, given her track record with men so far.

"Well, it just so happens I did ask Eric for the money back. At least some of it." Though she wasn't going to admit to her friend that it had been a half-hearted effort that was meant more to just get Eric off the phone the other night. And to make sure he didn't start harboring any illusions about the two of them reuniting in any way.

But Frannie had her figured out pretty well. Her next words confirmed it. "But you're not really going to fight for it, are you?"

Mel didn't bother to answer. She couldn't even think about Eric or what he owed her right now. Her thoughts were fully centered on Ray and the hurt of his betrayal.

"It's a cliché, but it's true," Frannie went on. "Some things are worth fighting for."

Mel clenched her hands. "And some fights are hardly worth

it. They leave you bloodied and bruised with nothing to show for it."

"You might be right," Frannie admitted. "Matters of love can be impossible to predict, regardless of the circumstances. I'm just saying you should at least fight for what belongs to you." She nodded toward the door, as if Ray had just this instant walked out, rather than over two hours ago.

"And that man's heart belongs to you."

CHAPTER FOURTEEN

RAY COULDN'T REMEMBER the last time he'd tried to sleep in. He wasn't terribly good at it. But he felt zero incentive to get out of bed this morning. For the past few days, he'd awoken each morning with the prospect of seeing or at least speaking with Mel.

That wasn't the case today. And wouldn't be the case from now on. Hard to believe just how much he would miss something he'd only experienced for a short while.

His cell phone rang and his father's number flashed on the screen. He had half a mind to ignore it but couldn't quite bring himself to do so. In all fairness, he was way past the point where he owed the king a status report.

He picked up the phone. "Hello, Father."

"Good morning, son."

"Morning."

"Is there anything you'd like to tell me?"

So it was clear his father had heard something. Ray rolled onto his back with the phone at his ear. "Which tabloid should I be looking at?"

"Take your pick," his father answered. "There's some American man who claims to have been at something known as a 'jamboree,' where you were in attendance. Apparently, he took plenty of photos and is now selling them to whoever will pay."

Ray pinched the bridge of his nose. "I apologize, Your Majesty. I was conducting myself with the utmost discretion. But I failed to anticipate an unexpected variable."

"I see. I hope you've resolved the matter with the young lady in question."

"I'm working on it, sir."

His father paused for several beats before continuing, "You do realize the depth of your responsibilities to Verdovia, don't you, Rayhan? Don't lose sight of who you are. Loose ends will not be tolerated, son."

Ray felt a bolt of anger settle in his core. The way his father referred to Mel as a loose end had him clenching the phone tight in his hand.

He hadn't wanted to do this over the phone, but he'd come to a few decisions over the past few days. Decisions he wasn't ready to back away from.

"With all the respect you're due, Your Majesty, I feel compelled to argue that the lady in question is far from a loose end."

The king's sharp intake of breath was audible across the line. Ray could clearly picture him frowning into the phone with disappointment. So be it.

"I'm not sure what that means, son. Nor, frankly, do I care. I simply ask that you remain mindful of who you are and of your duties."

Ray took a deep, steadying breath. He'd been hoping to wrap things up here and have this conversation with his father in person. But fate appeared to be forcing his hand.

"Since we're discussing this now, Father, I wondered if we might have something of a conversation regarding duty and responsibility to the sovereign."

Silence once again. Ray couldn't remember a time he had tested the king's patience in such a manner. Nor his authority.

"What kind of conversation? What exactly is it you would

like to communicate with me about responsibility and your honor-bound duties as prince?"

His father was throwing his words out as a challenge. Normally Ray would have been the dutiful, obedient son and simply acquiesced. But not this time. This time he felt the stakes too deeply.

"Thank you for asking, sir," Ray replied in his sincerest voice. "I'm glad to have an opportunity to explain."

His father sighed loudly once again. "If you must."

"I've been going over some numbers, sir."

"Numbers? What kind of numbers exactly?"

"I've been looking at our nation's holdings and overall wealth and how it impacts our citizens. Particularly since the time you yourself took over the throne. Followed by the growth experienced once I graduated university and began working for the royal house as a capitalist."

"And?" his father prompted. He sounded much less annoyed, less irritated. The discussion about figures and wealth had certainly gained his attention, just as Ray had known it would.

"And a simple analysis easily shows that the country has prospered very nicely since you started your reign, sir. And it continued that growth once I started acquiring investments on behalf of Verdovia. As a result, we've seen increased exports, higher wages overall for our citizens and extensions of most social benefits."

His father grunted, a sure sign that he was impressed. "Go on. Is there a point to all of this, son?"

"A simple point, sir. Maybe our duty shouldn't need to go any further than such considerations—to further the quality of life for our citizens and nationals. And that maybe we even owe a duty to ourselves as well, to ensure our own fulfillment and happiness. Despite being members of the royal house of al Saibbi."

Ray wouldn't blame her if she didn't open the door. He'd texted her last night to say he wanted to stop by this morning. She hadn't replied. Well, he was here anyway. On the off chance that she would give him one more opportunity and agree to see him.

The possibility of that seemed to lower with each passing second as he braced himself against the blowing wind, while standing on the concrete stoop outside her door.

He was just about to give up and turn around when he heard shuffling footsteps from the other side of the wood. Slowly, the lock unlatched and Mel opened the door.

She stepped aside to let him in.

"Thank you for seeing me, Mel. I know it's short notice."

She motioned toward the sofa in the center of the room. "I just brewed a pot of coffee. Can I get you some?"

"No. Thank you. I won't take up much of your time."

She walked over to the love seat across the sofa and sat as well, pulling her feet underneath her. Ray took a moment to study her. She looked weary, subdued. He saw no hint of the exuberant, playful woman he'd got a chance to know over the past week. He had no one but himself to blame for that.

"So you said you wanted to talk about a business matter? Do you have questions about the Newford Inn? If so, you could have called Myrna directly."

He shook his head. "This business matter involves you directly."

Her eyes scanned his face. "I hope you're not back to offer me another check. I told your associate I'm not interested in taking your money. Not when I didn't really do anything to earn it."

Ray leaned forward, braced his arms on his knees. "Well, we'll have to agree to disagree about whether you earned that money or not. But that's not why I'm here."

"Then why?"

"To put it simply—I'd like to offer you a position."

Mel's eyes narrowed on him, her gaze moving over his face. "Come again? Aren't you a royal prince, who'll eventually become king? What kind of position would someone like that offer a waitress?"

It was a valid question. "I am. The royal house is the largest employer in Verdovia. And a good chunk of the surrounding nations, in fact."

"Okay. What's that got to do with me? I'm a waitress in a diner."

At that comment, he wanted to take her by the shoulders and give her a mild shake. She was so much more than that.

"I mentioned to you earlier, that day at the diner, that we were looking to purchase several New England inns and B and Bs. I'd like to charge you with that. Your official title would be project manager."

Mel inhaled deeply and looked off to the side. "You're offering me a job? Is that it?"

He nodded. "Yes, I think you'd be perfect for it. You know the way these establishments operate and you know New England. The first part will be to get the Newford Inn purchased and renovated. That will give you a chance to slowly get your feet wet. What better way to ease into the job?"

When she returned her gaze to his face, a hardened glint appeared in her eyes. "It sounds ideal on the surface."

"But?"

"But I'm not sure what to tell you, Ray. What if you'd never accidentally met me that day? Would I be the person you would think of to fill such a position?"

Ray gave her a small shrug. "It's a moot point, isn't it? The fact that we met is the only reason these deals are happening."

"I guess there's a certain logic in that," she agreed.

He pressed his case further. "Why worry about what-ifs? I need someone to assist with these acquisitions, and I think you'd do well."

She chewed the inside of her lip, clearly turning the matter over in her mind.

"Please, just think about it, Mel."

"Sure," she said and stood. "I'll think about it."

Something in her tone and facial expression told him she was simply humoring him. But he'd done what he could.

She walked him to the door.

He turned to her before she could open it. "Mel, please understand. Cultural changes don't happen quickly. Especially in a country so small and so set in its ways."

"You don't have to explain, Ray. I understand the reality of it all. You're here to offer me the only thing you feel you can. A job in your employ."

Damn it, when she put it that way...

"Thank you for stopping by. I promise to give your proposal a lot of consideration." She cracked an ironic smile that didn't quite reach her eyes. "After all, it's not like I'm all that great a waitress."

Mel watched through the small slit in her curtains as Ray walked down her front steps to the vehicle waiting for him outside. He hesitated before pulling the car door open and turned to stare at her building. It would be so easy to lift the window and yell at him to wait. She wanted to run out to him before he could drive away, to accept his offer, to tell him she'd take anything he was willing to give her.

But the self-preserving part of her prevailed and she forced herself to stay still where she was. Eventually, Ray got in and his car pulled away and drove off. She didn't even have any tears left; she was all cried out. In hindsight, she had to admit to herself that none of this was Ray's doing. She was responsible for every last bit of it.

Melinda Osmon alone was responsible for not guarding her heart, for somehow managing to fall for a man so far out of her league, she wasn't even in the same stratosphere. To think, she'd believed him to be out of reach when she knew him as a businessman. Turned out he was a real live prince.

He'd had a point when he'd told her that he'd never lied to

her outright. He'd never led her on, never behaved inappropriately in any way.

And he'd just shown up at her apartment with the offer of a job opportunity because he knew she was disappointed and defeated.

Mel leaned back against the window, then sank to her knees. No. She had no one to blame but herself for all of it.

So now there was only one question that needed to be answered. What was she going to do about it? A part of her wanted so badly to take what she could get. To do anything she could to at least inhabit a spot in his orbit, however insignificant.

But that would destroy her. She wasn't wired that way. To have to watch him from a distance as he performed the duties of the throne, as he went about the business of being king one day.

As he committed himself to another woman.

And what of much later? Eventually, he would start a family with the lucky lady who ended up snaring him. Mel could never watch him become a father to someone else's children without shattering inside. Bad enough she would have to see it all from a distance.

Even the mere thought of it sent a stab of pain through her heart. She wouldn't survive having to watch it all from a front-row seat.

She knew Ray thought he'd found a workable solution. He'd offered her the only thing he could.

It just simply wasn't enough.

Ray sat staring at the same column of numbers he'd been staring at for the past twenty minutes before pushing the laptop away with frustration. He'd never had so much trouble focusing.

But right now, all he could think about was if he'd done the right thing by offering Mel a job. He might very well have crossed a line. But the alternative had been to do nothing, to walk out of her life completely. At least as an employee of Verdovia's royal house, he could be confident that she was being taken care of, that she had the backing of his family name and that of his nation. It was the best he could do until he figured out what to do about everything else.

One thing was certain. He wasn't going to go along with any kind of sham engagement. If there was anything he'd learned during these past few days in the States, it was that he was unquestionably not ready. If that meant upsetting the council, the king and even the constituency, then so be it.

The sharp ring of the hotel phone pulled him out of his reverie. The front desk was calling to inform him there was some sort of package for him that they would bring up if it was a convenient time. Within moments of him accepting, a knock sounded on the door.

The bellhop handed him a small cardboard box. Probably some type of promotional material from the various endeavors he was currently involved in. He was ready to toss it aside when the return address caught his eye.

Mel had sent him something.

With shaky fingers, he pulled the cardboard apart. He couldn't even begin to guess what the item might be. She still hadn't given him any kind of answer about the job.

The box contained a lush velvet satchel. He reached inside the bag and pulled out some type of glass figurine. A note was tied to it with a red satin ribbon, almost the identical color of the dress she'd worn the night of the mayor's charity ball. He carefully unwrapped the bow to remove the item.

And his breath caught in his throat.

A blown-glass sculpture of a couple dancing. It wasn't quite a replica of the one made of ice they'd seen in the town square after the storm. She'd put her own creative spin on it. This couple was wrapped in a tighter embrace, heads closer together.

Her talent blew him away. She'd somehow captured a singular moment in time when they were on the dance floor together, a treasured moment he remembered vividly.

He gently fingered the smooth surface with his thumb before straightening out her note to read it.

Ray,
Though I can't bring myself to accept your offer, I hope that you'll accept this small gift from me. I didn't realize while creating it that it was meant for you, but there is no doubt in my mind now that you were the intended recipient all along.

I hope it serves as a cherished souvenir to help you to remember.

As I will never forget.
M

Ray gently set the figurine and the note on the desk and then walked over to the corner standing bar to pour himself a stiff drink. After swallowing it in one swig, he viciously launched the tumbler against the wall with all the anger and frustration pulsing through his whole being.

It did nothing to ease his fury.

CHAPTER FIFTEEN

RAY STILL HADN'T cleaned up the broken glass by the time room service showed up the next morning with his coffee tray. The server took a lingering look at the mess but wisely asked no questions.

"I'll get Housekeeping to clean that up for you, sir," the man informed him as Ray signed off on a tip.

"There's no rush. It can wait until their regular rounds."

"Yes, sir."

So he was surprised when there came another knock on the door in less than twenty minutes.

Ray walked to the door and yanked it open. "I said there was no hur—"

But it wasn't a hotel employee standing on the other side. Far from it.

"Mother? Father? What are you two doing here?"

His mother lifted an elegant eyebrow. "Aren't you going to invite us in, darling?"

Ray blinked the shock out of his eyes and stepped aside. "I apologize. Please, come in."

The queen gave him an affectionate peck on the cheek as she entered, while the king acknowledged him with a nod.

He spoke after entering the room. "Your mother grew

quite restless with the girls away on their performance tour of Europe and you here in the States. She wanted to surprise you. So, surprise."

That it certainly was.

"How are you, dear?" his mother wanted to know. "You look a little ragged. Have you been getting enough sleep?"

Ray couldn't help but smile. Shelba al Saibbi might be a queen, but first and foremost she was a mother.

"I'm fine, Mother."

She didn't look convinced. "Really?"

"Really. But I can't help but think there must be more to this visit than your boredom or a simple desire to spring a surprise on your son." He looked from one to the other, waiting for a response.

"Very well," his mother began. "Your father has something he needs to discuss with you. After giving the matter much thought."

The king motioned to the one of the leather chairs around the working desk. Ray waited until his father sat down before taking a seat himself. The queen stood behind her husband, placing both hands on his shoulders.

"What's this about, Your Majesty?"

"Saleh called me a couple of days ago," his father began. "He wanted to make sure I was aware of certain happenings since you've arrived in the US."

Ray felt a throb in his temple. Why, the little snitching…

His mother guessed where his thoughts were headed. "He did it for your own good, dear. He's been very concerned about you, it seems."

"He needn't have been."

"Nevertheless, he called and we're here."

"Does this have anything to do with your impending engagement?" his father asked.

Ray bolted out of the chair, his patience stretched taut beyond its limits. Perhaps Saleh was right to be concerned about him. He'd never so much as raised his voice around his parents. "How can there be an engagement when I don't even really know the women I'm supposed to choose from? How can I simply tie myself to someone and simply hope that I grow fond of them later? What if it doesn't work out that way?" He took a deep breath before looking his father straight in the eye and continuing, "I can't do it. I'm sorry. I can't go forward with it. Even if means Councilman Riza continues to rabble-rouse, or that Verdovia no longer has the specter of a royal engagement to distract itself with."

"And what of your mother?" the king asked quietly, in a low, menacing voice.

Ray tried not to wince at the pang of guilt that shot through his chest. "Mother, I'm sorry. Maybe we can hire some more assistants to help you with your official duties. I can even take over some of the international visits myself. But I'm simply not ready to declare anyone a princess. I'm just now starting to figure out what type of relationship I might enjoy, the kind of woman I might want to spend my days with. It's not anyone back in Verdovia, I'm afraid."

His father stared at him in stunned silence. But to his utter shock, his mother's response was a wide, knowing grin.

"Well, goodness. You should have just told us that you've met someone."

Ray blinked at her. How could she possibly know that? Saleh might have called his parents out of concern, but Ray knew the other man would have never betrayed that much of a confidence.

"Is that so?" his father demanded to know. "Is all this turmoil because of that woman you were photographed dancing with?"

Ray forced himself to contain his ire. Not only were these people his parents, they were also his king and queen. "That woman's name is Melinda Osmon. And she happens to be the most dynamic, the most intriguing young lady I've ever met."

"I see." His father ran a hand down his face. "Is that your final say, then?"

Ray nodded. "I'm afraid so."

"You do realize that this will throw the whole country into a tailspin. Entire industries have been initiated based on speculation of an upcoming royal engagement and eventual wedding. Also, Councilman Riza will pounce on this as a clear and damning example of the royal family disappointing the people of Verdovia. A royal family he believes serves no real purpose and which is part of a system he believes should be abolished."

Ray swallowed and nodded. "I accept the consequences fully."

His mother stepped around the table to face her husband. "Farood, dear. You must think this through. We cannot have our only son bear the full brunt of this simply because he has no desire to be engaged. And we certainly can't have him miserable upon his return home."

She turned back to her son. "Do not worry about me, I can handle my duties just fine. Frankly, I'm getting a bit tired of all the fuss over my health. I'm not a fragile little doll that needs anyone's constant concern," she bit out, followed by a glare in her husband's direction.

Ray couldn't hide his smile. "I believe I've come across stone blocks more fragile than you are, Mother."

The queen reached over and gave her son an affectionate pat. "I believe there's someone you need to go see, no?" She indicated her husband with a tilt of her head. "Do not worry about what this one will have to say about it."

For several moments, none of them spoke. A thick tension filled the air. Ray clenched his hands at his sides. The king had never been challenged quite so completely before. But he refused to back down.

It was what the Americans liked to call a "game of chicken." Finally, his father threw his hands up in exasperation. "I don't know what the two of you expect me to do about any of this."

The queen lifted her chin. "May I remind you, dear, that you are in fact the king?"

The statement echoed what Saleh had said to him all those nights ago.

His mother then added in a clipped tone, "I'm sure you'll think of something."

Mel tried not to turn her nose at the morning's breakfast special as she carried it out to the latest customer to order it. Lobster-and-cheese omelet. It appeared to be a big hit among the regulars, but for the life of her, she couldn't fathom why.

The holiday shoppers supplied a steady flow of patrons into the diner, despite the wintry cold. The forecasters were predicting one of the whitest Christmases on record. Though she'd be remembering this year's holiday herself for entirely different reasons. How would she ever cope with the Christmas season ever again when everything about it would forever remind her of her prince?

The door opened as several more customers entered, bringing with them a brisk gust of December wind and a good amount of snow on their covered boots and coats.

She nearly dropped the plates she was carrying as she realized one of those customers happened to be a handsome, snow-covered royal.

Mel couldn't help her first reaction upon seeing him. Though she hadn't forgotten the hurt and anguish of those few days, she'd realized she missed him. Deeply. She set her load down quickly in front of the diners before making a complete mess. Then she blinked to make sure she wasn't simply seeing what her heart so desperately wanted to see. But it really was him. He really was here.

Ray walked up to her with a smile. "Hey."

"Hey, yourself."

He peeled his leather gloves off as he spoke. "So I was hoping you could help me order an authentic New England breakfast. Any recommendations?"

She laughed, though she could barely hear him over the pounding in her ears. "Definitely not the day's special."

He tapped her playfully on the nose. "Should you be discouraging people from ordering that? You're right, you're not that great a waitress."

"What are you doing here, Ray? I thought you'd be heading back home. Myrna mentioned that the deal has already been settled and signed."

"I came to offer you a proposition."

Mel's heart sank. The happiness she'd felt just a few short moments ago fled like an elusive doe. He was simply here to make her some other kind of job offer.

"I'm afraid I'm still not interested," she told him in a shaky voice. "I should get back to work."

He took her by the arm before she could turn away. The touch of his hand on her skin set her soul on fire. She'd give anything to go back to the morning when she'd woken up in his arms at the inn. And to somehow suspend that moment forever in time.

She tried to quell the shaking in the pit of her stomach. Seeing him again was wreaking havoc on her equilibrium. But she refused to accept his crumbs. She'd made that mistake once already to avoid being alone, and she wouldn't do it again. Not even for this man.

"I can't do it, Ray. Please don't ask me to work for you again. I don't want your job opportunity."

He steadfastly held on to her arm. "Don't you want to hear what it is first?" he asked with a tease in his voice.

Something about the lightness in his tone and the twinkle in his dark eyes gave her pause. Ray was up to something.

"All right."

He tapped the finger of his free hand against his temple. "I've come up with it completely myself. A brand-new position, which involves a lot of travel. You'll be accompanying a certain royal member of Verdovia to various functions and events throughout the world. Maybe even a holiday ball or two."

He couldn't mean… She wouldn't allow herself to hope. Could she? "Is that so?"

He nodded with a grin. "Definitely."

Oh, yeah, he was definitely up to something. "What else?" she prompted, now unable to keep the excitement out of her voice. Was he really here to say he wanted to spend time with her? That he wanted to be with her? Or was it possible that she had not actually woken up yet this morning and was still in the midst of the most wonderful dream.

Ray rubbed his chin. "I almost forgot. There'll be a lot of this—" Before she could guess what he meant, he pulled her to him and took her lips with his own. The world stood still. Her hands moved up to his shoulders as she savored the taste of him. It had been so long.

She couldn't tear herself away, though a diner full of people had to be watching them. This was all she'd been able to think about since the moment she'd first laid eyes on him on that Boston street.

Someone behind them whistled as another started a steady clap. Mel knew Greta and Frannie had to be the initiators of the cheers, but pretty soon the whole diner had joined in.

In response, Ray finally pulled away with a small chuckle and then twirled her around in a mini waltz around one of the empty tables in the center of the room.

"I miss dancing with you," he whispered against her ear and sent her heart near to bursting with joy.

The applause grew even louder. Catcalls and whistles loudly filled the air. But she could hardly hear any of it over the joyous pounding of her heart.

Ray dipped Mel in his arms in an elaborate ending to their mini waltz and gave her another quick kiss on the lips.

He turned to where Frannie and Greta stood over by the counter, grinning from ear to ear. He gave them both a small nod, which they each returned with an exaggerated curtsy that almost had Greta toppling over.

"If it's not all that busy, would you mind if my lady here takes the rest of the day off?"

Their answer was a loud, resounding "Yes," which was said in unison.

Mel laughed in his arms as he straightened, bringing her back up with him.

"Get your coat and come with me before I have to carry you out of here."

Behind them, Ray heard a voice that sounded vaguely familiar. "I'm telling you, these guys should sell tickets. It's better than going to the movies."

The man was right. This was so much better than any movie. And Ray knew without a doubt there'd be a happy ending.

EPILOGUE

"THOSE TWO MAKE for the most unconventional bridesmaids in the history of weddings," Ray said, laughing, motioning across the room to where Greta and Frannie sat with his two sisters at the bridesmaids' table.

Mel returned his chuckle as she took in the sight of the four of them.

"One would think those four have known each other for years."

"They certainly don't seem to mind the vast age difference," Mel added with a laugh of her own.

Ray took her hand in his on top of the table and rubbed his thumb along the inside of her palm. A ripple of arousal ran over her skin and she had to suck in a breath at her instant reaction. The merest touch still set her on fire, even after all these months together.

"They're pretty unconventional in lots of ways," she said with a smile, still trying to ignore the fluttering in her chest that was only getting stronger as Ray continued his soft caress of her hand.

Verdovia's version of a rehearsal dinner was certainly a grand affair, a sight straight out of a fairy tale—with a string quartet, tables loaded with extravagant foods and desserts, and even a champagne fountain. In fact, Mel felt like her whole life had turned into one big fantasy. She was actually sitting at a table with her fiancé, the crown prince, as his parents, the king and queen, sat beaming on either side of them.

Mel cast a glance at her future mother-in-law, who returned her smile with a wide one of her own. She looked the perfect picture of health and vibrancy. The king was equally fit and formidable. It didn't look like she and Ray would be ascending any throne anytime soon. A fact she was very grateful for. No one would ever be able to replace her real parents, Mel knew. But her future in-laws had so far shown her nothing but true affection and kindness. In fact, the whole country had received her with enthusiasm and acceptance—a true testament to the regard they felt for their prince and the royal family as a whole. And all despite Mel's utter unpreparedness for the rather bright proverbial spotlight she'd suddenly found herself in once her and Ray's engagement had been announced to the world.

Her fiancé pulled her out of her thoughts by placing a small kiss on the inside of her wrist. A sensation of pure longing gripped her core.

"I can't wait to be alone with you," he told her.

"Is that so?" she asked with a teasing grin. "What did you have in mind?"

He winked at her. "To dance with you, of course."

Mel gave in to the urge to rest her head against his strong shoulder. "There's no one else I'd rather dance with," she said, her joy almost too much to contain.

"And there's no one else I'd rather call my wife."

His words reminded her that the true fantasy had nothing to do with the myriad of parties being held for them over the next several weeks or even the extravagant wedding ceremony currently being planned. All that mattered was the complete and unfettered love she felt for this man.

Her husband-to-be was a prince in many more ways than one.

* * * * *

Unwrapping The Neurosurgeon's Heart

Charlotte Hawkes

MEDICAL

Pulse-racing passion

Books by Charlotte Hawkes

Harlequin Medical Romance

Hot Army Docs

Encounter with a Commanding Officer
Tempted by Dr. Off-Limits

The Army Doc's Secret Wife
The Surgeon's Baby Surprise
A Bride to Redeem Him
The Surgeon's One-Night Baby
Christmas with Her Bodyguard
A Surgeon for the Single Mom
The Army Doc's Baby Secret

Visit the Author Profile page
at millsandboon.com.au.

Dear Reader,

I can still remember the moment that, without warning, the Gunn brothers burst into my head. Malachi, the serious, responsible older brother, who had become a carer for both his mother and little brother at such a young age; and Solomon, the younger of the Gunn boys, who had carried the weight of his brother's expectations.

Now a fast-rising neurosurgeon—with a reputation as a playboy—I knew that Sol would need a very special heroine to be able to get past his layers of defenses. Only the most skilled, gentle, compassionate woman was ever going to stand a chance of landing the untamable Sol, but there was an issue—my heroine, Anouk, had her own past to confront and didn't want to play ball!

I had a blast writing Anouk and Sol's story, not least the fact that Sol loves Christmas while Anouk loathes it! They helped me to navigate the perfect way to allow them to connect and open up to each other—I really do hope you enjoy reading it just as much.

It's wonderful hearing from readers, so I'd love it if you dropped by my website at charlotte-hawkes.com, or meet me on Twitter @CHawkesUK.

Charlotte xx

To my very first hero, who introduced me to
mountains, maths and Marmite—love you, Dad xx

CHAPTER ONE

'ANOUK?' THE RESUS WARD'S sister poked her head around the Resus bay curtain. 'Are you running the seven-year-old casualty who fell off a climbing frame?'

'I am.' Anouk spun quickly around. 'Is she in?'

'Yes, the HEMS team are on the roof now.'

'Thanks.' Nodding grimly, Anouk turned back to her team for a final check. 'Everyone happy? Got your gear?'

The only thing she was missing was the neurosurgeon. The department had been paged ten minutes ago but they must be swamped up there. Still, she needed a neurosurgeon for the young kid. Sucking in a steadying breath, she ducked out of the bay, and slammed straight into Moorlands General's hottest commodity.

Solomon Gunn.

Six feet three of solid muscle, more suited to a Hollywood kickboxing stunt guy than the average neurosurgeon, didn't even shift under her flexing palms as the faintest hint of a woody, citrusy scent filled her nostrils.

Her skin prickled instantly. *How could it not?* It was all Anouk could do to snatch her arms down to her sides and take a step back, telling herself that the alien sensation currently rolling through her was nothing more than a basic physiological reaction.

Instinct. Nothing more.

She couldn't possibly be so unlucky as to have the Smoking Gun as the neurosurgeon on her case, could she? And, for the record, she didn't think much of the idiot who had bestowed that moniker on him. Not that it would be unlucky for the poor girl who had fallen, of course. As he was one of the up-and-coming stars of the region, the girl couldn't be in better hands than Sol's.

If only the guy weren't so devastating when it came to women who weren't in his care.

He practically revelled in his reputation as a demigod neurosurgeon and out-of-hours playboy. And still it seemed that almost every woman in the hospital wanted him.

Including, to Anouk's absolute shame, herself.

Not that she would ever, *ever* let another living soul know that fact. Solomon Gunn was the antithesis of absolutely everything she should want in a man.

Yet, caught in the rich, swirling, cognac-hued depth of his gaze, something inside her shifted and rolled deliciously, nonetheless.

She'd only been at Moorlands General for a couple of months and been in Resus when Sol had, but so far they'd never worked together on the same casualty. A traitorous part of her almost hoped that tonight was different.

'Dr Anouk Hart, I believe.'

'Yes. Are you here for my case?' Self-condemnation made her tone sharper than she might otherwise have intended.

'I don't know.' He grinned, as though he could see right through her. 'Which is your case?'

'Seven-year-old girl; climbing frame,' she bullet-pointed.

'Then I'd say you're in luck. I'm here for you.'

Her heart kicked. Anouk told herself it was frustration, nothing more.

'Lucky me,' she managed, rolling her eyes.

'Lucky both of us.'

He flicked his eyes up and down her in frank appraisal. On another man it would have appeared arrogant, maybe even lewd. But Sol wasn't *another man*; he pulled the act off in such a way that it left her body practically sizzling. An ache spearing its way right down through her until she felt it right *there*. Right between her legs.

What was the matter with her?

The man was damned near lethal.

'You might be accustomed to women throwing themselves at you.' She jerked her head over his shoulder to where a group of her colleagues was shamelessly clustered around the central desk and shooting him flirty smiles and applauding gestures. 'However, I certainly don't intend to be one of them.'

'Oh, they're just enjoying the home-made mince pies I brought in.'

'Sorry, what?'

'It *is* Christmas, Anouk.' His grin ramped up and she almost imagined she could feel those straight, white teeth against her skin. 'No need to be a Grinch.'

He couldn't have any idea quite how direct a hit his words were. She hated Christmas. It held no happy memories for her. It never had. Not that she was about to let Sol know that.

'Home-made? By whom? Your housekeeper?'

'My own fair hands.' He waggled them in her face and she tried not to notice how utterly masculine they looked. Not exactly the delicate hands people usually associated with a surgeon.

Those hands had worked magic on hundreds of patients. But it wasn't quite the same kind of magic she was imagining now.

Anouk blinked hard and tried to drag her mind back to the present.

'That's as may be, but I don't think it's your mince pies they're interested in.'

'Oh, I don't know. They're pretty good, if I do say so myself.'

'So modest.' She snorted. 'Well, if you've stopped playing *Great British Bake-Off* with your home-made mince pies...'

'"Playing *Great British Bake-Off*"?' He flashed a wolfish smile, which made her skin positively goosebump. 'I would ask if you're passive aggressive with everyone, or if it's just me, but, given the reputation you've already garnered amongst your colleagues in the few months you've been here, I fear I already know the answer.'

She shouldn't take the bait. She *mustn't*.

'And what reputation would that be?' she demanded, regretting it instantly.

His eyes gleamed mischievously. She half expected him not to answer her.

'Focussed, dedicated, a good doctor.'

'Oh.' She bit her lip. 'Well...then...thanks.'

'Even if you do walk around like you've got a stick up your behind.'

'I beg your pardon?' Heat flooded her cheeks. She could feel it.

'Sorry.' He held his hands up as though appeasing her. 'Their words, not mine. But you have to admit, you are a little bit uptight. A little *prim and proper*.'

She opened her mouth to reply, then snapped it closed again.

If she was honest, she'd heard worse about herself. At best, she was considered to be a good—even great—doctor to her patients, but cold and unapproachable to her colleagues. A bit aloof.

The only person who knew different was Saskia; her best friend since their Hollywood A-list mothers had declared each other their nemesis, over twenty-five years ago.

'Of course, *I* don't think that,' Sol continued, clearly enjoying himself. Not that she blamed him—he couldn't have any idea of her inner turmoil. 'But then, most women have a way of...melting around me.'

'How do you get away with that?' She shook her head. 'Do

you actually enjoy living up to all the worst stereotypes of your own Lothario reputation?'

'Let me guess, in your book that's wrong?'

'Oh, you're incorrigible,' Anouk snapped. 'Though I assume you'll take that as a compliment.'

'You mean it wasn't?' He clasped his hand over his heart, laughing. 'I'm cut to the quick.'

A deep, rich, sinful sound, which had no right to flood through her the way it did. She hated how her body reacted to him, despite every order from her brain to do the opposite. Tipping her head back, she jutted her chin out a fraction and ignored him.

'All we know so far is that we have a seven-year-old on her way having fallen approximately nine feet off a climbing frame in a park...'

'She landed on her head and suffered loss of consciousness for a minute or so,' he concluded. 'The heli-med team are on the roof now and our response team has gone to meet them.'

'Right.' She didn't do a very good job of covering her surprise. 'So, if you could just stop making eyes at the female contingent of our team long enough to concentrate on the casualty, that would be great.'

The amusement disappeared from his face in a split second. His tone was more than a little cool.

'I *always* put my patients ahead of anything else.'

She actually felt chastened.

'Yes... I... I know that.' Anouk flicked out a tongue to moisten her lips. 'I apologise, and I take it back. Your professional reputation is faultless.'

Better than faultless. He was an esteemed neurosurgeon, rapidly heading to the top of his field.

'It's just my personal reputation that languishes in muddier waters?' he asked, apparently reading her thoughts.

But at least the smile was back, his previous disapproval seemingly forgotten. Still, Anouk was grateful when the doors at the far end of the trauma area pulled open with a hiss and the helicopter team brought their patient in.

In an instant, Anouk was across the room and in the Resus bay, vaguely aware that Sol had fallen in quickly beside her.

'This is Isobel, she's seven years old and normally fit and well. No allergies or medications, and up to date with her jabs. Around one hour ago she was climbing on a rope basket climbing frame and was approximately nine feet up when she had an altercation with another child and fell, landing on her face or head with a loss of consciousness of perhaps one minute. She has a laceration above her left eyebrow and she has also lost two of her teeth.'

'Okay.' Anouk nodded, stepping forward. 'Thanks.'

'This is Isobel's sister, Katie.' The doctor turned to where another young girl was standing, and Anouk didn't know when Sol had moved but he was next to her. 'Katie was with her sister when she fell, and has accompanied her whilst Mum is on her way.'

Strangely, Katie lifted her head to Sol and offered a tiny, almost imperceptible shake of her head, but Anouk didn't have time to dwell on that; she needed to help her patient.

'Hi, Isobel, I'm Anouk, the doctor who is going to be looking after you. Do you remember what happened, sweetheart?' She turned to her team, who had already stepped into action. 'Two drips in, guys?'

Isobel muttered something incoherent.

'Can you open your eyes for me, Isobel?' Anouk asked, checking her young patient's pupils. 'Good, that's a good girl. Now, can you take a really big, deep breath and hold it for me?'

She palpitated the girl's chest and stomach.

'You're doing really well, sweetheart. Can you talk to me? Have you got any pain in your tummy?'

'No,' Isobel managed tearfully. 'Katie?'

'Your sister is right here, my love. We just need to check you over to see if you hurt yourself when you fell, and then she'll be able to come and talk to you.'

'Yep, got blood,' one of her team confirmed.

'Great. Okay, and let's give her two point five milligrams of morphine.' She looked back at the child. 'That will help with the pain, all right, sweetheart? Good girl.'

Quickly and efficiently Anouk and her team continued to deal with their patient, settling the girl, doing their observations, and making her as comfortable as they could. Finally, Anouk had a chance to update the girl's mum, but it was still only the sister, who couldn't have been more than ten or eleven herself, who was waiting outside the bay. Anouk remembered how Isobel had asked for Katie, and not her mum.

'Katie, isn't it?' Anouk asked softly, going over to the worried little girl and sitting on the plastic seat next to her.

The girl nodded.

'Mum isn't here yet?'

'No.' Katie shook her head before fixing Anouk with a direct gaze, her voice holding a level of maturity that set warning bells off in Anouk's head. 'But you can talk to me. I'm eleven and I can answer any questions you need me to about my sister. I'm responsible for her.'

An image of Sol and Katie exchanging a concerned look crossed her mind.

Was the girls' mum at work? Uninterested? She knew those feelings all too well. Still, she had her own protocol to follow now.

'I understand that, and you seem like a very good sister,' Anouk confirmed, standing back up. 'But I think it's better if I talk to your mum when she gets here.'

'No, wait.' Katie stood up quickly, glancing at her and then across to the team.

It took a moment for Anouk to realise that she wasn't looking at her sister so much as looking at Sol.

'You know each other?'

'I need to speak to him.' Katie nodded.

'He's just looking after your sister right now.'

'I know, he's a neurosurgeon.' The young girl clucked her tongue impatiently as though she thought Anouk was treating her like a baby. 'And you're probably going to be taking Izzy to scan her head and see if there is any damage from her fall.'

Anouk tried not to show her surprise.

'We will be.'

'Well, when he is free, Sol will come and talk to me,' Katie said confidently, but Anouk didn't miss the fear that flashed briefly in the girl's eyes.

As if sensing the moment, Sol lifted his head and looked straight at them. Then, with a quick word to one of the senior nurses in the team, he made his way over.

'You doing okay, Katie?'

Quiet, professional, compassionate. It had been one thing to see Sol working from across a ward, to know of his reputation as a good doctor, a good neurosurgeon, but it was another actually to witness it first-hand.

Her mother had always ranted about the beauty of a brilliant actor playing a different role from the one the world was used to them adopting. That moment when the audience suddenly realised that it had forgotten who the actor was and got lost in the character.

Watching Sol at work made it almost impossible to remember his reputation as a womaniser.

And it certainly wasn't helping to smother her inconvenient crush on him.

'The doctor won't tell me anything,' Katie replied flatly.

'I'd rather explain to Mum.' Anouk bit back her irritation as Katie and Sol exchanged a glance, hating the feeling that she was missing a vital piece of information.

'Bad day?' he asked Katie simply.

She bit her lip. 'She can't even get up today. But she was resting so I thought Izzy and I could have an hour at the park before we went back and started our chores. There's no way she will be able to get here on her own.'

'I'm on call so I can't leave.' He rubbed his face thoughtfully. 'But I could call Malachi. He can help if she'd be happy about that?'

'Yes.' Katie's relief was evident. 'Please call him. I'll text Mum.'

Shifting her weight from one foot to the other, Anouk tried to control her heart, which had decided to pick up its pace as she listened to the conversation. It was aggravating feeling as though she wasn't entirely following, but the tone of it seemed all too painfully familiar. Or was she just reading too much into it?

Still, she had nowhere else to be for the moment; a nurse was with Isobel and they were waiting on a few results before they could move her to CT.

'In the meantime,' Sol's voice dragged her back to the moment, 'let me try to explain to Dr Anouk here why she can speak to you.'

Katie narrowed her eyes uncertainly.

'You're going to have to trust her,' Sol cajoled. 'I do.'

They were just words to ease the concerns of a kid, Anouk knew that, and yet she was helpless to stop a burst of...*something* from going off inside her chest.

'The more I understand, Katie, the more I can help.' She fixed her gaze on the young girl, whose penetrating stare was unsettling.

'Okay,' Katie conceded at last, before turning back to Sol. 'But you'll call Malachi?'

'Right now,' Sol confirmed.

For a moment it looked as though her face was about to crumple, the pressure of the decisions clearly getting to her. But then she pulled herself together, sinking down onto her chair and fishing out a mobile phone to begin texting. As if there wasn't time for self-indulgent emotions.

As if she was a lot older than her years with far too much adult responsibility.

Anouk fought back the wave of grief that swelled inside her. All too familiar. All too unwelcome. Coming out of nowhere.

'Anouk.'

She snapped her head up to find that Sol was beckoning her, his eyes on Katie to ensure she was preoccupied as he moved across the room.

Wordlessly, Anouk followed, letting him lead her around the curtain and into the central area, keeping his voice low.

'Katie and Isobel are young carers. They look after their mum, who suffers from multiple sclerosis. Some days are good, some not so good. Today, unfortunately, is a bad day, which means Michelle can't even get out of bed without their help.'

'I see.' Anouk breathed in as deeply and as unobtrusively as she could and tried to fight back the sense of nausea that rushed her. Her own situation had been vastly different from the girls', but the similarities were there. 'Dad?'

'Died in an RTA two years ago. He'd just popped out to get cough mixture.'

She exhaled sharply, the injustice of it scraping at her.

'Who's Malachi?'

'My brother. He'll go round and help Michelle. See if there's anything he can do to get her here. Otherwise you keep me informed throughout and we'll agree as much as we can tell Katie. She's mature, but she's still only eleven and she has enough to deal with.'

'Isn't there anyone else?' She already knew the answer, but she still had to ask. 'Any other family member?'

'No. Let me see what I can do but there are a few people I could call as a last resort. They're from the centre and they can at least sit with Katie so that she isn't alone until my shift finishes or I can get someone to cover for me.'

'Why would you do that?' She folded her arms across her chest as though the action could somehow contain the churn of...*feelings* that were swirling inside her, so close to the surface that she was afraid they might spill out.

She wanted to pretend that it was just empathy for Katie, the familiarity of a young girl who had far too much responsibility for her tender age. But she had a feeling it was also to do with Sol. His obvious concern and care for the young girl and her sister and mother was irritatingly touching.

She was ashamed to admit that she'd been attracted enough to the man when she'd thought he was just a decent doctor but also a gargantuan playboy. Seeing this softer side to him was only making the attraction that much stronger.

'Why not do it?' He shrugged and the fact that he was clearly hiding something only made Anouk want to get to know him that much more.

It was galling, really.

Checking on little Isobel and consulting with her team was the opportunity Anouk needed to regroup, and as she worked she let the questions about Sol fall from her head, even as he worked alongside her. Her patient was her priority, as always. Soon enough it was time to take the girl to CT to scan her head and neck.

'Can I go with her and hold her hand?' asked Katie, the concern etched over her face jabbing into Anouk's heart.

She usually let parents go in to be with their child, but unnecessarily exposing an eleven-year-old to ionising radiation, however short a burst, was different.

'How about if I go in?' Sol announced over her shoulder. 'You can wait outside but I'll hold Izzy's hand for you?'

Katie eyed him slowly for a moment.

'Okay, thank you,' she conceded at length.

'Great, you walk with Anouk here and your sister. Okay?'

Something jolted in Anouk's chest at the weight of Sol's gaze on her.

'Fine with me. You're going to get leaded?'

'I thought I might. They probably won't let me in the room otherwise.'

He made it out to be a light-hearted joke, but Anouk knew better. Usually only parents were allowed to accompany their younger children into the room when the imaging was in progress.

'You don't have any patients up on Neurology?'

'I'll sort it. The only one I'm worried about right now is a Mrs Bowman, but I'll deal with that.'

The fact that Sol was putting himself into that position in lieu of the girls' mother said a lot more about him than Anouk expected.

She couldn't shake the impression that it was also more than he would normally like a colleague to know about him. Why did she feel compelled to suddenly test him?

'Boost your reputation around here to compassionate hero as well as playboy, huh?' she murmured discreetly, so only Sol heard.

He glanced at her sharply, then formed his mouth into something that most people might take to be a smile. She knew better.

'Something like that,' he agreed with deliberate cheerfulness that instantly revealed to Anouk that this was the last stunt he wanted to be pulling.

He didn't fool her. She couldn't have said how she knew it, but Sol was doing this for Isobel and for Katie, *despite* the fact that it was going to make him all the more eligible within the hospital's pool of bachelors, and not *because* of it. Which suggested there was more to Sol Gunn than she had realised.

Anouk wished fervently that the concept weren't such an appealing one.

'Right.' Shoving the knowledge from her head, she smiled brightly at Katie and then at her patient. 'Let's get you to CT, shall we, Izzy? Don't worry, your sister will be right beside you until you go in, and then again the moment you come back out.'

And that sharp jab behind her eyes as Katie slipped past her to walk next to the gurney and take her sister's hand in her own wasn't tears, Anouk told herself fiercely.

Just as she wasn't softening in her opinion of the Smoking Gun. She couldn't afford to soften, because that would surely render him more perilous than ever.

CHAPTER TWO

'WHAT'S THE STORY, *BRATIK*?'

Lost in his own thoughts, a plastic cup of cold, less than stellar vending-machine coffee cupped in his hands, Sol took a moment to regroup from the out-of-the-blue question from his big brother.

Then another to act as though he didn't know what Malachi was getting at.

'The scan revealed no evidence of any bleed on the brain and Izzy hadn't damaged her neck or broken her jaw in the fall, which we'd suspected, hence why she's been transferred to Paediatric Intensive Care. Maxillofacial are on their way to deal with the teeth in Izzy's mouth that are still loose. We have the two that came out in a plastic lunchbox someone gave to Izzy, but I think they're baby teeth so that shouldn't be too much of an issue. We won't know for sure until some of the swelling goes down.'

They had left Izzy with her mother and sister for some privacy, but, without having to exchange a word, both brothers had chosen to remain on hand. The girls' mother was going to need help, if nothing else.

'I know all that,' Malachi cut in gruffly, as though it pained him to ask. 'The paediatric doctor told me. I was asking what the story was with you, numb-nuts.'

An image of Anouk popped, unbidden, into Sol's head, but he shoved it aside.

'Don't know what you're talking about.'

It was only a partial lie.

He knew what his brother was getting at, which was surprising since they didn't *do* that *feelings* stuff, but he didn't know the answer to the question himself.

'You know exactly what I mean.' Malachi snorted. 'You forget I've practically raised you since we were kids. You can't fool me.'

Sol opened his mouth to jibe back, as he normally would. But tonight, for some inexplicable reason, the retort wouldn't come. He told himself it was the situation with Izzy. Or perhaps the fact that sitting on hard, plastic chairs, in a low-lit, deserted hospital corridor in the middle of the night, played with the mind.

He had a feeling it was more like the five-foot-seven blonde doctor who was resurrecting ghosts he'd thought long since buried. He had no idea what it was about her that so enthralled him, but she had been doing so ever since the first moment he'd met her.

It had been an evening in a nightclub where Saskia, already a doctor at Moorlands General, had brought Anouk along so that she could meet her new colleagues. The night before, he'd seen Anouk as a focussed, driven, dedicated doctor. And she'd been so uncomfortable that it had been clear that clubs definitely weren't her thing.

He'd seen her from across the room. She'd looked up and met his gaze and something unfamiliar and inexplicable had punched through him. Like a fist right to his chest. Or his gut.

If it had been any other woman he would have gone over, bought her a drink, probably spent the night with her. Uncomplicated, mutually satisfying sex between adults. What could be better? But as much as his body might have greedily wanted the pretty blonde across the room, possibly more than he'd wanted any woman, something had sounded a warning bell in his head, holding him back.

And then someone had spiked her drink—they must have done because he'd seen her go from responsible to disorientated in the space of half a drink—and he'd found himself swooping in to play some kind of knight in shining armour, before any of her colleagues could see her.

Sol couldn't have said how he knew that would have mattered to her more than almost anything else. There was no plausible explanation for the...*connection* he'd felt with her.

So he'd alerted the manager to the situation before pushing his way across the room, grabbing the dazed Anouk's bag and coat and putting his arm around her before anyone else could see her, and leading her out of the nightclub.

Only one person had challenged him on the way out, a belligerent, narrow-eyed, spotty kid he hadn't known, who he suspected had been the one to spike Anouk's drink. It hadn't taken more than a scowl from Sol to send the kid slinking back to the shadows.

He'd got Anouk home and made sure she was settled and safely asleep in bed before he'd left her. The way he knew Saskia would have been doing if she hadn't snuck away by that point. Along with his brother. Sol had seen them leave. Together. So wrapped up in each other that they hadn't even noticed anyone else.

He'd headed back to the club to advise them of the situation, before calling it a night; there had been a handful of women all more than willing to persuade him to stay. None of them had enticed him that night.

Or since. If he was being honest.

Not that Malachi knew that he knew any of it, of course, and he wasn't about to mention it to his big brother. Not here, anyway. Not now. Not when it included Saskia. If the pair of them had wanted him to know they'd ever got together then they wouldn't have pretended they didn't know each other back when Malachi had brought Izzy's mum up to the ward and Saskia had explained to her what was going on with the little girl.

He'd tackle Malachi about it some other time, when he could wind him up a little more about it. The way the two of them usually did.

Sol glowered into his coffee rather than meet Malachi's characteristically sharp gaze.

'I haven't forgotten anything.' He spoke quietly. 'I remember everything you went through to raise us, Mal. I know you sold your soul to the devil just to get enough money to buy food for our bellies.'

For a moment, he could feel his brother's eyes boring into him, but still Sol couldn't bring himself to look up.

'Bit melodramatic, aren't you, *bratik*?' Malachi gritted out. 'Is this about Izzy?'

'I guess.'

His second lie of the night to his brother.

'Yeah. Well,' Malachi bit out at length. 'No need to get soppy about it.'

'Right.'

Downing the last of the cold coffee and grimacing, Sol crushed the plastic cup and lobbed it into the bin across the hallway. The perfect drop shot. Malachi grunted his approval.

'You ever wondered what might have happened if we'd had a different life?' The question was out before he could stop himself. 'Not had a drug addict for a mother, or had to take care of her and keep her away from her dealer every spare minute?'

'No,' Malachi shut him down instantly. 'I don't. I don't ever think about it. It's in our past. Done. Gone.'

'What the hell kind of childhood was that for us?' Sol continued regardless. 'Our biggest concern should have been whether we wanted an Action Man or Starship Lego for Christmas, not keeping her junkie dealer away from her.'

'Well, it wasn't. I wouldn't have asked if I'd known you were going to get maudlin on me.'

'You were eight, Mal. I was five.'

'I know how old we were,' Malachi growled. 'What's got into you, Sol? It's history. Just leave it alone.'

'Right.'

Sol pressed his lips into a grim line as the brothers lapsed back into silence. Malachi could claim their odious childhood was in the rear-view mirror as much as he liked, but they both knew that if they'd really locked the door on their past then they wouldn't have founded Care to Play, their centre where young carers from the age of merely five up to sixteen could just unwind and be kids instead of responsible for a parent or a sibling.

If there had been anything like that around when he and Malachi had been kids, he liked to think it could have made a difference. Then again, he and Mal had somehow defied the odds, hadn't they?

Would the strait-laced Anouk think him less of an arrogant playboy if she knew *that* about him?

Geez, why did he even care?

Shooting to his feet abruptly, Sol shoved his hands in his pockets.

'I'm going to check on some of my patients upstairs, then I'll be back to see Izzy.'

He didn't wait for his brother to respond, but he could picture Malachi's head dip even as he strode down the corridor and through the fire door onto the stairwell.

He wasn't ready for Anouk to come bounding up the steps and, by the way she stopped dead when she saw him, she was equally startled.

'You're still here?' she faltered.

'Indeed.'

'I'd have thought you'd have gone home by now. I heard Izzy's mum arrived.'

She glanced nervously over his shoulder, as if checking no

one could see them talking. He could well imagine she didn't want to be seen as the next notch on his bedpost. He almost wanted to ask her how much free time she imagined a young neurosurgeon to have that he could possibly have made time for so many women.

He bit his tongue.

What did it matter to him if she believed he was as bad as all those stories? Besides, hadn't he played up to every one of them over the years? Better people thought him a commitment-phobe than realise the truth about him.

Whatever the truth even was.

'Mal and I stayed to help.'

'Mal?'

'Malachi.'

'That's right.' She clicked her fingers. 'Your brother. You did say he was collecting the girls' mother.'

'He's through there now.' A thought occurred to him. 'With Saskia.'

'Okay.' She nodded, but her eyes stayed neutral.

Interesting. She clearly didn't know that Saskia and Malachi had had a...*thing.* He wondered what, if anything, Anouk remembered from that night. The club? The drink? The fact that he'd been the one to escort her safely home? Did she not remember him at all from that night?

'Anyway, I have to go.'

'Women waiting for you?'

That prim note in her voice had no business tingling through him like that.

'Always.'

She shot him a deprecating look and he couldn't help grinning, even as he moved to the flight of stairs, heading down two at a time.

'See you around, Anouk.'

He was briefly aware of her grunt before she yanked open the door and shot through it. Waiting a few seconds to be sure the door closed behind her, Sol turned around and headed back upstairs to the neurology department to check on his patients.

He felt somehow oddly...*deflated*.

Anouk tapped her fingers agitatedly on her electronic pad as she waited for the lift.

Why did she keep letting Solomon Gunn get under her skin? It was ignominious enough that her body was clearly attracted to him but it was so much worse that she kept wanting him to be different from the playboy cliché—*imagining* that she saw glimpses of something deeper within him, for pity's sake.

She who, of all people, should surely have known better?

She'd spent her entire childhood managing her mother. Playing the grown-up opposite her childlike mother—a woman who had perfected all the drama and diva-like tendencies of the worst kind of Hollywood star stereotypes.

She had watched the stunning Annalise Hartwood chase playboy after playboy, fellow stars and movie directors alike, convinced that she would be the one to tame them. It was the same story every time. Of course each finale was as trite as the last. Her biological father had been the worst, by all accounts, but ultimately they'd all ended up using her, hurting her, dumping her.

And Anouk had been the one who'd had to pick up the pieces and put her mother's fragile ego back together.

Not that Annalise had ever thanked her for it.

Quite the opposite.

Anouk had never quite matched up to her mother's mental image of how she should be as the daughter of a famous movie star. She'd been too gawky, too lanky; too introverted and too geeky; too book-smart and too gauche.

It had taken decades—and Saskia—for Anouk to finally realise that the problem hadn't really been her. It had been her mother.

That deathbed confession had been the most desolating moment of all. The betrayal had been inconceivable. It had laid her to waste right where she'd stood.

That was the moment she'd realised she had to get away from her old life.

She'd changed her name, her backstory, and she'd come to the UK. And Saskia, loyal and protective, had dropped everything to come with her.

In over a decade in the UK no one had come close to getting under her skin and poking away at old wounds the way Sol had somehow seemed able to do.

The lift doors *pinged* and she stepped forward in readiness. The last person she expected to see inside was the cause of her current unease. This was the very reason she'd waited for the lift instead of returning via the staircase. For a moment, she almost thought he looked as unsettled as she felt.

But that was ridiculous. Nothing ever unsettled Sol.

'Have you decided against getting in after all?' he asked dryly when she'd hovered at the doors so long that he'd been compelled to step forward and press the button to hold them. 'Anyone would think you were avoiding me.'

No, they wouldn't. Not unless he'd equally been avoiding her, surely?

Her mind began to tick over furiously. Her school teachers had called her an over-thinker as a kid. They'd made it sound like a bad thing.

'I thought you were leaving? Women to meet.'

'I am.' He shrugged casually, leaning back against the lift wall and stretching impossibly long, muscled legs in front of him.

'Up in Neurology?' she challenged.

'I forgot something.'

She eyed him thoughtfully. No coat, no bag, no laptop.

'What?'

'Sorry?'

'What did you forget?' she pushed.

'What is this?'

He laughed convincingly and anyone else might have believed him. She probably *should* believe him.

'The Inquisition?'

'You were checking on your patients,' she realised, with a start.

Who was that patient he'd mentioned earlier? Ah, yes.

'Mrs Bowman, by any chance?'

He swiftly covered his surprise.

'My patient, my responsibility,' he commented briskly.

Anouk ignored him.

'And now you're going back to support Izzy and her family.'

'Is that so?'

Her heart thundered in Anouk's chest and she didn't know if it was at the realisation of what he was doing, or the fact that she was confronting him about it.

'You play the tough guy, the playboy, but you've actually got a bit of a softer side, haven't you?'

'Vicious rumour,' he dismissed.

'I don't think so.'

The lift bumped gently as they reached the ground floor and when she swayed slightly, Sol instinctively reached out to steady her. The unexpected contact was a jolt as though she'd grabbed hold of an electrical power cable with no Faraday suit to protect her.

It coursed through her, zinging from the top of her head to the tips of her toes.

His darkening eyes and flared nostrils confirmed that she wasn't the only one who felt it.

A little unsteadily, she made her way out of the lift with no choice but to walk together across the lobby or risk making things look all the more awkward.

The doors slid open and the cool night air hit her hard. In a matter of seconds he'd be gone, across the car park and into that low, muscled vehicle of his.

Any opportunity would have evaporated. For good.

She stopped abruptly at the kerbside.

'Can I ask you something?'

'Shoot,' he invited.

She opened her mouth but her courage deserted her abruptly.

'Those mince pies the other day…were you also the one who decorated the desk with tinsel?'

He grinned.

'Sometimes in a place like this—' he bobbed his head back to the hospital '—it can be easy to forget Christmas should be a celebration. Don't underestimate how much a bit of tinsel and a few mince pies can lift the spirits.'

'Blue and white tinsel hung like an ECG tracing,' she clarified.

'Festive and atmospheric all at once.' He grinned again, and another moment of awareness rippled over her skin.

'Right.'

'Indeed.'

They watched each other a moment longer. Neither speaking. Finally, Sol took a step forward.

'Well, goodnight, Anouk.'

'Can I ask you something else?'

He stopped and turned back to her as she drew in a deep breath.

'How is it you know this family so well? Well enough that you've saddled yourself with four of the worst shifts of the year just to get the night off to sit with those girls in there whilst your brother is helping their mum?'

A hundred witty comebacks danced on his tongue. She could practically feel them buzzing in the air around the two of them. But then he looked at her and seemed to bite them back.

'Malachi and I work with a young carers' group in town,' he heard himself saying. 'Katie and Isobel are two of about thirty kids who come to the centre.'

'So many?'

It was the bleak look in his eyes that gouged her the most.

'That's not even the half of it.' He shook his head. 'You've read the reports, probably around a quarter of a million kids are carers for a parent or other family member. All under sixteen, some as young as four or five. We want to reach them all but we've only just got the council on board. Sometimes the hardest bit is getting people to even acknowledge there's an issue.'

'*You're* raising awareness?' Her eyebrows shot up.

This really meant something to him? He truly cared?

He watched her carefully, wordless for a moment. As if he was waging some internal battle. She waited, holding her breath, although she didn't understand why.

'We're having a fundraiser on Saturday night, to throw a spotlight on the centre.'

'Solomon Gunn is throwing a charity gala?'

Something flitted across his eyes but then he grinned and offered a nonchalant shrug, and it was gone.

'What can I say? Lots of attractive, willing women to choose from, so I guess I get to kill the two proverbial birds with one stone.'

The silence pulled tighter, tauter.

A few hours ago she would have believed that. Now she knew it was an act. And that was what terrified her the most.

Was she being open-minded and non-judgemental? Or was she simply being gullible, seeing what she wished she could see?

'Come with me.'

She had a feeling the invitation had slipped out before he could stop himself.

She frowned.

'Sorry?'

For a moment she thought he was going to laugh it off.

'Be my guest at the gala.'

Something rocked her from the inside. Like thousands of butterflies all waking up from their hibernation, and beating their wings all at once.

She had never experienced anything like it.

'Like…a date?'

'Why not?' he asked cheerfully.

As though it was no big deal to him.

It probably wasn't.

'With you?'

'Your eagerness is a real ego boost for a man, you know that?'

She aimed a sceptical look in his direction.

'I hardly think a man like you needs any more ego massages. You have women practically throwing themselves at you at every turn.'

'I'm not asking them, though, am I?' he pointed out. 'I'm asking you.'

She schooled herself not to be sucked in. Not to fall into that age-old trap. But it wasn't as easy as it had been for all those other men who had flirted with her over the years.

Because those other guys hadn't been Sol, a small voice needled her.

Anouk gritted her teeth.

'Is that why you're inviting me? Because you don't like the fact that I'm not falling over myself to flirt with you?'

'That's exactly it,' he replied, deadpan. 'I find my ego can't take the knockback.'

'Sarcastic much?' she muttered, but a small smile tugged at her mouth despite herself.

'I'll pick you up at half-past seven.'

'I might be on duty.'

'You aren't.' He shrugged.

'I beg your pardon?'

'Relax. I was just checking the rotas before and I don't remember seeing your name.'

She told herself that it meant nothing. It was pure coincidence.

'What makes you think I want to go?'

'What else are you doing that night? It's fun, and, hey, you can do something for charity at the same time.'

He was impressively convincing.

'People will think I'm just the next notch on your bedpost.'

'Some women are happy to have that accolade.'

'I am not *some* women.'

'No,' he agreed. 'You are not.'

The compliment rolled through her, making long-dormant parts of her body unfurl and stretch languidly. Her head was rapidly losing this battle with her body.

'How about this?' he suggested. 'I'll give you my ticket and you can take Saskia, or whoever you want, as your plus one.'

'You would give me your ticket?'

'Sure. That way you won't feel like I'm trying to obligate you in any way.'

'And I could take anyone?'

'Of course.'

She narrowed her eyes.

'Even a date of my own?'

'Oof!' He clutched his stomach as though she'd delivered a punch to his gut, making her laugh exactly as he'd clearly intended. 'You know where to strike a man, don't you? Yes, even a date of your own.'

'And you would miss out? On something as important to you as you've suggested these young carers are?'

'Oh, I won't miss out,' he said airily. 'I'll just go as someone else's plus one.'

It shouldn't hurt to hear. Yet it did. Anouk arranged her features into what she hoped was a neutral expression.

'Of course. You must have a whole host of potential dates just waiting for you to call.'

'So many it can become exhausting at times,' he concurred blithely.

'I'll leave the tickets behind the Resus desk for you before your shift ends tomorrow.'

And then, before she could answer, or say anything uncharacteristically stupid, Sol walked away. The way they probably both should have done ten minutes earlier.

CHAPTER THREE

'THIS PLACE IS STUNNING,' Anouk breathed as she gazed up at the huge sandstone arches that lined either side of the gala venue, and then up again to the breathtaking vaulted ceiling.

'Isn't it?' Saskia demurred.

'I feel positively shabby by comparison.'

'Well, you don't look it.' Saskia laughed and Anouk wondered if she'd imagined the tension she'd noted in her friend over the past few months. 'You look like you're sparkling, and it isn't just the new dress. Although I'm glad you let me talk you into buying it.'

'I'm glad I let you talk me into buying it, too,' admitted Anouk, smoothing her hands over the glorious fabric.

It was amazing how much confidence the dress was giving her, from its fitted body and plunging sweetheart neckline to its mermaid hemline. Three strings of jewelled, off-the-shoulder straps swished over her upper arms whilst the royal-blue colour seemed to complement her blonde hair perfectly.

'You look totally Hollywood.'

'Don't.' Anouk shuddered, knowing Saskia was the one person she could be honest with. 'I think I've had enough of Hollywood to last me a lifetime.'

'Me, too. But still, the look is good.'

'Maybe I should have been in more festive colours.' She glanced at Saskia's own, stunning emerald dress, which had looked gorgeous on the rack, but on her friend's voluptuously feminine body seemed entirely bespoke, complementing Saskia's dark skin tone to perfection.

'I look like a Christmas tree.' Her friend laughed, before waving towards the glorious eighteen-foot work of art, complete with elegant decorations, that dominated the entrance. 'Although if I looked *that* amazing I'd be happy.'

'You look even better, and you know it.' Anouk laughed. 'You've only just walked in and you've turned a dozen heads.'

'They're probably looking at you, and, either way, I don't care. Tonight, Anouk, we're going to relax and enjoy ourselves.'

'We are?'

'We are.' Saskia was firm, taking a champagne flute from the tray of a passing waiter, her beam of thanks making the poor guy fall for her instantly. 'Starting with this.'

She passed the drink to Anouk.

'You still feeling sick?' Anouk frowned.

'Yeah.' Saskia pulled a rueful face but Anouk didn't miss the flush of colour staining her cheeks.

If she hadn't known better she might have suspected that Saskia was pregnant. But that surely wasn't possible? Up until ten months ago Saskia had been engaged and, for all Saskia's confidence and effervescent personality, Anouk knew her ex-fiancé had been only the second man her friend had ever slept with.

But he hadn't been as loyal, and Anouk had never really taken to him. Whenever she'd looked at him she'd seen yet another playboy—just like her mother's lovers.

Just like Sol, a voice whispered in her head.

'Relax.' Saskia nudged her gently. 'Enjoy your drink.'

'I don't really like...' Anouk began, but her friend shushed her.

'You do tonight.'

Anouk balked.

She still wasn't sure what had happened at that nightclub. She had the vaguest memory of starting to relax and trying to have a little fun, and then a sense of panic. After that it wasn't clear, but she'd ended up back home, in her own bed, alone.

Safe.

The popping bubbles looked innocuous enough—fun, even— but all Anouk could see was her mother, downing glasses and popping pills. Had anything else passed her lips in those final few years?

'One glass doesn't make you your mother.' Saskia linked her arm through Anouk's, reading her mind.

Anouk offered a rueful smile.

'That obvious, huh?'

'Only to me. Now go on, forget about your mother and enjoy this evening. You and I both deserve a bit of time off, and, anyway, we're supporting a good cause.'

'We are, aren't we?' Anouk nodded, dipping her head and taking a tentative sip.

It wasn't as bad as she'd feared. In fact, it was actually quite pleasant. Not the cheap plonk, at least, with no bitter aftertaste. Including that of her mother.

Sighing quietly, Anouk finally felt some of the tension begin to uncoil within her.

This was going to be a good evening. She was determined to enjoy it.

'I was beginning to think you weren't coming after all.'

His voice was like a lightning bolt moving through her, pinning her to the spot. Her mouth felt suddenly dry, and even her legs gave a traitorous tremor beneath the gorgeous blue fabric.

Gathering up all her will, Anouk made herself turn around, even as Saskia was sliding her arm from Anouk's and greeting Sol as if they were good friends.

Then again, they were. Saskia had been at Moorlands General for years. Admittedly a much nicer hospital than Moorlands Royal Infirmary, where she herself had trained. Why hadn't she made the transfer sooner?

She was so wrapped up in her thoughts that she only just caught Saskia murmuring something about going to check the seating plan, too late to stop her friend from slipping away into the faceless crowd.

And just like that she was alone with Sol.

As if the couple of hundred other people in the place didn't even exist.

It should have worried Anouk more that she felt that way.

'You look…breathtaking.'

Ridiculously, the fact that he had to reach for the word, as though it was genuine and not some well-trotted-out line, sent another bolt of brilliant light through her.

And heat.

So much heat.

Which was why he had a reputation for being fatal. He was the Smoking Gun, after all.

She would do well to remember that.

'You thought I wasn't coming?' she made herself ask, tipping her head to one side in some semblance of casualness.

'I did wonder.'

Some golden liquid swirled about an expensive-looking, crystal brandy glass in his hand. But it was the bespoke suit that really snagged her attention. Expensively tailored, it showcased Sol to perfection with his broad shoulders and strong chest, tapering to an athletic waist. The crisp white shirt with the bow tie that was already just a fraction too loose suggested a hint of debauchery, as though he was already on the brink of indulging where he shouldn't.

With her?

She went hot, then cold, then hot again at the thought. It was shameful that the idea should appeal so much. The simmering heat seemed to make her insides expand until she feared her flesh and bones wouldn't be able to contain her. He was simply too...*much*.

He isn't your type, she told herself forcefully. Only it didn't seem as though her body wanted to listen.

'I thought perhaps I could introduce you to some people.'

'Oh.' That surprised her. 'Is that why you came over, then?'

He hesitated, and then offered a grin that she supposed was meant to look rueful but just looked deliciously wicked instead.

'Not really.' He made it sound like a confession yet he deliberately didn't elaborate and Anouk wasn't about to play into his hands by asking him.

'I see,' she lied.

'Do you indeed?' he murmured. 'Then perhaps you might explain to me why I couldn't resist coming over here the instant I saw you walk in.'

Her chest kicked. Hard. It didn't matter how many times she silently chanted that he couldn't affect her, Anouk realised all too quickly that she was fighting a losing battle. She had no idea how she managed to inject a disparaging note into her voice.

'Does that line usually work?'

'I don't know, I've never used it before. I'll tell you next time I try.'

She bit her tongue to stop herself from asking when that next time would be. He was clearly baiting her, but what bothered her was that it was working.

'Besides...' his eyes skimmed her in frank, male appreciation, and everywhere his eyes moved she was sure she nearly scorched in response '...if I hadn't come over then some other bloke would have. You're much too alluring in that gown.'

'But not out of it?' she quipped.

His eyes gleamed black, his smile all the more wolfish. Too late, Anouk realised what she'd said.

'Is that an invitation? I have a feeling I would be breaking quite a few harassment in the workplace rules if I admitted to imagining you out of that dress.'

'I mean… I didn't mean… That isn't what I intended.'

'Then be careful what you say, *zolotse*, you can build a man up too quickly otherwise.'

'Zolotse?' she echoed. It sounded… Russian, maybe?

'Zolotse,' he confirmed.

It was the way his voice softened on that word—as if he hardly knew what he was saying himself as he moved closer, his body so tantalisingly close to hers and his breath brushing her neck—that sent a fresh awareness singing through her veins. It made her forget even to draw breath.

Her mind struggled to stay in control.

'You don't intend to elucidate?' She barely recognised her own voice, it was so laced with desire.

'I do not,' he muttered.

Now that she thought about it, Sol and Malachi both had a bit of a Russian look about them. But if they were Russian then it was something Sol didn't share with many other people. Certainly it wasn't common knowledge around the hospital.

Which only made her feel that much more unique.

Dammit, but the man was positively lethal.

Three hours had passed since she'd arrived.

Three hours!

It felt like a mere five minutes, and all because she'd been in Sol's company.

The man had turned out to be a revelation. She'd known he was intelligent, witty, devastatingly attractive, of course. The whole hospital talked about him often enough. But knowing it and *experiencing* it turned out to be two entirely different things.

He had a way of making her feel…special. And it didn't matter how many times she cautioned herself that this was his trick, every time he stared at her as though she were the only person in the entire room, an incredible thrill skewered her like a javelin hurtling through her body.

Even as he'd introduced her around the room—to contacts to whom many of the top consultants would have amputated their own limbs to be introduced—she'd had to fight to concentrate on what he was saying. The feel of his hand at the small of her back kept sending her brain into a tailspin.

She felt like a reed, bending and turning, twisting wherever the breeze took her, and right now that breeze took the form of Solomon Gunn. He was swaying her at will and yet all he was really doing was moving smoothly through the throng, his hand barely touching her searing flesh.

Still, she smiled and greeted and charmed, just as she'd learned to do at the knee of her Hollywood mother. And she made no objection to what Sol was doing.

Perhaps because a portion of her longed to wallow shamelessly in the glances cast their way?

Some admiringly. Others enviously. She'd been on the receiving end of enough sugar-coated scowls and underhanded digs to know that she wasn't the only one to have noticed Sol's attention to her. Or realise that this was more than just his usual behaviour towards a woman on his arm.

He was giving her his undivided attention and presenting her as though she were a proper date. Half of the room seemed to be more than conscious of his body standing so close to hers. As though she were more than just a colleague.

As though there were something intimate between them.

And yet she couldn't bring herself to care the way she suspected she might have cared a few days ago.

His gentleness and compassion with the young family the other night still played on her mind.

Sol might be renowned for caring about his patients, but she'd seen the way he'd stayed with that family even when he was off duty, helping the girls' mother even when he should have been getting much-needed rest.

Too natural, too easy. A world away from the playboy Lothario she'd once thought him to be. It fired her curiosity until she couldn't ignore it any longer.

'I must say that, whilst I don't know your brother all that well, I wouldn't have thought a gala ball to raise money for kids was something you'd be interested in. Let alone quite so heavily involved with. It begs the question of *why.*'

'If there is something you want to know, then ask. I am an open book, *zolotse.*' He shrugged breezily, and yet it tugged at Anouk.

Was there more going on behind his words than Sol was willing to reveal?

It was all she could do to stay brisk.

'Next you'll be telling me that you're misunderstood. That your playboy reputation is a terrible exaggeration.'

Was she really teasing him now?

'On the contrary.' He shook his head, his stunning smile cracking her chest and making her heart skip a beat or ten. 'My reputation is something for which I've never made any apologies.'

'You're proud of it,' she realised abruptly.

And there was no reason for the sharp stab of disappointment that lanced through her at that moment. No reason at all.

'I wouldn't say I was proud of it, but then I'm not ashamed of it either.'

His nonchalance was clear. She had only imagined there was another side to him because that was what she'd wanted to see. What her mother had always done with her own lovers.

It galled Anouk to realise that she was more like her mother than she'd ever wanted to admit.

'Perhaps you should be ashamed of it,' she challenged pointedly, but Sol simply flashed an even wider, heart-thumping grin.

'Perhaps. But you could argue that I'm better than many people because I'm above board. I don't pretend to be emotionally available and looking for a relationship to get a woman into bed, only to turn around and ghost her, or whatever.'

'No, but women practically throw themselves at your feet and you sleep with them anyway.'

'They're grown women, Anouk, it's *their* choice.'

Anouk snorted rather indelicately.

'You must know they're secretly hoping for more.'

'Some, maybe. But I make no false pretences. Why does this rile you so much, Anouk?' His voice softened suddenly. 'Is this about what happened with Saskia? Or did some bloke treat you that badly in the past?'

He might as well have doused her with a bucket of icy water.

What was she doing arguing with him about this? Letting him see how much it bothered her just as clearly as if she'd slid her heart onto her sleeve.

She fought to regroup. To plaster a smile on her face as though she weren't in the least bothered by the turn of conversation. But she feared it looked more like a grimace.

'No, I'm fortunate that I've never been treated that way.'

She didn't add that she'd watched her mother repeat the same mistake over and over enough times never to be caught out like that.

'Never?'

'Never,' she confirmed adamantly.

As though that would rewind the clock. Back to the start of the conversation when she hadn't been quite so revealing about herself. Or the start of the night before she'd let Saskia walk away and leave her alone with him. Or three days ago when they'd worked together on little Isobel and she'd arrogantly imagined she saw something in the man that no one else appeared to have noticed.

The worst of it was that there was some component of her that didn't want to rewind anything. Which, despite every grey cell in her brain screaming at her not to be such an idiot, was enjoying tonight. With Sol.

'In that case, there's something else you should bear in mind.' He leaned into her ear, his breath tickling her skin, and it was like a huge hand stealing into her chest and closing around her heart. 'There are plenty of women who enjoy no-strings sex just as much as I do.'

Don't imagine him in bed. Don't.

But it was too late.

Anouk wrinkled her nose in self-disgust.

'I get that in your twenties, but you're—what? Mid-thirties? Don't you think you might want to grow up some time? Settle down. Be an adult.' She cocked an eyebrow. 'You aren't Peter Pan.'

'That's a shame, because you'd make the perfect Tinker Bell.'

'I'm not a ruddy fairy,' she huffed crossly.

'See?' he teased, oblivious to the eddies now churning within her. 'You even have the Tinker Bell temper down flawlessly. Clearly we're perfectly matched.'

'We most certainly are not,' she gasped.

And he laughed whilst she pretended to be irritated, even though she still didn't try to pull away. So when Sol's hand didn't leave her, when his body remained so close to hers without actually invading her space or making her feel crowded in, and when he deftly steered her out of the path of a couple of rather glassy-eyed, lustful-looking men, she found it all such an intoxicating experience.

As though Sol wanted to keep her to himself.

No, she was being fanciful, not to mention ridiculous.

And still that knot sat there, in the pit of her stomach. Not *apprehension* so much as…anticipation. She was waiting for Sol to do something. More than that, she *wanted* him to.

Perhaps that was why, when reality cut harshly into the dream that the night had become, Anouk was caught completely off guard.

'Now, these are the Hintons,' he leaned in to whisper in her ear as a rather glamorous older-looking couple approached. 'She was a human rights lawyer whilst he was a top cardiothoracic surgeon. They're nice, too.'

'How lovely to meet you.' The older woman smiled at her, but her old eyes burned brightly as they looked her over thoughtfully. 'Anouk Hart... Hartwood... Hmm. You seem familiar, my dear?'

'No, I don't think so.' Anouk forced herself to smile back but her cheeks felt too frozen, her smile too false.

The woman peered closer and Anouk could feel the blood starting to drag through her veins even as her heart kicked with the effort of getting it moving again.

'Yes, definitely familiar.' She nudged her husband, who was still beaming at Anouk. 'Don't you think so, Jonathon?'

He pondered the question for a moment.

Anouk tried not to tense, not to react, but she could feel herself sway slightly. Not so much that a casual observer might notice, but enough that a man standing with his hand on her back might. Certainly enough that Sol did.

His head turned to look at her but she kept staring straight ahead, a tight smile straining her lips.

'Around the hospital, no doubt.' She had no idea how she injected that note of buoyancy into her voice. 'Or maybe I just have one of those faces.'

'Oh, no, my dear, you do not have *one of those faces*.' The woman chuckled.

'More like a screen icon,' her husband agreed, then his face cleared and Anouk's stomach plummeted. 'Like Annalise Hartwood.'

'Annalise Hartwood,' the woman echoed delightedly. 'And she had a daughter...what was her name, Jonathon? Was it Noukie?'

How she'd always hated that nickname. She was sure her mother had known it, too. It was why Annalise had used it all the more.

'Noukie...' He nodded slowly. 'Yes, I think it might have been. You're Noukie Hartwood.'

As if she didn't already know! They said it as if it were a nugget of gold, a little bit of information that they were giving her.

Anouk wanted to shout and bellow. Instead, she stood exactly where she was, her smile not slipping, muscles not twitching.

'Anouk Hart.' She tried to smile. 'Yes.'

'My goodness, I can hardly believe it. Annalise was such a screen icon in my day. But, my dear, you don't have any American accent at all, do you? How long have you been over here?'

How it hurt to keep smiling.

'My friend and I came to university over here…' she paused as if she were searching for the memory, when the truth was she knew practically to the week, the day '…so a little over ten years ago.'

The moment her mother had died and Anouk had finally felt free of her. What kind of person did that make her?

But then, after her mother's deathbed revelation, who could blame her? To realise that her mother, her grandmother, had been lying to her about her father for eighteen years.

What kind of people did that make *them*?

'It was awful what happened to your mother, dear. God rest her soul.'

Their sympathy was apparent, but all Anouk could feel was how relieved she'd been. It had been awful, but it had also been liberating.

What had felt awful had been getting to the UK, tracking down her father from an address on a fragment of paper, only to discover that he had died a few years earlier. Her eyes pricked, hot and painful, at the memory. It had been the moment she'd realised the truth had been buried from her, quite literally if she thought about it, for ever.

She hastily blinked away the inconvenient tears. This was no time for sentimental nonsense. Sol's eyes were boring into her. Seeing her in a new way. Or maybe seeing her in the old way, the way she hadn't wanted anyone to look at her ever again.

'Yes, well...' The smile was as rigid as ever but suddenly she felt like a sad, lonely, frightened kid all over again.

You are a successful doctor, she chanted silently to herself. *Successful*. That wasn't her life any more.

'I know it wasn't public knowledge, my dear. But we knew of the rumours. The things you did for her.'

'No... I...' The practised denial was on her lips but it had been so long. So many years.

'What a marvellous ambassador for the young carers you will be.' The woman brightened up, and it took Anouk a moment to realise what she was implying.

She opened her mouth to interject but the woman was already turning to her husband.

'Noukie, here, will make a wonderful role model. Don't you think, Jonathon?'

'Oh, quite, quite,' he agreed solemnly, completely oblivious of the turmoil their observations were churning within Anouk. 'Letting them know it doesn't matter what your background— even the glitz of Hollywood—being responsible for someone else, like a parent, can happen to anyone.'

She couldn't focus. They were still talking but the words were becoming more and more distant and muffled. Her brain was shutting down despite her attempts to fight it. She tried to tell them that they had it all wrong, that she wasn't anyone's role model, but they were caught up in their excitement and weren't listening.

She wasn't really aware of Sol taking charge, winding the conversation up in a natural, easy way, but she knew he must have done, because the next thing she knew he was guiding her gently but firmly through the crowds without commotion. Or, certainly, no one seemed to be paying her any more or less attention than they had been before.

It was only when she found herself in a quiet anteroom that she felt herself starting to come to.

CHAPTER FOUR

'SORRY.' SHE BARED her teeth in what she desperately hoped would pass for a wide smile. Her stiff cheeks screamed in protest. 'Don't know what happened there.'

'I think you do.'

It was soft, compassionate even. Something pulled, like a painful band, in her chest. She could deny it, but what would be the point?

'So, Noukie Hartwood? I never knew.'

She really didn't want to answer and yet she found herself speaking. Why was it so much easier to talk to Sol?

'I always hated Noukie,' she managed.

'And the surname?'

She lifted her shoulders.

'I shortened it to Hart when I came to the UK.'

'Why?'

'I don't know.' That was a lie. 'To put some distance between myself and my mother, I guess.'

'Because she'd died?'

'She took an overdose,' Anouk clarified brusquely as she shot him a sharp look. 'I thought everyone knew that.'

'I'm aware of the story,' he acknowledged after a moment.

There was no need for her to say anything else, and yet she found herself speaking, her voice high and harsh.

'Of course, she probably didn't mean to. She had a new movie coming out and I think it was her attempt at a publicity stunt gone wrong. That's who she was.'

She could practically feel the emotions dancing inside her. Or stomping inside her. Not that it made much difference; either way, they were having a field day.

What was she doing, bleating on?

'Anyway.' She shook her head back, straightening her shoulders. As if that could somehow make her feel stronger. 'I don't want to talk about this any longer.'

Whatever she'd expected him to say, it wasn't the quiet observation that he came out with.

'No one ever does, which is part of the problem. Why do you think we're here tonight, Anouk? At this obscenely lavish ball, which costs so much per head that we could probably fund a young carers' centre for a year?'

'Maybe because people have cared enough to come out?' she bit back.

'No, because too many people as rich as most of the guests here tonight would rather throw money at an issue and get back to enjoying themselves guilt-free, than actually look at a problem and talk about it.'

She couldn't say what it was about his tone that made her ears prick up.

'That sounds remarkably like someone who has come from nothing and been on the wrong side of those issues.' She eyed him curiously, glad of the opportunity to set her own personal problems aside for a moment. 'I thought you and Malachi were millionaires? Family money or something?'

'You're changing the subject.'

'And you're evading my question,' she countered.

He contemplated her for a long minute. The band was pulling tighter around her chest with each passing second. So tight that she could barely breathe. Anouk swung around, forcing one leg in front of the other, until she found herself by an exquisitely carved writing desk with a stunning leather inlay.

She reached out to pick up an unusual-looking paperweight as if it could distract her mind, and pretended to herself that her hands weren't shaking.

'I'm not changing the subject, I just don't want to discuss it. I put that chunk of my life behind me a long time ago.'

'If that were true then you wouldn't have gone so white in that ballroom that I feared you were about to keel over. Besides, you don't just lock it away and pretend it doesn't exist. It informs what you do in later life. It's why you're a doctor now.'

She hated that he sounded so logical.

'You think you know me so well,' she threw at him caustically.

'So tell me I'm wrong.'

The worst of it was that they both knew she couldn't do that. So, instead, she spluttered a little.

'Because of course, of all people, you'd understand.'

'More than you'd think.' His voice was still impossibly even whilst she felt scraped raw.

'Then *you* talk.'

'I'm not the one who is struggling right now.'

It was odd, but the more empathetic he sounded, the more she wanted to throw the damn paperweight at his head. Carefully, she used her free hand to prise it out of her clamped fingers and set it back down before turning around. Her teeth hurt from clenching them so she struggled to loosen her jaw, too.

'You think you can help me?' she managed testily.

'Maybe…' he shrugged '…but more likely just talking about it will allow you to help yourself.'

'It was a lifetime ago. It's dead and buried.' She jutted her chin out stubbornly, hoping her whole body wasn't shaking as much as she feared it was.

'I told you, it doesn't work that way. Don't underestimate the monsters inside, Anouk. They exist. They're real. They know where your vulnerable spots are and they know just when to hit you for maximum effect. If you can't even admit they are there, how will you ever defeat them?'

'That's the sort of thing I imagine you say to your patients. Do you really believe that? Have you ever actually practised what you preach, Sol?'

'I've never needed to.' His voice raked over her skin. 'I'm fortunate that my life has been...uneventful.'

She narrowed her eyes, trying to decide whether he was telling the truth. Something in her whispered that he wasn't but he looked so easy, so calm, that she thought she might be wrong. So if he *was* deceiving her then he had to be one of the most convincing liars in the world.

She wasn't sure which truth disappointed her the most.

She stared at him, not trusting herself. She hadn't talked about this in over a decade. The only person who knew the truth—or at least, the sanitised, abridged version—was Saskia.

Solomon Gunn should be the last person in the world she would *ever* talk to about her past. And yet there was a crazy part of her that wanted to open up and spill out every last truth. Right here, right now.

'The term is *confront to get closure*,' he added nonchalantly.

She wanted to gouge that part of her out with the letter opener lying on the desk behind her. And she hated that she felt this way. So out of control.

'The term—' she narrowed her eyes '—is *sod off*.'

He watched her for a moment, his eyes so intense that she had to drop her gaze to his mouth to protect herself from plunging right into them.

'You know it's funny, everyone says you're this gentle, sweet-natured, conservative person. They obviously don't see this other side of you, but I do. Why is that?'

She felt as if she'd been caught with her hand in the proverbial cookie jar. Her heart pounded loudly in her chest and all she could do was be thankful that he couldn't hear it.

'You don't know what you're talking about.' She was impressed at quite how haughty she managed to sound.

Sol, it seemed, was more amused than intimidated.

'Oh, trust me, I do. I know women well enough. I seem to push all your buttons, Anouk Hart.'

'You wouldn't know my buttons if I waved them in your face,' she retorted, congratulating herself on her quick wit.

It was only when he laughed—a deliciously rude and decidedly dirty sound—that she realised quite what she'd said.

Again.

'I do admire a good double entendre. First the invitation to get you out of that dress, and now this. I would say that I believe your subconscious is trying to tell you something, Anouk. But I see you've cleverly managed to manipulate the subject after all.'

'There is a silver lining, then,' she managed, perching on the edge of the desk, her legs stretched in front of her, her arms extended either side of her with her hands resting on the polished wood, too.

It had been a move intended to show she wasn't as cornered as she felt, but she hadn't been prepared for Sol's reaction.

His eyes dropped down her body, as though taking in every new curve she had inadvertently revealed, from the deep plunge of her dress to the way the fabric clung to her thighs. Even the skyscraper heels that she had borrowed from Saskia.

She folded her arms over her chest, realising too late how it made her cleavage appear to swell and threaten to spill over the glorious blue fabric. But then she saw the effect it was having on Sol and her entire body burned.

It was thrilling, the way his eyes raked over her as though he couldn't tear his gaze from her. As though he ached to do so much more than simply look.

It was empowering, too.

Anouk didn't think—she couldn't afford to talk herself out

of testing her theory—she just acted. And so what if she didn't believe it when she told herself that all she was trying to do was prevent him from asking any more questions?

Pushing herself up from the desk, she stood and faced him, and Sol didn't miss a moment. His eyes turned molten, his body—all six-foot-three of broad-shouldered, sculpted, wholly masculine beauty—looked suddenly taut and the room started practically humming with sexual tension.

The silence in the room was almost deafening.

Had she ever felt so desired? So confident? So reckless?

'Are you seducing me?' he demanded, the hoarseness of his tone making her blood actually tingle in her veins. 'Because if you are, I can tell you that you're going to need to be a little more persuasive.'

He was lying and they both knew it.

'That can be arranged,' she murmured before her brain even seemed to have kicked into gear.

It was as though someone completely separate to her had taken control of her body, a confident, sexually assertive persona that she herself had never felt in her life before.

It was exhilarating.

With exaggerated care, she reached around and unzipped the low back of the dress.

'What are you doing, Anouk? This isn't you.'

Another hit of triumph punched through her at the slightly raspy tone to his usually rich timbre.

'I'm shutting down any more of your conversations about my past, in the only way I know you'll respond to,' she replied, shocked at how controlled her voice sounded when inside it felt as if a thousand fizzing fireworks were all going off at once.

'I thought you told me you were only coming tonight on the premise that it wasn't a date, and that you wouldn't be sleeping with me?' he bit out, but she could see him clenching his fists at his sides.

As if he was trying so desperately to keep himself in place

and maintain that distance between them. Her heart hammered in her chest, every fibre of her body on edge.

'Oh, believe me, I have no intention of either of us doing any *sleeping*.'

She could see him, coiled and ready. Just about holding himself in place.

'This isn't who you are, or what you do, Anouk,' he growled. 'I'm trying to be a good man here, but there's a limit to how far you can push me.'

'So this isn't what you wanted tonight?' She flicked a tongue out over her dry lips.

She had expected him to break by now and seduction wasn't really one of her skills. How did she convince him that she wanted this, too?

'I'm sick of playing the good girl,' she bit out. 'The responsible girl.'

Noukie Hartwood, the reliable, responsible, *boring* child of the amazing Annalise. Tedious, joyless, a killjoy. And all the other words her mother had flung at her throughout her childhood that had suggested that she didn't have a fun, daring, spontaneous bone in her body.

'Maybe I've decided it's time I had a bit of fun.' She shrugged, almost starting when her dress slipped and threatened to expose her completely, but just about catching herself in time. 'With you.'

'Consider this your last warning, Anouk,' he growled, his gaze riveted on her gaping bodice.

With a final grasp of that confidence she seemed to have acquired for one night only, Anouk shimmied and let her dress slide gracefully down her body to puddle at her feet. She had no idea how she managed to make her legs move enough to step elegantly out of the pool of blue fabric, her eyes locked with Sol's.

'Duly considered,' she murmured.

He moved so fast she was barely aware of it, crossing the space between them to haul her to him.

'Don't say I didn't warn you, *zolotse*,' he growled.

And then suddenly his lips were on hers, only for a fraction of a second, brushing them softly, almost as if he was testing her. It was startling, and it was dangerous, not least because it didn't unsettle her so much as thrill her. Yet still she didn't pull away, not even when he laced his fingers through her hair, met her unblinking gaze again and held it as he slowly—torturously slowly—lowered his mouth to hers and everything…*shifted*.

It wasn't just a kiss. Or, at least, it wasn't like any kiss Anouk had ever known before. It was the most powerful, intense, head-rush kiss that she had ever believed possible. He was claiming her, teasing her, torturing her. There was something so primal, so raw in his tone that every thought melted out of Anouk's head and it seemed to go on for ever. Dipping and tasting, scraping and teasing. Electrifying her like nothing Anouk had ever experienced before.

But then, *Sol* was like no one she had ever kissed before. With every slide of his lips, hunger seared through her, white-hot, torrid. With every sweep of his tongue she was rent apart. With every graze of his teeth she struggled to control a slew of fracturing sensations, too many to contain. *Too much.*

With each drugging drag of his mouth, and every divinely wicked slide of his tongue, he detonated something inside her. Over and over. Until he angled his head for a better, deeper fit, his hands dropping down her back, skimming the skin, tracing her sides, spanning her lower chest, just under her breasts.

It was how she imagined an initial bump of ketamine would feel, giving her a sudden head rush, making her feel giddy and fluffy. And yet, inconsistently, she was also entirely too aware of herself.

Too hot. Too jumpy. Too *everything*.

He drew whorls on her bare skin, leaving the rest of her body resenting the material that barred him from drawing them everywhere else. And when he returned to cup her face, her entire body ached for him.

Sol was *too much*. And yet she simultaneously couldn't get enough. She placed her hands on his chest as if to anchor herself, realising too late her mistake. The solid wall of warm steel beneath her palms only served to detonate even more fireworks within her. It was impossible to stop her fingers from inching across, exploring and acquainting herself with all the care that her old grandmother used to take reading her braille books. Anouk's imagination filled in all the blanks of the utterly masculine body that lay beneath the slick, tailored suit. Every ridge, dip, and contour. In stunningly vivid technicolour.

How she longed to see it for herself. She felt helpless, and aching, and desperate. Her body entirely spring-loaded with a kind of wanton desire.

When had sex ever been quite like this? So charged, so full of expectation and need? She didn't have an abundance of experience, it was true; but she wasn't exactly an untried virgin, either.

Without quite knowing what she was doing, Anouk flattened her body to his, crushing her suddenly heavy breasts to his chest as though it might afford them some relief. And then Sol let one hand glide down her collarbone, over her chest, and all he did was gently graze one thumb pad over a straining peak and pleasure jolted through her as if he'd just shocked her.

She arched into him, a silent plea for more. She couldn't seem to get close enough. Perhaps she couldn't.

'If you carry on like that, we're not going to stop,' he warned, his mouth barely breaking from hers and yet she felt the loss acutely.

Looping her arms around his neck, Anouk pressed herself closer to him. If she was going to do something so outrageously out of character, then she was going to enjoy every single second of it.

'Promises, promises,' she muttered.

'Not a promise,' rasped Sol. 'Fair warning.'

'Warning taken,' she muttered, her lips tingling as his mouth continued to brush her. 'Now you just need to prove it.'

* * *

It was insanity.

Not the fact that he was in a side room at a party with a beautiful, practically naked woman in his arms—he shamefully had to admit this had happened many times in the past—but rather, the insanity was that he was here with Anouk and she was making him feel more out of control than he'd ever felt with anyone else.

As though he couldn't have resisted her inexperienced seduction even if he'd wanted to. As if she had that kind of power over him. Which, of course, was sheer nonsense.

But he wasn't about to put it to the test and try to pull away from her now. Not when his whole body was igniting at the feel of her smooth, silky skin and scraps of lace beneath his palms; the taste of her skin on his lips and tongue; the way she shivered so deliciously when he grazed his teeth down that long line of her neck.

Not to mention that sinful garter belt, which he really hadn't been expecting from prim Dr Hart. Did he take it off her, or leave it on?

His head couldn't keep track of all the ways he wanted this woman. He wanted her with an intensity, a fierceness that almost floored him. He thought it might kill him and he couldn't even bring himself to care. As long as he had her.

Lowering his head, he claimed her mouth again and again, tasting her with his lips and his tongue, whilst she met him stroke for stroke. He captured each one of her soft sighs in his mouth, emitted as though she was as driven by desire as he was.

He let his hands trail over her body, revelling in the way her body quivered beneath his touch, and every time she pressed herself against him. He relished the way she lifted her hands to fumble with his shirt buttons and then slid them inside to trace the ridges of his chest as if she was trying to commit them to memory merely by touch.

He didn't even remember when he'd lost his jacket or bow-tie. When he'd begun to cup that peachy backside to lift her up to sit on the desk, her hard nipples raking over his chest, his hips locked within the tight embrace of her incredible long, slender legs.

He was so hard, so ready he could barely think straight. *Barely.* But he could think enough to register that if she rocked against him much longer then he was going to be beyond help.

'Are you on the pill?' he muttered.

'Hmm?' She lifted her head to meet his gaze, her eyes glazed and overflowing with naked desire so that it was almost his undoing.

'I don't have any protection on me.' Every word felt as though it was being torn from Sol's throat, especially when he wouldn't have slept with any other woman without protection yet all he could think about with Anouk was burying himself deep inside her and driving them both to oblivion.

It made no sense.

'Oh.'

She flushed, and he couldn't help himself lowering his head and following the pretty flush with his lips.

She moaned softly and it went straight to his sex as surely as if she'd gripped him with her hands.

What the hell had he been saying?

'Protection,' he remembered hoarsely.

Another brief pause and then she shook her head.

'Oh, Lord…no. No pill.'

She loosened her legs from around his hips as though it was the hardest thing she'd ever had to do. But he wasn't about to give her up that easily.

He couldn't.

He might not be able to slide inside her but he had to do *something* to sate this storm that raged and howled inside him, demanding more of her. *Needing* more of her.

Dropping to his knees, he hooked the shred of lace to one side.

'Wait.' She struggled to sit up, breathless and flustered. 'What are you…?'

But he didn't give her time to finish, he wanted to taste her too badly. Sliding one of her legs over his shoulder, he lowered his head and licked his way straight into her. Her shaky cry, as her hands tangled into his hair, was all the validation he needed.

She tasted of slick, sweet honey, and Sol couldn't get enough. He played with her, toyed with her, drawing lazy whorls with his tongue all around her swollen, molten core, before sliding over her, sliding into her, sucking on her, making her hips meet his mouth with each thrust.

And then she was moving faster, her breathing more ragged than ever, and he gripped hold of her and held her fast, prolonging her agony and ecstasy.

'Sol…please…' she rasped out.

As if she was all his for the taking.

The thought lanced through him with more appeal than it had any right to do.

With one finger sliding inside her, he licked faster and sucked harder. Anouk cried out, bucked against him, and shattered on his tongue. Fragmenting all around him. But he wasn't finished. Over and over he pushed her past the edge until he knew she could fall no more and, reluctantly, he sat back.

He re-buttoned his shirt, locating his jacket and bow tie with surprisingly shaky hands. At least it gave him time to recover, lest he lose all sense of self and pull her onto him to sate them both, there and then.

He watched her as she finally began to come back to herself. God, but she was beautiful. The need to have her still pounded through him, leaving him edgy and restless in a way he'd never experienced before.

Her eyes flickered to him, seeming to focus.

'You're dressed?'

The distraught shadow in those blue pools caught at him, pulling into a tight band around his chest. Around his sex.

'I have to go back out to the gala,' he gritted out. 'It's my role to raise money. For the charity.'

'Of course.' She pulled her mouth into a semblance of a smile although he wondered what it cost her. 'This was sex. Just sex.'

And there was no reason for that to grate on him as it did.

'And tonight, I intend there to be much more of it,' he growled. 'Properly. When we can take our time.'

'More?' Her hand fluttered to her chest and he found he rather liked it.

'Much more,' he echoed firmly. 'Trust me, Anouk. That was just for starters.'

And then, before she could answer he spun around and left the room, not trusting himself. He had a duty to the charity, and the kids. But if he stayed another moment with Anouk, he wasn't sure he could trust himself not to give in to temptation in the form of this bright, focussed, driven doctor with the blonde hair that sparkled like a glorious beach, and the blue eyes that made him sink fathoms deep.

And, goodness, he could still taste her sweetness on his tongue; still smell her on his fingers. And it was driving him to distraction.

She was driving him to distraction.

Who would have thought that the demure, strait-laced Anouk Hart would have ended up being his kryptonite?

CHAPTER FIVE

Sol slammed his car door shut with a vicious whack of his arm and made his way across the hospital car park.

He'd been in a foul mood since the Gala.

Leaving Anouk in that room after such a teaser of her luscious body had been nearly impossible. Promising them both a night full of more carnal discoveries had been the only way he'd managed to get back out to the gala to carry out the role that had brought him there in the first place: to raise money and awareness for the young carers, the kids who already had enough responsibility for people in their lives, and he refused to let them down.

Even for Anouk.

But he couldn't have anticipated that things would become so chaotic with Malachi, who had had to leave. It hadn't occurred to him that the night with Anouk might not happen. But his body had been protesting it ever since.

Even this morning he'd woken in the early hours, his head full of images of Anouk, his body hard and ready. He would swear he could still taste her on his tongue; still close his eyes and feel the heat from her body against his chest. And decidedly lower.

As if he were an overeager adolescent.

When had any woman invaded his every thought like this? When had any woman made him...*pine* for her? It simply wasn't his usual style.

Yet worse than any of that had been the fact that he'd wanted to tell her that he wasn't as bad as his reputation painted him. Perhaps ten years ago he'd been a playboy, even eight years ago. But recently, between his career and the charity, he didn't have time to seduce the sheer volume of women the rumours would have Anouk believe.

But, to what end?

What would it change?

He might no longer have the time, or the same inclination, for one-night stands with an endless procession of pretty, eager partners—but that hardly meant he was suddenly going to turn into the kind of commitment-ready man that a woman like Anouk would demand.

She might still be haunting his brain, and his body, in a way that no other woman ever had, but that was surely just because that all too brief encounter in the office hadn't quite been enough to slake their desire for one another. He still couldn't offer her any more than no-strings sex.

So then why care whether his reputation was entirely accurate? It was close enough, wasn't it? What did it matter *what* Anouk Hart thought of him?

Disgusted with himself, he had thrown the bedsheets back and stomped down to his home gym, running, rowing and carrying out a brutal training routine designed to really push his body. As if it could drive out the gnawing hunger he felt inside.

He shouldn't want her with such hunger.

Attraction was one thing, but this desire he felt for Anouk was something infinitely more dangerous. It made him wonder, just for a moment, what a normal relationship would be like. And that was much too treacherous a path because he wasn't like most normal people. He didn't have that capacity for love that they had. Hadn't his childhood taught him that? When his mother had been at her most vulnerable, when she'd most needed his care, he'd resented her. Hated her, even.

He had never gone to visit her in that centre Malachi had managed to get her into when he'd been fifteen. He'd only gone to her funeral a year later because Malachi had practically dragged him there by his ear. And he had resented every single second of it. Hadn't he given that woman enough of his precious time and attention? Hadn't he sacrificed his childhood for her? And hadn't Malachi sacrificed even more?

All of which meant he wasn't the kind of man for a woman like Anouk. He didn't love a person, flaws and all. No, he honed in on any imperfections and magnified them until he couldn't see past them to the person beneath. He used those flaws against them and Anouk deserved better than that.

She deserved better than him. If he thought anything of her at all then he would stay away from her.

At least the punishing training regime of the last couple of days seemed to have distracted his body. Hopefully, the demands of a shift in Neurology would occupy his head, as well.

What he hadn't expected was to be called straight down to Resus only to find he was once again needed on Anouk's team.

As if fate were personally throwing them together, he griped, striding through the doors only to come face to face with the woman who occupied too much of his brain. She stared at him in shock for several long seconds before dropping her eyes and switching back into professional mode.

Just like Anouk. Sol couldn't help grinning to himself. He would have been disappointed if she hadn't done so but at least she seemed as disquieted about his appearance as he felt. That was perhaps some consolation.

She cleared her throat and he knew he didn't imagine that overly bossy tone was meant for him.

'Okay, team, can you gather round a moment, please? We have a twenty-month-old girl who fell frontwards down a flight of concrete steps. ETA five minutes. Blood loss, but breathing and conscious. Helipad response team have gone up to the roof now to meet the HEMS. We're just waiting for now.'

The team moved quickly, getting equipment, a fresh mattress, the right materials—a flurry of activity as they prepared for the new patient to arrive. And when it all stilled, he wasn't prepared for Anouk to be standing right in front of him, a startled look on her face as though she hadn't expected to turn around and find him there.

He tried reminding himself of all the reasons he should keep his distance, but suddenly he couldn't think of a single one of them.

'I see I'm not the only one to have been brightening up this place.'

Sol jerked his head to the two-foot counter-top Christmas tree, prettily decorated, on the centre computer tables. He had no idea where they came from, yet the words tripped off his tongue, low and teasing.

'I didn't do it,' she retorted quickly.

Perhaps a little too quickly. And the way she flushed a deep scarlet made him unexpectedly curious. Was there something more to the story? Something that made her blush like a school-girl in front of him? Sol discovered he rather liked that idea.

'Ah, but do you know who did?' He took a stab in the dark, delighted when it seemed to pay off as her blush didn't fade, but she did manage to look simultaneously murderous.

As well as ridiculously cute.

'No.'

'Isn't that odd? I don't think I believe you,' he offered soberly, earning him a long-suffering eye-roll.

It delighted him beyond all measure.

'Fine. Saskia did it,' she bit out. 'Now will you leave it alone?'

'And you let her?' he heard himself asking. Laughing.

'I let her?' Anouk folded her arms across her chest.

'You let her decorate Resus? After the go you had at me for

the bit of tinsel? Or did my words make you reconsider your rather military stance?'

Anouk scowled. He was obviously baiting her, so the last thing she should do was rise to it.

'You think a lot of yourself, don't you? And for the record, I don't control Saskia.'

'I never suggested you did.' He grinned, beginning to enjoy himself now. 'But she's your best friend. I dare say she wouldn't have done it if you'd asked her not to.'

She glowered, continuing to eye him silently, for several beats too long.

'Fine,' she conceded eventually, grudgingly. Rolling her eyes at him and sending a lick of heat straight through to his sex. 'I thought it might be nice.'

'Nice, huh?'

'For the patients,' she huffed. 'You really do need to stop being so arrogant. I didn't do it because *you* suggested it.'

'Heaven forbid.'

He didn't even attempt to conceal his chuckles.

'In fact, like I said, I didn't even do it at all.'

'No, of course not. It was your friend. And I'm guessing you didn't help her one bit.'

Her bristly demeanour gave her away, and Sol grinned broadly. It was nonsensical how much lighter and happier, Anouk made things—even when she was irritated with him she managed to flip some unseen switch to turn his day from aggravating to enjoyable.

Even when she was dealing with a casualty, he found his eyes lingered a fraction longer on Anouk. Something about her seeming to shine that little bit brighter than everyone else around her.

She was fascinating.

Which made her so much worse than simply *hot*.

Anouk had taken up residence in his head and was apparently claiming squatter's rights. He couldn't seem to eject her and the harder he tried, the deeper she seemed to insinuate herself.

Which left only one solution. A solution that he would never in his right mind have expected himself to consider, and that he couldn't imagine any other woman in the world bringing him to.

The only way to stop himself from thinking about Anouk Hart was to convince her that they hadn't finished what she'd started the other night. That they both wanted more. Which shouldn't be too hard, given the sexual chemistry still crackling between them right now.

But he refused to lead her on. Just because he would be breaking his rule about second dates—not that it had been a proper first date, given that she hadn't even let him take her to that ball—it didn't mean he was offering her anything more. He wasn't putting a relationship on the table.

Who are you trying to convince? The question popped, unbidden, into his head. *Anouk or yourself?*

He shoved it away for the nonsense it was, but its echo lingered, nonetheless.

He needed more of Anouk. He *craved* her. But it was clear that whatever madness—he flattered himself to think it was their intense attraction—had overcome her the night of the gala, she wasn't going to let it get to her a second time. Not without a fight.

She'd pulled down the *strait-laced* shutters and set up the blockades of *disapproval*. But she didn't quite manage to pull off *forbidding* with the same aplomb as before. There was a flash of memory in her expression, a spike of hunger in her glance.

He had no doubt that Anouk craved him every bit as much as he craved her. But her mind was trying to shut off all that her lush, rather wanton body was telling it.

Which meant that he was going to have to seduce her. *Court her*, as old Mrs Bowman would have said.

Old-fashioned, and prim.

But dammit all if a perverse portion of him didn't relish the thought a little bit too much.

* * *

Did she really have to let Solomon Gunn affect her like this?
Anouk thought shakily, her eyes locked on the doors at the end
of Resus, waiting for the HEMS team to walk in.

She had veered from horror at her lustful display the night
of the gala, to regret that they had only enjoyed one single,
fiery, sensational act that night and she yearned for more. For
the past two days it had been impossible to empty her head of
the most vivid, thrilling, X-rated dreams that had kept her entire body smouldering.

No wonder she could barely bring herself to look him in the
eye now, for fear that her every last wanton thought was etched
right across her face for him to read.

Even now her body pricked with awareness, and she folded
her arms over her chest as though she could dull the ache in
her heavy nipples, as she relived the feel of his thumb skimming over them.

Mercifully, the doors chose that moment to swing open and
the HEMS team hurried in.

'This is Rosie, twenty months old,' the HEMS doctor began
handover. 'Normally fit and well. Approximately one hour ago
she was in the park with her mum when she tumbled a metre
and a half down a flight of concrete steps. She has a laceration
above her right eye and has had altered GCS. GCS is eleven.
Primary diagnosis is that she has had concussion and a period
of observation will determine whether there are any inter-cranial injuries. She's had two hundred of paracetamol and one
milligram ondansetron.'

'Pupils?' Anouk checked.

'She won't open her eyes.' The HEMS doctor shook his head
gently.

'Right.' She nodded. 'Sol…'

There was little need to say anything. As the neurology spe-
cialist, he was already beginning his obs, his low, calm pitch

already reassuring the little girl who was beginning to respond to his gentle instruction.

She nodded to her team to begin a fresh set of obs, as they were already preparing to do, and turned back to the HEMS doctor.

'Mum came with her?'

'This is Mum.' He turned to locate the young girl's mother, who was looking ashen but keeping herself together well.

'Okay, Mum.' Anouk smiled reassuringly. 'We're just going to check Rosie over for now, perhaps give her some medication to make her more comfortable, and then we'll be taking her for a scan to see what's going on with her head and neck. You're absolutely fine to stay here with her, let her see you, talk to her.'

'My husband is on his way…?' The mum trailed off uncertainly.

'That's fine. If he goes to the desk someone will bring him straight through to Resus.

'Thank you.' She smiled weakly, her eyes darting straight back to her daughter and her smile becoming deliberately brighter, her voice more upbeat as she tried to reassure the baby girl looking so small on the dark blue mattress.

As soon as they had completed their initial assessment they could wrap her in a blanket, which would stop her from looking quite so tiny and helpless. But Anouk didn't need the neurosurgeon beside her to tell her that, given Rosie's age, her little bones were still quite soft and the concern was that there could be an internal bleed, which might cause pressure and push the child's brain down.

Her team worked quickly and methodically, focussed on their task, feeding the information back to Anouk as she mentally constructed a picture for herself of what was going on with Rosie before preparing to take her little patient to CT.

'You're happy for the mother to accompany the child?' Sol's voice suddenly rumbled, low and rich in her ear, spreading through her body like luxuriously sticky caramel.

Anouk told herself not to be so stupid.

'Yes, I asked her if she was happy to join us before, so they'll be getting her leaded up.'

'Good,' he confirmed simply.

And there was no reason for her body to goosebump at the way they apparently worked so harmoniously together. No reason at all.

She thanked the HEMS team and wrapped up handover before getting straight back to her little patient and preparing her for CT.

'Do you fancy some lunch?' Sol asked quietly a couple of hours later, making her turn her head so fast that her neck cracked painfully. She pretended that it hadn't. 'It's a surprisingly quiet day today. I think we might actually be able to give it a try eating a meal for once.'

'Lunch?'

'Yes, the thing normal people eat around midday.'

'As opposed to the packet of biscuits I usually just about get time to grab?' She tried laughing to conceal her shock.

If she hadn't known Sol better, it might have sounded like an actual date.

'Hence why I want to buy you lunch.'

The temptation to accept was shockingly strong.

'Why?' she demanded instead.

He didn't even blink.

'I thought that, perhaps after the other night, it might be nice to get to know each other a little better. That is to say, *with* our clothes on.'

'Shush,' Anouk hissed, spinning wildly around before bustling him into an empty side room. 'Someone might hear you.'

'They didn't. So, lunchtime?'

'Like…a date?' she demanded stiffly. 'I don't think that's a good idea.'

His mouth crooked upwards.

'Don't panic, it's just lunch. No date.'

'It isn't *just* anything. It's about the optics.'

'No one cares.'

She rolled her eyes at him.

'Lots of people care. And even if they didn't, *I* care.'

'That you're seen on a lunch date at work? Or that you're seen with me?'

'Both. And I thought you said it wouldn't be a date?'

His grin ramped up until it made her stomach tighten. And other things tighten, too.

'I lied.' He winked at her, making her tingle now, too.

She was pretty sure he knew exactly what he was doing. That he could read every embarrassing effect on her hot face.

'You're irredeemable,' she snapped.

'Thanks.'

'It wasn't a compliment.'

'Too late. I took it as one.' He rocked back and leant on the doorjamb, folding his arms over his chest in a way that he must surely know made him look all the more hewn and powerful. All male.

She cursed her faithless heart and the tattoo it was currently beating throughout every vein and nerve-ending in her body. His dark eyes—as glossy and mesmerising as a master chocolatier's darkest mirror glaze—rippled with something she couldn't read but traitorously wished she could.

She ought to back up and put a little distance between the two of them. Or, better yet, leave. Instead, she stayed exactly where she was. Within arm's reach of Sol. A silent invitation even as she pretended it wasn't.

The lazy, insouciant way he watched her warned her that he knew it was pretence. His eyes raked over her body and left it as tingling and *aware* as she'd been that night. Craving more. She couldn't tear her gaze from that mouth, wicked and expert all at once. The things it had done to her should be illegal.

She was glad they weren't.

Everything inside was still. Calm. Expectant.

'Is something wrong?' he demanded suddenly.

And Anouk was aware of an edge to his tone. A hint that he was teasing her, playing with her, but she didn't know what the joke was.

'Wrong?'

'You appear to be rather fixated.'

'Fixated?'

She was beginning to sound a little like the old neighbour's parrot that had had a habit of waking her and Saskia at ridiculous hours in the morning, despite the fact that it was a decent apartment and the walls weren't exactly thin.

'With my mouth?'

She snapped her eyes up.

'I'm not fixated with your mouth.'

'Indeed? Only, I was going to ask if there was something there. A mark perhaps. An ink stain. A crumb.'

God help her, but all she could think of now was that if it had been a crumb, she would have gladly licked it off.

'No crumb,' she managed briskly. 'Or anything else.'

'Shame.'

As though he could read her illicit thoughts.

'I should go.'

'You should,' he agreed.

It took a great effort to galvanise her legs, moving one in front of the other in a great imitation of a newborn foal. Was it any wonder then that as she reached Sol and he refused to budge to let her pass easily, she faltered slightly?

He caught her in an instant, not that she had been about to fall, and suddenly she was being hauled into his arms, and he was holding her there, and she couldn't breathe. All she could do was stare again at his fascinating mouth, silently begging it to come crashing down on hers as it had that night.

When it didn't, Anouk didn't see any other choice but to lean up and press her lips to his.

It was instant combustion. His arms encircled her, pulling her to him. Her soft, pliant body against his deliciously hard one. He dipped his head and tasted her, sampling as though she were some precious vintage wine, leaving Anouk feeling revered and rare.

He dipped in and out, making her arch to him for more, soft moans escaping her lips in spite of herself.

He let his fingers tangle in her hair, mumbling words like *glorious* and *spun-silk gold*.

'It's just hair,' she muttered against his mouth, half afraid that she would fall for his charms when she knew better, probably better than anyone.

'No,' he argued, drawing back from her and tangling his hands deep within the abundance. 'It's like running my fingers through the softest gallium.'

'I don't need the hollow compliments…' she began, but when he raked his thumb over her lower lip, apparently revelling in the feel of her shaky breath on his skin, she found she couldn't even remember what she'd been about to say.

All the while she wanted the moment to last an eternity, maybe two, and yet also wanted the journey to be over, so that he could finally take her to his apartment and release the madness that had been building ever since he'd pressed his head between her legs that night and showed her exactly what she'd been missing all these years. With her two perfectly nice, perfectly dull boyfriends.

He kissed her some more. Slowly, reverently, as though they had all the time in the world and as though they weren't in the middle of a busy hospital.

The hospital, the voice sounded dully through the fog of her brain.

Her shift.

She had no idea from where she found the strength to break his kiss. And then some more, to break his hold.

'This is what you do, isn't it?' she managed in a strangled voice.

'Does it matter? If we're both enjoying it?'

She couldn't tell him that *yes, it mattered*. Especially when he made her feel as though she were special, only to remember that she wasn't.

That a hundred girls had probably travelled this same road before.

Idiot that she was.

'I have work to do,' she bit out, whirling around and snatching open the door before she could do something as stupid as change her mind.

The last thing she expected was to hear his voice carry, deep and smooth, down the hall.

'Come with me to the centre.'

She shouldn't let him worm his way under her skin. She *shouldn't*.

'Say that again?' she demanded, stopping and turning slowly.

'Come with me to see the Care to Play centre. See what it's all about.'

He was offering to show her into his private world? His private life? She could hardly believe he would be that open with her. Or anyone, for that matter.

By the expression that fleetingly clouded Sol's face, he could hardly believe it either. If she didn't accept quickly, she feared he might rescind the invitation. And, despite all her promises to herself to steer clear of him after the gala, she desperately didn't want him to rescind anything.

Solomon Gunn.

He'd been worming his way under her skin ever since she'd met him. She'd staved him off initially by fixing on his playboy reputation. It hadn't been too difficult, not after watching her self-destructive mother make one poor choice after the next where bad boys were concerned.

Yet, she'd also seen flashes of another side of Sol. A compassionate side lacked by other top-flight surgeons she knew. The incident with young Izzy and her family, if she was going to be honest now, hadn't been the first. Nor the care for his old patient—Mrs Bowman.

But that didn't mean she had to be attracted to him, did it? She was supposed to be immune, for pity's sake.

Anouk was still giving herself a halfway decent talking-to when she heard her own voice replying.

'Okay.' No, not really *okay*, her brain screamed at her to take it back. 'I'd like to see the centre.'

'Then I'll bring you some forms to sign.'

'Forms?'

'Standard security. For being with the kids. As a doctor you'll be fine, but it protects the centre.'

'Right.'

By the book, Sol? Anouk said nothing but filed it away. It was yet another sign of how much this centre, and these kids, meant to him.

Reckless playboy? Or caring protector? Every time she thought she knew him, he morphed into something else. She couldn't pin him down.

It mattered to her more than it had any right to.

CHAPTER SIX

'WELL,' ANOUK MUTTERED to herself as she slapped her steering wheel lightly. 'You've been sitting out here for nearly half an hour. Here goes nothing.'

Yanking open her door, she jackknifed out of her car, clicked the lock button, and marched to the centre before she could talk herself out of anything.

She was barely through the doors before an older woman stopped her.

'Can I help you?'

'I'm Anouk,' she began. 'Anouk Hart. I…'

She trailed off. Should she say she was here to meet Sol? Or just that he'd given her forms to fill out the other day? Or perhaps she shouldn't mention him at all; she didn't want people to think she was just using the centre to somehow wheedle her way in with him.

'Oh, yes, Anouk.' The woman smiled. 'I'm Barbara. Sol has been telling us all about you. So have Izzy and Katie.'

'The girls are here?'

'Yes, Katie particularly, of course. Izzy only got out of hospital yesterday but the first thing she did was ask when you would be coming in.' Barbara laughed.

'It always amazes me how resilient kids are.' Anouk shook her head. 'Only a week ago she was in my Resus department.'

'Now she's home and already back to helping her mum,' the woman agreed. 'Inspirational. Just like so many of the kids I see come through those doors.'

'I can see why Sol cares so much about this place. I guess not everyone with a privileged childhood wants to see what other people have to go through.'

'I know. I like to think that's why Sol—and Malachi, for that matter—set up this place. They might be rich, influential men now, but neither of them has ever forgotten how appalling their own childhoods were.'

Anouk blinked. She fought to keep her expression neutral. 'Right.'

'I mean, not just as young carers themselves but how they had to drag themselves out of the gutter,' Barbara continued, clearly under the impression that this wasn't news to Anouk. 'Without them getting the message out, people with clout wouldn't even know about us. This centre, and the new one they are building, simply wouldn't exist.'

Anouk made a sound of acknowledgement, but her head was spinning.

Sol had been a young carer? He had dragged himself out of the gutter?

It didn't make any sense. But what confused her most was that Barbara didn't seem worried about discussing it. As though it was common knowledge.

As though she was talking about a completely different Solomon Gunn from the playboy neurosurgeon who relished his Smoking Gun nickname.

Was it possible that his colleagues didn't know the man at all?

Even she herself sometimes forgot how other people envied her childhood when they knew she was the daughter of a late Hollywood actress. They couldn't see the darker, uglier side of that life. Was it the same for Sol? People said he was a wealthy neurosurgeon, coming from money, and they made judgements. *She* had made judgements.

Would the real Solomon Gunn please step forward?

'So, anyway, we thought you might like to spend the afternoon with Libby. She's a friendly little girl, six, sole carer for her mother, although...' Barbara paused, half stating, half questioning '...you'll know that we don't discuss that side of things here?'

'Yes, I know. This is a place she can come and just be a child.'

The woman nodded her approval.

'At the moment Libby is making Father Christmas faces for the Christmas Fayre. Are you any good at crafting?'

'I'm not known for it.' Her laugh betrayed a hint of nerves, but that couldn't be helped. 'But I'm keen to learn. Sol isn't here?'

'There was a problem at the construction site. Besides, I think he thought you might find it easier getting to know the children in your own time.'

Without him looking over her shoulder, did he mean? Either way, it was odd but, taking the complication of having to interact with Sol out of the equation, she could practically *feel* some of her tension slipping from her shoulders, through her body to the floor, and away from her.

She exhaled quietly with relief.

'That probably would be better.'

Was it her imagination, or did Barbara's smile suddenly seem brighter? Wider?

'That will do just fine,' Barbara approved, leading her over to where a young girl sat, with a unicorn T-shirt and pink jeans, her hair plaited exceptionally neatly either side of her head.

'Libby, I've got another set of helping hands. This is Anouk. You remember Izzy and Katie mentioned her.'

A six-year-old girl glanced up with a wide, toothy smile.

'And Sol talked about her, too,' she added. 'You're just in time to help me decorate the next lot of faces to stick on the goodie bags. Can you bring those cotton-wool balls over there for the beard? I've got the googly eyes but we'll cut little red hats out of the felt and use a mini pom-pom for the bobble.'

Before she knew it, Barbara had gone, leaving Libby and Anouk alone. Not that it seemed to matter since Libby was quite happy to take charge.

'What if you cut the felt hats and I'll stick them on?' Libby suggested. 'Wait, no, not like that. Like this. Let me show you.'

Quickly, efficiently, Libby demonstrated what she wanted, talking Anouk through each step, not that it seemed particularly complicated. Yet the way the girl approached the crafting task with such meticulousness and attention to detail, in a way that was common in six-year-olds, reminded her of Libby's experience as a young carer.

Her chest kicked. It was an unexpected reminder of her own childhood, when she had organised her mother with care and discipline as though she were Annalise Hartwood's personal assistant rather than her daughter.

And verbal punching bag, of course.

Her brain skittered away from the unwanted memories.

'Are you looking forward to Christmas?' Anouk asked milliseconds before it occurred to her that it might not be the most appropriate question for someone like Libby.

For a moment, the little girl looked thoughtful and then, to Anouk's relief, she managed a slow bob of her head. Anouk hadn't realised she'd been holding her breath until that moment.

'Yes, I think so. It's a lot better now that I have this place to come to.'

'Right,' Anouk agreed, swallowing quickly. 'And these are for the Christmas Fayre?'

'Yep, it's a lot of fun. There are stalls and fairground games, and Sol and Malachi usually arrange something special. Like, one year it was an ice rink, and another it was fairground rides. It can be a chance for the centre to get out into the community and show them that we're good kids.'

'I understand.' Anouk bobbed her head, carefully concealing her surprise.

The maturity with which Libby spoke belied her six years. But then, that was likely a result of being a child carer for her parent. It was testament to her resilience how this little girl could talk so eloquently one moment, and be excited about making Father Christmas faces to stick on paper bags of stocking fillers.

'Plus, we raise money to help keep the centre running,' she added proudly. 'And to buy new pieces for our Christmas village scene.'

Anouk wasn't quite sure what that was, but before she could ask Libby was reaching for a small box beside her to lift up a handful of faces from Santa to Rudolph, and from elves to gingerbread men.

'I made these already.'

'They're amazing.'

Libby beamed, dropping her voice to a conspiratorial whisper.

'And, don't tell the younger girls, but I know that Father Christmas isn't real.'

'What makes you think that?' Anouk asked carefully. Most six-year-olds she knew still believed.

Libby shot her a cynical smile.

'Please. I know he isn't. Last year, when I was five, we went shopping together and Mummy bought me presents without me knowing. But over Christmas she got unwell again and couldn't get out of bed without my help so she couldn't put them out overnight. She tried to pretend that Father Christmas had got lost and left them under her bed by mistake.'

'That's entirely possible,' Anouk replied steadily, her eyes deliberately focussed on her task.

'You don't have to protect me. I'm not your average six-year-old,' Libby remonstrated softly, echoing words she must have heard people use time and again about her.

The matter-of-fact tone only tugged at Anouk's heart all the harder.

'The point is that Mummy was ill so I'd had to do the hoovering over Christmas. I knew the presents had been there for weeks. I tried to tell Mummy but she got upset and cross with herself so I pretended that I believed her.'

'It's still possible—'

Libby cut her off as though she hadn't spoken.

'But I wanted to tell someone and I like you. I think I can trust you.' She tipped her head on one side and eyed Anouk shrewdly. 'I can, can't I?'

The lump in her throat meant she might as well have been trying to swallow a golf ball.

'You can,' she choked out, and Libby just eyed her a little longer before bending her head back to her Father Christmas crafting and working diligently again. A companionable silence settled over them once more—as long as the little girl couldn't hear how hard and how fast Anouk's heart was beating for her, that was.

A good half-hour had to have passed before Libby spoke again.

'You know there's going to be an entertainer at the Christmas Fayre, maybe a magician or a puppet show?'

As if their previous conversation had never happened.

'Wow.' Anouk hoped she managed to inject just the right amount of sounding impressed but not condescending. 'That sounds like it will be fun.'

'It will.' The girl nodded enthusiastically. 'Especially when it's a real entertainer and not just Sol and Malachi dressed up in costumes. Although they're pretty funny, too. And so cool.'

'You think so?' She tried to sound chatty but her throat felt dry. Scratchy.

Libby's unbridled adoration didn't help Anouk in her fight not to let Sol get under her skin any more than he had already appeared to.

'Of course—' Libby snorted in a little-girl sort of way '—you could normally see it for yourself. They're usually always here. Or at least, they used to be before they started to build our new centre.'

Picking up another face to glue, Anouk tried to sound utterly casual.

'What makes them so cool, then?'

'Well, *everything*, I guess.' Libby looked up, her expression thoughtful. 'They were carers, too, just like all of us, only my mummy loves me and their mummy didn't. But they've still become rich and famous. When I grow up, I'm going to be just like them.'

'A surgeon like Sol?'

It was all she could do to sound normal. Another revelation about Sol. Another description that made him seem like a world away from the commitment-phobic playboy of the hospital gossip mill.

'Sol's a *neurosurgeon*,' Libby corrected. 'He saves lives. Or maybe I'll be an investor and become a millionaire like Malachi. I haven't decided yet, but they're both always saying that if you want something enough, and work hard enough for it, there's a good chance that you can achieve it.'

'Right.' Anouk grappled for something to say.

She wasn't sure if it was Libby's maturity or the fact that Sol was such an inspiration to the little girl that stole her breath away the most.

'Did you know they like to help to actually build the new centre?'

'Sorry?' Anouk snapped back to the present.

'Sol and Malachi?' Libby prompted. 'They are actually helping to build the new Care to Play. We saw them a lot in the summer when the centre organised rounders and football matches in the park. They were carrying bags off a builder's truck and cutting wood.'

'They did?' The image certainly didn't do anything to dampen the ache that constantly rolled inside her these days.

No wonder Sol always looked so healthy. Every time she had failed to push away memories of that mouth-watering physique, slick and hot under her hands, she'd consoled herself with the knowledge that he must spend countless hours in the gym. Her mother had enjoyed enough gym-junkie boyfriends for her to know that they loved themselves more than they would ever be able to love someone else.

She'd almost convinced herself that this fact therefore detracted from how good-looking Sol might otherwise seem. So discovering now that he had achieved that honed, utterly masculine body from genuine physical labour—and not just any labour, but building a centre for young carers—only made it that much harder to pretend there wasn't some empyreal fire to the man.

'Some of the older girls said they were hot.' Libby looked sceptical, all of her six years suddenly showing. 'But I think they were probably okay because they'd taken their tops off to cool down. They put them back on when we passed, though.'

'Right,' Anouk managed. Just about.

She imagined that the temperature of the brothers wasn't the kind of *hot* the older girls had meant. But the image of Sol shirtless wasn't one she was ready to deal with right at this moment.

'Sometimes we take them bottles of water to help cool them down.'

Despite herself, Anouk suppressed a grin.

'Very thoughtful of you.'

Libby, her eyes on her Santa face, didn't notice.

'Sol and Malachi look after us, it's only fair that we do a little for them. They're who we buy the Christmas village scenes for. It's special to them.'

'I'm pretty sure they're looking after you because you already take care of people,' Anouk said softly.

'Well…maybe, but they know exactly what we're going through, and that makes it easier to talk about.'

Another titbit of information. Anouk felt like a tiny bird, starving for every morsel dropped about Sol. She bit her lip.

'How did they come to be carers?'

She'd tried to sound casual, but the little girl glanced up sharply.

'That's their story to tell.' Libby shut down immediately, sounding for all the world like a young woman and not a six-year-old kid. 'Don't you think?'

It was all Anouk could do not to let it show how flustered she felt. She plastered a smile on her face. She wouldn't think about Sol Gunn a second longer.

'Okay, Libby, I've finished that batch of Father Christmas faces. What should I make now?'

And she wouldn't be going anywhere near the new building site, either.

Sol knew she was there even before he turned around. It was as though the entire air seemed to change and shift around him and where it had been peaceful before, now a kind of energy was pulsating through it.

He took a breath and took his time, turning slowly. She looked delicious standing there, all bundled up in a big coat, a Christmas pudding hat and a very green, Christmas-tree-patterned scarf.

'Anouk.' Even her name tasted absurdly good as it rolled off his tongue. 'Just passing?'

'Don't be fatuous,' she replied evenly. 'Libby said I could find you here. As I imagine you knew she would.'

He wanted to deny it but couldn't.

Libby was confident and talkative, a good kid who would have been able to show Anouk around without becoming tongue-tied. But he supposed there was a tiny piece of him that had also known the six-year-old would have told Anouk about the new centre.

He just hadn't known, until now, whether Anouk would have taken the bait and come to see him for herself. He tried to ignore the sense of satisfaction that punctured him.

'Ah, but you didn't have to come.'

'Of course that's what your response would be.' She drew her lips into a thin line.

Yet Sol couldn't help but notice that it wasn't a denial either. He was barely even aware of dropping his tools and making his way to her, feeling the heat start to come back to his frozen limbs as he stamped his way over the stony ground.

'So why *are* you here?'

'Libby mentioned that you and Malachi are helping to build the place. I had to come and see for myself, and here you are, hauling bags of...' she cocked her head to read the packaging that he still had hoisted on his shoulder '...plaster off a truck. Surely you have guys to do that for you?'

'Every bit Mal and I do means more money saved for the centre itself.'

Plus, the physical labour of it somehow...fulfilled him.

'I thought you were a millionaire playboy? You and your brother come from money. Isn't that what the hospital grapevine says?'

He opened his mouth to make one of his typical, non-committal responses, but found he couldn't. There was a new edge in her tone, almost as if she was testing him. But she couldn't possibly know the truth, could she?

Something dark and unfamiliar loomed in the shadows of his mind. A lesser man might have mistaken it for shame at his past. But he refused to be that lesser man. Malachi was right: it was done. It was history. No need to rake up the humiliation of their childhood for anyone, especially the daughter of a Hollywood starlet who had no doubt enjoyed a charmed upbringing.

Except that wasn't what the Hintons had said, was it?

He stuffed it down and forced himself to be upbeat.

'Mal and I can donate all we want, but these centres need to exist for themselves, support themselves—that way they can keep going long after we're gone. And if the model works then it can be replicated up and down the country.'

'You want more Care to Play centres,' she realised.

'Right. One centre is good, two centres is even better, but what we want is a business model which can be extended nationally.'

'I...didn't think of that.'

'Why would you?' he asked. 'Want a tour?'

Anouk looked surprised, before bouncing her Christmas pudding hat slowly and looking even more ridiculously cute.

'Sure. Why not?'

'So, what happened with that toddler who fell down the concrete steps?' he asked as he turned and headed into the building as if it made no difference to him whether she had followed or not. It was only as he lowered the plaster bag and heard her boots clicking on the concrete floor that he knew she had.

Why did it give him another jolt of victory?

How had this woman managed to insinuate her way under his skin? It was sheer insanity and he should walk away now.

Sol had the oddest sensation that if he didn't walk now, it would be too late.

And still he unlocked the padlock and unwound the heavy-link chain from around the temporary plywood doors.

'The twenty-month-old?' Anouk looked surprised.

'Yeah. Rosie, right?'

'Yes, Rosie. Believe it or not she was okay.' Anouk grinned, the miraculous recovery of kids never failing to amaze her. 'You knew there were no obvious signs of any breaks or fractures?'

'I did, but there was that inter-cranial bleed that needed to be monitored.'

'Yep, that's it. She stayed in for two nights before being cleared. She was discharged yesterday.'

'Lucky.' He smiled.

'Very.'

'Anyway, welcome to our new Care to Play centre.' He slid the chain through one door handle and pulled the other open to usher her inside. 'We should be in by the new year.'

Anouk walked through what would soon be the reception area, stopping dead practically in the doorway of the new hall. Then she glanced around, silently taking it all in. From the expansive, hi-tech-looking space with its spaghetti junction of wires, evidently in preparation for any number of new gadgets for the kids, and the large heaters to dry the plaster.

It was inexplicable how buoyed up he felt, showing her around and watching her reaction—this unique, complicated woman who pulled at something deep inside him—and he didn't know what name to put to it.

He didn't really want to try.

There was an attraction, certainly, but he'd been attracted to plenty of women in his time. A primal, sexual attraction.

This wasn't that.

He grappled for the word but the only thing he could come up with was...*connection*. And he knew better than to believe that.

Didn't he?

'What's going over there?' she asked, pointing to an area of the room where there was still a fair amount of work to do.

'A stage.' Sol smiled. 'You want to see the talent some of these kids have. They're just bursting for a forum in which they can showcase what they can do. Behind the wall there are a couple of soundproofed music rooms, too. We'll be putting instruments in them and the kids can set up their own bands if they want to. Or just sing, whatever they want.'

'Goodness, this place really is so much bigger than where they are now.'

'By a couple of hundred square metres,' Sol agreed. 'But it isn't just that, it's the way we've teched the place up.'

'I get that.' She smiled, with the kind of radiance that heated up a person's very bones. Heated up *his* very bones, anyway. 'It's incredible. The kids are going to be bowled over.'

'That's the hope. Come on, I'll show you the rest.'

He continued the tour to the new kitchens, the offices, the music rooms, and finally the small quiet rooms.

'Although the centre is built on the idea that kids can come in and talk about normal things, and just be a kid crafting, or playing, or singing, there are nonetheless times when kids *will* need to talk. Maybe a little group of them will get together.'

'And support each other,' Anouk offered.

'Exactly. Or sometimes someone might just need a quiet room for a one-on-one chat with an adult. We do get kids who have been self-harming and need something more to help them cope. They might have been struggling without any support and things have just got on top of them and they haven't known where to turn.'

He didn't miss the way Anouk dropped her eyes from his, that familiar stain creeping over her skin whenever she was embarrassed.

'Everything okay?'

'So Care to Play can be there for them and make sure they know that they're no longer alone?' she trotted out stiffly. 'That's great.'

Spinning around, she lunged for the door to leave and practically bumped into him.

Instinct made him reach out and grab her upper arms to steady her, before he could stop himself. There was clearly something more going on here and he felt oddly driven to find out what it was.

But the instant he made physical contact with her, electricity charged through him, practically fusing his hands in place. He was wholly unable to pull away. The need to learn more about this woman who had infiltrated his whole being in a matter of a week was almost visceral.

'What's going on, Anouk?' Urgency laced through his voice. 'What is it?'

These rooms were designed to feel closed off. A place where kids could talk about the things they might not even want to admit to themselves. *Safe.*

Right now, with Anouk up against his chest and his nostrils suddenly full of that fresh, faintly floral scent that he associated with her alone, Sol felt about as far from safe as it was possible to get.

He glanced down to see the pulse in her slender neck jolt then quicken, which didn't exactly help matters. The need to bend his head to hers and taste her lips again was almost overpowering.

Almost.

It was only the need to wait for her answer, to understand her better, that held him back. It made no sense and yet he ached to hear her talk to him as though he was someone other than a morally bankrupt tomcat willing to jump on anything in a skirt.

And yet, if she did, was he ready to answer her?

CHAPTER SEVEN

SHE GLANCED UP at him, though he got the impression that it cost her dearly to do so. She watched him for what seemed like an eternity and, for a moment, he believed she was actually going to talk. To tell him…something that counted.

And then the shutters slammed down with a clang.

'I don't know what you're talking about.' She forced a smile, trying to inch discreetly back a fraction. Not that there was anywhere to go in this tiny space.

'I don't believe that.'

She glowered at him, but he didn't miss the way she swallowed. Hard.

He could push her. He wanted to. But something told Sol that would be counterproductive.

The moments ticked by.

'Why would I?' she demanded suddenly.

'Why would you what?'

'Why would I talk to you? Open up to you?' Her voice sounded angry and pained, and raw all at once. It spoke to him in a way he recognised only too well. 'When you wouldn't dream of talking to me.'

'I have talked to you,' he lied. 'I've invited you here. You've spent time with the kids only today.'

He made himself step back, pretending that her soft, plump lips weren't still imprinted in his mind's eye. And that the feel of her arms didn't still sear through his palms. He reminded himself that it was purely physical, sexual attraction, even if it felt alien.

Because what else *could* it be?

'You've told me lots about the kids, and the centre. Between the gala, and my visit, you've given me plenty of information. You've explained how there are lots of charities out there for young carers, and lots of volunteers, really good people, and how your charity is different. You've shown how it still isn't enough. These kids need more.'

'They do.'

'I agree.' She lifted her eyes to his, her gaze almost too intense to bear. 'My point is, Sol, that, in all the talking you've done, the one subject you steer clear of is why you care so much.'

He hadn't seen it coming, but he should have. He should have been ready for the question. In a way, he was. And yet it still had the power to wind him.

His hands dropped from her arms and he swung away—the moment lost.

'Does it matter?' he managed, amazed at how calm, how cool, he sounded when inside his heart was pumping blood around his body as though he was a gold medal winning sprinter.

Behind him, she seemed to ponder for a moment. Though whether about how to phrase her questions, or how she had come to ask them in the first instance, Sol couldn't quite be certain.

'I don't know,' she admitted. 'I suppose that's what I'm asking. If it matters.'

'I don't think I follow.'

'No,' she conceded, pulling her lips together as if she wasn't even sure what she was saying. 'It's just that *this* you isn't the image you tend to put forward of yourself. Solomon Gunn the playboy is well known, but it doesn't fit with all of...*this*.'

She waved her hand around the construction site that was the centre.

'I suppose I want to know which version of the man is really you. And if it's this one, then wouldn't you rather be Solomon Gunn, tireless advocate for young carers?'

'No.'

She blinked.

'Why not?'

Because it invited too many questions, too much scrutiny, his own childhood would inevitably come out and that wasn't a side of his life he wanted people to see when they looked at him.

As it was threatening to do now.

It was odd the way he wanted her to know he was more than just that playboy—as inexplicable as that was—but when it came to telling her, showing her, the truth, he found he couldn't contend with that either.

Because the truth made him feel ashamed. Lacking. It was a chunk of his life he would readily burn down, if only he could.

'Because I like my playboy lifestyle,' he lied with an aplomb that had been perfected over more than a decade.

And, possibly for the first time, he hated himself for it.

'Do you really?' she asked softly. 'Only, I'm beginning to wonder, from all the things I've been hearing about you today, how you have much time at all for quite the number of amorous conquests your reputation suggests.'

'I'm a skilled multitasker.' He feigned a laugh.

Anyone else would have bought into it. Anouk stared at him, unfazed.

'You'd have to be in two places at once. No one is that good at multitasking.'

It was as though she could see down to his soul.

He reminded himself that even if she did know some scraps of truth about him, that was all she knew. Scraps. Not the whole picture, and it would stay that way. However much he might loathe what he was about to do.

'Trust me, Anouk, you're not the first woman I've slept with who has mistaken sexual intimacy for a more profound connection, and thought it meant they *understood* me. But it's just sex, nothing more.'

She blanched, making him feel the cad he knew he was.

Better that than this irrational ache he had to buy into her better opinion of him.

As the silence tightened around him, seemingly weighed down with anticipation, the last thing he expected was for Anouk to rally.

'I suspect you care about these kids because you understand them better than you'd have your moneyed gala guests believe.'

'Not really,' he denied.

'Of course you do.' She held his gaze, refusing to cow to him. 'Because you were a young carer, too, Sol.'

Of all the things he'd expected Anouk might say, that certainly wasn't one of them. For one brief, heart-stopping moment, he wondered if he could bluff her.

He had the oddest sensation that he wouldn't be able to. She would see right through his façade. The realisation needled him.

Or was he more galled at the idea that some traitorous element of himself wanted her to see through it?

He had no idea how he kept his tone neutral.

'You've been talking to Barbara.'

She shook her head but he didn't believe her and determined to make no bones about it.

'I've warned her about sharing personal information before,' he growled. 'No matter who it's about, or who to.'

'It wasn't Barbara.' Anouk raised her eyebrows.

'Of course it was. It had to be.'

'Actually, Libby told me,' Anouk bit out finally. 'She also told me that you and your brother were young carers. For your mother.'

He couldn't answer. Couldn't even speak.

'What else did she say?' he gritted out when he felt as if he'd finally managed to work his tongue loose.

'That it was your story to tell, not hers,' Anouk admitted.

His short, sharp laugh—if that was what it could be called—bounced off the freshly plastered walls.

'That sounds like Libby.'

There was another beat of silence, which Anouk only broke after it had become more than awkward.

'So, it's true?'

He didn't answer. If he denied it he would feel as though he was betraying a six-year-old girl. At the same time, he had no idea what else to say.

'How young?' Anouk added at last.

He'd answered this question a thousand times to different kids over the years, or considered it not to be the business of any of his hospital colleagues. But somehow it was different with Anouk. He couldn't bring himself to send her home, yet he had no intention of sharing something so personal with her.

Even if a component of him wanted to.

All of a sudden he had to get out of there. This conversation—or perhaps the last few—with Anouk had left him feeling battered and bruised, as though he couldn't work out what he wanted from her.

It was an unfamiliar, unwelcome sensation.

Mostly.

He should leave, but he found that he wanted to spend more time with her and therein lay the issue. The more Sol thought about it, the more he came to the conclusion that he only wanted her because he hadn't had her yet.

As distasteful as it was, there was no other explanation. No other reason why she should have him tied up in such knots.

The solution was to remedy that situation. To convince Anouk that it was in both their interests to finish what they'd started the night of the gala. Once they had indulged their mutual desire, the sweeping need would at last abate.

Surely it was inevitable?

'There's no electricity in this place yet,' he stated abruptly. 'Except for the temporary generator powering the heaters. But there's a decent coffee house on the high street.'

She stood still as they watched each other for a beat too long. He waited for her to make her excuses and leave, and he told himself that he didn't care either way.

And then, abruptly, she grabbed her bag and threw it onto her shoulder.

'Let's go, then.'

'I swear I've heard this Christmas song in the shops since November,' Anouk muttered as they opened the doors to the coffee house only to be blasted by the heat, the gorgeous smells, and the music.

She wasn't even sure what she was doing here. Only that her chest was tight with some nonsensical notion that Solomon Gunn might actually…open up to her. As much as she knew it was ridiculous, she couldn't eject it from her head.

'Or October.' Sol laughed, his earlier unease having apparently melted away as soon as they'd left the centre and she'd dropped her questions. 'Okay, you get the table, I'll get the drinks. Just tell me what you want.'

Anouk tried not to feel deflated. It shouldn't matter that he didn't want to trust her. She shouldn't let it bother her. Just as she hadn't let that moment back in the new centre get to her. When he'd held her so close that she'd been convinced he was going to kiss her again.

When she'd *ached* for him to kiss her again.

But he hadn't. He'd just dropped her as though the moment hadn't crept under his skin even a fraction of the way it had slunk under hers.

And then she'd badgered him about his life, his childhood, being a young carer. As if that could reveal a side of him that she could understand, relate to, trust. But to what end? It wasn't as if she wanted a relationship with him. She wasn't naïve enough to think any woman could tame a perennial playboy, and yet… there was something about him that simply didn't seem to fit with the reputation.

Or perhaps that was what she was telling herself to justify her incongruously wanton forwardness the night of the gala. The night she *still* couldn't bring herself to regret. Even though she knew she ought to.

Maybe wanting to trust him was more about herself than Sol. Perhaps it was her wanting to vindicate that uncharacteristic one-night stand—if you could even call it that—to explain her sudden foray into seductress territory.

And still, it ate away at her that the Sol whom the kids at the centre loved so much was so very different from the bad boy the hospital knew.

She coveted knowing that man, too.

Yet she couldn't push him. The harder she tried, the more she could see the shutters coming down and still she couldn't seem to make herself walk away.

'I'm going for the Christmas cinnamon roast coffee,' he concluded after perusing the board for a moment. 'What would you like?'

'Tea. Nothing fancy, just a plain one, please.'

He raised his eyebrows at her.

'This can't be a manifestation of your aversion to Christmas?'

'It isn't an aversion,' she denied awkwardly.

'You really hate this time of year that much?'

He was turning the tables so casually that she couldn't be sure if it was deliberate or if he really couldn't help it. Nevertheless, she opened her mouth to tell him that *of course she didn't*.

'Pretty much.' She shrugged, the words popping out of their own volition. 'I know you don't feel the same. With your home-baked mince pies, and your gorgeous tree, and the Christmas village scene.'

Instantly his face changed and she sucked in a breath, not sure what she'd said.

'What about the Christmas village scene?'

His tone was too careful.

'I'm not sure,' she admitted cautiously. 'I don't actually know what Libby meant, she just told me that the kids from the centre do all they can to get together enough money to buy you and Malachi a new piece every year.'

She waited for him to push her on the subject, but instead his expression cleared and he dipped his head before striding to the counter, leaving her to find an available table. And remind herself to stop reading too much into everything that concerned Solomon Gunn.

'What are we doing here, Sol?' Curiosity made her drop the question even before he'd finished sliding the tray onto their table. 'I can't imagine you bring *dates* here. At least, not *after* you've already stripped them bare on the desk in an opulent study. Though perhaps before, when you're still trying to seduce them.'

He didn't answer straight away, sliding his coat off and dropping into the seat opposite her to stir his drink thoughtfully.

'I find myself as mystified as you are by this continuing... draw,' he answered enigmatically, sending her mind into a whirl analysing what he might mean by it.

So much for not reading too much into everything he said or did, she snorted quietly to herself.

'Which means what, exactly?'

'I'm debating that,' he told her. 'And I'm rapidly coming to the conclusion that these drawn-out, skirting-the-issue games don't appear to be getting us anywhere.'

'I'm not playing games.' Her indignation wasn't as sharp as she might have expected it to be.

'Therefore, I would like to propose something else,' he continued, as though she hadn't spoken. 'I contend that allowing it to play out seems to be the most logical conclusion.'

She couldn't quite dislodge the pocket of air blocking her throat.

'Play out?' she asked faintly. 'As in…?'

His smile was lethal enough to make her fear for her sanity. 'Sex.'

The statement sliced through the air between them, its simplicity robbing her of all thought for a moment; sending delicious shivers all the way down her spine.

'One night of pure, unrestrained pleasure,' he repeated, as though she might not have understood his meaning the first time—but for the wicked smile carved into his handsome face. 'A conclusion of that night at the gala.'

It was useless to pretend that a restlessness didn't roll right through her at the audacity of the man. Along with the rudest images of the hot, devilish expression on his face moments before he'd dipped his head between her legs and greedily drunk her in.

It was why, although every grey cell in her head was screaming at her to decline, she could only sit there, her body tense and…*needy*, as she stared at him in silence.

'But if we do, Anouk. Then there will have to be ground rules.'

'Ground rules?' she echoed faintly.

'To avoid confusion at a later date.'

'Avoiding confusion is good,' she conceded, her voice sounding thick and slow.

She felt as though she were outside her own body.

She ought to be telling him *no*. Instead, she just wanted to get the so-called ground rules agreed so they could get onto the meatier portion of the conversation.

Who was this strange woman inhabiting her body? And what had Sol done to the real her that night? She should be disgusted with herself; at how easily she seemed to be falling in with what Sol was suggesting.

Her weak acquiescence was all too reminiscent of her desperate mother.

And yet something niggled at Anouk, even if she couldn't quite place her finger on it.

Something in the way Sol sat, slightly more upright than usual. Or the way he appeared to be choosing his words deliberately. Or the intent look in his eyes. It all gave the impression that he wasn't nearly as blasé about it as he wanted her to believe.

Or possibly it was just in her imagination.

Either way, Anouk made the decision there and then to accept it at face value. When would she ever get the chance to act so daringly with someone who thrilled her the way that Sol did?

'Let me guess, the ground rules are that it's just sex?' she managed hoarsely. 'That it's just for the one night? That there are no troublesome, wild emotions complicating things afterwards?'

'Yes, to all three,' he growled. 'Except for the wild part.'

'Oh?' she managed.

'I intend it to get very wild,' he promised, his voice low and practically pulsing through her. 'And very hot. And very lustful.'

She thought she might have swallowed her tongue for a moment.

'I'd be disappointed if it was anything less,' she managed, at last.

She didn't quite recall moving, but suddenly they were both standing and Sol was helping her into her coat before enveloping her hand in his and leading her outside. They didn't stop, or debate it any longer, but he pulled Anouk close to him and began threading his way through the streets spilling over with Christmas shoppers.

Streets that were still slick and wet from the rain that had fallen whilst they'd been inside but that had now stopped. As if just for them. The darkness enclosed them, the coldness not able to bite into her.

She didn't know when it occurred to her that something wasn't right. Possibly around the same time that Sol slowed down, scanning all around them with a grim expression on his face.

'Something is going on,' he ruminated. 'The roads are too busy, even for this time of year.'

'And the traffic is going the wrong way,' Anouk concurred, twisting around to look. 'A road traffic accident, maybe? A main road closed? Diversions?'

It was one of the side-effects of being an A & E doctor: she could perceive a potential major accident like a sixth sense. Things just didn't…sit right.

'More than one road, I'd say, given the volume of traffic.'

'So a multiple-car RTA?'

'Something.' He nodded, sliding his phone out of his back pocket as they exchanged a glance.

'I don't have to make the call. If they need me, they'll call.'

'It's work,' she raised her eyebrows. 'We both know you're itching to make that call. Anyway, call it a sign.'

'I don't believe in signs,' he scoffed. 'You and I getting together is inevitable, Anouk. We both know it. We can't out run it, and however hard we try it will catch up with us. That need will wrap itself around us and topple us to the ground.'

'Then I'll just have to run faster.'

He laughed. An oddly sensuous sound.

'The faster you run, the further you get, the harder the fall will ultimately be.'

He hadn't even begun to make the call when it rang.

'Here goes.' Raising his eyebrows, Sol took the call.

When he let go of her hand, it felt too much like a loss. All Anouk could do was try to glean all she could from his terse responses. When he started moving, she hurried to keep up.

'It's a major incident,' he bit out, snapping his phone shut a few moments later. 'Some kind of gas explosion on Beechmoor

Street. Multiple casualties; they're splitting them between us and the Royal.'

Saskia.

'That's around the corner from where I live,' Anouk cried. 'I have to get back there.'

He stopped momentarily, swinging back to her.

'It isn't safe. The area has apparently been evacuated.'

'I have to get home.' She stepped onto the kerb with the intention of hailing a taxi.

'You won't get a taxi,' Sol told her. 'They said it's gridlock towards the hospital. If we head around the north side on foot, we should make it to the hospital.'

Should she go? For a moment, Anouk wondered whether following Sol was sensible or not. But if people were injured…?

'Okay.' She dipped her head, hurrying after him as he raced ahead.

She hadn't been called, but if things were that serious then extra hands could only be welcome.

And then, her phone began ringing, too.

CHAPTER EIGHT

'Blood gas is back,' Anouk announced to her team. 'She's got a pH of seven point zero four with a lactate of nine.'

'Bicarb?' her colleague asked.

She checked the screen.

'Eight. Basics are minus twenty. Okay, guys, let's go back to the beginning. Airway?'

She waited for her team to communicate that it was unobstructed before moving on.

'Breathing?'

The pause felt like a lifetime, and Anouk knew even before her colleague spoke that the breathing that had been weak before was now absent. Instantly she began CPR.

The casualty had arrived in a bad way. How the crew had even got her from the scene of the explosion to the hospital without losing her was a testament to them, but she could tell this wasn't likely to go the way she would want. And she hated that. She hated losing a patient.

Any patient. Every *patient*.

She knew in this case she was fighting the inevitable, but did it matter? As long as she fought for the young woman lying in front of her?

She completed several rounds of CPR before her head finally reined in her heart.

'Pulse check?'

Even as her colleagues were checking one source, she was checking another.

'No pulse.'

No, not for her either. Anger and frustration coursed through Anouk as she lifted her head to the clock and announced the time of death.

'We didn't stand a chance,' one of her colleagues muttered, tapping her lightly on the shoulder as she passed.

Anouk dipped her head. Much as she knew that, it didn't always help. She reached for the curtains. There wasn't time to stop and grieve; the casualties were coming in thick and fast. No sooner would she step out than there would be another emergency to deal with.

Normally this was what she thrived on—not the losses, of course, but the challenge, the wins, the lives saved. But tonight there were too many other fears racing around her brain, and not all to do with Sol.

In some ways she was almost grateful for the distraction. Perhaps she'd been impulsive thinking that she could have a one-night stand with Sol. With anyone. Maybe it was a good thing they hadn't ended up back at his apartment. At least now she had time to think and realise what a bad decision that would have been.

Wouldn't it?

So why could she only think about surrendering to the temptation that had been haunting her ever since their intimate encounter?

Her head was reeling.

She told herself it was the fear of knowing that the explosion was so close to her and Saskia's apartment block. She'd tried calling her friend on the way to the hospital, but it had gone straight to voicemail. She had no way of knowing if Saskia was all right. Or even where she was.

So that was definitely a concern. But it wasn't what filled her mind with such a confusion of thoughts.

No, she suspected that tangle was more to do with the man who she would have been with, *right now*, if that accident hadn't happened.

It was why she needed a good save more than anything. She needed Saskia and she needed the high of saving lives to push the unwelcome thoughts of Sol from her brain. Given the emergencies flooding in, and not enough staff yet able to get to the hospital, there was plenty for her to do.

As the porters dealt with the deceased patient in the bay, Anouk pushed the loss out of her head and moved on to the next bay, only for Sol to catch her before she went in.

For an instant her heart jolted madly and everything seemed to come into sharper focus.

'What are you doing here?'

'Someone paged Neuro,' he replied evenly. 'A thirty-two-year-old cyclist with T12 and L1 fractures?'

'That's one of my cases.' Whatever her body might be feeling, her brain flipped immediately, locking back into professional mode. 'In here.'

He followed her quickly into a bay, nodding a brief greeting to the girl who was sitting, terrified, at the bedside of her injured boyfriend.

'This is Jared,' Anouk told Sol. 'He came in earlier and we've already had him up to CT.'

'He was caught in the blast?'

'Yes, we understood from witnesses who spoke to the air ambulance team that Jared went over the handlebars and was thrown into another vehicle. He was wearing a crash helmet. The head to pelvis CT scan showed fractured third and fourth ribs with a right-sided pneumothorax. Fractured T12 and L1 with possible evidence of neuro-compromise. He had a deep gash on his right thigh, which we have dealt with. He's had a total of around fourteen mils morphine.'

'Understood,' Sol agreed. 'I need to look at the imaging and decide what to do about the spine.'

'Agreed. I was working on the basis that if he has broken vertebrae at T12 and L1 there are likely to be depressional fractures through the endplates.'

It shouldn't have surprised her how well, how slickly, the two of them were working together. Almost as if the gala evening had never happened.

'Get it to me,' confirmed Sol, already jogging to his next call.

Little wonder the demand on the neuro team would be ridiculously high tonight.

For several hours Anouk worked steadily, hurrying between patients. She struggled to find beds for the unending stream of casualties injured in the blast. Still, she hadn't realised how much time had passed until she dashed from her current patient in order to call Neuro again, only for Sol to appear as she lifted the receiver.

'I've just been looking for you.'

'Thank goodness.' Dropping down the receiver, Anouk pulled a grimace as she turned to him. 'I thought no one was going to be able to get here.'

'About Jared? The cyclist with the T12 and L1 fractures?'

'Sorry?'

'I'm satisfied that the fractures are stable and that no intervention by us is necessary. I'm also confident that there is no neuro deficit so you can admit him to trauma team care, but he doesn't need to be transferred to Neuro.'

'Right.' Anouk hailed one of the nurses to relay the message and ensure the transfer happened quickly to free up a precious resus bed, simultaneously grabbing Sol's lapels as he made to move away.

'Anouk?' he growled as he swung back to her, his dark gaze taking in her hands still gripping his clothing.

She didn't even have time to feel abashed.

'I need you to look at this patient. It's urgent.'

'I came down to give you the results. I have another patient to see. You're probably on Ali's list—she'll be on her way as soon as she's finished with her patient upstairs.'

'There isn't time to wait for Ali.' Anouk shook her head, ushering him to the screen and calling up a new set of images.

Vaguely, it occurred to her that he could have objected. He could have focussed on his next assigned patient, but he was trusting her that this was critical.

'Her name is Jocelyn,' Anouk explained, still bringing up the images. 'She was right outside the building when the explosion occurred and the blast wave knocked her across the road and into a wall. She had a loss of consciousness for approximately ten minutes. On arrival of paramedics she had a GCS of three, which transitioned to a GCS of eleven. Very aggressive and we have confirmed with her husband that it's out of character. The patient was put into a medically induced coma and taken to CT.'

She flashed the images up on the screen.

'A large extradural haematoma.' Sol pursed his lips. 'Very large, in fact.'

'Yes,' Anouk agreed. 'Midline shift.'

'And it has shifted more?' he confirmed.

'Yes.'

They both knew that immediate surgery was imperative. Best case would be that the neurosurgeons could drain the blood and that the brain could move back into place and heal over. Most likely it would never be the same, but the faster they moved, the more chance there was.

Worst case, Jocelyn would die.

'I'll take her,' Sol confirmed after verifying the images for himself. 'I'll push my patient to Ali—he isn't as critical.'

'Thanks.'

With a nod, Sol straightened and moved away quickly, and Anouk couldn't help feeling warm.

She could pretend it was because she knew that her patient was in the very best hands. But she knew that wasn't all it was.

The night flew by, exhausting and chaotic, but with enough saves to bolster Anouk and her team as twelve hours went by, then eighteen, then twenty-four and the casualties had finally thinned out, the wail of ambulances subsiding.

And Anouk could finally go home. She tried not to think of where she might have been now if the gas explosion had never happened. Would she still be at Sol's, or would he have found a way to subtly eject her from his apartment rather than have her stay the night? Somehow, she couldn't imagine it. Playboy or not, it just didn't seem... *Sol-like*.

Then again, what was she doing imagining *anything*?

She rounded the corner, straight into Saskia. They had seen each other in Resus, passing as they darted into different bays but, incredibly, their cases hadn't coincided all evening. But now, without even uttering a word, her friend hugged her tightly.

'I was so relieved when I heard you were safe.'

'Why wouldn't I be?' Anouk laughed. 'And never mind me, the hospital is practically buzzing with some gossip that you arrived by helicopter?'

Saskia thrust her away, her eyes searching Anouk.

'You haven't heard, then?' Saskia demanded, ignoring the comment.

A sense of unease began to creep through Anouk.

'Heard what?'

'That the explosion affected Kings Boulevard?'

'That's us.' Anouk frowned.

'Yes. The whole area has been cordoned off until they can determine which buildings are structurally intact and which aren't. We can't go home.' Anouk couldn't answer as Saskia hugged her again. 'At least we're both safe.'

'We should…book a hotel, then.' Anouk fought off the daze that had settled over her. 'I'll call now.'

'Not for me.' Her friend placed her hand over Anouk's as she reached into her locker for her mobile. 'I'm… I have some-where to be.'

'Where?'

'I… I'm staying with Malachi,' Saskia apologised.

'With Malachi?'

Sol's brother?

It didn't make much sense but Saskia was already changing her shoes and closing her bag.

'Saskia? Are you in here?' Sol's voice only seemed to ramp up the tension in the room.

Or perhaps it was just her, Anouk thought, flustered.

'Oh, Anouk.' Was it her imagination or did he pause for a fraction of a second when he spotted her, before addressing Saskia again? 'Mal says you need to get going. His heli is on the roof and they want it cleared in case an emergency has to come in.'

'I should go,' Saskia muttered.

Sol looked at her.

'If you're calling for a hotel, Anouk, you're too late. I heard a couple of guys complaining an hour ago that every hotel in the city was booked out. The cordon is quite extensive—lots of apartment blocks have been evacuated.'

'Great.' She gritted her teeth as Saskia hovered, still not leav-ing. Worry etched in her face.

'You could find an on-call room.'

'I'm guessing they'll be taken, too,' Sol told them. 'They're setting up temporary beds in community centres around the place.'

'Oh,' Anouk bit out as Saskia grabbed her hand.

'I could speak to Malachi? See if you could come with us?'

'Or you could just stay with me,' Sol cut in, quietly, firmly.

He didn't finish the sentence. He didn't need to. It hung there, in the silence between them.

She could stay with Sol…*as she had been going to do before the explosion had happened.*

Only it wasn't twenty-odd hours ago and things had shifted since that reckless moment in the coffee shop. That moment had gone. They could pretend it was just exhaustion from the chaotic shift; she would be happy with that.

'Thanks, but I don't think it's a good idea.'

They both knew what she meant by it. But her objection was drowned out by her friend who, Anouk was sure, cast Sol a grateful look.

'That's a great idea.'

What was going on here?

'I'm sorry, I do have to go,' Saskia muttered, squeezing her hand again.

'I don't understand, Sask?'

'It's complicated. I'll explain everything when I can.'

Then Saskia hurried out of the room, leaving Anouk staring as the door closed behind her friend. The flashback to her teenage years was as sudden as it was unexpected. The moment she'd first realised that people were moving on whilst she was standing still. Too caught up in her mother's dramas to have time for a life of her own.

Was it possible she'd been standing still ever since?

'Do you know what that was about?' she asked Sol before she could stop herself.

He shoved his hands into his pockets and leaned back against the wall. He looked ridiculously model-like. And dammit if a thrilling shiver didn't dance down her spine.

'Possibly.'

'But you aren't going to tell me?'

'I don't know anything for sure.' He shrugged. 'When they want us to know, they'll tell us.'

'There's a *they*?'

She wasn't surprised when he didn't elaborate.

'I don't believe it's my business,' he said calmly. 'Now, do you want a place to stay or not?'

He just waited calmly, as though offering her a place to stay when there was nowhere else was no big deal. Yet she wouldn't take it, not because she was afraid of what might happen between them, but because she was afraid that she *wanted* it too much.

And if it did, what was the worst that could happen? They'd enjoy a night, maybe a few nights, of intimacy. Even the memory of that night at the gala was enough to have her...*aching*. Just as she'd been ever since.

And hadn't she already considered that maybe it was a good thing she hadn't ended up at his house twenty-four hours ago? That maybe it was *fate*?

Maybe that argument had worked when her mind had been preoccupied by her patients. Her job. Only now the ready-made excuse was gone, it seemed that she wasn't as eager to head somewhere alone, after all. Not when Sol was standing, in all his six-three, honed glory in front of her.

Not when he'd acted as a dashing knight in blue scrubs on several occasions for her patients tonight.

'What happened to Jocelyn?' she demanded abruptly.

'Two hours in surgery. We'll keep her in an induced coma for the next few days and see what happens when she wakes up.'

'And then you take it from there?'

He lifted a shoulder in acknowledgement.

Nothing was certain in this life. But if it had been a test as to whether he cared enough about his patients to know their names, he had passed. With flying colours.

She was going home with him. It was inexorable.

'I'm not one of your conquests.' The words spilled out before she could stop them. 'That is, I'm only agreeing to this if you promise me that no one will find out.'

'Agreeing to *this*?' he challenged, his face a picture of innocence.

She sucked in a deep breath and quelled her irritation.

'You know what I'm saying.'

'I don't believe that I do.' He raised his eyebrows but amusement tugged at that sinful mouth. 'Elucidate.'

Anouk huffed.

But if she couldn't even say the word then how was she going to manage to do it?

'Casual sex,' she clarified stiffly.

'Indeed?' He grinned wolfishly and she felt it like teeth against her soul. 'Forgive me if I'm wrong, but I seem to recall simply offering you a place to stay since there was nowhere else. I don't recall sex ever being a detail of the discussion.'

Heat flooded her body.

'I… You…' She faltered, hardly able to believe her own *faux pas*.

What was it about Sol that had her acting so out of character? So recklessly? First at the gala, and now *this*. Shame chased through her, and then something else.

It took her a moment to realise that it was anger. She grabbed hold of it. At least it gave her a sense of courage, even if it was a false sensation.

'You're right, you didn't. I assumed,' she ground out. 'But then, we both know that's where we will end up. Look where we were headed before we got called in last night.'

'I seem to remember you muttering something about it being a sign.' He smirked. 'Though personally, I've never believed in that nonsense.'

'No, you told me as much,' she reminded him crossly. 'You also told me that it was inevitable. That however much I tried to outrun it, it would catch up with me sooner or later and topple me to the ground. That the faster and further I ran, the fall would be all the harder as a result.'

'I didn't realise you were paying such close attention to every word I was saying.' Sol stretched his legs out languorously. 'Not that I am complaining, you understand.'

'You're playing games aren't you?' she realised, disappointment plummeting through her.

The air around them turned cooler in an instant, as Sol pushed himself off the wall.

'Contrary to the low opinion you hold about me, Anouk, I don't play games every moment of every conversation.'

'Common consensus is that you do,' she rallied.

She wasn't sure what else to do, his reaction was so unexpected. As though she'd hit a nerve, even though she'd never known him to have a nerve when it came to the way he revelled in his reputation. So obviously that couldn't be right.

'You're right,' he managed flatly, moving past her and heading for the door. 'But let's just say that it has been a long, exhausting twenty-four hours, and frankly I'm too weary for game-playing.'

'I see.' Not seeing at all, Anouk grabbed her bag and hurried after him.

Actually, he did look rather…out of character.

'So, for tonight at least, you're safe. All I'm offering you is a place to sleep and nothing more. We'll have to walk; the car is still by the new carers' centre. Does that suit you?'

'Perfectly,' she confirmed. Lying through her teeth.

CHAPTER NINE

'DID SOMETHING HAPPEN with one of your patients?' she ventured after they'd been walking for a while.

'Why?'

'Because you're acting…differently. And I think I get that way, every now and again, when one particular patient gets under my skin.'

He slowed, but didn't stop.

'It was, wasn't it?' she pressed him gently.

They continued walking in silence. Everywhere oddly quiet after weathering that storm in the hospital.

'A baby boy. Nineteen months,' was all Sol said, after what seemed like an age.

She didn't answer. Instead she simply fell into step with him, and hoped that it was enough. She understood only too well.

It was another age before he spoke again.

'It's odd, the way it gets to you sometimes, don't you think?' he said, his head down and his hands thrust into his pockets.

The question was more rhetorical than anything, Anouk knew that, but she answered anyway.

'You mean loss? Death?'

'We deal with it every day. It's so easy to become desensitised to it.' He shrugged. 'But after an incident like that…'

'Yes,' she whispered. 'I think it's the sheer volume of it. All at once. It makes it feel too much.'

Again, they walked in companionable silence for minutes—though it felt like a lifetime, lost as she was in her thoughts. It was only when he stopped at a shop window that she realised they had made it to the lower part of the town. Slowing down, she backed up, but she wasn't prepared.

'What is this, Sol?'

'You asked me about the Christmas village scene.'

'This is it?'

'This is it.'

She turned to take in the scene. Even through her loathing of this time of year, she could at least admit it was spectacular. Little trains ran in circles around the quaintest village set-up; a snow-covered village green with tiny figures walking, ice-skating, or simply strolling the wintry streets in the warm glow of the orange/yellow lights.

Little old-fashioned shops lined the painstakingly constructed hillside road, which, if she looked closely, Anouk thought might be polystyrene blocks, but they looked for all the world like snowy inclines. Meanwhile, a miniature cable car ran up and down another polystyrene hill scene.

'This is what the kids work so hard to raise the money to buy,' Anouk murmured. 'For you, and for Malachi. Why?'

There was a beat of silence.

'Why, Sol?' She pressed her fingers to the glass, as if proximity could solve the riddle she was sure existed.

'It's become a tradition,' he offered simply.

'What makes it so traditional?' she repeated.

There was no logical explanation for why it should matter to her to know.

Yet it did.

The still night began to hum with anticipation. She turned her head to watch him but his gaze was fixed on the scene, not on her.

'Please, Sol?

He scowled, drawing in a deep breath before answering.

'Malachi and I were kids when we first saw a village like this,' he began, falteringly at first. He hadn't told this story in... well, ever. 'There was a toyshop in town which had one every Christmas—not that we were ever allowed in, of course. The owner would chase us down the road if we even peered into the window, for steaming it up with our snotty noses.'

'He really said that?'

'He said a sight worse than that. Even clipped our legs with the back of a broom handle on more than one occasion.' Sol shrugged. 'Anyway, sometimes we would wait until it was dark and sneak out of the house if we could leave Mum for long enough. There was a guy with a sugared doughnut stall and if he was still there cleaning up, he used to give us any leftovers, which would otherwise get thrown away.'

'That's nice.' Anouk smiled as though her chest was tight and painful at the thought of Sol's childhood.

She'd had no idea. But then, no one did. Clearly that was the way Sol liked it.

'He was a decent guy. Years later, when Mal had made his first real money as a boxer, he bought the business from the guy for about five times its worth, just to repay him.'

'Did he know?'

'Yeah, he was so damned grateful, it was really nice to do. Mal then gave the business to a couple of kids he knew would appreciate it, from the first centre we built. They ended up getting four stalls between them and they're still going strong.'

'Wow.'

She thought Sol was going to say more but suddenly he caught himself. As if he didn't know why he'd told her that. Possibly it had all been stuffed down in the same box for so many years that now she'd sprung the lid, random snippets were springing out left and right, completely out of his control and in no logical order.

Or maybe he was just playing her.

'Anyway. Mal and I used to sneak down to watch the little trains going around, and the carousel, and the people going in and out of buildings on that turntable. And we vowed that we would make it through to the other side and we'd buy every damned piece of that village in existence. We swore we'd become the kind of people who idiots like that toyshop owner would fawn over. Never again would we get chased from a shop doorway or window.'

'You guys must have had the kind of money to buy a village *world* years ago. Several times over. But you didn't?' Anouk eyed him thoughtfully. The deep blue pools were fathoms deep.

'We did, as it happens.' He smiled a genuine smile. 'We bought the lot. Just to know what it felt like.'

'And?'

'And it felt good.' He laughed suddenly. 'A bit surreal, that first time we set it up. Young adults reliving a childhood moment that had once been denied them. But after that we felt like we'd made our point, if only to ourselves. So we split it out and sent a bundle to each of about five or six kids' community centres.'

'And one of them was Care to Play?' Anouk guessed.

'Yeah. Once the kids there found out, they decided that was what they wanted to do for us, buy a new piece every year. It's a matter of pride to them, to do something to raise money for a new toyshop, or ride, or ice-skating rink.'

'That's really nice.' She glanced around ruefully. 'Even I bought into the idea. I thought you'd love this, but you just do it for the kids.'

'Why not? They get pleasure from it, too.'

'That's another thing which confused me,' she admitted. 'At the centre you're an inspiration for making good from nothing. At the hospital, the rumour is that you both came from money?'

'At the hospital it's just that,' he growled. 'A rumour. Malachi has become a multimillionaire thanks to his boxing, but I'm not.'

'You must earn a decent salary as a neurosurgeon?'

He raised an eyebrow at her.

'Did I say I was complaining?'

'Well, no,' she conceded. 'So why not just tell people that?'

'Why bother? It isn't any of their business and because it would invite questions, more interest, delving into my past—and Malachi's.'

'Surely that's a good thing? Two boys, with humble beginnings, have done incredibly well for themselves. It's the fairy tale, people would have lapped it up. You'd have had even more women falling at your feet.'

She hadn't intended to sound so cross when she'd made that latter observation.

'I told you,' he cut across her, 'it would have been an invitation for people to rifle through our lives like they're some kind of public property.'

Surprisingly, Anouk was beginning to realise just how protective both Sol, and particularly Malachi, were about their private lives.

Who would have thought it?

But she couldn't ask anything more, she didn't dare. Not after he'd effectively shut down that line of conversation. And still, his gaze held hers and she couldn't move. He might not have told her a lot, but, given his driving need for privacy, she felt as though he'd told her more than she could have hoped he would.

As though she was significant.

'Did you know that ridiculous pudding hat of yours was on inside out?' he told her, lifting it gently and turning it right side out before lowering it back on her head. Infinitely tender, infinitely thrilling.

She waited, pinned to the spot, as he released her hat and cupped her face instead, like a blast of heat in the cold winter air.

'Sol?' she breathed, when neither of them had moved and it was clear that neither of them was going to move.

Still, they both remained motionless. And then, just when

Anouk had finished telling herself that she had to be the one to step back, to break the contact, however much she railed against it, he bent his head and brushed her lips with his.

It ignited a fire in an instant, sending the surrounding people, the coffee shop, the entire street, reeling into the background.

With a low moan, she stepped towards him, her arms raised to grab his jacket with her hands. Whether she deepened the kiss or Sol did, it hardly mattered.

His mouth was hot and demanding, his taste every bit as exhilarating as she remembered. It confirmed the one truth she'd suspected since the gala ball—one night with him hadn't been enough. She wanted more. She *needed* more.

He kissed her with ruinous skill, turning her inside out and upside down. He plundered and claimed, teasing her with his lips, his tongue, his teeth; he pulled her body to him until she was sure she could feel every last muscled ridge of that washboard body that had stamped itself so indelibly in her mind, and he made a low sound as he kissed her as if, like her, he needed more.

And she was lost. As enchanted by the man as every other woman before her had been.

She who should know better.

'My place?' he broke contact long enough to mutter.

Anouk didn't even try to speak, she just nodded.

They barely even made it through the door of his apartment before they were undressing each other.

Sol's touch was fire over every millimetre of her skin, smouldering over her wherever he trailed those expert fingers of his. Setting her ablaze every time he lowered his head, and that skilful mouth, to brand her somewhere new.

Her neck, her shoulder, the rise of her breast. One hand laced itself through her hair, cupping the nape of her neck and making her feel cherished and precious, whilst the other hand played a wicked concerto on her body as if it were the most exquisite instrument.

And with every accomplished stroke the fire inside her grew hotter and brighter, until it was too painful to look at. And so Anouk closed her eyes and gave herself over to the sheer beauty of it. She was singing in her head, arias she had never known before. Certainly not like this.

Again and again Sol moved his fingers, his hand, his mouth, over her body, testing her and tasting her. Paying homage to every inch of her, he supported her neck with one hand while the other skimmed over her back and then spanned the hollow at the base of her spine with enviably long, strong fingers, making her feel infinitely delicate.

He took his time, as though they were in no rush. As though there was no end goal, trailing his fingers up one side and down again, leaving shivers of delight in his wake.

Up and down.

Up again, and down again.

Pleasing and punishing her, until every molecule of her pulsed with burning, intense need. All she could do was respond to him. As if she'd been waiting for this moment for ever. As if she were his to command.

As if she were *his*.

Time stood still for Anouk. She stayed there in his arms, letting all this desire swirl around, and move through her as Sol branded her with every touch, leaving her feeling as though she would never be the same again.

This is his skill, a tiny voice urged silently in her head. *He makes you feel special, unique, and as long as you don't fall for him, it will be fine.*

But the voice was too hazy, too muffled, too deliberately easy for the sensations tearing through her to drown out. Or perhaps it was more that she wanted to drown *in* the sensations. To drown in Sol.

It was only when she heard the loud, delectably rude sound

of a zip sliding that she realised he had unfastened her jeans and was sliding his fingers under the material.

They hadn't even made it to the bedroom.

'Do you want to… I mean…here?' she began weakly, the words catching in her throat as, without warning, he brushed one finger tantalisingly over the front of her underwear.

Then the damned man lifted his head and shot her the most devilish grin.

'Sorry, what were you saying?'

But it was the dark, oddly intent look in his eyes that snagged at her the most. As though he wasn't quite as in control as he wanted to appear. As if she was affecting him that little bit more than he wanted to reveal.

It was a heady thought. And then, before she could find her voice, he hooked the material back and repeated the action, this time with no barrier between them.

'Did you want me to stop?'

There was no mistaking the rawness in his voice just then, but before she could answer he let his fingers move over her, stroking her once, twice, before dipping into her heat.

Everything in her clenched in delicious anticipation. But then her eyes flew open as he drew his hand back up, and she was powerless to prevent a small sound of objection from escaping her lips.

'Relax,' he commanded, his tone purely hedonistic. 'I'm not going anywhere. Except here.'

And before she could say a word he lifted his finger to his mouth and licked it. Very deliberately.

'What…' she managed to find her voice, as jagged as it sounded '…are you doing?'

He fixed her with a lazy, hooded look.

'Tasting you.' His voice was thick, loaded. 'And you are as intoxicating as I remember.'

She had no idea how she managed to speak; her whole body was jolting with need.

'You've been remembering this?'

'Yes,' he growled, sliding his hand back into her trousers and his cool, wet finger straight over where she needed him most. 'And I've been imagining a hell of a lot more. So, let me ask you again, shall I continue or did you want me to stop?'

Her eyes fluttered slightly and it was all Anouk could do to bite her lip and shake her head. He'd stolen her voice again with a flick of his fingers, as if he were some wicked sorcerer using his clever fingers to wind the most magical of spells around her.

'Say it,' he growled.

It was an effort to open her heavy eyelids. Even more of one to speak. So instead she lifted her bottom, just a fraction, to brush his hand.

Yet it seemed he was one step ahead of her, and as she moved his hand shifted out of reach. Barely. She could still feel the heat from him rolling over her, but she couldn't make contact.

'I find I want to hear the words from you,' Sol ground out.

The man was a fiend!

She swallowed. Hard.

'Continue,' she managed hoarsely. 'Definitely, continue.'

Sol seemed only too happy to oblige.

'So wet,' he growled in a voice so carnal that it sent another ache slicing through her right to her core.

Anouk tried to answer, but speech was impossible. Even before he slid those expert fingers around to caress her.

It took her a moment to realise that the low moans she heard were her own. This—what Sol was doing to her right now—was like nothing she'd ever known before.

So adrift, so out of her own body, and yet so wholly at its mercy all at the same time. She was vaguely aware of moving her head so that she could fit her mouth back to Sol's, every slip and slide of his tongue mirroring what his fingers were doing, stoking that fire higher with each passing moment.

He moved his other hand from the nape of her neck to cup her cheek, cradling it almost tenderly, if she hadn't known that to be ridiculous. Still, when he angled his head for a deeper fit, she poured more into that kiss than she'd ever known possible.

It was incredible, the sensations rushing through her body from her mouth to her core and back again, everywhere that Sol was; the devastating rhythm he was building inside her. She would be ruined for any other man. She was sure of it. Solomon Gunn would make sure that no other man would ever be able to satisfy her again.

She didn't think she cared—just as long as he never stopped doing what he was doing now.

She sighed, a sound of deep longing, causing Sol to wrench his mouth from hers, his eyes seeking her out and staring at her as though trying to see something in them. Either that, or conveying some silent message that she couldn't understand. She wanted to ask him, but it wasn't in her to speak, his dexterous fingers leaving her only just able to breathe; tracing her shape, holding her, cradling her and then, finally, slipping inside her slick heat. She felt the shudder roll through her even before she heard her needy moan.

His eyes went almost black with desire.

'You respond so perfectly, *zoloste*,' he murmured, his gravelly voice the perfect telltale.

She bit her lip and nodded, unable to speak. Not that it mattered, she wouldn't know what to say even if she could. His fingers were still moving over her, around her, inside her. And she couldn't get enough. Especially when he lowered his head, placing his wicked mouth on her neck and driving her wild with his clever tongue and devilish teeth.

She didn't know when she began moving against his palm, urging him to quicken the pace when he seemed to want to take it at his own leisurely pace—to stretch out the blissful agony in her that much longer—she only knew she could feel herself hurtling along, and the abyss coming up on her so quickly she thought she might hurtle down for ever and ever and ever.

And she wanted Sol inside her. Properly. She reached down

his body to his belt buckle, her fingers fumbling in her haste. She could feel him. Steel straining behind the denim, as though he wanted her just as badly. It was a thrilling thought. If only she could work the damned belt.

The driving rhythm didn't stop or even slow for an instant, but with his free hand Sol caught her wrists and moved her away.

'There's time enough for that,' he muttered, every word dancing across her skin as his fingers continued their devastating concerto. 'Right now, this is about you.'

She'd never felt so worshipped, so powerful, or so confident in her own body.

Finally it broke over her, as if every nerve ending in her entire body were fizzing and popping, from the top of her head right down to her very toes, and then he twisted his wrist skilfully, in a way she'd never known before, and she felt herself catapult into the air. Higher and higher, further and longer, soaring spectacularly on a wave of shimmering, magical sensation that she thought might never end.

She certainly never wanted it to. And still Sol touched her, held her. So that as the wave finally began to slow, and drop, she found herself tumbling straight onto another, which took her soaring back up again.

Time after time.

Finally, sated and spent, she felt herself tumbling, her body sagging into Sol's, her breathing rapid and harsh.

And all she could do was hope that he broke her fall when she finally hit the ground.

Anouk was in his bed by the time she started coming back to herself. Right where he'd been imagining her for too long now. As nonsensical as that notion was. He watched her, half amused, half ravenous, as she blinked and tried to focus on her new surroundings.

'Oh.' The small sound escaped her lips and he was powerless

to do anything but lower his head and try to catch the sound in his own mouth.

'I took the liberty of bringing you to my bed,' he managed. Then, as her eyes wandered down to his naked form, he added, 'I also took the liberty of stripping. Is that a problem?'

'On the contrary.' Her voice was thick, hoarse, and he liked that she couldn't conceal her need for him. 'I find I rather like that.'

And then, as if to prove her point, she stretched beneath him, parting her legs to settle him against her wet heat, and Sol almost lost it there and then.

'There's no rush, *zolotse*,' he chided gently, as though he himself weren't so perilously close to the edge.

But then Anouk looped her arms around his neck and her legs around his body and shot him a daring, cheeky grin.

'Are you quite sure about that?'

Before he could answer, she lifted her hips and drew him inside her, as taut, scorching need knotted in his belly.

It stole his breath from his very lungs.

With a low moan, he thrust inside her, revelling in her answering shudder. The way she locked her legs tighter around him, and lifted her hips to meet him. He made himself slide out of her slowly, then back in again, setting a deliberate pace and fighting the driving urge to take her there and then.

He had no idea how he kept it going. Whether he even managed it for long at all. But then he found he was moving faster, harder, deeper, and Anouk was matching him stroke for stroke. And he could feel it building inside her, just as it was inside him.

When her breath came in shallower gasps, he hooked his hand under her and angled her perfectly, reaching between them to find the very centre of her need, and then he sent her over the edge, the sound of her crying his name far more potent than it should have been.

And Sol, unable to bear it any longer, followed her.

CHAPTER TEN

HE KNEW SHE was gone even before his eyes had adjusted to the pitch-black of the room. He could sense it. The bed felt...empty without her. And an irrational sense of anger rolled through him that she should have snuck out, like some kind of thief, whilst he slept. He who never slept soundly.

Throwing back the sheet and stabbing his legs into a pair of night-time joggers, he stomped out of the bedroom and down the hallway. And stopped abruptly.

The light to the living area was on and he could hear the sound of cutlery on porcelain. It was insane how glad that sound made him.

Wandering through, he leaned on the doorjamb and watched her, perched on the granite worktop, one of his T-shirts swamping her delectable body, eating his cereal.

'Hungry?'

She jumped instantly.

'It was a long shift and...an energetic night.' She offered him a sheepish grin. 'I didn't mean to wake you.'

'You didn't.'

Stepping in, he opened the cupboards and retrieved his own cereal bowl, filling it up and pouring on the milk she had left on the counter, before putting the bottle away.

'I didn't realise you were a neat freak,' she teased.

'I didn't consider that you were a slob.' He laughed.

She straightened up indignantly.

'I am not, I was going to clean up as soon as I'd finished, so you can take that back.'

'Fair enough.' He took a spoonful of the cereal, watching her wriggle off the counter-top and potter around his kitchen.

He had no idea what rippled through him at the sight but he didn't care to analyse it too deeply.

'So…do I come back to…your bed? Or do I…go to the guest room?'

Ah, so the new, bold Anouk had taken cover again and the old, reserved Anouk was back.

'Come back to bed.' He didn't even bother to keep the amusement from his tone.

'It's all very well for you to laugh.' She bristled. 'But I'm not used to…*this*.'

'I know I have a reputation as a playboy, Anouk. But I'm not a complete bastard. Just because I'm not cut out for relationships, or love, or any of that mumbo jumbo, doesn't mean I throw women out in the middle of the night as soon as the sex is over.'

'About that,' Anouk announced, loudly if a little shakily. 'I think that's utter tosh, as it happens.'

'Say that again?'

To say he was incredulous didn't cut it. Anouk moistened her lips nervously and he had to force himself not to let his eyes linger.

'I think you use sex as a distraction,' she declared.

'Is that so?'

'Yes.' Clearly warming to her subject, she drew herself a little taller and eyed him determinedly. 'I think you use sex as a distraction to stop you from getting too close to anyone.'

Anger and something else—something someone who didn't know him might have categorised as fear—spread through his mind.

'This idea that you're not cut out for relationships, or love is nonsense.'

'Careful, *zoloste*, you're wandering into precarious territory.'

A lesser woman would have backed away at the dangerous edge in his voice.

But then, Anouk wasn't a lesser anything.

'Someone has to,' defiance laced her tone.

'Why? Because you want me to tell you that I love you?'

'No!' she actually looked horrified. 'Not me. Of course not. That's...insane.'

'Of course it's insane,' Sol couldn't pinpoint what charged through him in that millisecond. He didn't want to. 'Because I'm not a man who believes in 'love'. I certainly can't offer it.'

'I think you *are* capable of love.' The panic was gone and her defiance was back again. 'The way you are with your patients, and those young carers, and even your relationship with your brother Malachi. You care, in everything that you do.'

He hated the way she thought he was a better man than he was. It only made it more apparent to him that he wasn't that man.

'You're trying to make me into something I'm not to suit your own agenda, *zolotse*,' he gritted out, suddenly angry. Because anger was easier than these other emotions that threatened to churn inside him. 'Because you hate yourself for a one-night stand with me and you want to make yourself feel better by claiming I can be more than that. But that isn't me. I'm not built that way, Anouk. I don't want to be. I warned you about that.'

She hated hearing those words; he could see it in her stiff stance, and the belligerent tilt of her head.

'That isn't what I'm doing, Sol,' she snapped. 'I'm telling you that I think you're a different man from the image of yourself you put out there, and I don't know if it's because you want others to believe that's all there is to you, or if you actually really do believe it's the truth. But, whatever the truth is, that's for you to know. It has no bearing on me, either way.'

'Your eagerness to change me suggests otherwise.'

If his cereal had contained broken glass, it couldn't have shredded him inside any worse. But Anouk didn't reply straight away. She just watched him, a solemn expression in those arresting blue eyes.

He couldn't help wishing he knew what she was thinking.

'Did I ever tell you that the reason I came to the UK was to find my father?' she asked, just as he was about to give up thinking she was going to speak again.

They both knew the answer to that. Her eyes were too bright, too flitting. He doubted she'd ever told anyone, expect maybe Saskia. Still, he could play the game for her, if that was what she needed.

He realised his previous anger had begun to dissipate.

'No.' He feigned a casualness. 'I don't think you did.'

'Just before my mother...died...' she faltered '...she told me that she had once received a letter from my father.'

'You hadn't known him?'

'Not at all. Only the story she'd told me about him not wanting to be around for us.' Her strained tone suggested that wasn't all there was to it, but Sol didn't press her on it. It was shocking enough that she was telling him this much. 'I didn't know he'd ever contacted us. Her. Me.'

'What did he say?'

'I don't know.' She looked angry for a moment, but then smoothed it away quickly, efficiently. 'Apparently she'd thrown it on the fire in a pique of temper. By the time she'd changed her mind, most of it was gone. She just about managed to retrieve part of an address.'

'To his home in the UK?'

Anouk eyed him speculatively for several long moments. There was patently more to the story than she was willing to reveal to him. And he shouldn't be so desperate to know the truth. To understand it more.

He shouldn't be so wrapped up in the abridged version she was feeding him now. It shouldn't matter to him.

'You came all the way from America because he lives in the UK.'

'Not just the UK. Moorlands itself,' she bit out, at length.

That was why she'd come here?

'Did you track him down?' He couldn't help himself.

What the hell was it about this woman that slid, so devilishly slickly, under his skin?

An internal war waged within Sol and for seconds, minutes, maybe hours, he couldn't breathe. He had no idea what would win.

There was another pause, before she nodded.

'Eight years ago. With Saskia.'

'And?'

'He'd died about five years before that. There was a young family living in the house, but the neighbours confirmed it.'

'You're sure it was him.'

'There's no doubt about it, Sol.' She offered a wan smile. 'I even visited his grave.'

'I'm so sorry,' he told her sincerely.

What more was there to say?

She leaned on the counter, her arms folded defensively across her chest.

'I'm not after pity, Sol. I just wanted you to know that I wasn't telling you that I think you're capable of love because I want you to love *me*. I know our deal was just sex. It's the only reason I agreed to it, so I'm not about to change the rules now. I don't want love in my life either. I don't trust it. I never have.'

Some seething thing slunk around inside him. But the anger wasn't directed *at* Anouk any more. Or himself. It was directed at those people who had never deserved her care in the first place. Who had hurt her. Who had destroyed something as fragile and precious as her trust in anyone who could love her.

'You trusted the wrong people,' he gritted out, realising that he wanted to reach out and pull her to him.

To tell her that she was beautiful, and caring, and lovable. Especially because it was only now occurring to him that she didn't know that for herself. How had he not seen that before? He was usually skilled at reading others.

'Of course, I trusted the wrong people,' she agreed flatly. 'But who would have thought that my mother and my grandmother were those wrong people? They lied to me my whole life. In the end I think my mother only told me the truth to get one final dig at me. To prove to me that she'd had the upper hand right up until her moment of death.'

'That doesn't mean you should still let her get to you now. You can trust people. You can trust me.'

Her eyebrows shot up.

'Said the spider to the fly.'

It was a fair point. Maybe that was why it grated on him. Maybe that was why, instead of shutting her question down as he would have done had any other woman asked, he found himself answering the question she'd once put to him.

'I was five when Malachi started to become a carer.'

She blinked.

'You don't have to do this, Sol. I wasn't telling you about me just to make you feel obliged to do the same.'

'He became a carer for me, and for our mum, when she needed it,' he continued, as if she hadn't spoken.

She only hesitated for a moment.

'She was ill?'

If you could call being a drug addict ill. Some people called it an illness. Having lived through it, borne the brunt of it, he and Malachi had always been considerably less charitable. Not that Sol was about to say any of that aloud.

'Something like that.' He tried not to spit it out in distaste.

Clearly he didn't do a very good job; the expression on her face said enough. Less shock, more a tired understanding. As though she hadn't expected it from him, but, now that he'd said it, she wasn't entirely surprised.

Or maybe he was just projecting. This woman made him re-think things of which he'd long since stopped taking notice. He blinked as he realised she was still talking to him.

'Sol? I asked about your dad.'

'Dead. That's why she became…ill.'

'So he cared for you before that?' She was trying to put it together, like one of the jigsaws at the carers' centre, only it was a jigsaw of his life and he hadn't given her all the pieces.

With anyone else, he wouldn't have wanted to.

'*Cared* is a bit too generous a description,' Sol ground out. 'He was a former Russian soldier.'

'Your parents were Russian?'

'Not my mother,' he clarified. 'My father was medically dis-charged due to injury; he had street smarts but no education so he earned a living taking work on the docks when it was avail-able, or as a pub fighter otherwise.'

'Did he hit you and Malachi?'

'No. He wasn't exactly the best father but he didn't hit us, except the odd clip around the ear as many kids got back them, not bad for a man who had been systematically used as a punch-ing bag by his own father. Though he did teach us to fight, from toddlers really, but particularly Mal because he was older. It was his way of bonding with us, I guess.'

'So that's how Malachi became the skilled fighter he is now.'

'I doubt he'd ever have believed it would make Mal a mil-lionaire.' Sol shook his head. 'Love wasn't something our father was good at. Even his relationship with our mother was more passionate and volatile than loving. She showed us some love as kids, and he put food on the table and a roof over our heads.'

'How did he die?'

'Bad fight.' Sol laughed but it was a hollow, scraping sound. 'Brain bleed. And yes, I know all the psychology arguments about that being the reason why I became a neurosurgeon. The point is that my mother fell apart. Started doing drugs to numb the pain. It wasn't a far reach from the world in which we lived back then. The love went pretty fast, then.'

'How old was Malachi?'

'Eight.' He shrugged as Anouk drew her lips into a thin line. 'By the time he was ten, she was a full-on addict and Mal was full-time carer for us both, whilst he also earned money for us to eat and live.'

'He was earning money at ten?' Anouk blew out a breath. 'Doing what? Surely no one would employ him.'

'Local gangs.'

'Gangs?' She looked momentarily stunned. 'So…what did he do?'

Sol crossed his arms over his chest. Even now, over two decades on, it still rattled him that he didn't know exactly what his brother had been compelled to do just to keep the two— three—of them together.

Like holding their lives together with sticking plaster. No, not even something so expensive. His ten-year-old brother had been holding their lives together with a bit of discarded string he'd found blowing about in the filthy street outside their tiny terraced house.

He didn't even understand why he was telling Anouk any of this, and yet he couldn't seem to stop. She drew it out of him, with all the patience and compassion that he had used on the young carers in his centre.

It was odd, the tables being turned on him. And, strangely, not entirely unpleasant.

'Errands like drugs?' she pressed gently.

He emitted another harsh laugh. Given the state of their mother, drug gangs were people Malachi had never, ever worked for.

'No, never drugs. I don't know everything he did, you'd have to ask Mal, but things like being a runner for bookies. They trusted him because of our dad. Maybe he did things which were a bit dodgy but not outright illegal. Even as a kid Mal was always unshakeable on that.'

'He seems so quiet.' Anouk shook her head, evidently trying to absorb it all.

No judgement. No false sympathy or drama. Just…*her*. Listening. Caring. It should have concerned him more that he was letting her get so close, but he couldn't bring himself to back away. Even emotionally.

He told himself that he knew what he was doing.

'Mal isn't as quiet as people think. He has this inner core of steel, I'm telling you. Even as a kid he handled himself with those guys. Enough to make sure that I kept going to school. Believe it or not, I was always better with the discipline than he was.'

'Sol, the playboy, a good schoolboy?'

She offered him a soft smile and he realised she was teasing him. It was like a lick of heat.

'Amazing, isn't it?'

'So how did he get away with not going?'

'Mal has a true eidetic memory. He didn't really need to be in lessons to keep up with school. I used to…persuade some lads in his year to get copies of the work.'

'Persuade as in employ some of the fighting techniques your father had taught you?' she guessed.

'Only in the beginning.' Sol made no apologies. Not even to this woman. 'With those ten- or eleven-year-old lads who had trouble accepting a polite request from an eight-year-old. They rarely had trouble the next time.'

'I never realised.'

'Why would you?' Sol pointed out evenly. 'The point is that we got by, and if he hadn't done all of that I wouldn't have stayed in school, and without him I wouldn't be in medicine, let alone a neurosurgeon.'

Neither of them could have imagined even a half of what they had today. Or just how far the two of them would pull themselves out of the gutter. Together. The way it had always been.

'What happened with your mum?'

He tensed; it was impossible not to.

'He got her the help she needed, but it turned out it still wasn't enough. She died when I was seventeen.'

'I'm sorry.'

'Don't be.' He shrugged, ignoring the odd scraping sensation deep inside his stomach. One that he was sure had more to do with the soft way that Anouk was looking at him than anything else. 'In some ways her death set Mal and me free.'

She stared at him for another long moment and he had to fight the urge to turn away lest she see right down to his soul. Down to where he still felt like that socially awkward, ashamed, inadequate kid.

'Is that where the playboy image came from? Not wanting to commit to someone, or settle down, or have kids because of your experience with your mum?'

Sol didn't answer.

He couldn't. Or wouldn't. Either way, the net result was the same.

He swung away to stare at the tiled wall, his hands resting on either side of him on the counter top. Behind him, he heard her slide off the granite surface. He could sense her approaching him and he turned, unable to help himself.

Suddenly they were facing each other, everything rending apart as Anouk placed her hands on either side of his face as if to make him look at her. He definitely didn't want to talk any more.

He forgot that he'd been doing all this to make her trust him. That he'd been waiting for her to need him so badly that she begged him, as she had the night of the gala.

'Confession time is over, *zolotse*,' he growled, snaking his arms to her waist and hauling her to him.

She didn't object. Especially not when he snagged her mouth with his.

Sol's whole body combusted in that one second. The woman was mouth-watering. Every slide of her tempting mouth, every shift of her delectable body, every tiny groan as he swept his finger over her sinfully hard nipples. He'd never *ached* so much before to bury himself inside a woman. Not aside from the primal, physical urge, that was.

Anouk was dynamite where before he'd only known black powder.

CHAPTER ELEVEN

'WHAT IS THE matter with you, *bratik*?' Malachi challenged from across the expansive, luxury office just as Sol was filling his mug with hot, rich coffee from his brother's coffee maker.

'What?' Sol cocked an eyebrow, selecting a couple of Danish pastries to put onto a napkin and striding over to flop in a comfortable chair.

The last week had been unparalleled. So much for a one-night stand. He hadn't wanted to let Anouk go and she had been more than happy to stay. There hadn't been a room in his penthouse they hadn't used as their personal playground.

'You're full of the joys of spring,' sniped Malachi.

'And you're grouchy and on edge.' Sol eyed him shrewdly. 'More so than usual, that is. Though I wouldn't have thought that was possible.'

'Funny,' Malachi bit out.

'Thanks.'

'Idiot.'

Sol shrugged, wholly unconcerned, and wolfed down the second pastry before speaking again.

'Hungry by any chance?'

'Always.' Sol grinned, glancing around the room.

'*Vkusno!* So, what's the Christmas tree all about?'

He didn't think he'd ever seen so much as a bauble in his brother's offices before. Only Anouk had been more resistant to festive decorations than his brother always had been. Sol didn't know why, but he found himself staring at it a little harder. It looked remarkably similar to the one in Resus. The one that Anouk had said her friend Saskia had decorated.

He practically heard the clang as the penny hit the floor of his brain.

'I realised it's good for morale,' Malachi sidestepped. 'I'm not the only one who works here, you know. Listen, I've got a board meeting to prepare for, so do you want to tell me why you really schlepped across town to see me?'

Sol stared at his brother wordlessly. That tree had nothing to do with morale; it was about Saskia, plain and simple. Suddenly, he wondered if she was doing for Malachi anything like what Anouk was doing for him. Making him feel whole when he hadn't before recognised how broken he'd been? And, if so, didn't they all deserve this chance?

'You and I have always said that we weren't built for commitment, or love. That everything *she* put us through destroyed that in us. But what if we're wrong, Mal? What if you and I have always been capable of love?'

'This discussion is over,' Malachi ground out. But still, he didn't move.

'There's always been a love between you and me.' What had Anouk said? 'It may be a different kind of love, but it's love nonetheless.'

'Where did those pearls of wisdom come from?' Malachi snorted, but Sol noted that it lacked the level of scorn he might have expected from his big brother. He also noticed that Malachi wasn't outright dismissing him.

Or was he just reading too much into it because of the way Anouk had made him re-evaluate his own priorities?

'I don't know,' he answered honestly.

'A woman?'

'No,' he denied. Then, 'Maybe.'

'Anouk?'

Reality bit hard, and for a moment Sol thought about denying it. What if talking about her with Malachi spoiled what he and Anouk had? *Might* have. Not that he even knew what they were—these...*feelings* that sloshed around inside him like sand and cement and water in a mixer.

'Are you going to take the proverbial?' He glowered at Malachi.

Their brotherly banter was inevitable, joshing each other, but for a moment, Malachi didn't say anything.

'Maybe next time.'

That was unexpected.

'Yeah, then,' Sol admitted. 'Anouk.'

'Something is going on between you both?'

Malachi didn't need to spell out that 'something going on' meant more than just him and Anouk having sex. His brother had mocked him for his playboy reputation plenty of times in the past.

'I don't know. Maybe.'

'Serious?'

Was it? If it wasn't, would he even be here? Doing this for her? He didn't care to examine that too deeply.

'Maybe. She's the reason I came here today, at least.'

His brother studied him, cool and perceptive.

'What do you need?' Malachi asked at length.

'You have people who can track stuff down for you, right?'

Malachi inclined his head.

'I want you to track down all you can on this man.' Sol flicked through his phone and found the notepad where he'd copied down the details from the scrap of paper in Anouk's picture frame, leaning forward to spin it across the desk to his brother. 'He died thirteen years ago, but he used to live there.'

Wordlessly, Malachi read the screen and made a note of the information. He didn't even question it and, not for the first time, Sol wondered how different his life would have been if he hadn't had his brother.

Anouk was right. Their relationship with their mother might have been destructive and damaging, but the two brothers had always believed in each other, loved each other. In their own fierce way.

How was it that she—a relative stranger—had understood even when he hadn't really been able to see it? He doubted Malachi had either.

What was that saying about not seeing the wood for the trees?

'Do you think you can do this without hurting her, Sol?' Malachi demanded suddenly.

'Sorry?' Sol was instantly on alert.

'Settling down with Anouk. Do you think you, the perennial playboy, can do that?'

'I'm not settling down,' Sol denied.

'Then why care? I mean, I get that you care about your patients, and the kids at the centre. But I've never known you to care about a woman enough to ask for my help.'

'She's...different.' He chose his words circumspectly. 'But that doesn't mean there's anything serious between us.'

'Right.'

Malachi pushed his chair back abruptly and stood up, moving to the window to look out, and it struck Sol that they were so alike, he and his brother.

Perhaps that was why, when he felt the disapproval radiating from Malachi's stiff back, Sol knew it wasn't actually directed at him. Rather, his brother was censuring himself. Which was why he took the plunge into the dangerous waters of asking personal questions.

'Who is she, Mal?'

Malachi swung around but said nothing. The silence seemed to arc between them, dangerous and electric, so many emotions charging over his brother's usually closed face that Sol could barely keep up. But he recognised anger, and he recognised fear.

What the hell could ever make his big, tough brother afraid?

'I think I prefer the Sol who just beds women and moves on,' Malachi said at length. 'You're acting like a lost puppy. Anouk's lost puppy, to be exact.'

But despite the way he bit out the words Sol knew his brother well enough to read that there was no malice behind them, and so he didn't take offence.

'Sod off.' He stood slowly and deliberately, then sauntered over to the sideboard and selected another pastry. A show of nonchalance. 'I'm no one's puppy.'

'Not usually, no.' Malachi shrugged. 'You're usually fending them off with a stick.'

'What? Puppies?' Sol quipped.

'Puppies, women, little old ladies.' Malachi folded his arms over his chest and shrugged. 'But I've never seen you look at anyone the way I saw you look at that one the night of the gala.'

'Her name's Anouk,' Sol corrected instinctively, before realising that Malachi was baiting him. His brother knew her name perfectly well. He'd already used it several times. 'And I didn't look at her any particularly special way.'

Malachi twitched one eyebrow upwards, but said nothing.

'No clever quip?' Sol demanded when he couldn't stand the heavy silence any longer.

'I told you, not this time.'

Sol sized up his big brother. There was something odd about Malachi, and it came back to the fact that the guy was more on edge than usual.

'What's going on, Mal?'

'Nothing.'

'You're being cagey.'

'Not really.' Mal dismissed it casually. Arguably a little too casually. 'No more so than you, anyway.'

'You're kidding, right?' Sol shook his head in disbelief.

'Not particularly.'

'Fine.' Leaning back on the sideboard, Sol eyed his brother.

'Time to tell me something I don't know, Mal. If you've got the balls for it.'

And just like that, they were two kids again, and Sol was pressing his brother on where he'd been that first time he'd done a job for the Mullen brothers.

Just as he began to think it wasn't going to work, Malachi opened his mouth.

'I always thought a wife, a family, wasn't for us. Not after everything with *her*.' Sol didn't answer; they both knew he meant their mother. 'I always thought I'd done that bit. I'd endured that responsibility. I never wanted to do it again.'

'But now?' Sol prompted.

'Lately... I don't know.' Malachi swung around from the window almost angrily. 'Forget it. I'm just... Forget I said anything.'

In all these years, they hadn't talked about what had happened. Or about feelings. They were the Gunn brothers. That wasn't the way they handled their issues. But suddenly, something was different. Not Anouk, of course.

He told himself that would be taking it too far. But...*something*. Maybe a delayed reaction to hitting his thirties. The incident with Izzy and her family. The responsibility of the centre.

'Are we capable of it, do you think, Mal?'

His brother frowned. 'Of what?'

'Of...love.'

'You love Anouk?'

'Don't be stupid,' Sol scoffed. 'I'm not saying that. It's just hypothetical.'

He hated himself for not sounding more convincing. It ought to—it was the truth after all. There was no way he could be *in love* with anyone. Let alone Anouk. Whatever they shared between the two of them, it wasn't love. Was it?

Sol waited for the harmless jeering but it didn't come. Instead, Malachi eyed him morosely.

'Hypothetically, I don't even know if we have that capacity,' Malachi gritted out unexpectedly. 'But maybe the question should be, do we deserve it?'

Sol didn't know how to answer, but it didn't matter because his brother was speaking again.

'More pertinently, does any woman deserve to be subjected to our love, *bratik*? Such as we know what that is.'

If his brother had punched him in the gut Sol couldn't have felt any more winded. As if the air had been sucked from his very lungs.

Was Mal right? Would his love be more of a curse than any sort of a gift?

His mind was so full of conflicting thoughts that he simply let them jostle, his eyes scanning the room almost as a distraction. Which was when they alighted again on the Christmas tree.

'So, you and Saskia?'

'I don't wish to discuss it.' Malachi cut him off harshly.

'But you need to,' Sol answered. He rarely stood up to his brother, he rarely needed to. This, he felt, was different. This mattered. To both of them. 'Right here, right now. Our mother ruined both of our childhoods. It's time we both decided whether we're going to let her ruin our futures, too.'

'What have we got?' Sol asked, rounding the corner to the bay. It had been a hectic shift so far, but he thrived on that.

The young doctor running the case looked relieved.

'Darren, nineteen, he suffers from epilepsy and this morning he had two back-to-back seizures, which is out of the norm for him. Full tonic-clonic seizures usually months apart and often only if there's already something going on in the body, like an infection.'

'Has he got an infection?' Sol checked.

'I think an ear infection.'

'And you've started a course of antibiotics?'

'Yes.'

'So, possibly not neuro at this point. But keep me in the loop,' Sol confirmed. 'Okay, let me go and check in the next bay. I had a call for them, as well.'

He slipped around the curtain just as Anouk glanced up. Surprise swept over her face for a moment but she regrouped quickly.

'This is Jack, twenty-five. He was drinking and playing football in the park with a group of mates when he collided with a tree. Loss of consciousness for about five minutes. Pupils are unequal and reactive and he's agitated. We're taking him up to CT now.'

'I'll come with you,' Sol confirmed.

Unequal pupils suggested a bleed on the brain, which might be pushing against the brain itself.

'Great.' Anouk nodded, turning back to her team and issuing her final instructions. 'Let's go.'

'He isn't responding to us verbally, although he does react physically if we ask him to do something. I don't know if the verbal is about the alcohol or a possible injury.'

'Are you going to the centre tonight?' she asked quietly as they strode along the corridors behind the patient.

'Yes, why?'

'I was thinking of going.'

'Do you need a lift?' He frowned, not liking her caginess.

It felt like a huge step backwards, but he couldn't pinpoint why.

'No, I just thought that…maybe you'd prefer it if we weren't there together.'

'Why not?'

It shouldn't gnaw at him the way it did. He understood why she might think it should bother him.

'If that was going to be an issue then I wouldn't have invited you to visit in the first instance,' he told her.

Except he still didn't know what had motivated him to ask her. He refused to accept that it was some uncharacteristic need to have her see a different side to him. That didn't make sense.

Although it seemed the most logical conclusion.

'I just wasn't sure.' She lowered her voice even further as the team reached the CT department and people began to congregate. 'After our...one-night stand.'

Her sudden whisper almost made him laugh. Any other time it probably would have done. But Sol was too busy thinking how dismal the term sounded on Anouk's lips. It felt inadequate to describe either of their encounters that way.

One-night stand—admittedly lasting longer than just the one 'night' sounded, frankly, a little pitiful.

What was happening to him? Why was he reading so much into everything? They'd had a good time together. Twice. Surely he should be more than happy to accept it for what it was?

'I'm heading down there after work,' he informed her. 'I'll drive you, too.'

'Oh, it's okay, I can walk.'

'I'll come down to the department when I'm done. If I'm caught up with a case, wait for me, we'll go together.'

It wasn't a request and they both knew it.

Still, when she flashed him a shy smile it twisted inside him, like a ribbon on a maypole. Delicate and pretty.

Sol snorted to himself as he stepped into the room. He was going to have to watch himself. If he wasn't careful then he risked Anouk wrapping herself around him in more ways than either of them could ever have anticipated.

CHAPTER TWELVE

THE CENTRE MIGHT as well have been Santa's grotto itself, Sol thought, surveying the scene in front of him—a hive of excitement and activity, it felt like the very epicentre of Christmas for the whole of Moorlands Wood.

And there, sitting on the floor, with Libby firmly wedged on one side of her and Katie on the other, pressing against her as though each claiming her as their own, was Anouk. It struck him that the girls' easy acceptance of her said more about Anouk than anything a person could say. These kids dealt with so much at such a young age that they often seemed to develop sixth senses about people.

This had to explain why he had let her slip under his skin without realising it. As he'd told Malachi, it wasn't anything as nonsensical as *love*.

Nevertheless, there was a draw there, a magnetism that pulled him in despite his vows to keep his distance. Which meant that, even now, he couldn't tear his gaze away.

Anouk looked totally engrossed in what she was doing. And what she was doing, he realised after a few moments' scrutiny, was measuring chocolate balls into a jar, before gluing reindeer antlers, funny eyes, and a big red nose onto the glass.

By the look of the full box in front of them, the trio had been working together for some time and were so focussed on the task in hand that none of them noticed him. And so he was free to stand and admire this fascinating woman who appeared, bizarrely, to have so captured his attention.

Without warning, Anouk looked up and her eyes—wide with surprise—locked with his. He didn't think, he didn't consider, he just reacted, flashing her a wide grin; something bursting inside him as she responded instinctively with a hint of a smile, her cheeks taking on a delicately pink hue.

Before he realised where he was, he had crossed the room and was standing in front of the trio. Still, it took him a supreme effort to tear his gaze from Anouk and greet the two young girls still nestled so lovingly on either side of her, as though seeking protection from her metaphorical wings.

'So we're making reindeer chocolate jars, are we?' he managed brightly.

'We've just finished.' Katie cast her arm over the full box solemnly. 'Now we're going to make beaded friendship bracelets for each other.'

'*Kruto!* Wow, they look amazing. Can I join in?' He felt Anouk's sharp gaze but he kept his eyes fixed on the girls, gratified when they nodded excitedly and got to their feet.

'We'll go and get the beads and the thread.' Libby grabbed Katie's arm. 'Why don't we use all green and red, like a Christmas theme?'

'Okay, but we should still have silver thread—that will make it brighter,' Katie advised as the two of them hurried off, lost in the carefree happiness of the moment and oblivious to the undertones that swirled around Sol and Anouk.

He settled himself on the floor next to her leaving a decent foot between them, but he still noticed her pulse leap at her throat as she deliberately avoided eye contact with him, inching another fraction away, as though she couldn't trust them to be so close to each other. It offered him a perverse kind of exultation.

At least he wasn't the only one feeling undercut by the intensity of the last week.

'Did you know this thing between Saskia and my brother is serious?'

He hadn't intended to say anything, but Malachi's revelations were still bubbling in his head and he couldn't help but wonder how much Anouk knew.

'Saskia and Malachi? No, how could I know?' Anouk frowned. 'I've been with you, and when I did return home she wasn't there.'

There was no reason for his body to tauten at the mere memory, surely?

'I hope he doesn't hurt her,' continued Anouk, obliviously. 'Saskia isn't as airy and tough as she might appear.'

'Funny, I was going to say the same thing about Malachi.'

She arched her eyebrows at him, waiting for some punchline. But he didn't have one. He was worried about his brother for the first time in for ever.

They weren't prepared for this...thing. Whatever it was. He might not have a name for it yet but he knew it was powerful. It assailed him at the most inopportune moments. Punching through him like a fist through wet paper. Like when he'd seen the naked sadness in her eyes when Anouk had told him about her father, or yesterday when he'd caught sight of her caring for her patient from across the ward, or today when she'd been so caught up with the girls that she hadn't even noticed anyone else in the room.

It wasn't love, but Sol imagined it was something in that family. He certainly *cared* for Anouk. So if whatever Mal felt for Saskia was anything like it, then he pitied his brother.

'Malachi won't hurt her. He isn't like me.'

The words came out automatically. Because he might once have believed them, although now he wasn't so sure.

'Because he isn't a playboy like you are, you mean?'

Why was it that it sounded so...hollow, coming off her

tongue? Especially after the conversation they'd had in his apartment that night. It occurred to him that she might be testing him, but he had no idea how he was supposed to answer.

'You could say that,' he conceded, shocked at how much it cost him to sound so nonchalant.

'The Smoking Gun,' she added, and she didn't need to add a roll of her eyes. Her words spoke loud and clear all on their own. As if she was reminding herself of his reputation. Cautioning herself.

And it bothered him. Especially after their time together.

For years he had revelled in his reputation as a playboy, had been proud of the fact that he'd come out of his childhood with such a strong sense of self. He had never pretended to be something he wasn't. He loved being with women, but he had always hated the idea of a relationship with them—how much more honest could a man be?

Yet now, something had shifted and the names sounded toneless, even uncomfortable. Like a familiar old jacket that no longer suited—or fitted—him, but that he'd been trying to hold onto nonetheless.

His head was unusually hazy. As if some of its connections had been unexpectedly broken and it was trying to rewire itself using different paths.

He still wasn't quite sure what it meant.

'Great nickname, wasn't it?' he challenged, but the words seemed to leave an unpleasant, metallic taste in his mouth.

This was absurd.

The…*thing* he felt for Anouk was absurd.

With her sweet smile and gentle demeanour she had succeeded in hooking him in a way he would not have believed possible a mere week ago. If he wasn't careful, she was the kind of woman who could easily tame him long enough to put him on a leash. But what had Malachi warned him? That a leopard didn't change its spots? That he was under some kind of spell now, but that when he came around again, all hell would break loose and the person he would most likely end up hurting would be Anouk herself?

And the idea of hurting her made him feel physically sick.

He needed to get up and move away. Now. Before it was too late.

Instead, he sat, perfectly still, not making even a sound. And still something swirled around them. He could feel it and he knew she could, too.

'We got loads of beads,' Libby's excited voice reached his ears from across the room.

Just one more night, he promised himself. Just one last time with Anouk, and then he'd find a way to end it without anyone getting hurt.

And when his eyes caught hers, widening a fraction, the pulse leaping at her throat, he knew she was thinking the same thing.

'Come home with me.' His voice was low and urgent, more a command than a request.

Anouk nodded, seconds before the girls raced back across the gallery floor to rejoin them, and he'd never wished for two hours to pass so expediently.

Last time they had barely got through the door before Sol had pulled her to him. This time, they barely made it to the lift.

Sol claimed her with such reverent kisses it was as though he was committing every detail of her touch to memory. Inscribing himself on her soul and she couldn't seem to get enough of him.

She could never seem to get enough. And that was the essential problem.

Even now, as he peeled off her clothing to kiss every last millimetre of her body, laying waste to her resolve and tearing down every last barrier between them, she couldn't do anything but let him.

A slave to him. Or a slave to her desire for him. Either way, it amounted to the same thing. He was making her forget their arrangement. He was making her want more.

And more again.

Worse, Anouk couldn't bring herself to care. So when he scooped her up to carry her through to the bedroom, muttering hoarsely about *not making it past the hallway otherwise*, all she could do was cling to him, pressing her body to his and meeting his possessive mouth with her own, greedy demands.

It was all she could do to ignore the tight emotions that tumbled through her when he laid her down so very reverently on the bed, removing the last of her clothes until she was naked before him, and rolling back to gaze at her, spread out before him as if she was his own personal feast.

'I've waited for this all day, *zolotse*,' he muttered, before lowering his mouth to her neck, kissing and licking the column of her throat, and fitting his palms to her breasts as if he couldn't bear not to touch her a moment longer.

He trailed scorching little kisses down her neck and to the sensitive hollow at the base, taking his time, until she was urging him on with little moans. He moved across her shoulder and over the swell of her chest, inch by exquisite inch, as if he didn't want to skip over a single millimetre of her body until finally—*finally*—his mouth took over from his hands.

First he sucked one hard, aching nipple into his mouth, grazing his teeth over it gently but not too gently, flicking over it with his tongue, lavishing attention on her. And only when he seemed truly satisfied did he turn his attention to the other side, to repeat the same, adoring process.

And Anouk arched up to him as though to offer up more of herself, her whole body feeling heavy and restless and wanting more. So much more. But he held her in place, deliberately trapping her legs so she couldn't part them around him, couldn't draw him against her, couldn't nestle him where she burned for him most.

Like some kind of exquisite torture.

But if he didn't slide inside her soon, filling her up where all these wild sensations jousted in her, she didn't know if she could survive it.

Anouk didn't know when it occurred to her that if he could torment her so wantonly, then surely she, too, could tease him?

Slowly, carefully, she ran her hands over his back, indulging, just for a moment or two, in reacquainting herself with those hewn muscles that not even his bespoke suit and waistcoat could conceal.

And when he murmured his approval, he answered her long and low, reverberating through her breasts and into her already molten core.

With deliberate care she slid one hand around his waist and wrapped her fingers delicately around his sex. The effect was instantaneous, making her feel womanly and powerful all at once.

'If you do that, you'll find this won't last anywhere as long as it could,' he growled, and she loved the rawness in his tone.

'That's the idea,' she whispered. 'Because I don't think I can hold out much longer.'

A primal sound slipped from his throat as he shifted from her, easing down her body and using his hand to move her legs apart.

'At last,' she sighed, waiting for him to settle between them.

But instead of his body, he edged down with his shoulders, lifting his head only long enough for her to see the wicked gleam in his eyes.

'You can last,' he rasped. 'I insist on it.'

And then he buried his mouth, his tongue, into her heat, before she could answer, and she heard herself cry out.

Anouk had no idea how long he stayed there, paying homage to her as she could only clutch at his hair, his head, his shoulders, her raspy breath and abandoned cry the only sounds to break the silence. His murmurs of approval echoed through her, against her, as he feasted all the more making her shatter once, twice against his tongue then his fingers.

You are ruined, a voice whispered. *You will never, ever meet another man like Sol. There* is *no other man like Solomon Gunn.*

But she couldn't allow herself such thoughts. That path only led to misery. And so she ejected the unwelcome voice from her head and wriggled out from under Sol, pushing him onto his back, her eyes locking with his as she knelt over him and drew him deep into her mouth.

He was big and hot, like silky steel, and she forgot that she was meant to be distracting herself from the intimacy of his mouth on her body and instead lost herself in the intimacy of her tongue swirling over and around him. She was tormenting him and pleasuring him with every second. The way she'd learned to do this past week. The way she never seemed to tire of doing. She probably never would.

She shut the errant thought down once again, concentrating on the moment. Reminding herself that this was just about sex. Only ever about sex.

There could be nothing more.

Lifting her eyes, she made herself focus on Sol. The intensity of his gaze and the unmistakeable shudder of need that took over his body made her feel powerful, and wicked. And all woman. She sucked him in deeper, wanting to lose herself inside that power, in a way she'd never enjoyed with any man before Sol.

Only Sol.

But apparently he wasn't prepared to let things end on her terms. With a low, primal groan, he pulled himself from her mouth and flipped her onto her back as he moved his body to cover hers. His hands traced every inch of her as though she was a revelation to him. It was incredible how precious, how *special*, she always felt when she was in his arms. Yet she was too hot, too needy, for any more play.

As though reading her mind, Sol shifted, nestling between her legs until she could feel his blunt end dipping into her.

'Please, Sol,' she breathed, desperate to lose herself in the primitive sensations that might drown out the other, more dangerous emotions that tumbled in her chest.

Emotions she told herself she had no name for.

Even as she was altogether too afraid that she could name them. Every last one.

And when Sol finally thrust inside her, deep and slow and sure, his gaze holding hers, she refused to let her eyes slide from him. She held her breath, for fear the words she refused to face might fall from them.

Sol moved, pulling out of her before driving home again. Deeper, tighter, hungrier. Driving her faster and faster towards the top. When she finally catapulted over the edge, and heard herself cry out his name, his eyes still holding hers as he followed her, she knew the truth in her heart but she still wasn't prepared to hear Sol say it out loud.

Clear and raw, as though the words had been ripped from the very depths of his soul.

'I love you, *zolotse*.'

'No,' she choked out. Then, louder, *'No!'*

'I'm in love with you, Anouk.' He tried the words again, rolling them around on his tongue, still in shock.

He was in shock. He hadn't intended to say them, much less repeat them, and yet the inexplicable thing was that the more he said them out loud, the easier it felt. The more he liked the way they tasted in his mouth, the way they sounded to his ears.

Like a melody he'd thought he would never want to hear.

'You can't say that.' She was furious. 'I won't hear it. Take it back.'

'Not possible,' he managed. 'It's out there and it can't be taken back.'

She stared at him as though he had physically wounded her.

'Why are you doing this?'

Her evident confusion clawed at his heart. It wasn't as if he understood completely himself. And yet, each time he said it, it made more sense.

Everything made more sense.

'I swore I would never fall in love with any woman. Ever. But here I am. And I know you feel the same way about me.'

'I don't,' she choked, scrambling to get off him.

Away from him.

He let her, even as he emitted a laugh at the irony of it.

He, who had spent over a decade steering clear of relationships with women who would inevitably declare themselves in love with him, was now in love.

It seemed only fitting that *he* should be the one saying it whilst the woman he loved didn't want to accept it. As if it was a test of his own making. He'd never failed a damned test in his entire career, he wasn't about to start now.

'Our deal was sex. Pure and simple,' she cried, spinning around searching for her clothes. 'You're the king of one-night stands.'

'I was. Until you came along.'

He watched her locate her T-shirt and pull it on, then flail around for her jeans. He didn't try to stop her, he didn't want her to feel trapped or cornered, but he didn't share her fluster. He just felt calm. At peace.

It was odd, the way the minute he'd admitted that he loved her, everything had seemed to start slotting into place, piece by piece. He felt somehow...*whole*.

'You said it yourself—I used sex as a distraction.' He shrugged. 'That I just needed to meet the right person. Turns out you were right.'

'No. No, I wasn't.' She shoved her feet into her jeans, first one and then the other, before yanking them up those slender legs that had spent so much of the night wrapped around him. 'You told me that I didn't know the first thing about you. That I was reading too much into it because I wanted you to be a better man than you really are.'

'Turns out I was wrong.'

'No!' Her voice sounded mangled, wretched, and his heart actually ached for her.

'You can deny it as many times as you like, Anouk. It won't change it, believe me. I've been pretending to myself that there was nothing more than sex between us—just like you are now—but I can't pretend any longer.'

'Then try,' she half choked, half bit out.

She looked wounded, and fragile, and even more beautiful than ever. As if finally acknowledging the truth had infused his whole world with a more vivid colour.

How had he ever thought that love was destructive? How had he failed to realise just how glorious it could be?

'More to the point,' he told her quietly, 'I don't want to pretend that it's just sex any more.'

'This is about the chase. You only think you love me because I'm the first woman who made you work for it. Because you had to give a little of yourself, telling me about your childhood and your hardships, in order to get closer to me.'

'You're wrong, Anouk.' At one time her words would have got under his skin, clawing at him, leaving scars. All he felt now was calm acceptance. It was enough to steal his breath away.

'You've confused lust for love.'

'I've never confused lust for anything.' He smiled. 'I always welcomed it, indulged in it. I don't love you because you are the first woman who made me work for you. I love you because you're the only woman who has ever made me *want* to work for it.'

'I don't want this.' She shook her head, sounding as if she was trying to swallow a sob. 'You can't do this to me.'

He stood with deliberate care, so as not to startle her. And despite all her protestations she froze, her eyes fixed on his body, the naked longing in them belying every word she was trying to tell him.

'I think you *do* want this, Anouk.' He reached for his own jeans, pulling them on slowly. Controlled. 'And I think that's what you're most afraid of. That, and the fact that it means trusting another person for the first time in your life.'

'I trust Saskia,' she shot back.

'This is different. *Love* is different. We both know that.'

'I can't offer you that.' Stumbling to the door, she gripped the handle so tightly that her knuckles went white. 'I can't offer you anything. I don't have the capacity for it.'

'Did I ask for anything? I told you I love you; I never demanded that you say it back. But, for what it's worth, you *do* have the capacity for it and one day you will realise it. Trust me. But until that day comes, I have enough love for both of us.'

He watched her stop, sucking in one deep breath after another and straightening her shoulders.

When she turned to him, he could see the forged steel in her eyes. But, behind the steel, stuffed as far back as she could manage, he could also see a desperate yearning to believe.

'You don't know what love is, Sol. Any more than I do. You don't care. Right now, it's thrilling because I've made you feel something you've never felt before. But whatever it is, it isn't love.'

'It's love, Anouk,' he assured her, calmly and quietly, because he'd never been so sure of anything in his life. 'I thought I wasn't capable of it. It turns out I just wasn't capable of it with anybody but you.'

'They're just hollow words,' she gasped, and even as she tried to argue he knew she was struggling to stay standing. 'I know that even if you don't, which is why I'm leaving now. And one day, in the not too distant future, no doubt, you'll thank me for it.'

'I want you to do whatever it is that you need to do, Anouk. I won't thank you for leaving, but neither will I blame you for it. Just as long as you remember you can come back.'

'You're so sure of yourself, aren't you? So arrogant.' She blinked, apparently not realising she'd raised her voice until she heard it echoing back at her.

'I've never apologised for who I am.' He kept his voice even. 'So yes, I'm willing to bet on myself. You'll come back to me. It's inevitable.'

'I'll never come back,' she gritted out.

Then she opened the door and lurched out, leaving him where he stood.

Sol had no idea how long he stood there, not moving, barely even daring to breathe. Waiting for Anouk to walk back through the doorway.

But she didn't. The truth was that he didn't know if she ever would. Yet he regretted nothing. He loved her.

He had never loved any other woman. He knew he never would.

All he could do was hope that she was as strong as he thought she was. That she would be able to trust herself and admit what he already knew to be true.

Anouk loved him, too.

And he could hope that, one day, he would have the chance to *prove* to her that he cared. That his actions would tell her he loved her in a way that she could believe, even if she couldn't accept his words.

Maybe it would take days, perhaps weeks. It could even take years. But he had to believe it would happen.

And when it did, he wouldn't miss his chance.

CHAPTER THIRTEEN

'This is Adam. He's eight years old and he fell approximately eight feet over the retaining wall at the bottom of his garden and onto grass below. He is normally fit and well with no allergies. He's not on any meds and he's up to date with all his jabs. He was playing at the bottom of the garden with his sister when the fence gave way and he fell down to the grass below, landing on his face and knocking out two teeth and there are a couple more loose in his mouth. He suffered a loss of consciousness of approximately one minute. Mum travelled in the helicopter with us, and Dad is on his way by car.'

'You have the teeth?'

'In some milk in there.' The HEMS doctor indicated a plastic fruit box his colleague was carrying.

'Okay, thank you.' Anouk bobbed her head. 'Okay, guys, let's get started.'

As her colleagues worked to set up the drips and take the bloods for testing, Anouk concentrated on the young boy.

'Adam? Can you hear me, sweetie? My name is Anouk and I'm the doctor who will be making you better. Can you tell me what happened, at all?' She turned to her team. 'Let's give him two point five mil of morphine, try to make him more comfortable.'

'Sure.' Her colleague nodded. 'Do you want me to get Maxillofacial?'

'Good idea,' she agreed. 'Give them a shout. Okay, let's get this little boy comfortable so that we can get him for a CT scan and check what's going on in his head.'

Even as she spoke, the monitors began to bleep, and her colleagues around the boy simultaneously declared the patient was becoming breathless.

'He's going tachycardic,' Anouk warned. 'Let's bag him.'

'Do you want to intubate?'

Anouk frowned. Adam's airway was at risk because if one of those loose teeth dislodged and he inhaled it, it could potentially block off his airway.

'He hasn't stopped breathing,' she confirmed. 'Let's see if we can't give OMS a chance to see him first.'

And the sooner she could get the little boy to the scanner to check his brain, the better.

'You've been avoiding me.'

Anouk jumped at the quiet voice by her shoulder. She didn't look up from the screen but she could no longer see a single word or image that was now swimming in front of her eyes.

'No,' she tried to deny it. 'I've just been…busy.'

It was partially true. She had been busy. Mostly she'd been busy trying not to relive his declaration to her, because she honestly didn't know how she felt about it.

She was supposed to not believe in love. She had spent years telling herself what love looked like and it had been an ugly, selfish, cruel image that she'd painted in her own head.

But the minute those very same words had come out of Sol's mouth, they had erased all of it, leaving something so beautiful, and precious, almost ethereal in their stead. Almost too perfect to be real.

So how could she trust it?

'I don't regret saying it,' he announced softly, as though he could read her thoughts.

The worst thing about it was that she so wanted to believe him.

'I'm sorry… I can't.' She shook her head, her words almost lost between her voice box and her ears. 'They're just words. They don't prove anything.'

'You need to come with me.'

'I'm working.'

'The place is quiet. In an hour it probably won't be, but, for now, you have half an hour. Come with me.'

She didn't need to hear him move to sense that he was leaving without her. She ought to let him.

Rising from her stool, with just another quick glance around to check that all was okay, Anouk followed him out of Resus.

'Where are we going?'

The winding nature of the old part of the hospital seemed to conspire with Sol to add to the sense of suspense today.

It had been a good day. Even her young patient, Adam, had defied the odds to avoid any serious injuries.

'You'll see.' Sol didn't slow his pace.

She tried not to dwell on the fact that he sounded so serious and intent. It was just her second-guessing herself. Not wanting to give away the fact that she'd realised she was doing something as wholly and utterly stupid as falling for the man.

She'd have to be an idiot to forget who she was dealing with.

And the worst thing about it was that she seemed to be exactly that idiot.

Where *was* Sol leading?

'We're going to the cafeteria?' she guessed, as she stretched out her stride trying to keep up with him.

He seemed sharper, edgier than usual.

'Yes.'

'Sol, it's been a long shift. I don't want to eat here. I'd rather just finish my shift and go home.'

'You're not eating here.' He stopped, taking her chin in his hands and tilting her head up to his.

The look he shot her was altogether too hot, and she shivered at the naughty thoughts that he could stir up with just a glance.

Her breath caught in her chest. Almost painful as it lodged there.

'What's going on, Sol?'

He turned her so that she was looking in through the internal cafeteria window.

'Can you see that woman sitting at the table over there? Sixties to seventies? Red coat on the back of the chair?'

Anouk scanned the room, focussing on the area where he was pointing. There was no reason in the world for her heart to thump. But it did.

'Why? Who is she?'

'That's your grandmother, Anouk. Your father's mother. Mal found her.'

Something dark, and angry, and...*panicky* rolled through her.

'Malachi did?' She could hear things crashing around her. It took a moment to realise it was in her head. 'You had your brother *track her down*?'

How could Sol have contacted her grandmother behind her back? How could he have brought her here? How could he have ambushed her like this?

Anouk didn't know how long she stood there. Probably only a few seconds but it felt like days. Her hands were clenched so tightly that her fingernails scored marks deep into her palms. And then she was spinning around, plunging back across the room, knocking chairs flying outside a consultation room, but wholly unable to stop, or turn, or pick them back up.

Sol caught up with her as she tore along the corridor away from the dining area.

'Anouk, stop. *Stop*. Don't run away.'

'Don't run away?' she snapped, her voice just about managing to work again. 'Don't *run away*?'

This time it was louder. She felt Sol's hands on her shoulders and she shrugged them off with a violence she would never have thought she possessed.

'Anouk—'

'How *dare* you do that to me?' she roared, because it was either that or give into this thing spiralling inside her that would make her crumple and fold.

She was dimly aware of Sol checking up and down the corridor as staff moved curiously through, before he tested a few doors and then pulled her into a consultation room. She didn't know whose. She didn't care.

Fear and anger duelled inside her, and she couldn't risk letting the former win.

'You just need to hear her out, Anouk.' Even the black look on his face couldn't deter her.

'Why, because *you* think I should? I'm not ready to do that yet. And you don't get to be the one to order me otherwise.'

'I'm trying to help you,' he growled.

The worst of it was that a part of her believed him. She barked out a hollow, unpleasant laugh, all the better to drown out the pounding of her blood through her veins.

'By dictating to me? My, how lucky am I?'

'You're twisting what's happening here.' Sol reached out as though he was going to take hold of her shoulders again, then thought better of it and rammed his hands in his pockets.

Half of her gave herself a satisfied air-punch whilst the other half lamented the loss. She felt twisted inside out, as if she didn't know who or where she was. Everything was wrong. Unsettled.

'And here, of all places?'

'It's neutral territory. You're a skilled doctor. This is where you feel safe and confident. It will translate into the conversation.'

'No, it won't,' she gritted out. 'Because there isn't going to be a conversation.'

'Anouk, don't be scared...'

'I'm not scared,' she cried, the lie mocking her even as it hung in the air. 'I'm an idiot but I'm not scared.'

'You are and you're lashing out. And that's fine. But you don't need to be frightened. I'm here to support you.'

'Support me? You?' She laughed, a brittle, harsh sound. 'You can't support me, or anyone. I was wrong when I said that you knew how to care for someone, how to love them. You don't have it in you to think of anyone but yourself. Deciding you know what's best for me without thinking to discuss it with me for one single second. My God, you even said the words to me. But you don't know what they mean. You don't know what it is to love someone. You're every bit as selfish and arrogant as you said you were.'

And before she could fall apart completely in front of him, Anouk whirled herself around and ran—as fast as she possibly could.

Sol watched her go, her words stinging him as if every one had been a knife going into his heart.

He'd hoped that bringing her here would resolve the impasse between them. He'd hoped it would show her that he was sincere. That he wanted to be worthy of her.

He loved her.

It had been almost a week since he'd told her. Since he'd heard himself say the words out loud. And oddly, it was getting easier and easier to accept, with each passing day. He'd always thought love was something to fear but Anouk made it seem like something special. Something new. Something to *aspire* to, rather than dread.

Unlike any other woman he had dated, he knew, he just knew, that Anouk understood why he had to be a part of centres like Care to Play. She would never pout, or complain, or moan that the kids got more of his time than she did. Or that she would rather be going to a fancy, high-society gala than another football-and-barbecue-in-the-park event. In fact, Anouk would most likely be right there beside him. Organising every single event.

She made everything shift and change when she was around. People, places, situations. They all sparkled that little brighter under her touch. And Sol wanted, more desperately than he could remember wanting anything for such a long time, to be a part of her life.

It made no sense, yet here he was fighting every instinct to go after her and *make* her listen to him.

He had to let her go—for now. The best thing he could do would be to take a leaf out of the book of the woman sitting in that cafeteria back there. The woman who was so utterly desperate to meet her granddaughter for the first time, and who had longed for this moment for over three decades yet still had the patience to wait that little bit longer.

Turning around, Sol strode back down the corridor. For one thing, he owed the older woman an apology and, for a second, she was the closest thing to a source he had on Anouk.

He could give Anouk her space, but still, the more he understood this complex and enigmatic woman who had somehow crept inside the heart he'd thought locked down for good, the better.

At least he knew one thing. Tracking down Anouk's grandmother had been the right thing to do. Whether Anouk wanted to accept the truth or not, it was clear that she needed to meet her other grandmother and learn what had really happened between her father and her mother.

Until Anouk had closure, for better or for worse, she was never going to be able to move past it and into a relationship with anyone.

With *him*.

Anouk had no idea how long she stood at the bright green front door, her eyes locked balefully onto the Christmas wreath and her hand poised to knock but her heart clattering much too wildly against her ribs to let her. So when the door opened, almost cautiously, she almost stumbled back down the steps.

'Hello, Anouk.'

It took a moment for Anouk to realise that she was still standing with her arm raised. She lowered it—it felt like in slow motion—but still couldn't work her mouth enough to answer.

'You've been standing there for the better part of ten minutes. Would you like to come in?'

Would she? Her mind felt split in two.

Stiffly, she bobbed her head, trying not to allow the older woman's soft smile to work its way inside her, and let herself be ushered carefully into the house.

A string of Christmas cards adorned the hallway, testament to how popular this new grandmother of hers appeared to be, and a decent, prettily decorated tree stood proudly in one corner of the living room.

'Your father decorated it every year. For me,' she was told by this older woman whom Anouk supposed was her grandmother. 'I don't think he ever had one at his own home. He always said Christmas was for the children, and he'd enjoy it when he had you to share it with.'

Anouk didn't know how to respond.

A couple of minutes later they were sitting in silence at a small, glossy, yew dining table with quaint coasters in front of them and a teapot, cups and saucers, and a quintessential plate of biscuits. It was so utterly English that Anouk had to swallow a faintly hysterical gurgle.

'I got the bag,' she managed awkwardly after what felt like an age. Maybe two.

Someone—presumably Sol—had left it in Resus for her the next day. But he hadn't been to see her.

She told herself it was for the best.

Her companion nodded and offered an encouraging smile. It occurred to Anouk that the older woman—it was hard to think of her as her paternal grandmother—was as nervous as she was, if not more so.

Somehow, the knowledge bolstered her.

'It meant a lot. I never…knew…'

'There are more bags like that,' her grandmother said sadly. 'Full up. Every Christmas, every birthday, without fail. We gave up sending them to you—they always got returned. But we never gave up on you.'

'I didn't even know you wrote to me,' she managed, her voice thick. 'I only knew about one letter, but I didn't know what it said, or when it had been sent.'

'We wrote to you all the time. Letters at first, as you saw in that bag. But diaries after a while.'

'Oh.' Anouk took a sip of tea by way of distracting herself, but suddenly it was impossible to swallow.

'Do you want to see them?'

Her grandmother pushed her chair back and Anouk almost fell over herself to stop her.

'No.' She hadn't meant to make the older woman jump. 'No. Sorry. It's just…'

'Too much to take at once,' her grandmother guessed. 'Another time, perhaps.'

'Another time,' Anouk agreed, surprised to realise that she really meant it.

She still hadn't processed the emotions that had crashed over her, threatening to overwhelm her, when she'd looked into that bag and found a selection of gifts from when she was a baby, to this very year.

The letters that had accompanied them—the first few marked *Return to Sender* in her mother's unmistakeable loopy handwriting—had been like a sledgehammer to her heart. Every word thumping painfully into her. Words she'd longed to hear as a kid but which her self-obsessed mother had never once uttered to her.

Her father and her grandmother had each penned letters that

had been so heartfelt, so pained, that Anouk couldn't have denied their veracity even if she'd wanted to. Which she didn't.

They spoke about how much they loved her, how the dimples on her baby cheeks, or the gurgle of her laugh, had filled them with such pride, such joy, and such a feeling of completeness. And the only thing that had undercut it all had been the fact that the two of them had been compelled to snatch every snippet they could from the magazine articles, or the news items, or the TV interviews, in which her mother had trotted her out with the sole reason of making herself look like a good and doting mother.

It had taken Anouk almost two days to track down a VHS player so that she could see the recordings her father had made on the two occasions he'd travelled to the States to try to speak to Annalise Hartwood, only for her security team to practically manhandle him away.

So much for her mother's claims that her father had wanted nothing to do with them.

'He wanted to be with you from the moment he knew Annalise was pregnant.' Her grandmother shook her head when Anouk voiced her thoughts out loud. 'He even proposed.'

'My father proposed?' Anouk felt her stomach twist. All the stories her mother had told her seemed more and more like lies. The worst of it was that she knew, instantly, that the version of events this relative stranger was recounting made more sense than anything Annalise had ever said.

'But your mother didn't want to know. She was rich and famous and he was nobody. Even when you came along there was nothing he could do. She refused to acknowledge him as the father, let alone allow him to have contact. But he did try, you must know that.'

'I do now,' Anouk murmured.

At least Annalise had never tried to pretend her father was someone else. The one consolation she had was that the identity of her father had remained constant throughout the years, even if only to her.

'He was so proud of the way you were growing up. He would have been over the moon to know you'd become a doctor. And that you'd come over to the UK.'

'I wish I had tried to make contact sooner. I just... I always thought... I was led to believe...'

'That he didn't want to know you,' her grandmother supplied.

Incredibly there was no bitterness or rancour to the older woman's tone, just a deep kind of grief, even as they both silently knew that Annalise had been the one to pour all that poison.

'It couldn't have been further from the truth.' Her eyes shimmered and Anouk ducked her head for a moment, pretending she didn't notice.

She didn't want to succumb, as well. There seemed little point in telling the woman—her grandmother—that she'd gone to his house years ago. That could be a discussion for another time.

'You have a good one there, you know.'

'A good one?' Anouk frowned as her grandmother smiled warmly.

'Solomon. The young man you're courting...or I should say dating, shouldn't I?'

'Oh. No. We're just friends.' She could feel the blush creeping up her neck and she knew her grandmother's surprisingly sharp eyes hadn't missed it.

Even the older woman's smile was suddenly faintly delighted.

'You don't go to the lengths your young man went to, or talk about a young lady the way he talked about you, if you're just friends. Take my word for it.'

'You're wrong.' Anouk flushed, but she could feel the tiny smile playing at the corners of her mouth, the spearhead of hope working its way around her heart like a sharp screwdriver prying the lid off an old tin of paint.

For the rest of the conversation, Anouk listened as her grandmother recounted some stories about her father, revelling in their obviously close relationship and trying not to resent her mother for keeping her from such a loving home.

She learned how her father had never married, his heart always belonging to her mother and herself, as cruelly as Annalise had treated him. Anouk didn't know if that made him single-minded or, frankly, a bit of a wet lettuce, but she liked to think of him as loyal and loving. And for now, that would work.

Her grandmother had an unexpectedly naughty sense of humour, which began to shine through once their initial nervousness had been overcome. And, Anouk discovered to her shock, the older woman had been very happily married three times. Widowed all three times.

'I was a bit of a saucy young lady,' her grandmother told her, 'but I loved each one of them very dearly. And I was always a good and faithful wife.'

And then the older woman twinkled in a way that Anouk suddenly realised was all too familiar. She had caught a glimpse of it in herself every now and then over the years, usually when Saskia had convinced her to relax on those rare nights out, but especially recently when Sol had been a part of her life.

Was it possible that Sol, like this woman with the twinkling eyes, had been a *bit saucy* until he'd found his soul mate? Could it be that she was Sol's? That Sol really did love her?

Anouk filed that little nugget in a box to dissect later. When she was alone. When she had the courage.

Still, the afternoon was emotionally exhausting. No doubt even more so for her grandmother.

'Maybe I should go,' Anouk hazarded after a while. 'I think I need to…absorb some of this.'

Her grandmother's eyes raked over her. The evident need for time to regroup obviously warring with the fear of never seeing her new granddaughter again.

'I'll come back,' Anouk added quickly. 'If you're happy for that, of course.'

A slender hand covered hers instantly, its grasp surprisingly strong.

'Do you promise me?'

It was so small a gesture, yet so strong, making something kick hard in her chest.

'I do,' she choked out.

'And you'll thank that young man of yours?'

Despite herself, Anouk couldn't help but smile.

'I told you, he isn't my young man.'

'He is if you want him to be,' came the surprising response.

For a moment, Anouk turned the idea over in her head.

Was he?

She wrinkled her nose and tried not to reveal her emotions. Everything seemed to be running so close to the surface these days, it was so unlike her usual self.

'No. I don't know if it really was once the case,' she heard herself confessing. 'But, if it was, it isn't any more.'

'That's up to you, my flower. I know enough about men to know that one is yours for the taking. If you want him, go and get him.'

Anouk wasn't sure if it was the grandmotherly advice or the term of endearment that tugged at her the most, but all of a sudden she had to fight the urge to break down. Right there and then.

But on the way home, her mind couldn't stop spinning. The events of the past hour, and the past few weeks, all whirling around her head. She was a mess.

She was never a mess.

But was it because of her father? Her grandmother? Or just Sol? And, more significantly, how was she going to sort it—and herself—out? Whatever this thing was inside her, this gnawing, empty, hollow thing, it needed Sol to assuage it. She wasn't prepared to go back to the life she'd had before him. She needed him. And whatever the hell that meant—they would work it out together.

If Sol really was hers for the taking, how on earth was she to even set about doing such a thing?

And then it came to her. What had Libby once said about Christmas Eve being the most magical time? First, she was going to need to take a detour to the Care to Play centre.

CHAPTER FOURTEEN

SOMETHING WAS DIFFERENT.

His home was...*changed*.

He had spent the entire day looking for Anouk. Checking her apartment, the hospital, the centre, even phoning Saskia so many times that an irritated Malachi had told him to give it up and go home for the night.

He hadn't wanted to.

The moment he'd heard that Anouk had approached Malachi for her grandmother's address, the need to find Anouk and ensure that she was okay had been overwhelming. He had no idea what her grandmother had ultimately told her and the fear that she was somewhere, alone and hurting, tore him up in a way he would never have believed possible.

If she was traumatised, then it would be his fault. He'd never intended for her to be ambushed by the knowledge of a grandmother she'd never met. He'd expected to be with her when they first met. And now he couldn't find Anouk anywhere. She had to be somewhere.

All he could do was head home and try again tomorrow. She couldn't hide out from him for ever. He wouldn't let her. He couldn't.

Sol stood, the front door still open behind him, as he tried to work out what it was. Slowly, as if his mind couldn't believe what his body already sensed, he kicked the door to and moved carefully to the archway.

The scene beyond was like something out of his childhood.

The main lights were low, and the place was illuminated with pretty, twinkling Christmas lights whilst a miniature winter, Christmas village covered the entire room, from little shops and houses to ice-skating rinks, Ferris wheels and small-gauge trains.

Beyond it all, Anouk stood, her hands twisted together and her face set in an anxious expression.

'What *is* this?' he demanded, his voice thick through his constricted throat.

He told himself not to believe, not to hope. He needed to wait, and hear the words.

'An apology.' Her voice was ragged, no better than his, and he allowed himself a moment to take that in.

To some degree it made him feel better. Still, he jammed his fists into his pockets as if that might stop him from striding across the room and reaching out for her the way he wanted to.

He moved further inside, wanting to kiss her. Claim her.

But by the way her arms were in front of her chest, her fingers knotting together, he had a feeling she needed to explain herself. Though perhaps not before babbling nervously a little first.

He could let her have that, too. After all, he wasn't entirely sure he knew what to say, himself.

'I went to see my grandmother today,' she breathed, a note of awe in her voice. 'She told me that I had to thank you.'

'I shouldn't have ambushed you at the hospital that day.' He exhaled sharply. 'I just thought that maybe the location would be the best place for you to feel in control. Strong.'

'It's okay.' She jerked forward, as though she was going to step up to him, before stopping awkwardly. 'I owe you an apology, for all those awful things I said. They were horrible, unkind. I'm so, so sorry.'

'Forget about them.' Closing the gap he caught her hands, trying to make her look at him. If she did, then he might be able to convince her that it really didn't matter.

She'd been frightened and cornered and she'd lashed out. Hell, he knew that feeling only too well.

'I can't. I didn't mean them…'

'I know. Anouk, look at me.' He crooked his finger under her chin. 'Forget it. Really.'

'I can hardly believe you did that for me.' Anouk smiled wanly, and, to Sol, even that was like the sunshine cracking through the heaviest sky after a thunderstorm. 'I can hardly believe you *cared* enough to do it.'

'It wasn't a big deal.'

'It was to me,' she said earnestly. 'No one has ever bothered to do anything like that for me before. Not unless they thought they could get something out of it. Usually access to my mother.'

'She did quite a number on you, didn't she?' Sol frowned as Anouk pulled away from him abruptly.

'My mother was…manipulative,' she confessed unexpectedly, her frankness taking him by surprise. 'She treated me like a precious daughter in public, but in private I was an inconvenient burden she couldn't stand to look at. And I was so desperate for her affection that I spent my whole life, whilst she was alive, turning myself inside out trying to win it. I even made myself sick trying to do everything I could for her. For her love.'

'The fault was never yours,' Sol said, shoving his clenched fists into his pockets just so that he wouldn't haul her into his arms.

He mustn't crowd her. She would come to him fully when she was ready.

'I know that. Logically.' She pulled a wry face. 'But I grew up in Hollywood, where there are altogether too many sycophants willing to excuse my mother's behaviour and agree that she was a saint and I was a problem child. And I was too young, too needy, too naïve to argue.'

'So you ended up believing them?'

'I saw a twisted kind of relationship where people used each other, all the while bandying about the word *love*. So I learned it can be a flawed, cruel concept more effective as a weapon than any kind of gift.'

Anger barrelled through him that someone as sweet, intelligent, and kind as Anouk could have allowed people who were *nothing* to drag her down and think less of herself. She seemed so strong, so sure, it was hard to believe it was just an act.

And yet…not hard at all. Because he saw her. Her virtues and her flaws. And he loved her despite them, or maybe *for* them.

'I know you don't believe me when I tell you that I love you, but it's true, Anouk. I love you with every fibre of who I am and, if you'll let me, I'll spend the rest of our lives trying to make you believe that.'

It felt like an eternity that she stood, watching him, immobile. And then suddenly she took his hand in her smaller ones.

'That's the point, Sol.' She smiled. 'I already believe you.'

It was like a thousand victories all spiralling through him at once.

'What changed?' He couldn't help but ask.

'You, contacting my grandmother. It showed you listened to me, you cared, and you understood.'

'I'll always listen to you, Anouk.'

'I think I really believe that,' she agreed. 'It's why I came back, and why I did this,'

He followed her head as it scanned the room, encompassing the entire Christmas scene, not realising that he was pulling her back, closer to him, as he did so.

And, what was more, she was letting him.

'I love it,' he murmured, not entirely sure which bit he was talking about.

'It was the one thing I could think of to show you I had listened, too,' Anouk babbled. 'Even if you and Malachi aren't into it any more, except for the kids.'

'Shh. I love that you wanted to do something for me. I love that you thought about this, especially when I know how much you hate Christmas. It makes it all the more special that you did this for me.'

'It wasn't as bad as I'd feared,' she admitted.

'That's good.'

'It is?'

'Sure.' He grinned suddenly. 'It bodes well for any kids we might have.'

'You want children with me?' Anouk breathed in wonder.

'If you'd like that.' He slid his fingers to her chin, tilting her head up until they were eye to eye.

Deep down, she'd always wondered if she would ever want to be a mother. She'd doubted she had it in her. Her life had been about her career as a doctor and nothing else had ever pulled at her.

And then Sol had slammed into her life and everything had changed. She might not have considered babies with him before, but the moment he had mentioned it there had been no doubt in Anouk's mind that she wanted nothing more than to start a life—and a family—with him.

'I want children with you,' she managed, then seemed to draw in a deep breath. 'And, as for Christmas, it turns out my father always wanted to celebrate the holiday with me. He might not be here, but maybe I can do it in memory of him? Maybe you can help me?'

He felt his mouth crook, a sense of triumph punching its way through him. Who would have thought it would feel this good to be wanted by a woman like Anouk? To want her back?

Before he could answer, she was speaking again. Suddenly serious. 'And you were right, of course. I was running away.'

'Understandable,' he growled. 'Given the circumstances.'

She shook her head.

'You misunderstand me.' She ran her tongue over her teeth, her nerves clearly threatening to get the better of her in a way that touched him deeply. 'I wasn't just running away from my grandmother. Or my fear that whatever she or my late father had to say, it wouldn't match up to the fantasy in my head. I was also running away from you. Or, more to the point, my growing feelings for you.'

It was more than he'd thought she would say. More than he could have hoped she would say. He couldn't bite his tongue any longer.

'Whatever you were worried about, don't be. I love you, Anouk Hart, with all that I am.'

It was the look of wonder in her eyes that made his heart swell so wildly that he feared his chest couldn't contain it.

'You still love me?' she whispered, her eyes scanning his, almost in disbelief.

'I will *always* love you. You had to know that, otherwise why come here?' He arced his arm around the room. 'Why do all of this?'

'Because *I* love *you*, you idiot.' She snorted, half laughing, half sobbing.

The words spun around him, lifting him and making him feel somehow complete.

'I can't believe you did all this yourself,' he told her at length when the breath in his chest finally felt like his again.

'Not all myself.' Anouk offered a wry smile. 'I had a little help. Quite a bit, in fact.'

'Is that so?'

'Libby, Katie and Isobel.'

He groaned loudly, but only half-heartedly.

'You realise those girls will for ever be able to say that I was wrong and they were right?'

'I do.' Her eyes twinkled mischievously, sending a streak of desire straight through him. 'Just as I know you won't begrudge them a moment of it.'

'I won't,' he murmured, revelling in the way Anouk's body was finally moulding to him.

As if she'd always been meant to be there.

'I love you,' he repeated, just because it felt incredible to say it. Because he couldn't get enough of hearing it. Because he didn't think he'd ever tire of basking in the tender glow of her sapphire gaze when he told her how he felt about her.

Now that her barriers had finally dropped.

'I love you, too, Solomon Gunn,' she whispered fiercely, all her tentativeness put aside in that moment. 'And I will continue loving you for the rest of my life.'

'I intend to hold you to that,' he managed gruffly, 'because I think it will take a lifetime to prove to you how much I love you, too.'

'Just the one?' she teased.

'Trust me, that's all we'll need, you and I. Together.'

He couldn't hold back a moment longer. Lowering his head, he claimed her mouth with his, letting her wind her arms around his neck, and lifting her up so that she could wrap her legs around his hips, as her heat poured through him.

And then he laid her down within their twinkling, magical Christmas village scene, and they welcomed in the first perfect Christmas of the rest of their lives together.

* * * * *